JOHN W. CAMPBELL ANTHOLOGY

John W. Campbell Anthology

With Introductions by
Lester del Rey and Isaac Asimov

DOUBLEDAY & COMPANY, INC., GARDEN CITY, NEW YORK, 1973

THE BLACK STAR PASSES, Copyright, 1953, by John W. Campbell, Jr. Copyright, 1930, by Experimenter Publications, Inc.

ISLANDS OF SPACE, Copyright, 1956, by John W. Campbell, Jr. Copyright, 1930, by Experimenter Publications, Inc.

INVADERS FROM THE INFINITE, Copyright, 1961, by John W. Campbell, Jr. An earlier version Copyright, 1932, by Experimenter Pub. Co.

ISBN: 0-385-06819-0
Library of Congress Catalog Card Number 72–89301
Copyright © 1973 by Doubleday & Company, Inc.
All Rights Reserved
Printed in the United States of America
First Edition

CONTENTS

The Sense of Wonder
by Isaac Asimov

I read John Campbell's "Arcot, Wade, and Morey" stories when I was still a pre-teener, and it is impossible for me to forget the sense of wonder with which they filled me. I saw visions of time and space that have haunted me ever since.

Yet Campbell was not exactly ancient himself. He wrote the stories when he was still in his early twenties, the first part when he was not yet old enough to vote.

The stories reflect Campbell's youth and possess the virtues and flaws inseparable from that fact. They are the joyful fantasies of a man young enough to dream without limit and not old enough to have learned of complications.

At the start of the epic, man has not yet ventured into space; the advance of science has taken him only to giant airplanes—propeller-driven although the year is 2126.

But then we meet Arcot and Morey (and later Wade). They are young heroes who fear no dangers and recognize no limitations. Never are they troubled by uncertainty, never hampered by ignorance. For them, to think is to solve, and to solve is to build, and to build is to win.

By the end of the three novels here included, which cover a period of no more than five years, the three friends (with the occasional help of a few others, both human and non-human) have driven from end to end of the Universe, have encountered creatures of superior technology from whom they have quickly learned and whom they have quickly surpassed, and have ended with powers like gods.

Never once in those five years of terrific (and virtually single-handed) advance is there any indication that there might be social resistance, bureaucratic bumbling, honest opposition, even simple differences in point of view. In fact, the human race does not exist—only Arcot, Wade, and Morey, and those occasional few who impinge upon them here and there.

In particular, women do no exist. Search from end to end of these stories and you will find neither wives nor mothers; neither sweethearts nor daughters. Not only are women not physically present; they are almost never in the words or thoughts of any of the characters—human or non-human. It is the masculine world par excellence of early magazine science fiction.

Campbell all his life deified mankind—or at least his vision of mankind, which was that of the tall, muscular, blond man of northwestern European heritage (very much like himself). You will find that vision not only in Arcot, Wade, and Morey, but in all the intelligent non-humans he portrays. They, too, are strong, and differ from mankind only in minor physical ways, leaving their northwestern European origin (at least spiritually) clearly visible.

And mankind always wins. No matter how far behind they may be technologically, they catch up and forge ahead. And the non-humans recognize human superiority, too. To be sure, this superiority seems to express itself largely in military technology. Every new advance dreamed up by Arcot (and the technological time-lag, from first flush of theory to finished machine in action, seems to be about six days) is a new weapon of destruction. The ethics of the matter never concern anyone.

What's more, Campbell's universe is one of peculiar violence. All the intelligent races (including mankind itself) are violent, and their one method of interaction is to make war. When Arcot, Wade, and Morey reach Venus, they naturally find it in the middle of an implacable war, and they (equally naturally) at once take sides, choosing their side with no consideration of the issues involved, but only because a city threatened with destruction is pretty.

And a fearsomely savage set of wars they are, too. It is all a matter of sheer force; there is neither diplomacy nor strategy; it is merely the head-on collision of energy versus energy, each side escalating until one side (Earth) blasts the other out of existence. And to Campbell all fighting is mindless and to the death. Each side withstands endless damage with no thought of surrender or even negotiations. The fight continues, at whatever cost, to absolute destruction (of non-humans).

But a peculiarly bloodless set of wars they are, too. We get no view of the fighters and how they feel, of their savage triumph at victory or their despairing woe at defeat. The adversaries (except for Arcot, Wade, and Morey) are machines only. Even when an entire planet is destroyed, one gets no feeling of the lost humanity or non-humanity involved. The planet is simply destroyed.

What's more, Campbell freely violates the most fundamental laws of nature. He extracts enormous quantities of work from a uniform heat sink, despite the second law of thermodynamics; produces matter out of solidified photons in the teeth of Einstein; and introduces new metals in defiance of the periodic table.

Why, then, in the light of all this, are Campbell's old novels required reading for those interested in science fiction?—For the simple reason that, shining through all the flaws, is the working of a brilliant imagination, together with a drive and enthusiasm that carries the reader along despite himself.

I have just reread them before writing this introduction and although four decades separates me from the boy who first read them, I find, once again, the vision of time and space that haunted me then, and I find, once again, that old sense of wonder.

Campbell's "Arcot, Wade, and Morey" stories are an example of the old "super-science epic" and with all the faults of narration, with all the absence of real humanity, with all the empty noise of empty wars—they remain the best of their kind, and to read them is an enriching experience.

Of Destiny and Wonder
by Lester del Rey

John W. Campbell was almost certainly the first man to decide that the field of science fiction should be his life's work; without question, he was the first to succeed in that goal. He was still in school when he sold his first story, but within a year or so, he had become one of the two most respected writers in the field. His reputation was made in the series of stories about Arcot, Wade, and Morey which are presented here.

These are stories of man's early dreams of human destiny, of his limitless frontiers, and of his ability to conquer space and go out to the ends of the known universe. They are also stories of the wonders of the wonderful machine, through which his destiny was to be shaped.

At the time when Campbell's stories first appeared, many men were in love with the machine. It was this love which first inspired the writing and publishing of that field of literature which came to be called science fiction. It should probably then have been called technological fiction, since the achievements of engineering were almost everything to it, while science was used only as a means to let man learn how to build greater and more wonderful machinery.

Such an attitude may seem strange now, but it was natural enough for those years. It was a time when the machine had shaped the world. Within little more than a generation, men had first conquered the sea in the submarine; had overcome the distances of land by the spread of automobiles so cheap that almost every family could own one, and had learned to master the air in airplanes that could put nearly two hundred miles behind them in a single hour. Lindbergh had crossed the Atlantic, Byrd had mastered the Poles. Radio had spread across the country, reduced from a crude mystery to a means of nightly entertain-

ment. And already, men had begun to see from Einstein's statement that E=mc² the possibility of drawing limitless power
from converting matter directly to energy. Oberth and others
had proven that flight through space was merely a matter of
applying known methods to engineering reality.

At that time, there was no talk of pollution. There had been
no dropping of atomic doom to put the fear of technology into
politics and daily life. The machine seemed all good, without
evil except as evil men tried to use it. There seemed to be no
limit to what man could do with the aid of the machine. To
know the power of the machine was to love it, so far as could
be determined by the young men like Campbell who were coming out of the colleges to spread its influence.

In a way, however, the love of the machine and its wonders
was only a symptom of a deeper feeling. The spirit of Invictus
was still fresh and strong. Human destiny seemed to have no
limits, save the fears of those who could not grasp it fully. Mankind had conquered the Earth and all that lay thereon. A man
was no longer bound to any one place or art. He could begin to
understand the universe, from the fire of the stars to the nature
of the atom. The neutron had just been discovered, to explain
what seemed mysterious about the atom before. Physics reigned
over the land. With its knowledge, the last mysteries were to be
removed, leaving man almost a god.

Again, particularly in America, this should not be surprising.
We had conquered a continent in five generations, beginning
from a tiny strip along the Eastern coast. America—at least in
its own mind—was not only the richest country in the world,
but also the greatest. When Europe had begun butchering itself
in war, we had been forced to make the world "safe for Democ-
racy." There was no question but that our system was the right
one, and it was our duty to teach it to all others. Manifest Destiny
was not just a phrase, but the emblem of the future.

Oh, there were still some signs of trouble. There was something called the Depression. But our leaders assured us that this
was just a temporary thing, and that prosperity was just around
the corner. When these stories were written, the real dangers
in our economy were not yet fully seen. The Industrial Revolu-
tion and the great system of Free Enterprise had proved themselves and would go on and on, gathering greater glories forever.

Our difficulties might be said to be only the fault of those who had not fully realized our true birthright.

Men looked forward to a Golden Age to come. And those with the greatest imagination foresaw it as nothing but wonder piled on wonder. The future was an endless panorama of marvels.

John W. Campbell was the son of an engineer, educated in science, with more knowledge than most of what could be made of the discoveries of the past two decades. And his sense of wonder was greater than that of most writers. He also had the fire and enthusiasm of youth.

It is this wonder and ethusiasm which are the basis for the stories he was writing then, and it instilled a sense of that wonder in all who read his tales, as nothing else had done so well—either before or after. These are the ultimate stories of wonder and of destiny. As such, they may well be the greatest stories of their kind ever written.

The faults are easy to find. As Dr. Asimov has indicated, they are often too strongly tinged with attitudes we have abandoned, though they were taken as unquestioned truths at the time.

They are probably chauvinistic, as read now. They were never meant to be, however. There are no women in the stories, in any real sense of the importance of women. That is unquestionably true. Yet when these were written, that seemed logical enough. These are stories of engineers, the ones best suited to developing and using the machines. And in those days, engineers were men, living in a man's world. That is more true than otherwise, even today; so far, women have only begun to invade the world of engineering, though they are proving themselves capable indeed. And in the field of technical warfare, the warriors then were men —as they still are in most countries.

Racial chauvinism is not quite so simple. It's easy to find that in these stories, of course. Every major human character is waspish to a major degree. But science fiction was no more guilty there than other fields of fiction. Nor was it, perhaps, as guilty. Science fiction had existed as a separate thing for only five years; yet already it had built a sort of body of folklore that was common property. And in that folklore, it was somehow understood that the races of man would begin to mingle; many stories had already told of the fusion of races and colors, until it was taken for granted. Campbell said nothing of this, and may not have meant it. But many writers of the time who seem equally chauvinistic were assuming that all differences in race would vanish in the next century or so; and yet, the names of the characters were equally waspish, probably because such names were most acceptable to the readers.

After all, the ones who read the magazines where these stories appeared were mostly quite young—under twenty, perhaps. They were not interested in family stories or love stories in this type of reading; they could get that elsewhere, in a plethora of family magazines that no longer exist. They were largely waspish themselves in attitude and background, and they were looking for stories that might have happened to them, had they been born later into the great age that was just dawning.

(Even today, the mass of people who attend science fiction conventions are not too different. I know that many of the readers are black, yet very few of these seem to belong to the fans who attend such get-togethers. Why this should be remains a mystery, since today I know of no group which has less race prejudice, on the average.)

The other flaws are minor, I feel. True, the fiction of the time disregarded the difficulty of putting new developments into production. They had no thought that the riches of an entire nation would be needed to build vessels to conquer space. All seemed simple, then. Yet this was based on no necessary ignorance, but on optimism that may have been displaced, but seemed justified. Writers simply assumed that such difficulties would be eliminated with later developments. The first automobiles had been difficult to produce; but Henry Ford had conquered that, to turn out seemingly instant cars so cheaply that a new one might be had for about $400. That was only the beginning. Mass production would create new technologies, until no engineering-to-production problems would remain.

Such things as unlimited energy requirements posed no problem, either. True, the laws of thermodynamics—which Campbell knew well—said that taking the energy out of the random distribution of energy in warm air was not possible. But even Maxwell postulated a demon who could control such a process. It seemed that all that was needed was greater knowledge to find other laws that led around the law that was a stumbling block—as radioactivity proved that the law of conservation of mass was not inevitably valid. The seeming impossibility of speeds greater than that of light was also known—Campbell was well aware of Special Relativity—but it was taken for granted then that some answer to this would be found. It is still so taken by modern writers.

Perhaps flaws can be found in the writing itself, when the stories are judged by the higher standards required today. The writing is simple, and the characters seem even simpler. Yet part of that was intentional, certainly. These characters are not intended to stand in the way of the wonders to be seen; they are almost used as myth types of great engineers, and the real characterization lay behind them, in the dreams of the readers of that day. Campbell himself later went on to show that such writing was not necessarily typical of him. In later stories (under the pseudonym of Don A. Stuart) he used a much different style and approach to writing in which he set a standard so high that few could achieve its equal for another generation. And as an editor, he did more to raise the level of writing and characterization in science fiction than any other man.

Grant then the faults. To me, they are not important. These are stories of a type which has been lost in later cynicism, but which we still need. They are adventures in wonder and destiny, where there was no limit to man's ability to achieve, no doubt as to which side was right. The dreams are still vital. And the more we despair now in many ways, the more we must be reminded of such dreams, and must learn again the thrills that are to be found in what may still be largely possible.

No man ever offered greater possibilities. No man ever carried destiny further for mankind than did John W. Campbell. No man ever told us that the limits of our ability were the limits of our imagination more eloquently. In all of science fiction, there is no greater reach of the imagination than in the great battle where Arcot can make and destroy universes with the power of his thoughts.

I loved these stories as a very young man. I love them still in my latest rereading of them. And I should have been a much poorer human being for the last forty years without them. There are only a few other pieces of any literature about which I can say that.

JOHN W. CAMPBELL ANTHOLOGY

THE BLACK STAR PASSES

INTRODUCTION

These stories were written nearly a quarter of a century ago, for the old *Amazing Stories* magazine. The essence of any magazine is not its name, but its philosophy, its purpose. That old *Amazing Stories* is long since gone; the magazine of the same name today is as different as the times today are different from the world of 1930.

Science-fiction was new, in 1930; atomic energy was a dream we believed in, and space-travel was something we tried to understand better. Today, science-fiction has become a broad field, atomic energy—despite the feelings of many present adults!—is no dream. (Nor is it a nightmare; it is simply a fact, and calling it a nightmare is another form of effort to push it out of reality.)

In 1930, the only audience for science-fiction was among those who were still young enough in spirit to be willing to hope and speculate on a new and wider future—and in 1930 that meant almost nothing but teen-agers. It meant the brightest group of teen-agers, youngsters who were willing to *play* with ideas and understandings of physics and chemistry and astronomy that most of their contemporaries considered "too hard work."

I grew up with that group; the stories I wrote over the years, and, later, the stories I bought for *Astounding Science Fiction* changed and grew more mature too. *Astounding Science Fiction* today has many of the audience that read those early stories; they're not high school and college students any more, of course, but professional engineers, technologists and researchers now. Naturally, for them we need a totally different kind of story. In growing with them, I and my work had to lose much of the enthusiastic scope that went with the earlier science fiction.

When a young man goes to college, he is apt to say, "I want to be a scientist," or "I want to be an engineer," but his concepts are broad and generalized. Most major technical schools, well knowing this, have the first year course for *all* students the same.

Only in the second and subsequent years does specialization start.

By the sophomore year, a student may say, "I want to be a *chemical* engineer."

At graduation, he may say, "I'm going into chemical engineering *construction*."

Ten years later he may explain that he's a chemical engineer specializing in the construction of corrosion-resistant structures, such as electroplating baths and pickling tanks for stainless steel.

Year by year, his knowledge has become more specialized, and much deeper. He's better and better able to do the important work the world needs done, but in learning to do it, he's necessarily lost some of the broad and enthusiastic scope he once had.

These are early stories of the early days of science-fiction. Radar hadn't been invented; we missed that idea. But while these stories don't have the finesse of later work—they have a bounding enthusiasm that belongs with a young field, designed for and built by young men. Most of the writers of those early stories were, like myself, college students. (*Piracy Preferred* was written while I was a sophomore at M.I.T.)

For old-timers in science-fiction—these are typical of the days when the field was starting. They've got a fine flavor of our own younger enthusiasm.

For new readers of science-fiction—these have the stuff that laid the groundwork of today's work, they're the stories that were meant for young imaginations, for people who wanted to think about the world they had to build in the years to come.

Along about sixteen to nineteen, a young man has to decide what is, for him, that Job That Needs Doing—and get ready to get in and pitch. If he selects well, selects with understanding and foresight, he'll pick a job that *does* need doing, one that will return rewards in satisfaction as well as money. No other man can pick that for him; he must choose the Job that *he* feels fitting.

Crystal balls can be bought fairly reasonably—but they don't work well. History books can be bought even more cheaply, and they're moderately reliable. (Though necessarily filtered through the cultural attitudes of the man who wrote them.) But they don't work well as predicting machines, because the world is changing too rapidly.

The world today, for instance, needs engineers desperately.

There are a lot of jobs that the Nation would like to get done that can't even be started; not enough engineers available.

Fifty years ago the engineering student was a sort of Second Class Citizen of the college campus. Today the Liberal Arts are fighting for a come-back, the pendulum having swung considerably too far in the other direction.

So science-fiction has a very real function to the teen-agers; it presents varying ideas of what the world in which he will live his adult life will be interested in.

This is 1953. My son will graduate in 1955. The period of his peak earning power should be when he's about forty to sixty— about 1970, say, to 1990. With the progress being made in understanding of health and physical vigor, it's apt to run beyond 2000 A.D., however.

Anyone want to bet that people will be living in the same general circumstances then? That the same general social and cultural and material standards will apply?

I have a hunch that the history books are a poor way of planning a life today—and that science-fiction comes a lot closer.

There's another thing about science-fiction yarns that is quite conspicuous; it's so difficult to pick out the villains. It might have made quite a change in history if the ballads and tales of the old days had been a little less sure of who the villains were. Read the standard boy's literature of forty years ago; tales of Crusaders who were always right, and Saracens who were always wrong. (The same Saracens who taught the Christians to respect the philosophy of the Greeks, and introduced them to the basic ideas of straight, self-disciplined thinking!)

Life's much simpler in a thatched cottage than in a dome on the airless Moon, easier to understand when the Villains are all pure black-hearted villains, and the Heroes are all pure White Souled Heroes. Just look how simple history is compared with science-fiction! It's simple—but is it good?

These early science-fiction tales explored the Universe; they were probings, speculations, as to where we *could* go. What we *could* do.

They had a sweep and reach and exuberance that belonged. They *were* fun, too. . . .

JOHN W. CAMPBELL, JR.
Mountainside, N.J.
April, 1953

BOOK ONE

PIRACY PREFERRED

Prologue

High in the deep blue of the afternoon sky rode a tiny speck of glistening metal, scarcely visible in the glare of the sun. The workers on the machines below glanced up for a moment, then back to their work, though little enough it was on these automatic cultivators. Even this minor diversion was of interest in the dull monotony of green. These endless fields of castor bean plants had to be cultivated, but with the great machines that did the work it required but a few dozen men to cultivate an entire county.

The passengers in the huge plane high above them gave little thought to what passed below, engrossed with their papers or books, or engaged in casual conversation. This monotonous trip was boring to most of them. It seemed a waste of time to spend six good hours in a short 3,500 mile trip. There was nothing to do, nothing to see, except a slowly passing landscape ten miles below. No details could be distinguished, and the steady low throb of the engines, the whirring of the giant propellers, the muffled roar of the air, as it rushed by, combined to form a soothing lullaby of power. It was all right for pleasure seekers and vacationists, but businessmen were in a hurry.

The pilot of the machine glanced briefly at the instruments, wondered vaguely why he had to be there at all, then turned, and leaving the pilot room in charge of his assistant, went down to talk with the chief engineer.

His vacation began the first of July, and as this was the last of June, he wondered what would have happened if he had done as he had been half inclined to do—quit the trip and let the assistant take her through. It would have been simple—just a few levers to manipulate, a few controls to set, and the instruments would have taken her up to ten or eleven miles, swung her into the great westward air current, and leveled her off at five hundred and sixty or so an hour toward 'Frisco.' They would hold her on the radio beam better than he ever could. Even the landing would have been easy. The assistant had never landed a big plane, but he knew the routine, and the instruments would have done the work. Even if he hadn't been there, ten minutes after they had reached destination, it would land automatically—if an emergency pilot didn't come up by that time in answer to an automatic signal.

He yawned and sauntered down the hall. He yawned again, wondering what made him so sleepy.

He slumped limply to the floor and lay there breathing ever more and more slowly.

The officials of the San Francisco terminus of The Transcontinental Airways company were worried. The great Transcontinental express had come to the field, following the radio beam, and now it was circling the field with its instruments set on the automatic signal for an emergency pilot. They were worried and with good reason, for this flight carried over 900,000 dollar's worth of negotiable securities. But what could attack one of those giant ships? It would take a small army to overcome the crew of seventy and the three thousand passengers!

The great ship was landing gently now, brought in by the emergency pilot. The small field car sped over to the plane rapidly. Already the elevator was in place beside it, and as the officials in the car drew up under the giant wing, they could see the tiny figure of the emergency pilot beckoning to them. Swiftly the portable elevator carried them up to the fourth level of the ship.

What a sight met their eyes as they entered the main salon! At first glance it appeared that all the passengers lay sleeping in their chairs. On closer examination it became evident that they were not breathing! The ear could detect no heartbeat. The members of the crew lay at their posts, as inert as the passengers! The assistant pilot sprawled on the floor beside the instrument panel—apparently he had been watching the record of the flight. There was no one conscious—or apparently living—on board!

"Dead! Over three thousand people!" The field manager's voice was hoarse, incredulous. "It's impossible—how could they have done it? Gas, maybe, drawn in through the ventilator pumps and circulated through the ship. But I can't conceive of any man being willing to kill three thousand people for a mere million! Did you call a doctor by radio, Pilot?"

"Yes, sir. He is on his way. There's his car now."

"Of course they will have opened the safe—but let's check anyway. I can only think some madman has done this—no sane man would be willing to take so many lives for so little." Wearily the men descended the stairs to the mail room in the hold.

The door was closed, but the lock of the door was gone, the magnesium-beryllium alloy burned away. They opened the door and entered. The room seemed in perfect order. The guard lay motionless in the steel guard chamber at one side; the thick, bullet-proof glass made his outlines a little blurred, and the color of his face was green—but they knew there too must be that same pallor they had seen on the other faces. The delicate instruments had brought in the great ship perfectly, but it was freighted with a cargo of dead!

They entered the room and proceeded to the safe, but it was opened as they had expected. The six-inch tungsto-iridium wall had been melted through. Even this unbelievable fact no longer surprised them. They only glanced at the metal, still too hot to touch, and looked about the room. The bonds had been taken. But now they noticed that over the mail-clerk's desk there had been fastened a small envelope. On it was printed:

To the Officials of the San Francisco Airport

Inside was a short message, printed in the same sharp, black letters:

Gentlemen:
     This plane should land safely. If it doesn't, it is your fault, not mine, for the instruments that it carries should permit it. The passengers are NOT dead! They have been

put in a temporary state of suspended animation. Any
doctor can readily revive them by the injection of seven
c.c. of decinormal potassium iodide solution for every 100
pounds of weight. Do NOT use higher concentrations.
Lower concentrations will act more slowly.

You will find that any tendency toward leprosy or cancer
will have been destroyed. It will kill any existing cancer,
and cure it in about one week. I have not experimented with
leprosy beyond knowing that it is cured very quickly.

This is an outside job. Don't annoy the passengers with
questions.

The gas used cannot be stopped by any material I know
of. You can try it with any mask—but don't use the C-32L.
It will react with the gas to kill. I would advise that you
try it on an animal to convince yourselves.

I have left stock in my new company to replace the bonds
I have taken.

Piracy Incorporated is incorporated under my own laws.

THE PIRATE

On the desk beneath the note was a small package which
contained a number of stock certificates. They totalled $900,000
face value of "Piracy Preferred", the preferred stock of a corpora-
tion, "Piracy, Inc."

"Piracy! Pirates in the air!" The field manager forced an
unnatural laugh. "In 2126 we have pirates attacking our air
lines. *Piracy Preferred!* I think I'd prefer the bonds myself.
But thank God he did not kill all those people. Doctor, you
look worried! Cheer up. If what this pirate says is true, we can
resuscitate them, and they'll be better off for the experience!"

The doctor shook his head. "I've been examining your
passengers. I'm afraid that you'll never be able to bring these
people back to life again, sir. I can't detect any heart action
even with the amplifier. Ordinary heart action sounds like a
cataract through this instrument. I can see nothing wrong with
the blood; it has not coagulated as I expected, nor is there
any pronounced hydrolysis as yet. But I'm afraid I'll have to
write out the death warrants for all these men and women.
One of the people on that ship was coming to see me. That's
how I happened to be on the field. For her, at least, it may

be better so. The poor woman was suffering from an incurable cancer."

"In this case, Doctor, I hope and believe you are wrong. Read this note!"

It was two hours before the work of reviving the passengers could be started. Despite all the laws of physics, their body temperature had remained constant after it had reached seventy-four, showing that some form of very slow metabolism was going on. One by one they were put into large electric blankets, and each was given the correct dose of the salt. The men waited anxiously for results—and within ten minutes of the injection the first had regained consciousness!

The work went forward steadily and successfully. Every one of the passengers and crew was revived. And the Pirate had spoken the truth. The woman who had been suffering from cancer was free from pain for the first time in many months. Later, careful examination proved she was cured!

The papers were issuing extras within five minutes of the time the great plane had landed, and the radio news service was broadcasting the first "break" in a particularly dead month. During all of June the news had been dead, and now July had begun with a bang!

With time to think and investigate, the airport officials went over the ship with the Air Guard, using a fine-tooth comb. It was soon evident that the job had been done from the outside, as the Pirate had said. The emergency pilot testified that when he entered the ship, he found a small piece of wire securing the air lock from the outside. This had certainly been put on while the ship was in flight, and that meant that whoever had done this, had landed on the great ship with a small plane, had somehow anchored it, then had entered the plane through the air lock at the ten mile height. He had probably flown across the path of the plane, leaving a trail of gas in its way to be drawn in through the ventilator pumps. It had been washed out by the incoming good air later, for the emergency pilot had not been affected.

Now the investigation led them to the mail-room. Despite the refractory nature of the metal, the door had been opened by melting or burning out the lock. And an opening had been burned into the safe itself! Opened by melting it through!

A bond shipment was due the next day, and the airline officials planned to be on the watch for it. It would get through safely, they were sure, for men were put on board in steel chambers hermetically welded behind them, with oxygen tanks and automatic apparatus sealed within to supply them with clean air. The front of the tanks were equipped with bullet-proof glass windows, and by means of electrically operated controls the men inside could fire machine guns. Thus they were protected from the Pirate's gas and able to use their weapons.

The ship was accompanied by a patrol of Air Guardsmen. Yet, despite this, cancer cases were aboard with the hope of being gassed.

When the plane reached the neighborhood of San Francisco, there had been no sign of an attack. The Pirate might well retire permanently on a million, if he were alone, as the singular signature indicated; but it seemed much more probable that he would attempt another attack in any case. Well, that just meant watching all the planes from now on, a tremendous job for the Air Guard to handle.

The leader of the patrol turned in an easy bank to descend the ten miles to earth, and his planes followed him. Then suddenly through the communicator came an unmistakable sound. *The plane automatically signaling for an emergency pilot!* That could only mean that the plane had been gassed under the very eyes of his men!

The bonds were gone and the passengers gassed, and incredibly, the men in the steel tanks were as thoroughly gassed as the rest.

The note was brief, and as much to the point as was the absence of the bonds.

To the Officials of the Airport:

Restore as usual. The men in the tanks are asleep also—I said the gas would penetrate *any* material. It does. A mask obviously won't do any good. Don't try that C-32L mask. I warn you it will be fatal. My gas reacts to produce a virulent poison when in contact with the chemicals in the C-32L.

THE PIRATE

I

On the thirty-ninth floor of a large New York apartment two young men were lounging about after a strenuous game of tennis. The blue tendrils of smoke from their pipes rose slowly, to be drawn away by the efficient ventilating system. The taller of the two seemed to be doing most of the talking. In the positions they had assumed it would have been rather difficult to be sure of which was the taller, but Robert Morey was a good four inches taller than Richard Arcot. Arcot had to suffer under the stigma of "runt" with Morey around—he was only six feet tall.

The chosen occupation of each was physical research, and in that field Arcot could well have called Morey "runt", for Arcot had only one competitor—his father. In this case it had been "like father, like son". For many years Robert Arcot had been known as the greatest American physicist, and probably the world's greatest. More recently he had been known as the father of the world's greatest physicist. Arcot junior was probably one of the most brilliant men the world had ever seen, and he was aided in all his work by two men who could help him in a way that amplified his powers a thousand fold. His father and his best friend, Morey, were the complimentary and balancing minds to his great intelligence. His father had learned through years of work the easiest and best ways of performing the many difficult feats of laboratory experimentation. Morey could develop the mathematical theory of a hypothesis far more readily than Arcot could. Morey's mind was more methodical and exact than Arcot's, but Arcot could grasp the broad details of a problem and get the general method of solution developed with a speed that made it utterly impossible for his friend even to follow the steps he suggested.

Since Arcot junior's invention of the multiple calculus, many new ramifications of old theories had been attained, and many developments had become possible.

But the factor that made Arcot so amazingly successful in his line of work was his ability to see practical uses for things, an ability that is unfortunately lacking in so many great physicists. Had he collected the royalties his inventions merited, he would have been a billionaire twice or thrice over. Instead he had made contracts on the basis that the laboratories he owned be kept in condition, and that he be paid a salary that should be whatever he happened to need. Since he had sold all his inventions to Transcontinental Airways, he had been able to devote all his time to science, leaving them to manage his finances. Perhaps it was the fact that he did sell these inventions to Transcontinental that made these lines so successful; but at any rate, President Arthur Morey was duly grateful, and when his son was able to enter the laboratories he was as delighted as Arcot.

The two had become boon companions. They worked, played, lived, and thought together.

Just now they were talking about the Pirate. This was the seventh day of his discovery, and he had been growing steadily more menacing. It was the great Transcontinental Airways that had suffered most repeatedly. Sometimes it was the San Francisco Flyer that went on without a pilot, sometimes the New York-St. Louis expresses that would come over the field broadcasting the emergency signal. But always the people were revived with little difficulty, and each time more of the stock of "Piracy, Inc." was accumulated. The Air Guard seemed helpless. Time and time again the Pirate slipped in undetected. Each time he convinced them that it was an outside job, for the door was always sealed from the outside.

"Dick, how do you suppose he gets away with the things he does right under the eyes of those Air Guardsmen? He must have some system; he does it every time."

"I have a vague idea," Arcot answered. "I was going to ask you today, if your father would let us take passage on the next liner carrying any money. I understand the insurance rates have been boosted so high that they don't dare to send any cash by air any more. They've resorted to the slow land routes. Is there any money shipment in sight?"

Morey shook his head. "No, but I have something that's just as good, if not better, for our purpose. The other day several men came into Dad's office, to charter a plane to San Francisco, and Dad naturally wondered why they had been referred to the president of the company. It seems the difficulty was that they wanted to hire the ship so they could be robbed! A large group of medical men and cancer victims were going for the 'treatment'. Each one of the twenty-five hundred going was to bring along one hundred dollars. That meant a total of a quarter of a million dollars, which is to be left on the table. They hoped the Pirate would gas them and thus cure them! Dad couldn't officially do this, but told them that if there were too many people for the San Francisco express, two sections would be necessary. I believe they are going on that second section. Only one hundred dollars! A low price for cancer cure!

"Another thing: Dad asked me to tell you that he'd appreciate your help in stopping this ultra-modern pirate. If you go down to see him in the morning, you'll doubtless be able to make the necessary arrangements."

"I'll do so gladly. I wonder, though, if you know more about this than I do. Did they try that C-32L mask on an animal?"

"The Pirate was telling the truth. They tried it on a dog and he went to sleep forever. But do you have any idea how that gas does all it does?"

Now Arcot shook his head. "I don't know what the gas is, but have a lead on how it works. You may know that carbon monoxide will seep through a solid plate of red-hot steel. That has been known for some three hundred years now, and I have to hand it to this Pirate for making use of it. Even in the war of 2075 they didn't find any practical application for the principal. He has just found some gas that induces sleep in very low concentrations, and at the same time is able to penetrate to an even greater extent than carbon monoxide."

"I was wondering how he stores that stuff," Morey commented. "But I suppose he makes it as fast as he uses it, by allowing two or more constituents to react. It might well be simple enough to store them separately, and the airstream blowing past him would carry the gas behind him, permitting him to lay a stream of it in front of the big plane. Is that about it?"

"That was about what I had figured. One of the things I want to do when I go with that Invalid Special tomorrow is to get some samples for analysis."

"That's a pretty big order, isn't it, Dick? How are you going to handle it, or even get it into your apparatus?"

"Easily enough as far as getting the sample goes. I have already had some sample bottles made. I have one of them in the lab—excuse me a moment." Arcot left the room, to return a few minutes later with a large aluminum bottle, tightly closed. "This bottle has been pumped out to a very good vacuum. I then swept it out with helium gas. Then it was pumped out again. I hope to take this into some gas-filled region, where the gas will be able to leak in, but the air won't. When it comes to going out again, the gas will have to fight air pressure, and will probably stay in."

"Hope it works. It would help if we knew what we were bucking."

The next morning Arcot had a long conference with President Morey. At the end of it, he left the office, ascended to the roof, and climbed into his small helicopter. He rose to the local traffic level, and waiting his chance, broke into the stream of planes bound for the great airfields over in the Jersey district. A few minutes later he landed on the roof of the Transcontinental Airways shops, entered them, and went to the office of the Designing Engineer, John Fuller, an old schoolmate. They had been able to help each other before, for Fuller had not paid as much attention to theoretical physics as he might have, and though he was probably one of the outstanding aeronautical designers, he often consulted Arcot on the few theoretical details that he needed. Probably it was Arcot who derived the greatest benefit from this association, for the ability of the designer had many times brought his theoretical successes to practical commercial production. Now, however, he was consulting Fuller, because the plane he was to take that afternoon for San Francisco was to be slightly changed for him.

He stayed in Fuller's office for the better part of an hour, then returned to the roof and thence to his own roof, where Morey junior was waiting for him.

"Hello, Dick! I heard from Dad that you were going this afternoon, and came over here. I got your note and I have the things fixed up here. The plane leaves at one, and it's ten-thirty now. Let's eat lunch and then start."

It was half-past eleven when they reached the flying field. They went directly to the private office which had been assigned to them aboard the huge plane. It was right next to the mailroom, and through the wall between the two a small hole had been cut. Directly beneath this hole was a table, on which the two men now set up a small moving picture camera they had brought with them.

"How many of the gas sample bottles did you bring, Bob?" asked Arcot.

"Jackson had only four ready, so I brought those. I think that will be enough. Have we got that camera properly placed?"

"Everything's O.K., I believe. Nothing to do now but wait."

Time passed—then they heard a faint whir; the ventilator machinery had started. This drew air in from outside, and pumped it up to the necessary pressure for breathing in the ship, no matter what the external pressure might be. There was a larger pump attached similarly to each of the engines to supply it with the necessary oxygen. Any loss in power by pumping the air in was made up by the lower back pressure on the exhaust. Now the engines were starting—they could feel the momentary vibration—vibration that would cease as they got under way. They could visualize the airtight door being closed; the portable elevator backing off, returning to the field house.

Arcot glanced at his watch. "One o'clock. The starting signal is due."

Morey sank back into a comfortable chair. "Well, now we have a nice long wait till we get to San Francisco and back, Dick, but you'll have something to talk about then!"

"I hope so, Bob, and I hope we can return on the midnight plane from San Francisco, which will get us in at nine o'clock tomorrow morning, New York time. I wish you'd go right to your father's office and ask him over to our place for supper, and see if Fuller can come too. I think we'll be able to use that molecular controller on this job; it's almost finished, and with it we'll need a good designing engineer. Then our little movie show will no doubt be of interest!"

There was a low rumble that quickly mounted to a staccato roar as the great propellers began whirling and the engines took up the load. The ground began to flash behind them; then suddenly, as flying speed was reached, there was a slight start, the roaring bark of the engine took on a deeper tone, the rocking stopped and the ground dropped away. Like some mighty wild bird, the plane was in the air, a graceful, sentient thing, wheeling in a great circle as it headed for San Francisco. Now the plane climbed steadily in a long bank; up, up, up she went, and gradually the terrific roar of the engine died to a low throbbing hum as the low pressure of the air silenced the noise.

Below them the giant city contracted as the great ship rode higher. The tiny private helicops were darting about below them like streams of nigh invisible individuals, creeping black lines among the buildings of the city. The towering buildings shone in the noon sun in riotous hues as the colored tile facing reflected the brilliant sunlight with glowing warmth of color.

It was a city of indescribable beauty now. It was one of the things that made this trip worthwhile.

Now the shining city dropped behind them, and only the soft green of the Jersey hills, and the deep purple-black of the sky above were visible. The sun blazed high in the nigh-black heavens, and in the rarefied air, there was so little diffusion that the corona was readily visible with the aid of a smoked glass. Around the sun, long banners in space, the Zodiacal light gleamed dimly. Here and there some of the brighter stars winked in the dark sky.

Below them the landscape swung slowly by. Even to these men who had made the trip dozens of times, the sight was fascinating, inspiring. It was a spectacle which had never been visible before the development of these super-planes. Whole flying observatories had been made that had taken photographs at heights of fifteen miles, where the air was so rarefied that the plane had to travel close to eight hundred miles an hour to remain aloft.

Already ahead of them Arcot and Morey could see the great splotch of color that was Chicago, the mightiest city on Earth. Situated as it was in the heart of the North American continent, with great water and ground landing facilities and broad plains about it, it made a perfect airport. The sea no longer meant much, for it was now only a source of power, recreation and food. Ships were no longer needed. Planes were faster and more economical; hence seacoast cities had declined in importance. With its already great start toward ascendancy, Chicago had rapidly forged ahead, as the air lines developed with the great super-planes. The European planes docked here, and it was the starting point of the South American lines. But now, as they swung high above it, the glistening walls of soft-colored tiles made it a great mass of changing, flashing color beneath them. Now they could see a great air liner, twice the size of their plane, taking off for Japan, its six giant propellers visible only as flashing blurs as it climbed up toward them. Then it was out of sight.

It was over the green plains of Nebraska that the Pirate usually worked, so there the men became more and more alert, waiting for the first sign of abnormal drowsiness. They sat quietly, not talking, listening intently for some new note, but knowing all the while that any sound the Pirate might make would be concealed by the whirring roar of the air sweeping past the giant airfoils of the plane.

Suddenly Arcot realized he was unbearably sleepy. He glanced drowsily toward Morey who was already lying down. He found it a tremendous effort of the will to make himself reach up and close the switch that started the little camera whirring almost noiselessly. It seemed he never pulled his arm back—he just—lay there—and—

A white uniformed man was bending over him as he opened his eyes. To one side of him he saw Morey smiling down at him.

"You're a fine guard, Arcot. I thought you were going to stay awake and watch them!"

"Oh, no, I left a much more efficient watchman! *It* didn't go to sleep—I'm willing to bet!"

"No, it may not have gone to sleep, but the doctor here tells me it has gone somewhere else. It wasn't found in our room when we woke up. I think the Pirate found it and confiscated it. All our luggage, including the gas sample bottles, is gone."

"That's all right. I arranged for that. The ship was brought down by an emergency pilot and he had instructions from father. He took care of the luggage so that no member of the pirate's gang could steal it. There might have been some of them in the ground crew. They'll be turned over to us as soon as we see the emergency man. I don't have to lie here any longer, do I, doctor?"

"No, Dr. Arcot, you're all right now. I would suggest that for the next hour or so you take it easy to let your heart get used to beating again. It stopped for some two hours, you know. You'll be all right, however."

II

Five men were seated about the Morey library, discussing the results of the last raid, in particular as related to Arcot and Morey. Fuller, and President Morey, as well as Dr. Arcot, senior, and the two young men themselves, were there. They had consistently refused to tell what their trip had revealed, saying that pictures would speak for them. Now they turned their attention to a motion picture projector and screen that Arcot junior had just set up. At his direction the room was darkened; and he started the projector. At once they were looking at the three dimensional image of the mail-room aboard the air liner.

Arcot commented: "I have cut out a lot of useless film, and confined the picture to essentials. We will now watch the pirate at work."

Even as he spoke they saw the door of the mail-room open a bit, and then, to their intense surprise, it remained open for a few seconds, then closed. It went through all the motions of opening to admit someone, yet no one entered!

"Your demonstration doesn't seem to show much yet, son. In fact, it shows much less than I had expected," said the senior Arcot. "But that door seemed to open easily. I thought they locked them!"

"They did, but the pirate just burned holes in them, so to save property they leave 'em unlocked."

Now the scene seemed to swing a bit as the plane hit an unusually bad air bump, and through the window they caught a glimpse of one of the circling Air Guardsmen. Then suddenly there appeared in the air within the room a point of flame. It hung in the air above the safe for an instant, described a strangely complicated set of curves; then, as it hung for an instant in mid-air, it became a great flare. In an instant this condensed to a point of intensely brilliant crimson fire. This described a complex series of curves and touched the top of the safe. In an inconceivably short time, the eight-inch thickness of tungsto-iridium alloy flared incandescently and began to flow sluggishly. A large circle of the red flame sprang out to surround the point of brilliance, and this blew the molten metal to one side, in a cascade of sparks.

In moments, the torch had cut a large disc of metal nearly free; seemingly on the verge of dropping into the safe. Now the flame left the safe, again retracting itself in that uncanny manner, no force seeming either to supply it with fuel or to support it thus, though it burned steadily, and worked rapidly and efficiently. Now, in mid-air, it hung for a second.

"I'm going to work the projector for a few moments by hand so that you may see this next bit of film." Arcot moved a small switch and the machine blinked, giving a strange appearance to the seemingly solid images that were thrown on the screen.

The pictures seemed to show the flame slowly descending till it again touched the metal. The tungsto-iridium glowed briefly; then, as suddenly as the extinguishing of a light, the safe was gone! It had disappeared into thin air! Only the incandescence of the metal and the flame itself were visible.

"It seems the pirate has solved the secret of invisibility. No wonder the Air Guardsmen couldn't find him!" exclaimed Arcot, senior.

The projector had been stopped exactly on the first frame, showing the invisibility of the safe. Then Arcot backed it up.

"True, Dad," he said, "but pay special attention to this next frame."

Again there appeared a picture of the room, the window beyond, the mail clerk asleep at his desk, everything as before, except that where the safe had been, *there was a shadowy, half visible safe,* the metal glowing brightly. Beside it there was visible a shadowy man, holding the safe with a shadowy bar of some sort. And through both of them the frame of the window was perfectly visible, and, ironically, an Air Guardsman plane.

"It seems that for an instant his invisibility failed here. Probably it was the contact with the safe that caused it. What do you think, Dad?" asked Arcot, junior.

"It does seem reasonable. I can't see off-hand how his invisibility is even theoretically possible. Have you any ideas?"

"Well, Dad, I have, but I want to wait till tomorrow night to demonstrate them. Let's adjourn this meeting, if you can all come tomorrow."

The next evening, however, it seemed that it was Arcot himself who could not be there. He asked Morey, junior, to tell them he would be there later, when he had finished in the lab.

Dinner was over now, and the men were waiting rather impatiently for Arcot to come. They heard some noise in the corridor, and looked up, but no one entered.

"Morey," asked Fuller, "what did you learn about that gas the pirate was using? I remember Arcot said he would have some samples to analyze."

"As to the gas, Dick found out but little more than we had already known. It is a typical organic compound, one of the metal radical type, and contains one atom of thorium. This is a bit radioactive, as you know, and Dick thinks that this may account in part for its ability to suspend animation. However, since it was impossible to determine the molecular weight, he could not say what the gas was, save that the empirical formula was $C_{62}TH H_{39}O_{27}N_5$. It broke down at a temperature of only 89° centigrade. The gases left consisted largely of methane, nitrogen, and methyl ether. Dick is still in the dark as to what the gas is." He paused, then exclaimed: "Look over there!"

The men turned with one accord toward the opposite end of the room, looked, and seeing nothing particularly unusual, glanced back rather puzzled. What they then saw, or better, failed to see, puzzled them still more. Morey had disappeared!

"Why—why where—ohhh! Quick work, Dick!" The senior Arcot began laughing heartily, and as his astonished and curious companions looked toward him, he stopped and called out, "Come on, Dick! We want to see you now. And tell us how it's done! I rather think Mr. Morey here—I mean the visible one—is still a bit puzzled."

There was a short laugh from the air—certainly there could be nothing else there—then a low but distinct click, and both Morey and Arcot were miraculously present, coming instantaneously from nowhere, if one's senses could be relied on. On Arcot's back there was strapped a large and rather hastily wired mechanism—one long wire extending from it out into the laboratory. He was carrying a second piece of apparatus, similarly wired. Morey was touching a short metal bar that Arcot held extended in his hand, using a table knife as a connector, lest they get radio frequency burns on making contact.

"I've been busy getting the last connection of this portable apparatus rigged up. I have the thing in working order, as you see—or rather, didn't see. This other outfit here is the thing that is more important to us. It's a bit heavy, so if you'll clear a space, I'll set it down. Look out for my power supply there—that wire is carrying a rather dangerously high E.M.F. I had to connect with the lab power supply to do this, and I had no time to rig up a little mechanism like the one the pirate must have.

"I have duplicated his experiment. He has simply made use of a principle known for some time, but as there was no need for it, it hasn't been used. It was found back in the early days of radio, as early as the first quarter of the twentieth century, that very short wavelengths effected peculiar changes in metals. It was shown that the plates of tubes working on very short waves became nearly transparent. The waves were so short, however, that they were economically useless. They would not travel in usable paths, so they were never developed. Furthermore, existing apparatus could not be made to handle them. In the last war they tried to apply the idea for making airplanes invisible, but they could not get their tubes to handle the power needed, so they had to drop it. However, with the tube I recently got out on the market, it is possible to get down there. Our friend the pirate has developed this thing to a point where he could use it. You can see that invisibility, while interesting, and a good thing for a stage and television entertainment, is not very much of a commercial need. No one wants to be invisible in any honest occupation. Invisibility is a tremendous weapon in war, so the pirate just started a little private war, the only way he could make any money on his invention. His gas, too, made the thing attractive. The two together made a perfect combination for criminal operations.

"The whole thing looks to me to be the work of a slightly unbalanced mind. He is not violently insane; probably just has this one particular obsession. His scientific bump certainly shows no sign of weakness. He might even be some new type of kleptomaniac. He steals things, and he has already stolen far more than any man could ever have any need of, and he leaves in its place a 'stock' certificate in his own company. He is not violent, for hasn't he carefully warned the men not to use the C-32L mask? You'll remember his careful instructions as to how to revive the people!

"He has developed this machine for invisibility, and naturally he can fly in and out of the air guard, without their knowing he's there, provided their microphonic detectors don't locate him. I believe he uses some form of glider. He can't use an internal combustion engine, for the explosions in the cylinders would be as visible as though the cylinders were made of clear quartz. He cannot have an electric motor, for the storage cells would weigh too much. Furthermore, if he were using any sort of prop, or a jet engine, the noise would give him away. If he used a glider, the noise of the big plane so near would be more than enough to kill the slight sounds. The glider could hang above the ship, then dive down upon it as it passed beneath. He has a very simple system of anchoring the thing, as I discovered to my sorrow. It's a powerful electro-magnet which he turns on when he lands. The landing deck of the big plane was right above our office aboard, and I found my watch was doing all sorts of antics today. It lost an hour this morning, and this afternoon it gained two. I found it was very highly magnetized—I could pick up needles with the balance wheel. I demagnetized it; now it runs all right.

"But to get back, he anchors his ship, then, leaving it invisible, he goes to the air lock, and enters. He wears a high altitude suit, and on his back he has a portable invisibility set and the fuel for his torch. The gas has already put everyone to sleep, so he goes into the ship, still invisible, and melts open the safe.

"His power supply for the invisibility machine seems to be somewhat of a problem, but I think I would use a cylinder of liquid air, and have a small air turbine to run a high voltage generator. He probably uses the same system on a larger scale to run his big machine on the ship. He can't use an engine for that either.

"That torch of his is interesting, too. We have had atomic hydrogen welding for some time, and atomic hydrogen releases some 100,000 calories per mole of molecular hydrogen; two grains of gas give one hundred thousand calories. Oxygen has not been prepared in any commercial quantity in the atomic state. From watching that man's torch, from the color of the flame and other indications, I gather that he uses a flame of atomic oxygen-atomic hydrogen for melting, and surrounds it with a preheating jacket of atomic hydrogen. The center flame probably develops a temperature of some 4000° centigrade, and will naturally make that tungsten alloy run like water.

"As to the machine here—it is, as I said, a machine which impresses very high frequencies on the body it is connected with. This puts the molecules in vibration at a frequency approaching that of light, and when the light impinges upon it, it can pass through readily. You know that metals transmit light for short distances, but in order that the light pass, the molecules of metal must be set in harmonic vibration at a rate approaching the frequency of light. If we can impress such a vibration on a piece of matter, it will then transmit light very freely. If we impress this vibration on the matter, say the body, electrically, we get the same effect and the body becomes perfectly transparent. Now, since it is the vibration of the molecules that makes the light pass through the material, it must be stopped if we wish to see the machine. Obviously it is much easier to detect me here among solid surroundings, than in the plane high in the sky. What chance has one to detect a machine that is perfectly transparent when there is nothing but perfectly transparent air around it? It is a curious property of this vibrational system of invisibility that the index of refraction is made very low. It is not the same as that of air, but the difference is so slight that it is practically within the limits of observation error; so small is the difference that there is no 'rainbow' effect. The difference of temperature of the air would give equal effect.

"Now, since this vibration is induced by radio impulse, is it not possible to impress another, opposing radio impulse, that will overcome this tendency and bring the invisible object into the field of the visible once more? It is; and this machine on the table is designed to do exactly that. It is practically a beam radio set, projecting a beam of a wavelength that alone would tend to produce invisibility. But in this case it will make me visible. I'm going to stand right here, and Bob can operate that set."

Arcot strode to the middle of the room, and then Morey turned the reflector of the beam set on him. There was a low snap as Arcot turned on his set, then he was gone, as suddenly as the coming of darkness when a lamp is extinguished. He was there one moment, then they were staring at the chair behind him, knowing that the man was standing between them and it and knowing that they were looking through his body. It gave them a strange feeling, an uncomfortable tingling along the spine. Then the voice—it seemed to come from the air, or some disembodied ghost as the invisible man called to Morey.

"All right, Bob, turn her on slowly."

There was another snap as the switch of the disrupter beam was turned on. At once there was a noticeable fogginess in the air where Arcot had been. As more and more power was turned into the machine, they saw the man materialize out of thin air. First he was a mere shadowy outline that was never fully above the level of conscious vision. Then slowly the outlines of the objects behind became dimmer and dimmer, as the body of the man was slowly darkened, till at last there was only a wavering aura about him. With a snap Morey shut off his machine and Arcot was gone again. A second snap and he was solid before them. He had shut off his apparatus too.

"You can see now how we intend to locate our invisible pirate. Of course we will depend on directional radio disturbance locating devices to determine the direction for the invisibility disrupter ray. But you are probably marvelling at the greatness of the genius who can design and construct this apparatus all in one day. I will explain the miracle. I have been working on short wave phenomena for some time. In fact, I had actually made an invisibility machine, as Morey will testify, but I realized that it had no commercial benefits, so I didn't experiment with it beyond the laboratory stunt stage. I published some of the theory in the Journal of the International Physical Society—and I wouldn't be surprised to learn that the pirate based his discovery on my report.

"I am still working on a somewhat different piece of apparatus that I believe we will find very relevant to this business. I'll ask you to adjourn after tonight's meeting for another twenty-four hours till I can finish the apparatus I am working on. It is very important that you be here, Fuller. I am going to need you in the work to follow. It will be another problem of design if this works out, as I hope it will."

"I'll certainly make every effort to be here, Arcot," Fuller assured him.

"I can promise you a tough problem as well as an interesting one." Arcot smiled. "If the thing works, as I expect it to, you'll have a job that will certainly be a feather for your cap. Also it will be a change."

"Well, with that inducement, I'll certainly be here. But I think that pirate could give us some hints on design. How does he get his glider ten miles up? They've done some high-altitude gliding already. The distance record took someone across the Atlantic in 2009, didn't it? But it seems that ten miles straight up is a bit too steep for a glider. There are no vertical air currents at that height."

"I meant to say that his machine is not a true glider, but a semi-glider. He probably goes up ten miles or more with the aid of a small engine, one so small it probably takes him half a day to get there. And it would be easy for a plane to pass through the lower traffic lanes, then, being invisible, mount high and wait for the air liner. He can't use a very large engine, for it would drag him down, but one of the new hundred horsepower jobs would weigh only about fifty pounds. I think we can draw a pretty good picture of his plane from scientific logic. It probably has a tremendous wingspread and a very high angle of incidence to make it possible to glide at that height, and the engine and prop will be almost laughably small."

The next evening the men got together for dinner, and there was considerable speculation as to the nature of the discovery that Arcot was going to announce, for even his father had no knowledge of what it was. The two men worked in separate laboratories, except when either had a particularly difficult problem that might be solved by the other. All knew that the new development lay in the field of short wave research, but they could not find out in what way it concerned the problem in hand.

At last the meal was over, and Arcot was ready to demonstrate.

"Dad, I believe that you have been trying to develop a successful solar engine. One that could be placed in the wings of a plane to generate power from the light falling on that surface. In all solar engines what is the greatest problem to be solved?"

"Well, the more I investigate the thing, the more I wonder which is the greatest. There are a surprising number of annoying problems to be met. I should say, though, that the one big trouble with all solar engines, eliminating the obvious restriction that they decidedly aren't dependable for night work, is the difficulty of getting an area to absorb the energy. If I could get enough area, I could use a very low efficiency and still have cheap power, for the power is absolutely free. The area problem is the greatest difficulty, no doubt."

"Well," Arcot junior said quietly, "I think you have a fairly good area to use, if you can only harness the energy it absorbs. I have really developed a very efficient solar engine. The engine itself requires no absorbing area, as I want to use it; it takes advantage of the fact that the earth is absorbing quintillions of horse-power. I have merely tapped the power that the earth has already absorbed for me. Come here."

He led the way down the corridor to his laboratory, and switched on the lights. On the main laboratory bench was set up a complicated apparatus of many tubes and heavy bus bar connectors. From the final tube two thin wires ran to a long tubular coil. To the left of this coil was a large relay switch, and a rheostat control.

"Turn on the relay, Dad, then slowly rotate the controller to the left. And remember that it is rather powerful. I know this doesn't look like a solar engine, and nine o'clock at night seems a peculiar hour to demonstrate such a thing, but I'll guarantee results—probably more than you expect."

Dr. Arcot stepped up to the controls and closed the switch. The lights dimmed a bit, but immediately brightened again, and from the other end of the room came a low, steady hum as the big transformer took up the load.

"Well, from the sound of that ten K.W. transformer there, if this engine is very efficient we ought to get a terrific amount of power out of it." Dr. Arcot was smiling amusedly at his son. "I can't very well control this except by standing directly in front of it, but I suppose you know what you're doing."

"Oh, this is a laboratory model, and I haven't gotten the thing into shape really. Look at the conductors that lead to the coil; they certainly aren't carrying ten K.W."

Dr. Arcot slowly rotated the rheostat. There was a faint hum from the coil; then it was gone. There seemed to be no other result. He rotated it a bit more; a slight draught sprang up within the room. He waited, but when nothing more startling occurred, he gave the rheostate a sharp turn. This time there was absolutely no doubt as to the result. There was a roar like a fifty-foot wind tunnel, and a mighty blast of cold air swept out of that coil like a six-inch model of a Kansas cyclone. Every loose piece of paper in the laboratory came suddenly alive and whirled madly before the blast of air that had suddenly leaped out. Dr. Arcot was forced back as by a giant hand; in his backward motion his hand was lifted from the relay switch, and with a thud the circuit opened. In an instant the roar of sound was cut off, and only a soft whisper of air told of the furious blast that had been there a moment before.

The astonished physicist came forward and looked at the device a moment in silence, while each of the other men watched him. Finally he turned to his son, who was smiling at him with a twinkle in his eye.

"Dick, I think you have 'loaded the dice' in a way that is even more lucrative than any other method ever invented! If the principle of this machine is what I think it is, you have certainly solved the secret of a sufficiently absorbing area for a solar engine."

"Well," remarked the elderly Morey, shivering a bit in the chill air of the room, "loaded dice have long been noted for their ability to make money, but I don't see how that explains that working model of an Arctic tornado. Burr—it's still too cold in here. I think he'll need considerable area for heat absorption from the sun, for that engine certainly does cool things down! What's the secret?"

"The principle is easy enough, but I had considerable difficulty with the application. I think it is going to be rather important though—"

"Rather important," broke in the inventor's father, with a rare display of excitement. "It will be considerably more than that. It's the biggest thing since the electric dynamo! It puts airplanes in the junk heap! It means a new era in power generation. Why, we'll never have to worry about power! It will make interplanetary travel not only possible, but commercially economical."

Arcot junior grinned broadly. "Dad seems to think the machine has possibilities! Seriously, I believe it will antiquate all types of airplanes, prop or jet. It's a direct utilization of the energy that the sun is kindly supplying. For a good many years now men have been trying to find out how to control the energy of atoms for air travel, or to release the energy of the constitution of matter.

"But why do it at all? The sun is doing it already, and on a scale so gargantuan that we could never hope nor desire to approach it. Three million tons of matter go into that colossal furnace every second of time, and out of that comes two and a half decillion ergs of energy. With a total of two and a half million billion billion billions of ergs to draw on, man will have nothing to worry about for a good many years to come! That represents a flood of power vaster than man could comprehend. Why try to release any more energy? We have more than we can use; we may as well tap that vast ocean of power.

"There is one thing that prevents us getting it out, the law of probability. That's why Dad mentioned loaded dice, for dice, as you know, are the classical example of probability when they aren't loaded. Once they are loaded, the law still holds, but the conditions are now so changed that it will make the problem quite different."

Arcot paused, frowning, then resumed half apologetically, "Excuse the lecture—but I don't know how else to get the thought across. You are familiar with the conditions in a liter of helium gas in a container—a tremendous number of molecules, each dashing along at several miles a second, and an equal number dashing in the opposite direction at an equal speed. They are so thickly packed in there, that none of them can go very far before it runs into another molecule and bounces off in a new direction. How good is the chance that all the molecules should happen to move in the same direction at the same time? One of the old physicists of Einstein's time, a man named Eddington, expressed it very well:

'If an army of monkeys were playing on typewriters they might write all the books in the British Museum. The chance of their doing so is decidedly more favorable than the chance that all the molecules in a liter of gas should move in the same direction at the same time.'

The very improbability of this chance is the thing that is making our problem appear impossible.

"But similarly it would be improbable—impossible according to the law of chance—to throw a string of aces indefinitely. It is impossible—unless some other force influences the happening. If the dice have bits of iridium stuck under the six spots, they will

throw aces. Chance makes it impossible to have all the molecules of gas move in the same direction at the same time—unless
we stack the chances. If we can find some way to influence
them, they may do so.

"What would happen to a metal bar if all the molecules in it
decided to move in the same direction at the same time? Their
heat motion is normally carrying them about at a rate of several
miles a second, and if now we have them all go in one way, the
entire bar must move in that direction, and it will start off at a
velocity as great as the velocity of the individual molecules.
But now, if we attach the bar to a heavy car, it will try to start
off, but will be forced to drag the car with it, and so will not be
able to have its molecules moving at the same rate. They will be
slowed down in starting the mass of the car. But slowly moving
molecules have a definite physical significance. Molecules move
because of temperature, and lack of motion means lack of heat.
These molecules that have been slowed down are then cold;
they will absorb heat from the air about them, and since the
molecule of hydrogen gas at room temperature is moving at
about seven miles a second, when the molecules of the confined
gas in our car, or the molecules of the metal bar are slowed
down to but a few hundred miles an hour, their temperature
drops to some hundreds of degrees below zero, and they absorb
energy very rapidly, for the greater the difference in temperature, the greater the rate of heat absorption.

"I believe we will be able to accelerate the car rapidly to a
speed of several miles a second at very high altitudes, and as we
will be able to use a perfectly enclosed streamlined car, we
should get tremendous speeds. We'll need no wings, of course,
for with a small unit pointed vertically, we'll be able to support
the car in the air. It will make possible a machine that will
be able to fly in reverse and so come to a quick stop. It will
steer us or it will supply us with electrical power, for we
merely have to put a series of small metal bars about the cir-
cumference of the generator, and get a tremendously powerful
engine.

"For our present need, it means a tremendously powerful
engine—and one that we can make invisible.

"I believe you can guess the source of that breeze we had
there? It would make a wonderful air-conditioning unit."

"Dick Arcot," began Morey, his voice tight with suppressed excitement, "I would like to be able to use this invention. I know enough of the economics of the thing, if not its science, to know that the apparatus before us is absolutely invaluable. I couldn't afford to buy the rights on it, but I want to use it if you'll let me. It means a new era in transcontinental air travel!"

He turned sharply to Fuller. "Fuller, I want you to help Arcot with the ship to chase the Pirate. You'll get the contract to design the new airliners. Hang the cost. It'll run into billions—but there will be no more fuel bills, no oil bills, and the cost of operation will be negligible. Nothing but the Arcot short waves tubes to buy—and each one good for twenty-five thousand hours service!"

"You'll get the rights on this if you want them, of course," said Arcot quietly. "You're maintaining these laboratories for me, and your son helped me work it out. But if Fuller can move over here tomorrow, it will help things a lot. Also I'd like to have some of your best mechanics to make the necessary machines, and to start the power units."

"It's done," Morey snapped.

III

Early the next morning Fuller moved his equipment over to the laboratory and set up his table for work. There Arcot and Morey joined him, and the designing of the new machine was started.

"First, let's get some idea of the most advisable shape," Fuller began methodically. "We'll want it streamlined, of course; roughly speaking, a cylinder modified to fit the special uses to which it will be put. But you probably have a general plan in mind, Arcot. Suppose you sketch it for us."

The big physicist frowned thoughtfully. "Well, we don't know much about this yet, so we'll have to work it out. You'll have plenty of fun figuring out strains in this machine, so let's be safe and use a factor of safety of five. Let's see what we'll need.

"In the first place, our machine must be proof against the Pirate's gas, for we won't be riding a beam with instruments to guide us safely, if we pass out. I've thought that over, and I think that the best system is just what we used in the sample bottles— a vacuum. His gas is stopped by nothing, so to speak, but there is no substance that will stop it! It will no doubt penetrate the outer shell, but on reaching the vacuum, it will tend to stay there, between the inner and outer walls. Here it will collect, since it will be fighting air pressure in going either in or out. The pressure inside will force it back, and the pressure outside will force it in. If we did not pump it out, it would soon build up pressure enough to penetrate the interior wall. Now, since the stuff can leak through any material, what kind of a pump shall we use? It won't be pushed by a piston, for it will leak through either the cylinder walls or the piston. A centrifugal pump would be equally ineffective. A mercury vapor pump will take it out, of course, and keep a high vacuum, but we'd never make any progress.

"Our new machine gives us the answer. With it we can just have a number of openings in the wall of the outer shell, and set in them one of these molecular motion directors, and direct the molecules into the outside air. They can't come in through it, and they will go out!"

"But," Morey objected, "the vacuum that keeps out the gas will also keep out heat, as well! Since our generator is to run on heat energy, it will be rather chilly inside if we don't remedy that. Of course, our power units could be placed outside, where the blast of air will warm them, but we really won't have a very good streamline effect if we hang a big electric generator outside."

"I've thought of that too," Arcot answered. "The solution is obvious—if we can't bring the generator to the air, we must bring the air to it." He began sketching rapidly on the pad before him, "We'll have all the power equipment in this room here in the back, and the control room up in front, here. The relays for controlling will be back here, so we can control electrically the operation of the power equipment from our warm, gas-tight room. If it gets too warm in there, we can cool it by using a little of the heat to help accelerate the ship. If it is too cold, we can turn on an electric heater run by the generator. The air for the generator can come in through a small sort of scoop on top, and leave through a small opening in the rear. The vacuum at the tail will assure us a very rapid circulation, even if the centrifugal pump action of the enclosed generator isn't enough."

His thoughts began moving more rapidly than his words.

"We'll want the generator greatly over power to run tests over a greater range. Won't need more than one hundred kilowatts altogether, but should install about a thousand—A.C., of course. Batteries in the keel for starting the generator . . . Self-supporting when it's rolling . . .

"But let's set down some actual figures on this."

For the rest of the day the three men were working on the general plan of the new ship, calculating the strengths needed, supplementing mathematics with actual experiments with the machines on hand. The calculating machines were busy continuously, for there were few rules that experience could give them. They were developing something entirely new, and though they were a designing staff of three of the foremost mathematicians in the world, it was a problem that tested their ingenuity to the utmost.

By the evening of the first day, however, they had been able to give the finished designs for the power units to the mechanics who were to make them. The order for the storage battery and the standard electrical equipment had been placed at once. By the time they had completed the drawings for the mail casting, the materials were already being assembled in a little private camp that Morey owned, up in the hills of Vermont. The giant freight helicopters could land readily in the wide field that had been cleared on the small plateau, in the center of which nestled a little blue lake and a winding trout brook.

The mechanics and electrical engineers had been sent up there already—officially on vacation. The entire program could be carried out without attracting the least attention, for such orders from the great Transcontinental lines were so frequent that no importance was attached to them.

Four days after the final plans had been completed the last of the supplies were being assembled in the portable metal shed that was to house the completed machine. The shining tungsto-steel alloy frame members were rapidly being welded in place by cathode ray welding torches in the hands of skilled artisans.

Already at the other end of the shop the generator had been arranged for use with the molecular motion power units. The many power units to drive and support the ship were finished and awaiting installation as the crew quit work on the fourth evening. They would be installed on the frame in the morning, and the generator would be hoisted into place with the small portable crane. The storage batteries were connected, and in place in the hull. The great fused quartz windows rested in their cases along one wall, awaiting the complete application of the steel alloy plates. They were to be over an inch thick, an unnecessary thickness, perhaps, but they had no need to economize weight, as witnessed by their choice of steel instead of light metal alloys throughout the construction.

The three men had arrived late that afternoon in a small helicopter, and had gone directly to the shops to see what progress had been made. They had been forced to remain in New York to superintend the shipment of the necessary supplies to the camp site, and since no trouble was anticipated in the making of the steel framework, they had not felt it necessary to come. But now they would be needed to superintend the more delicate work.

"She's shaping up nicely, isn't she?" Arcot gazed at the rapidly rounding frame with a critical eye. Unhindered as they were by the traditional shapes, by wings or other protuberances, they had been able to design a machine of striking beauty. The ship was to retain its natural metallic sheen, the only protection being a coat of "passivity paint"—a liquid chemical that could be brushed or sprayed on iron, chromium, nickel or cobalt alloys, rendering them passive to practically all chemical agents. The new "paint" left the iron or steel as brilliantly glossy as ever, but overcast with a beautiful iridescence, and immune to the most powerful reagents.

The three men walked around the rapidly growing hull, and looked with excited interest at the heavy welded joints and the great beams. The ship seemed capable of withstanding a fall of several hundred feet with little damage. The location of the power units was plainly visible and easily recognized, for at each point there came together four or five great beams, welded into one great mass of tough metal, and in it there were set heavy tungsten bolts that would hold the units in place.

They inspected each joint minutely for signs of flaws, using a small portable X-ray fluoroscope to see the interior of the metal. Each joint seemed perfect. They retired, satisfied that everything was ready for the work of the next day.

The morning began early with a long swim in the lake, and a

hearty breakfast of country cured ham and eggs. Then the work on the great framework was continued, and that day saw the power units bolted in place, removable if change was thought advisable. Each power unit was equipped with long streamlined copper fins lying close to the rounded hull, that they might absorb heat more rapidly.

Day by day the structure drew nearer completion, and, with the large crew of highly skilled workers, the craft was practically complete within a week. Only the instruments remained to be installed. Then at last even these had been put in place, and with the aid of Fuller, Morey junior, and his own father, Arcot had connected their many complicated circuits.

"Son," remarked Arcot senior, looking critically at the great switchboard, with its maze of connections, its many rheostats and controls, and its heavy busbar connectors behind it, "no one man can keep an eye on all those instruments. I certainly hope you have a good-sized crew to operate your controls! We've spent two days getting all those circuits together, and I'll admit that some of them still have me beat. I don't see how you intend to watch all those instruments, and at the same time have any idea what's going on outside."

"Oh," laughed Arcot junior, "these aren't intended for constant watching. They're merely helps in a lot of tests I want to make. I want to use this as a flying laboratory so I can determine the necessary powers and the lowest factor of safety to use in building other machines. The machine is very nearly completed now. All we need is the seats—they are to be special air-inflated gyroscopically controlled seats, to make it impossible for a sudden twist of the ship to put the strain in the wrong direction. Of course the main gyroscopes will balance the ship laterally, horizontally, and vertically, but each chair will have a separate gyroscopic mounting for safety."

"When do you expect to start after the Pirate?" Fuller asked.

"I plan to practice the manipulation of the machine for at least four days," Arcot replied, "before I try to chase the Pirate. I'd ordinarily recommend the greatest haste, but the man has stolen close to ten million already, and he's still at it. That would not be done by anyone in his right mind. I suppose you've heard, the War Department considers his new gas so important that they've obtained a pardon for him on condition they be permitted to have the secret of it. They demand the return of the money, and I have no doubt he has it. I am firmly convinced that he is a kleptomaniac. I doubt greatly if he will stop taking money before he is caught. Therefore it will be safe to wait until we can be sure of our ability to operate the machine smoothly. Any other course would be suicidal. Also, I am having some of those tool-makers make up a special type of molecular motion machine for us as a machine gun. The bullets are steel, about three inches long, and as thick as my thumb. They will be perfectly streamlined, except for a little stabilizer at the tail, to guide 'em. They won't spin as a rifle bullet does, and so there will be no gyroscopic effect to hold them nose on, but the streamlining and the stabilizer will keep them on their course. I expect them to be able to zipp right through many inches of armour plate, since they will have a velocity of over four miles a second.

"They'll be fed in at the rate of about two hundred a minute—faster if I wish, and started by a small spring. They will instantly come into the field of a powerful molecular motion-director, and will be shot out with terrific speed. It will be the first rifle ever made that could shoot bullets absolutely parallel to the ground.

"But that is all we can do today. The guns will be mounted outside, and controlled electrically, and the charts will be installed tomorrow. By the day after tomorrow at eight A.M. I plan to take off!"

The work the next day was rushed to completion far earlier than Arcot had dared to hope. All the men had been kept isolated at the farm, lest they accidentally spread the news of the new machine. It was with excited interest that they helped the machine to completion. The guns had not been mounted as yet, but that could wait. Mid-afternoon found the machine resting in the great construction shed, completely equipped and ready to fly!

"Dick," said Morey as he strode up to him after testing the last of the gyroscopic seats, "she's ready! I certainly want to get her going—it's only three-thirty, and we can go around to the sunlight part of the world when it gets dark at the speeds we can travel. Let's test her now!"

"I'm just as anxious to start as you are, Bob. I've sent for a

U. S. Air Inspector. As soon as he comes we can start. I'll have to put an 'X' license indication on her now. He'll go with us to test it—I hope. There will be room for three other people aboard, and I think you and Dad and I will be the logical passengers."

He pointed excitedly. "Look, there's a government helicopter coming. Tell the men to get the blocks from under her and tow her out. Two power trucks should do it. Get her at least ten feet beyond the end of the hangar. We'll start straight up, and climb to at least a five mile height, where we can make mistakes safely. While you're tending to that, I'll see if I can induce the Air Inspector to take a trip with us."

Half an hour later the machine had been rolled entirely out of the shed, on the new concrete runway.

The great craft was a thing of beauty shimmering in the bright sunlight. The four men who were to ride in it on its maiden voyage stood off to one side gazing at the great gleaming metal hull. The long sweeping lines of the sides told a story of perfect streamlining, and implied high speed, even at rest. The bright, slightly iridescent steel hull shone in silvery contrast to the gleaming copper of the power units' heat-absorption fins. The great clear windows in the nose and the low, streamlined air intake for the generator seemed only to accentuate the graceful lines of the machine.

"Lord, she's a beauty, isn't she, Dick!" exclaimed Morey, a broad smile of pleasure on his face.

"Well, she did shape up nicely on paper, too, didn't she. Oh, Fuller, congratulations on your masterpiece. It's even better looking than we thought, now the copper has added color to it. Doesn't she look fast? I wish we didn't need physicsts so badly on this trip, so you could go on the first ride with us."

"Oh, that's all right, Dick, I know the number of instruments in there, and I realize they will mean a lot of work this trip. I wish you all luck. The honor of having designed the first ship like that, the first heavier-than-air ship that ever flew without wings, jets, or props—that is something to remember. And I think it's one of the most beautiful that ever flew, too."

"Well, Dick," said his father quietly, "let's get under way. It should fly—but we don't really know that it will!"

The four men entered the ship and strapped themselves in the gyroscopic seats. One by one they reported ready.

"Captain Mason," Arcot explained to the Air Inspector, "these seats may seem to be a bit more active than one generally expects a seat to be, but in this experimental machine, I have provided all the safety devices I could think of. The ship itself won't fall, of that I am sure, but the power is so great it might well prove fatal to us if we are not in a position to resist the forces. You know all too well the effect of sharp turns at high speed and the results of the centrifugal force. This machine can develop such tremendous power that I have to make provision for it.

"You notice that my controls and the instruments are mounted on the arm of the chair really; that permits me to maintain complete control of the ship at all times, and still permits my chair to remain perpendicular to the forces. The gyroscopes in the base here cause the entire chair to remain stable if the ship rolls, but the chair can continue to revolve about this bearing here so that we will not be forced out of our seats. I'm confident that you'll find the machine safe enough for a license. Shall we start?"

"All right, Dr. Arcot," replied the Air Inspector. "If you and your father are willing to try it, I am."

"Ready, Engineer?" asked Arcot.

"Ready, Pilot!" replied Morey.

"All right—just keep your eye on the meters, Dad, as I turn on the system. If the instruments back there don't take care of everything, and you see one flash over the red mark—yank open the main circuit. I'll call out what to watch as I turn them on."

"Ready, son."

"Main gyroscopes!" There was a low snap, a clicking of relays in the rear compartment, and then a low hum that quickly ran up the scale. "Main generators!" Again the clicking switch, and the relays thudding into action, again the rising hum. "Seat-gyroscopes." The low click was succeeded by a quick shrilling sound that rose in moments above the range of hearing as the separate seat-gyroscopes took up their work. "Main power tube bank!" The low hum of the generator changed to a momentary roar as the relays threw on full load. In a moment the automatic controls had brought it up to speed.

"Everything is working perfectly so far. Are we ready to start now, son?"

"Main vertical power units!" The great ship trembled throughout its length as the lift of the power units started. A special instrument had been set up on the floor beside Arcot, that he might be able to judge the lift of his power units; it registered the apparent weight of the ship. It had read two hundred tons. Now all eyes were fixed on it, as the pointer dropped quickly to 150-100-75-50-40-20-10—there was a click and the instrument flopped back to 300—it was registering in pounds now! Then the needle moved to zero, and the mighty structure floated into the air, slowly moving down the field as a breeze carried it along the ground.

The men outside saw it rise swiftly into the sky, straight toward the blue vault of heaven. In two or three minutes it was disappearing. The glistening ship shrank to a tiny point of light; then it was gone! It must have been rising at fully three hundred miles an hour!

To the men in the car there had been a tremendous increase in weight that had forced them into the air cushions like leaden masses. Then the ground fell away with a speed that made them look in amazement. The house, the construction shed, the lake, all seemed contracting beneath them. So quickly were they rising that they had not time to adjust their mental attitude. To them all the world seemed shrinking about them.

Now they were at a tremendous height; over twenty miles they had risen into the atmosphere; the air about them was so thin that the sky seemed black, the stars blazed out in cold, unwinking glory, while the great fires of the sun seemed reaching out into space like mighty arms seeking to draw back to the parent body the masses of the wheeling planets. About it, in far flung streamers of cold fire shone the mighty zodiacal light, an Aurora on a titanic scale. For a moment they hung there, while they made readings of the meters.

Arcot was the first to speak and there was awe in his voice. "I never began to let out the power of this thing! What a ship! When these are made commercially, we'll have to use about one horsepower generators in them, or people will kill themselves trying to see how fast they can go."

Methodically the machine was tried out at this height, testing various settings of the instruments. It was definitely proven that the values that Arcot and Morey had assigned from purely theoretical calculations were correct to within one-tenth of one percent. The power absorbed by the machine they knew and had calculated, but the terrific power of the driving units was far beyond their expectations.

"Well, now we're off for some horizontal maneuvers," Arcot announced. "I'm sure we agree the machine can climb and can hold itself in the air. The air pressure controls seem to be working perfectly. Now we'll test her speed."

Suddenly the seats swung beneath them; then as the ship shot forward with ever greater speed, ever greater acceleration, it seemed that it turned and headed upward, although they knew that the main stabilizing gyroscopes were holding it level. In a moment the ship was headed out over the Atlantic at a speed no rifle bullet had ever known. The radio speedometer needle pushed farther and farther over as the speed increased to unheard of values. Before they left the North American shoreline they were traveling faster than a mile a second. They were in the middle of the Atlantic before Arcot gradually shut off the acceleration, letting the seats drop back into position.

A hubbub of excited comments rose from the four men. Momentarily, with the full realization of the historical importance of this flight, no one paid any attention to anyone else. Finally a question of the Air Inspector reached Arcot's ears.

"What speed did we attain, Dr. Arcot? Look—there's the coast of Europe! How fast are we going now?"

"We were traveling at the rate of three miles a second at the peak," Arcot answered. "Now it has fallen to two and a half."

Again Arcot turned his attention to his controls. "I'm going to try to see what the ultimate ceiling of this machine is. It must have a ceiling, since it depends on the operation of the generator to operate the power units. This, in turn, depends on the heat of the air, helped somewhat by the sun's rays. Up we go!"

The ship was put into a vertical climb, and steadily the great machine rose. Soon, however, the generator began to slow down. The readings of the instruments were dropping rapidly. The temperature of the exceedingly tenuous air outside was so close to absolute zero that it provided very little energy.

"Get up some forward speed," Morey suggested, "so that you'll have the aid of the air scoop to force the air in faster."

"Right, Morey." Arcot slowly applied the power to the forward propulsion units. As they took hold, the ship began to move forward. The increase in power was apparent at once. The machine started rising again. But at last, at a height of fifty-one miles, her ceiling had been reached.

The cold of the cabin became unbearable, for every kilowatt of power that the generator could get from the air outside was needed to run the power units. The air, too, became foul and heavy, for the pumps could not replace it with a fresh supply from the near-vacuum outside. Oxygen tanks had not been carried on this trip. As the power of the generator was being used to warm the cabin once more, they began to fall. Though the machine was held stable by the gyroscopes, she was dropping freely; but they had fifty miles to fall, and as the resistance of the denser air mounted, they could begin to feel the sense of weight return.

"You've passed, but for the maneuvers, Dr. Arcot!" The Air Inspector was decidedly impressed. "The required altitude was passed so long ago—why we are still some miles above it, I guess! How fast are we falling?"

"I can't tell unless I point the nose of the ship down, for the apparatus works only in the direction in which the ship is pointed. Hold on, everyone, I am going to start using some power to stop us."

It was night when they returned to the little field in Vermont. They had established a new record in every form of aeronautical achievement except endurance! The altitude record, the speed record, the speed of climb, the acceleration record—all that Arcot could think of had been passed. Now the ship was coming to dock for the night. In the morning it would be out again. But now Arcot was sufficiently expert with the controls to maneuver the ship safely on the ground. They finally solved the wind difficulty by decreasing the weight of the ship to about fifty pounds, thus enabling the three men to carry it into the hangar!

The next two days were devoted to careful tests of the power factors of the machine, the best operating frequency, the most efficient altitude of operation, and as many other tests as they had time for. Each of the three younger men took turns operating, but so great were the strains of the sudden acceleration, that Arcot senior decided it would be wisest for him to stay on the ground and watch.

In the meantime reports of the Pirate became fewer and fewer as less and less money was shipped by air.

Arcot spent four days practicing the manipulation of the machine, for though it handled far more readily than any other craft he had ever controlled, there was always the danger of turning on too much power under the stress of sudden excitement.

The night before, Arcot had sailed the ship down and alighted on the roof of Morey senior's apartment, leaving enough power on to reduce the weight to but ten tons, lest it fall through the roof, while he went down to see the President of the Lines about some "bait" for the Pirate.

"Send some cash along," said Arcot, when he saw Morey senior, "say a quarter of a million. Make it more or less public knowledge, and talk it up so that the Pirate may think there's a real haul on board. I am going to accompany the plane at a height of about a quarter of a mile above. I will try to locate him from there by means of radar, and if I have my apparatus on, I naturally can't locate him. I hope he won't be scared away—but I rather believe he won't. At any rate, you won't lose on the try!"

IV

Again Morey and Arcot were looking at the great Jersey aerodrome, out on the fields that had been broad marshes centuries before. Now they had been filled in, and stretched for miles, a great landing field, close to the great city across the river.

The men in the car above were watching the field, hanging inert, a point of glistening metal, high in the deep velvet of the purple sky, for fifteen miles of air separated them from the Transcontinental machine below. Now they saw through their field glasses that the great plane was lumbering slowly across the field, gaining momentum as it headed westward into the breeze. Then it seemed to be barely clearing the great skyscrapers that towered twenty-four hundred feet into the air, arching over four or five city blocks. From this height they were toys made of colored paper, soft colors glistening in the hot noon sunlight, and around and about them wove lines of flashing, moving helicopters, the individual lost in the mass of the million or so swiftly moving machines. Only the higher, steadily moving levels of traffic were visible to them.

"Just look at that traffic! Thousands and thousands coming back into the city after going home to lunch—and every day the number of helicopters is increasing! If it hadn't been for your invention of this machine, conditions would soon be impossible. The airblast in the cities is unbearable now, and getting worse all the time. Many machines can't get enough power to hold themselves up at the middle levels; there is a down current over one hundred miles an hour at the 400-foot level in downtown New York. It takes a racer to climb fast there!

"If it were not for gyroscopic stabilizers, they could never live in that huge airpocket. I have to drive in through there. I'm always afraid that somebody with an old worn-out bus will have stabilizer failure and will really smash things." Morey was a skillful pilot, and realized, as few others did, the dangers of that downward airblast that the countless whirring blades maintained in a constant roar of air. The office buildings now had double walls, with thick layers of sound absorbing materials, to stop the roar of the cyclonic blast that continued almost unabated twelve hours a day.

"Oh, I don't know about that, Morey," replied Arcot. "This thing has some drawbacks. Remember that if we had about ten million of these machines hung in the air of New York City, there would be a noticeable drop in the temperature. We'd probably have an Arctic climate year in and year out. You know, though, how unbearably hot it gets in the city by noon, even on the coldest winter days, due to the heating effect of the air friction of all those thousands of blades. I have known the temperature of the air to go up fifty degrees. There probably will have to be a sort of balance between the two types of machines. It will be a terrific economic problem, but at the same time it will solve the difficulties of the great companies who have been fermenting grain residues for alcohol. The castor bean growers are also going to bring down their prices a lot when this machine kills the market. They will also be more anxious to extract the carbon from the cornstalks for reducing ores of iron and of other metals."

As the ship flew high above the Transcontinental plane, the

men discussed the economic values of the different applications of Arcot's discoveries from the huge power stations they could make, to the cooling and ventilating of houses.

"Dick, you mentioned the cooling effect on New York City; with the millions on millions of these machines that there will be, with huge power plants, with a thousand other different applications in use, won't the terrific drain of energy from the air cause the whole world to become a little cooler?" asked Fuller.

"I doubt it, Bob," said Arcot slowly. "I've thought of that myself. Remember that most of the energy we use eventually ends up as heat anyway. And just remember the decillions of ergs of energy that the sun is giving off! True, we only get an infinitesimal portion of that energy—but what we do get is more than enough for us. Power houses can be established very conveniently in the tropics, where they will cool the air, and the energy can be used to refine metals. That means that the surplus heat of the tropics will find a use. Weather control will also be possible by the direction-control of great winds. We could set huge director tubes on the tops of mountains, and blow the winds in whatever direction best suited us. Not the blown wind itself, but the vast volume of air it carried with it, would be able to cool the temperate zones in the summer from the cold of the poles, and warm it in winter with the heat of the tropics."

After a thoughtful silence, Arcot continued, "And there is another thing it may make possible in the future—a thing that may be hard to accept as a commercial proposition. We have a practically inexhaustible source of energy now, but we have no sources of minerals that will last indefinitely. Copper is becoming more and more rare. Had it not been for the discoveries of the great copper fields of the Sahara and in Alaska, we wouldn't have any now. Platinum is exhausted, and even iron is becoming more and more valuable. We are facing a shortage of metals. Do you realize that within the next two centuries we will be unable to maintain this civilization unless we get new sources of certain basic raw materials?

"But we have one other chance now. The solution is—there are nine planets in this solar system! Neptune and Uranus are each far vaster than Earth; they are utterly impossible for life as we know it, but a small colony might be established there to refine metals for the distant Earth. We might be able to build domed and sealed cities. But first we could try the nearer planets—Mars, Venus, or some satellites such as our Moon. I certainly hope that this machine will make it possible."

For some time they sat in silence as they sped along, high above the green plains of Indiana. Chicago lay like some tremendous jewel far off on the horizon to the right and ahead. Five miles below them the huge bulk of the Transcontinental plane seemed a toy as it swung slowly across the fields—actually traveling over six hundred miles an hour. At last Morey spoke.

"You're right, Arcot. We'll have to think of the interplanetary aspects of this some day. Oh, there's Chicago! We'd better start the vacuum gas protector. And the radar. We may soon see some action."

The three men immediately forgot the somewhat distant danger of the metal shortage. There were a number of adjustments to be made, and these were quickly completed, while the machine forged evenly, steadily ahead. The generator was adjusted to maximum efficiency, and the various tubes were tested separately, for though they were all new, and each good for twenty-five thousand hours, it would be inconvenient, to say the least, if one failed while they were in action. Each tested perfect; and they knew from the smooth functioning of the various relays that governed the generator, as the loads on it varied, that it must be working perfectly, at something less than one-half maximum rating.

Steadily they flew on, waiting tensely for the first sign of a glow from the tiny neon tube indicator on the panel before Morey.

"This looks familiar, Dick," said Morey, looking about at the fields and the low line of the blue mountains far off on the western horizon. "I think it was about here that we took our little nap in the 'Flying Wheel chair', as the papers called it. It would be about here th— LOOK! It is about here! Get ready for action, Fuller. You're taking the machine gun, I'll work the invisibility disrupter, and Arcot will run the ship. Let's go!"

On the board before him the tiny neon tube flickered dully, glowed briefly like a piece of red-hot iron, then went out. In a moment it was glowing again, and then quickly its brilliance mounted till it was a line of crimson. Morey snapped the switch from the general radar to the beam receiver, that he might locate the machine exactly. It was fully a minute before the neon tube flashed into life once more. The pirate was flying just ahead of the big plane, very likely gassing them. All around him were the Air Guardsmen, unaware that the enemy was so near. As the disrupter beam could be projected only about a mile, they would have to dive down on the enemy at once; an instant later the great plane beneath them seemed to be rushing upward at a terrific speed.

The two radar beams were kept focused constantly on the Pirate's craft. When they were about two miles from the two planes, the neon tube blazed brilliantly with a clash of opposing energy. The Pirate was trying to maintain his invisibility, while the rapidly growing strength of the machine above strove to batter it down. In moments the ammeter connected with the disrupter beam began to rise so rapidly that Morey watched it with some concern. Despite the ten-kilowatt set being used to project the beam, the resistance of the apparatus on board the pirate ship was amazing.

Abruptly the three became aware of a rapidly solidifying cloud before them. The interference of the beam Morey was sending had begun breaking down the molecular oscillation that permitted the light to pass freely through the pirate's craft. Suddenly there was a circle of blue light about the shadow form, and a moment later the ionized air relapsed into normal condition as the pirate's apparatus broke down under the strain. At once Morey shut off his apparatus, convinced by the sudden change that the pirate's apparatus had blown out. He glanced up quickly as Arcot called to him, "Morey—look at him go!"

Too late. Already the plane had shot off with terrific speed. It had flashed up and to their left, at a rate of climb that seemed unbelievable—except that the long trail of flaming gas told the story! The plane was propelled by rockets! The terrific acceleration carried it out of their range of vision in an instant, and as Arcot swung the ship to bring him again within sight of the windows, they gasped, for already he was many miles away.

There was a terrific wrench as Arcot threw on all the power he dared, then quickly leveled the machine, following the pirate at lightning speed. He increased the acceleration further as the men grew accustomed to the force that weighed them down. Ahead of them the pirate was racing along, but quickly now they were overhauling him, for his machine had wings of a sort! They produced a tremendous amount of head resistance at their present velocity, for already the needle of the radio speedometer had moved over to one mile a second. They were following the fleet plane ahead at the rate of 3600 miles an hour. The roar of the air outside was a tremendous wave of sound, yet to them, protected by the vacuum of the double walls, it was detectable only by the vibration of the car.

Rapidly the pirate's lead was cut down. It seemed but a moment before he would be within range of their machine gun. Suddenly he nosed down and shot for the ground, ten miles below, in a power dive. Instantly Arcot swung his machine in a loop that held him close to the tail of the pirate. The swift maneuvers at this speed were a terrific strain on both men and machines—the acceleration seemed crushing them with the weight of four men, as Arcot followed the pirate in a wide loop to the right that ended in a straight climb, the rocket ship standing on its tail, the rocket blast roaring out behind a stream of fire a half mile long.

The pirate was climbing at a speed that would have distanced any other machine the world had ever seen, but the tenacious opponent behind him clung ever tighter to the tiny darting thing. He had released great clouds of his animation suspending gas. To his utter surprise, the ship behind him had driven right through it, entirely unaffected! He, who knew most about the gas, had been unable to devise a material to stop it, a mask or a tank to store it, yet in some way these men had succeeded! And that hurtling, bullet-shaped machine behind! Like some miniature airship it was, but with a speed and an acceleration that put even his ship to shame! It could twist, turn, dive, rise and shoot off on the straight-away with more flashing speed than anything aloft. Time and again he tried complicated maneuvers that strained him to the utmost, yet that machine always followed after him!

There was one more thing to do. In outer space his rockets would support him. In a straight climb he shot up to the blazing sun above, out into space, while the sky around him grew black, and the stars shone in solemn splendor around him. But he had eyes for only one thing, the shining car that was rising with more than equal speed behind him. He knew he must be climbing over two thousand miles an hour, yet the tracker came ever closer. Just out of sighting range for the machine gun now . . . in a moment . . . but, she was faltering!

The men in the machine behind sat white-lipped, tense, as the whirling shocks of sudden turns at terrific speed twisted the gyroscopic seats around like peas in a rolling ball. Up, down, left, right, the darting machine ahead was twisting with un-believable speed. Then suddenly the nose was pointed for the zenith again, and with a great column of flame shooting out behind him, he was heading straight toward space!

"If he gets there, I lose him, Morey!" said Arcot. The terrific acceleration of the climb seemed to press them to their seats with a deadly weight. It was labor to talk—but still the car ahead shot on—slowly they seemed to be overhauling him. Now that the velocities were perforce lowered by the effects of gravity, and the air resistance of the atmosphere was well nigh gone, only the acceleration that the human body could stand was considered. The man ahead was pushing his plane ahead with an acceleration that would have killed many men!

Slowly the acceleration of the machine was falling. Arcot pushed the control over to the last ampere, and felt the slight surge, as greater power rushed through the coils momentarily. Soon this was gone too, as the generator behind faltered. The driving power of the atmospheric heat was gone. More than sixty miles below them they could see the earth as a greenish brown surface, slightly convex, and far to the east they could distinguish a silvery line of water! But they had no eyes but for the column of shooting flame that represented the fleeing raider! Out in airless space now, he was safe from them. They could not follow. Arcot turned the plane once more, parallel to the earth, watching the plane above through the roof window. Slowly the machine sank to the fifty-mile level, where there was just sufficient air to maintain it in efficient operation.

"Well, he beat us! But there is only one thing for us to do. He must hang there on his rockets till we leave, and we can hang here indefinitely, if we can only keep this cabin decently warm. He has no air to cool him, and he has the sun to warm him. The only thing that is worrying him right now is the heat of his rock-ets. But he can throw most of that out with the gases. Lord, that's some machine! But eventually his rockets will give out, and down he will come, so we'll just hang here beneath him and—whoa—not so fast—he isn't going to stay there, it seems; he is angling his ship off a bit, and shooting along, so that, besides, holding himself up, he is making a little forward progress. We'll have to follow! He's going to do some speeding, it seems! Well, we can keep up with him, at our level."

"Dick, no plane ever made before would have stood the terrific pulls and yanks that his plane got. He was steering and twisting on the standard type air rudders, and what strains he had! The unique type of plane must be extremely strong. I never saw one shaped like his before, though—it is the obvious shape at that! It was just a huge triangular arrowhead! Did you ever see one like it?"

"Something like it, yes, and so have you. Don't you recognize that as the development of the old paper gliders you used to throw around as a kid? It has the same shape, the triangular wings with the point in the lead, except that he undoubtedly had a slight curve to the wings to increase the efficiency. Something like the flying wings of fifty years ago. I hope that man is only a kleptomaniac, because he can be cured of that, and I may then have a new laboratory partner. He has some exceedingly intelligent ideas!

"He's an ingenious man, but I wish he didn't store quite so much fuel in his rocket tubes! It's unbearably cold in here, and I can't sacrifice any power just for comfort. The rocket ship up there seems to be getting more and more acceleration in the level. He has me dropping steadily to get air to run the generator. He is going fast enough!"

They followed beneath the pirate, faster and faster as the rockets of the ship began to push it forward more and more.

"Dick, why is it he didn't use all his rockets at first instead of gradually increasing the power this way?"

"If you were operating the ship, Morey, you'd understand. Look at the speedometer a moment and see if you can figure it out."

"Hmmm—4.5 miles per second—buzzing right along—but I don't see what that—good Lord! We never will get him at this rate! How do you expect to get him?"

"I have no idea—yet. But you missed the important point. He is going 4.5 miles a second. When he reaches 5 miles a second he will never come down from his hundred and fifty mile high perch! He will establish an orbit! He has so much centrifugal force already that he has very little weight. We are staying right beneath him, so we don't have much either. Well, there he goes in a last spurt. We are falling behind pretty fast—there we are catching up now—no—we are just holding parallel! He's done it! Look!"

Arcot pulled out his watch and let go of it. It floated motionless in the air for a moment, then slowly drifted back toward the rear of the room. "I am using a bit of acceleration—a bit more than we need to maintain our speed. We are up high enough to make the air resistance almost nothing, even at this velocity, but we still require some power. I don't know—"

There was a low buzz, repeated twice. Instantly Morey turned the dials of the radio receiving set—again the call signal sounded. In a moment a voice came in—low, but distinct. The power seemed fading rapidly.

"I'm Wade—the Pirate—help if you can. Can you get outside the atmosphere? Exceed orbital speed and fall out? Am in an orbit and can't get out. Fuel reserve gauge stuck, and used all my rockets. No more power. Cannot slow down and fall. I am running out of compressed air and the generator for this set is going —will take animation suspending gas—will you be able to reach me before entering night?"

"Quick, Morey—answer that we will."

"We will try, Pirate—think we can make it!"

"O.K.—power about gone—"

The last of his power had failed! The pirate was marooned in space! They had seen his rockets go out, leaving the exhaust tube glowing for a moment before it, too, was dark, and only the sun shining on the silvery ship made it visible.

"We have to hurry if we want to do anything before he reaches night! Radio the San Francisco fields that we will be coming in soon, and we need a large electro-magnet—one designed to work on about 500 volts D.C., and some good sized storage cells; how many will have to be decided later, depending on the room we will have for them. I'll start decelerating now so we can make the turn and circle back. We are somewhere west of Hawaii, I believe, but we ought to be able to do the trick if we use all the power we can."

Morey at once set to work with the radio set to raise San Francisco airport. He was soon in communication with them, and told them that he would be there in about an hour. They promised all the necessary materials; also that they would get ready to receive the pirate once he was finally brought in to them.

It was nearer an hour and a quarter later that the machine fell to the great San Francisco landing field, where the mechanics at once set to work bolting a huge electro-magnet on the landing skids on the bottom of the machine. The most serious problem was connecting the terminals electrically without making holes in the hull of the ship. Finally one terminal was grounded, and the radio aerial used as the other. Fuller was left behind on this trip, and a large number of cells were installed in every possible position. In the power room, a hastily arranged motor generator set was arranged, making it possible to run the entire ship from the batteries. Scarcely had these been battened down to prevent sliding under the accelerations necessary, than Arcot and Morey were off. The entire operation had required but fifteen minutes.

"How are you going to catch him, Arcot?"

"I'll overtake him going west. If I went the other way I'd meet him going at 10 miles a second in relation to his machine. He had the right idea. He told me to fall out to him at a greater than orbital speed. I will go just within the earth's atmosphere till I get just under him, holding myself in the air by means of a downward acceleration on the part of the regular lifting power units. I am going to try to reach eight miles a second. We will be overhauling him at three a second, and the ship will slow down to the right speed while falling out to him. We must reach him before he gets into the shadow of the earth, though, for if he reaches 'night' he will be without heat, and he'll die of cold. I think we can reach him, Dick!"

"I hope so. Those spare cells are all right, aren't they? We'll need them! If they don't function when we get out there, we'll fall clear off into space! At eight miles a second, we would leave earth forever!"

The ship was accelerating steadily at the highest value the men aboard could stand. The needle of the speedometer crept steadily across the dial. They were flying at a height of forty miles that they might have enough air and still not be too greatly hindered by air resistance. The black sky above them was spotted with points of glowing light, the blazing stars of space. But as they flew along, the sensation of weight was lost; they had reached orbital speed, and as the car steadily increased its velocity, there came a strange sensation! The earth loomed gigantic above them! Below them shone the sun! The direction of up and down was changed by the terrific speed! The needle of the speedometer was wavering at 7.8 miles a second. Now it held steady!

"I thought you were going to take it up to eight miles a second, Dick?"

"Air resistance is too great! I'll have to go higher!"

At a height of fifty miles they continued at 8.1 miles a second. It seemed hours before they reached the spot where the pirate's machine should be flying directly above them, and they searched the black sky for some sign of the shining dot of light. With the aid of field glasses they found it, far ahead, and nearly one hundred miles above.

"Well, here we go! I'm going to fall up the hundred miles or so, till we're right in his path; the work done against gravity will slow us down a little, so I'll have to use the power units somewhat. Did you notice what I did to them?"

"Yes, they're painted a dull black. What's the idea?"

"We'll have no air from which to get heat for power out here, so we'll have to depend on the sunlight they can absorb. I'm using it now to slow us down as much as possible."

At last the tiny silver dot had grown till it became recognizable as the pirate plane. They were drawing up to it now, slowly, but steadily. At last the little machine was directly beneath them, and a scant hundred yards away. They had long since been forced to run the machine on the storage batteries, and now they applied a little power to the vertical power units. Sluggishly, as they absorbed the sun's heat, the machine was forced lower, nearer to the machine below. At last a scant ten feet separated them.

"All right, Morey."

There was a snap, as the temporary switch was closed, and the current surged into the big magnet on the keel. At once they felt the ship jump a little under the impulse of the magnet's pull on the smaller machine. In a moment the little plane had drifted up to the now idle magnet, touched it and was about to bounce off, when Morey again snapped the switch shut and the two machines were locked firmly together!

"I've got him, Dick!" Morey exclaimed. "Now slow down till it falls. Then we can go and wait for it. Being a glider, it ought to be quite manageable!"

Now the energy of the power units on the roof of the machine began to slow down the two machines, the magnet grinding slightly as the momentum of the plane was thrust upon it. They watched the speedometer drop. The speed was sinking very slowly, for the area of the absorbing fins was not designed to absorb the sun's heat directly, and was very inefficient. The sun was indeed sinking below their horizon; they were just beginning to watch that curious phenomenon of seeing dawn backward, when they first struck air dense enough to operate the power units noticeably. Quickly the power was applied till the machines sank rapidly to the warmer levels, the only governing factor being the tendency of the glider to break loose from the grip of the magnet.

At fifty miles the generator was started, and the heaters in the car at once became more active. There was no heat in the car below, but that was unavoidable. They would try to bring it down to warm levels quickly.

"Whew, I'm glad we reached the air again, Dick. I didn't tell you sooner, for it wouldn't have done any good, but that battery was about gone! We had something like twenty amp-hours left! I'm giving the recharge generator all she will take. We seem to have plenty of power now."

"I knew the cells were low, but I had no idea they were as low as that! I noticed that the magnet was weakening, but thought it was due to the added air strain. I am going to put the thing into a nose dive and let the glider go down itself. I know it would land correctly if it had a chance. I am going to follow it, of course, and since we are over the middle of Siberia we'd better start back."

The return trip was necessarily in the lower level of the atmosphere, that the glider might be kept reasonably warm. At a height of but two miles, in the turbulent atmosphere, the glider was brought slowly home. It took them nearly twenty hours to go the short distance of twelve thousand miles to San Francisco, the two men taking turns at the controls. The air resistance of the glider forced them to go slowly; they could not average much better than six hundred an hour despite the fact that the speed of either machine alone was over twelve hundred miles an hour.

At last the great skyscrapers of San Francisco appeared on their horizon, and thousands of private planes started out to meet them. Frantically Arcot warned them away, lest the air blast from their props tear the glider from the magnet. At last, however, the Air Guard was able to force them to a safe distance and clear a lane through one of the lower levels of the city traffic. The great field of the Transcontinental lines was packed with excited men and women, waiting to catch a glimpse of two of the greatest things the country had heard of in the century— Arcot's molecular motion machine and the Air Pirate!

The landing was made safely in the circle of Air Guardsmen. There was a small hospital plane standing beside it in a moment, and as Arcot's ship released it, and then hung motionless, soundless above it, the people watched it in wonder and excitement. They wanted to see Arcot perform; they clamored to see the wonderful powers of this ship in operation. Air Guardsmen who had witnessed the flying game of tag between these two super-air machines had told of it through the press and over the radio.

Two weeks later, Arcot stepped into the office of Mr. Morey, senior.

"Busy?"

"Come on in; you know I'm busy—but not *too* busy for you. What's on your mind?"

"Wade—the pirate."

"Oh—hmm. I saw the reports on his lab out on the Rockies, and also the psychomedical reports on him. And most particularly, I saw the request for his employment you sent through channels. What's your opinion on him? You talked with him."

Arcot frowned slightly. "When I talked to him he was still two different identities dancing around in one body. Dr. Ridgely says the problem's settling down; I believe him. Ridgely's no more of a fool in his line than you and Dad are in your own lines, and Ridgely's business is healing mental wounds. We agreed some while back that the Pirate must be insane, even before we met him.

"We also agreed that he had a tremendously competent and creative mind. As a personality in civilization, he'd evidently slipped several cogs. Ridgely says that is reparable.

"You know, Newton was off the beam for about two years. Faraday was in a complete breakdown for nearly five years—and after his breakdown, came back to do some monumental work.

"And those men didn't have the help of modern psychomedical techniques.

"I think we'd be grade A fools ourselves to pass up the chance to get Wade's help. The man—insane or not—figured out a way of stabilizing and storing atomic hydrogen for his rockets. If he could do that in the shape he was then in . . . !

"I'd say we'd be smart to keep the competition in the family."

Mr. Morey leaned back in his chair and smiled up at Arcot. "You've got a good case there. I'll buy it. When Dr. Ridgely says Wade's got those slipped cogs replaced—offer him a job in your lab staff.

"I'm a bit older than you are; you've grown up in a world where the psychomedical techniques really work. When I was growing up, psychomedical techniques were strictly rule of thumb—and the doctors were all thumbs." Mr. Morey sighed. Then, "In this matter, I think your judgment is better than mine."

"I'll see him again, and offer him the job. I'm pretty sure he'll take it, as I said. I have a suspicion that, within six months, he'll be a lot saner than most people around. The ordinary man doesn't realize what a job of rechecking present techniques can do—and Wade is, naturally, getting a very thorough overhaul.

"Somewhat like a man going in for treatment of a broken arm; in any decent hospital they'll also check for any other medical problems, and he'll come out healthier than if he had never had the broken arm.

"Wade seems to have had a mind that made friends with molecules, and talked their language. After Ridgely shows him how to make friends with people—I think he'll be quite a man on our team!"

BOOK TWO

SOLARITE

I

The lights of great Transcontinental Airport were blazing in cheering splendor. Out there in the center of the broad field a dozen men were silhouetted in the white brilliance, looking up at the sky, where the stars winked cold and clear on the jet background of the frosty night. A slim crescent of moon gleamed in the west, a sickle of light that in no way dimmed the cold flame of the brilliant stars.

One point of light now moved across the motionless field of far-off suns, flashing toward the airport in a long, swift curve. The men on the field murmured and pointed up at it as it swept low over the blazing lights of New York. Lower it swooped, the towering city behind it. Half a mile into the air the buildings rose in shining glory of colored tile that shone brightly in the sweeping play of floodlights.

One of them picked out the descending machine, and it suddenly leaped out of the darkness as a shining, streamlined cylinder, a cylinder with a great halo of blue fire, as the beam of the searchlight set it off from the jet black night.

In moments the ship was vast before the eyes of the waiting men; it had landed gently on the field, was floating smoothly, gracefully toward them.

Twenty-four men climbed from the great ship, shivering in the icy blast that swept across the field, spoke a moment with the group awaiting their arrival, then climbed quickly into the grateful warmth of a field car. In a moment they were speeding toward the lights of the field house, half a mile off.

Behind them the huge ship leaped into the sky, then suddenly pointed its nose up at an angle of thirty degrees and shot high into the air at an unbelievable speed. In an instant it was gone.

At the field house the party broke up almost immediately. "We want to thank you, Mr. Morey, for your demonstration of the new ship tonight, and you, Dr. Arcot, for answering our many questions about it. I am sure we all appreciate the kindness you have shown the press." The reporters filed out quickly, anxious to get the news into the morning editions, for it was after one o'clock now. Each received a small slip of paper from the attendant standing at the exit, the official statement of the company. At last all had left but the six men who were responsible for the new machine.

This night had witnessed the official demonstration of the first of the Arcot-Morey molecular motion ships. Small as she was, compared to those that were to come, yet she could carry over three thousand passengers, as many as could any existing winged plane, and her speed was immensely greater. The trip from the west coast to the eastern had been made in less than one hour. At a speed close to one mile a second the great ship had shot through the thin air, twenty-five miles above the earth.

In this vessel a huge bar of metal could be affected by an ultra-high-frequency generator. When so affected, its molecules all moved forward, taking the ship with them. Thus, a molecular-motion-drive vessel could, theoretically, approach the velocity of light as a limit.

"Arcot," said Morey, senior, after the pressmen had left the room, "as president of this company I certainly want to thank you for the tremendous thing you have given us to use. You have 'sold' us this machine—but how can we repay you? Before this, time and time again, you have sold us your inventions, the ideas that have made it possible for Transcontinental to attain its present high position in world transportation. All you have ever accepted is the laboratory you use, its upkeep, and a small annual income. What can we do to show our appreciation this time?"

"Why," answered Arcot smiling, "you haven't stated the terms correctly. Actually, I have a fully equipped lab to putter around in, all the time I want for my own amusement, and all the money I want. What more could I ask?"

"I suppose that's all true—but you draw only about six thou-

sand a year for personal expenses—a good clerk could get that—
and you, admittedly the most brilliant physicist of the earth, are
satisfied! I don't feel we're paying you properly!"

Arcot's expression became suddenly serious. "You can repay
me this time," he said, "for this latest discovery has made a new
thing possible. I've always wanted to be able to visit other
planets—as has many a scientist for the last three centuries. This
machine has made it possible. If you are willing—we could start
by the spring of 2117. I'm quite serious about this. With your
permission, I want to start work on the first interplanetary ship.
I'll need Fuller's help, of course. The proposition will be expensive, and that's where I must ask you to help me. I think, however, that it may be a paying proposition, at that, for there will
certainly be something of commercial value on the other planets."

They had walked out to the shed where Arcot's private
molecular motion car stood, the first machine ever built that
used the heat of the sun to drive it. Thoughtfully the president
of the great Transcontinental Lines looked at it. It was small
compared with the great machine that had just brought them
east, but of the same swift type. It was a thing of graceful
beauty even on the ground, its long curving streamlines giving it
wonderful symmetry. They stood in thoughtful silence for a
minute—the young men eager to hear the verdict of their pro-
spective backer. Morey, always rather slow of speech, took an
unusually long time to answer.

"If it were only money you asked for, Arcot, I'd gladly give you
double the sum, but that isn't the case. I know perfectly well that
if you do go, my son will go with you, and Fuller and Wade will
naturally go too." He looked at each in turn. "Each of you has
come to mean a lot to me. You and Fuller have known Bob
since college days. I've known Wade only three months, but
every day I grow to like him more. There's no denying the fact
that any such trip is a terrifically dangerous proposition. But if
you were lost, there would be more than my personal loss. We
would lose some of the most brilliant men on earth. You, for
instance, are conceded as being the world's most brilliant physicist; Fuller is one of the greatest designing engineers; Wade is
rapidly rising into prominence as a chemist and as a physicist;
and my son is certainly a good mathematician."

He paused, frowning, weighing the situation. "But you men

should know how to get out of scrapes just that much better. Certainly there are few men on Earth who would not be willing to back such a group of men—or any one of you, for that matter! I'll back your trip!" His words became more facetious. "I know that Arcot and you, Bob, can handle a gun fairly well. I don't know so much about Wade and Fuller. What experience have you two had?"

Fuller shook his head. "I think I'll fit best in the galley on the trip, Mr. Morey. I've done the cooking on a number of camping trips, and food is an important factor in the success of any expedition. I can shoot a bit, too."

Wade spoke rather hesitantly. "I come from the west, and have had a good bit of fun with a gun in the Rockies; there are still some mountain lions and some deer there, you know. I also have a sneaking acquaintance with the new gun, which Arcot developed in connection with his molecular motion. But there is so little you know about me—and most if it bad—I don't see how I really get in on this opportunity—but," he added hastily, "I certainly don't intend to keep the old boy knocking—I'm with you, since I'm invited!"

Arcot smiled. "Then you'll definitely support us?"

"Yes, I will," replied Morey, senior, seriously, "for I think it's worth doing."

The four young men climbed into the ship, to start for their apartment. Arcot was piloting, and under his sure touch the ship sped out into the cold night air, then up through the atmosphere, till they hung poised at a height of fifty miles on the upper edge of the airy blanket. They looked out in silent thought at the magnificent blazing stars of space. Here, where the dust-laden air could no longer mask their true colors, the stars shone unwinkingly, steadily, and in a glory that earth-bound men had never seen before. They shone in a wondrous riot of color, as varied and as beautiful as the display of colored floodlights in some great city. They were tiny pinpoints of radiance, red, green, orange, and yellow, shining with intense brilliance.

Slowly Arcot let the machine settle to the blazing city miles below.

"I love to come out here and look at those cold, pinpoint lights; they seem to draw me—the lure of other worlds. I've always had a sense of unfulfilled longing—the desire to go out there—and it's

always been so hopeless. Now—I'll be out there by next spring!"
Arcot paused and looked up at the mighty field of stars that
arched over his head to be lost on either horizon. A wonderful
night!

"Where shall we go first, Dick?" asked Wade softly as he
gazed out at the far-off suns of space, his voice unconsciously
hushed by the grandeur of the spectacle.

"I've thought of that for the last four months, and now that
we are definitely going to go, we'll have to make a decision.
Actually, it won't be too hard to decide. Of course we can't
leave the solar system. And the outer planets are so far away that
I think we had better wait till later trips. That leaves the choice
really between Mars, Venus, and Mercury. Mercury isn't practical since it's so close to the sun. We know a fair bit about Mars
from telescopic observation, while Venus, wrapped in perpetual
cloud, is a mystery. What do you vote?"

"Well," said Morey, "it seems to me it's more fun to explore a
completely unknown planet than one that can be observed
telescopically. I vote Venus." Each of the others agreed with
Morey that Venus was the logical choice.

By this time the machine had sunk to the roof of their apartment, and the men disembarked and entered. The next day they
were to start the actual work of designing the space ship.

II

"When we start this work," Arcot began next morning, "we
obviously want to design the ship for the conditions we expect
to meet, and for maximum convenience and safety. I believe
I've thought about this trip longer than the rest of you, so I'll
present my ideas first.

"We don't actually *know* anything about conditions on Venus,
since no one has actually been there. Venus is probably a younger
planet than earth. It's far nearer the sun than we are, and it
gets twice the heat we do. In the long-gone time when the
planets were cooling I believe Venus required far longer than
earth, for the inpouring heat would retard its cooling. The surface
temperature is probably about 150 degrees Fahrenheit.

"There is little land, probably, for with the cloud-mass covering
Venus as it does, it's logical to visualize tremendous seas. What

life has developed must be largely aquatic, and the land is probably far behind us in evolution. Of course, Venus is the planet of mystery—we don't know; we can only guess. But we do know what things we are going to need to cross space.

"Obviously, the main driving force will be the power units. These will get their energy from the rays of the sun by absorbing them in copper discs about twelve feet in diameter—the ship will have to be more of a disc than a cylinder. I think a ship a hundred and eighty feet long, fifty feet wide, and twenty feet deep will be about the best dimensions. The power units will be strung along the top of the ship in double rows—one down each side of the hull. In the middle will be a series of fused quartz windows, opening into a large room just under the outer shell. We'll obviously need some source of power to activate the power tubes that run the molecular motion power units. We'll have a generator run by molecular motion power units in here, absorbing its heat from the atmosphere in this room. The air will be heated by the rays of the sun, of course, and in this way we'll get all our power from the sun itself.

"Since this absorption of energy might result in making the ship too cool, due to the radiation of the side away from the sun, we'll polish it, and thus reduce the unlighted side's radiation.

"The power units will not be able to steer us in space, due to their position, and those on the sides, which will steer us in the atmosphere by the usual method, will be unable to get the sun's power; they'll be shaded. For steering in space, we'll use atomic hydrogen rockets, storing the atomic gas by the Wade method in tanks in the hold. We'll also have a battery down there for starting the generator and for emergencies.

"For protection against meteors, we'll use radar. If anything comes within a dozen miles of us, the radar unit covering that sector will at once set automatic machinery in operation, and the rockets will shoot the ship out of the path of the meteor."

All that day Arcot and the others discussed the various pieces of apparatus they would need, and toward evening Fuller began to draw rough sketches of the different mechanisms that had been agreed upon.

The next day, by late afternoon, they had planned the rough details of the ship and had begun the greater task of calculating the stresses and the power factors.

"We won't need any tremendous strength for the ship while it is in space," Arcot commented, "for then there will be little strain on it. It will be weightless from the start, and the gentle acceleration will not strain it in the least, but we must have strength, so that it can maneuver in the atmosphere.

"We'll leave earth by centrifugal force, for I can make much better speed in the atmosphere where there is plenty of power to draw on; outside I must depend solely on sunlight. We'll circle the earth, forming an orbit just within the atmosphere, at five miles a second. We'll gradually increase the speed to about ten miles a second, at which point the ship would normally fly off into space under its own centrifugal force. With the power units we'll prevent its release until the proper moment. When we release it, it will be entirely free of earth, and no more work will be needed to overcome earth's pull."

The planning continued with exasperating slowness. The details of the work were complex, for all the machines were totally new. Several weeks passed before even the power units could be ordered and the first work on the ship started. After that orders for materials left the office daily. Still, it was late in November before the last order was sent out.

Now they must begin work on other phases of the expedition—food supplies and the standard parts of the equipment.

In the interval Arcot had decided to make a special ventilated suit for use on Venus. This was to make use of a small molecular motion director apparatus to cool the air, and blow it through the suit. The apparatus consisted of a small compressed air-driven generator and a power tube bank that could be carried on the back.

"Arcot," Wade said when he saw the apparatus completed and the testing machine ready, "I've just noticed how similar this is to the portable invisibility apparatus I developed as the Pirate. I wonder if it might not be handy at times to be invisible—we could incorporate that with a slight change. It wouldn't add more than five pounds, and those tubes you are using I'm sure are easily strong enough to carry the extra load."

"Great idea, Wade," said Arcot. "It might be very useful if we met hostile natives. The disappearance stunt might makes us gods or something to primitive beings. And now that you mention it, I think we can install the apparatus in the ship. It will require almost no power, and might save our lives some time."

The work went forward steadily at the great Transcontinental Shops where the space ship was being built. Its construction was being kept as much of a secret as possible, for Arcot feared the interference of the crowds that would be sure to collect if the facts were known, and since the shops directly joined the airfield, it meant that there would be helicopters buzzing about the Transatlantic and Transcontinental planes.

The work to be done required the most careful manipulation and workmanship, for one defect could mean death. They calculated six weeks for the trip, and in the time before they could reach either planet, much might happen to a crippled ship.

To the men who were making the trip, the waiting seemed most exasperating, and they spent the days before they could begin the installation of the electrical apparatus in purchasing the necessary standard equipment; the standard coils, tubes, condensers, the canned food supplies, clothes, everything that they could imagine as of possible utility. They were making the ship with a great deal of empty storage space, for Arcot hoped the trip would be a financial success, particularly supplying much-needed metals. Many vital elements were already excessively scarce, and no satisfactory substitutes had been found.

On the outward trip some of this space would be filled with the many things they would consume en route. In addition they were carrying a great many spare parts, spare tubes, spare power units, spare condensers—a thousand and one odd parts. Arcot intended that they should be able to make an entire new power switchboard and motion director unit if anything should go wrong, and he certainly had all the apparatus.

At last came the day when the final connection had been soldered, and the last joint welded. The atomic hydrogen tanks were full, and under the ship's own power the oxygen tanks were filled and the batteries charged. They were ready for a test flight!

The great ship rested on the floor of the shed now, awaiting the start.

"Oh fellows—come here a minute!" Arcot called to the other members of the party. "I want to show you something."

The three walked quickly to the bow where Arcot stood, and following the line of his vision, looked in wonder to see that everything was right. They watched curiously as he drew from his coat a large glass bottle, tightly sealed.

"What's that for?" asked Wade curiously.

"We're about to start on the first cruise, and I've been wondering if it isn't time we gave the ship a name."

"Great—I'd been thinking of that too—what are we going to name her?"

"Well," said Arcot, "I had been thinking of Alexander—he longed for other worlds to conquer!"

"Not bad," Morey commented. "I have been thinking of naming it too—I guess we all have—but I was thinking of Santa Maria —the first ship to discover the New World."

"I was thinking more of its home," said Wade. "How about calling it Terrestrian?"

"Well—it's your turn, Fuller—you designed it. What do you suggest for your masterpiece?" asked Arcot.

"I was thinking also of its home—the home it will never leave. I like to think that we might find people on Venus, and I would like to have a name on it that might be translatable into more friendly and less foreign terms—why not call it Solarite?"

"Solarite—a member of the solar system—it will be that, always. It will be a world unto itself when it makes its trips—it will take up an orbit about the sun—a true member of the solar system. I like it!" Arcot turned to the others. "How about it?" It was agreed upon unanimously.

"But I'm still curious about that glass bottle, so carefully sealed," Morey commented with a puzzled smile. "What's in it? Some kind of gas?"

"Wrong—no gas—practically nothing at all, in fact. What more appropriate for christening a space ship than a bottle of hard vacuum?

"We can't have a pretty girl christen this ship, that's sure. A flying bachelor's apartment christened by a mere woman? Never! We will have the foreman of the works here do that. Since we can't have the ship slide down the ways or anything, we will get inside and move it when he smashes the bottle. But in the meantime, let's have a symbol set in contrasting metal on the bow. We can have a blazing sun, with nine planets circling it, the earth indicated conspicuously; and below it the word SOLARITE."

III

It was shortly after noon when the newly christened *Solarite* left on its first trip into space. The sun was a great ball of fire low in the west when they returned, dropping plummet-like from the depths of space, the rush of the air about the hull, a long scream that mounted from a half-heard sound in the outer limits of the earth's atmosphere, to a roar of tortured air as the ship dropped swiftly to the field and shot into the hangar. Instantly the crew darted to the side of the great cylinder as the door of the ship opened.

Fuller appeared in the opening, and at the first glimpse of his face, the hangar crew knew something was wrong. "Hey, Jackson," Fuller called, "get the field doctor—Arcot had a little accident out there in space!" In moments the man designated returned with the doctor, leading him swiftly down the long metal corridor of the *Solarite* to Arcot's room aboard.

There was a mean-looking cut in Arcot's scalp, but a quick, sure examination by the doctor revealed that there appeared to be no serious injury. He had been knocked unconscious by the blow that made the cut, and he had not yet recovered his senses.

"How did this happen?" asked the doctor as he bathed the cut and deftly bandaged it.

Morey explained: "There's a device aboard whose job it is to get us out of the way of stray meteors, and it works automatically. Arcot and I were just changing places at the controls. While neither of us was strapped into our seats, a meteor came within range and the rocket tubes shot the car out of the way. We both went tumbling head over heels and Arcot landed on his ear. I was luckier, and was able to break my fall with my hands, but it was a mean fall—at our speed we had about double weight, so, though it was only about seven feet, we might as well have fallen fourteen. We took turns piloting the ship, and Arcot was about to bring us back when that shock just about shook us all over the ship. We will have to make some changes. It does its job—but we need warning enough to grab hold."

The doctor was through now, and he began to revive his patient. In a moment he stirred and raised his hand to feel the sore spot. In ten minutes he was conversing with his friends, apparently none the worse except for a very severe headache. The doctor gave him a mild opiate, and sent him to bed to sleep off the effects of the blow.

With the ship fully equipped, tested and checked in every possible way, the time for leaving was set for the following Saturday, three days off. Great supplies of stores had to be carried aboard in the meantime. Care had to be exercised in this work, lest the cargo slip free under varying acceleration of the *Solarite,* and batter itself to bits, or even wreck some vital part of the ship. At noon on the day chosen, the first ship ever to leave the bounds of the earth's gravity was ready to start!

Gently the heavily laden *Solarite* rose from the hangar floor, and slowly floated out into the bright sunshine of the early February day. Beside it rode the little ship that Arcot had first built, piloted by the father of the inventor. With him rode the elder Morey and a dozen newsmen. The little ship was badly crowded now as they rose slowly, high into the upper reaches of the Earth's atmosphere. The sky about them was growing dark—they were going into space!

At last they reached the absolute ceiling of the smaller ship, and it hung there while the *Solarite* went a few miles higher; then slowly, but ever faster and faster they were plunging ahead, gathering speed.

They watched the radio speedometer creep up—1-2-3-4-5-6—steadily it rose as the acceleration pressed them hard against the back of the seats—8-9—still it rose as the hum of the generator became a low snarl—10-11-12—they were rocketing at twelve miles a second, the tenuous air about the ship shrieking in a thin scream of protest as it parted on the streamlined bow.

Slowly the speed rose—reached fifteen miles a second. The sun's pull became steadily more powerful; they were falling toward the fiery sphere, away from the earth. A microphone recessed in the outer wall brought them the fading whisper of air from outside. Arcot shouted a sudden warning:

"Hold on—we're going to lose all weight—out into space!"

There was a click, and the angry snarl of the overworked generator died in an instant as the thudding relays cut it out of the circuit. Simultaneously the air scoop which had carried air to the generator switched off, transferring to solar heat as a source of power. They seemed to be falling with terrific and ever-increasing speed. They looked down—saw the earth shrinking visibly as they shot away at more than five miles a second; they were traveling fifteen miles a second ahead and five a second straight up.

The men watched with intensest interest as the heavens opened up before them—they could see stars now a scant degree from the sun itself, for no air diffused its blinding glory. The heat of the rays seemed to burn them; there was a prickling pleasantness to it now, as they looked at the mighty sea of flame through smoked glasses. The vast arms of the corona reached out like the tentacles of some fiery octopus through thousands of miles of space—huge arms of flaming gas that writhed out as though to reach and drag back the whirling planets to the parent body. All about the mighty sphere, stretching far into space, a wan glow seemed to ebb and flow, a kaleidoscope of swiftly changing color. It was the zodiacal light, an aurora borealis on a scale inconceivable!

Arcot worked rapidly with the controls, the absence of weight that gave that continued sense of an unending fall, aiding him and his assistants in their rapid setting of the controls.

At last the work was done and the ship flashed on its way under the control of the instruments that would guide it across all the millions of miles of space and land it on Venus with unerring certainty. The photo-electric telescopic eye watched the planet constantly, keeping the ship surely and accurately on the course that would get them to the distant planet in the shortest possible time.

Work thereafter became routine requiring a minimum of effort, and the men could rest and use their time to observe the beauties of the skies as no man had ever seen them during all the billions of years of time that this solar system has existed. The lack of atmosphere made it possible to use a power of magnification that no terrestrial telescope may use. The blurred outlines produced by the shifting air prohibits magnifications of more than a few hundred diameters, but here in space they could use the greatest power of their telescope. With it they could look at Mars and see it more clearly than any other man had ever seen it, despite the fact that it was now over two hundred million miles away.

But though they spent much time taking photographs of the planets and of the moon, and in making spectrum analyses of the sun, time passed very slowly. Day after day they saw measured on the clocks, but they stayed awake, finding they needed little sleep, for they wasted no physical energy. Their weightlessness eliminated fatigue. However, they determined that during the twelve hours before reaching Venus they must be thoroughly alert, so they tried to sleep in pairs. Arcot and Morey were the first to seek slumber—but Morpheus seemed to be a mundane god, for he did not reward them. At last it became necessary for them to take a mild opiate, for their muscles refused to permit their tired brains to sleep. It was twelve hours later when they awoke, to relieve Wade and Fuller.

They spent most of the twelve hours of their routine watch in playing games of chess. There was little to be done. The silver globe before them seemed unchanging, for they were still so far away it seemed little larger than the moon does when seen from earth.

But at last it was time for the effects of the mild drug to wear off, and for Wade and Fuller to awaken from their sleep.

"Morey—I've an idea!" There was an expression of perfect innocence on Arcot's face—but a twinkle of humor in his eyes. "I wonder if it might not be interesting to observe the reactions of a man waking suddenly from sleep to find himself alone in space?" He stared thoughtfully at the control that would make the ship perfectly transparent, perfectly invisible.

"I wonder if it would?" said Morey grasping Arcot's idea. "What do you say we try it?" Arcot turned the little switch—and where there had been the ship, it was no more—it was gone!

Fuller stirred uneasily in his bed, tightly strapped as he was. The effects of the drug were wearing off. Sleepily he yawned—stretched, and blindly, his heavy eyes still closed, released the straps that held him in bed. Yawning widely he opened his eyes—with a sudden start sat upright—then, with an excellent imitation of an Indian on the warpath, he leaped from his bed, and started to run wildly across the floor. His eyes were raised to the place where the ceiling should have been—he called lustily in alarm—then suddenly he was flying up—and crashed heavily against the invisible ceiling! His face was a picture of utter astonishment as he fell lightly to the floor—then slowly it changed, and took on a chagrined smile—he understood!

He spun around as loud cries suddenly resounded from Wade's room across the hall—then there was a dull thud, as he too, forgetting the weightlessness, jumped and hit the ceiling. Then the cries were gone, like the snuffing of a candle. From the control room there rose loud laughter—and a moment later they felt more normal, as they again saw the four strong walls about them.

Wade sighed heavily and shook his head.

They were approaching the planet visibly now. In the twelve hours that had passed they had covered a million miles, for now they were falling toward the planet under its attraction. It glowed before them now in wondrous splendor, a mighty disc of molten silver.

For the last twenty-four hours they had been reducing their speed relative to Venus, to insure their forming an orbit about the planet, rather than shoot around it and back into space. Their velocity had been over a hundred miles a second part of the way, but now it had been reduced to ten. The gravity of the planet was urging them forward at ever increasing speed, and their problem became more acute moment by moment.

"We'll never make it on the power units alone, out here in space," said Arcot seriously. "We'll just shoot around the planet. I'll tell you how we can do it, though. We'll circle around it, entering its atmosphere on the daylight side, and shoot into the upper limits of its atmosphere. There the power units can find some heat to work on, and we can really slow down. But we'll have to use the rocket tubes to get the acceleration we'll need to drive the ship into the air."

There was a sudden clanging of a bell, and everyone dived for a hold, and held on tightly. An instant later there was a terrific wrench as the rocket jets threw the plane out of the way of a meteor.

"We're getting near a planet. This is the third meteor we've met since we were more than a million miles from Earth. Venus and Earth and all the planets act like giant vacuum cleaners of space, pulling into themselves all the space debris and meteors within millions of miles by their gravitational attraction."

Swiftly the planet expanded below them—growing vaster with each passing moment. It had changed from a disc to a globe, and now, as the molten silver of its surface seemed swiftly clouding, it turned gray; then they saw its true appearance, a vast field of rolling, billowing clouds!

The *Solarite* was shooting around the planet now at ten miles a second, far more than enough to carry them away from the planet again, out into space once more if their speed was not checked.

"Hold on everybody," Arcot called. "We're going to turn toward the planet now!" He depressed a small lever—there was a sudden shock, and all the space about them seemed to burst into huge, deep-red atomic hydrogen flames.

The *Solarite* reeled under the sudden pressure, but the heavy gyroscopic stabilizers caught it, held it, and the ship remained on an even keel. Then suddenly there came to the ears of the men a long drawn whine, faint—almost inaudible—and the ship began slowing down. The *Solarite* had entered the atmosphere of Venus—the first man-made machine to thus penetrate the air of another world!

Quickly Arcot snapped open the control that had kept the rockets flaming, turning the ship to the planet—driving it into the atmosphere. Now they could get their power from the air that each instant grew more dense about them.

"Wade—in the power room—emergency control post—Morey—control board there—hang on, for we'll have to use some husky accelerations."

Instantly the two men sprang for their posts—literally diving, for they were still almost weightless.

Arcot pulled another lever—there was a dull snap as a relay in the power room responded—the lights wavered—dimmed—then the generator was once more humming smoothly—working on the atmosphere of Venus! In a moment the power units were again operating, and now as they sucked a plentitude of power from the surrounding air, they produced a force that made the men cling to their holds with almost frantic force. Around them the rapidly increasing density of the air made the whine grow to a roar; the temperature within the ship rose slowly, warmed by friction with the air, despite the extreme cold at this altitude, more than seventy-five miles above the surface of the planet.

They began dropping rapidly now—their radio-speedometer had fallen from ten to nine—then slowly, but faster and faster as more heat could be extracted from the air, it had fallen 8—7—6—5—4. Now they were well below orbital speed, falling under the influence of the planet. The struggle was over—the men relaxed. The ship ran quietly now, the smooth hum of the air rushing over the great power units coming softly through the speaker to their ears, a humming melody—the song of a new world.

IV

Suddenly the blazing sun was gone and they were floating in a vast world of rolling mists—mists that brushed the car with tiny clicks, which, with the millions of particles that struck simultaneously, merged into a steady roar.

"Ice—ice clouds!" Morey exclaimed.

Arcot nodded. "We'll drop below the clouds; they're probably miles deep. Look, already they're changing—snow now—in a moment it will be water—then it'll clear away and we'll actually see Venus!"

For ten miles—an endless distance it seemed—they dropped through clouds utterly impenetrable to the eye. Then gradually the clouds thinned; there appeared brief clear spots, spots into which they could see short distances—then here and there they caught glimpses of green below. Was it water—or land?

With a suddenness that startled them, they were out of the clouds, shooting smoothly and swiftly above a broad plain. It seemed to stretch for endless miles across the globe, to be lost in the far distance to end and west; but to the north they saw a low range of hills that rose blue and misty in the distance.

"Venus! We made it!" Morey cried jubilantly. "The first men ever to leave earth—I'm going to start the old sender and radio back home! Man—look at that stretch of plain!" He jumped to his feet and started across the control room. "Lord—I feel like of ton of lead now—I sure am out of condition for walking after all that time floating!"

Arcot raised a restraining hand. "Whoa—wait a minute there, Morey—you won't get anything through to them now. The earth is on the other side of Venus—it's on the night side, remember —and we're on the day side. In about twelve hours we'll be able to send a message. In the meantime, take the controls while I make a test of the air here, will you?"

Relieved of the controls, Arcot rose and walked down the corridor to the power room where the chemical laboratory had been set up. Wade had already collected a dozen samples of air, and was working on them.

"How is it—what have you tested for so far?" asked Arcot.

"Oxygen and CO_2. The oxygen is about twenty-two per cent, or considering the slightly lower air pressure here, we will have just about the right amount of oxygen. The CO_2 is about one-tenth of one per cent. The atmosphere is O.K. for terrestrial life apparently; that mouse there is living quite happily. Whatever the other seventy-five per cent or so of diluting gas is, I don't know, but it isn't nitrogen."

Briefly Arcot and Wade discussed the unusual atmosphere, finally deciding that the inert gas was argon.

"No great amount of nitrogen," Arcot concluded. "That means that life will have a sweet time extracting it from the air—but wherever there is life, it finds a way to do the impossible. Test it more accurately, will you—you try for nitrogen and I'll try the component inert gases."

They ran the analyses rapidly, and in a very short time—less than an hour—their results stood at 23 per cent oxygen, .1 per cent carbon dioxide, 68 per cent argon, 6 per cent nitrogen, 2 per cent helium, 5 per cent neon, .05 per cent hydrogen, and the rest krypton and xenon apparently. The analyses of these inert gases had to be done rather roughly in this short time, but it was sufficient to balance fairly accurately.

The two chemists reported back to the control cabin.

"Well, we'll be able to breathe the atmosphere of Venus with ease. I believe we can go on now. I have been surprised to see no water in sight, but I think I see my mistake now. You know the Mississippi has its mouth further from the center of the earth than its source; it flows up hill! The answer is, of course, that the centrifugal force of the earth's spin impels it to flow that way. Similarly, I am sure now that we will find that Venus has a vast belt of water about the middle, and to the north and south there will be two great caps of dry land. We are on the northern cap.

"We have the microphone turned way down. Let's step up the power a bit and see if there are any sounds outside," said Arcot and walked over to the power control switch. An instant later a low hum came from the loud-speaker. There was a light breeze blowing. In the distance, forming a dull background for the hum, there came a low rumbling that seemed punctuated now and then by a greater sound.

"Must be a long way off," said Arcot, a puzzled frown on his face. "Swing the ship around so we can see in what direction the sound is loudest," he suggested.

Slowly Morey swung the ship around on its vertical axis. Without a doubt, something off in the direction of the hills was making a considerable noise.

"Arcot, if that's a fight between two animals—two of those giant animals that you said might be here—I don't care to get near them!" Fuller's narrowed eyes strove to penetrate the haze that screened the low hills in the blue distance.

The microphone was shut off while the *Solarite* shot swiftly forward toward the source of the sound. Quickly the hills grew, the blue mistiness disappearing, and the jagged mounds revealing themselves as bleak harsh rock. As they drew nearer they saw beyond the hills, intermittent flashes of brilliant light, heard shattering blasts of sound.

"A thunderstorm!" Wade began, but Arcot interrupted.

"Not so fast, Wade—Fuller's animal *is* there—the only animal in all creation that can make a noise like that! Look through the telescope—see those dots wheeling about there above the flashing lights? The only animal that can make that racket is man! There are men over there—and they aren't in a playful mood! Turn on the invisibility while we can, Morey—and let's get nearer!"

"Look out—here we go!" Morey began to close a tiny switch set in one side of the instrument panel—then, before the relay below could move, he had flipped it back.

"Here, you take it, Arcot—you always think about two steps ahead of me—you're quicker and know the machine better anyway."

Quickly the two men exchanged places.

"I don't know about that, Morey," said a voice from vacancy, for Arcot had at once thrown the ship into invisibility. "The longer we're here, the more mistakes I see we made in our calculations. I see what put me off so badly on my estimate of the intelligence of life found here! The sun gives it a double dose of heat—but also a double dose of other radiations—some of which evidently speed up evolution. Anyway, we may be able to find friends here more quickly if we aid one side or the other in the very lively battle going on there. Before we go any further, what's our decision?"

"I think it is a fine idea," said Fuller. "But which side are we to aid—and what are the sides? We haven't even seen them yet. Let's go nearer and take a good look."

"Yes—but are we going to join either side after looking?"

"Oh, that's unanimous!" said Wade, excitedly.

The invisible ship darted forward. They sped past the barrier of low hills, and were again high above a broad plain. With a startled gasp, Arcot cut their speed. There, floating high in the air, above a magnificent city, was a machine such as no man had ever before seen! It was a titanic airplane—monstrous, gargantuan, and every other word that denoted immensity. Fully three-quarters of a mile the huge metal wings stretched out in the dull light of the cloudy Venerian day; a machine that seemed to dwarf even the vast city beneath it. The roar of its mighty propellers was a rumbling thunder to the men in the *Solarite*. From it came the flashing bursts of flame.

On closer inspection, the watchers saw what seemed to be a swarm of tiny gnats flying about the mighty plane. They appeared to be attacking the giant as vainly as gnats might attack an eagle, for they could not damage the giant machine. The flashing bombs burst in blasts of yellow flame as harmlessly as so many firecrackers.

All that mighty plane was covered with heavy metal plates, fully ten inches thick, and of metal so tough that when the powerful bombs hit it they made no impression, though they blasted tremendous craters in the soil below. From it poured a steady stream of bombs that burst with a great flash of heat and light, and in an instant the tiny planes they struck streaked down as incandescent masses of metal.

Yet the giant seemed unable to approach the city—or was it defending it? No, for it was from the city that the vainly courageous little ships poured out. But certainly it was not these ships that kept the titanic battleship of the air at bay!

Tensely the men watched the uneven conflict. The rain of bombs continued, through all fell short of the city. But slowly around the metropolis there appeared an area of flaring, molten lava, and steadily this moved toward the beautiful buildings. Suddenly the battleship turned toward the city and made a short dash inward on its circling path. As though awaiting this maneuver, a battery of hissing, flaming swords of white light flashed upward, a few hundred feet from the ring of molten rock. As the titanic plane rolled, side-slipped out of the way, they passed, harmlessly, barely missing a monstrous wing.

"Which?" Arcot demanded. "I say the city. No one should destroy anything so magnificent."

Not a dissenting voice was raised, so Arcot sent the *Solarite* nearer.

"But what in the world can we do to that huge thing?" Fuller's voice came eerily out of the emptiness. "It has perfect invulnerability through size alone."

There was sudden silence among the Terrestrials as one of the tiny planes darted forward and dove at full speed directly toward one of the giant's propellors. There were fifty of these strung along each great wing. If enough of them could be destroyed, the plane must crash. There came a terrific crash—a flare of light— and splintered fragments of flaming wreckage plummeted down. Yet the mighty blades continued whirling as smoothly as ever!

What could the *Solarite* do against the giant monoplane? Evidently Arcot had a plan. Under his touch their machine darted high into the sky above the great plane. There was a full mile between them when he released the sustaining force of the *Solarite* and let it drop, straight toward the source of the battle— falling freely, ever more and more rapidly. They were rushing at the mighty plane below at a pace that made their hearts seem to pause—then suddenly Arcot cried out, "Hold on—here we stop!"

They seemed a scant hundred feet from the broad metal wings of the unsuspecting plane, when suddenly there was a tremendous jerk, and each man felt himself pressed to the floor beneath a terrific weight that made their backs crack with the load. Doggedly they fought to retain their senses; the blackness receded.

Below them they saw only a mighty sea of roaring red flames —a hell of blazing gas that roared like a score of bombs set off at once. The *Solarite* was sitting down on her rocket jets! All six of the rocket tubes in the base of the ship had been opened wide, and streaming from them in a furious blast of incandescent gas, the atomic hydrogen shot out in a mighty column of gas at 3500 degrees centigrade. Where the gas touched it, the great plane flared to incandescence; and in an immeasurable interval the fall of the *Solarite* ended, and it rebounded high into the air. Arcot, struggling against the weight of six gravities, pulled shut the little control that had sent those mighty torches blasting out. An instant later they sped away lest the plane shoot toward the gas columns.

From a safe distance they looked back at their work. No longer was the mighty plane unscathed, invulnerable, for now in its top gaped six great craters of incandescent metal that almost touched and coalesced. The great plane itself reeled, staggering, plunging downward; but long before it reached the hard soil below, it was brought into level flight, and despite many dead engines, it circled and fled toward the south. The horde of small planes followed, dropping a rain of bombs into the glowing pits in the ship, releasing their fury in its interior. In moments the beings manning the marauder had to a large extent recovered from the shock of the attack and were fighting back. In a moment—just before the ship passed over the horizon and out of sight—the Terrestrians saw the great props that had been idle, suddenly leap into motion, and in an instant the giant had left its attackers behind—fleeing from its invisible foe.

Under Arcot's guidance the ship from earth, still invisible, returned to the approximate spot where they had destroyed the invulnerability of the Giant. Then suddenly, out of nothing, the *Solarite* appeared. In an instant a dozen of the tiny two-man planes darted toward it. Just that they might recognize it, Arcot shot it up a bit higher with the aid of the keel rockets at one-third power. The typical reddish flame of atomic hydrogen, he knew, would be instantaneously recognizable.

Little these planes were, but shaped like darts, and swifter than any plane of Earth. They shot along at 1000 miles an hour readily, as Arcot soon found out. It was not a minute before they had formed a long line that circled the *Solarite* at minimum speed, then started off in the direction of the city. On impulse Arcot followed after them, and instantly the planes increased their velocity, swiftly reaching 1000 miles per hour.

The city they were approaching was an inspiring sight. Mighty towers swept graceful lines a half mile in the air, their brightly colored walls gleaming in rainbow hues, giving the entire city the aspect of a gigantic jewel—a single architectural unit. Here was symmetry and order, with every unit in the city built around the gigantic central edifice that rose, a tremendous tower of black and gold, a full half mile in the air.

The outer parts of the city were evidently the residential districts, the low buildings and the wide streets with the little green lawns showing the care of the individual owner. Then came the apartment houses and the small stores; these rose in gentle slopes, higher and higher, merging at last with the mighty central pinnacle of beauty. The city was designed as a whole, not in a multitude of individually beautiful, but inharmonious units, like some wild mixture of melodies, each in itself beautiful, but mutually discordant.

V

The Terrestrians followed their escort high above these great buildings, heading toward the great central tower. In a moment they were above it, and in perfect order the ships of the Venerians shot down to land smoothly, but at high speed. On the roof of the building they slowed with startling rapidity, held back by electromagnets under the top dressing of the roof landing, as Arcot learned later.

"We can't land on that—this thing weighs too much—we'd probably sink right through it! The street looks wide enough for us to land there." Arcot maneuvered the *Solarite* over the edge of the roof, and dropped it swiftly down the half mile to the ground below. Just above the street, he leveled off, and descended slowly, giving the hurrying crowds plenty of time to get from beneath it.

Landing finally, he looked curiously at the mass of Venerians who had gathered in the busy street, coming out of buildings where they evidently had sought shelter during the raid. The crowd grew rapidly as the Terrestrians watched them—people of a new world.

"Why," exclaimed Fuller in startled surprise, "they look almost like us!"

"Why not?" laughed Arcot. "Is there any particular reason why they shouldn't look like us? Venus and Earth are very nearly the same size, and are planets of the same parent sun. Physical conditions here appear to be very similar to conditions back home, and if there's anything to Svend Arrehenius' theory of life spores being sent from world to world by sunlight, there's no reason why humanoid races cannot be found throughout the universe. On worlds, that is, suitable for the development of such life forms."

"Look at the size of 'em," Fuller commented.

Their size was certainly worth noting, for in all that crowd only the obviously young were less than six feet tall. The average seemed to be seven feet—well-built men and women with unusually large chests, who would have seemed very human indeed, but for a ghastly, death-like blue tinge to their skin. Even their lips were as bright a blue as man's lips are red. The teeth seemed to be as white as any human's, but their mouths were blue.

"They look as if they'd all been eating blueberries!" laughed Wade. "I wonder what makes their blood blue? I've heard of blue-blooded families, but these are the first I've ever seen!"

"I think I can answer that," said Morey slowly. "It seems odd to us—but those people evidently have their blood based on hemocyanin. In us, the oxygen is carried to the tissues, and the carbon dioxide carried away by an iron compound, hemo-globin, but in many animals of Earth, the same function is performed by a copper compound, hemocyanin, which is an intense blue. I am sure that that is the explanation for these strange people. By the way, did you notice their hands?"

"Yes, I had. They strike me as having one too many fingers—look there—that fellow is pointing—why—his hand hasn't too many fingers, but too many thumbs! He has one on each side of his palm! Say, that would be handy in placing nuts and bolts, and such fine work, wouldn't it?"

Suddenly a lane opened in the crowd, and from the great black and gold building there came a file of men in tight-fitting green uniforms, a file of seven-foot giants. Obviously they were soldiers of some particular branch, for in the crowd there were a number of men dressed in similar uniforms of deep blue.

"I think they want one or more of us to accompany them,"

Arcot said. "Let's flip a coin to decide who goes—two better stay here, and two go. If we don't come back inside of a reasonable period of time, one of you might start making inquiries; the other can send a message to Earth, and get out of harm's way till help can come. I imagine these people are friendly now, however—else I wouldn't go."

The leader of the troop stepped up to the door of the *Solarite*, and coming to what was obviously a position of attention, put his left hand over his right breast in an equally obvious salute, and waited.

The coin was flipped with due ceremony—it would decide which of them were to have the distinction of being the first Terrestrians to set foot on Venus. Arcot and Morey won, and they quickly put on the loose-fitting ventilated cooling suits that they might live comfortably in the hot air outside—for the thermometer registered 150°!

The two men quickly walked over to the airlock, entered, closed it behind them, and opened the outer door. There was a slight rush of air, as the pressure outside was a bit lower than that inside. There was a singing in their ears, and they had to swallow several times to equalize the pressure.

The guards at once fell into a double row on either side of them, and the young officer strode ahead. He himself had curbed his curiosity after the single startled glance he had given these strange men. Only their hands were visible, for the cooling suits covered them almost completely, but the strange pink color must indeed have been startling to the eyes; also their dwarf stature, and the strange suits they wore. The men of his little troop, however, as well as the people in the crowd about them, were not so disinterested. They were looking in eager amazement at these men who had just saved their city, these strange small men with their queer pink skin. And most surprising of all, perhaps, the inner thumb was missing from each hand!

But soon they had passed beyond the sight of the crowd, which was held in check by a handful of the deep blue uniformed men.

"Those fellows would never hold such a Terrestrial crowd back if visitors from another planet landed!" remarked Morey wonderingly.

"How do they know we are visitors from another planet?" Arcot objected. "We suddenly appeared out of nowhere—they don't even know our direction of approach. We might be some strange race of Venerians as far as they know."

They walked briskly up to the massive gold and black entrance, and passed through the great doors that seemed made of solid copper, painted with some clear coating that kept the metal lustrous, the rich color shining magnificently. They stood open wide now, as indeed they always were. Even the giant Venerians were dwarfed by these mighty doors as they passed through into an equally vast hall, a tremendous room that must have filled all the front half of the ground floor of the gigantic building, a hall of graceful columns that hid the great supporting members. The stone, they knew, must serve the Venerians as marble serves us, but it was a far more handsome stone. It was a rich green, like the green of thick, heavy grass in summer when the rain is plentiful. The color was very pleasing to the eye, and restful too. There was a checker-board floor of this green stone, alternated with another, a stone of intense blue. They were hard, and the colors made a very striking pattern, pleasingly different from what they had been accustomed to, but common to Venus, as they later learned.

At last the party had crossed the great hall, and stopped beside a large doorway. The officer halted for a moment, and gestured toward two of his men, who remained, while the others walked quickly away. The diminished party stepped through the doorway into a small room whose walls were lined with copper, and an instant later, as the officer pushed a small button, there was a low hiss of escaping air, and a copper grating sprang quickly up across the opening of the elevator. He touched another button, and there was the familiar sinking feeling as the car rose, a low hum seeming to come from its base.

The elevator rose swiftly through a very considerable distance —up—up, endlessly.

"They must have some wonderfully strong cables here on Venus!" Morey exclaimed. "The engineers of Terrestrial buildings have been wondering for some time how to get around the difficulty of shifting elevators. The idea of changing cars doesn't appeal to me, either—but we must have risen a long way!"

"I should say so—I wonder how they do it. We've been rising for a minute and a half at a very fair clip—there we are; end of the line—I want to look at this car!" Arcot stepped over to the control board, looked at it closely, then stepped out and peered down between the car and the shaft as the copper grating fell, simultaneously pulling down with it the door that had blocked off the hall-way.

"Come here, Morey—simple system at that! It would be so, of course. Look—they have tracks, and a regular trolley system, with cog rails alongside, and the car just winds itself up! They have a motor underneath, I'll bet, and just run it up in that way. They have never done that on Earth because of the cost of running the car up without too much power. I think I see the solution—the car has electro-dynamical brakes, and descending, just slows itself down by pumping power into the line to haul some other car up. This is a mighty clever scheme!"

As Arcot straightened, the officer beckoned to him to follow, and started down the long corridor which was lined on either side with large doorways, much like a very exotic earthly office building. Passing through a long series of branching corridors they at last reached one that terminated in a large office, into which the young officer led them. Snapping to attention, he spoke briefly and rapidly, saluted and retired with his two men.

The man before whom the Terrestrians stood was a tall, kindly-faced old gentleman. His straight black hair was tinged with bluish gray, and the kindly face bore the lines of age, but the smiling eyes, and the air of sincere interest gave his countenance an amazingly youthful air. It was warm and friendly despite its disconcerting blueness. He looked curiously, questioningly at the two men before him, looked at their hands, his eyes widening in surprise; then he stepped quickly forward, and extended his hand, at the same time looking toward Arcot.

Smiling, Arcot extended his own. The Venerian grasped it—then with an exclamation on the part of each, they mutually released each other, Arcot feeling an uncomfortable sensation of heat, just as the Venerian felt a flash of intense cold! Each stared from his hand to the hand of the other in surprise, then a smile curved the blue lips of the Venerian as he very emphatically put his hand at his side. Arcot smiled in turn, and said to Morey in an animated tone:

"They have a body temperature of at least 170° Fahrenheit. It would naturally be above room temperature, which is 150° here, so that they are most unpleasantly hot to us. Marvelous how nature adapts herself to her surroundings!" He chuckled. "I hope these fellows don't have fevers. They'd be apt to boil over!"

The Venerian had picked up a small rectangle of black material, smooth and solid. He drew quickly upon it with what appeared to be a pencil of copper. In a moment he handed the tablet to Arcot, who reached out for it, then changed his mind, and motioned that he didn't want to burn his fingers. The old Venerian held it where Arcot could see it.

"Why, Morey, look here—I didn't think they had developed astronomy to any degree, because of the constant clouds, but look at this. He has a nice little map of the solar system, with Mercury, Venus, Earth, the Moon, Mars, and all the rest on it. He has drawn in several of the satellites of Jupiter and of Saturn too."

The Venerian pointed to Mars and looked inquisitively at them. Arcot shook his head and pointed quickly to Earth. The Venerian seemed a bit surprised at this, then thought a moment and nodded in satisfaction. He looked at Arcot intently. Then to the latter's amazement, there seemed to form in his mind a thought—at first vague, then quickly taking definite form.

"Man of Earth," it seemed to say, "we thank you—you have saved our nation. We want to thank you for your quick response to our signals. We had not thought that you could answer us so soon." The Venerian seemed to relax as the message was finished. It obviously had required great mental effort.

Arcot looked steadily into his eyes now, and tried to concentrate on a message—on a series of ideas. To him, trained though he was in deep concentration on one idea, the process of visualizing a series of ideas was new, and very difficult. But he soon saw that he was making some progress.

"We came in response to no signals—exploration only—we saw the battle—and aided because your city seemed doomed, and because it seemed too beautiful to be destroyed."

"What's it all about, Arcot?" asked Morey wonderingly, as he watched them staring at each other.

"Mental telepathy," Arcot answered briefly. "I'm terribly thick from his point of view, but I just learned that they sent signals to Earth—why, I haven't learned—but I'm making progress. If I don't crack under the strain, I'll find out sooner or later—so wait and see." He turned again to the Venerian.

The latter was frowning at him rather dubiously. With sudden decision he turned to his desk, and pulled down a small lever. Then again he looked intently at Arcot.

"Come with me—the strain of this conversation is too great—I see you do not have thought transference on your world."

"Come along, Morey—we're going somewhere. He says this thought transference is too much for us. I wonder what he is going to do?"

Out into the maze of halls they went again, now led by the kindly seven-foot Venerian. After walking through a long series of halls, they reached a large auditorium, where already there had gathered in the semi-circle of seats a hundred or so of the tall, blue-tinged Venerians. Before them, on a low platform, were two large, deeply-cushioned chairs. To these chairs the two Terrestrians were led.

"We will try to teach you our language telepathically. We can give you the ideas—you must learn the pronunciation, but this will be very much quicker. Seat yourselves in these chairs and relax."

The chairs had been designed for the seven-footers. These men were six feet and six feet four, respectively, yet it seemed to them, as they sank into the cushions, that never had they felt such comfortable chairs. They were designed to put every muscle and every nerve at rest. Luxuriously, almost in spite of themselves, they relaxed.

Dimly Arcot felt a wave of sleepiness sweep over him; he yawned prodigiously. There was no conscious awareness of his sinking into a deep slumber. It seemed that suddenly visions began to fill his mind—visions that developed with a returning consciousness—up from the dark, into a dream world. He saw a mighty fleet whose individual planes were a mile long, with three-quarters of a mile wingspread—titantic monoplanes, whose droning thunder seemed to roar through all space. Then suddenly they were above him, and from each there spurted a great stream of dazzling brilliance, an intense glow that reached down, and touched the city. An awful concussion blasted his ears. All the world about him erupted in unimaginable brilliance; then darkness fell.

Another vision filled his mind—a vision of the same fleet hanging over a giant crater of molten rock, a crater that gaped angrily in a plain beside low green hills—a crater that had been a city. The giants of the air circled, turned, and sped over the horizon. Again he was with them—and again he saw a great city fuse in a blazing flash of blinding light—again and yet again—until around all that world he saw smoking ruins of great cities, now blasted crimson craters in a world of fearful desolation.

The destroyers rode up, up, up—out of the clouds—and he was with them. Out beyond the swirling mists, where the cold of space seemed to reach in at them, and the roaring of the mighty propellers was a thin whine—then suddenly that was gone, and from the tail of each of the titanic machines there burst a great stream of light, a blazing column that roared back, and lit all space for miles around—rocket jets that sent them swiftly across space!

He saw them approaching another world, a world that shone a dull red, but he saw the markings and knew that it was Earth, not Mars. The great planes began falling now—falling at an awful speed into the upper air of the planet, and in an instant the rocket flares were gone, fading and dying in the dense air. Again there came the roar of the mighty propellers. Then swiftly the fleet of giants swooped down, lower and lower. He became aware of its destination—a spot he knew must be New York—but a strangely distorted New York—a Venerian city, where New York should have been. And again, the bombs rained down. In an instant the gigantic city was a smoking ruin.

The visions faded, and slowly he opened his eyes, looked about him. He was still in the room of the circle of chairs—he was still on Venus—then with sudden shock, understanding came. He knew the meaning of these visions—the meaning of that strangely distorted New York, of that red earth. It meant that this was what the Venerians believed was to happen! They were trying to show him the plans of the owners and builders of those gigantic ships! The New York he had seen was New York as these men imagined it.

Startled, confused, his forehead furrowed, he rose unsteadily to his feet. His head seemed whirling in the throes of a terrific headache. The men about him were looking anxiously at him. He glanced toward Morey. He was sleeping deeply in the seat, his features now and again reflecting his sensations. It was his turn to learn this new language and see the visions.

The old Venerian who had brought them there walked up to Arcot and spoke to him in a softly musical language, a language that was sibilant and predominated in liquid sounds; there were no gutturals, no nasals; it was a more musical language than Earth men had ever before heard, and now Arcot started in surprise, for he understood it perfectly; the language was as familiar as English.

"We have taught you our language as quickly as possible—you may have a headache, but you must know what we know as soon as possible. It may well be that the fate of two worlds hangs on your actions. These men have concentrated on you and taught you very rapidly with the massed power of their minds, giving you visions of what we know to be in preparation. You must get back to your wonderful ship as quickly as possible; and yet you must know what has happened here on our world in the last few years, as well as what happened twenty centuries ago.

"Come with me to my office, and we will talk. When your friend has also learned, you may tell him."

Quickly Arcot followed the Venerian down the long corridors of the building. The few people they met seemed intent on their own business, paying little attention to them.

At last they seated themselves in the office where Arcot had first met his escort; and there he listened to a new history—the history of another planet.

"My name is Tonlos," the old man said. "I am a leader of my people—though my title and position are unimportant. To explain would entail a prolonged discussion of our social structure, and there is no time for that. Later, perhaps—but now to our history.

"Twenty centuries ago," Tonlos continued, "there were two great rival nations on this planet. The planet Turo is naturally divided so that there would be a tendency toward such division. There are two enormous belts of land around the globe, one running from about 20 degrees north of the equator to about 80 degrees north. This is my country, Lanor. To the south there is a similar great belt of land, of almost identical size, Kaxor. These two nations have existed for many thousands of our years.

"Two thousand years ago a great crisis arose in the affairs of the world—a great war was in process of starting—but a Lanorian developed a weapon that made it impossible for the Kaxorians to win—and war was averted. The feeling was so strong, however, that laws were passed which stopped all intercourse between the two nations for these thousands of years. By devious ways we've learned that Kaxor has concentrated on the study of physics, perhaps in hopes of finding a weapon with which they could threaten us once more. Lanor has studied the secrets of the human mind and body. We have no disease here any longer; we have no insanity. We are students of chemistry, but physics has been neglected to a great extent. Recently, however, we have again taken up this science, since it alone of the main sciences had not received our study. Only twenty-five years have been spent on these researches, and in that short time we cannot hope to do what the Kaxorians have done in two thousand.

"The secret of the heat ray, the weapon that prevented the last war, had been almost forgotten. It required diligent research to bring it to life again, for it is a very inefficient machine—or was. Of late, however, we have been able to improve it, and now it is used in commerce to smelt our ores. It was this alone that allowed this city to put up the slight resistance that we did. We were surely doomed. This is the capitol of Lanor, Sonor. We—and the nation—would have fallen but for you.

"We have had some warning that this was coming. We have spies in Kaxor now, for we learned of their intentions when they flew the first of their giant planes over one of our cities and dropped a bomb! We have been trying, since we discovered the awful scope of their plans, to send you a warning if you could not help us. That you should come here at this particular time is almost beyond belief—a practically impossible coincidence—but perhaps there is more than coincidence behind it? Who knows?" He paused briefly; went on with a heavy sigh: "Since you drove that plane away, we can expect a new raid at any moment, and we must be prepared. Is there any way you can signal your planet?"

"Yes—we can signal easily," Arcot answered; he struggled with the newly acquired language. "I do not know the word in your tongue—it may be that you do not have it—radio we call it—it is akin to light, but of vastly longer wavelength. Produced electrically, it can be directed like light and sent in a beam by means of a reflection. It can penetrate all substances except metals, and can leak around them, if it be not directional. With it I can talk readily with the men of earth, and this very night I will."

Arcot paused, frowning thoughtfully, then continued, "I know there's definite need for haste, but we can't do anything until Morey has received the knowledge you've given me. While we're waiting here, I might just as well learn all I can about your planet. The more I know, the more intelligently I'll be able to plan for our defense."

In the conversation which followed, Arcot gained a general knowledge of the physical makeup of Venus. He learned that iron was an exceedingly rare element on the planet, while platinum was relatively plentiful. Gold, though readily available, was considered a nuisance, since it was of no practical value due to its softness, excessive weight and its affinity for many catalysts. Most of the other metallic elements were present in quantities approximating those of Earth, except for an element called "morlus". When Tonlos mentioned this, Arcot said:

"Morlus—I have the word in your language—but I do not know the element. What is it?"

"Why—here is some!"

Tonlos handed Arcot a small block of metal that had been used as a weight on a table in one corner of the room. It seemed fairly dense, about as heavy as iron, but it had a remarkably bluish tint. Obviously, it was the element that composed the wings of the airplane they had seen that afternoon. Arcot examined it carefully, handicapped somewhat by its heat. He picked up a small copper rod and tried to scratch it but there was no noticeable effect.

"You cannot scratch it with copper," said Tonlos. "It is the second hardest metal we know—it is not as hard as chromium, but far less brittle. It is malleable, ductile, very very strong, very tough, especially when alloyed with iron, but those alloys are used only in very particular work because of iron's rarity."

Indicating the bluish block, Arcot said, "I'd like to identify this element. May I take it back to the ship and test it?"

"You may, by all means. You will have considerable difficulty getting it into solution, however. It is attacked only by boiling selenic acid which, as you must know, dissolves platinum readily. The usual test for the element is to so dissolve it, oxidize it to an acid, then test with radium selenate, when a brilliant greenish blue salt is—"

"Test with radium selenate!" Arcot exclaimed. "Why, we have no radium salts whatever on Earth that we could use for that purpose. Radium is exceedingly rare!"

"Radium is by no means plentiful here," Tonlos replied, "but we seldom have to test for morlus, and we have plenty of radium salts for that purpose. We have never found any other use for radium—it is so active that it combines with water just as sodium does; it is very soft—a useless metal, and dangerous to handle. Our chemists have never been able to understand it—it is always in some kind of reaction no matter what they do, and still it gives off that very light gas, helium, and a heavy gas, niton, and an unaccountable amount of heat."

"Your world is vastly different from ours," Arcot commented. He told Tonlos of the different metals of Earth, the non-metals, and their occurrence. But try as he would, he could not place the metal Tonlos had given him.

Morey's arrival interrupted their discussion. He looked very tired, and very serious. His head ached from his unwonted mental strain, just as Arcot's had. Briefly Arcot told him what he had learned, concluding with a question as to why Morey thought the two planets, both members of the same solar family, should be so different.

"I have an idea," said Morey slowly, "and it doesn't seem *too* wacky. As you know, by means of solar photography, astronomers have mapped the sun, charting the location of the different elements. We've seen hydrogen, oxygen, silicon and others, and as the sun aged, the elements must have been mixed up more and more thoroughly. Yet we have seen the vast areas of single elements. Some of those areas are so vast that they could easily be the source of an entire world! I wonder if it is not possible that Earth was thrown off from some deposit rich in iron, aluminum and calcium, and poor in gold, radium and those other metals—and particularly poor in one element. We have located in the sun the spectrum of an element we have named coronium —and I think you have a specimen of coronium in your hand there! I'd say Venus came from a coronium-rich region!"

The discussion ended there, for already the light outside had deepened to a murky twilight. The Terrestrians were led quickly down to the elevator, which dropped them rapidly to the ground. There was still a large crowd about the *Solarite,* but the way was quickly cleared for them. As the men passed through the crowd, a peculiar sensation struck them very forcibly. It seemed that everyone in the crowd was wishing them the greatest success—the best of good things in every wish.

"The ultimate in applause! Morey, I'll swear we just received a silent cheer!" exclaimed Arcot, as they stood inside the airlock of the ship once more. It seemed home to them now! In a moment they had taken off the uncomfortable ventilating suits and stepped once more into the room where Wade and Fuller awaited them.

"Say—what were you fellows doing?" Wade demanded. "We were actually getting ready to do some inquiring about your health!"

"I know we were gone a long time—but when you hear the reason you'll agree it was worth it. See if you can raise Earth on the radio, Morey, will you, while I tell these fellows what happened? If you succeed, tell them to call in Dad and your father, and to have a couple of tape recorders on the job. We'll want a record of what I have to send. Say that we'll call back in an hour." Then, while Morey was busy down in the power room sending the signals out across the forty million miles of space that separated them from their home planet, Arcot told Wade and Fuller what they had learned.

Morey finally succeeded in getting his message through, and returned to say that they would be waiting in one hour. He had had to wait eight minutes after sending his message to get any answer, however, due to time required for radio waves to make the two-way trip.

"Fuller," Arcot said, "as chef, suppose you see what you can concoct while Wade and I start on this piece of coronium and see what there is to learn."

At the supper table Wade and Arcot reported to the others the curious constants they had discovered for coronium. It was not attacked by any acid except boiling selenic acid, since it formed a tremendous number of insoluble salts. Even the nitrate violated the long-held rule that "all nitrates are soluble"—it wouldn't dissolve. Yet it was chemically more active than gold.

But its physical constants were the most surprising. It melted at 2800° centigrade, a very high melting point indeed. Very few metals are solid at that temperature. But the tensile strength test made with a standard bar they finally turned out by means of a carbaloy tool, gave a reading of more than one million, three hundred thousand pounds per square inch! It was far stronger than iron—stronger than tungsten, the strongest metal heretofore known. It was twice as strong as the Earth's strongest metal!

Fuller whistled in awe. "No wonder they can make a plane like that when they have such a metal to work with." The designing engineer had visions of a machine after his own heart—one in which half the weight was *not* employed in holding it together!

It was a little later that they got communication through to Earth, and the men went to the power room. The television screen was struggling to form a clear image despite the handicap of forty million miles of space. In a moment it had cleared, though, and they saw the face of Dr. Arcot. He showed plainly that he was worried about the startling news that had reached him already, sketchy though it was. After brief though warm greetings, his son rapidly outlined to him the full extent of their discoveries, and the force that Earth would have to meet.

"Dad, these Kaxorians have planes capable of far more than a thousand miles an hour in the air. For some reason the apparatus they use to propel them in space is inoperative in air, but their propellers will drive them forward faster than any plane Earth ever saw. You must start at once on a fleet of these molecular motion planes—and a lot of the gas Wade developed—you know how to make it—the animation suspending gas. They don't have it—and I believe it will be useful. I'll try to develop some new weapon here. If either of us makes any progress along new lines —we'll report to the other. I must stop now—a Lanorian delegation is coming." After a few words of farewell, Arcot severed connections with the Earth and arose to await the arrival of the visitors.

Since the return of the Terrestrians to the *Solarite*, a great crowd of Venerians had gathered around it, awaiting a glimpse of the men, for the news had spread that this ship had come from Earth. Now, the crowd had divided, and a group of men was approaching, clothed in great heavy coats that seemed warm enough to wear in Terrestrial arctic regions!

"Why—Arcot—what's the idea of the winter regalia?" asked Fuller in surprise.

"Think a moment—they are going to visit a place whose temperature is seventy degrees colder than their room temperature. In the bargain, Venus never has any seasonal change of temperature, and a heavy bank of clouds that eternally cover the planet keeps the temperature as constant as a thermocouple arrangement could. The slight change from day to night is only appreciable by the nightly rains—see—the crowd is beginning to break up now. It's night already, and there is a heavy dew settling. Soon it will be rain, and the great amount of moisture in the air will supply enough heat, in condensing, to prevent a temperature drop of more than two or three degrees. These men are not used to changes in temperature as we are and hence they must protect themselves far more fully."

Three figures now entered the air-lock of the *Solarite*, and muffled in heavy garments as they were, large under any conditions, they had to come through one at a time.

Much that Arcot showed them was totally new to them. Much he could not explain to them at all, for their physics had not yet reached that stage.

But there was one thing he could show them, and he did. There were no samples of the liquids he wanted, but their chemistry was developed to a point that permitted the communication of the necessary data and Arcot told them the formula of Wade's gas. It's ability to penetrate any material at ordinary temperatures, combined with its anesthetic properties, gave it obvious advantages as a weapon for rendering the opposing forces defenseless.

Since it was able to penetrate all substances, there was no means of storing it. Hence it was made in the form of two liquids which reacted spontaneously and produced the gas, which was then projected to the spot where needed.

Arcot asked now that the Venerian chemists make him a supply of these two liquids; and they promptly agreed. He felt he would have a fighting chance in combatting the enemy if he could but capture one of their flying forts. It seemed a strange task! Capturing so huge a machine with only the tiny *Solarite*— but Arcot felt there was a good possibility of his doing it if he but had a supply of that gas.

There was one difficulty—one step in the synthesis required a considerable quantity of chlorine. Since chlorine was rare on Venus, the men were forced to sacrifice most of their salt supply; but this chlorine so generated could be used over and over again.

It was quite late when the Venerians left, to go again into the scalding hot rain, rain that seemed to them to be a cold drizzle. After they had gone, the Terrestrians turned in for the night, leaving a telephone connection with the armed guard outside.

The dull light of the Venerian day was filtering in through the windows the next morning when the Terrestrians awoke. It was eight o'clock, New York time, but Sonor was working on a twenty-three hour day. It happened that Sonor and New York had been in opposition at midnight two nights ago, which meant that it was now ten o'clock Sonorian time. The result was that Arcot left the car to speak to the officer in charge of the guard about the ship.

"We need some pure water—water free of copper salts. I think it would be best if you can get me some water that has been distilled. That is, for drinking. Also we need about two tons of water of any kind—the ship's tanks need recharging. I'd like about a ton of the drinking water." Arcot had to translate the Terrestrian measures into the corresponding Venerian terms, of course, but still the officer seemed puzzled. Such a large amount of water would create a real problem in transportation. After apparently conferring by telepathic means with his superiors, the officer asked if the *Solarite* could be moved to some more accessible place.

Arcot agreed to have it moved to a spot just outside the city, where the water could be procured directly from a stream. The drinking water would be ready when he returned to the city.

The *Solarite* was moved to the bank of the little river and the electrolysis apparatus was set up beside it. During the previous day, and ever since they had landed on Venus, all their power had been coming from the storage cells, but now that the electrolysis apparatus was to establish such a heavy and constant drain, Arcot started the generator, to both charge the cells, and to do the work needed.

Throughout the day there could be heard the steady hum of the generator, and the throb-throb-throb of the oxygen pump, as the gas was pumped into the huge tanks. The apparatus they were using produced the gas very rapidly, but it was near nightfall before the huge tanks had again been filled. Even then there was a bit more room for the atomic hydrogen that was simultaneously formed, although twice as much hydrogen as oxygen was produced. Its task completed, the *Solarite* rose again and sped toward the distant city.

A soft red glow filled the sky now, for even through the miles of clouds the intense sun was able to force some direct rays, and all the city was lighted with that warm radiance. The floodlights had not yet been turned on, but the great buildings looming high in the ruddy light were wonderfully impressive, the effect being heightened by the planned construction, for there were no individual spires, only a single mass that grew from the ground to tower high in the air, like some man-made mountain.

Back at the Capital the *Solarite* again settled into the broad avenue that had been cut off to traffic now, and allotted to it as its resting place. Tonlos met them shortly after they had settled into place, and with him were five men, each carrying two large bottles.

"Ah-co," as Tonlos pronounced the Terrestrian name, "we have not been able to make very much of the materials needed for your gas, but before we made any very great amount, we tried it out on an animal, whose blood structure is the same as ours, and found it had the same effect, but that in our case the iodide of potassium is not as effective in awakening the victim as is the sorlus. I do not know whether you have tried that on Terrestrial animals or not. Luckily sorlus is the most plentiful of the halogen groups; we have far more of it than of chlorine, bromine or iodine."

"Sorlus? I do not know of it—it must be one of the other elements that we do not have on Earth. What are its properties?"

"It, too, is much like iodine, but heavier. It is a black solid melting at 570 degrees; it is a metallic looking element, will conduct electricity somewhat, oxidizes in air to form an acidic oxide, and forms strong oxygen acids. It is far less active than iodine, except toward oxygen. It is very slightly soluble in water. It does not react readily with hydrogen, and the acid where formed is not as strong as HI."

"I have seen so many new things here, I wonder if it may not be the element that precedes niton. Is it heavier than that?"

"No," replied Tonlos; "it is just lighter than that element you call niton. I think you have none of it."

"Then," said Arcot, "it must be the next member of the halogen series, Morey. I'll bet they have a number of those heavier elements."

The gas was loaded aboard the *Solarite* that evening, and when Wade saw the quantity that they had said was "rather disappointingly small" he laughed heartily.

"Small! They don't know what that gas will do! There's enough stuff there to gas this whole city. Why, with that, we can bring down any ship! But tell them to go on making it, for we can use it on the other ships."

Again that night they spoke with Earth, and Morey, senior, told them that work was already under way on a hundred small ships. They were using all their own ships already, while the Government got ready to act on the idea of danger. It had been difficult to convince them that someone on Venus was getting ready to send a force to Earth to destroy them; but the weight of their scientific reputation had turned the trick. The ships now under construction would be ready in three weeks. They would be unable to go into space, but they would be very fast, and capable of carrying large tanks of the gas-producing chemicals.

It was near midnight, Venerian time, when they turned in. The following day they planned to start for the Kaxorian construction camp. They had learned from Tonlos that there were but five of the giant planes completed now, but there were fifteen more under construction, to make up the fleet of twenty that was to attack Earth. These fifteen others would be ready in a week—or less. When they were ready, the *Solarite* would stand small chance. They must capture one of the giants and learn its secrets, and then, if possible, with the weapons and knowledge of two worlds, defeat them. A large order!

Their opportunity came sooner than they had hoped for—or wanted. It was about three o'clock in the morning when the telephone warning hummed loudly through the ship. Arcot answered.

Far to the east and south of them the line of scout planes that patrolled all the borders of Lanor had been broken. Instantaneously, it seemed, out of the dark, its lights obscured, the mighty Kaxorian craft had come, striking a tiny scout plane head on, destroying it utterly before the scout had a chance to turn from the path of the titanic ship. But even as the plane spun downward, the pilot had managed to release a magnesium flare, a blindingly brilliant light that floated down on a parachute, and in the blaze of the white light it gave off, the other scouts at a few miles distance had seen the mighty bulk of the Kaxorian plane. At once they had dropped to the ground and then, by telephone lines, had sent their report to far off Sonor.

In moments the interior of the *Solarite* became a scene of swift purposeful activity. All day the Terrestrians had been able to do so little in preparation for the conflict they knew must come, the battle for two worlds. They had wanted action, but they had no weapons except their invisibility and the atomic hydrogen. It would not sink a plane. It would only break open its armor, and they hoped, paralyze its crew. And on this alone they must pin their hopes.

VI

Arcot lifted the *Solarite* at once high into the air, and started toward the point on the border, where the plane had been seen crossing. In a short time Wade relieved him at the controls while he dressed.

They had been flying on in silence for about an hour, when suddenly Wade made out in the distance the great bulk of the plane, against the dull gray of the clouds, a mile or so above them. It seemed some monstrous black bat flying there against the sky, but down to the sensitive microphone on the side of the *Solarite* came the drone of the hundred mighty propellers as the great plane forged swiftly along.

Just how rapidly these giants moved, Arcot had not appreciated until he attempted to overtake this one. It was going over a mile a second now—a speed that demanded only that it move its own length in about five-eighths of a second! It made this tremendous speed by streamlining and through sheer power.

The *Solarite* hovered high above the dark ship at length, the roar of the terrific air blast from its propellers below coming up to them as a mighty wave of sound that made their own craft tremble! The hundred gigantic propellers roaring below, however, would distribute their gas perfectly.

"We're going invisible," Arcot exclaimed. "Look out!" There was a click as the switch shut, and the *Solarite* was as transparent as the air above it. Arcot drove his ship swiftly, above and ahead of the mighty colossus, then released the gas. There was a low hiss from the power room, barely detectable despite the vacuum that shut them off from the roar of the Kaxorian plane. The microphone had long since been disconnected. Out of the gas vent streamed a cloud of purplish gas, becoming faintly visible as it left the influence of the invisibility apparatus, but only to those who knew where to look for it. The men in that mighty plane could not see it as their machine bore down into the little cloud of gas.

Tensely the Terrestrians waited. Moments—and the gigantic plane wobbled! There was a sudden swerve that ended in a nose dive, straight toward Venus seven miles below.

That the ship should crash into the ground below was not at all Arcot's plan, and he was greatly relieved when it flattened its dive and started to climb, its incalculable mass rapidly absorbing its kinetic energy. Down from its seven mile height it glided, controlling itself perfectly as Arcot released the last of the first four containers of the liquid gas makers, putting to sleep the last man on the ship below.

In a long glide that carried it over many miles, the great ship descended. It had sunk far, and gone smoothly, but now there loomed ahead of it a range of low hills! It would certainly crash into the rocky cliffs ahead! Nearer and nearer drew the barrier while Arcot and the others watched with rigid attention. It might skim above those low hills at that—just barely escaping . . . The watchers cringed as head on, at nearly two thousand miles an hour, the machine crashed into the rocks. Arcot had snapped the loud speaker into the circuit once more, and now as they looked at the sudden crash below, there thundered up to them mighty waves of sound!

The giant plane had struck about twenty feet from the top of a nearly perpendicular cliff. The terrific crash was felt by seismographs in Sonor nearly two thousand miles away! The mighty armored hull plowed into the rocks like some gigantic meteor, the hundreds of thousands of tons crushing the rocky precipice, grinding it to powder, and shaking the entire hill. The cliff seemed to buckle and crack. In moments the plane had been brought to rest, but it had plowed through twenty feet of rock for nearly an eighth of a mile. For an instant it hung motionless, perched perilously in the air, its tail jutting out over the little valley, then slowly, majestically it sank, to strike with a reverberating crash that shattered the heavy armor plate!

For another instant the great motors continued turning, the roar of the propellers like some throbbing background to the rending crashes as the titanic wreck came to rest. Suddenly, with a series of roaring explosions, the bank of motors in the left wing blew up with awful force. There was a flash of indescribable brilliance that momentarily blinded the watching Terrestrians; then there came to the microphone such waves of sound as it could not reproduce.

From the rock on which rested the fused mass of metal that they knew had been the wing, rose a great cloud of dust. Still the motors on the other side of the ship continued roaring and the giant propellers turned. As the blast of air blew the dust away, the Terrestrians stared in unbounded amazement. Up from the gaping, broken wing lanced a mighty beam of light of such dazzling intensity that Arcot swiftly restored them to visibility that they might shut it out. There was a terrific hissing, crackling roar. The plane seemed to wobble as it lay there, seemingly recoiling from that flaming column. Where it touched the cliff there was intense incandescence that made the rock glow white hot, then flow down in a sluggish rivulet of molten lava! For five minutes longer this terrific spectacle lasted, while Arcot withdrew the *Solarite* to a safer distance.

The fifty motors of the remaining wing seemed slowing down now—then suddenly there was such a crash and towering flash of light as no human being had ever seen before! Up—up into the very clouds it shot its mighty flame, a blazing column of light that seemed to reach out into space. The *Solarite* was hurled back end over end, tumbling, falling. Even the heavy gyroscopes could not hold it for an instant, but quickly the straining motors brought them to rest in air that whirled and whined about them. They were more than twenty miles from the scene of the explosion, but even at that distance they could see the glow of the incandescent rock. Slowly, cautiously they maneuvered the *Solarite* *back* to the spot, and looked down on a sea of seething lava!

Morey broke the awed silence. "Lord—what power that thing carries! No wonder they could support it in the air! But—how can they control such power? What titanic forces!"

Slowly Arcot sent the *Solarite* away into the night—into the kindly darkness once more. His voice when he spoke at last was oddly restrained.

"I wonder what those forces were—they are greater than any man has ever before seen! An entire hill fused to molten, incandescent rock, not to mention the tons and tons of metal that made up that ship.

"And such awful forces as these are to be released on our Earth!" For an interminable period they sat silent as the panorama of hills glided by at a slow two-hundred miles an hour. Abruptly Arcot exclaimed, "We *must* capture a ship. We'll try again—we'll either destroy or capture it—and either way we're ahead!"

Aimlessly they continued their leisurely course across a vast plain. There were no great mountains on Venus, for this world had known no such violent upheaval as the making of a moon. The men were lost in thought, each intent on his own ideas. At length Wade stood up, and walked slowly back to the power room.

Suddenly the men in the control room heard his call:

"Arcot—quick—the microphone—and rise a mile!"

The *Solarite* gave a violent lurch as it shot vertically aloft at tremendous acceleration. Arcot reached over swiftly and snapped the switch of the microphone. There burst in upon them the familiar roaring drone of a hundred huge propellers. No slightest hum of motor, only the vast whining roar of the mighty props.

"Another one! They must have been following the first by a few minutes. We'll get this one!" Arcot worked swiftly at his switches. "Wade—strap yourself in the seat where you are—don't take time to come up here."

They followed the same plan which had worked so well before. Suddenly invisible, the *Solarite* flashed ahead of the great plane. The titanic wave of rushing sound engulfed them—then again came the little hiss of the gas. Now there were no hills in sight, as far as the eye could see. In the dim light that seemed always to filter through these gray clouds they could see the distant, level horizon.

Several dragging minutes passed before there was any evident effect; the men from Earth were waiting for that great ship to waver, to wobble from its course. Suddenly Arcot gave a cry of surprise. Startled amazement was written all over his face, as his companions turned in wonderment to see that he was partially visible! The *Solarite*, too, had become a misty ghost ship about them; they were becoming visible! Then in an instant it was gone—and they saw that the huge black bulk behind them was wavering, turning; the thunderous roar of the propellers fell to a whistling whine; the ship was losing speed! It dipped, and shot down a bit—gained speed, then step by step it glided down—down—down to the surface below. The engines were idling now, the plane running more and more slowly.

They were near the ground now—and the watchers scarcely breathed. Would this ship, too, crash? It glided to within a half mile of the plain—then it dipped once more, and Arcot breathed his relief as it made a perfect landing, the long series of rollers on the base of the gigantic hull absorbing the shock of the landing. There were small streams in the way—a tree or two, but these were obstacles unnoticed by the gargantuan machine. Its mighty propellers still idling slowly, the huge plane rolled to a standstill.

Swooping down, the *Solarite* landed beside it, to be lost in the vast shadows of the mighty metal walls.

Arcot had left a small radio receiver with Tonlos in Sonor before he started on this trip, and had given him directions on how to tune in on the *Solarite*. Now he sent a message to him, telling that the plane had been brought down, and asking that a squadron of planes be sent at once.

Wade and Arcot were elected to make the first inspection of the Kaxorian plane, and clad in their cooling suits, they stepped from the *Solarite*, each carrying, for emergency use, a small hand torch, burning atomic hydrogen, capable of melting its way through even the heavy armor of the great plane.

As they stood beside it, looking up at the gigantic wall of metal that rose sheer beside them hundreds of feet straight up, it seemed impossible that this mighty thing could fly, that it could be propelled through the air. In awed silence they gazed at its vast bulk.

Then, like pygmies beside some mighty prehistoric monster, they made their way along its side, seeking a door. Suddenly Wade stopped short and exclaimed: "Arcot, this is senseless—we can't do this! The machine is so big that it'll take us half an hour of steady walking to go around it. We'll have to use the *Solarite* to find an entrance!"

It was well that they followed Wade's plan, for the only entrance, as they later learned, was from the top. There, on the back of the giant, the *Solarite* landed—its great weight having no slightest effect on the Kaxorian craft. They found a trap-door leading down inside. However, the apparatus for opening it was evidently within the hull, so they had to burn a hole in the door before they could enter.

What a sight there was for these men of Earth. The low rumble of the idling engines was barely audible as they descended the long ladder.

There was no resemblance whatever to the interior of a flying machine; rather, it suggested some great power house, where the energies of half a nation were generated. They entered directly into a vast hall that extended for a quarter of a mile back through the great hull, and completely across the fuselage. To the extreme nose it ran, and throughout there were scattered little globes that gave off an intense white light, illuminating all of the interior. Translucent bull's-eyes obscured the few windows.

All about, among the machines, lay Venerians. Dead they seemed, the illusion intensified by their strangely blue complexions. The two Terrestrians knew, however, that they could readily be restored to life. The great machines they had been operating were humming softly, almost inaudibly. There were two long rows of them, extending to the end of the great hall. They suggested mighty generators twenty feet high. From their tops projected two-feet-thick cylinders of solid fused quartz. From these extended other rods of fused quartz, rods that led down through the floor; but these were less bulky, scarcely over eight inches thick.

The huge generator-like machines were disc-shaped. From these, too, a quartz rod ran down through the floor. The machines on the further row were in some way different; those in the front half of the row had the tubes leading to the floor below, but had no tubes jutting into the ceiling. Instead, there were many slender rods connected with a vast switchboard that covered all of one side of the great room. But everywhere were the great quartz rods, suggesting some complicated water system. Most of them were painted black, though the main rods leading from the roof above were as clear as crystal.

Arcot and Wade looked at these gigantic machines in hushed awe. They seemed impossibly huge; it was inconceivable that all this was but the power room of an airplane!

Without speaking, they descended to the level below, using a quite earthly appearing escalator. Despite the motionless figures everywhere, they felt no fear of their encountering resistance. They knew the effectiveness of Wade's anesthetic.

The hall they entered was evidently the main room of the plane. It was as long as the one above, and higher, yet all that vast space was taken by one single, titanic coil that stretched from wall to wall! Into it, and from it there led two gigantic columns of fused quartz. That these were rods, such as those smaller ones above was obvious, but each was over eight feet thick!

Short they were, for they led from one mighty generator such as they had seen above, but magnified on a scale inconceivable! At the end of it, its driving power, its motor, was a great cylindrical case, into which led a single quartz bar ten inches thick. This bar was alive with pulsing, glowing fires, that changed and maneuvered and died out over all its surface and through all its volume. The motor was but five feet in diameter and a scant seven feet long, yet obviously it was driving the great machine, for there came from it a constant low hum, a deep pitched song of awful power. And the huge quartz rod that led from the titanic coil-cylinder was alive with the same glowing fires that played through the motor rod. From one side of the generator, ran two objects that were familiar, copper bus-bars. But even these were *three feet thick!*

The scores of quartz tubes that came down from the floor above joined, coalesced, and ran down to the great generator, and into it.

They descended to another level. Here were other quartz tubes, but these led down still further, for this floor contained individual sleeping bunks, most of them unoccupied, unready for occupancy, though some were made up.

Down another level; again the bunks, the little individual rooms.

At last they reached the bottom level, and here the great quartz tubes terminated in a hundred smaller ones, each of these leading into some strange mechanism. There were sighting devices on it, and there were ports that opened in the floor. This was evidently the bombing room.

With an occasional hushed word, the Terrestrians walked through what seemed to be a vast city of the dead, passing sleeping officers, and crewmen by the hundreds. On the third level they came at last to the control room. Here were switchboards, control panels, and dozens of officers, sleeping now, beside their instruments. A sudden dull thudding sound spun Arcot and Wade around, nerves taut. They relaxed and exchanged apologetic smiles. An automatic relay had adjusted some mechanism.

They noted one man stationed apart from the rest. He sat at the very bow, protected behind eight-inch coronium plates in which were set masses of fused quartz that were nearly as strong as the metal itself. These gave him a view in every direction except directly behind him. Obviously, here was the pilot.

Returning to the top level, they entered the long passages that led out into the titanic wings. Here, as elsewhere, the ship was brightly lighted. They came to a small room, another bunk room. There were great numbers of these down both sides of the long corridor, and along the two parallel corridors down the wing. In the fourth corridor near the back edge of the wing, there were bunk rooms on one side, and on the other were bombing posts.

As they continued walking down the first corridor, they came to a small room, whence issued the low hum of one of the motors. Entering, they found the crew sleeping, and the motor idling.

"Good Lord!" Wade exclaimed. "Look at that motor, Arcot! No bigger than the trunk of a man's body. Yet a battery of these sends the ship along at a mile a second! What power!"

Slowly they proceeded down the long hall. At each of the fifty engine mountings they found the same conditions. At the end of the hall there was an escalator that led one level higher, into the upper wing. Here they found long rows of the bombing posts and the corresponding quartz rods.

They returned finally to the control room. Here Arcot spent a long time looking over the many instruments, the controls, and the piloting apparatus.

"Wade," he said at last, "I think I can see how this is done. I am going to stop those engines, start them, then accelerate them till the ship rolls a bit!" Arcot stepped quickly over to the pilot's seat, lifted the sleeping pilot out, and settled in his place.

"Now, you go over to that board there—that one—and when I ask you to, please turn on that control—no, the one below—yes —turn it on about one notch at a time."

Wade shook his head dubiously, a one-sided grin on his face. "All right, Arcot—just as you say—but when I think of the powers you're playing with—well, a mistake might be unhealthy!"

"I'm going to stop the motors now," Arcot announced quietly. All the time they had been on board, they had been aware of the barely inaudible whine of the motors. Now suddenly, it was gone, and the plane was still as death!

Arcot's voice sounded unnaturally loud. "I did it without blowing the ship up after all! Now we're going to try turning the power on!"

Suddenly there was a throaty hum; then quickly it became the low whine; then, as Arcot turned on the throttle before him, he heard the tens of thousands of horsepower spring into life—and suddenly the whine was a low roar—the mighty propellers out there had became a blur—then with majestic slowness the huge machine moved off across the field!

Arcot shut off the motors and rose with a broad, relieved smile, "Easy!" he said. They made their way again up through the ship, up through the room of the tremendous cylinder coil, and then into the power room. Now the machines were quiet, for the motors were no longer working.

"Arcot, you didn't shut off the biggest machine of all down there. How come?"

"I couldn't, Wade. It has no shut-off control, and if it did have, I wouldn't use it. I will tell you why when we get back to the *Solarite*."

At last they left the mighty machine; walked once more across its broad metal top. Here and there they now saw the ends of those quartz cylinders. Once more they entered the *Solarite*, through the air lock, and took off the cumbersome insulating suits.

As quickly as possible Arcot outlined to the two who had stayed with the *Solarite*, the things they had seen, and the layout of the great ship.

"I think I can understand the secret of all that power, and it's not so different from the *Solarite*, at that. It, too, draws its power from the sun, though in a different way, and it stores it within itself, which the *Solarite* does not try to do.

"Light of course, is energy, and therefore, has mass. It exerts pressure, the impact of its moving units of energy—photons. We have electrons and protons of matter, and photons of light. Now we know that the mass of protons and electrons will attract other protons and electrons, and hold them near—as in a stone, or in a solar system. The new idea here is that the photons will attract each other ever more and more powerfully, the closer they get. The Kaxorians have developed a method of getting them so close together, that they will, for a while at least, hold themselves there, and with a little 'pressure', will stay there indefinitely.

"In that huge coil and cylinder we found there we saw the main power storage tank. That was full of gaseous light-energy held together by its own attraction, plus a little help of the generator!"

"A little help?" Wade exclaimed. "Quite a little! I'll bet that thing had a million horsepower in its motor!"

"Yes—but I'll bet they have nearly fifty pounds of light condensed there—so why worry about a little thing like a million horsepower? They have plenty more where that comes from.

"I think they go up above the clouds in some way and collect the sun's energy. Remember that Venus gets twice as much as Earth. They focus it on those tubes on the roof there, and they, like all quartz tubes, conduct the light down into the condensers where it is first collected. Then it is led to the big condenser downstairs, where the final power is added, and the condensed light is stored.

"Quartz conducts light just as copper conducts electricity—those are bus-bars we saw running around there.

"The bombs we've been meeting recently are, of course, little knots of this light energy thrown out by that projector mechanism we saw. When they hit anything, the object absorbs their energy —and is very promptly volatilized by the heat of the absorption.

"Do you remember that column of hissing radiance we saw shooting out of the wrecked plane just before it blew up? That was the motor connection, broken, and discharging free energy. That would ordinarily have supplied all fifty motors at about full speed. Naturally, when it cut loose, it was rather violent.

"The main generator had been damaged, no doubt, so it stopped working, and the gravitational attraction of the photons wasn't enough, without its influence to hold them bound too long. All those floods of energy were released instantaneously, of course.

"Look—there come the Lanorians now. I want to go back to Sonor and think over this problem. Perhaps we can find something that will release all that energy—though honestly I doubt it."

Arcot seemed depressed, overawed perhaps, by the sheer magnitude of the force that lay bound up in the Kaxorian ship. It seemed inconceivable that the little *Solarite* could in any way be effective against the incredible machine.

The Lanorian planes were landing almost like a flock of birds, on the wings, the fuselage, the ground all about the gigantic ship. Arcot dropped into a chair, gazing moodily into emptiness, his thoughts on the mighty giant, stricken now, but only sleeping. In its vast hulk lay such energies as intelligence had never before controlled; within it he knew there were locked the powers of the sun itself. What could the *Solarite* do against it?

"Oh, I almost forgot to mention it." Arcot spoke slowly, dejectedly. "In the heat of the attack back there it went practically unnoticed. Our only weapon beside the gas is useless now. Do you remember how the ship seemed to lose its invisibility for an instant? I learned why when we investigated the ship. Those men are physicists of the highest order. We must realize the terrible forces, both physical and mental that we are to meet. They've solved the secret of our invisibility, and now they can neutralize it. They began using it a bit too late this time, but they had located the radio-produced interference caused by the ship's invisibility apparatus, and they were sending a beam of interfering radio energy at us. We are invisible only by reason of the vibration of the molecules in response to the radio impressed oscillations. The molecules vibrate in tune, at terrific frequency, and the light can pass perfectly. What will happen, however, if someone locates the source of the radio waves? It'll be simple for them to send out a radio beam and touch our invisible ship with it. The two radio waves impressed on us now will be out of step and the interference will instantly make us visible. We can no longer attack them with our atomic hydrogen blast, or with the gas—both are useless unless we can get close to them, and we can't come within ten miles of them now. Those bombs of theirs are effective at that distance."

Again he fell silent, thinking—hoping for an idea that would once more give them a chance to combat the Kaxorians. His three companions, equally depressed and without a workable idea, remained silent. Abruptly Arcot stood up.

"I'm going to speak with the Commander-in-Field here. Then we can start back for Sonor—and maybe we had better head for home. It looks as though there is little we can do here."

Briefly he spoke to the young Venerian officer, and told him what he had learned about the ship. Perhaps they could fly it to Sonor; or it could be left there undestroyed if he would open a certain control just before he left. Arcot showed him which one— it would drain out the power of the great storage tank, throwing it harmlessly against the clouds above. The Kaxorians might destroy the machine if they wanted to—Arcot felt that they would not wish to. They would hope, with reason, that they might recapture it! It would be impossible to move that tremendous machine without the power that its "tank" was intended to hold.

VII

Slowly they cruised back to Sonor, Arcot still engrossed in thought. Would it be that Venus would fall before the attack of the mighty planes, that they would sweep out across space, to Earth—to Mars—to other worlds, a cosmic menace? Would the mighty machines soon be circling Earth? Guided missiles with atomic warheads could combat them, perhaps, as could the molecular motion machines. Perhaps these could be armored with twenty-inch steel walls, and driven into the great propellers, or at miles a second, into the ship itself! But these ships would require long hours, days, even weeks to build, and in that time the

Kaxorian fleet would be ready. It would attack Earth within six days now! What hope was there to avert incalculable destruction—if not outright defeat?

In despair Arcot turned and strode quickly down the long hallway of the *Solarite*. Above him he could hear the smooth, even hum of the sweetly functioning generator, but it only reminded him of the vastly greater energies he had seen controlled that night. The thudding relays in the power room, as Wade maneuvered the ship, seemed some diminutive mockery of the giant relays he had seen in the power room of the Kaxorian plane.

He sat down in the power room, looking at the stacked apparatus, neatly arranged, as it must be, to get all this apparatus in this small space. Then at last he began to think more calmly. He concentrated on the greatest forces known to man—and there were only two that even occurred to him as great! One was the vast energies he had that very night learned of; the other was the force of the molecules, the force that drove his ship.

He had had no time to work out the mathematics of the light compression, mathematics that he now knew would give results. There remained only the molecular motion. What could he do with it that he had not done?

He drew out a small black notebook. In it were symbols, formulas, and page after page of the intricate calculus that had ended finally in the harnessing of this great force that was even now carrying him smoothly along.

Half an hour later he was still busy—covering page after page with swiftly written formulas. Before him was a great table of multiple integers, the only one like it known to exist in the System, for the multiple calculus was an invention of Arcot's. At last he found the expression he wanted, and carefully he checked his work, excitedly though now, with an expression of eager hope —it seemed logical—it seemed correct—

"Morey—oh, Morey," he called, holding his enthusiasm in check, "if you can come here—I want you to check some math for me. I've done it—and I want to see if you get the same result independently!" Morey was a more careful mathematician than he, and it was to him Arcot turned for verification of any new discovery.

Following the general directions Arcot gave him, Morey went through the long series of calculations—and arrived at the same results. Slowly he looked up from the brief expression with which he had ended.

It was not the formula that astonished him—it was its physical significance.

"Arcot—do you think we can make it?"

There was a new expression in Arcot's eyes, a tightness about his mouth.

"I hope so, Morey. If we don't, Lanor is lost beyond a doubt—and probably Earth is, too. Wade—come here a minute, will you? Let Fuller take the controls, and tell him to push it. We have to get to work on this."

Rapidly Arcot explained their calculations—and the proof he had gotten.

"Our beam of molecular motion-controlling energy directs all molecular motion to go at right angles to it. The mechanism so far has been a field inside a coil really, but if these figures are right, it means that we can project that field to a considerable distance even in air. It'll be a beam of power that will cause all molecules in its path to move at right angles to it, and in the direction we choose, by reversing the power in the projector. That means that no matter how big the thing is, we can tear it to pieces; we'll use its own powers, its own energies, to rip it, or crush it.

"Imagine what would happen if we directed this against the side of a mountain—the entire mass of rock would at once fly off at unimaginable speed, crashing ahead with terrific power, as all the molecules suddenly moved in the same direction. Nothing in all the Universe could hold together against it! It's a disintegration ray of a sort—a ray that will tear, or crush, for we can either make one half move away from the other—or we can reverse the power, and make one half drive toward the other with all the terrific power of its molecules! It is omnipotent—hmmm—" Arcot paused, narrowing his eyes in thought.

"It has one limitation. Will it reach far in the air? In vacuum it should have an infinite range—in the atmosphere all the molecules of the air will be affected, and it will cause a terrific blast of icy wind, a gale at temperatures far below zero! This will be even more effective here on Venus!

"But we must start designing the thing at once! Take some of the Immorpho and give me some, and we can let the sleep ac-

cumulate till we have more time! Look—we're in Sonor already!
Land us, Fuller—right where we were, and then come back here.
We're going to need you!"

The gorgeous display of a Venerian dawn was already coloring
the East as the great buildings seemed to rise silently about them.
The sky, which had been a dull luminous gray, a gray that rapidly grew brighter and brighter, was now like molten silver,
through which were filtering the early rays of the intense sun. As
the sun rose above the horizon, though invisible for clouds, it
still was traceable by the wondrous shell pink that began to suf-
fuse the ten mile layer of vapor. The tiny droplets were, however,
breaking the clear light into a million rainbows, and all about the
swiftly deepening pink were forming concentric circles of blue,
of green, orange, and all the colors of the rainbow, repeated time
after time—a wondrous halo of glowing color, which only the
doubly intense sun could create.

"It's almost worth missing the sun all day to see their sunrises
and sunsets," Fuller commented. The men were watching it,
despite their need for haste. It was a sight the like of which no
Earthman had ever before seen.

Immediately, then, they plunged into the extremely complex
calculation of the electrical apparatus to produce the necessary
fields. To get the effect they wanted, they must have two separate fields of the director ray, and a third field of a slightly different nature, which would cause the director ray to move in one
direction only. It would be disconcerting, to say the least, if the
director ray, by some mistake, should turn upon them!

The work went on more swiftly than they had considered possible, but there was still much to be done on the theoretical end
of the job alone when the streets about them began to fill. They
noticed that a large crowd was assembling, and shortly after they
had finished, after some of these people had stood there for more
than an hour and a half, the crowd had grown to great size.

"From the looks of that collection, I should say we are about
to become the principals in some kind of a celebration that we
know nothing about. Well, we're here, and in case they want us,
we're ready to come."

The guard that always surrounded the *Solarite* had been doubled, and was maintaining a fairly large clear area about the
ship.

Shortly thereafter they saw one of the high officials of Lanor come down the walk from the governmental building, walking toward the *Solarite*.

"Time for us to appear—and it may as well be all of us this time. I'll tell you what they say afterward, Wade. They've evidently gone to considerable trouble to get up this meeting, so let's cooperate. I hate to slow up the work, but we'll try to make it short."

The four Terrestrians got into their cooling suits, and stepped outside the ship. The Lanorian dignitary left his guard, walked up to the quartet from Earth with measured tread, and halted before them.

"Earthmen," he began in a deep, clear voice, "we have gathered here this morning to greet you and thank you for the tremendous service you have done us. Across the awful void of empty space you have journeyed forty million miles to visit us, only to discover that Venerians were making ready to attack your world. Twice your intervention has saved our city.

"There is, of course, no adequate reward for this service; we can in no way repay you, but in a measure we may show our appreciation. We have learned from the greatest psychologist of our nation, Tonlos, that in your world aluminum is plentiful, but gold and platinum are rare, and that morlus is unknown. I have had a small token made for you, and your friends. It is a little plaque, a disc of morlus, and on it there is a small map of the Solar System. On the reverse side there is a globe of Venus, with one of Earth beside it, as well as our men could copy the small globe you have given us. The northern hemisphere of each is depicted—America, your nation, and Lanor, ours, thus being shown. We want you, and each of your friends, to accept these. They are symbols of your wonderful flight across space!" The Venerians turned to each of the Terrestrians and presented each with a small metal disc.

Arcot spoke for the Terrestrians.

"On behalf of myself and my friends here, two of whom have not had an opportunity to learn your language, I wish to thank you for your great help when we most needed it. You, perhaps, have saved more than a city—you may have made it possible to save a world—our Earth. But the battle here has only begun.

"There are now in the Kaxorian camp eighteen great ships. They have been badly defeated in the three encounters they have had with the *Solarite* so far. But no longer will they be vulnerable to our earlier methods of attack. Your spies report that the first plane, the plane which was first attacked by the *Solarite,* is still undergoing repairs. These will be completed within two days, and then, when they can leave a base guard of two ships, they will attack once more. Furthermore, they will attack with a new weapon. They have destroyed the usefulness of our weapon, invisibility, and in turn, now have it to use against us! We must seek out some new weapon. I hope we are on the right track now, but every moment is precious, and we must get back to the work. This address must be short. Later, when we have completed our preliminary work, we will have to give plans to your workmen, which you will be able to turn into metal, for we lack the materials. With this help we may succeed, despite our handicap."

The address was terminated at once. The Lanorians were probably disappointed, but they fully realized the necessity for haste.

"I wish Terrestrian orators spoke like that," remarked Morey as they returned to the ship. "He said all there was to say, but he didn't run miles of speech doing it. He was a very forceful speaker, too!"

"People who speak briefly and to the point generally are," Arcot said.

It was nearly noon that day before the theoretical discussion had been reduced to practical terms. They were ready to start work at once, but they had reason to work cheerfully now. Even through air they had found their ray would be able to reach thirty-five miles! They would be well out of the danger zone while attacking the gigantic planes of Kaxor.

Morey, Wade and Arcot at once set to work constructing the electrical plant that was to give them the necessary power. It was lucky indeed that they had brought the great mass of spare apparatus! They had more than enough to make all the electrical machinery. The tubes, the coils, the condensers, all were there. The generator would easily supply the power, for the terrific forces that were to destroy the Kaxorian ships were to be generated in the plane itself. It was to destroy itself; the *Solarite* would merely be the detonator to set it off!

While the physicists were busy on this, Fuller was designing the mechanical details of the projector. It must be able to turn through a spherical angle of 180 degrees, and was necessarily controlled electrically from the inside. The details of the projector were worked out by six that evening, and the numerous castings and machined pieces that were to be used were to be made in the Venerian machine shops.

One difficulty after another arose and was overcome. Night came on, and still they continued work. The Venerian workmen had promised to have the apparatus for them by ten o'clock the next morning—or what corresponded to ten o'clock.

Shortly after three o'clock that morning they had finished the apparatus, had connected all the controls, and had placed the last of the projector directors. Except for the projector they were ready, and Morey, Wade and Fuller turned in to get what sleep they could. But Arcot, telling them there was something he wished to get, took another dose of Immorpho and stepped out into the steaming rain.

A few minutes after ten the next morning Arcot came back, followed by half a dozen Venerians, each carrying a large metal cylinder in a cradle. These were attached to the landing gear of the *Solarite* in such fashion that the fusing of one piece of wire would permit the entire thing to drop free.

"So *that's* what you hatched out, eh? What is it?" asked Wade as he entered the ship.

"Just a thing I want to try out—and I'm going to keep it a deep, dark secret for a while. I think you'll get quite a surprise when you see those bombs in action! They're arranged to be released by turning current into the landing lights. We'll have to forgo lights for the present, but I needed the bombs more.

"The mechanics have finished working on your projector parts, Fuller, and they'll be over here in a short time. Here comes the little gang I asked to help us. You can direct them." Arcot paused and scowled with annoyance. "Hang it all—when they drill into the outer wall, we'll lose the vacuum between the two walls, and all that hot air will come in. This place will be roasting in a short time. We have the molecular motion coolers, but I'm afraid they won't be much good. Can't use the generator—it's cut off from the main room by vacuum wall.

"I think we'd better charge up the gas tanks and the batteries as soon as this is done. Then tonight we'll attack the Kaxorian construction camp. I've just learned that no spy reports have been coming in, and I'm afraid they'll spring a surprise."

Somewhat later came the sound of drills, then the whistling roar as the air sucked into the vacuum, told the men inside that the work was under way. It soon became uncomfortably hot as, the vacuum destroyed, the heat came in through all sides. It was more than the little molecular coolers could handle, and the temperature soon rose to about a hundred and fifteen. It was not as bad as the Venerian atmosphere, for the air seemed exceedingly dry, and the men found it possible to get along without cooling suits, if they did not work. Since there was little they could do, they simply relaxed.

It was nearly dark before the Lanorians had finished their work, and the gas tanks had been recharged. All that time Arcot had spent with Tonlos determining the position of the Kaxorian construction camp. Spy reports and old maps had helped, but it was impossible to do very accurate work by these means.

It was finally decided that the Kaxorian construction camp was about 10,500 miles to the southwest. The *Solarite* was to start an hour after dark. Traveling westward at their speed, they hoped to reach the camp just after nightfall.

VIII

The *Solarite* sped swiftly toward the southwest. The sky slowly grew lighter as the miles flashed beneath them. They were catching up with the sun. As they saw the rolling ocean beneath them give way to low plains, they realized they were over Kaxorian land. The *Solarite* was flying very high, and as they showed no lights, and were not using the invisibility apparatus, they were practically undetectable. Suddenly they saw the lights of a mighty city looming far off to the east.

"It's Kanor. Pass well to the west of it. That's their capital. We're on course." Arcot spoke from his position at the projector, telling Wade the directions to follow on his course to the berth of the giant planes.

The city dropped far behind them in moments, followed by another, and another. At length, veering southward into the dusk, they entered a region of low hills, age-old folds in the crust of the planet, rounded by untold millennia of torrential rains.

"Easy, Wade. We are near now." Mile after mile they flashed ahead at about a thousand miles an hour—then suddenly they saw far off to the east a vast glow that reached into the sky, painting itself on the eternal clouds miles above.

"There it is, Wade. Go high, and take it easy!"

Swiftly the *Solarite* climbed, hovering at last on the very rim of the cloud blanket, an invisible mote in a sea of gray mist. Below them they saw a tremendous field carved, it seemed, out of the ancient hills. From this height all sense of proportion was lost. It seemed but an ordinary field, with eighteen ordinary airplanes resting on it. One of these now was moving, and in a moment it rose into the air! But there seemed to be no men on all the great field. They were invisibly small from this height.

Abruptly Arcot gave a great shout. "That's their surprise! They're ready far ahead of the time we expected! If all that armada gets in the air, we're done! Down, Wade, to within a few hundred feet of the ground, and close to the field!"

The *Solarite* flashed down in a power dive—down with a sickening lurch. A sudden tremendous weight seemed to crush them as the ship was brought out of the dive not more than two hundred feet from the ground. Close to blacking out, Wade nevertheless shot it in as close to the field as he dared. Anxiously he called to Arcot, who answered with a brief "Okay!" The planes loomed gigantic now, their true proportions showing clearly against the brilliant light of the field. A tremendous wave of sound burst from the loudspeaker as the planes rolled across the ground to leap gracefully into the air—half a million tons of metal!

From the *Solarite* there darted a pale beam of ghostly light, faintly gray, tinged with red and green—the ionized air of the beam. It moved in a swift half circle. In an instant the whirr of the hundreds, thousands of giant propellers was drowned in a terrific roar of air. Great snowflakes fell from the air before them; it was white with the solidified water vapor. Then came a titanic roar and the planet itself seemed to shake! A crash, a snapping and rending as a mighty fountain of soil and rock cascaded skyward, and with it, twisting, turning, hurled in a dozen directions at once, twelve titanic ships reeled drunkenly into the air!

For a barely perceptible interval there was an oppressive silence as the ray was shut off. Then a bedlam of deafening sound burst forth anew, a mighty deluge of unbearable noise as the millions of tons of pulverized rock, humus and metal fell back. Some of it had ascended for miles; it settled amid a howling blizzard—snow that melted as it touched the madly churned airfield.

High above there were ten planes flying about uncertainly. Suddenly one of these turned, heading for the ground far below, its wings screaming their protest as the motors roared, ever faster, with the gravity of the planet aiding them. There was a rending, crackling crash as the wings suddenly bent back along the sides. An instant later the fuselage tore free, rocketing downward; the wings followed more slowly—twisting, turning, dipping in mile-long swoops.

The *Solarite* shot away from the spot at maximum speed—away and up, with a force that nailed the occupants to the floor. Before they could turn, behind them flared a mighty gout of light that struck to the very clouds above, and all the landscape, for miles about, was visible in the glare of the released energy.

As they turned, they saw on the plain below a tremendous crater, in its center a spot that glowed white and bubbled like the top of a huge caldron.

Nine great planes were circling in the air; then in an instant they were gone, invisible. As swiftly the *Solarite* darted away with a speed that defied the aim of any machine.

High above the planes they went, for with his radar Arcot could trace them. They were circling, searching for the *Solarite*.

The tiny machine was invisible in the darkness, but its invisibility was not revealed by the Kaxorian's radio detectors. In the momentary lull, Fuller asked a question.

"Wade, how is it that those ships can be invisible when they are driven by light, and have the light stored in them? They're perfectly transparent. Why can't we see the light?"

"They are storing the light. It's bound—it can't escape. You can't see light unless it literally hits you in the eye. Their stored light can't reach you, for it is held by its own attraction and by the special field of the big generators."

They seemed to be above one of the Kaxorian planes now. Arcot caught the roar of the invisible propellers.

"To the left, Wade—faster—hold it—left—ah!" Arcot pushed a button.

Down from the *Solarite* there dropped a little canister, one of the bombs that Arcot had prepared the night before. To hit an invisible target is ordinarily difficult, but when that target is far larger than the proverbial side of a barn, it is not very difficult, at that. But now Arcot's companions watched for the crash of the explosion, the flash of light. What sort of bomb was it that Arcot hoped would penetrate that tremendous armor?

Suddenly they saw a great spot of light, a spot that spread with startling rapidity, a patch of light that ran, and moved. It flew through the air at terrific speed. It was a pallid light, green and wan and ghostly, that seemed to flow and ebb.

For an instant Morey and the others stared in utter surprise. Then suddenly Morey burst out laughing.

"Ho—you win, Arcot. That was one they didn't think of, I'll bet! Luminous paint—and by the hundred gallon! Radium paint, I suppose, and no man has ever found how to stop the glow of radium. That plane sticks out like a sore thumb!"

Indeed, the great luminous splotch made the gigantic plane clearly evident against the gray clouds. Visible or not, that plane was marked.

Quickly Arcot tried to maneuver the *Solarite* over another of the great ships, for now the danger was only from those he could not see. Suddenly he had an idea.

"Morey—go back to the power room and change the adjustment on the meteorite avoider to half a mile!" At once Morey understood his plan, and hastened to put it into effect.

The illuminated plane was diving, twisting wildly now. The *Solarite* flashed toward it with sickening speed, then suddenly the gigantic bulk of the plane loomed off to the right of the tiny ship, the great metal hull, visible now, rising in awesome might. They were too near; they shot away to a greater distance—then again that ghostly beam reached out—and for just a fraction of a second it touched the giant plane.

The titanic engine of destruction seemed suddenly to be in the grip of some vastly greater Colossus—a clutching hand that closed! The plane jumped back with an appalling crash, a roar of rending metal. For an instant there came the sound like a mighty buzz-saw as the giant propellers of one wing cut into the body of the careening plane. In that instant, the great power storage tank split open with an impact like the bursting of a world. The *Solarite* was hurled back by an explosion that seemed to rend the very atoms of the air, and all about them was a torrid blaze of heat and light that seemed to sear their faces and hands with its intensity.

Then in a time so brief that it seemed never to have happened, it was gone, and only the distant drone of the other ships' propellers came to them. There was no luminous spot. The radium paint had been destroyed in the only possible way—it was volatilized through all the atmosphere!

The Terrestrians had known what to expect; had known what would happen; and they had not looked at the great ship in that last instant. But the Kaxorians had naturally been looking at it. They had never seen the sun directly, and now they had been looking at a radiance almost as brilliant. They were temporarily blinded; they could only fly a straight course in response to the quick order of their squadron commander.

And in that brief moment that they were unable to watch him, Arcot dropped two more bombs in quick succession. Two bright spots formed in the black night. No longer did these planes feel themselves invulnerable, able to meet any foe! In an instant they had put on every last trace of power, and at their top speed they were racing west, away from their tiny opponent—in the only direction that was open to them.

But it was useless. The *Solarite* could pick up speed in half the time they could, and in an instant Arcot again trained his beam on the mighty splotch of light that was a fleeing plane.

Out of the darkness came a ghostly beam, for an instant of time so short that before the explosive shells of the other could be trained on it, the *Solarite* had moved. Under that touch the mighty plane began crumbling, then it splintered beneath the driving blow of the great wing, as it shot toward the main body of the plane at several miles a second—driving into and through it! The giant plane twisted and turned as it fell swiftly downward into the darkness—and again there came that world-rocking explosion, and the mighty column of light.

Again and yet again the *Solarite* found and destroyed Kaxorian super-planes, protected in the uneven conflict by their diminutive size and the speed of their elusive maneuvering.

But to remind the men of the *Solarite* that they were not alone, there came a sudden report just behind them, and they turned to see that one of the energy bombs had barely fallen short! In an instant the comparative midget shot up at top speed, out of danger. It looped and turned, hunting, feeling with its every detector for that other ship. The great planes were spread out now. In every direction they could be located—and all were leaving the scene of the battle. But one by one the *Solarite* shot after them, and always the speed of the little ship was greater.

Two escaped. They turned off their useless invisibility apparatus and vanished into the night.

The *Solarite,* supported by her vertical lift units, coasted toward a stop. The drone of the fleeing super-planes diminished and was gone, and for a time the thrum of the generator and the tap-dance of relays adjusting circuits was the only sound aboard.

Wade sighed finally. "Well, gentlemen, now we've got it, what do we do with it?"

"What do you mean?" Morey asked.

"Victory. The Jack-pot. Having the devices we just demonstrated, we are now the sole owners, by right of conquest, of one highly disturbed nation of several million people. With that gadget there, we can pick it up and throw it away.

"Personally, I have a feeling that we've just won the largest white elephant in history. We don't just walk off and leave it, you know. We don't want it. But we've got it.

"Our friends in Sonor are not going to want the problem either; they just wanted the Kaxorians combed out of their hair.

"As I say—we've got it, now—but what do we do with it?"

"It's basically their problem, isn't it?" protested Fuller.

Morey looked somewhat stricken, and thoroughly bewildered. "I hadn't considered that aspect very fully; I've been too darned busy trying to stay alive."

Wade shook his head. "Look, Fuller—it was their problem before, too, wasn't it? How'd they handle it? If you just let them alone, what do you suppose they'll do with the problem this time?"

"The same thing they did before," Arcot groaned. "I'm tired. Let's get some sleep first, anyway."

"Sure; that makes good sense," Wade agreed. "Sleep on it, yes. But go to sleep on it—well, that's what the not-so-bright Sonorans tried doing.

"And off-hand, I'd say we were elected. The Kaxorians undoubtedly have a nice, two thousand year old hatred for the Sonorans who so snobbishly ignored them, isolated them, and considered them unfit for association. The Sonorans, on the other hand, are now thoroughly scared, and will be feeling correspondingly vindictive. They won this time by a fluke—our coming. I can just see those two peoples getting together and settling any kind of sensible, long-term treaty of mutual cooperation!"

Arcot and Morey both nodded wearily. "That is so annoyingly correct," Morey agreed. "And you know blasted well none of us is going to sleep until we have some line of attack on this white elephant disposal problem. Anybody any ideas?"

Fuller looked at the other three. "You know, in design when two incompatible materials must be structurally united, we tie each to a third material that is compatible with both.

"Sonor didn't win this fight. Kaxor didn't win it. Earth—in the *persona* of the *Solarite*—did. Earth isn't mad at anybody, hasn't been damaged by anybody, and hasn't been knowingly ignoring anybody.

"The Sonorans want to be let alone; it won't work, but they can learn that. I think if we run the United Nations in on this thing, we may be able to get them to accept our white elephant for us.

"They'll be making the same mistake Sonor did if they don't—knowingly ignoring the existence of a highly intelligent and competent race. It doesn't seem to work, judging from history both at home and here."

The four looked at each other, and found agreement.

"That's something more than a problem to sleep on," Morey said. "I'll get in touch with Sonor and tell 'em the shooting is over, so they can get some sleep too.

"It's obvious a bunch of high-power research teams are going to be needed in both countries. Earth has every reason to respect Sonoran mental sciences as well as Kaxorian light-engineering. And Earth—as we just thoroughly demonstrated—has some science of her own. Obviously, the interaction of the three is to the maximum advantage of each—and will lead to a healing of the breach that now exists."

Arcot looked up and yawned. "I'm putting this on auto-pilot at twenty miles up, and going to sleep. We can kick this around for a month anyway—and this is not the night to start."

"The decision is unanimous," Wade grinned.

BOOK THREE

THE BLACK STAR PASSES

Prologue

Taj Lamor gazed steadily down at the vast dim bulk of the ancient city spread out beneath him. In the feeble light of the stars its mighty masses of up-flung metal buildings loomed strangely, like the shells of some vast race of crustacea, long extinct. Slowly he turned, gazing now out across the great plaza, where rested long rows of slender, yet mighty ships. Thoughtfully he stared at their dim, half-seen shapes.

Taj Lamor was not human. Though he was humanoid, Earth had never seen creatures just like him. His seven foot high figure seemed a bit ungainly by Terrestrial standards, and his strangely white, hairless flesh, suggesting unbaked dough, somehow gave the impression of near-transparency. His eyes were disproportionately large, and the black disc of pupil in the white corneas was intensified by contrast. Yet perhaps his race better deserved the designation *homo sapiens* than Terrestrians do, for it was wise with the accumulated wisdom of uncounted eons.

He turned to the other man in the high, cylindrical, dimly lit tower room overlooking the dark metropolis, a man far older than Taj Lamor, his narrow shoulders bent, and his features grayed with his years. His single short, tightfitting garment of black plastic marked him as one of the Elders. The voice of Taj Lamor was vibrant with feeling:

"Tordos Gar, at last we are ready to seek a new sun. Life for our race!"

A quiet, patient, imperturbable smile appeared on the Elder's face and the heavy lids closed over his great eyes.

"Yes," he said sadly, "but at what cost in tranquility! The discord, the unrest, the awakening of unnatural ambitions—a dreadful price to pay for a questionable gain. Too great a price, I think." His eyes opened, and he raised a thin hand to check the younger man's protest. "I know—I know—in this we do not see as one. Yet perhaps some day you will learn even as I have that to rest is better than to engage in an endless struggle. Suns and planets die. Why should races seek to escape the inevitable?" Tordos Gar turned slowly away and gazed fixedly into the night sky.

Taj Lamor checked an impatient retort and sighed resignedly. It was this attitude that had made his task so difficult. Decadence. A race on an ages-long decline from vast heights of philosophical and scientific learning. Their last external enemy had been defeated millennia in the past; and through easy forgetfulness and lack of strife, ambition had died. Adventure had become a meaningless word.

Strangely, during the last century a few men had felt the stirrings of long-buried emotion, of ambition, of a craving for adventure. These were throwbacks to those ancestors of the race whose science had built their world. These men, a comparative handful, had been drawn to each other by the unnatural ferment within them; and Taj Lamor had become their leader. They had begun a mighty struggle against the inertia of ages of slow decay, had begun a search for the lost secrets of a hundred-million-year-old science.

Taj Lamor raised his eyes to the horizon. Through the leaping curve of the crystal clear roof of their world glowed a blazing spot of yellow fire. A star—the brightest object in a sky whose sun had lost its light. A point of radiance that held the last hopes of an incredibly ancient race.

The quiet voice of Tordos Gar came through the semi-darkness of the room, a pensive, dreamlike quality in its tones.

"You, Taj Lamor, and those young men who have joined you in this futile expedition do not think deeply enough. Your vision is too narrow. You lack perspective. In your youth you cannot think on a cosmic scale." He paused as though in thought, and when he continued, it seemed almost as though he were speaking to himself.

"In the far, dim past fifteen planets circled about a small, red sun. They were dead worlds—or rather, worlds that had not yet lived. Perhaps a million years passed before there moved about on three of them the beginnings of life. Then a hundred million years passed, and those first, crawling protoplasmic masses had become animals, and plants, and intermediate growths. And they fought endlessly for survival. Then more millions of years passed, and there appeared a creature which slowly gained ascendancy over the other struggling life forms that fought for the warmth of rays of the hot, red sun.

"That sun had been old, even as the age of a star is counted, before its planets had been born, and many, many millions of years had passed before those planets cooled, and then more eons sped by before life appeared. Now, as life slowly forced its way upward, that sun was nearly burned out. The animals fought, and bathed in the luxury of its rays, for many millennia were required to produce any noticeable change in its life-giving radiations.

"At last one animal gained the ascendancy. Our race. But though one species now ruled, there was no peace. Age followed age while semi-barbaric peoples fought among themselves. But even as they fought, they learned.

"They moved from caves into structures of wood and stone— and engineering had its beginning. With the buildings came little chemical engines to destroy them; warfare was developing. Then came the first crude flying-machines, using clumsy, inefficient engines. Chemical engines! Engines so crude that one could watch the flow of their fuel! One part in one hundred thousand million of the energy of their propellents they released to run the engines, and they carried fuel in such vast quantities that they staggered under its load as they left the ground! And warfare became worldwide. After flight came other machines and other ages. Other scientists began to have visions of the realms beyond, and they sought to tap the vast reservoirs of Nature's energies, the energies of matter.

"Other ages saw it done—a few thousand years later there passed out into space a machine that forced its way across the void to another planet! And the races of the three living worlds became as one—but there was no peace.

"Swiftly now, science grew upon itself, building with ever

faster steps, like a crystal which, once started, forms with incalculable speed.

"And while that science grew swiftly greater, other changes took place, changes in our universe itself. Ten million years passed before the first of those changes became important. But slowly, steadily our atmosphere was drifting into space. Through ages this gradually became apparent. Our worlds were losing their air and their water. One planet, less favored than another, fought for its life, and space itself was ablaze with the struggles of wars for survival.

"Again science helped us. Thousands of years before, men had learned how to change the mass of matter into energy, but now at last the process was reversed, and those ancestors of ours could change energy into matter, any kind of matter they wished. Rock they took, and changed it to energy, then that energy they transmuted to air, to water, to the necessary metals. Their planets took a new lease of life!

"But even this could not continue forever. They must stop that loss of air. The process they had developed for reformation of matter admitted of a new use. Creation! They were now able to make new elements, elements that had never existed in nature! They designed atoms as, long before, their fathers had designed molecules. At last their problem was solved. They made a new form of matter that was clearer than any crystal, and yet stronger and tougher than any metal known. Since it held out none of the sun's radiations, they could roof their worlds with it and keep their air within!

"This was a task that could not be done in a year, nor a decade, but all time stretched out unending before them. One by one the three planets became tremendous, roofed-in cities. Only their vast powers, their mighty machines made the task possible, but it was done."

The droning voice of Tordos Gar ceased. Taj Lamor, who had listened with a mixture of amusement and impatience to the recital of a history he knew as well as the aged, garrulous narrator, waited out of the inborn respect which every man held for the Elders. At length he exclaimed: "I see no point—"

"But you will when I finish—or, at least, I hope you will." Tordos Gar's words and tone were gently reproving. He continued quietly:

"Slowly the ages drifted on, each marked by greater and greater triumphs of science. But again and again there were wars. Some there were in which the population of a world was halved, and all space for a billion miles about was a vast caldron of incandescent energy in which tremendous fleets of space ships swirled and fused like ingredients in some cosmic brew. Forces were loosed on the three planets that sent even their mighty masses reeling drunkenly out of their orbits, and space itself seemed to be torn by the awful play of energies.

"Always peace followed—a futile peace. A few brief centuries or a few millennia, and again war would flame. It would end, and life would continue.

"But slowly there crept into the struggle a new factor, a darkening cloud, a change that came so gradually that only the records of instruments, made during a period of thousands of years, could show it. Our sun had changed from bright red to a deep, sullen crimson, and ever less and less heat poured from it. It was waning!

"As the fires of life died down, the people of the three worlds joined in a conflict with the common menace, death from the creeping cold of space. There was no need for great haste; a sun dies slowly. Our ancestors laid their plans and carried them out. The fifteen worlds were encased in shells of crystal. Those that had no atmosphere were given one. Mighty heating plants were built—furnaces that burned matter, designed to warm a world! At last a state of stability had been reached, for never could conditions change—it seemed. All external heat and light came from far-off stars, the thousands of millions of suns that would never fail.

"Under stress of the Great Change one scarcely noticed, yet almost incredible, transformation had occurred. We had learned to live with each other. We had learned to think, and enjoy thinking. As a species we had passed from youth into maturity. Advancement did not stop; we went on steadily toward the goal of all knowledge. At first there was an underlying hope that we might some day, somehow, escape from these darkened, artificial worlds of ours, but with the passing centuries this grew very dim and at length was forgotten.

"Gradually as millennia passed, much ancient knowledge was also forgotten. It was not needed. The world was unchanging, there was no strife, and no need of strife. The fifteen worlds were warm, and pleasant, and safe. Without fully realizing it, we had entered a period of rest. And so the ages passed; and there were museums and libraries and laboratories; and the machines of our ancestors did all necessary work. So it was—until less than a generation ago. Our long lives were pleasant, and death, when it came, was a sleep. And then—"

"And then," Taj Lamor interrupted, a sharp edge of impatience in his tone, "some of us awakened from our stupor!"

The Elder sighed resignedly. "You cannot see—you cannot see. You would start that struggle all over again!" His voice continued in what Taj Lamor thought of as a senile drone, but the younger man paid scant attention. His eyes and thoughts were centered on that brilliant yellow star, the brightest object in the heavens. It was that star, noticeably brighter within a few centuries, that had awakened a few men from their mental slumbers.

They were throwbacks, men who had the divine gift of curiosity; and sparked by their will to know, they had gone to the museums and looked carefully at the ancient directions for the use of the telectroscope, the mighty electrically amplified vision machine, had gazed through it. They had seen a great sun that seemed to fill all the field of the apparatus with blazing fire. A sun to envy! Further observation had revealed that there circled about the sun a series of planets, five, definitely; two more, probably; and possibly two others.

Taj Lamor had been with that group, a young man then, scarcely more than forty, but they had found him a leader and they had followed him as he set about his investigation of the ancient books on astronomy.

How many, many hours had he studied those ancient works! How many times had he despaired of ever learning their truths, and gone out to the roof of the museum to stand in silent thought looking out across the awful void to the steady flame of the yellow star! Then quietly he had returned to his self-set task.

With him as teacher, others had learned, and before he was seventy there were many men who had become true scientists, astronomers. There was much of the ancient knowledge that these men could not understand, for the science of a million centuries is not to be learned in a few brief decades, but they mastered a vast amount of the forgotten lore.

They knew now that the young, live sun, out there in space, was speeding toward them, their combined velocities equaling more than 100 miles each second. And they knew that there were not seven, but nine planets circling about that sun. There were other facts they discovered; they found that the new sun was far larger than theirs had ever been; indeed, it was a sun well above average in size and brilliance. There were planets, a hot sun—a home! Could they get there?

When their ancestors had tried to solve the problem of escape they had concentrated their work on the problem of going at speeds greater than that of light. This should be an impossibility, but the fact that the ancients had tried it, seemed proof enough to their descendants that it was possible, at least in theory. In the distant past they had needed speeds exceeding that of light, for they must travel light years; but now this sun was coming toward them, and already was less than two hundred and fifty billion miles away!

They would pass that other star in about seventy years. That was scarcely more than a third of a man's lifetime. They could make the journey with conceivable speeds—but in that brief period they must prepare to move!

The swift agitation for action had met with terrific resistance. They were satisfied; why move?

But, while some men had devoted their time to arousing the people to help, others had begun doing work that had not been done for a long, long time. The laboratories were reopened, and workshops began humming again. They were making things that were new once more, not merely copying old designs.

Their search had been divided into sections, search for weapons with which to defend themselves in case they were attacked, and search for the basic principles underlying the operation of their space ships. They had machines which they could imitate, but they did not understand them. Success had been theirs on these quests. The third section had been less successful. They had also been searching for secrets of the apparatus their forefathers had used to swing the planets in their orbits, to move worlds about at will. They had wanted to be able to take not only their space ships, but their planets as well, when they went to settle on these outer worlds and in this other solar system.

But the search for this secret had remained unrewarded. The secret of the spaceships they learned readily, and Taj Lamor had designed these mighty ships below there with that knowledge. Their search for weapons had been satisfied; they had found one weapon, one of the deadliest that their ancestors had ever invented. But the one secret in which they were most interested, the mighty force barrage that could swing a world in its flight through space, was lost. They could not find it.

They knew the principles of the driving apparatus of their ships, and it would seem but a matter of enlargement to drive a planet as a ship, but they knew this was impossible; the terrific forces needed would easily be produced by their apparatus, but there was no way to apply them to a world. If applied in any spot, the planet would be torn asunder by the incalculable strain. They must apply the force equally to the entire planet. Their problem was one of application of power. The rotation of the planet made it impossible to use a series of driving apparatus, even could these be anchored, but again the sheer immensity of the task made it impossible.

Taj Lamor gazed down again at the great ships in the plaza below. Their mighty bulks seemed to dwarf even the huge buildings about them. Yet these ships were his—for he had learned their secrets and designed them, and now he was to command them as they flew out across space in that flight to the distant star.

He turned briefly to the Elder, Tordos Gar. "Soon we leave," he said, a faint edge of triumph in his voice. "We will prove that our way is right."

The old man shook his head. "You will learn—" he began, but Taj Lamor did not want to hear.

He turned, passed through a doorway, and stepped into a little torpedo-shaped car that rested on the metal roof behind him. A moment later the little ship rose, and then slanted smoothly down over the edge of the roof, straight for the largest of the ships below. This was the flagship. Nearly a hundred feet greater was its diameter, and its mile and a quarter length of gleaming metal hull gave it nearly three hundred feet greater length than that of the ships of the line.

This expedition was an expedition of exploration. They were prepared to meet any conditions on those other worlds—no atmosphere, no water, no heat, or even an atmosphere of poisonous gases they could rectify, for their transmutation apparatus would permit them to change these gases, or modify them; they knew well how to supply heat, but they knew too, that that sun would warm some of its planets sufficiently for their purposes.

Taj Lamor sent his little machine darting through the great airlock in the side of the gigantic interstellar ship and lowered it gently to the floor. A man stepped forward, opened the door for the leader, saluting him briskly as he stepped out; then the car was run swiftly aside, to be placed with thousands of others like it. Each of these cars was to be used by a separate investigator when they reached those other worlds, and there were men aboard who would use them.

Taj Lamor made his way to a door in the side of a great metal tube that threaded the length of the huge ship. Opening the door he sat down in another little car that shot swiftly forward as the double door shut softly, with a low hiss of escaping air. For moments the car sped through the tube, then gently it slowed and came to rest opposite another door. Again came the hissing of gas as the twin doors opened, and Taj Lamor stepped out, now well up in the nose of the cruiser. As he stepped out of the car the outer and inner doors closed, and, ready now for other calls, the car remained at this station. On a ship so long, some means of communication faster than walking was essential. This little pneumatic railway was the solution.

As Taj Lamor stepped out of the tube, a half-dozen men, who had been talking among themselves, snapped quickly to attention. Following the plans of the long-gone armies of their ancestors, the men of the expedition had been trained to strict discipline; and Taj Lamor was their technical leader and the nominal Commander-in-Chief, although another man, Kornal Sorul, was their actual commander.

Taj Lamor proceeded at once to the Staff Cabin in the very nose of the great ship. Just above him there was another room, walled on all sides by that clear, glass-like material, the control cabin. Here the pilot sat, directing the motions of the mighty ship of space.

Taj Lamor pushed a small button on his desk and in a

moment a gray disc before him glowed dimly, then flashed into life and full, natural color. As though looking through a glass porthole, Taj Lamor saw the interior of the Communications Room. The Communications Officer was gazing at a similar disc in which Taj Lamor's features appeared.

"Have they reported from Ohmur, Lorsand, and Throlus, yet, Morlus Tal?" asked the commander.

"They are reporting now, Taj Lamor, and we will be ready within two and one half minutes. The plans are as before; we are to proceed directly toward the Yellow Star, meeting at Point 71?"

"The plans are as before. Start when ready."

The disc faded, the colors died, and it was gray again. Taj Lamor pulled another small lever on the panel before him, and the disc changed, glowed, and was steady; and now he saw the preparations for departure, as from an eye on the top of the great ship. Men streamed swiftly in ordered columns all about and into the huge vessels. In an incredibly short time they were in, and the great doors closed behind them. Suddenly there came a low, dull hum through the disc, and the sound mounted quickly, till all the world seemed humming to that dull note. The warning!

Abruptly the city around him seemed to blaze in a riot of colored light! The mighty towering bulks of the huge metal buildings were polished and bright, and now, as the millions of lights, every color of the spectrum, flashed over all the city from small machines in the air, on the ground, in windows, their great metal walls glistening with a riot of flowing color. Then there was a trembling through all the frame of the mighty ship. In a moment it was gone, and the titanic mass of glistening metal rose smoothly, quickly to the great roof of their world above them. On an even keel it climbed straight up, then suddenly it leaped forward like some great bird of prey sighting its victim. The ground beneath sped swiftly away, and behind it there came a long line of ships, quickly finding their position in the formation. They were heading toward the giant airlock that would let them out into space. There was but one lock large enough to permit so huge a ship to pass out, and they must circle half their world to reach it.

On three other worlds there were other giant ships racing

thus to meet beyond their solar system. There were fifty ships coming from each planet; two hundred mighty ships in all made up this Armada of Space, two hundred gargantuan interstellar cruisers.

One by one the giant ships passed through the airlock and out into space. Here they quickly reformed as they moved off together, each ship falling into its place in the mighty cone formation, with the flagship of Taj Lamor at the head. On they rushed through space, their speed ever mounting. Suddenly there seemed to leap out of nowhere another mass of shining machines that flew swiftly beside them. Like some strange, shining ghosts, these ships seemed to materialize instantly beside and behind their fleet. They fell in quickly in their allotted position behind the Flagship's squadron. One—two more fleets appeared thus suddenly in the dark, and together the ships were flashing on through space to their goal of glowing fire ahead!

Hour after hour, day after day the ships flashed on through the awful void, the utter silence relieved by the communications between themselves and the slowly weakening communications from the far-off home planets.

But as those signals from home grew steadily weaker, the sun before them grew steadily larger. At last the men began to feel the heat of those rays, to realize the energy that that mighty sea of flame poured forth into space, and steadily they watched it grow nearer.

Then came a day when they could make out clearly the dim bulk of a planet before them, and for long hours they slowed down the flying speed of the ships. They had mapped the system they were approaching; there were nine planets of varying sizes, some on the near and some on the far side of the sun. There were but three on the near side; one that seemed the outermost of the planets, about 35,000 miles in diameter, was directly in their path, while there were two more much nearer the sun, about 100,000,000 and 70,000,000 miles distant from it, each about seven to eight thousand miles in diameter, but they were on opposite sides of the sun. These more inviting and more accessible worlds were numbers two and three of the planetary system. It was decided to split the expedition into two parts; one part was to go to planet two, and the other to three. Taj Lamor was to lead his group of a hundred ships to the nearer planet at once.

In a very brief time the great ships slanted down over what seemed to be a mighty globe of water. They were well in the northern hemisphere, and they had come near the planet first over a vast stretch of rolling ocean. The men had looked in wonder at such vast quantities of the fluid. To them it was a precious liquid, that must be made artificially, and was to be conserved, yet here they saw such vast quantities of natural water as seemed impossible. Still, their ancient books had told of such things, and of other strange things, things that must have been wondrously beautiful, though they were so old now, these records, that they were regarded largely as myths.

Yet here were the strange proofs! They saw great masses of fleecy water vapor, huge billowy things that seemed solid, but were blown lightly in the wind. And natural air! The atmosphere extended for hundreds of miles off into space; and now, as they came closer to the surface of this world the air was dense, and the sky above them was a beautiful blue, not black, even where there were stars. The great sun, so brilliantly incandescent when seen from space, and now a glowing globe of reddish-yellow.

And as they came near land, they looked in wonder at mighty masses of rock and soil that threw their shaggy heads high above the surrounding terrain, huge masses that rose high, like waves in the water, till they towered in solemn grandeur miles into the air! What a sight for these men of a world so old that age long erosion had washed away the last traces of hills, and filled in all of the valleys!

In awe they looked down at the mighty rock masses, as they swung low over the mountains, gazing in wonder at the green masses of the strange vegetation; strange, indeed, for they for uncounted ages had grown only mushroom-like cellulose products, and these mainly for ornament, for all their food was artificially made in huge factories.

Then they came over a little mountain lake, a body of water scarcely large enough to berth one of their huge ships, but high in the clear air of the mountains, fed by the melting of eternal snows. It was a magnificent sapphire in a setting green as emerald, a sparkling lake of clear water, deep as the sea, high in a cleft in the mountains.

In wonder the men looked down at these strange sights. What a marvelous home!

Steadily the great machines proceeded, and at last the end of the giant mountain was reached, and they came to a great plain. But that plain was strangely marked off with squares, as regularly as though plotted with a draftsman's square. This world must be inhabited by intelligent beings!

Suddenly Taj Lamor saw strange specks off in the far horizon to the south, specks that seemed to grow in size with terrific velocity; these must be ships, the ships of these people, coming to defend their home. The strangely pallid face of Taj Lamor tightened into lines of grim resolution. This was a moment he had foreseen and had dreaded. Was he to withdraw and leave these people unmolested, or was he to stand and fight for this world, this wonderfully beautiful home, a home that his race could live in for millions of years to come? He had debated this question many times before in his mind, and he had decided. There would never, never be another chance for his people to gain a new home. They must fight.

Swiftly he gave his orders. If resistance came, if an attack were made, they were to fight back at once, with every weapon at their disposal.

The strangers' ships had grown swiftly larger to the eye, but still, though near now, they seemed too small to be dangerous. These giant interstellar cruisers were certainly invulnerable to ships so small; their mere size would give them protection! These ships were scarcely as long as the diameter of the smaller of the interstellar ships—a bare two hundred and fifty feet for the largest.

The interstellar cruisers halted in their course, and waited for the little ships to approach. They were fast, for they drew alongside quickly, and raced to the front of the flagship. There was one small one that was painted white, and on it there was a large white banner, flapping in the wind of its passage. The rest of the ships drew off as this came forward, and stopped, hanging motionless before the control room of the giant machine. There were men inside—three strange men, short and oddly pink-skinned—but they were gesturing now, motioning that the giant machine settle to the ground beneath. Taj Lamor was considering whether or not to thus parley with the strangers, when suddenly there leaped from the white craft a beam of clear white—a beam that was directed toward the ground, then swung up toward the great cruiser in a swift arc!

As one, a dozen swift beams of pale red flared out from the giant and bathed the pigmy craft. As they reached it, the white ray that had been sweeping up suddenly vanished, and for an instant the ship hung poised in the air; then it began to swing crazily, like the pendulum of a clock—swung completely over— and with a sickening lurch sped swiftly for the plain nearly five miles below. In moments there came a brief flare, then there remained only a little crater in the soft soil.

But the red beams had not stopped with the little ship; they had darted out to the other machines, trying to reach them before they could bring those strange white rays into play. The cruisers obviously must win, for they carried dozens of projectors, but they might be damaged, their flight delayed. They must defeat those strangers quickly. The rays of Taj Lamor's ship lashed out swiftly, but almost before they had started, all the other ships, a full hundred, were in action, and the flagship was darting swiftly up and away from the battle. Below, those pale red rays were taking a swift toll of the little ships, and nearly twenty of them rolled suddenly over, and dashed to destruction far below.

But now the little ships were in swift darting motion. Because of their small size, they were able to avoid the rays of the larger interstellar cruisers, and as their torpedo-shaped hulls flashed about with bewildering speed, they began to fight back. They had been taken utterly by surprise, but now they went into action with an abandon and swiftness that took the initiative away from the gigantic interstellar liners. They were in a dozen places at once, dodging and twisting, unharmed, out of the way of the deadly red beams, and were as hard to hit as so many dancing feathers suspended over an air jet.

And if the pilots were skillful in avoiding enemy rays, their ray men were as accurate in placing theirs. But then, with a target of such vast size, not so much skill was necessary.

These smaller vessels were the ships of Earth. The people of the dark star had entered the solar system quite unannounced, except that they had been seen in passing the orbit of Mars, for a ship had been out there in space, moving steadily out toward

Neptune, and the great interstellar cruisers, flashing in across space, away from that frigid planet, had not seen the tiny wanderer. But he had seen those mighty hulks, and had sent his message of danger out on the ether, warning the men of Earth. They had relayed it to Venus, and the ships that had gone there had received an equally warm reception, and were even now finding their time fully occupied trying to beat off the Interplanetary Patrol.

The battle ended as swiftly as it began, for Taj Lamor, in his machine high above, saw that they were outclassed, and ordered them to withdraw at once. Scarcely ten minutes had elapsed, yet they had lost twenty-two of their giant ships.

The expedition that had gone to Venus reported a similarly active greeting. It was decided at once that they should proceed cautiously to the other planets, to determine which were inhabited and which were not, and to determine the chemical and physical conditions on each.

The ships formed again out in space, on the other side of the sun, however, and started at once in compact formation for Mercury.

Their observations were completed without further mishap, and they set out for their distant home, their number depleted by forty-one ships, for nineteen had fallen on Venus.

I

The Terrestrian and Venerian governments had met in conference, a grim, businesslike discussion with few wasted words. Obviously, this was to be a war of science, a war on a scale never before known on either world. Agreements were immediately drawn up between the two worlds for a concerted, cooperative effort. A fleet of new and vastly more powerful ships must be constructed—but first they must have a complete report on the huge invading craft that had fallen in western Canada, and on Venus, for they might conceivably make their secrets their own.

They called for the scientists whose work had made possible their successful resistance of the marauders: Arcot, Morey and Wade. They found them working in the Arcot Laboratories.

"Wade," called Arcot tensely as he snapped the switch of the televisophone, "bring Morey and meet me at the machine on the roof at once. That was a call from Washington. I'll explain as soon as you get there."

On the roof Arcot opened the hangar doors, and entered the five-passenger molecular-motion ship inside. Its sleek, stream-lined sides spoke of power and speed. This was a special research model, designed for their experiments, and carrying mechanisms not found in commercial crafts. Among these were automatic controls still in the laboratory stage, but permitting higher speed, for no human being could control the ship as accurately as these.

It took the trio a little less than a quarter of an hour to make the 5000 mile trip from New York to the battlefield of Canada. As they sped through the air, Arcot told them what had transpired. The three were passed through the lines at once, and they settled to the ground beside one of the huge ships that lay half buried in the ground. The force of the impact had splashed the solid soil as a stone will splash soft mud, and around the ship there was a massive ridge of earth. Arcot looked at the titanic proportions of this ship from space, and turned to his friends:

"We can investigate that wreck on foot, but I think it'll be far more sensible to see what we can do with the car. This monster is certainly a mile or more long, and we'd spend more time in walking than in investigation. I suggest, we see if there isn't room for the car inside. This beats even those huge Kaxorian planes for size." Arcot paused, then grinned. "I sure would have liked to mix in the fight they must have had here— nice little things to play with, aren't they?"

"It would make a nice toy," agreed Wade as he looked at the rows of wicked-looking projectors along the sides of the metal hull, "and I wonder if there might not be some of the crew alive in there? If there are, the size of the ship would prevent their showing themselves very quickly, and since they can't move the ship, it seems to me that they'll let us know shortly that they're around. Probably, with the engines stopped, their main weapons are useless, but they would doubtless have some sort of guns. I'm highly in favor of using the car. We carry a molecular director ray, so if the way is blocked, we can make a new one."

Wade's attention was caught by a sudden flare of light a few miles across the plain. "Look over there—that ship is still flaming—reddish, but almost colorless. Looks like a gas flame, with a bit of calcium in it. Almost as if the air in the ship were combustible. If we should do any exploring in this baby, I suggest we use altitude suits—they can't do any harm in any case."

Three or four of the great wrecks, spread over a wide area, were burning now, hurling forth long tongues of colorless, intensely hot flame. Several of the ships had been only slightly damaged; one had been brought down by a beam that had torn free the entire tail of the ship, leaving the bow in good condition. Apparently this machine had not fallen far; perhaps the pilot had retained partial control of the ship, his power failing when he was only a comparatively short distance from Earth. This was rather well to one side of the plain, however, and they decided to investigate it later.

The ship nearest them had crashed nose first, the point being crushed and shattered. Arcot maneuvered his craft cautiously toward the great hole at the nose of the ship, and they entered the mighty vessel slowly, a powerful spotlight illuminating the interior. Tremendous girders, twisted and broken by the force of impact, thrust up about them. It soon became evident that there was little to fear from any living enemies, and they proceeded more rapidly. Certainly no creature could live after the shock that had broken these huge girders! Several times metal beams blocked their path, and they were forced to use the molecular director ray to bend them out of the way.

"Man," said Arcot as they stopped a moment to clear away a huge member that was bent across their path, "but those beams do look as if they were built permanently! I'd hate to ram into one of them! Look at that one—if that has anywhere near the strength of steel, just think of the force it took to bend it!"

At last they had penetrated to the long tube that led through the length of the ship, the communication tube. This admitted the small ship easily, and they moved swiftly along till they came to what they believed to be about the center of the invader. Here Arcot proposed that they step out and see what there was to be seen.

The others agreed, and they at once put on their altitude suits of heavy rubberized canvas, designed to be worn outside the ship when at high altitude, or even in space. They were supplied with oxygen tanks that would keep the wearer alive for about six hours. Unless the atmosphere remaining in the alien ship was excessively corrosive, they would be safe. After a brief discussion, they decided that all would go, for if they met opposition, there would be strength in numbers.

They met their first difficulty in opening the door leading out of the communication tube. It was an automatic door, and resisted their every effort—until finally they were forced to tear it out with a ray. It was impossible to move it in any other way. The door was in what was now the floor, since the ship seemed to have landed on one side rather than on its keel.

They let themselves through the narrow opening one at a time, and landed on the sloping wall of the corridor beyond.

"Lucky this wasn't a big room, or we'd have had a nice drop to the far wall!" commented Wade. The suits were equipped with a thin vibrating diaphragm that made speech easy, but Wade's voice came through with a queerly metallic ring.

Arcot agreed somewhat absently, his attention directed toward their surroundings. His hand light pierced the blackness, finally halting at a gaping opening, apparently the entrance to a corridor. As they examined it, they saw that it slanted steeply downward.

"It seems to be quite a drop," said Wade as he turned his light into it, "but the surface seems to be rather rough. I think we can do it. I notice that you brought a rope, Morey; I think it'll help. I'll go first, unless someone else wants the honor."

"You go first?" Arcot hesitated briefly. "But I don't know—if we're all going, I guess you had better, at that. It would take two ordinary men to lower a big bulk like you. On the other hand, if anybody is going to stay, you're delegated as elevator boy!

"Hold everything," continued Arcot. "I have an idea. I think none of us will need to hold the weight of the others with the rope. Wade, will you get three fairly good-sized pieces of metal, something we can tie a rope to? I think we can get down here without the help of anyone else. Morey, will you cut the rope in three equal pieces while I help Wade tear loose that girder?"

Arcot refused to reveal his idea till his preparations were complete, but worked quickly and efficiently. With the aid of Wade, he soon had three short members, and taking the rope that Morey had prepared, he tied lengths of cord to the pieces of metal, leaving twenty foot lengths hanging from each. Now he carefully tested his handiwork to make sure the knots would not slip.

"Now, let's see what we can do." Arcot put a small loop in one end of a cord, thrust his left wrist through this, and grasped the rope firmly with his hand. Then he drew his ray pistol, and adjusted it carefully for direction of action. The trigger gave him control over power. Finally he turned the ray on the block of metal at the other end of the rope. At once the metal pulled vigorously, drawing the rope taut, and as Arcot increased the power, he was dragged slowly across the floor.

"Ah—it works." He grinned broadly over his shoulder. "Come on, boys, hitch your wagon to a star, and we'll go on with the investigation. This is a new, double action parachute. It lets you down easy, and pulls you up easier! I think we can go where we want now." After a pause he added, "I don't have to tell you that too much power will be very bad!"

With Arcot's simple brake, they lowered themselves into the corridor below, descending one at a time, to avoid any contact with the ray, since the touch of the beam was fatal.

The scene that lay before them was one of colossal destruction. They had evidently stumbled upon the engine room. They could not hope to illuminate its vast expanse with their little hand lights, but they could gain some idea of its magnitude, and of its original layout. The floor, now tilted at a steep angle, was torn up in many places, showing great, massive beams, buckled and twisted like so many wires, while the heavy floor plates were crumpled like so much foil. Everywhere the room seemed covered with a film of white silvery metal; it was silver, they decided after a brief examination, spattered broadcast over the walls of the room.

Suddenly Morey pointed ceilingward with his light. "That's where the silver came from!" he exclaimed. A network of heavy bars ran across the roof, great bars of solid silver fully three feet thick. In one section gaped a ragged hole, suggesting the work of a disintegration ray, a hole that went into the metal roof above, one which had plainly been fused, as had the great silver bars.

Arcot looked in wonder at the heavy metal bars. "Lord—bus-bars three feet thick! What engines they must have! Look at the way those were blown out! They were short circuited by the crash, just before the generator went out, and they were volatilized! Some juice!"

With the aid of their improvised elevators, the three men attempted to explore the tremendous chamber. They had scarcely begun, when Wade exclaimed:

"Bodies!"

They crowded around his gruesome find and caught their first glimpse of the invaders from space. Anatomical details could not be distinguished since the bodies had been caught under a ram of crushing beams, but they saw that they were not too different from both Terrestrians and Venerians—though their blood seemed strangely pallid, and their skin was of a ghastly whiteness. Evidently they had been assembled before an unfamiliar sort of instrument panel when catastrophe struck; Morey indicated the dials and keys.

"Nice to know what you're fighting," Arcot observed. "I've a hunch that we'll see some of these critters alive—but not in this ship!"

They turned away and resumed their examination of the shattered mechanisms.

A careful examination was impossible; they were wrecks, but Arcot did see that they seemed mainly to be giant electrical machines of standard types, though on a gargantuan scale. There were titanic masses of wrecked metal, iron and silver, for with these men silver seemed to replace copper, though nothing could replace iron and its magnetic uses.

"They are just electrical machines, I guess," said Arcot at last. "But what size! Have you seen anything really revolutionary, Wade?"

Wade frowned and answered, "There are just two things that bother me. Come here." As Arcot jumped over, nearly suspended by his ray pistol, Wade directed his light on a small machine that had fallen in between the cracks in the giant mass of broken generators. It was a little thing, apparently housed in a glass case. There was only one objection to that assumption. The base of a large generator lay on it, metal fully two feet thick, and that metal was cracked where it rested on the case, and the case, made of material an inch and a half thick, was not dented!

"Whewww—that's a nice kind of glass to have!" Morey commented. "I'd like to have a specimen for examination. Oh—I wonder—yes, it must be! There's a window in the side up there toward what was the bow that seemed to me to be the same stuff. It's buried about three feet in solid earth, so I imagine it must be."

The three made their way at once to where they had seen the window. The frame appeared to be steel, or some such alloy, and it was twisted and bent under the blow, for this was evidently the outer wall, and the impact of landing had flattened the rounded side. But that "glass" window was quite undisturbed! There was, as a further proof, a large granite boulder lying against it on the outside—or what had been a boulder, though it had been shattered by the impact.

"Say—that's some building material!" Arcot indicated the transparent sheet. "Just look at that granite rock—smashed into sand! Yet the window isn't even scratched! Look how the frame that held it is torn—just torn, not broken. I wonder if we can tear it loose altogether?" He stepped forward, raising his pistol. There was a thud as his metal bar crashed down when the ray was shut off. Then, as the others got out of the way, he stepped toward the window and directed his beam toward it. Gradually he increased the power, till suddenly there was a rending crash, and they saw only a leaping column of earth and sand and broken granite flying up through the hole in the steel shell. There was a sudden violent crash, then a moment later a second equally violent crash as the window, having flown up to the ceiling, came thumping back to the floor.

After the dust had settled they came forward, looking for the window. They found it, somewhat buried by the rubbish, lying off to one side. Arcot bent down to tilt it and sweep off the dirt; he grasped it with one hand, and pulled. The window remained where it was. He grasped it with both hands and pulled harder. The window remained where it was.

"Uh—say, lend a hand will you, Wade." Together the two men pulled, but without results. That window was about three feet by two feet by one inch, making the total volume about one-half a cubic foot, but it certainly was heavy. They could not begin to move it. An equal volume of lead would have weighed about four hundred pounds, but this was decidedly more than four hundred pounds. Indeed, the combined strength of the three men did not do more than rock it.

"Well—it certainly is no kind of matter we know of!" observed Morey. "Osmium, the heaviest known metal, has a density of twenty-two and a half, which would weigh about 730 pounds. I think we could lift that, so this is heavier than anything we know. At least that's proof of a new system. Between Venus and Earth we have found every element that occurs in the sun. These people must have come from another star!"

"Either that," returned Arcot, "or proof of an amazing degree of technological advancement. It's only a guess, of course—but I have an idea where this kind of matter exists in the solar system. I think you have already seen it—in the gaseous state. You remember, of course, that the Kaxorians had great reservoirs for storing light-energy in a bound state in their giant planes. They had bound light, light held by the gravitational attraction for itself, after condensing it in their apparatus, but they had what amounted to a gas—gaseous light. Now suppose that someone makes a light condenser even more powerful than the one the Kaxorians used, a condenser that forces the light so close to itself, increases its density, till the photons hold each other permanently, and the substance becomes solid. It will be matter, matter made of light—light matter—and let us call it a metal. You know that ordinary matter is electricity matter, and electricity matter metals conduct electricity readily. Now why shouldn't our 'light matter' metal conduct light? It would be a wonderful substance for windows."

"But now comes the question of moving it," Wade interposed. "We can't lift it, and we certainly want to examine it. That means we must take it to the laboratory. I believe we're about through here—the place is clearly quite permanently demolished. I think we had better return to the ship and start to that other machine we saw that didn't appear to be so badly damaged. But—how can we move this?"

"I think a ray may do the trick." Arcot drew his ray pistol, and stepped back a bit, holding the weapon so the ray would direct the plate straight up. Slowly he applied the power, and as he gradually increased it, the plate stirred, then moved into the air.

"It works! Now you can use your pistol, Morey, and direct it toward the corridor. I'll send it up, and let it fall outside, where we can pick it up later." Morey stepped forward, and while

Arcot held it in the air with his ray, Morey propelled it slowly with his, till it was directly under the corridor leading upward. Then Arcot gave a sudden increase in power, and the plate moved swiftly upward, sailing out of sight. Arcot shut off his ray, and there came to their ears a sudden crash as the plate fell to the floor above.

The three men regained their ropes and "double action parachutes" as Arcot called them, and floated up to the next floor. Again they started the process of moving the plate. All went well till they came to the little car itself. They could not use the ray on the car, for fear of damaging the machinery. They had to use some purely mechanical method of hoisting it in.

Finally they solved the problem by using the molecular director ray to swing a heavy beam into the air, then one man pulled on the far end of it with a rope, and swung it till it was resting on the door of the ship on one end, and the other rested in a hole they had torn in the lining of the tube.

Now they maneuvered the heavy plate till it was resting on that beam; then they released the plate, and watched it slide down the incline, shooting through the open doorway of the car. In moments the job was done. The plate at last safely stowed, the three men climbed into the car, and prepared to leave.

The little machine glided swiftly down the tube through the mighty ship, finally coming out through the opening that had admitted them. They rose quickly into the air, and headed for the headquarters of the government ships.

II

A great number of scientists and military men were already gathered about the headquarters ship. As Arcot's party arrived, they learned that each of the wrecks was being assigned to one group. They further learned that because of their scientific importance, they were to go to the nearly perfect ship lying off to the west. Two Air Patrolmen were to accompany them.

"Lieutenant Wright and Lieutenant Greer will go with you," said the Colonel. "In the event of trouble from possible—though unlikely—survivors, they may be able to help. Is there anything further we can do?"

"These men are armed with the standard sidearms, aren't they?" Arcot asked. "I think we'll all be better off if I arm them with some of the new director-ray pistols. I have several in my boat. It will be all right, I suppose?"

"Certainly, Dr. Arcot. They are under your command."

The party, increased to five now, returned to the ship, where Arcot showed the men the details of the ray pistols, and how to use them. The control for direction of operation was rather intricate in these early models, and required considerable explanation. The theoretical range of even these small hand weapons was infinity in space, but in the atmosphere the energy was rather rapidly absorbed by ionization of the air, and the dispersion of the beam made it ineffective in space over a range of more than thirty-five miles.

Again entering the little molecular-motion car, they went at once to the great hull of the fallen ship. They inspected it cautiously from overhead before going too close, for the dreadnought, obviously, had landed without the terrific concussion that the others had experienced, and there was a possibility that some of the crew had survived the crash. The entire stern of the huge vessel had been torn off, and evidently the ship was unable to rise, but there were lights glowing though the portholes on the side, indicating that power had not failed completely.

"I think we'd better treat that monster with respect," remarked Wade, looking down at the lighted windows. "They have power, and the hull is scarcely dented except where the stern was caught by a beam. It's lucky we had those ray projector ships! They've been in service only about four months, haven't they, Lieutenant?"

"Just about that, sir," the Air Patrolman replied. "They hadn't gotten the hand weapons out in sufficient quantities to be issued to us as yet."

Morey scowled at the invader. "I don't like this at all. I wonder why they didn't greet us with some of their beams," he said in worried tones. It did seem that there should be some of the rays in action now. They were less than a mile from the fallen giant, and moving rather slowly.

"I've been puzzled about that myself," commented Arcot, "and I've come to the conclusion that either the ray projectors are fed by a separate system of power distribution, which has been destroyed, or that the creatures from space are all dead."

They were to learn later, in their exploration of the ship, that the invaders' ray projectors were fed from a separate generator, which produced a special form of alternating current wave for them. This generator had been damaged beyond use.

The little machine was well toward the stern of the giant now, and they lowered it till it was on a level with the torn metal. It was plain that the ship had been subjected to some terrific tension. The great girders were stretched and broken, and the huge ribs were bent and twisted. The central tube, which ran the length of the ship, had been drawn down to about three quarters of its original diameter, making it necessary for them to use their ray to enter. In moments their speedster glided into the dark tunnel. The searchlight reaching ahead filled the metal tunnel with a myriad deceptive reflections. The tube was lighted up far ahead of them, and seemed empty. Cautiously they advanced, with Arcot at the controls.

"Wade—Morey—where will we stop first?" he asked. "The engines? They'll probably be of prime importance. We know their location. What do you say?"

"I agree," replied Wade, and Morey nodded his approval.

They ran their craft down the long tube till they reached the door they knew must be the engine room landing, and stepped out, each wearing an altitude suit. This ship had landed level, and progress would be much easier than in the other one. They waited a moment before opening the door into the engine room, for this led into a narrow corridor where only one could pass. Caution was definitely in order. The Air Patrolmen insisted on leading the way. They had been sent along for the express purpose of protecting the scientists, and it was their duty to lead. After a brief argument Arcot agreed.

The two officers stepped to the door, and standing off to one side, tore it open with a ray from their pistols. It fell with a clatter to the rounded metal floor of the tube, and lay there vibrating noisily, but no rays of death lanced out from beyond it. Cautiously they peered around the corner of the long corridor, then seeing nothing, entered. Wade came next, then Arcot, followed by Morey.

The corridor was approximately thirty feet long, opening

into the great engine room. Already the men could hear the smooth hum of powerful machines, and could see the rounded backs of vast mechanisms. But there was no sign of life, human or otherwise. They halted finally at the threshold of the engine room.

"Well," Arcot said softly. "We haven't seen anyone so far, and I hope no one has seen us. The invaders may be behind one of those big engines, quite unaware of us. *If* they're there, and they see us, they'll be ready to fight. Now remember, those weapons you have will tear loose anything they hit, so take it easy. You know something about the power of those engines, so don't put them out of commission, and have them splash us all over the landscape.

"But look out for the crew, and get them if they try to get you!"

Cautiously but quickly they stepped out into the great room, forming a rough half circle, pistols ready for action. They walked forward stealthily, glancing about them—and simultaneously the enemies caught sight of each other. There were six of the invaders, each about seven feet tall, and surprisingly humanoid. They somewhat resembled Venerians, but they weren't Venerians, for their skin was a strange gray-white, suggesting raw dough. It seemed to Arcot that these strange, pale creatures were advancing at a slow walk, and that he stood still watching them as they slowly raised strange hand weapons. He seemed to notice every detail: their short, tight-fitting suits of some elastic material that didn't hamper their movements, and their strange flesh, which just seemed to escape being transparent. Their eyes were strangely large, and the black spot of the pupil in their white corneas created an unnatural effect.

Then abruptly their weapons came up—and Arcot responded with a sudden flick of his ray, as he flung himself to one side. Simultaneously his four companions let their beams fly toward the invaders. They glowed strangely red here, but they were still effective. The six beings were suddenly gone—but not before they had released their own beams. And they had taken toll. Lieutenant Wright lay motionless upon the floor.

The Terrestrians scarcely had a chance to notice this, for immediately there was a terrific rending crash, and clean daylight came pouring in through a wide opening in the wall of

the ship. The five rays had not stopped on contact with the
enemy, but had touched the wall behind them. An irregular
opening now gaped in the smooth metal.

Suddenly there came a second jarring thud, a dull explosion;
then a great sheet of flame filled the hole—a wall of ruddy flame
swept rapidly in. Arcot swung up his ray pistol, pointing it at the
mass of flaming gas. A mighty column of air came through the
narrow corridor from the tube, rushing toward the outside, and
taking the flame with it. A roaring mass of gas hovered outside of
the ship.

"Lieutenant," said Arcot, swiftly, "turn your ray on that hole,
and keep it there, blowing that flame outside with it. You'll find
you can't put the fire out, but if you keep it outside the ship, I
believe we'll be reasonably safe." The Patrolman obeyed instantly, relieving Arcot.

Wade and Morey were already bending over the fallen man.
"I'm afraid there's nothing we can do for him," the latter said
grimly, "and every moment here is dangerous. Let's continue our
investigation and carry him back to the ship when we leave."
Arcot nodded silently.

Solemnly they turned away from the motionless figure on the
floor and set out on their investigation.

"Arcot," began Morey after a moment, "why is that gas burning like that? Can't we put it out?"

"Let's get through with this job first," replied Arcot somewhat tersely. "The discussion comes after."

The bodies of the invaders were gone, so they could not
examine them now. That was a matter for the doctors and
biologists, anyway. The engines were their main interest, huge
things which overshadowed everything about them.

It must have been the concealment afforded by the engines
that permitted three of the enemy to get so close. The only
warning the Terrestrians had was a faint pink haze as they
stepped around the corner of an engine; and a sudden feeling of
faintness swept over them. They leaped back, out of sight,
peering around the corner with nerves and muscles tensed. There
was no sign of movement.

As they watched, they saw a pallid hand reaching out with a
ray gun; and Wade swiftly pointed his own weapon. There
came a sudden crash of metal, a groan and quiet. Two other

aliens leaped from behind the great engine just as the Terrestrians dodged further back; as swiftly, they too found concealment.

Arcot swung his ray up, and was about to pull the trigger that would send the huge engine toppling over upon them, when he saw that it was running. He thought of the unknown energies in the machine, the potential destruction, and he shook his head. Cautiously he looked around the edge of the towering mass, waiting—his beam flashed out, and there was a snapping sound as the ray caught a reaching hand and hurled its owner against a mighty transformer of some sort. For an instant the huge mass tottered, then was still. In the low concentration of power that Arcot had used, only a small portion had been touched, and the molecules of this portion had not been enough to tip over its tremendous weight.

Only one enemy remained; and Arcot learned swiftly that he was still in action, for before he could dodge back there came that now-familiar pink haziness. It touched Arcot's hand, outstretched as it had been when he fired, and a sudden numbness came over it. His pistol hand seemed to lose all feeling of warmth or cold. It was there; he could still feel the weapon's deadened weight. Reflex action hurled him back, his hand out of range of the ray. In seconds feeling began to return, and in less than ten his hand was normal again.

He turned to the others with a wry grin. "Whew—that was a narrow squeak! I must say their ray is a gentlemenly sort of thing. It either kills you, or doesn't injure you at all. There it goes again!"

A shaft of pink radiance reached the end of the engine, just grazing it, evidently absorbed by its mass. "Pinning us down," Wade grated. They certainly couldn't step out into the open space—but they couldn't stay where they were indefinitely, either. Reinforcements might arrive!

"Look," Wade pointed with his pistol, "he's under that big metal bar—up there in the roof—see it? I'll pull it down; he may get nervous and come into sight." Swiftly Arcot sprang forward and caught his arm.

"Lord—don't do that, Wade—there's too much stuff here that we don't know anything about. Too much chance of your smashing us with him. I'm going to try to get around to the other side of this machine and see what I can do, while you fellows keep him occupied."

Arcot disappeared around the black humming giant. Interminably the others waited for something to happen; then suddenly the beam that had been playing at irregular intervals across the end of the machine, swung quickly to the other side; and simultaneously another ray seemed to leap from the machine itself. They met and crossed. There came a momentary crashing arc, then both went dead, as the apparatus that generated them blew out under terrific overload.

The invader evidently carried a spare, for the watchers saw him dart from concealment, clawing at his pocket pouch. They turned their rays on him, and just as his projector came free, a ray hurled him violently to the left. He crashed into a huge motor, and the result was not nice.

The projector had been jerked from his hand and lay off to the side. Arcot ran to it and picked it up just as they heard the Lieutenant call an alarmed inquiry.

"I think we're okay now," Arcot answered. "I hope there are no more—but by all means stay where you are, and use as little power as possible in blowing that flame outside. It uses up the atmosphere of the ship, and though we don't need it, I think we'd better take things easy. Call us if anything looks odd to you."

For several minutes the three scientists looked about them in awe-struck wonder. They were the first men of Earth to see the driving equipment of one of the tremendous Kaxorian planes, and they felt tiny beside its great bulk; but now, as they examined this engine room, they realized that even the huge plane shrank into insignificance beside this interstellar cruiser.

All about them loomed the great rounded backs of giant electric motor-generators of some sort. Across the roof ran a network of gigantic metal bars, apparently conductors, but so large that they suggested heavy structural members. The machines they ran into loomed fully thirty feet into the air; they were longer than cylinders, thirty feet in diameter, and there was a group of four main machines fully a hundred twenty feet long! There were many smaller mechanisms—yet these smaller ones would easily have constituted a complete power supply for the average big city. Along each wall ran a bank of transformers, cast in the same heroic mold. These seemed connected with the smaller machines, there being four conductors leading into each of the minor units, two intake, and two, apparently, output leads, suggesting rotary converters. The multiple units and the various types and sizes of transformers made it obvious that many different frequencies were needed. Some of the transformers had air cores, and led to machines surrounded with a silvery white metal instead of the usual iron. These apparently, were generating current at an extremely high frequency.

"Well," Morey commented, "they ought to have power enough. But do you notice that those four main units have their leads radiating in different directions? The one on the left there seems to lead to that big power board at the front—or better, bow. I think it would be worth investigating."

Arcot nodded. "I had the same idea. You notice that two of the main power units are still working, but that those other two have stopped? Probably the two dead ones have something to do with the motion of the ship. But there's one point I think is of even greater interest. All the machines we have seen, all the conspicuous ones, are secondary power sources. There are no primary sources visible. Notice that those two main conduits lead over to the right, and toward the bow. Let's check where they go to."

As they talked they followed the huge conductors back to their point of convergence. Suddenly they rounded one of the huge main power units, and saw before them, at the center of square formed by these machines, a low platform of transparent light-metal. At the exact center of this platform, which was twenty feet in diameter, there was a table, about seven feet across and raised about five feet above the level of the platform on stout light-metal legs. On the table were two huge cubes of solid silver, and into these cubes ran all the conductors they had seen.

In the space of about six inches left between the blocks of metal, there was a small box constructed of some strange new material. It was the most perfect reflecting surface that any of the men had ever imagined. Indeed, it was so perfect a reflector that they were unable to see it, but could detect its presence only by the mirror images, and the fact that it blotted out objects behind it.

Now they noticed that through the huge blocks of metal there were two small holes, and two thin wires of this same reflecting material led into those holes. The wires led directly up to the roof, and, suspended on three-foot hangers of the light-metal, continued on toward the bow.

Could this be the source of power for the entire ship? It seemed impossible, yet there were many other seeming impossible things here, among them that strangely reflecting matter.

There was a low railing about the central platform, apparently intended to keep observers at a safe distance, so they decided against any more detailed investigation. As they were about to discuss their unusual find, the Lieutenant called that he heard sounds behind him.

At once the three ran rapidly toward the narrow corridor that had given them entrance. The flaming gas was still shooting through the hole in the wall of the ship, and the rush of air through the corridor made it difficult to hear any sounds there, and exceedingly difficult to walk.

"Turn on more power, Lieutenant, and see if we can't draw out the enemy," suggested Arcot, while they braced themselves around the tube exit.

As the Patrolman increased the power of his beam, the moan of the air through the corridor increased suddenly to a terrific roar, and a cyclonic gale swept through. But none of the invaders were drawn out.

After the Lieutenant had shut off the blast from his pistol at Arcot's signal, the latter said: "I don't think anything less than a war tank could stand that pressure. It's probable that we'll be attacked if we stay here much longer, though—and we may not be able to get out at all. I think, Lieutenant, I'll ask you to stay here while we go out and get the ship ready to leave." He paused, grinning. "Be sure to keep that flame outside. You'll be in the position of Hercules after Atlas left him holding the skies on his shoulders. You can't shut off the ray for long or we'll have a first-rate explosion. We'll signal when we're ready by firing a revolver, and you make it to the ship as fast as you can travel."

Arcot's expression became solemn. "We'll have to carry Wright back to the ship. He was a brave man, and he certainly deserves burial in the soil of his own world. And, Morey, we'll have to look up his family. Your father's company will have to take care of them if they need help."

Slowly the men forced their way back toward their ship, fighting against the roaring column of air, their burden hindering them somewhat; but at last they reached the open tunnel. Even here the air was in violent motion.

They got into their boat as quickly as possible, and set the controls for reverse flight. Then Wade fired the signal shot. In moments they saw Lieutenant Greer bucking against the current of air, continuing under its own momentum.

By the time he was in the ship an ominous calm had fallen. Swiftly they sped down the corridor, and had almost reached the open air, when suddenly there was a dull rumble behind them, and they were caught on a wave of pressure that hurled them along at terrific speed. In a flash they sped into the open air, the great tunnel with its thick walls and flared opening acting like a gigantic blunderbus, with the ship as its bullet. Arcot made no attempt to slow down the little craft, but pressed his foot heavily on the vertical accelerator. The ship rocketed up with terrific speed, and the acceleration pinned the men down to their seats with tripled weight.

Anxiously they watched the huge invader as they sped away from it. At Arcot's direction Morey signaled the other groups of scientists to get out of danger with all speed, warning of the impending blow-up. As the moments sped by the tension mounted. Arcot stared fixedly into the screen before him, keeping the giant space ship in focus. As they sped mile upon miles away from it, he began to relax a bit.

Not a word was spoken as they watched and waited. Actually, very little time passed before the explosion, but to the watchers the seconds dragged endlessly. Then at twenty-seven miles, the screen flared into a sheet of blind white radiance. There was a timeless instant—then a tremendous wave of sound, a roaring, stunning concussion smote the ship, shaking it with unrestrained fury—to cease as abruptly as it came.

Immediately they realized the reason. They were rushing away from the explosion faster than the sound it made, hence could not hear it. After the first intolerable flash, details became visible. The great ship seemed to leap into countless tremendous fragments, each rushing away from the point of the blow-up.

They did not go far; the force was not sustained long enough, nor was it great enough to overcome the inertia of so vast a mass for more than moments. Huge masses rained to earth, to bury themselves in the soil.

There came a momentary lull. Then suddenly, from the mass which evidently held the wrecked engine room, there shot out a beam of intense white light that swept around in a wide, erratic arc. Whatever it touched fused instantly into a brilliantly glowing mass of liquid incandescence. The field itself, fragments of the wreckage, fused and mingled under its fury. The beam began to swing, faster and faster, as the support that was holding it melted; then abruptly it turned upon itself. There came a sudden blast of brilliance to rival that of the sun—and the entire region became a molten lake. Eyes streaming, temporarily blinded, the men turned away from the screen.

"That," said Arcot ruefully, "is that! It seems that our visitors don't want to leave any of their secrets lying around for us to investigate. I've an idea that all the other wrecks will go like this one did." He scowled. "You know, we really didn't learn much. Guess we'd better call the headquarters ship and ask for further instructions. Will you attend to it, Lieutenant Greer?"

III

Swiftly Arcot's sleek cruiser sped toward New York and the Arcot Laboratories. They had halted briefly at the headquarters ship of the Earth-Venus forces to report on their experience; and alone again, the three scientists were on their way home.

With their course set, Arcot spoke to the others. "Well, fellows, what are your opinions on—what we've seen? Wade, you're a chemist—tell us what you think of the explosion of the ship, and of the strange color of our molecular ray in their air."

Wade shook his head doubtfully. "I've been trying to figure it out, and I can't quite believe my results. Still, I can't see any other explanation. That reddish glow looked like hydrogen ions in the air. The atmosphere was certainly combustible when it met ours, which makes it impossible for me to believe that their air contained any noticeable amount of oxygen, for anything above twenty per cent oxygen and the rest hydrogen would be violently explosive. Apparently the gas had to mix liberally with our air to reach that proportion. That it didn't explode when ionized, showed the absence of hydro-oxygen mixture.

"All the observed facts except one seem to point to an atmosphere composed largely of hydrogen. That one—there are beings living in it! I can understand how the Venerians might adapt to a different climate, but I can't see how anything approaching human life can live in an atmosphere like that."

Arcot nodded. "I have come to similar conclusions. But I don't see too much objection to the thought of beings living in an atmosphere of hydrogen. It's all a question of organic chemistry. Remember that our bodies are just chemical furnaces. We take in fuel and oxidize it, using the heat as our source of power. The invaders live in an atmosphere of hydrogen. They eat oxidizing fuels, and breathe a reducing atmosphere; they have the two fuel components together again, but in a way different from our method. Evidently, it's just as effective. I'm sure that's the secret of the whole thing."

"Sounds fairly logical," Wade agreed. "But now I have a question for you. Where under the sun did these beings come from?"

Arcot's reply came slowly. "I've been wondering the same thing. And the more I wonder, the less I believe they did come from—under our sun. Let's eliminate all the solar planets—we can do that at one fell swoop. It's perfectly obvious that those ships are by no means the first crude attempts of this race to fly through space. We're dealing with an advanced technology. If they have had those ships even as far away as Pluto, we should certainly have heard from them by now.

"Hence, we've got to go out into interstellar space. You'll probably want to ram some of my arguments down my throat—I know there is no star near enough for the journey to be made in anything less than a couple of generations by all that's logical; and they'd freeze in the interstellar cold doing it. There is no *known* star close enough—but how about unknowns?"

"What have they been doing with the star?" Morey snorted. "Hiding it behind a sun-shade?"

Arcot grinned. "Yes. A shade of old age. You know a sun can't radiate forever; eventually they die. And a dead sun would be quite black, I'm sure."

"And the planets that circle about them are apt to become a wee bit cool too, you know."

"Agreed," said Arcot, "and we wouldn't be able to do much about it. But give these beings credit for a little higher order of intelligence. We saw machines in that space ship that certainly are beyond us! They are undoubtedly heating their planets with the same source of energy with which they are running their ships.

"I believe I have confirmation of that statement in two things. They are absolutely colorless; they don't even have an opaque white skin. Any living creature exposed to the rays of a sun, which is certain to emit some chemical rays, is subject to coloration as a protection against those rays. The whites, who have always lived where sunlight is weakest, have developed a skin only slightly opaque. The Orientals, who live in more tropical countries, where less clothes and more sun is the motto, have slightly darker skins. In the extreme tropics Nature has found it necessary to use a regular blanket of color to stop the rays. Now extrapolating the other way, were there no such rays, the people would become a pigmentless race. Since most proteins are rather translucent, at least when wet, they would appear much as these beings do. Remember, there are very few colored proteins. Hemoglobin, such as in our blood, and hemo-cyanin, like that in the blue blood of the Venerians, are practically unique in that respect. For hydrogen absorption, I imagine the blood of these creatures contains a fair proportion of some highly saturated compound, which readily takes on the element, and gives it up later.

"But we can kick this around some more in the lab."

Before starting for New York, Arcot had convinced the officer in charge that it would be wise to destroy the more complete of the invaders' ships at once, lest one of them manage to escape. The fact that none of them had any rays in operation was easily explained; they would have been destroyed by the Patrol if they had made any show of weapons. But they might be getting some ready, to be used in possible escape attempts. The scientists were through with their preliminary investigations. And the dismembered sections would remain for study, anyway.

The ships had finally been rayed apart, and when the three had left, their burning atmosphere had been sending mighty tongues of flame a mile or more into the air. The light gas of the alien atmosphere tended to rise in a great globular cloud, a ball that quickly burned itself out. It had not taken long for the last of the machines to disintegrate under the rays. There would be no more trouble from them, at any rate!

Now Morey asked Arcot if he thought that they had learned all they could from the ships; would it not have been wiser to save them, and investigate more fully later, taking a chance on stopping any sudden attack by surviving marauders by keeping a patrol of Air Guards there.

To which Arcot replied, "I thought quite a bit before I suggested their destruction, and I conferred for a few moments with Forsyth, who's just about tops in biology and bacteriology. He said that they had by no means learned as much as they wished to, but they'd been forced to leave in any event. Remember that pure hydrogen, the atmosphere we were actually living in while on the ship, is quite as inert as pure oxygen—when alone. But the two get very rough when mixed together. The longer those ships lay there the more dangerously explosive they became. If we hadn't destroyed them, they would have wrecked themselves. I still think we followed the only logical course.

"Dr. Forsyth mentioned the danger of disease. There's a remote possibility that we might be susceptible to their germs. I don't believe we would be, for our chemical constitution is so vastly different. For instance, the Venerians and Terrestrians can visit each other with perfect freedom. The Venerians have diseases, and so do we, of course; but there are things in the blood of Venerians that are absolutely deadly to any Terrestrian organism. We have a similar deadly effect on Venerian germs. It isn't immunity—it's simply that our respective constitutions are so different that we don't need immunity. Similarly, Forsyth thinks we would be completely resistant to all diseases brought by the invaders. However, it's safer to remove the danger, if any, first, and check afterward."

The three men sped rapidly back to New York, flying nearly sixty miles above the surface of the earth, where there would be no interfering traffic, till at length they were above the big city, and dropping swiftly in a vertical traffic lane.

Shortly thereafter they settled lightly in the landing cradle at the Arcot Laboratories. Arcot's father, and Morey's, were there, anxiously awaiting their return. The elder Arcot had for many years held the reputation of being the nation's greatest physicist, but recently he had lost it—to his son. Morey senior was the president and chief stockholder in the Transcontinental Air Lines. The Arcots, father and son, had turned all their inventions over to their close friends, the Moreys. For many years the success of the great air lines had been dependent in large part on the inventions of the Arcots; these new discoveries enabled them to keep one step ahead of competition, and as they also made the huge transport machines for other companies, they drew tremendous profits from these mechanisms. The mutual interest, which had begun as a purely financial relationship, had long since become a close personal friendship.

As Arcot stepped from his speedster, he called immediately to his father, telling of their find, the light-matter plate.

"I'll need a handling machine to move it. I'll be right back." He ran to the elevator and dropped quickly to the heavy machinery lab on the lower floor. In a short time he returned with a tractor-like machine equipped with a small derrick, designed to get its power from the electric mains. He ran the machine over to the ship. The others looked up as they heard the rumble and hum of its powerful motor. From the crane dangled a strong electro-magnet.

"What's that for?" asked Wade, pointing to the magnet. "You don't expect this to be magnetic, do you?"

"Wait and see!" laughed Arcot, maneuvering the handling machine into position. One of the others made contact with the power line, and the crane reached into the ship, lowering the magnet to the plate of crystal. Then Arcot turned the power into the lifting motor. The hum rose swiftly in volume and pitch till the full load began to strain the cables. The motor whined with full power, the cables vibrating under the tension. The machine pulled steadily, until, to Arcot's surprise, the rear end of the machine rose abruptly from the floor, tipping forward.

"Well—it *was* magnetic, but how did you know?" asked the surprised Wade. Since the ship was made of the Venerian metal, coronium, which was only slightly magnetic, the plate was obviously the magnet's only load.

"Never mind. I'll tell you later. Get an I-beam, say about

twenty feet long, and see if you can't help lift that crazy mass. I think we ought to manage it that way."

And so it proved. With two of them straddling the I-beam, the leverage was great enough to pull the plate out. Running it over to the elevator, they lowered the heavy mass, disconnected the cable, and rode down to Arcot's laboratory. Again the I-beam and handling machine were brought into play, and the plate was unloaded from the car. The five men gathered around the amazing souvenir from another world.

"I'm with Wade in wondering how you knew the plate was magnetic, son," commented the elder Arcot. "I can accept your explanation that the stuff is a kind of matter made of light, but I know you too well to think it was just a lucky guess. How did you know?"

"It really was pretty much of a guess, Dad, though there was some logic behind the thought. You ought to be able to trace down the idea! How about you, Morey?" Arcot smiled at his friend.

"I've kept discreetly quiet," replied Morey, "feeling that in silence I could not betray my ignorance, but since you ask me, I can guess too. I seem to recall that light is affected by a powerful magnet, and I can imagine that that was the basis for your guess. It has been known for many years, as far back as Clerk Maxwell, that polarized light can be rotated by a powerful magnet."

"That's it! And now we may as well go over the whole story, and tell Dad and your father all that happened. Perhaps in the telling, we can straighten out our own ideas a bit."

For the next hour the three men talked, each telling his story, and trying to explain the whys and wherefores of what he had seen. In the end all agreed on one point: if they were to fight this enemy, they *must* have ships that could travel though space with speed to match that of the invaders, ships with a self-contained source of power.

During a brief lull in the conversation, Morey commented rather sarcastically: "I wonder if Arcot will now kindly explain his famous invisible light, or the lost star?" He was a bit nettled by his own failure to remember that a star could go black. "I can't see what connection this has with their sudden attack. If they were there, they must have developed when the star was bright, and as a star requires millions of years to cool down, I can't see how they could suddenly appear in space."

Before answering, Arcot reached into a drawer of his desk and pulled out an old blackened briar pipe. Methodically he filled it, a thoughtful frown on his face; then carefully lighting it, he leaned back, puffing out a thin column of gray smoke.

"Those creatures must have developed on their planets before the sun cooled." He puffed slowly. "They are, then, a race millions of years old—or so I believe. I can't give any scientific reason for this feeling; it's merely a hunch. I just have a feeling that the invaders are old, older than our very planet! This little globe is just about two billion years old. I feel that that race is so very ancient they may well have counted the revolutions of our galaxy as, once every twenty or thirty million years, it swung about its center.

"When I looked at those great machines, and those comparatively little beings as they handled their projectors, they seemed out of place. Why?" He shrugged. "Again, just a hunch, an impression." He paused again, and the slow smoke drifted upward.

"If I'm granted the premise that a black, dead star is approaching the Solar System, then my theorizing may seem more logical. You agree?" The listeners nodded and Arcot continued. "Well—I had an idea—and when I went downstairs for the handling machine, I called the Lunar Observatory." He couldn't quite keep a note of triumph out of his voice. "Gentlemen—some of the planets have been misbehaving! The outermost planets, and even some of those closer to the sun have not been moving as they should. A celestial body of appreciable mass *is* approaching the System; though thus far nothing has been seen of the visitor!"

A hubbub of excited comment followed this startling revelation. Arcot quieted them with an upraised hand. "The only reason you and the world at large haven't heard about this as yet is the fact that the perturbation of the planets is so very slight that the astronomers figured they might have made an error in calculation. They're rechecking now for mistakes.

"To get back to my visualization—— It must have been many millions of years ago that life developed on the planets of the black star, a warm sun then, for it was much younger. It was probably rather dim as suns go even its younger days. Remember, our own sun is well above average in brilliance and heat radiation.

"In those long-gone ages I can imagine a race much like ours developing, differing chemically, in their atmosphere of hydrogen; but the chemical body is not what makes the race, it's the thought process. They must have developed, and then as their science grew, their sun waned. Dimmer and dimmer it became, until their planets could not maintain life naturally. Then they had to heat them artificially. There is no question as to their source of power; they had to use the energy of matter—socalled atomic energy—for no other source would be great enough to do what had to be done. It is probable that their science had developed this long before their great need arose.

"With this must also have come the process of transmutation, and the process they use in driving their interstellar cruisers. I am sure those machines are driven by material energy.

"But at last their star was black, a closed star, and their cold, black planets must circle a hot, black sun forever! They were trapped for eternity unless they found a way to escape to some other stellar system. They could not travel as fast as light, and they could escape only if they found some near-by solar system. Their star was dead—black. Let's call it Nigra—the Black One—since like every other star it should have a name. Any objection?"

There was none, so Arcot continued:

"Now we come to an impossibly rare coincidence. That two suns in their motion should approach each other is beyond the point of logic. That both suns have a retinue of planets approaches the height of the ridiculous. Yet that is what is happening right now. And the Nigrans—if that's the correct term —have every intention of taking advantage of the coincidence. Since our sun has been visible to them for a long, long time, and the approaching proximity of the suns evident, they had lots of time to prepare.

"I believe this expedition was just an exploratory one; and if they can send such huge machines and so many of them, for mere exploration, I'm sure they must have quite a fleet to fight with.

"We know little about their weapons. They have that death

ray, but it's not quite as deadly as we might have feared, solely because our ships could outmaneuver them. Next time, logically, they'll bring with them a fleet of little ships, carried in the bellies of those giants, and they'll be a real enemy. We'll have to anticipate their moves and build to circumvent them.

"As for their ray, I believe I have an idea how it works. You're all familiar with the catalytic effects of light. Hydrogen and chlorine will stand very peacefully in the same jar for a long time, but let a strong light fall on them, and they combine with terrific violence. This is the catalytic effect of a vibration, a wave motion. Then there is such a thing as negative catalysis. In a certain reaction, if a third element or compound is introduced, all reaction is stopped. I believe that's the principle of the Nigran death ray; it's a catalyst that simply stops the chemical reactions of a living body, and these are so delicately balanced that the least resistance will upset them."

Arcot halted, and sat puffing furiously for a moment. During his discourse the pipe had died to an ember; with vigorous puffing he tried to restore it. At last he had it going and continued.

"What other weapons they have we cannot say. The secret of invisibility must be very old to them. But we'll guard against the possibility by equipping our ships against it. The only reason the patrol ships aren't equipped already is that invisibility is useless with modern criminals; they all know the secret and how to fight it."

Morey interrupted with a question.

"Arcot, it's obvious that we have to get out into space to meet the enemy—and we'll have to have freedom of movement there. How are we going to do it? I was wondering if we could use Wade's system of storing the atomic hydrogen in solution. That yields about 100,000 calories for every two grams, and since this is a method of storing heat energy, and your molecular motion director is a method of converting heat into mechanical work with 100 per cent efficiency, why not use that? All we need, really, is a method of storing heat energy for use while we're in space."

Arcot exhaled slowly before answering, watching the column of smoke vanish into the air.

"I thought of that, and I've been trying to think of other, and if possible, better, cheaper, and quicker ways of getting the necessary power.

"Let's eliminate the known sources one by one. The usual ones, the ones men have been using for centuries, go out at once. The atomic hydrogen reaction stores more energy per gram than any other chemical reaction known. Such things as the storage battery, the electro-static condenser, the induction coil, or plain heat storage, are worthless to us. The only other method of storing energy we know of is the method used by the Kaxorians in driving their huge planes.

"They use condensed light-energy. This is efficient to the ultimate maximum, something no other method can hope to attain. Yet they need huge reservoirs to store it. The result is still ineffective for our purpose; we want something we can put in a small space; we want to condense the light still further. That will be the ideal form of energy storage, for then we will be able to release it directly as a heat ray, and so use it with utmost efficiency. I think we can absorb the released energy in the usual cavity radiator."

A queer little smile appeared on Arcot's face. "Remember— what we want is light in a more condensed form, a form that is naturally stable, and that does not need to be held in a bound state, but actually requires urging to bring about the release of energy. For example—"

A shout from Wade interrupted him. "That's really rare! *Whoo*—I have to hand it to you! That takes all the prizes!" He laughed delightedly. In puzzled wonder Morey and the two older men looked at him, and at Arcot who was grinning broadly now.

"Well, I suppose it must be funny," Morey began, then hesitated. "Oh—I see—say, that *is* good!" He turned to his father. "I see now what he's been driving at. It's been right here under our noses all the time.

"The light-matter windows we found in the wrecked enemy ships contain enough bound light-energy to run all the planes we could make in the next ten years! We're going to have the enemy supply us with power we can't get in any other way. I can't decide, Arcot, whether you deserve a prize for ingenuity, or whether we should receive booby-prizes for our stupidity."

Arcot senior smiled at first, then looked dubiously at his son.

"There's definitely plenty of the right kind of energy stored there—but as you suggested, the energy will need encouragement to break free. Any ideas?"

"A couple. I don't know how they'll work, of course; but we can try." Arcot puffed at his pipe, serious now as he thought of the problems ahead.

Wade interposed a question. "How do you suppose they condense that light energy in the first place, and, their sun being dead, whence all the light? Back to the atom, I suppose."

"You know as much as I do, of course, but I'm sure they must break up matter for its energy. As for the condensation problem, I think I have a possible solution of that too—it's the key to the problem of release. There's a lot we don't know now—but we'll have a bigger store of knowledge before this war is over—if we have anything at all!" he added grimly. "It's possible that man may lose knowledge, life, his planets and sun—but there's still plenty of hope. We're not finished yet."

"How do you think they got their energy loose?" asked Wade. "Do you think those big blocks of what appeared to be silver were involved in the energy release?"

"Yes, I do. Those blocks were probably designed to carry away the power once it was released. How the release was accomplished, though, I don't know. They couldn't use material apparatus to start their release of material energy; the material of the apparatus might 'catch fire' too. They had to have the disintegrating matter held apart from all other matter. This was quite impossible, if you are going to get the energy away by any method other than by the use of fields of force. I don't think that is the method. My guess is that a terrific current of electricity would accomplish it if anything would.

"How then are we going to get the current to it? The wires will be subject to the same currents. Whatever they do to the matter involved, the currents will do to the apparatus—except in one case. If that apparatus is made of *some other kind of matter*, then it wouldn't be affected. The solution is obvious. Use some of the light-matter. What will destroy light-matter, won't destroy electricity-matter, and what will destroy electricity-matter, won't disturb light-matter.

"Do you remember the platform of light-metal, clear as crystal? It must have been an insulating platform. What we started as our assumptions in the case of the light-metal, we can now carry further. We said that electricity-metals carried electricity, so light-metals would carry or conduct light. Now we know that there is no substance which is transparent to light, that will carry electricity by metallic conduction. I mean, of course, that there is no substance transparent to light, and at the same time capable of carrying electricity by electronic transmission. True, we have things like NaCl solutions in ordinary H_2O which will carry electricity, but here it's ionic conduction. Even glass will carry electricity very well when hot; when red hot, glass will carry enough electricity to melt it very quickly. But again, glass is not a solid, but a viscous liquid, and it is again carried by ionic conduction. Iron, copper, sodium, silver, lead—all metals carry the current by means of electron drift through the solid material. In such cases we can see that no transparent substance conducts electricity.

"Similarly, the reverse is true. No substance capable of carrying electricity by metallic conduction is transparent. All are opaque, if in any thickness. Of course, gold is transparent when in leaf form—but when it's that thin it won't conduct very much! The peculiar condition we reach in the case of the invisible ship is different. There the effects are brought about by the high frequency impressed. But you get my point.

"Do you remember those wires that we saw leading to that little box of the reflecting material? So perfectly reflecting it was that we didn't see it. We only saw where it must be; we saw the light it reflected. That was no doubt light-matter, a non-metal, and as such, non-conductive to light. Like sulphur, an electric non-metal, it reflected the base of which it was formed. Sulphur reflects the base of which it was formed. Sulphur reflects electricity and—in the crystalline form—passes light. This light-non-metal did the same sort of thing; it reflected light and passed electricity. It was a conductor.

"Now we have the things we need, the matter to disintegrate, and the matter to hold the disintegrating material in. We have two different types of matter. The rest is obvious—but decidedly not easy. They have done it, though; and after the war is over, there should be many of their machines drifting about in space waiting to give up their secrets."

Arcot senior clapped his son on the back. "A fair foundation on which to start, anyway. But I think it's time now that you got working on your problem; and since I'm officially retired. I'm going downstairs. You know I'm working in my lab on a method to increase the range and power of your projector for the molecular motion field. Young Norris is helping me, and he really has ideas. I'll show you our math later."

The party broke up, the three younger men staying in their own labs, the older men leaving.

IV

The three immediately set to work. At Arcot's suggestion, Wade and Morey attacked the plate of crystal in an attempt to tear off a small piece, on which they might work. Arcot himself went into the televisophone room and put through a second call to the Tychos Observatory, the great observatory that had so recently been established on the frigid surface of the Moon. The huge mirror, twenty feet in diameter, allowed an immense magnification, and stellar observations were greatly facilitated, for no one bothered them, and the "seeing" was always perfect.

However, the great distance was rather a handicap to the ordinary televisophone stations, and all calls put through to the astronomers had to be made through the powerful sending station in St. Louis, where all interplanetary messages were sent and received, while that side of the Earth was facing the station; and from Constantinople, when that city faced the satellite. These stations could bridge the distance readily and clearly.

For several minutes Arcot waited while connections were being made with the Moon; then for many more minutes he talked earnestly with the observer in this distant station, and at last satisfied, he hung up.

He had outlined his ideas concerning the black star, based upon the perturbation of the planets; then he had asked them to investigate the possibilities, and see if they could find any blotting out of stars by a lightless mass.

Finally he returned to Morey and Wade who had been working on the crystal plate. Wade had an expression of exasperation on his face, and Morey was grinning broadly.

"Hello, Arcot—you missed all the fun! You should have seen

Wade's struggle with that plate!" The plate, during his absence, had been twisted and bent, showing that it had undergone some terrific stresses. Now Wade began to make a series of highly forceful comments about the properties of the plate in language that was not exactly scientific. It had value, though, in that it seemed to relieve his pent-up wrath.

"Why, Wade, you don't seem to like that stuff. Maybe the difficulty lies in your treatment, rather than in the material itself. What have you tried?"

"Everything! I took a coronium hack saw that will eat through molyodenum steel like so much cheese, and it just wore its teeth off. I tried some of those diamond rotary saws you have, attached to an electric motor, and it wore out the diamonds. That got my goat, so I tried using a little force. I put it in the tension testing machine, and clamped it—the clamp was good for 10,000,000 pounds—but it began to bend, so I had to quit. Then Morey held it with a molecular beam, and I tried twisting it. Believe me, it gave me real pleasure to see that thing yield under the pressure. But it's not brittle; it merely bends.

"And I can't cut it, or even get some shavings off the darned thing. You said you wanted to make a Jolly balance determination of the specific gravity, but the stuff is so dense you'd need only a tiny scrap—and I can't break it loose!" Wade looked at the plate in thorough disgust.

Arcot smiled sympathetically; he could understand his feelings, for the stuff certainly was stubborn. "I'm sorry I didn't warn you fellows about what you'd run into, but I was so anxious to get that call through to the Moon that I forgot to tell you how I expected to make it workable. Now, Wade, if you'll get another of those diamond-tooth rotary saws, I'll get something that may help. Put the saw on the air motor. Use the one made of coronium."

Wade looked after the rapidly disappearing Arcot with raised eyebrows, then, scratching his head, he turned and did as Arcot had asked.

Arcot returned in about five minutes with a small handling machine, and a huge magnet. It must have weighed nearly half a ton. This he quickly connected to the heavy duty power lines of the lab. Now, running the handling machine into position, he quickly hoisted the bent and twisted plate to the poles of the magnet, with the aid of the derrick. Then backing the handling machine out of the way, he returned briskly to his waiting associates.

"Now we'll see what we will see!" With a confident smile Arcot switched on the current of the big magnet. At once a terrific magnetic flux was set up through the light-metal. He took the little compressed-air saw, and applied it to the crystal plate. The smooth hiss of the air deepened to a harsh whine as the load came on it, then the saw made contact with the re-fractory plate.

Unbelievingly Wade saw the little diamond-edge saw bite its way slowly but steadily into the plate. In a moment it had cut off a little corner of the light-matter, and this fell with a heavy thud to the magnet pole, drawn down by the attraction of the magnet and by gravity.

Shutting off the magnet, Arcot picked up a pair of pliers and gripped the little fragment.

"Whew—light-metal certainly isn't light metal! I'll bet this little scrap weighs ten pounds! We'll have to reduce it considerably before we can use it. But that shouldn't be too difficult."

By using the magnet and several large diamond faceplates they were able to work the tough material down to a thin sheet; then with a heavy press, they cut some very small fragments, and with these, determined the specific gravity.

"Arcot," Wade asked finally, "just how does the magnet make that stuff tractable? I'm not physicist enough to figure out what takes place inside the material."

"Magnetism worked as it did," Arcot explained, "because in this light-matter every photon is affected by the magnetism, and every photon is given a new motion. That stuff can be made to go with the speed of light, you know. It's the only solid that could be so affected. This stuff should be able, with the aid of a molecular motion beam, which will make all the photons move in parallel paths, to move at the full speed of each photon— 186,000 miles a second. The tremendous speed of these individual photons is what makes the material so hard. Their kinetic impulse is rather considerable! It's the kinetic blow that the molecules of a metal give that keeps other metal from penetrating it. This simply gives such powerful impulse that even diamonds wouldn't cut it.

"You know that an iron saw will cut platinum readily, yet if both are heated to say, 1600 degrees, the iron is a liquid, and the platinum very soft—but now the platinum cuts through the iron!

"Heat probably won't have any effect on this stuff, but the action of the magnet on the individual photons corresponds to the effect of the heat on the individual atoms and molecules. The mass is softened, and we can work it. At least, that's the way I figure it out.

"But now, Wade, I wish you'd see if you can determine the density of the stuff. You're more used to those determinations and that type of manipulation than we are. When you get through, we may be able to show you some interesting results ourselves!"

Wade picked up a tiny chip of the light-metal and headed for his own laboratory. Here he set up his Jolly balance, and began to work on the fragment. His results were so amazing that he checked and rechecked his work, but always with the same answer. Finally he returned to the main lab where Arcot and Morey were busy at the construction of a large and complicated electro-static apparatus.

"What did you find?" called out Arcot, as he saw Wade re-enter the room. "Hold your report a second and give us a hand here, will you? I have a laboratory scale apparatus of the type the Kaxorians used in the storage of light. They've known, ever since they began working with them, that their machines would release the energy with more than normal violence, if certain changes were made in them. That is, the light condenser, the device that stored the photons so close to each other, would also serve to urge them apart. I've made the necessary changes, and now I'm trying to set up the apparatus to work on solid light-matter. It was developed for gaseous material, and it's a rather tricky thing to change it over. But I think we've almost got it.

"Wade, will you connect that to the high frequency oscillator there—no—through that counterbalanced condenser. We may have to change the oscillator frequency quite a bit, but a variable condenser will do that.

"Now, what results did you get?"

Wade shook his head doubtfully. "We all know it's amazing stuff—and of course, it must be heavy—but still—well, anyway, I got a density of 103.5!"

"Whewww—103.5! Lord! That's almost five times as heavy as the heaviest metal hitherto known. There's about half a cubic foot of the material; that would mean about 4000 pounds for the whole mass, or two tons. No wonder we couldn't lift the plate!"

They stopped their work on the Kaxorian apparatus to discuss the amazing results of the density test, but now they fell to again, rapidly assembling the device, for each was a trained experimenter. With all but the final details completed, Arcot stood back and surveyed their handiwork.

"I think we'll have enough urge to cause disintegration right here," he said, "but I want to make sure, and so, before we set up the case over it. I think we may as well put that big magnet in place, and have it there to help in the work of disintegration, if need be."

At last the complete apparatus was set up, and the tiny bit of light-matter they were to work on was placed on the table of a powerful Atchinson projector microscope, the field of view being in the exact center of the field of both the magnet and the coil. Carefully, then, step by step, Arcot, Morey and Wade went over their work, checking and rechecking.

"Well, we're ready," said Arcot finally, as he placed the projector screen in position and dimmed the lights in the room. A touch of the switch, and the projection screen was illuminated with the greatly enlarged image of the tiny scrap of light-metal.

With his hand on the switch, Arcot spoke to the other two. "I won't say there's *no* danger, since we haven't done this before; and if all the energy should be released at once, it'll blow the top out of the building. But I'm reasonably sure that it will work safely. Any objections?"

Wade shook his head, and Morey said: "I can't see any flaws in our work."

Arcot nodded, and unconsciously tensing, he closed the switch. This put the powerful Arcot oscillator tubes into action, and the power was ready for application.

Slowly he closed the rheostat and put the power into the coil.

The little sliver of metal on the slide seemed to throb a bit, and its outline grew hazy; but at last, with full power on, the release was so slow as to be imperceptible.

"Guess we need the magnet after all; I'll put it on this time."

He opened the coil circuit and closed the magnet circuit at half voltage, then again he increased the current through the rheostat. This time the plate throbbed quite violently, it took the appearance of a bit of iodine. Dense vapors began pouring from it, and instantly those vapors became a blindingly brilliant flood of light. Arcot had snapped open the switch the moment he saw this display start, and it had had little time to act, for the instant the circuit was opened, it subsided. But even in that brief time, the light aluminum screen had suddenly become limp and slumped down, molten! The room was unbearably hot, and the men were half blinded by the intensity of the light.

"It works!" yelled Wade. "It works! That sure was hot, too—it's roasting in here." He flung open a window. "Let's have some air."

Arcot and Morey gripped hands with a broad grin. That display meant that Earth and Venus would have space ships with which to fight space ships. Reason enough for their joy.

Though they had made an unusual amount of progress already, there was still a great deal of development work to be done. Fuller was needed, Arcot decided, so he called the elder Morey and requested his services if he could be spared from his present work. He could, and would arrive later that day.

When Fuller appeared about mid-afternoon, he found the three friends already at work on the development of a more compact apparatus than the makeshift hookup used in making that first release mechanism.

"And so you can see," said Arcot as he finished his summary of their work to that point, "we still have quite a job ahead of us. I'm now trying to find some data for you to work on, but I can tell you this: We'll need a ship that has plenty of strength and plenty of speed. There will be the usual power plant, of course; the generators, the power-tube board, and the electro-magnetic relays for the regular molecular motion controls. Then, in addition, we must have controls for the ray projector, though that must wait a while, for Dad is working on a method of doubling our range . . . Oh yes, the driving units will be inside the ship now, for all our power will come from the energy of the light-matter."

They spent the next hour in discussing the manifold details involved in the design of their space ship: the mechanism involved in transferring the light-energy to the drivers; a means of warming the ship in interstellar space; a main horizontal drive for forward and backward motion as well as braking; three smaller vertical power units to give them freedom of direction in climb or descent; other smaller horizontal power units for turning and moving sideways.

The ships, they decided, must be capable of six or seven thousand miles a second. They would need three types of ships: a small single-man speedster, without bunk or living quarters, simply a little power plant and weapon. Designed for speed and mobility, it would be very hard to hit, and because of its own offensive power would be dangerous to the enemy. They would need a fleet of mother ships—ships that would hold both the speedsters and their pilots—say thirty to a cruiser. There would also be some ten-man scouts, operating in the same manner as the larger cruisers, but with a smaller fleet of speedsters dependent on them.

"For defense," Arcot concluded, "we'll have to depend on armor as heavy as we can make and still remain within the bounds of practical construction. I don't believe we'll be able to build up enough mass to insulate against their negative catalysis ray. We'll have to depend on mobility and offense.

"But now let's get back to work. I think, Fuller, that you might call in the engineers of all the big aircraft and machine tool manufacturers and fabricators, and have them ready to start work at once when the plans are finally drawn up. You'd better get in touch with the Venerian producers, too. Those new works in Sorthol, Kaxor, will certainly be able to help a lot.

"I suppose the Interplanetary Patrol men will have something to say, so they better be called in. Likewise the Venerian Council. Morey, maybe your dad can handle some of this."

As one they arose and set to work on their respective tasks —the planning and building of the Earth-Venus war fleet.

V

Despite their utmost endeavor and the hard work of the industrial might of two worlds, it was nearly six weeks before the fleet had grown to a thing of importance. The tests to which they subjected the tiny speedsters had been more than satisfactory. They behaved wonderfully, shooting about at terrific speed, and with all the acceleration a pilot could stand. These speedsters were literally piloted projectiles, and their amazing mobility made them a powerful arm of offense.

There came into being a special corps dubbed, oddly enough, the "Rocket Squad", a group of men who could stand plenty of "G's". This "Rocket Squad" was composed solely of Terrestrians, for they were accustomed to the gravity of Earth and could stand greater acceleration strains than could the Venerians. The pick of the Air Patrol formed the nucleus of this new military organization; and in short order, so great is the appeal of the new and novel, the cream of the young men of the planet were competing for a place among the Rocketeers.

Each ship, both speedster and mother craft, was equipped with an invisibility locator, a sensitive short-wave directional receiver, that would permit the operator to direct his rays at invisible targets. The ships themselves could not be made invisible, since they depended in their very principle on the absorption of light-energy. If the walls of every part of the ship were perfectly transparent, they could absorb no energy at all, and they would still be plainly visible—even more so than before! They must remain visible, but they could also force the enemy to remain visible.

Each ten-man ship carried an old-fashioned cannon that was equipped to hurl canisters carrying the luminous paint. They decided that these would have advantages, even if the invaders did not use invisibility, for in space a ship is visible only because it reflects or emits light. For this reason the ships were not equipped with any portholes except in the pilot room and at the observation posts. No light could escape. To reduce the reflection to the absolute minimum, the ships had each been painted with a 99% absorptive black. In space they would be exceedingly difficult targets.

The heating effect of the sun on the black pigment when near the great star was rather disagreeably intense, and to cool the speedsters they had installed molecular director power units, which absorbed the heat and used the energy to drive the ship. Heaters offset the radiation loss of the black surface when too far from the sun.

Each of the speedsters was equipped with a small machine-gun shooting luminous paint bullets. One of these, landing on another craft, made it visible for at least two hours, and since they could cover an area of about thirty feet, they were decidedly effective.

It was found that ray practice was rather complicated. The government had ranges set up in great mountain districts away from any valuable property, but they soon found that spatial warplay could not be carried on on earth. The rays very quickly demolished the targets, and in a short time made good progress toward demolishing the mountains as well. The problem was solved by using the barren surface of the moon and the asteroid belt beyond Mars as a proving ground.

The ships were sent out in squadrons as fast as they could be finished and the men could be brought together and trained. They were establishing a great shield of ships across all that section of the system where the Nigrans had appeared, and they hoped to intercept the next attack before it reached Earth, for they were certain the next attack would be in full force.

Arcot had gone to the conference held on Venus with the other men who had investigated the great wrecks, and each scientist had related his view of things and had offered suggestions. Arcot's idea of the black star was not very favorably received. As he later told Wade and Morey, who had not gone, there was good reason for their objection to his idea. Though the scientists were willing to admit that the invaders must have come from a great distance, and they agreed that they lived in an atmosphere of hydrogen, and judging from their pale skins, that they were not used to the rays of a sun, they still insisted on the theory of an outer planet of Sol.

"You remember," explained Arcot, "several years ago there was considerable discussion about the existence of a planet still further out from the sun than Pluto. It is well known that there are a number of irregularities in the orbits of Neptune and Pluto that can't be caused by known planets, and an outer planet could have the necessary mass and orbit to account for them.

"This attack from outer space was immediately taken as proof of that theory, and it was very easily supported, too. My one good point that stood for any length of time under their attacks was the fact that those ships weren't developed in a year, nor a century, and that the chemical constitution of the men was so different. There were no new elements discovered, except the light-matter, but they are rather wondering about the great difference of earthly chemical constitution and the constitution of these invaders.

"They had one argument that was just about enough to throw mine out, though they pointed to the odds against the thing happening. You know, of course, how planets are formed? They are the results of tidal action on two passing suns.

"You can imagine two mighty stars careening through space and then drawing slowly nearer, till at last they come within a few billion miles of each other, and their gigantic masses reach out and bind them with a mighty chain of gravity. Their titanic masses swing about each other, each trying to pull free, and continue its path about the center of the galactic system. But as their huge bulks come nearer, the chains that bind them become stronger and stronger, and the tremendous pull of the one gargantuan fire ball on the other raises titanic tides of flame. Great streamers of gas shoot out, and all the space about is lighted by the flaming suns. The pull of gravity becomes more and more intense, and as the one circles the other, the tide is pulled up, and the mighty ball of fire, which, for all its existence has been practically motionless as far as rotation goes, begins to acquire a greater and greater rotational speed as the tidal drag urges it on. The flames begin to reach higher and higher, and the tides, now urged from the sun by centrifugal force, rise into an ever greater crest, and as the swinging suns struggle to break loose, the flaming gas is pulled up and up, and becomes a mighty column of fire, a column that reaches out across three—four—a dozen millions of miles of space and joins the two stars at last, as stalactites and stalagmites grow together. A flaming tie of matter joins them, two titanic suns, and a mighty rope of fire binds them, while far mightier chains of gravity hold them together.

"But now their original velocity reasserts itself, and having spiraled about each other for who can say how long—a year—a million years seems more probable—but still only an instant in the life of a star—they begin to draw apart, and the flaming column is stretched out, and ever thinner it grows, and the two stars at last separate. But now the gas will never fall back into the sun. Like some giant flaming cigar it reaches out into space and it will stay thus, for it has been set in rotation about the sun at such a speed as is needed to form an orbit. The giant mass of gas is, however, too cool to continue to develop energy from matter, for it was only the surface of the sun, and cool. As it cools still further, there appear in it definite condensations, and the beginnings of the planets are there. The great filament that stretched from the sun to sun was cigar-shaped, and so the matter is more plentiful toward the center, and larger planets develop. Thus Jupiter and Saturn are far larger than any of the others. The two ends are tapering, thus Earth is larger than Venus, which is larger than Mercury, and Uranus and Neptune are both smaller than Saturn, Pluto being smaller than either.

"Mars and the asteroids are hard to explain. Perhaps it is easier to understand when we remember that the planets thus formed must necessarily have been rotating in eccentric orbits when they were first born, and these planets came too near the sun while gaseous, or nearly so, and Mars lost much of its matter, while the other, which now exists only as the asteroids, broke up.

"But now that other flaming star has retired, wandering on through space. The star has left its traces, for behind it there are planets where none existed before. But remember that it, too, must have planets now.

"All this happened some 2,000 million years ago.

"But in order that it might happen, it required that two stars pass within the relatively short distance of a few billion miles of each other. Space is not overcrowded with matter, you know. The density of the stars has been compared with twenty tennis balls roaming about 8,000-mile sphere that the Earth fills up—twenty tennis balls in some 270 billion cubic miles of space. Now imagine two of those tennis balls—with plenty of room to wander in—passing within a few yards of each other.

The chances are about as good as the chances of two stars passing close enough to make planets.

"Now let us consider another possibility.

"The Black Star, as I told you, has planets. That means that it must have thus passed close to another star. Now we have it coming close to another sun that has been similarly afflicted. The chances of that happening are inconceivably small. It is one chance in billions that the planets will form. Two stars must pass close to each other, when they have all space to wander about in. Then those afflicted stars separate, and one of them passes close by a new star, which has thus been similarly afflicted with that one chance in billions—well, that is then a chance in billions of billions.

"So my theory was called impossible. I don't know but what it is. Besides, I thought of an argument the other men didn't throw at me. I'm surprised they didn't, too—the explanation of the strange chemical constitution of these men of a solar system planet would not be so impossible. It is quite possible that they live on a planet revolving about the sun which is, nevertheless, a planet of another star. It is quite conceivable to me that the chemical constitution of Neptune and Pluto will be found to be quite different from that of the rest of our planets. The two filaments drawn out from the suns may not have mingled, though I think they did, but it is quite conceivable that, just before parting, our sun tore one planet, or even two or three, from the other star.

"And that would explain these strange beings.

"My other ideas were accepted. The agreed-on plan for the release of energy, and the source of the power." Arcot puffed on his pipe meditatively for several moments, then stood up and stretched.

"Ho—I wish they'd let me go on active duty with the space fleet! A scientific reputation can be an awful handicap at times," he grinned. He had been rejected very emphatically when he had tried to enlist. The Interplanetary governments had stated flatly that he was too important as a scientist to be risked as a pilot of a space ship.

On two worlds the great construction plants were humming with activity. Civilian production of all but the barest essentials had been put aside for the duration of the emergency. Space ships were being turned out at top speed, getting their fuel from the wrecks of the invaders' cruisers. Each ship needed only a small amount of the light-metal, for the energy content was tremendous. And those ships had been gigantic.

Already there was a fleet of speedsters and mother ships out there in space, and with every passing hour others left the home planets, always adding to the fighting force that was to engage the attackers deep in space, where no stray ships might filter through to destroy the cities of Earth or Venus. Assembly lines were now turning out ships so rapidly that the training of their operators was the most serious problem. This difficulty had finally been overcome by a very abbreviated training course in the actual manipulation of the controls on the home planets, and subsequent training as the squadrons raced on their outward courses.

It was soon decided that there must be another service beside that of the ordinary ships. One plant was devoted to making huge interstellar liners. These giants, made on Venus, were nearly a quarter of a mile long, and though diminutive in comparison with the giant Nigran ships, they were still decidedly large. Twelve of these could be completed within the next month, it was found; and one was immediately set aside as an officers' headquarters ship. It was recognized that the officers must be within a few hundred thousand miles of the actual engagements, for decisions would have to be made without too much loss of time in the transmission of reports.

The ship must not be brought too near the front lest the officers be endangered and the entire engagement lost for want of the organizing central headquarters. The final solution had been the huge central control ship.

The other large vessels were to be used to carry food and supplies. They were not to enter the engagement, for their huge size would make them as vulnerable to the tiny darting mites of space as the Nigran ships had been to the Interplanetary Patrol. The little ships could not conveniently stock for more than a week of engagement, then drop back to these warehouses of space, and go forward again for action.

Throughout the long wait the officers of the Solarian forces organized their forces to the limit of their ability, planning each move of their attack. Space had been marked off into a great three-dimensional map, and each ship carried a small replica, the planets moving as they did in their orbits. The space between the planets was divided off into definite points in a series of Cartesian co-ordinates, the sun being the origin, and the plane of the elliptic being the X-Y plane.

The OX line was taken pointing toward one of the brightest of the fixed stars that was in the plane of the elliptic. The entire solar system was thus marked off as had been the planets long ages before, into a system of three dimensional latitude and longitude. This was imperative, in order to assure the easy location of the point of first attack, and to permit the entire fleet to come into position there. A scattered guard was to remain free, to avoid any false attacks and a later attack from a point millions of miles distant. Earth and Venus were each equipped with gigantic ray projectors, mighty weapons that could destroy anything, even a body as large as the Moon, at a distance of ten thousand miles. Still, a ship might get through, and with the death ray—what fearful toll might be exacted from a vast city such as Chicago—with its thirty millions! Or Karos, on Venus, with its fifteen and one half millions!

The tension became greater and greater as with each passing day the populace of two worlds awaited the call from the far-flung guard. The main bulk of the fleet had been concentrated in the center of their great spherical shell of ships. They could only wait—and watch—and prepare! Hundreds of miles apart, yet near enough so that no ship except perhaps a one-man craft could pass them undetected; and behind them were ships with delicate apparatus that could detect any foreign body of any size whatever within a hundred thousand miles of them.

The Solar System was prepared to repel boarders from the vast sea of space!

VI

Taj Lamor gazed down at the tremendous field below him. In it lay close packed a great mass of ships, a concourse of Titans of Space, dreadnoughts that were soon to set out to win—not a nation, not even a world, but to conquer a solar system, and to win for their owners a vast new sun, a sun that would light them and heat them for long ages to come.

Momentarily Taj Lamor's gaze followed the retreating figure of Tordos Gar, the Elder; a figure with stooped shoulders and bowed head. His quiet yet vibrant parting words still resounded in his ears:

"Taj Lamor, remember what I tell you. If you win this awful war—you lose. As will our race. Only if you lose will you win."

With a frown Taj Lamor stared down at the vast metal hulls glistening softly in the dull light of far-off stars, the single brightly beaming star that was their goal, and the dim artificial lighting system. From the distance came to him the tapping and humming of the working machines below as they strove to put the finishing touches to the great ships.

He raised his eyes toward the far-off horizon, where a great yellow star flamed brilliantly against the black velvet of space. He thought of that planet where the sky had been blue—an atmosphere of such intensity that it colored the sky!

Thoughtfully he gazed at the flaming yellow point.

He had much to consider now. They had met a new race, barbarians in some ways, yet they had not forgotten the lessons they had learned; they were not decadent. Between his eon-old people and their new home stood these strange beings, a race so young that its age could readily be counted in millennia, but withal a strong, intelligent form of life. And to a race that had not known war for so many untold ages, it was an unthinkable thing that they must kill other living, intelligent beings in order that they might live.

They had no need of moving, Tordos Gar and many others had argued; they could stay where they were forever, and never find any need for leaving their planet. This was the voice of decadence, Taj Lamor told himself; and he had grown to hate that voice.

There were other men, men who had gone to that other solar system, men who had seen vast oceans of sparkling water, showering from their ruffled surfaces the brilliant light of a great, hot sun. They had seen towering masses of mountains that reached high into the blue sky of a natural atmosphere, their mighty flanks clothed with green growth; natural plants in abundance.

And best of all, they had fought and seen action, such as no member of their race had known in untold ages. They knew Adventure and Excitement, and they had learned things that no member of their ancient race had known for millennia. They had learned the meaning of advancement and change. They had a new ardor, a new strength, a new emotion to drive them, and those who would have held them back became enthusiasts themselves. Enthusiasm may be contagious, but the spirit of their decadence was rapidly failing before this new urge. Here was their last chance and they must take it; they would!

They had lost many men in that battle on the strange world, but their race was intelligent; they learned quickly; the small ships had been very hard targets, while their big ships were too easy to strike. They must have small ships, yet they must have large ships for cargo, and for the high speed driving apparatus. The small ships were not able to accelerate to the terrific speed needed. Once their velocity had been brought up to the desired value, it was easy to maintain it with the infinitely small friction of space as the only retarding force; one atom per cubic inch was all they must meet. This would not hold them up, but the great amount of fuel and the power equipment needed to accelerate to the desired speed could not be packed into the small ship. Into the vast holds of the huge ships the smaller ones were packed, long shining rows of little metal projectiles. Tiny they were, but they could dart and twist and turn as swiftly as could the ships they had met on that other world—tiny ships that flashed about with incredible suddenness, a target that seemed impossible to hit. These ships would be a match for those flashing motes of the Yellow Sun. Now it might be that their great transport and battle ships could settle down to those worlds and arrange them for their own people!

And they had discovered new weapons, too. One of their mightiest was a very old apparatus, one that had been forgotten for countless ages. A model of it was in existence in some forgotten museum on a deserted planet, and with it long forgotten tomes that told of its principles, and of its consequences. Invisibility was now at their command. It was an ancient weapon, but might be exceedingly effective!

And one other. They had developed a new thing! They had not learned of it in books, it was their invention! They did not doubt that there were other machines like it in their museums, but the idea was original with them. It was a beam of electrical oscillatory waves, projected with tremendous energy, and it would be absorbed by any conductor. They could melt a ship with this!

And thus that great field had been filled with Giants of Space! And in each of these thousand great warships there nestled three thousand tiny one-man ships.

Here was a sight to inspire any race!

Taj Lamor watched as the last of the working machines dragged its slow way out of the great ships. They were finished! The men were already in them, waiting to start, and now there was an enthusiasm and an activity that had not been before; now the men were anxious to get that long journey completed and to be there, in that other system!

Taj Lamor entered his little special car and shot swiftly down to the giant cruisers. He stepped out of his little craft and walked over to the tube conveyor ready for the trip to the nose of the great vessel. Behind him attendants quickly moved his car to a locked cradle berth beside long rows of similar vehicles.

A short while later those who were to remain on the dark planet saw the first of the monsters of space rise slowly from the ground and leap swiftly forward; then as methodically as though released by automatic machinery, the others leaped in swift pursuit, rushing across half a world to the tremendous space lock that would let them out into the void. In a long, swift column they rushed on. Then one at a time they passed out into the mighty sea of space. In space they quickly formed and set out.

As though by magic, far to the left of their flight, there suddenly appeared a similiar flight of giant ships, and then to the right, and above them, another seemed to leap out of nothingness as the ships of other planets came into sight. Quickly they formed a vast cone about their leader's ship, a protecting screen, yet a powerful offensive formation.

Endlessly, it seemed, they sped on through the darkness. Then as the yellow star flamed brighter and brighter before them, they slowed their ships till the small fliers could safely be released into space.

Like a swarm of insects flying about giant birds of space the little ships circled the mighty masses of the battle cruisers. So huge were they, that in the combined mass of the fleet there rested sufficient gravitational attraction to force the little fliers to form orbits about them. And so they sped on through the void, the vast conical fleet with its slowly circling belt of little ships. A fleet whose counterpart had never entered the Solar System.

It was well beyond the orbit of Pluto that the first of the Solarian scouts detected the approaching invasion fleet. The tension that had gripped Earth and Venus and their guardian ships for so long a time suddenly snapped; and like a great machine set into sudden motion, or a huge boulder, balanced, given the last push that sends it spinning with destructive violence down a slope, the fleet went into action.

It was merely a little scout, a ten-man cruiser, that sent in the message of attack, and then, upon receiving headquarters' permission, went into action. Some of the tacticians had wanted to try to get the entire fleet into battle range for a surprise attack in power; but others felt that this could not possibly succeed. Most important, they decided, was the opportunity of learning if the invaders had any new weapons.

The Nigrans had no warning, for a ten-man cruiser was invisible to them, though the vast bulk of their own ships stood out plainly, lighted by a blazing sun. No need here to make the sun stand still while the battle was finished! There was no change out here in all time! The first intimation of attack that the Nigrans had was the sudden splitting and destruction of the leading ship. Then, before they could realize what was happening, thirty-five other destructive molecular motion beams were tearing through space to meet them! The little ten-man cruiser and its flight of speedsters was in action! Twenty-one great ships crumpled and burst noiselessly in the void, their gases belching out into space in a great shining halo of light as the sun's light struck it.

Unable to see their tiny enemies, who now were striking as swiftly, as desperately as possible, knowing that death was practically certain, hoping only to destroy a more equal number of the giants, they played their beams of death about them, taking care to miss their own ships as much as possible.

Another ship silently crumpled, and suddenly one cruiser right in the line of the flight was brought to a sudden halt as all its molecules were reversed. The ships behind it, unable to stop so suddenly, piled up on it in chaotic wreckage! A vast halo of shining gas spread out fifty thousand miles about, blinding further the other ships, the radiance about them making it impossible to see their tiny enemies.

Now other of the Solarian ships were coming swiftly to the attack. Suddenly a combination of three of the ten-man cruisers stopped another of the great ships instantaneously. There was another soundless crash, and the giant mass of wreckage that heaped suddenly up glowed dully red from the energy of impact.

But now the little ships of the invaders got into action. They had been delayed by the desperate attempts of the dreadnoughts to wipe out their enemies with the death rays, and they could not cover the great distances without some delay.

When a battle spreads itself out through a ten-thousand mile cube of space—through a thousand billion cubic miles of space—it is impossible to cover it instantaneously with any machine.

Already nearly a hundred and fifty of the giant liners had gone into making that colossal mass of junk in space. They must protect the remaining cruisers! And it was that flight of small ships that did protect them. Many of the Solarians went down to death under their rays. The death rays were exceedingly effective, but the heat rays were not able to get quite as long a range, and they were easily detected by the invisibility locaters, which meant certain destruction, for a molecular motion ray would be there in moments, once they had been located.

The main fleet of the Solar System was already on its way, and every moment drew closer to this running battle, for the great ships of the Nigrans had, although they were entering the system cautiously, been going at a very high speed, as interplanetary speeds are measured. The entire battle had been a running encounter between the two forces. The Solarian force, invisible because of its small size, was certainly getting the better of the encounter thus far, but now that the odds were changing, now that the small ships had come into the fray, engaging them at close range, they were not having so easy time of it.

It would be many hours before the full strength of the Solarian fleet could be brought to bear on the enemy. They were not able to retire and await their arrival, for they *must* delay the Nigran fleet. If even one of those great ships should safely reach the two planets behind them—!

But within a half hour of the original signal, the Rocket Squad had thrown itself into the battle with a fervor and abandon that has given that famous division a name that will last forever.

The small fliers of the Nigrans were beginning to take an appalling toll in the thinning ranks of the Solarians. The coming of the Rocket Squad was welcome indeed! They were able to maneuver as swiftly as the enemy; the speedsters were harder to spot than the Solarian ten-man and thirty-man boats. The Solarian speedsters were even smaller than the comparable Nigran craft, and some of these did a tremendous amount of damage. The heat ray was quite ineffective against the ten-man ships, even when working at full capacity, when produced by the small generators of the Nigran one-man boats. The cruisers could absorb the heat and turn it into power faster than the enemy could supply it. Beams from the monster interstellar liners were another matter, of course.

But the one-man speedsters had a truly deadly plan of attack against the liners. The plan was officially frowned upon because of the great risks the pilots must take. They directed their boats at one of the monster ships, all the power units on at full drive. As close to target as possible the man jumped from his ship, clothed, of course, in an altitude suit equipped with a radio transmitter and receiver.

Death rays could not stop the speedsters, and with their momentum, the invaders could not make it less deadly with their heat beam, for, molten, it was still effective. A projectile weighing twenty-two tons, moving a hundred miles a second, can destroy anything man can lift off a planet! Their very speed made it impossible to dodge them, and usually they found their mark. As for the risk, if the Solarian forces were victorious, the pilots could be picked up later, provided too long a time had not elapsed!

In the midst of the battle, the Solarians began to wonder why the Nigran fleet was decreasing so rapidly—certainly they had not caused all that damage! Then suddenly they found the answer. One of their ships—then another—and another fell victim to a pale red ray that showed up like a ghostly pillar of luminosity coming from nowhere and going nowhere! The answer? The invaders' ships were becoming invisible! The invisibility detectors were being overloaded now, and the hunt was hard, while the Nigrans were slipping past them and silently destroying Solarian ships! The molecular motion rays were quite effective on an invisible ship—once it had been found. They were destroying the Nigrans as rapidly as they were being destroyed, but they were letting some of them slip past! The luminous paint bombs and bullets were now called into play. All enemy ships were shot at with these missiles, and invisibility was forestalled.

At long last the dark bulk of the main fleet approached, a scarcely visible cloud of tiny darting metal ships. The battle so far had been a preliminary engagement. The huge ships of the Nigrans were forced to stop their attack, and releasing the last of the fliers, to retire to a distance, protected by a screen of small ships, for they were helpless against the Solarian speedsters. Invisibility fell into disfavor, too, now that there were plenty of Solarian ships, for the Nigrans were more conspicuous when invisible than when visible. The radio detector could pick them out at once.

The entire Nigran fleet was beginning to reveal the disorder and uncertainty that arose from desperation, for they were cornered in the most undesirable position possible. They were outside the Solarian fleet, and their ships were lighted by the glare of the sun. The defenders, on the other hand, were in such a position that the enemy could see only the "night" side of them—the shadowed side—and, as there was no air to diffuse the light, they were exceedingly hard to find. In the bargain, the radium paint was making life for the Nigrans a brief and flitting thing!

The invaders began to pay an awful toll in this their first real engagement. They lacked the necessary power to cover the entire Solarian fleet with their death rays, and their heat weapons were of little help. The power of the small ships did not count for much—and the big liners could not use their weapons effectively for their small fliers must be between them and their adversary. Despite this, however, the Nigrans so greatly outnumbered the

Earth-Venus forces that it looked as though a long and costly war lay ahead.

At last the Solarian generals tried a ruse, a ruse they hoped would work on these beings; but they who never before had to plan a war in space, were not sure that their opponents had not had experience in the art. True, the Nigrans hadn't revealed any especially striking generalship—had, in fact, committed some inexcusable blunders—but they couldn't be sure. Though they didn't know it, the Solarians had the advantage of thousands of years of planetary warfare to rely on. This stood them in good stead now.

The Nigrans were rallying rapidly. To their surprise, the forces of the Solarians were dwindling, and no matter how desperately this remnant fought, they could not hold back the entire force of the Nigran fliers. At last it appeared certain that the small ships could completely engage the Solarian fleet!

Quickly the giant cruisers formed a great dense cone of attack, and at a given signal, the fliers cleared a hole for them through the great disc-shaped shield of the defenders. And with all their rays fanned out in a 100 per cent overlap ahead of them, the Nigran fleet plunged through the disc of ships at close to four hundred miles per second. They broke through—were on their way to the unprotected planets!

The Solarian ships closed the gap behind them, and eighteen of the giant ships burst into wreckage as powerful beams found them, but for the most part the remnant of the defending forces were far too busy with the fliers to attack the large ships. Now, as the monster engines of destruction raced on toward the planets still approximately two billion miles away, they knew that, far behind them, their fliers were engaging the Solarians. They had left their guard—but the guard was keeping the enemy occupied while they were free to drive in!

Then from nowhere came the counterattack! Nearly five thousand thirty-man ships of Earth and Venus, invisible in the darkness of space, suddenly leaped into action as the dreadnoughts sped past. Their destroying rays played over the nigh-helpless giants, and the huge ships were crumbling into colossal derelicts. With the last of their guard stripped from them, they fell easy prey to the attackers. Faster than they could keep count they were losing their warships of space!

The ruse had worked perfectly! Nearly all of the ten-man and one-man ships had been left behind them in the original disc, while all the thirty-man light cruisers, and a few hundred each of the ten-man and one-man crafts sped away to form a great ring twenty thousand miles farther back. The Nigran fleet had flown blindly into the ambush.

There was only one thing left for them to do. They were defeated. They must return to their far-off black star and leave the Solarians in possession of their worlds. For all battle purposes their great force was nearly wiped out, only the fliers remained in force; and these could no longer be carried in the remnant of the great liners. Swiftly they fell back, passing again through the disc, losing thirty more vessels, then raced swiftly away from the fleet of their enemies.

The Solarians, however, were not content. Their ships were forming in a giant hollow cylinder, and as the sphere of the Nigrans retreated, their beams playing behind them, the cylinder moved forward until it surrounded them, and they raced together toward the distant lightless sun. The Solar end of the cylinder swiftly closed, blocked by a group of huge ships which had taken no visible part in the battle. The Nigrans had stopped using their rays; and the Solarians followed in armed readiness, not molesting as long as they were not molested.

Many days this strange flight lasted, till at last the great yellow sun, Sol, had faded in the distance to an unusually brilliant star. Then, suddenly visible out of the darkness, a strange black world loomed ahead, and the Nigran ships settled swiftly toward it. Through the airlocks the great liners settled to their planet. No action was taken so long as the Solarian ships were not menaced, but for eight long months the darting ships hung above the four englobed worlds of Nigra.

Then at last the astronomers of Earth and Venus sent through the billions of miles of ether their message of safety. The guard could return home, for the sun they had been guarding would soon be too far from Earth or Venus to make any attack logical. Despite this, for years to come the fleet would guard the rim of the System, just to be sure; but it appeared that the suns had passed, never again to meet.

A strange thing had happened during the passing of the stars. Pluto no longer circled Sol; it had been captured by Nigra! The great fleet returned to a changed Solar system. Sol was still at its center, but there were now ten planets, including two new ones that the sun had captured from Nigra in return for Pluto; and all the planets had shifted a bit in their orbits.

What the ultimate effect on the planets will be, we cannot say as yet. The change thus far is certainly not very great, though a somewhat warmer climate exists now on Earth, and it is a bit cooler on Venus. The long-range difference, however, will be exceedingly interesting.

The Solar System has just passed through an experience which is probably unique in all the history of the mighty nebula of which our sun is an infinitesimal part. The chances that one star, surrounded by a system of planets, should pass within a hundred billion miles of another star, similarly accompanied, was one in billions of billions. That both systems should have been inhabited by intelligent races—

It is easy to understand why the scientists could not believe Arcot's theory of attack from another sun until they had actually seen those other worlds.

In that war between two solar systems we learned much and lost much. Yet, in all probability we gained more than we lost, for those two new-old planets will mean tremendous things to us. Already scientists are at work in the vast museums and ancient laboratories that are on them, and every day new things are being discovered. We lost many men, but we saved our worlds, and we learned many invaluable secrets from the invaders. In addition, we have but scratched the surface of a science that is at least a thousand million years old!

Epilogue

Taj Lamor looked out across the void of space toward a fading point of yellow light. Far in the distance it glowed, and every second moved it many more miles farther from him. They had lost their struggle for life and a new sun, he had thought when he turned back, defeated, from that distant sun. But time had brought new hope.

They had lost many men in that struggle, and their dwindling resources had been strained to the limit, but now there was hope, for a new spirit had been born in their race. They had fought, and lost, but they had gained a spirit of adventure that had been dormant for millions of years.

Below him, in the great dim mass that was their city, he knew that many laboratories were in the full swing of active work. Knowledge and its application were being discovered and re-discovered. New uses were being found for old things, and their daily life was changing. It was again a race awake, rejuvenated by a change!

As the great sea of yellow fire that was that strange sun had faded behind their fleeing ships, leaving their dead planets still circling a dead sun, he had thought their last chance was gone forever. But hope had reawakened, with the birth of new ideas, new ways of doing things.

Tordos Gar had been right! They had lost—but in the losing, they had won!

Taj Lamor shifted his gaze to a blazing point of light, where a titanic sea of flame was burning with a brilliance and power that, despite the greater distance, made the remote yellow sun seem pale and dim. The blue-white glow told of a monster star, a star far brighter than the one they had just left. It had become the brightest star in their heavens. On their ancient star charts it was listed as a red giant, named Tongsil -239-e, which meant it was of the fifth magnitude and very distant. But in the long ages that had passed since it was classified, it had become a mighty sun—a star in its prime.

How were they to reach it? It was eight and one half light years away!

Their search for the force that would swing a world from its orbit had at last been successful. The knowledge had come too late to aid them in their fight for the yellow sun, but they might yet use it—they might even tear their planets from their orbits, and drive them as free bodies across the void. It would take ages to make the trip—but long ages had already passed as their dark planet swung through the void. What difference would it make if they were or were not accompanied by a dead star?

True, the star that was now their goal was a double star; their planets could not find orbits about it, but they might remedy that—they could tear one star free and hurl it into space, making the remaining sun suitable for their use.

But they *would* escape this dead sun.

ISLANDS OF SPACE

Prologue

In the early part of the Twenty Second Century, Dr. Richard Arcot, hailed as "the greatest living physicist", and Robert Morey, his brilliant mathematical assistant, discovered the so-called "molecular motion drive", which utilized the random energy of heat to produce useful motion.

John Fuller, designing engineer, helped the two men to build a ship which used the drive in order to have a weapon to seek out and capture the mysterious Air Pirate whose robberies were ruining Transcontinental Airways.

The Pirate, Wade, was a brilliant but neurotic chemist who had discovered, among other things, the secret of invisibility. Cured of his instability by modern psychomedical techniques, he was hired by Arcot to help build an interplanetary vessel to go to Venus.

The Venusians proved to be a humanoid race of people who used telepathy for communication. Although they were similar to Earthmen, their blue blood and double thumbs made them enough different to have caused distrust and racial friction, had not both planets been drawn together in a common bond of defense by the passing of the Black Star.

The Black Star, Nigra, was a dead, burned-out sun surrounded by a planetary system very much like our own. But these people had been forced to use their science to produce enough heat and light to stay alive in the cold, black depths of interstellar space. There was nothing evil or menacing in their attack on the Solar System; they simply wanted a star that gave off light and heat. So they attacked, not realizing that they were attacking beings equal in intelligence to themselves.

They were at another disadvantage, too. The Nigrans had spent long millennia fighting their environment and had had no time to fight among themselves, so they knew nothing of how to wage a war. The Earthmen and Venusians knew only too well, since they had a long history of war on each planet.

Inevitably, the Nigrans were driven back to the Black Star.

The war was over. And things became dull. And the taste of adventure still remained on the tongues of Arcot, Wade, and Morey.

I

Three men sat around a table which was littered with graphs, sketches of mathematical functions, and books of tensor formulae. Beside the table stood a Munson-Bradley intergraph calculator which one of the men was using to check some of the equations he had already derived. The results they were getting seemed to indicate something well above and beyond what they had expected.

And anything that surprised the team of Arcot, Wade, and Morey was surprising indeed.

The intercom buzzed, interrupting their work.

Dr. Richard Arcot reached over and lifted the switch. "Arcot speaking."

The face that flashed on the screen was businesslike and determined. "Dr. Arcot, Mr. Fuller is here. My orders are to check with you on all visitors."

Arcot nodded. "Send him up. But from now on, I'm not in to anyone but my father or the Interplanetary Chairman or the elder Mr. Morey. If they come, don't bother to call, just send 'em up. I will not receive calls for the next ten hours. Got it?"

"You won't be bothered, Dr. Arcot."

Arcot cut the circuit and the image collapsed.

Less than two minutes later, a light flashed above the door. Arcot touched the release, and the door slid aside. He looked at the man entering and said, with mock coldness:

"If it isn't the late John Fuller. What did you do—take a plane? It took you an hour to get here from Chicago."

Fuller shook his head sadly. "Most of the time was spent in getting past your guards. Getting to the seventy-fourth floor of the Transcontinental Airways Building is harder than stealing the Taj Mahal." Trying to suppress a grin, Fuller bowed low. "Besides, I think it would do your royal highness good to be kept waiting for a while. You're paid a couple of million a year to putter around in a lab while honest people work for a living. Then, if you happen to stub your toe over some useful gadget, they increase your pay. They call you scientists and spend the resources of two worlds to get you anything you want—and apologize if they don't get it within twenty-four hours.

"No doubt about it; it will do your majesties good to wait."

With a superior smile, he seated himself at the table and shuffled calmly through the sheets of equations before him.

Arcot and Wade were laughing, but not Robert Morey. With a sorrowful expression, he walked to the window and looked out at the hundreds of slim, graceful aircars that floated above the city.

"My friends," said Morey, almost tearfully, "I give you the great Dr. Arcot. These countless machines we see have come from one idea of his. Just an idea, mind you! And who worked it into mathematical form and made it calculable, and therefore useful? I did!

"And who worked out the math for the interplanetary ships? I did! Without me they would never have been built!" He turned dramatically, as though he were playing King Lear. "And what do I get for it?" He pointed an accusing finger at Arcot. "What do I get? *He* is called 'Earth's most brilliant physicist', and I, who did all the hard work, am referred to as 'his mathematical assistant'." He shook his head solemnly. "It's a hard world."

At the table, Wade frowned, then looked at the ceiling. "If you'd make your quotations more accurate, they'd be more trustworthy. The news said that Arcot was the '*System's* most brilliant physicist', and that you were the brilliant mathematical assistant who showed great genius in developing the mathematics of Dr. Arcot's new theory'." Having delivered his speech, Wade began stoking his pipe.

Fuller tapped his fingers on the table. "Come on, you clowns, knock it off and tell me why you called a hard-working man away from his drafting table to come up to this play room of yours. What have you got up your sleeve this time?"

"Oh, that's too bad," said Arcot, leaning back comfortably in his chair. "We're sorry you're so busy. We were thinking of going out to see what Antares, Betelguese, or Polaris looked like at close range. And, if we don't get too bored, we might run over to the giant model nebula in Andromeda, or one of the others. Tough about your being busy; you might have helped us by designing the ship and earned your board and passage. Tough." Arcot looked at Fuller sadly.

Fuller's eyes narrowed. He knew Arcot was kidding, but he also knew how far Arcot would go when he was kidding—and this sounded like he meant it. Fuller said: "Look, teacher, a man named Einstein said that the velocity of light was tops over two hundred years ago, and nobody's come up with any counter evidence yet. Has the Lord instituted a new speed law?"

"Oh, no," said Wade, waving his pipe in a grand gesture of importance. "Arcot just decided he didn't like that law and made a new one himself."

"Now *wait* a minute!" said Fuller. "The velocity of light is a property of space!"

Arcot's bantering smile was gone. "Now you've got it, Fuller. The velocity of light, just as Einstein said, is a property of space. What happens if we change space?"

Fuller blinked. "Change space? How?"

Arcot pointed toward a glass of water sitting nearby. "Why do things look distorted through the water? Because the light rays are bent. Why are they bent? Because as each wave front moves from air to water, *it slows down*. The electromagnetic and gravitational fields between those atoms are strong enough to increase the curvature of the space between them. Now, what happens if we reverse that effect?"

"Oh," said Fuller softly. "I get it. By changing the curvature of the space surrounding you, you could get any velocity you wanted. But what about acceleration? It would take years to reach those velocities at any acceleration a man could stand."

Arcot shook his head. "Take a look at the glass of water again. What happens when the light comes *out* of the water? It speeds up again *instantaneously*. By changing the space around a spaceship, you instantaneously change the velocity of the ship to a comparable velocity in that space. And since every particle is accelerated at the same rate, you wouldn't feel it, any more than you'd feel the acceleration due to gravity in free fall."

Fuller nodded slowly. Then, suddenly, a light gleamed in his eyes. "I suppose you've figured out where you're going to get the energy to power a ship like that?"

"He has," said Morey. "Uncle Arcot isn't the type to forget a little detail like that."

"Okay, give," said Fuller.

Arcot grinned and lit up his own pipe, joining Wade in an attempt to fill the room with impenetrable fog.

"All right," Arcot began, "we needed two things: a tremendous source of power and a way to store it.

"For the first, ordinary atomic energy wouldn't do. It's not controllable enough and uranium isn't something we could carry by the ton. So I began working with high-density currents.

"At the temperature of liquid helium, near absolute zero, lead becomes a nearly perfect conductor. Back in nineteen twenty, physicists had succeeded in making a current flow for four hours in a closed circuit. It was just a ring of lead, but the resistance was so low that the current kept on flowing. They even managed to get six hundred amperes through a piece of lead wire no bigger than a pencil lead.

"I don't know why they didn't go on from there, but they didn't. Possibly it was because they didn't have the insulation necessary to keep down the corona effect; in a high-density current, the electrons tend to push each other sideways out of the wire.

"At any rate, I tried it, using *lux* metal as an insulator around the wire."

"Hold it!" Fuller interrupted. "What, may I ask, is *lux* metal?"

"That was Wade's idea," Arcot grinned. "You remember those two substances we found in the Nigran ships during the war?"

"Sure," said Fuller. "One was transparent and the other was a perfect reflector. You said they were made of light—photons so greatly condensed that they were held together by their gravitational fields."

"Right. We called them light-metal. But Wade said that was too confusing. With a specific gravity of 103.5, light-metal was certainly not a light metal! So Wade coined a couple of words. *Lux* is the Latin for light, so he named the transparent one *lux* and the reflecting one *relux*."

"It sounds peculiar," Fuller observed, "but so does every coined word when you first hear it. Go on with your story."

Arcot relit his pipe and went on. "I put a current of ten thousand amps through a little piece of lead wire, and that gave me a current density of 10^{10} amps per square inch.

"Then I started jacking up the voltage, and modified the thing with a double-polarity field somewhat similar to the molecular motion field except that it works on a sub-nucleonic level. As a result, about half of the lead fed into the chamber became contraterrene lead! The atoms just turned themselves inside out, so to speak, giving us an atom with positrons circling a negatively charged nucleus. It even gave the neutrons a reverse spin, converting them into anti-neutrons.

"Result: total annihilation of matter! When the contraterrene lead atoms met the terrene lead atoms, mutual annihilation resulted, giving us pure energy.

"Some of this power can be bled off to power the mechanism itself; the rest is useful energy. We've got all the power we need —power, literally by the ton."

Fuller said nothing; he just looked dazed. He was well beginning to believe that these three men could do the impossible and do it to order.

"The second thing," Arcot continued, "was, as I said, a way to store the energy so that it could be released as rapidly or as slowly as we needed it.

"That was Morey's baby. He figured it would be possible to use the space-strain apparatus to store energy. It's an old method; induction coils, condensers, and even gravity itself are storing energy by straining space. But with Morey's apparatus we could store a lot more.

"A torus-shaped induction coil encloses all its magnetic field within it; the torus, or 'doughnut' coil, has a perfectly enclosed magnetic field. We built an enclosed coil, using Morey's principle, and expected to store a few watts of power in it to see how long we could hold it.

"Unfortunately, we made the mistake of connecting it to the city power lines, and it cost us a hundred and fifty dollars at a quarter of a cent per kilowatt hour. We blew fuses all over the place. After that, we used the relux plate generator.

"At any rate, the gadget can store power and plenty of it, and it can put it out the same way."

Arcot knocked the ashes out of his pipe and smiled at Fuller. "Those are the essentials of what we have to offer. We give you the job of figuring out the stresses and strains involved. We want a ship with a cruising radius of a thousand million light years."

"Yes, sir! Right away, sir! Do you want a gross or only a dozen?" Fuller asked sarcastically. "You sure believe in big orders! And whence cometh the cold cash for this lovely dream of yours?"

"That," said Morey darkly, "is where the trouble comes in. We have to convince Dad. As President of Transcontinental Airways, he's my boss, but the trouble is, he's also my father. When he hears that I want to go gallivanting off all over the Universe with you guys, he is very likely to turn thumbs down on the whole deal. Besides, Arcot's dad has a lot of influence around here, too, and I have a healthy hunch he won't like the idea, either."

"I rather fear he won't," agreed Arcot gloomily.

A silence hung over the room that felt almost as heavy as the pall of pipe smoke the air conditioners were trying frantically to disperse.

The elder Mr. Morey had full control of their finances. A ship that would cost easily hundreds of millions of dollars was well beyond anything the four men could get by themselves. Their inventions were the property of Transcontinental, but even if they had not been, not one of the four men would think of selling them to another company.

Finally, Wade said: "I think we'll stand a much better chance if we show them a big, spectacular exhibition; something really impressive. We'll point out all the advantages and uses of the apparatus. Then we'll show them complete plans for the ship. They might consent."

"They might," replied Morey smiling. "It's worth a try, anyway. And let's get out of the city to do it. We can go up to my place in Vermont. We can use the lab up there for all we need. We've got everything worked out, so there's no need to stay here.

"Besides, I've got a lake up there in which we can indulge in a little atavism to the fish stage of evolution."

"Good enough," Arcot agreed, grinning broadly. "And we'll need that lake, too. Here in the city it's only eighty-five because the aircars are soaking up heat for their molecular drive, but out in the country it'll be in the nineties."

"To the mountains, then! Let's pack up!"

II

The many books and papers they had collected were hastily put into the briefcases, and the four men took the elevator to the landing area on the roof.

"We'll take my car," Morey said. "The rest of you can just leave yours here. They'll be safe for a few days."

They all piled in as Morey slid into the driver's seat and turned on the power.

They rose slowly, looking below them at the traffic of the great city. New York had long since abandoned her rivers as trade routes; they had been covered solidly by steel decks which were used as public landing fields and ground car routes. Around them loomed titanic structures of glistening colored tile. The sunlight reflected brilliantly from them, and the contrasting colors of the buildings seemed to blend together into a great, multi-colored painting.

The darting planes, the traffic of commerce down between the great buildings, and the pleasure cars above, combined to give a series of changing, darting shadows that wove a flickering pattern over the city. The long lines of ships coming in from Chicago, London, Buenos Aires and San Francisco, and the constant flow from across the Pole—from Russia, India, and China, were like mighty black serpents that wound their way into the city.

Morey cut into a Northbound traffic level, moved into the high-speed lane, and eased in on the accelerator. He held to the traffic pattern for two hundred and fifty miles, until he was well past Boston, then he turned at the first break and fired the ship toward their goal in Vermont.

Less than forty-five minutes since they had left New York, Morey was dropping the car toward the little mountain lake that offered them a place for seclusion. Gently, he let the ship glide smoothly into the shed where the first molecular motion ship had been built. Arcot jumped out, saying:

"We're here—unload and get going. I think a swim and some sleep is in order before we start work on this ship. We can begin tomorrow." He looked approvingly at the clear blue water of the little lake.

Wade climbed out and pushed Arcot to one side. "All right,

out of the way, then, little one, and let a man get going." He headed for the house with the briefcases.

Arcot was six feet two and weighed close to two hundred, but Wade was another two inches taller and weighed a good fifty pounds more. His arms and chest were built on the same general plan as those of a gorilla. He had good reason to call Arcot little.

Morey, though still taller, was not as heavily formed, and weighed only a few pounds more than Arcot, while Fuller was a bit smaller than Arcot.

Due to several factors, the size of the average human being had been steadily increasing for several centuries. Only Wade would have been considered a "big" man by the average person, for the average man was over six feet tall.

They relaxed most of the afternoon, swimming and indulging in a few wrestling matches. At wrestling, Wade consistently proved himself not only built like a gorilla but muscled like one; but Arcot proved that skill was not without merit several times, for he had found that if he could make the match last more than two minutes, Wade's huge muscles would find an insufficient oxygen supply and tire quickly.

That evening, after dinner, Morey engaged Wade in a fierce battle of chess, with Fuller as an interested spectator. Arcot, too, was watching, but he was saying nothing.

After several minutes of uneventful play, Morey stopped suddenly and glared at the board. "Now why'd I make that move? I intended to move my queen over there to check your king on the red diagonal."

"Yeah," replied Wade gloomily, "that's what I wanted you to do. I had a sure checkmate in three moves."

Arcot smiled quietly.

They continued play for several moves, then it was Wade who remarked that something seemed to be influencing his play.

"I had intended to trade queens. I'm glad I didn't, though; I think this leaves me in a better position."

"It sure does," agreed Morey. "I was due to clean up on the queen trade. You surprised me, too; you usually go in for trades. I'm afraid my position is hopeless now."

It was. In the next ten moves, Wade spotted the weak points in every attack Morey made; the attack crumbled disastrously and white was forced to resign, his king in a hopeless position.

Wade rubbed his chin. "You know, Morey, I seemed to know exactly why you made every move, and I saw every possibility involved."

"Yeah—so I noticed," said Morey with a grin.

"Come on, Morey, let's try a game," said Fuller, sliding into the chair Wade had vacated.

Although ordinarily equally matched with Fuller, Morey again went down to disastrous defeat in an amazingly short time. It almost seemed as if Fuller could anticipate every move.

"Brother, am I off form today," he said, rising from the table. "Come on, Arcot—let's see you try Wade."

Arcot sat down, and although he had never played chess as extensively as the others, he proceeded to clean Wade out lock, stock, and barrel.

"Now what's come over you?" asked Morey in astonishment as he saw a very complicated formation working out, a formation he knew was far better than Arcot's usual game. He had just worked it out and felt very proud of it.

Arcot looked at him and smiled. "That's the answer, Morey!"

Morey blinked. "What—what's the answer to what?"

"Yes—I meant it—don't be so surprised—you've seen it done before. I have—no, not under him, but a more experienced teacher. I figured it would come in handy in our explorations."

Morey's face grew more and more astonished as Arcot's strange monologue continued.

Finally, Arcot turned to Wade, who was looking at him and Morey in wide-eyed wonder. And this time, it was Wade who began talking in a monologue.

"You *did?*" he said in a surprised voice. "When?" There was a long pause, during which Arcot stared at Wade with such intensity that Fuller began to understand what was happening.

"Well," said Wade, "if you've learned the trick so thoroughly, try it out. Let's see you project your thoughts! Go ahead!"

Fuller, now understanding fully what was going on, burst out laughing. "He *has* been projecting his thoughts! He hasn't said a word to you!" Then he looked at Arcot. "As a matter of fact, you've said so little that I don't know how you pulled this telepathic stunt—though I'm quite convinced that you did."

"I spent three months on Venus a while back," said Arcot, "studying with one of their foremost telepathists. Actually, most of that time was spent on theory; learning how to do it isn't a difficult proposition. It just takes practice.

"The whole secret is that everyone has the power; it's a very ancient power in the human brain, and most of the lower animals possess it to a greater degree than do humans. When Man developed language, it gave his thoughts more concreteness and permitted a freer and more clearly conceived type of thinking. The result was that telepathy fell into disuse.

"I'm going to show you how to do it because it will be invaluable if we meet a strange race. By projecting pictures and concepts, you can dispense with going to the trouble of learning the language.

"After you learn the basics, all you'll need is practice, but watch yourself! Too much practice can give you the great-granddaddy of all headaches! Okay, now to begin with . . ."

Arcot spent the rest of the evening teaching them the Venerian system of telepathy.

They all rose at nine. Arcot got up first, and the others found it expedient to follow his example shortly thereafter. He had brought a large Tesla coil into the bedroom from the lab and succeeded in including sufficient voltage in the bedsprings to make very effective, though harmless, sparks.

"Come on, boys, hit the deck! Wade, as chief chemist, you are to synthesize a little coffee and heat-treat a few eggs for us. We have work ahead today! Rise and shine!" He didn't shut off the coil until he was assured that each of them had gotten a considerable distance from his bed.

"Ouch!" yelled Morey. "Okay! Shut it off! I want to get my pants! We're all up! You win!"

After breakfast, they all went into the room they used as a calculating room. Here they had two different types of integraph calculators and plenty of paper and equipment to do their own calculations and draw graphs.

"To begin with," said Fuller, "let's decide what shape we want to use. As designer, I'd like to point out that a sphere is the strongest, a cube easiest to build, and a torpedo shape the most efficient aerodynamically. However, we intend to use it in space, not air.

"And remember, we'll need it more as a home than as a ship during the greater part of the trip."

"We might need an aerodynamically stable hull," Wade interjected. "It came in mighty handy on Venus. They're darned useful in emergencies. What do you think, Arcot?"

"I favor the torpedo shape. Okay, now we've got a hull. How about some engines to run it? Let's get those, too. I'll name the general things first; facts and figures can come later.

"First: We must have a powerful mass-energy converter. We could use the cavity radiator and use cosmic rays to warm it, and drive the individual power units that way, or we can have a main electrical power unit and warm them all electrically. Now, which one would be the better?"

Morey frowned. "I think we'd be safer if we didn't depend on any one plant, but had each as separate as possible. I'm for the individual cavity radiators."

"Question," interjected Fuller. "How do these cavity radiators work?"

"They're built like a thermos bottle," Arcot explained. "The inner shell will be of rough relux, which will absorb the heat efficiently, while the outer one will be of polished relux to keep the radiation inside. Between the two we'll run a flow of helium at two tons per square inch pressure to carry the heat to the molecular motion apparatus. The neck of the bottle will contain the atomic generator."

Fuller still looked puzzled. "See here; with this new space strain drive, why do we have to have the molecular drive at all?"

"To move around near a heavy mass—in the presence of a strong gravitational field," Arcot said. "A gravitational field tends to warp space in such a way that the velocity of light is lower in its presence. Our drive tries to warp or strain space in the opposite manner. The two would simply cancel each other out and we'd waste a lot of power going nowhere. As a matter of fact, the gravitational field of the sun is so intense that we'll have to go out beyond the orbit of Pluto before we can use the space strain drive effectively."

"I catch," said Fuller. "Now to get back to the generators. I think the power units would be simpler if they were controlled from one electrical power source, and just as reliable. Anyway, the molecular motion power is controlled, of necessity, from a single generator, so if one is apt to go bad, the other is, too."

"Very good reasoning," smiled Morey, "but I'm still strong for decentralization. I suggest a compromise. We can have the main power unit and the main verticals, which will be the largest, controlled by individual cosmic ray heaters, and the rest run by electric power units. They'd be just heating coils surrounded by the field."

"A good idea," said Arcot. "I'm in favor of the compromise. Okay, Fuller? Okay. Now the next problem is weapons. I suggest we use a separate control panel and a separate generating panel for the power tubes we'll want in the molecular beam projectors."

The molecular beam projector simply projected the field that caused molecular motion to take place as wanted. As weapons, they were terrifically deadly. If half a mountain is suddenly thrown into the air because all the random motion of its molecules becomes concentrated in one direction, it becomes a difficult projectile to fight. Or touch the bow of a ship with the beam; the bow drops to absolute zero and is driven back on the stern, with all the speed of its billions of molecules. The general effect is similar to that produced by two ships having a head-on collision at ten miles per second.

Anything touched by the beam is broken by its own molecules, twisted by its own strength, and crushed by its own toughness. Nothing can resist it.

"My idea," Arcot went on, "was that since the same power is used for both the beams and the drive, we'll have two separate power-tube banks to generate it. That way, if one breaks down, we can switch to the other. We can even use both at once on the drive, if necessary; the molecular motion machines will stand it if we make them of relux and anchor them with lux metal beams. The projectors would be able to handle the power, too, using Dad's new system.

"That will give us more protection, and, at the same time, full power. Since we'll have several projectors, the power needed to operate the ship will be about equal to the power required to operate the projectors.

"And I also suggest we mount some heat beam projectors."

"Why?" objected Wade. "They're less effective than the molecular rays. The molecular beams are instantly irresistible, while the heat beams take time to heat up the target. Sure, they're unhealthy to deal with, but no more so than the molecular beam."

"True enough," Arcot agreed, "but the heat beam is more spectacular, and we may find that a mere spectacular display will accomplish as much as actual destruction. Besides, the heat beams are more local in effect. If we want to kill an enemy and spare his captive, we want a beam that will be deadly where it hits, not for fifty yards around."

"Hold it a second," said Fuller wearily. "Now it's heat beams. Don't you guys think you ought to explain a little bit to the poor goon who's designing this flying battlewagon? How did you get a heat beam?"

Arcot grinned. "Simple. We use a small atomic cavity radiator at one end of which is a rough relux parabolic filter. Beyond that is a lux metal lens. The relux heats up tremendously, and since there is no polished relux to reflect it back, the heat is radiated out through the lux metal lens as a powerful heat beam."

"Okay, fine," said Fuller. "But stop springing new gadgets on me, will you?"

"I'll try not to," Arcot laughed. "Anyway, let's get on to the main power plant. Remember that our condenser coil is a gadget for storing energy in space; we are therefore obliged to supply it with energy to store. Just forming the drive field alone will require two times ten to the twenty-seventh ergs, or the energy of about *two and a half tons* of matter. That means a whale of a lot of lead wire will have to be fed into our conversion generators; it would take several hours to charge the coils. We'd better have two big chargers to do the job.

"The controls we can figure out later. How about it? Any suggestions?"

"Sounds okay to me," said Morey, and the others agreed.

"Good enough. Now, as far as air and water go, we can use the standard spacecraft apparatus, Fuller, so you can figure that in any way you want to."

"We'll need a lab, too," Wade put in. "And a machine shop with plenty of spare parts—everything we can possibly think of. Remember, we may want to build some things out in space."

"Right. And I wonder—" Arcot looked thoughtful. "How about

the invisibility apparatus? It may prove useful, and it won't cost much. Let's put that in, too."

The apparatus he mentioned was simply a high-frequency oscillator tube of extreme power which caused vibrations approaching light frequency to be set up in the molecules of the ship. As a result, the ship became transparent, since light could easily pass through the vibrating molecules.

There was only one difficulty; the ship was invisible, all right, but it became a radio sender and could easily be detected by a directional radio. However, if the secret were unknown, it was a very effective method of disappearing. And, since the frequency was so high, a special detector was required to pick it up.

"Is that all you need?" asked Fuller.

"Nope," said Arcot, leaning back in his chair. "Now comes the kicker. I suggest that we make the hull of foot-thick lux metal and line it on the inside with relux wherever we want it to be opaque. And we want relux shutters on the windows. Lux is too doggone transparent; if we came too close to a hot star, we'd be badly burned."

Fuller looked almost goggle-eyed. "A—foot—of—lux! Good Lord, Arcot! This ship would weigh a quarter of a million tons! That stuff is *dense!*"

"Sure," agreed Arcot, "but we'll need the protection. With a ship like that, you could run through a planetoid without hurting the hull. We'll make the relux inner wall about an inch thick, with a vacuum between them for protection in a warm atmosphere. And if some tremendous force did manage to crack the outer wall, we wouldn't be left without protection."

"Okay, you're the boss," Fuller said resignedly. "It's going to have to be a big ship, though. I figure a length of about two hundred feet and a diameter of around thirty feet. The interior I'll furnish with aluminum; it'll be cheaper and lighter. How about an observatory?"

"Put it in the rear of the ship," Wade suggested. "We'll mount one of the Nigran telectroscopes."

"Control room in the bow, of course," Morey chipped in.

"I've got you," Fuller said. "I'll work the thing out and give you a cost estimate and drawings."

"Fine," said Arcot, standing up. "Meanwhile, the rest of us

will work out our little exhibition to impress Mr. Morey and Dad. Come on, lads, let's get back to the lab."

III

It was two weeks before Dr. Robert Arcot and his old friend Arthur Morey, president of Transcontinental Airways, were invited to see what their sons had been working on.

The demonstration was to take place in the radiation labs in the basements of the Transcontinental building. Arcot, Wade, Morey, and Fuller had brought the equipment in from the country place in Vermont and set it up in one of the heavily-lined, vault-like chambers that were used for radiation experiments.

The two older men were seated before a huge eighty-inch three-dimensional television screen several floors above the level where the actual demonstration was going on.

"There can't be anyone in the room, because of radiation burns," explained Arcot, junior. "We could have surrounded the thing with relux, but then you couldn't have seen what's going on.

"I'm not going to explain anything beforehand; like magic, they'll be more astounding before the explanation is given."

He touched a switch. The cameras began to operate, and the screen sprang into life.

The screen showed a heavy table on which was mounted a small projector that looked something like a searchlight with several heavy cables running into it. In the path of the projector was a large lux metal crucible surrounded by a ring of relux, and a series of points of relux aimed into the crucible. These points and the ring were grounded. Inside the crucible was a small ingot of coronium, the strong, hard, Venerian metal which melted at twenty-five hundred degrees centigrade and boiled at better than four thousand. The crucible was entirely enclosed in a large lux metal case which was lined, on the side away from the projector, with roughened relux.

Arcot moved a switch on the control panel. Far below them, a heavy relay slammed home, and suddenly a solid beam of brilliant bluish light shot out from the projector, a beam so brilliant that the entire screen was lit by the intense glow, and the spectators thought that they could almost feel the heat.

It passed through the lux metal case and through the coronium bar, only to be cut off by the relux liner, which, since it was rough, absorbed over ninety-nine percent of the rays that struck it.

The coronium bar glowed red, orange, yellow, and white in quick succession, then suddenly slumped into a molten mass in the bottom of the crucible.

The crucible was filled now with a mass of molten metal that glowed intensely white and seethed furiously. The slowly rising vapors told of the rapid boiling, and their settling showed that their temperature was too high to permit them to remain hot— the heat radiated away too fast.

For perhaps ten seconds this went on, then suddenly a new factor was added to the performance. There was a sudden crashing arc and a blaze of blue flame that swept in a cyclonic twisting motion inside the crucible. The blaze of the arc, the intense brilliance of the incandescent metal, and the weird light of the beam of radiation shifted in a fantastic play of colors. It made a strange and impressive scene.

Suddenly the relay sounded again; the beam of radiance disappeared as quickly as it had come. In an instant, the blue violet glare of the relux plate had subsided to an angry red. The violent arcing had stopped, and the metal was cooling rapidly. A heavy purplish vapor in the crucible condensed on the walls into black, flakey crystals.

The elder Arcot was watching the scene in the screen curiously. "I wonder—" he said slowly. "As a physicist, I should say it was impossible, but if it did happen, I should imagine these would be the results." He turned to look at Arcot junior. "Well, go on with your exhibition, son."

"I want to know your ideas when we're through, though, Dad," said the younger man. "The next on the program is a little more interesting, perhaps. At least it demonstrates a more commercial aspect of the thing."

The younger Morey was operating the controls of the handling robots. On the screen, a machine rolled in on caterpillar treads, picked up the lux case and its contents, and carried them off.

A minute later, it reappeared with a large electromagnet and a relux plate, to which were attached a huge pair of silver bus-bars. The relux plate was set in a stand directly in front of the projector, and the big electromagnet was set up directly behind the relux plate. The magnet leads were connected, and a coil, in the form of two toruses intersecting at right angles enclosed in a form-fitting relux case, had been connected to the heavy terminals of the relux plate. An ammeter and a heavy coil of coronium wire were connected in series with the coil, and a kilovoltmeter was connected across the terminals of the relux plate.

As soon as the connections were completed, the robot backed swiftly out of the room, and Arcot turned on the magnet and the ray projector. Instantly, there was a sharp deflection of the kilovoltmeter.

"I haven't yet closed the switch leading into the coil," he explained, "so there's no current." The ammeter needle hadn't moved.

Despite the fact that the voltmeter seemed to be shorted out by the relux plate, the needle pointed steadily at twenty-two. Arcot changed the current through the magnet, and the reading dropped to twenty.

The rays had been on at very low power, the air only slightly ionized, but as Arcot turned a rheostat, the intensity increased, and the air in the path of the beam shone with an intense blue. The relux plate, subject now to eddy currents, since there was no other path for the energy to take, began to heat up rapidly.

"I'm going to close the switch into the coil now," said Arcot. "Watch the meters."

A relay snapped, and instantly the ammeter jumped to read 4500 amperes. The voltmeter gave a slight kick, then remained steady. The heavy coronium spring grew warm and began to glow dully, while the ammeter dropped slightly because of the increased resistance. The relux plate cooled slightly, and the voltmeter remained steady.

"The coil you see is storing the energy that is flowing into it," Arcot explained. "Notice that the coronium resistor is increasing its resistance, but otherwise there is little increase in the back E.M.F. The energy is coming from the rays which strike the polarized relux plate to give the current."

He paused a moment to make slight adjustments in the controls, then turned his attention back to the screen.

The kilovoltmeter still read twenty.

"Forty-five hundred amperes at twenty thousand volts," the elder Arcot said softly. "Where is it going?"

"Take a look at the space within the right angle of the torus coils," said Arcot junior. "It's getting dark in there despite the powerful light shed by the ionized air."

Indeed, the space within the twin coils was rapidly growing dark; it was darkening the image of the things behind it, oddly blurring their outlines. In a moment, the images were completely wiped out, and the region within the coils was filled with a strange solid blackness.

"According to the instruments," young Arcot said, "we have stored fifteen thousand kilowatt hours of energy in that coil and there seems to be no limit to how much power we can get into it. Just from the power it contains, that coil is worth about forty dollars right now, figured at a quarter of a cent per kilowatt hour.

"I haven't been using anywhere near the power I can get out of this apparatus, either. Watch." He threw another switch which shorted around the coronium resistor and the ammeter, allowing the current to run into the coil directly from the plate.

"I don't have a direct reading on this," he explained, "but an indirect reading from the magnetic field in that room shows a current of nearly a *hundred million amperes!*"

The younger Morey had been watching a panel of meters on the other side of the screen. Suddenly, he shouted: "Cut it, Arcot! The conductors are setting up a secondary field in the plate and causing trouble."

Instantly, Arcot's hand went to a switch. A relay slammed open, and the ray projector died.

The power coil still held its field of enigmatic blackness.

"Watch this," Arcot instructed. Under his expert manipulation, a small robot handler rolled into the room. It had a pair of pliers clutched in one claw. The spectators watched the screen in fascination as the robot drew back its arm and hurled the pliers at the black field with all its might. The pliers struck the blackness and rebounded as if they had hit a rubber wall. Arcot caused the little machine to pick up the pliers and repeat the process.

Arcot grinned. "I've cut off the power to the coil. Unlike the ordinary induction coil, it isn't necessary to keep supplying power to the thing; it's a static condition.

"You can see for yourself how much energy it holds. It's a handy little gadget, isn't it?" He shut off the rest of the instruments and the television screen, then turned to his father.

"The demonstration is over. Got any theories, Dad?"

The elder Dr. Arcot frowned in thought. "The only thing I can think of that would produce an effect like that is a stream of positrons—or contraterrene nuclei. That would explain not only the heating, but the electrical display.

"As far as the coil goes, that's easy to understand. Any energy storage device stores energy the strain in space; here you can actually see the strain in space." Then he smiled at his son. "I see my ex-laboratory assistant has come a long way. You've achieved controlled, usable atomic energy through total annihilation of mass. Right?"

Arcot smiled back and nodded. "Right, Dad."

"Son, I wonder if you'd give me your data sheet on that process. I'd like to work out some of the mathematical problems involved."

"Sure, Dad. But right now—" Arcot turned toward the elder Mr. Morey. "—I'm more interested in the mathematics of finance. We have a proposition to put to you, Mr. Morey, and that proposition, simply stated, is—"

Perhaps it was simply stated, but it took fully an hour for Arcot, Wade, and Morey to discuss the science of it with the two older men, and Fuller spent another hour over the carefully drawn plans for the ship.

At last, the elder Mr. Morey settled back and looked vacantly at the ceiling. They were seated now in the conference room of Transcontinental Airways.

"Well, boys," said Mr. Morey, "as usual, I'm in a position where I'm forced to yield. I might refuse financial backing, but you could sell any one of those gadgets for close to a billion dollars and finance the expedition independently, or you could, with your names, request the money publicly and back it that way." He paused a moment. "I am, however, thinking more in terms of your safety than in terms of money." There was another long pause, then he smiled at the four younger men.

"I think, however, that we can trust you. Armed with cosmic and molecular rays, you should be able to put up a fair scrap anywhere. Also, I have never detected any signs of feeblemindedness in any of you; I don't think you'll get yourselves in a jam you can't get out of. I'll back you."

"I hate to interrupt your exuberance," said the elder Dr. Arcot, "but I should like to know the name of this remarkable ship."

"What?" asked Wade. "Name? Oh, it hasn't any."

The elder Morey shook his head sadly. "That is indeed an important oversight. If a crew of men can overlook so fundamental a thing, I wonder if they *are* to be trusted."

"Well, what are we going to call it, then?" asked Arcot.

"*Solarite II* might do," suggested Morey. "It will still be from the Solar System."

"I think we should be more broadminded," said Arcot. "We aren't going to stay in this system—not even in this galaxy. We might call it the *Galaxian.*"

"Did you say broadminded?" asked Wade. "Let's really be broad and call it the *Universite* or something like that. Or, better yet, call it *Flourine!* That's everywhere in the universe and the most active element there is. This ship will go everywhere in the universe and be the most active thing that ever existed!"

"A good name!" said the elder Morey. "That gets my vote!"

Young Arcot looked thoughtful. "That's mighty good—I like the idea—but it lacks ring." He paused, then, looking up at the ceiling, repeated slowly:

> *"Alone, alone, all, all alone;*
> *Alone on a wide, wide sea;*
> *Nor any saint took pity on*
> *My soul in agony."*

He rose and walked over to the window, looking out where the bright points of light that were the stars of space rode high in the deep violet of the moonlit sky.

"The sea of all space—the sea of vastness that lies between the far-flung nebulae—the mighty void—alone on a sea, the vastness of which no man can imagine—alone—alone where no other man has been; alone, so far from all matter, from all mankind, that not even light, racing at billions of miles each day, could reach home in less than a million years." Arcot stopped and stood looking out of the window.

Morey broke the silence. "*The Ancient Mariner.*" He paused.

"'Alone' will certainly be right. I think that name takes all the prizes."

Fuller nodded slowly. "I certainly agree. *The Ancient Mariner.* It's kind of long, but it is *the* name."

It was adopted unanimously.

IV

The *Ancient Mariner* was built in the big Transcontinental shops in Newark; the power they needed was not available in the smaller shops.

Working twenty-four hours a day, in three shifts, skilled men took two months to finish the hull according to Fuller's specifications. The huge walls of lux metal required great care in construction, for they could not be welded; they had to be formed in position. And they could only be polished under powerful magnets, where the dense magnetic field softened the lux metal enough to allow a diamond polisher to do the job.

When the hull was finished, there came the laborious work of installing the power plant and the tremendous power leads, the connectors, the circuits to the relays—a thousand complex circuits.

Much of it was standard: the molecular power tubes, the molecular ray projectors, the power tubes for the invisibility apparatus, and many other parts. All the relays were standard, the gyroscopic stabilizers were standard, and the electromagnetic braking equipment for the gyros was standard.

But there would be long days of work ahead for Arcot, Wade, and Morey, for only they could install the special equipment; only they could put in the complicated wiring, for no one else on Earth understood the circuits they had to establish.

During the weeks of waiting, Arcot and his friends worked on auxiliary devices to be used with the ship. They wanted to make some improvements on the old molecular ray pistols, and to develop atomic powered heat projectors for hand use. The primary power they stored in small space-strain coils in the handgrip of the pistol. Despite their small size, the coils were capable of storing power for thirty hours of continuous operation of the rays. The finished weapon was scarcely larger than a standard molecular ray pistol.

Arcot pointed out that many of the planets they might visit would be larger than Earth, and they lacked any way of getting about readily under high gravity. Since something had to be done about that, Arcot did it. He demonstrated it to his friends one day in the shop yard.

Morey and Wade had just been in to see Fuller about some details of the ship, and as they came out, Arcot called them over to his work bench. He was wearing a space suit without the helmet.

The modern space suit is made of woven lux metal wires of extremely small diameter and airproofed with a rubberoid flurocarbon plastic, and furnished with air and heating units. Made as it was, it offered protection nothing else could offer; it was almost a perfect insulator and was resistant to the attack of any chemical reagent. Not even elemental fluorine could corrode it. And the extreme strength of the lux metal fiber made it stronger, pound for pound, than steel or coronium.

On Arcot's back was a pack of relux plated metal. It was connected by relux web belts to a broad belt that circled Arcot's waist. One thin cable ran down the right arm to a small relux tube about eight inches long by two inches in diameter.

"Watch!" Arcot said, grinning.

He reached to his belt and flipped a little switch.

"So long! See you later!" He pointed his right arm toward the ceiling and sailed lightly into the air. He lowered the angle of his arm and moved smoothly across the huge hangar, floating toward the shining bulk of the rapidly forming *Ancient Mariner*. He circled the room, rising and sinking at will, then headed for the open door.

"Come out and watch me where there's more room," he called.

Out in the open, he darted high up into the air until he was a mere speck in the sky. Then he suddenly came dropping down and landed lightly before them, swaying on his feet and poised lightly on his toes.

"Some jump," said Morey, in mock surprise.

"Yeah," agreed Fuller. "Try again."

"Or," Wade put in, "give me that weight annihilator and I'll beat you at your own game. What's the secret?"

"That's a cute gadget. How much load does it carry?" asked Morey, more practically.

"I can develop about ten tons as far as it goes, but the human body can't take more than five gravities, so we can only visit planets with less than that surface gravity. The principle is easy to see; I'll show you."

He unhooked the cables and took the power pack from his back. "The main thing is the molecular power unit here, electrically heated and mounted on a small, massive gyroscope. That gyro is necessary, too. I tried leaving it out and almost took a nosedive. I had it coupled directly to the body and leaned forward a little bit when I was in the air. Without a gyro to keep the drive upright, I took a loop and started heading for the ground. I had to do some fancy gymnastics to keep from ending up six feet under—literally.

"The power is all generated in the pack with a small power plate and several storage coils. I've also got it hooked to these holsters at my belt so we can charge the pistols while we carry them.

"The control is this secondary power cable running down my arm to my hand. That gives you your direction, and the rheostat here at the belt changes the velocity.

"I've only made this one so far, but I've ordered six others like it. I thought you guys might like one, too."

"I think you guessed right!" said Morey, looking inside the power case. "Hey! Why all the extra room in the case?"

"It's an unperfected invention as yet; we might want to put some more stuff in there for our own private use."

Each of the men tried out the apparatus and found it quite satisfactory.

Meanwhile, there was other work to be done.

Wade had been given the job of gathering the necessary food and anything else in the way of supplies that he might think of. Arcot was collecting the necessary spare parts and apparatus. Morey was gathering a small library and equipping a chemistry laboratory. Fuller was to get together the necessary standard equipment for the ship—tables, seats, bunks, and other furniture.

It took months of work, and it seemed it would never be finished, but finally, one clear, warm day in August, the ship was completely equipped and ready to go.

On the last inspection, the elder Dr. Arcot and the elder Mr.

Morey went with the four younger men. They stood beside the great intergalactic cruiser, looking up at its shining hull.

"We came a bit later than we expected, son," said Dr. Arcot, "but we still expect a good show." He paused and frowned. "I understand you don't intend to take any trial trip. What's the idea?"

Arcot had been afraid his father would be worried about that, so he framed his explanation carefully. "Dad, we figured this ship out to the last decimal place; it's the best we can make it. Remember, the molecular motion drive will get a trial first; we'll give it a trial trip when we leave the sun. If there's any trouble, naturally, we'll return. But the equipment is standard, so we're expecting no trouble.

"The only part that would require a trial trip is the space-control apparatus, and there's no way to give that a trial trip. Remember, we have to get far enough out from the sun so that the gravitational field will be weak enough for the drive to overcome it. If we tried it this close, we'd just be trying to neutralize the sun's gravity. We'd be pouring out energy, wasting a great deal of it; but out away from the sun, we'll get most of the energy back.

"On the other hand, when we do get out and get started we will go faster than light, and we'd be hopelessly beyond the range of the molecular motion drive in an instant. In other words, if the space-control drive doesn't work, we can't come back, and if it does work, there's no need to come back.

"And if anything goes wrong, we're the only ones who could fix it, anyway. If anything goes wrong, I'll radio Earth. You ought to be able to hear from me in about a dozen years." He smiled suddenly. "Say! We might go out and get back here in time to hear ourselves talking!

"But you can see why we felt that there was little reason for a trial trip. If it's a failure, we'll never be back to say so; if it isn't, we'll be able to continue."

His father still looked worried, but he nodded in acquiescence. "Perfect logic, son, but I guess we may as well give up the discussion. Personally, I don't like it. Let's see this ship of yours."

The great hull was two hundred feet long and thirty feet in diameter. The outer wall, one foot of solid lux metal, was separated from the inner, one-inch relux wall by a two inch gap which would be evacuated in space. The two walls were joined in many places by small lux metal crossbraces. The windows consisted of spaces in the relux wall, allowing the occupants to see through the transparent lux hull.

From the outside, it was difficult to detect the exact outline of the ship, for the clear lux metal was practically invisible and the foot of it that surrounded the more visible part of the ship gave a curious optical illusion. The perfect reflecting ability of the relux made the inner hull difficult to see, too. It was more by absence than presence that one detected it; it blotted out things behind it.

The great window of the pilot room disclosed the pilot seats and the great switchboard to one side. Each of the windows was equipped with a relux shield that slid into position at the touch of a switch, and these were already in place over the observatory window, so only the long, narrow portholes showed the lighted interior.

For some minutes, the elder men stood looking at the graceful beauty of the ship.

"Come on in—see the inside," suggested Fuller.

They entered through the airlock close to the base of the ship. The heavy lux door was opened by automatic machinery from the inside, but the combination depended on the use of a molecular ray and the knowledge of the correct place, which made it impossible for anyone to open it unless they had the ray and knew where to use it.

From the airlock, they went directly to the power room. Here they heard the soft purring of a large oscillator tube and the indistinguishable murmur of smoothly running AC generators powered by large contraterrene reactors.

The elder Dr. Arcot glanced in surprise at the heavy-duty ammeter in a control panel.

"Half a billion amperes! Good Lord! Where is all that power going?" He looked at his son.

"Into the storage coils. It's going in at ten kilovolts, so that's a five billion kilowatt supply. It's been going for half an hour and has half an hour to run. It takes two tons of matter to charge the coil to capacity, and we're carrying twenty tons of fuel—enough for ten charges. We shouldn't need more than three tons if all goes well, but 'all' seldom does.

"See that large black cylinder up there?" Arcot asked, pointing.

Above them, lying along the roof of the power room, lay a great black cylinder nearly two feet in diameter and extending out through the wall in the rear. It was made integral with two giant lux metal beams that reached to the bow of the ship in a long, sweeping curve. From one of the power switchboards, two heavy cables ran up to the giant cylinder.

"That's the main horizontal power unit. We can develop an acceleration of ten gravities either forward or backward. In the curve of the ship, on top, sides, and bottom, there are power units for motion in the other two directions.

"Most of the rest of the stuff in this section is old hat to you, though. Come on into the next room."

Arcot opened the heavy relux door, leading the way into the next room, which was twice the size of the power room. The center of the floor was occupied by a heavy pedestal of lux metal upon which was a huge, relux-encased, double torus storage coil. There was a large switchboard at the opposite end, while around the room, in ordered groups, stood the familiar double coils, each five feet in diameter. The space within them was already darkening.

"Well," said Arcot, senior, "that's some battery of power coils, considering the amount of energy one can store. But what's the big one for?"

"That's the main space control," the younger Arcot answered. "While our power is stored in the smaller ones, we can shoot it into this one, which, you will notice, is constructed slightly differently. Instead of holding the field within it, completely enclosed, the big one will affect all the space about it. We will then be enclosed in what might be called a hyperspace of our own making."

"I see," said his father. "You go into hyperspace and move at any speed you please. But how will you see where you're going?"

"We won't, as far as I know. I don't expect to see a thing while we're in that hyperspace. We'll simply aim the ship in the direction we want to go and then go into hyperspace. The only thing we have to avoid is stars; their gravitational fields would drain the energy out of the apparatus and we'd end up in the center of a white-hot star. Meteors and such, we don't have to worry about; their fields aren't strong enough to drain the coils, and since we won't be in normal space, we can't hit them."

The elder Morey looked worried. "If you can't see your way back you'll get lost! And you can't radio back for help."

"Worse than that!" said Arcot. "We couldn't receive a signal of any kind after we get more than three hundred light years away; there weren't any radios before that.

"What we'll do is locate ourselves through the sun's light. We'll take photographs every so often and orient ourselves by them when we come back."

"That sounds like an excellent method of stellar navigation," agreed Morey senior. "Let's see the rest of the ship." He turned and walked toward the farther door.

The next room was the laboratory. On one side of the room was a complete physics lab and on the other was a well-stocked and well-equipped chemistry lab. They could perform many experiments here that no man had been able to perform due to lack of power. In this ship they had more generating facilities than all the power stations of Earth combined!

Arcot opened the next door. "This next room is the physics and chemistry storeroom. Here we have a duplicate—in some cases, six or seven duplicates—of every piece of apparatus on board, and plenty of material to make more. Actually, we have enough equipment to make a new ship out of what we have here. It would be a good deal smaller, but it would work.

"The greater part of our materials is stored in the curvature of the ship, where it will be easy to get at if necessary. All our water and food is there, and the emergency oxygen tanks.

"Now let's take the stairway to the upper deck."

The upper deck was the main living quarters. There were several small rooms on each side of the corridor down the center; at the extreme nose was the control room, and at the extreme stern was the observatory. The observatory was equipped with a small but exceedingly powerful telectroscope, developed from those the Nigrans had left on one of the deserted planets Sol had captured in return for the loss of Pluto to the Black Star. The arc commanded by the instrument was not great, but it was easy to turn the ship about, and most of their observations could be made without trouble.

Each of the men had a room of his own; there was a small

galley and a library equipped with all the books the four men could think of as being useful. The books and all other equipment were clamped in place to keep them from flying around loose when the ship accelerated.

The control room at the nose was surrounded by a hemisphere of transparent lux metal which enabled them to see in every direction except directly behind, and even that blind spot could be covered by stationing a man in the observatory.

There were heat projectors and molecular ray projectors, each operated from the control room in the nose. To complete the armament, there were more projectors in the stern, controlled from the observatory, and a set on either side controlled from the library and the galley.

The ship was provisioned for two years—two years without stops. With the possibility of stopping on other planets, the four men could exist indefinitely in the ship.

After the two older men had been shown all through the intergalactic vessel, the elder Arcot turned to his old friend. "Morey, it looks as if it was time for us to leave the *Ancient Mariner* to her pilots!"

"I guess you're right. Well—I'll say goodbye—but you all know there's a lot more I could say." Morey senior looked at them and started toward the airlock.

"Goodbye, son," said the elder Arcot. "Goodbye, men. I'll be expecting you any time within two years. We can have no warning, I suppose; your ship will outrace the radio beam. Goodbye." Dr. Arcot joined his old friend and they went outside.

The heavy lux metal door slid into place behind them, and the thick plastic cushions sealed the entrance to the airlock.

The workmen and the other personnel around the ship cleared the area and stood well back from the great hull. The two older men waved to the men inside the ship.

Suddenly the ship trembled, and rose toward the sky.

V

Arcot, at the controls of the *Ancient Mariner*, increased the acceleration as the ship speared up toward interplanetary space. Soon, the deep blue of the sky had given way to an intense violet, and this faded to the utter black of space as the ship drew away from the planet that was its home.

"That lump of dust there is going to look mighty little when we get back," said Wade softly.

"But," Arcot reminded him, "that little lump of dust is going to pull us across a distance that our imaginations can't conceive of. And we'll be darned happy to see that pale globe swinging in space when we get back—provided, of course, that we do get back."

The ship was straining forward now under the pull of its molecular motion power units, accelerating at a steady rate, rapidly increasing the distance between the ship and Earth.

The cosmic ray power generators were still charging the coils, preventing the use of the space strain drive. Indeed, it would be a good many hours before they would be far enough from the sun to throw the ship into hyperspace.

In the meantime, Morey was methodically checking every control as Arcot called out the readings on the control panel. Everything was working to perfection. Their every calculation had checked out in practice so far. But the real test was yet to come.

They were well beyond the orbit of Pluto when they decided they would be safe in using the space strain drive and throwing the ship into hyperspace.

Morey was in the hyperspace control room, watching the instruments there. They were ready!

"Hold on!" called Arcot. "Here we go—if at all!" He reached out to the control panel before him and touched the green switch that controlled the molecular motion machines. The big power tubes cut off, and their acceleration ceased. His fingers pushed a brilliant red switch—there was a dull, muffled thud as a huge relay snapped shut.

Suddenly, a strange tingling feeling of power ran through them—space around them was suddenly black. The lights dimmed for an instant as the titanic current that flowed through the gigantic conductors set up a terrific magnetic field, reacting with the absorption plates. The power seemed to climb rapidly to a maximum—then, quite suddenly, it was gone.

The ship was quiet. No one spoke. The meters, which had

flashed over to their limits, had dropped back to zero once more, except those which indicated the power stored in the giant coil. The stars that had shone brilliantly around them in a myriad of colors were gone. The space around them glowed strangely, and there was a vast cloud of strange, violet or pale green stars be-fore them. Directly ahead was one green star that glowed big and brilliant, then it faded rapidly and shrank to a tiny dot—a distant star. There was a strange tenseness about the men; they seemed held in an odd, compelled silence.

Arcot reached forward again. "Cutting off power, Morey!" The red tumbler snapped back. Again space seemed to be charged with a vast surplus of energy that rushed in from all around, coursing through their bodies, producing a tingling feeling. Then space rocked in a gray cloud about them; the stars leaped out at them in blazing glory again.

"Well, it worked once!" breathed Arcot with a sigh of relief. "Lord, I made some errors in calculation, though! I hope I didn't make any more! Morey—how was it? I only used one-sixteenth power."

"Well, don't use any more, then," said Morey. "We sure trav-eled! The things worked perfectly. By the way, it's a good thing we had all the relays magnetically shielded; the magnetic field down here was so strong that my pocket kit tried to start run-ning circles around it.

"According to your magnetic drag meter, the conductors were carrying over fifty billion amperes. The small coils worked per-fectly. They're charged again; the power went back into them from the big coil with only a five percent loss of power—about twenty thousand megawatts."

"Hey, Arcot," Wade said. "I thought you said we wouldn't be able to see the stars."

Arcot spread his hands. "I did say that, and all my apologies for it. But we're not seeing them by light. The stars all have pro-jections—shadows—in this space because of their intense gravita-tional fields. There are probably slight fluctuations in the field, perhaps one every minute or so. Since we were approaching them at twenty thousand times the speed of light, the Doppler effect gives us what looks like violet light.

"We saw the stars in front of us as violet points. The green ones were actually behind us, and the green light was tremendously reduced in frequency. It certainly can't be anything less than gamma rays and probably even of greater frequency.

"Did you notice there were no stars off to the side? We weren't approaching them, so they didn't give either effect."

"How did you know which was which?" asked Fuller skeptically.

"Did you see that green star directly ahead of us?" Arcot asked. "The one that dwindled so rapidly? That could only have been the sun, since the sun was the only star close enough to show up as a disc. Since it was green and I knew it was behind us, I decided that all the green ones were behind us. It isn't proof, but it's a good indication."

"You win, as usual," admitted Fuller.

"Well, where are we?" asked Wade. "I think that's more important."

"I haven't the least idea," confessed Arcot. "Let's see if we can find out. I've got the robot pilot on, so we can leave the ship to itself. Let's take a look at Old Sol from a distance that no man ever reached before!"

They started for the observatory. Morey joined them and Arcot put the view of Sol and his family on the telectroscope screen. He increased the magnification to maximum, and the four men looked eagerly at the system. The sun glowed brilliantly, and the planets showed plainly.

"Now, if we wanted to take the trouble, we could calculate when the planets were in that position and determine the distance we have come. However, I notice that Pluto is still in place, so that means we are seeing the Solar System as it was before the passing of the Black Star. We're at least two light years away."

"More than that," said Morey. He pointed at the screen. "See here, how Mars is placed in relation to Venus and Earth? The planets were in that configuration seven years ago. We're seven light years from Earth."

"Good enough!" Arcot grinned. "That means we're within two light years of Sirius, since we were headed in that direction. Let's turn the ship so we can take a look at it with the telectroscope."

Since the power had been cut off, the ship was in free fall, and the men were weightless. Arcot didn't try to walk toward the control room; he simply pushed against the wall with his feet and made a long, slow dive for his destination.

The others reached for the handgrips in the walls while Arcot swung the ship gently around so that its stern was pointed toward Sirius. Because of its brilliance and relative proximity to Sol, Sirius is the brightest star in the heavens, as seen from Earth. At this much lesser distance, it shone as a brilliant point of light that blazed wonderfully. They turned the telectroscope toward it, but there was little they could see that was not visible from the big observatory on the Moon.

"I think we may as well go nearer," suggested Morey, "and see what we find on close range observation. Meanwhile, turn the ship back around and I'll take some pictures of the sun and its surrounding star field from this distance. Our only way of getting back is going to be this series of pictures, so I think we had best make it complete. For the first light century, we ought to take a picture every ten light years, and after that one each light century until we reach a point where we are only getting diminishing pictures of the local star cluster. After that, we can wait until we reach the edge of the Galaxy."

"Sounds all right to me," agreed Arcot. "After all, you're the astronomer, I'm not. To tell you the truth, I'd have to search a while to find Old Sol again. I can't see just where he is. Of course, I could locate him by means of the gyroscope settings, but I'm afraid I wouldn't find him so easily visually."

"Say! You sure are a fine one to pilot an expedition in space!" cried Wade in mock horror. "I think we ought to demote him for that! Imagine! He plans a trip of a thousand million light years, and then gets us out seven light years and says he doesn't know where he is! Doesn't even know where home is! I'm glad we have a cautious man like Morey along." He shook his head sadly.

They took a series of six plates of the sun, using different magnifications.

"These plates will help prove our story, too," said Morey as he looked at the finished plates. "We might have gone only a little way into space, up from the plane of the ecliptic and taken plates through a wide angle camera. But we'd have had to go at least seven years into the past to get a picture like this."

The new self-developing short-exposure plates, while not in perfect color balance, were more desirable for this work, since they took less time on exposure.

Morey and the others joined Arcot in the control room and

strapped themselves into the cushioned seats. Since the space strain mechanism had proved itself in the first test, they felt they needed no more observations than they could make from the control room meters.

Arcot gazed out at the spot that was their immediate goal and said slowly: "How much bigger than Sol is that star, Morey?"

"It all depends on how you measure size," Morey replied. "It is two and a half times as heavy, has four times the volume, and radiates twenty-five times as much light. In other words, one hundred million tons of matter disappear each second in that star.

"That's for Sirius A, of course. Sirius B, its companion, is a different matter; it's a white dwarf. It has only one one-hundred-twenty-five-thousandths the volume of Sirius A, but it weighs *one third* as much. It radiates more per square inch than our sun, but, due to its tiny size, it is very faint. That star, though almost as massive as the sun, is only about the size of Earth."

"You sure have those statistics down pat!" said Fuller, laughing. "But I must say they're interesting. What's that star made of, anyway? Solid lux metal?"

"Hardly!" Morey replied. "Lux metal has a density of around 103, while this star has a density so high that one cubic inch of its matter would weigh a ton on Earth."

"Wow!" Wade ejaculated. "I'd hate to drop a baseball on my toe on that star!"

"It wouldn't hurt you," Arcot said, smiling. "If you could lift the darned thing, you ought to be tough enough to stand dropping it on your toe. Remember, it would weigh about two hundred tons! Think you could handle it?"

"At any rate, here we go. When we get there, you can get out and try it."

Again came the shock of the start. The heavens seemed to reel about them; the bright spot of Sirius was a brilliant violet point that swelled like an expanding balloon, spreading out until it filled a large angle.

Then again the heavens reeled, and they were still. The control room was filled with a dazzling splendor of brilliant blue-white light, and an intense heat beat in upon them.

"Brother! Feel that heat," said Arcot in awe. "We'd better watch ourselves; that thing is giving off plenty of ultraviolet. We

could end up with third-degree sunburns if we're not careful."
Suddenly he stopped and looked around in surprise. "Hey!
Morey! I thought you said this was a double star! Look over
there! That's no white dwarf—*it's a planet!*"

"Ridiculous!" snapped Morey. "It's impossible for a planet to
be in equilibrium about a double star! But—" He paused, bewildered. "But it is a planet! But—but it can't be! We've made too
many measurements on this star to make it possible!"

"I don't give a hang whether it can or not," Wade said coolly,
"the fact remains that it is. Looks as if that shoots a whole flock
of holes in that bedtime story you were telling us about a superdense star."

"I make a motion we look more closely first," said Fuller, quite
logically.

But at first the telectroscope only served to confuse them
more. It was most certainly a planet, and they had a strange,
vague feeling of having seen it before.

Arcot mentioned this, and Wade launched into a long, pedan-
tic discussion of how the left and right hemispheres of the brain
get out of step at times, causing a sensation of having seen a
thing before when it was impossible to have seen it previously.

Arcot gave Wade a long, withering stare and then pushed himself into the library without saying a word. A moment later, he
was back with a large volume entitled: *"The Astronomy of the
Nigran Invasion,"* by *D. K. Harkness.* He opened the volume to
a full-page photograph of the third planet of the Black Star as
taken from a space cruiser circling the planet. Silently, he
pointed to it and to the image swimming on the screen of the
telectroscope.

"Good Lord!" said Wade in astonished surprise. "It's impossible! We came here faster than light, and that planet got here
first!"

"As you so brilliantly remarked a moment ago," Arcot pointed
out, "I don't give a hang whether it can or not—it is. How they
did it, I don't know, but it does clear up a number of things. According to the records we found, the ancient Nigrans had a force
ray that could move planets from their orbits. I wonder if it
couldn't be used to break up a double star? Also, we know their
scientists were looking for a method of moving faster than light;

if we can do it, so could they. They just moved their whole system of planets over here after getting rid of the upsetting influence of the white dwarf."

"Perfect!" exclaimed Morey enthusiastically. "It explains everything."

"Except that we saw that companion star when we stopped back there, half an hour ago," said Fuller.

"Not half an hour ago," Arcot contradicted. "Two years ago. We saw the light that left the companion before it was moved. It's rather like traveling in time."

"If that's so," asked Fuller, suddenly worried, "what is our time in relation to Earth?"

"If we moved by the space-strain drive at all times," Arcot explained, "we would return at exactly the same time we left. Time is passing normally on Earth as it is with us right now, but whenever we use the space-strain, we move instantaneously from one point to another as far as Earth and the rest of the universe is concerned. It seems to take time to us because we are within the influence of the field.

"Suppose we were to take a trip that required a week. In other words, three days traveling in space-strain, a day to look at the destination, and three more days coming back. When we returned to Earth, they would insist we had only been gone one day, the time we spent out of the drive. See?"

"I catch," said Fuller. "By the way, shouldn't we take some photographs of this system? Otherwise, Earth won't get the news for several years yet."

"Right," agreed Morey. "And we might as well look for the other planets of the Black Star, too."

They made several plates, continuing their observations until all the planets had been located, even old Pluto, where crews of Nigran technicians were obviously at work, building giant structures of lux metal. The great cities of the Nigrans were beginning to bloom on the once bleak plains of the planet. The mighty blaze of Sirius had warmed Pluto, vaporizing its atmosphere and thawing its seas. The planet that the Black Star had stolen from the Solar System was warmer than it had been for two billion years.

"Well, that's it," said Arcot when they had finished taking the necessary photographs. "We can prove we went faster than light easily, now. The astronomers can take up the work of classifying the planets and getting details of the orbits when we get back.

"Since the Nigrans now have a sun of their own, there should be no reason for hostility between our race and theirs. Perhaps we can start commercial trade with them. Imagine! Commerce over quintillions of miles of space!"

"And," interrupted Wade, "they can make the trip to this system in less time than it takes to get to Venus!"

"Meanwhile," said Morey, "let's get on with our own exploration."

They strapped themselves into the control seats once more and Arcot threw in the molecular drive to take them away from the sun toward which they had been falling.

When the great, hot disc of Sirius had once more diminished to a tiny white pinhead of light, Arcot turned the ship until old Sol once more showed plainly on the crosshairs of the aiming telescope in the rear of the vessel.

"Hold on," Arcot cautioned, "here we go again!"

Again he threw the little red tumbler that threw a flood of energy into the coils. The space about them seemed to shiver and grow dim.

Arcot had thrown more power into the coils this time, so the stars ahead of them instead of appearing violet were almost invisible; they were radiating in the ultra-violet now. And the stars behind them, instead of appearing to be green, had subsided to a dull red glow.

Arcot watched the dull red spark of Sirius become increasingly dimmer. Then, quite suddenly, a pale violet disc in front of them ballooned out of nowhere and slid off to one side.

The spaceship reeled, perking the men around in the control seats. Heavy safety relays thudded dully; the instruments flickered under a suddenly rising surge of power—then they were calm again. Arcot had snapped over the power switch.

"That," he said quietly, "is not so good."

"Threw the gyroscopes, didn't it?" asked Morey, his voice equally as quiet.

"It did—and I have no idea how far. We're off course and we don't know which direction we're headed."

VI

"What's the matter?" asked Fuller anxiously.

Arcot pointed out the window at a red star that blazed in the distance. "We got too near the field of gravity of that young giant and he threw us for a loss. We drained out three-fourths of the energy from our coils and lost our bearings in the bargain. The attraction turned the gyroscopes and threw the ship out of line, so we no longer know where the sun is.

"Well, come on, Morey; all we can do is start a search. At this distance, we'd best go by Sirius; it's brighter and nearer." He looked at the instrument panel. "I was using the next lowest power and I still couldn't avoid that monster. This ship is just a little *too* hot to handle."

Their position was anything but pleasant. They must pick out from the vast star field behind them the one star that was home, not knowing exactly where it was. But they had one tremendous help—the photographs of the star field around Sol that they had taken at the last stop. All they had to do was search for an area that matched their photographs.

They found the sun at last, after they had spotted Sirius, but they had had to rotate the ship through nearly twenty-five degrees to do it. After establishing their bearings, they took new photographs for their files.

Meanwhile, Wade had been recharging the coils. When he was finished, he reported the fact to Arcot.

"Fine," Arcot said. "And from now on, I'm going to use the least possible amount of power. It certainly isn't safe to use more."

They started for the control room, much relieved. Arcot dived first, with Wade directly behind him. Wade decided suddenly to go into his room and stopped himself by grabbing a handhold. Morey, following close behind, bumped into him and was brought to rest, while Wade was pushed into his room.

But Fuller, coming last, slammed into Morey, who moved forward with new velocity toward the control room, leaving Fuller hanging at rest in the middle of the corridor.

"Hey, Morey!" he laughed. "Send me a skyhook! I'm caught!" Isolated as he was in the middle of the corridor, he couldn't push on anything and remained stranded.

"Go to sleep!" advised Morey. "It's the most comfortable bed you'll find!"

Wade looked out of his room just then. "Well, if it isn't old Weakmuscles Fuller! Weighs absolutely nothing and is still so weak he can't push himself around."

"Come on, though, Morey—give me a hand—I got you off dead center." Fuller flailed his hand helplessly.

"Use your brains, if you have any," said Morey, "and see what you can do. Come on, Wade—we're going."

Since they were going to use the space control, they would remain in free fall, and Fuller would remain helplessly suspended in mid-air.

The air of the ship suddenly seemed supercharged with energy as the space around them became gray; then the stars were all before them. The ship was moving forward again.

"Well, old pals," said Fuller, "at least I have traffic blocked fairly well if I feel like it, so eventually you'd have to help me. However—" He floundered clumsily as he removed one of his foam-rubber space-boots. "—my brains tell me that action is equal and opposite to reaction!" And he threw the boot with all possible velocity toward Morey!

The reaction of the motion brought him slowly but surely to a handhold in the wall.

In the meantime, the flying boot caught Morey in the chest with a pronounced *smack!* as he struggled vainly to avoid it. Handicapped by the lack of friction, his arms were not quite powerful enough to move his mass as quickly as his legs might have done, for his inertia was as great as ever, so he didn't succeed in ducking.

"Round one!" called Arcot, laughing. "Won by Kid Fuller on a TKO! It appears he has brains and knows how to use them!"

"You win," laughed Morey. "I concede the battle!"

Arcot had cut off the space-strain drive by the time Fuller reached the control room, and the men set about making more observations. They took additional photographs and turned on the drive again.

Time passed monotonously after they had examined a few stars. There was little difference; each was but a scene of flaming matter. There was little interest in this work, and, as Fuller remarked, this was supposed to be a trip of exploration, not observation. They weren't astronomers; they were on a vacation. Why all the hard work? They couldn't do as good a job as an experienced astronomer, so they decided to limit their observations to those necessary to retrace their path to Earth.

"But we want to investigate for planets to land on, don't we?" asked Morey.

"Sure," agreed Fuller. "But do we have to hunt at random for them? Can't we look for stars like our own sun? Won't they be more apt to have planets like Sol's?"

"It's an idea," replied Morey.

"Well, why not try it then?" Fuller continued logically. "Let's pick out a G-O type sun and head for it."

They were now well out toward the edge of the Galaxy, some thirty thousand light years from home. Since they had originally headed out along the narrow diameter of the lens-shaped mass of stars that forms our Island Universe, they would reach the edge soon.

"We won't have much chance of finding a G-O this far out," Arcot pointed out. "We're about out of stars. We've left most of the Galaxy behind us."

"Then let's go on to another of the galactic nebulae," said Morey, looking out into the almost unbroken night of intergalactic space. Only here and there could they see a star, separated from its nearest neighbor by thousands of light years of empty space.

"You know," said Wade slowly, "I've been wondering about the progress along scientific lines that a race out here might make. I mean, suppose that one of those lonely stars had planets, and suppose intelligent life evolved on one of those planets. I think their progress would be much slower."

"I see what you mean," Arcot said. "To us, of Earth, the stars are gigantic furnaces a few light years away. They're titanic test tubes of nature, with automatic reading devices attached, hung in the sky for us to watch. We have learned more about space from the stars than all the experiments of the physicists of Earth ever secured for us. It was in the atoms of the suns that we first counted the rate of revolutions of the electrons about their nuclei."

"Couldn't they have watched their own sun?" Fuller asked.

"Sure, but what could they compare it with? They couldn't

see a white dwarf from here. They couldn't measure the paralax to the nearest star, so they would have no idea of stellar distances. They wouldn't know how bright S Doradus was. Or how dim Van Maanen's star was."

"Then," Fuller said speculatively, "they'd have to wait until one of their scientists invented the telectroscope."

Arcot shook his head. "Without a knowledge of nuclear physics, the invention of the telectroscope is impossible. The lack of opportunity to watch the stars that might teach them something would delay their knowledge of atomic structure. They might learn a great deal about chemistry and Newtonian physics, and go quite a ways with math, but even there they would be handicapped. Morey, for instance, would never have developed the autointegral calculus, to say nothing of tensor and spinor calculus, which were developed two hundred years ago, without the knowledge of the problems of space to develop the need. I'm afraid such a race would be quite a bit behind us in science.

"Suppose, on the other hand, we visit a race that's far ahead of us. We'd better not stay there long; think what they might do to us. They might decide our ship was too threatening and simply wipe us out. Or they might even be so far advanced that we would mean nothing to them at all—like ants or little squalling babies." Arcot laughed at the thought.

"That isn't a very complimentary picture," objected Fuller. "With the wonderful advances we've made, there just isn't that much left to be able to say we're so little."

"Fuller, I'm surprised at you!" Arcot said. "Today, we are only opening our eyes on the world of science. Our race has only a few thousand years behind it and hundreds of millions yet to come. How can any man of today, with his freshly-opened eyes of science, take in the mighty pyramid of knowledge that will be built up in those long, long years of the future? It's too gigantic to grasp; we can't imagine the things that the ever-expanding mind of man will discover."

Arcot's voice slowed, and a far-off look came in his eyes.

"You might say there can be no greater energy than that of matter annihilation. I doubt that. I have seen hints of something new—an energy so vast—so transcendently tremendous—that it frightens me. The energies of all the mighty suns

of all the galaxies—of the whole cosmos—in the hand of man!
The energy of a billion billion billion suns! And every sun
pouring out its energy at the rate of quintillions of horsepower
every instant!

"But it's too great for man to have—I am going to forget it,
lest man be destroyed by his own might."

Arcot's halting speech told of his intense thought—of a dream
of such awful energies as man had never before conceived. His
eyes looked unseeing at the black velvet of space with its few,
scattered stars.

"But we're here to decide which way to go," he added with
a sudden briskness as he straightened his shoulders. "Every now
and then, I get a new idea and I—I sort of dream. That's when
I'm most likely to see the solution. I think I know the solution
now, but unless the need arises, I'm never going to use it. It's too
dangerous a toy."

There was silence for a moment, then Morey said, quietly:

"I've got a course plotted for us. We'll leave this Galaxy at a
steep angle—about forty-five degrees from the Galactic plane—
to give us a good view of our own Galaxy. And we can head for
one of the nebulae in that general area. What do you say?"

"I say," remarked Fuller, "that some of the great void without seems to have leaked into my own poor self. It's been thirty
thousand years since I am going to have a meal this morning
—whatever it is I mean—and I want another." He looked mean-
ingfully at Wade, the official cook of the expedition.

Arcot suddenly burst out laughing. "So that's what I've been
wanting!" It had been ten chronometer hours since they had
eaten, but since they had been outracing light, they were now
thirty thousand years in Earth's past.

The weightlessness of free fall makes it difficult to recognize
normally familiar sensations, and the feeling of hunger is one of
them. There was little enough work to be done, so there was no
great need for nourishment, but the ordinary sensation of hunger
is not caused by lack of nourishment, but an empty stomach.

Sleep was another problem. A restless body will not permit
a tired brain to sleep, and though they had done a great deal of
hard mental work, the lack of physical fatigue made sleep
difficult. The usual "day" in space was forty hours, with thirty-
hour waking periods and ten hours of sleep.

"Let's eat, then," Arcot decided. "Afterwards, we'll take a few photographs and then throw this ship into high and really make time."

Two hours later, they were again seated at the control board. Arcot reached out and threw the red switch. "I'm going to give her half power for ten seconds." The air about them seemed suddenly snapping with unprecedented power—then it was gone as the coil became fully charged.

"Lucky we shielded those relays," Arcot muttered. The tremendous surge of current set up a magnetic field that turned knives and forks and, as Wade found to his intense disgust, stopped watches that were not magnetically shielded.

Space was utterly black about them now; there wasn't the slightest hint of light. The ten seconds that Arcot had allowed dragged slowly. Then at last came the heavy crashing of the huge relays; the current flowed back into the storage coils, and space became normal again. They were alone in the blackness.

Morey dove swiftly for the observatory. Before them, there was little to see; the dim glow of nebulae millions of light years away was scarcely visible to the naked eye, despite the clarity of space.

Behind them, like a shining horizon, they saw the mass of the Galaxy for the first time as free observers.

Morey began to make swift calculations of the distance they had come by measuring the apparent change in diameter of the Galaxy.

Arcot floated into the room after him and watched as Morey made his observations and began to work swiftly with pencil and paper. "What do you make?" Arcot asked.

"Mmmmm. Let's see." Morey worked a moment with his slide rule. "We made good time! Twenty-nine light years in ten seconds! You had it on at half power—the velocity goes up as the cube of the power—doubling the power, then, gives us eight times the velocity—Hmmmmmm." He readjusted the slide rule and slid the hairline over a bit. "We can make ten million light years in a little less than five days at full power.

"But I suggest we make another stop in six hours. That will put us about five radii, or half a million light years from the

Galaxy. We'll need to take some more photographs to help us retrace our steps to Earth."

"All right, Morey," Arcot agreed. "It's up to you. Get your photos here and we'll go on. By the way, I think you ought to watch the instruments in the power room; this will be our first test at full power. We figured we'd make twenty light years per second, and it looks as if it's going to be closer to twenty-four."

A few minutes later, Arcot seated himself at the control board and flipped on the intercom to the power room. "All ready, Morey? I just happened to think—it might be a good idea to pick out our galaxy now and start toward it."

"Let's wait," cautioned Morey. "We can't make a very careful choice at this distance, anyway; we're beyond the enlarging power range of the telectroscope here. In another half million light years, we'll have a much better view, and that comparatively short distance won't take us much out of our way."

"Wait a minute," said Fuller. "You say we're beyond the magnification range of the telectroscope. Then why would half a million light years out of ten million make that much difference?"

"Because of the limit of amplification in the tubes," Arcot replied. "You can only have so many stages of amplification; after that, you're amplifying noise. The whole principle of the vacuum tube depends on electronic emission; if you get *too much* amplification, you can hear every single electron striking the plate of the first tube by the time the thing reaches the last amplifying stage! In other words, if your incoming signal is weaker than the minimum noise level on the first amplifying stage, no amount of amplification will give you anything but more noise.

"The same is true of the telectroscope image. At this distance, the light signal from those galaxies is weaker than the noise level. We'd only get a flickering, blurred image. But if we go on another half million light years, the light signal from the nearer nebulae will be *stronger* than the base noise level, and full amplification will give us a good image on the screen."

Fuller nodded. "Okay, then let's go that additional half million light years. I want to take a look at another galaxy."

"Right." Arcot turned to the intercom. "Ready, Morey?"

"Anytime you are."

"Here goes!" said Arcot. He pushed over the little red control.

At full power, the air filled with the strain of flowing energy and actually broke down in spots with the terrific electrical energy of the charge. There were little snapping sparks in the air, which, though harmless electrically, were hot enough to give slight burns, as Wade found to his sorrow.

"Yike! Say, why didn't you tell us to bring lightning rods?" he asked indignantly as a small spark snapped its way over his hand.

"Sorry," grinned Arcot, "but most people know enough to stay out of the way of those things. Seriously, though, I didn't think the electrostatic curvature would be so slow to adjust. You see, when we build up our light-rate distortion field, other curvatures are affected. We get some gravity, some magnetic, and some electrostatic field distortion, too. You can see what happens when they don't leak their energy back into the coil.

"But we're busy with the instruments; leave the motorman alone!"

Morey was calling loudly for tests. Although the ship seemed to be behaving perfectly, he wanted check tests to make sure the relays were not being burned, which would keep them from responding properly. By rerouting the current around each relay, Arcot checked them one by one.

It was just as they had finished testing the last one that Fuller yelled.

"Hey! *Look!*" He pointed out the broad viewport in the side of the ship.

Far off to their left and far to their right, they saw two shining ships paralleling their course. They were shining, sleek ships, their long, longitudinal windows glowing with white light. They seemed to be moving at exactly the same speed, holding grimly to the course of the *Ancient Mariner*. They bracketed the ship like an official guard, despite the terrific velocity of the Earthmen's ship.

Arcot stared in amazement, his face suddenly clouded in wonder. Morey, who had come up from the power room, stared in equal wonder.

Quickly, Wade and Fuller slid into the ray control seats. Their long practice with the rays had made them dead shots, and they had been chosen long before as the ship's official ray operators.

"Lord," muttered Morey as he looked at the ships, "where can they have come from?"

VII

Silently, the four men watched the two ships, waiting for any hostile movement. There was a long, tense moment, then something happened for which three of them were totally unprepared.

Arcot burst into sudden laughter.

"Don't—ho—hoh-ho—oh—don't shoot!" he cried, laughing so hard it was almost impossible to understand him. "Ohoh—space —curved!" he managed to gasp.

For a moment more, Morey looked puzzled—then he was laughing as hard as Arcot. Helplessly, Wade and Fuller looked at them, then at each other. Then, suddenly, Wade caught the meaning of Arcot's remark and joined the other two in laughter.

"All right," said Fuller, still mystified, "when you half-witted physicists recover, please let me in on the joke!" He knew it had something to do with the mysterious ships, so he looked closely at them in hopes that he would get the point, too. When he saw it, he blinked in amazement. "Hey! What is this? Those ships are exact duplicates of the *Ancient Mariner!*"

"That—that's what I was laughing at," Arcot explained, wiping his eyes. "Four big, brave explorers, scared of their own shadows!"

"The light from our own ship has come back to us, due to the intense curvature of the space which encloses us. In normal space, a light ray would take hundreds of millions of years to travel all the way around the Universe and return to its point of origin. Theoretically, it would be possible to photograph our own Galaxy as it was thousands of millennia ago by the light which left it then and has traveled all the way around the curvature of space.

"But our space has such terrific curvature that it only takes a fraction of a second for light to make the trip. It has gone all the way around our little cosmos and come back again.

"If we'd shot at it, we would have really done ourselves in! The ray beam would go around and hit us from behind!"

"Say, that is a nice proposition!" laughed Fuller. "Then we'll be accompanied by those ghosts all the way? There goes the spirit 'nine fathoms deep' which moves the ship—the ghosts that work the sails. This will be a real *Ancient Mariner* trip!"

It was like that famed voyage in another way, too. The men found little to do as they passed on at high speed through the vast realm of space. The chronometer pointed out the hours with exasperating slowness. The six hours that were to elapse before the first stop seemed as many days. They had thought of this trip as a wonderful adventure in itself, but the soundless continued monotony was depressing. They wandered around, aimlessly. Wade tried to sleep, but after lying strapped in his bunk for half an hour, he gave up in despair.

Arcot saw that the strain of doing nothing was not going to be good for his little crew and decided to see what could be done about it.

He went down to the laboratory and looked for inspiration. He found it.

"Hey! Morey! Wade! Fuller! Come on down here! I've got an idea!" he called.

They came to find him looking meditatively at the power pack from one of the flying suits he had designed. He had taken the lux metal case off and was looking at the neat apparatus that lay within.

"These are equipped for use with the space suits, of course," Morey pointed out, "and that gives us protection against gases. But I wonder if we might install protection against mechanical injury—with intent to damage aforethought! In other words, why not equip these suits with a small invisibility apparatus? We have it on the ship, but we might need personal protection, too."

"Great idea," said Wade, "provided you can find room in that case."

"I think we can. We won't need to add anything but a few tuning devices, really, and they don't take a whale of a lot of power."

Arcot pointed out the places where they could be put; also,

he replaced some of the old induction coils with one of his new storage cells and got far higher efficiency from the tubes.

But principally, it was something to do.

Indeed, it was so thoroughly something to do that the six hours had almost elapsed before they realized it. In a very short time, they returned again to the control room and strapped themselves in.

Arcot reached toward the little red switch that controlled the titanic energies of the huge coil below and pulled it back a quarter of the way.

"There go the ghosts!" he said. The images had quickly disappeared, seemingly leaping away from them at terrific speed as the space in which the ship was enclosed opened out more and more and the curvature decreased. They were further away from themselves!

Easing back a quarter at a time, to prevent sparks again flying about in the atmosphere of the ship, Arcot cut the power to zero, and the ship was standing still once more.

They hurriedly dived to the observatory and looked eagerly out the window.

Far, far behind them, floating in the marvelous, soft, utter blackness of space, was a shining disc made up of myriads of glowing points. And it didn't seem to be a huge thing at a great distance, but simply a small glowing object a few feet outside the window.

So perfectly clear was their view through the lux metal wall and the black, empty space that all sense of distance was lost. It seemed more a miniature model of their universe—a tiny thing that floated close behind them, unwavering, shining with a faint light, a heatless illumination that made everything in the darkened observatory glow very faintly. It was the light of three hundred million suns seen at a distance of three million million million miles! And it seemed small because there was nothing with which to compare it.

It was an amazingly beautiful thing, that tiny floating disc of light.

Morey floated over to the cameras and began to take pictures.

"I'd like to take a color shot of that," he said a few minutes later, "but that would require a direct shot through the reflector telescope and a time exposure. And I can't do that; the ship is moving."

"Not enough to make any difference," Arcot contradicted. "We're moving away from it in a straight line, and that thing is three quintillion miles away. We're not moving fast enough to cause any measurable contraction in a time exposure. As for having a steady platform, this ship weighs a quarter of a million tons and is held by gyroscopes. We won't shake it."

While Morey took the time exposure, Arcot looked at the enlarged image in the telectroscope and tried to make angular measurements from the individual stars. This he found impossible. Although he could spot Betelgeuse and Antares because of their tremendous radiation, they were too close together for measurements; the angle subtended was too small.

Finally, he decided to use the distance between Antares and S Doradus in the Lesser Magellanic Cloud, one of the two clouds of stars which float as satellites to the Galaxy itself.

To double-check, he used the radius of the Galaxy as base to calculate the distance. The distances checked. The ship was five hundred thousand light years from home!

After all the necessary observations were made, they swung the ship on its axis and looked ahead for a landing place.

The nebulae ahead were still invisible to the naked eye except as points, but the telectroscope finally revealed one as decidedly nearer than the rest. It seemed to be a young Island Universe, for there was still a vast cloud of gas and dust from which stars were yet to be born in the central whorl—a single titanic gas cloud that stretched out through a million billion miles of space.

"Shall we head for that?" asked Arcot at last, as Morey finished his observations.

"I think it would be as good as any—there are more stars there than we can hope to visit."

"Well, then, here we go!"

Arcot dived for the control room, while Morey shut off the telectroscope and put the latest photographs in the file.

Suddenly space was snapping about him—they were off again. Another shock of surging energy—another—the ship leaped forward at tremendous speed—still greater—then they were rushing at top speed, and beside them ran the ghost ships of the *Ancient Mariner*.

Morey pushed himself into the control room just as Arcot, Wade, and Fuller were getting ready to start for the lab.

"We're off for quite a while, now," he said. "Our goal is about five days away. I suggest we stop at the end of four days, make more accurate measurements, then plan a closer stop.

"I think from now on we ought to sleep in relays, so that there will be three of us awake at all times. I'll turn in now for ten hours, and then someone else can sleep. Okay?"

It was agreed, and in the meantime the three on duty went down to the lab to work.

Arcot had finished the installation of the invisibility apparatus in his suit at the end of ten hours, much to his disappointment. He tested it, then cast about for something to do while Wade and Morey added the finishing touches to theirs.

Morey came down, and when Wade had finished his, which took another quarter of an hour, he took the off duty shift.

Arcot had gone to the library, and Morey was at work down below. Fuller had come up, looking for something to do, and had hit upon the excellent idea of fixing a meal.

He had just begun his preparations in the kitchen when suddenly the *Ancient Mariner* gave a violent leap, and the men, not expecting any weight, suddenly fell in different ways with terrific force!

Fuller fell half the length of the galley and was knocked out by the blow. Wade, asleep in bed, was awakened violently by the shock, and Morey, who had been strapped in his chair, was badly shaken.

Everyone cried out simultaneously—and Arcot was on his way to the control room. The first shock was but a forerunner of the storm. Suddenly the ship was hurled violently about; the air was shot through with great burning sparks; the snapping hiss of electricity was everywhere, and every pointed metal object was throwing streamers of blue electric flame into the air! The ship rocked, heaved, and cavorted wildly, as though caught in the play of titanic forces!

Scrambling wildly along the handholds, Arcot made his way toward the control room, which was now above, now below, and now to one side of him as the wildly variable acceleration shook the ship. Doggedly, he worked his way up, frequently getting severe burns from the flaming sparks.

Below, in the power room, the relays were crashing in and out wildly.

Then, suddenly, a new sound was added just as Arcot pulled himself into the control chair and strapped himself down. The radiation detector buzzed out its screaming warning!

"COSMIC RAYS!" Arcot yelled. "HIGH CONCENTRATION!"

He slapped at the switch which shot the heavy relux screens across every window in the ship.

There was a sudden crash and a fuse went out below—a fuse made of a silver bar two feet thick! In an instant, the flames of the burning sparks flared up and died. The ship cavorted madly, shaking mightily in the titanic, cosmic forces that surrounded it—the forces that made the highest energy form in the universe!

Arcot knew that nothing could be done with the power coil. It was drained; the circuit was broken. He shifted in the molecular drive, pushing the acceleration to four gravities, as high as the men could stand.

And still the powerful ship was being tossed about, the plaything of inconceivable forces. They lived only because the forces did not try to turn the ship more violently, not because of the strength of the ship, for nothing could resist the awful power around them.

As a guide, Arcot used the compass gyroscope, the only one not twisted far out of its original position; with it, he managed to steer a fairly straight course.

Meanwhile, in the power room, Wade and Morey were working frantically to get the space-strain drive coil recharged. Despite the strength-sapping strain of working under four gravities of acceleration, they managed to get the auxiliary power unit into operation. In a few moments, they had it pouring its energies into the coil-bank so that they could charge up the central drive coil.

Another silver bar fuse was inserted, and Wade checked the relays to make sure they were in working order.

Fuller, who had regained consciousness, worked his way laboriously down to the power room carrying three spacesuits. He had stopped in the lab to get the power belts, and the three men quickly donned them to help them overcome the four-gravity pull.

Another half hour sped by as the bucking ship forced its way through the terrific field in space.

Suddenly they felt a terrific jolt again—then the ship was moving more smoothly, and gradually it was calm. They were through!

"Have we got power for the space-strain drive yet?" Arcot called through the intercom.

"Enough," Morey cried. "Try it!"

Arcot cut off the molecular motion drive, and threw in all the space-control power he had. The ship was suddenly supercharged with energy. It jarred suddenly—then was quiet. He allowed ten minutes to pass, then he cut off the drive and allowed the ship to go into free fall.

Morey's voice came over the intercom. "Arcot, things are really busted up down here! We had to haywire half the drive together."

"I'll be right down. Every instrument on the ship seems to be out of kilter!"

It was a good thing they had plenty of spare parts; some of the smaller relays had burned out completely, and several of the power leads had fused under the load that had been forced through them.

The space-strain drive had been leaking energy at a terrific rate; without further repair, it could not function much longer.

In the power room, Arcot surveyed the damage. "Well, boys, we'd better get to work. We're stranded here until we get that drive repaired!"

VIII

Forty hours later, Arcot was running the ship smoothly at top speed once again. The four men had gone to bed after more than thirty hours of hard work. That, coupled with the exhaustion of working under four gravities, as they had while the ship was going through the storm, was enough to make them sleep soundly.

Arcot had awakened before the others and had turned on the drive after resetting their course.

After that was done, there was little to do, and time began to hang heavily on Arcot's hands. He decided to make a thorough inspection of the hull when the others awoke. The terrific strain might have opened cracks in the lux metal hull that would not be detectable from the inside because the inner wall was separated from the outer envelope.

Accordingly, he got out the spacesuits, making sure the oxygen tanks were full and all was ready. Then he went into the library, got out some books, and set about some calculations he had in mind.

When Morey woke, some hours later, he found Arcot still at work on his calculations.

"Hey!" he said, swinging himself into the chair beside Arcot, "I thought you'd be on the lookout for more cosmic rays!"

"Curious delusion, wasn't it?" asked Arcot blandly. "As a matter of fact, I've been busy doing some figuring. I think our chance of meeting another such region is about one in a million million million million. Considering those chances, I don't think we need to worry. I don't see how we ever met one— but the chances of hitting one are better than hitting two."

Just then Fuller stuck his head in the door.

"Oh," he said, "so you're at it already? Well, I wonder if one of you could tell me just what it was we hit? I've been so busy I haven't had a chance to think."

"Don't take the chance now, then," grinned Morey. "You might strain your brain."

"*Please!*" Fuller pleaded, wincing. "Not before breakfast. Just explain what that storm was."

"We simply came to a region in space where cosmic rays are created," explained Arcot.

Fuller frowned. "But there's nothing out here to generate cosmic rays!"

Arcot nodded. "True. I think I know their real source, but I believe I'll merely say they are created here. I want to do more work on this. My idea for an energy source greater than any other in the universe has been confirmed.

"At any rate, they are created in that space, a perfect vacuum, and the space there is distorted terrifically by the titanic forces at work. It is bent and twisted far out of the normal, even curvature, and it was that bumpy spot in space that threw us about so.

"When we first entered, using the space-strain drive, the space around the ship, distorted as it was, conflicted with the region of the cosmic ray generation and the ship lost out. The curvature of space that the ship caused was sometimes reinforced and sometimes canceled out by the twisted space around it, and the tremendous surges of current back and forth from the main power coil to the storage coils caused the electric discharges that kept burning through the air. I notice we all got a few burns from that. The field was caused by the terrific surges of current, and that magnetic field caused the walls of the ship to heat up due to the generation of electric current in the walls."

Fuller looked around at the walls of the ship. "Well, the *Ancient Mariner* sure took a beating."

"As a matter of fact, I was worried about that," said Arcot. "Strong as that hull is, it might easily have been strained in that field of terrific force. If it happened to hit two 'space waves' at once, it might have given it an acceleration in two different directions at once, which would strain the walls with a force amounting to thousands of tons. I laid out the suits up front, and I think we might reasonably get there and take a look at the old boat. When Wade gets up—well, well—speak of the devil! My, doesn't he look energetic?"

Wade's huge body was floating in through the library door. He was yawning sleepily and rubbing his eyes. It was evident he had not yet washed, and his growing beard, which was heavy and black on his cheeks, testified to his need for a shave. The others had shaved before coming into the library.

"Wade," said Arcot, "we're going outside, and we have to have someone in here to operate the airlock. Suppose you get to work on the hirsute adornment; there's an atomic hydrogen cutting torch down in the lab you can use, if you wish. The rest of us are going outside." Then Arcot's voice became serious. "By the way, don't try any little jokes like starting off with a little acceleration. I don't think you would—you've got good sense —but I like to make certain. If you did, we'd be left behind, and you'd never find us in the vast immensity of intergalactic space."

It wasn't a pleasant idea to contemplate. Each of the suits had a radio for communication with each other and with the ship, but they would only carry a few hundred miles. A mere step in space!

Wade shook his head, grinning. "I have no desire to be left all by myself on this ship, thank you. You don't need to worry."

A few minutes later, Arcot, Morey, and Fuller stepped out of the airlock and set to work, using power flashlights to examine the outer hull for any signs of possible strain.

The flashlights, equipped as they were with storage coils for power, were actually powerful searchlights, but in the air-lessness of space the rays were absolutely invisible. They could only be seen when they hit the relux inner wall at such an angle that they were reflected directly into the observer's eyes. The lux metal wall, being transparent, was naturally invisible, and the smooth relux, reflecting one hundred percent of the incident light, did not become illuminated, for illumination is the result of the scattering of light.

It was necessary to look closely and pass the beams over every square inch of the surface. However, a crack would be rough, and hence would scatter light and be even more readily visible than otherwise.

To their great relief, after an hour and a half of careful inspection, none of them had found any signs of a crack, and they went back into the ship to resume the voyage.

Again they hurled through space, the twin ghost ships following them closely. Hour after hour the ship went on. Now they had something else to do. They were at work calculating some problems that Arcot had suggested in connection with the velocities of motion that had been observed in the stars at the edge of the island universe they were approaching. Since these stars revolved about the mass of the entire galaxy, it was possible to calculate the mass of the entire universe by averaging the values from several stars. Their results were not exact, but they were reliable enough. They found the universe to have a mass of two hundred and fifty million suns, only a little less than the home Galaxy. It was an average-sized nebula.

Still the hours dragged as they came gradually nearer their goal—gradually, despite their speed of twenty-four light years per second!

At the end of the second day after their trouble with the cosmic ray field, they stopped for observation. They were now so near the Island Universe that the stars spread out in a huge disc ahead of them.

"About three hundred thousand light years distant, I should guess," said Morey.

"We know our velocity fairly accurately," said Wade. "Why can't we calculate the distance between two of these stars and then go on in?"

"Good idea," agreed Arcot. "Take the angle, will you, Morey? I'll swing the ship."

After taking their measurements, they advanced for one hour. Knowing this distance from experience, they were able to calculate the diameter of this galaxy. It turned out to be on the order of ninety thousand light years.

They were now much closer; they seemed, indeed, on the very edge of the giant universe. The thousands of stars flamed bright below them, stretching across their horizon more and more—a galaxy the eyes of men had never before seen at such close range! This galaxy had not yet condensed entirely to stars, and in its heart there still remained the vast gas cloud that would eventually be stars and planets. The vast misty cloud was plainly visible, glowing with a milky light like some vast frosted light bulb.

It was impossible to conceive the size of the thing; it looked only like some model, for they were still over a quarter of a million light years from it.

Morey looked up from his calculations. "I think we should be there in about three hours. Suppose we go at full speed for about two hours and then change to low speed?"

"You're the astronomical boss, Morey," said Arcot. "Let's go!"

They swung the ship about once more and started again. As they drew nearer to this new universe, they began to feel more interest in the trip. Things were beginning to happen!

The ship plunged ahead at full speed for two hours. They could see nothing at that velocity except the two ghost ships that were their ever-present companions. Then they stopped once more.

About them, they saw great suns shining. One was so close they could see it as a disc with the naked eye. But they could not see clearly; the entire sky was misty and the stars that were not close were blotted out. The room seemed to grow warm.

"Hey! Your calculations were off!" called Arcot. "We're getting out of here!"

Suddenly the air snapped and they were traveling at low speed under the drive of the space-strain apparatus. The entire space about them was lit with a dim violet glow. In ten minutes, the glow was gone and Arcot cut the drive.

They were out in ordinary dark space, with its star-studded blackness.

"What was the matter with my calculations?" Morey wanted to know.

"Oh, nothing much," Arcot said casually. "You were only about thirty thousand light years off. We landed right in the middle of the central gas cloud, and we were plowing through it at a relative velocity of around sixteen thousand miles per second! No wonder we got hot!

"We're lucky we didn't come near any stars in the process; if we had, we would have had to recharge the coil."

"It's a wonder we didn't burn up at that velocity," said Fuller.

"The gas wasn't dense enough," Arcot explained. "That gas is a better vacuum that the best pump could give you on Earth; there are fewer molecules per cubic inch than there are in a radio tube.

"But now that we're out of that, let's see if we can find a planet. No need to take photographs going in; if we want to find the star again, we can take photos as we leave. If we don't want to find it, we would just waste film.

"I'll leave it to Morey to find the star we want."

Morey set to work at once with the telescope, trying to find the nearest star of spectral type G-O, as had been agreed upon. He also wanted to find one of the same magnitude, or brilliance. At last, after investigating several such suns, he discovered one which seemed to fulfill all his wishes. The ship was turned, and they started toward the adventure they had really hoped to find.

As they rushed through space, the distorted stars shining vividly before them, they saw the one which was their goal. A bright, slowly changing violet point on the crosshairs of the aiming telescope.

"How far is it?" asked Arcot.

"About thirty light centuries," replied Morey, watching the star eagerly.

They drove on in silence. Then, suddenly, Morey cried out: "Look! It's gone!"

"What happened?" asked Arcot in surprise.

Morey rubbed his chin in thought. "The star suddenly flared brightly for an instant, then disappeared. Evidently, it was a G-O giant which had burned up most of the hydrogen that stars normally use for fuel. When that happens, a star begins to collapse, increasing in brilliance due to the heat generated by the gas falling toward the center of the star.

"Then other nuclear reactions begin to take place, and, due to the increased transparency of the star, a supernova is produced. The star blows away most of its gaseous envelope, leaving only the superdense core. In other words, it leaves a white dwarf." He paused and looked at Arcot. "I wonder if that star did have any planets?"

They all knew what he meant. What was the probable fate of beings whose sun had suddenly collapsed to a tiny, relatively cold point in the sky?

Suddenly, there loomed before them the dim bulk of the star, a disc already, and Arcot snapped the ship over to the molecular motion drive at once. He knew they must be close. Before them was the angry disc of the flaming white star.

Arcot swung the ship a bit to one side, running in close to the flaming star. It was not exceedingly hot, despite the high temperature and intense radiation, for the radiating surface was too small.

They swung about the star in a parabolic orbit, for, at their velocity, the sun could not hold them in a planetary orbit.

"Our velocity, relative to this star, is pretty high," Arcot announced. "I'm swinging in close so that I can use the star's attraction as a brake. At this distance, it will be about six gravities, and we can add to that a molecular drive braking of four gravities.

"Suppose you look around and see if there are any planets. We can break free and head for another star if there aren't."

Even at ten gravities of deceleration, it took several hours to reduce their speed to a point which would make it possible to head for any planet of the tiny sun.

Morey went to the observatory and swept the sky with the telectroscope.

It was difficult to find planets because the reflected light from the weak star was so dim, but he finally found one. He took angular readings on it and on the central sun. A little later, he took more readings. Because of the changing velocity of the ship, the readings were not too accurate, but his calculations showed it to be several hundred million miles out.

They were decelerating rapidly, and soon their momentum had been reduced to less than four miles a second. When they reached the planet, Arcot threw the ship into an orbit around it and began to spiral down.

Through the clear lux windows of the control room, the men looked down upon a bleak, frozen world.

IX

Below the ship lay the unfamiliar panorama of an unknown world that circled, frozen, around a dim, unknown sun, far out in space. Cold and bleak, the low, rolling hills below were black, bare rock, coated in spots with a white sheen of what appeared to be snow, though each of the men realized it must be frozen air. Here and there ran strange rivers of deep blue which poured into great lakes and seas of blue liquid. There were mighty mountains of deep blue crystal looming high, and in the hollows and cracks of these crystal mountains lay silent, motionless seas of deep blue, unruffled by any breeze in this airless world. It was a world that lay frozen under a dim, dead sun.

They continued over the broad sweep of the level, crystalline plain as the bleak rock disappeared behind them. This world was about ten thousand miles in diameter, and its surface gravity about a quarter greater than that of Earth.

On and on they swept, swinging over the planet at an altitude of less than a thousand feet, viewing the unutterably desolate scene of the cold, dead world.

Then, ahead of them loomed a bleak, dark mass of rock again. They had crossed the frozen ocean and were coming to land again—a land no more solid than the sea.

Everywhere lay the deep drifts of snow, and here and there, through valleys, ran the streams of bright blue.

"Look!" cried Morey in sudden suprise. Far ahead and to their left loomed a strange formation of jutting vertical columns, covered with the white burden of snow. Arcot turned a powerful searchlight on it, and it stood out brightly against the vast snowfield. It was a dead, frozen city.

As they looked at it, Arcot turned the ship and headed for it without a word.

It was hard to realize the enormity of the catastrophe that had brought a cold, bleak death to the population of this world— death to an intelligent race.

Arcot finally spoke. "I'll land the ship. I think it will be safe for us all to leave. Get out the suits and make sure all the tanks are charged and the heaters working. It will be colder here than in space. Out there, we were only cooled by radiation, but those streams are probably liquid nitrogen, oxygen, and argon, and there's a slight atmosphere of hydrogen, helium and neon cooled to about fifty degrees Absolute. We'll be cooled by conduction and convection."

As the others got the suits ready, he lowered the ship gently to the snowy ground. It sank into nearly ten feet of snow. He turned on the powerful searchlight and swept it around the ship. Under the warm beams, the frozen gases evaporated, and in a few moments he had cleared the area around the ship.

Morey and the others came back with their suits. Arcot donned his, and adjusted his weight to ten pounds with the molecular power unit.

A short time later, they stepped out of the airlock onto the ice field of the frozen world. High above them glowed the dim, blue-white disc of the tiny sun, looking like little more than a bright star.

Adjusting the controls on the suits, the four men lifted into the tenuous air and headed toward the city, moving easily about ten feet above the frozen wastes of the snow field.

"The thing I don't understand," Morey said as they shot toward the city, "is why this planet is here at all. The intense radiation from the sun when it went supernova should have vaporized it!"

Arcot pointed toward a tall, oddly-shaped antenna that rose

from the highest building of the city. "There's your answer. That antenna is similar to those we found on the planets of the Black Star; it's a heat screen. They probably had such antennas all over the planet.

"Unfortunately, the screen's efficiency goes up as the fourth power of the temperature. It could keep out the terrific heat of a supernova, but couldn't keep in the heat of the planet after the supernova had died. The planet was too cool to make the screen work efficiently!"

At last they came to the outskirts of the dead city. The vertical walls of the buildings were free of snow, and they could see the blank, staring eyes of the windows, and within, the bleak, empty rooms. They swept on through the frozen streets until they came to one huge building in the center. The doors of bronze had been closed, and through the windows they could see that the room had been piled high with some sort of insulating material, evidently used as a last-ditch attempt to keep out the freezing cold.

"Shall we break in?" asked Arcot.

"We may as well," Morey's voice answered over the radio. "There may be some records we could take back to Earth and have deciphered. In a time like this, I imagine they would leave some records, hoping that some race *might* come and find them."

They worked with molecular ray pistols for fifteen minutes tearing a way through. It was slow work because they had to use the heat ray pistols to supply the necessary energy for the molecular motion.

When they finally broke through, they found they had entered on the second floor; the deep snow had buried the first. Before them stretched a long, richly decorated hall, painted with great colored murals.

The paintings displayed a people dressed in a suit of some soft, white cloth, with blond hair that reached to their shoulders. They were shorter and more heavily built than Earthmen, perhaps, but there was a grace to them that denied the greater gravity of their planet. The murals portrayed a world of warm sunlight, green plants, and tall trees waving in a breeze—a breeze of air that now lay frozen on the stone floors of their buildings.

Scene after scene they saw—then they came to a great hall. Here they saw hundreds of bodies; people wrapped in heavy cloth blankets. And over the floor of the room lay little crystals of green.

Wade looked at the little crystals for a long time, and then at the people who lay there, perfectly preserved by the utter cold. They seemed only sleeping—men, women, and children, sleeping under a blanket of soft snow that evaporated and disappeared as the energy of the lights fell on it.

There was one little group the men looked at before they left the room of death. There were three in it—a young man, a fair, blonde young woman who seemed scarcely more than a girl, and between them, a little child. They were sleeping, arms about each other, warm in the arms of Death, the kindly Reliever of Pain.

Arcot turned and rose, flying swiftly down the long corridor toward the door.

"That was not meant for us," he said. "Let's leave."

The others followed.

"But let's see what records they left," he went on. "It may be that they wanted us to know their tragic story. Let's see what sort of civilization they had."

"Their chemistry was good, at least," said Wade. "Did you notice those green crystals? A quick, painless poison gas to relieve them of the struggle against the cold."

They went down to the first floor level, where there was a single great court. There was no pillars, only a vast, smooth floor.

"They had good architecture," said Morey. "No pillars under all the vast load of that building."

"And the load is even greater under this gravity," remarked Arcot.

In the center of the room was a great, golden bronze globe resting on a platform of marble. It must have been new when this world froze, for there was no sign of corrosion or oxidation. The men flew over to it and stood beside it, looking at the great sphere, nearly fifteen feet in diameter.

"A globe of their world," said Fuller, looking at it with interest.

"Yes," agreed Arcot, "and it was set up after they were sure the cold would come, from the looks of it. Let's take a look at it." He flew up to the top of it and viewed it from above. The whole globe was a carefully chiseled relief map, showing seas, mountains, and continents.

"Arcot—come here a minute," called Morey. Arcot dropped down to where Morey was looking at the globe. On the edge of one of the continents was a small raised globe, and around the globe, a circle had been etched.

"I think this is meant to represent this globe," Morey said. "I'm almost certain it represents this very spot. Now look over here." He pointed to a spot which, according to the scale of the globe, was about five thousand miles away. Projecting from the surface of the bronze globe was a little silver tower.

"They want us to go there," continued Morey. "This was erected only shortly before the catastrophe; they must have put relics there that they want us to get. They must have guessed that eventually intelligent beings would cross space; I imagine they have other maps like this in every large city.

"I think it's our duty to visit that cairn."

"I quite agree," assented Arcot. "The chance of other men visiting this world is infinitely small."

"Then let's leave this City of the Dead!" said Wade.

It gave them a sense of depression greater than that inspired by the vast loneliness of space. One is never so lonely as when he is with the dead, and the men began to realize that the original *Ancient Mariner* had been more lonely with strange companions than they had been in the depths of ten million light years of space.

They went back to the ship, floating through the last remnants of this world's atmosphere, back through the chill of the frozen gases to the cheering, warm interior of the ship.

It was a contrast that made each of them appreciate more fully the gift that a hot, blazing sun really is. Perhaps that was what made Fuller ask: "If this happened to a star so much like our sun, why couldn't it happen to Sol?"

"Perhaps it may," said Morey softly. "But the eternal optimism of man keeps us saying: 'It can't happen here.' And besides—" He put a hand on the wall of the ship. "—we don't ever have to worry about anything like that now. Not with ships like this to take us to a new sun—a new planet."

Arcot lifted the ship and flew over the cold, frozen ground beneath them, following the route indicated on the great globe in the dead city. Mile after mile of frozen ice fields flew by as they shot over it at three miles per second.

Suddenly, the bleak bulk of a huge mountain loomed gigantic before them. Arcot reversed the power and brought the ship to a stop. With the powerful searchlight, he swept the area, looking for the tower he knew should be here. At last, he made it out, a pyramid rather than a tower, and coated over with ice. They soon thawed out the frozen gases by playing the energy of three powerful searchlights upon them, and in a few minutes the glint of gold showed through the melting ice and snow.

"It looks," said Wade, "as though they have an outer wall of gold over a strong wall of iron or steel to protect it from corrosion. Certainly gold doesn't have enough tensile strength to hold itself up under this gravity—not in such masses as that."

Arcot brought the ship down beside the tower and the men once more went out through the airlock into the cold of the almost airless world. They flew across to the pyramid and looked for some means of entrance. In several places, they noticed hieroglyphics carved in great, foot-high characters. They searched in vain for a door until they noticed that the pyramid was not perfect, but truncated, leaving a flat area on top. The only joint in the walls seemed to be there, but there was no handle or visible methods of opening the door.

Arcot turned his powerful light on the surface and searched carefully for some opening device. He found a bas-relief engraving of a hand pointing to a corner of the door. He looked more closely and found a small jewel-like lens set in the metal.

Suddenly the men felt a vibration! There was a heavy click, and the door panel began to drop slowly.

"Get on it!" Arcot cried. "We can always break our way out if we're trapped!"

The four men leaped on it and sank slowly with it. The massive walls of the tower were nearly five feet thick, and made of some tough, white metal.

"Pure iron!" diagnosed Wade. "Or perhaps a silicon-iron alloy. Not as strong as steel, but very resistant to corrosion."

When the elevator stopped, they found themselves in a great chamber that was obviously a museum of the lost race. All around the walls were arranged models, books, and diagrams.

"We can never hope to take all this in our ship!" said Arcot, looking at the great collection. "Look—there's an old winged airplane! And a steam engine—and that's an electric motor! And that thing looks like some kind of an electric battery."

"But we can't take all that stuff," objected Fuller.

"No," Morey agreed. "I think our best bet would be to take all the books we can—making sure we get the introductory ones, so we can read the language.

"See—over there—they have marked those shelves with a single vertical mark. The ones next to them have two vertical marks, and next ones three. I suggest we load up with those books and take them to the ship."

The rest agreed, and they began carrying armloads of books, flying out through the top of the pyramid to the ship and back for more.

Instead of flying back to the pyramid for the last load, Arcot announced that he was going to leave a note for anyone who might come here later. While the others went back for the last load, he worked at drawing the "note".

"Let's see your masterpiece," said Morey as the three men returned to the ship with the last of the books.

Arcot had used a piece of tough, heavy plastic which would resist any corrosion the cold, almost airless world might have to offer.

Near the top, he had drawn a representation of their ship, and beneath it a representation of the route they had taken from universe to universe. The galaxy they were in was represented by a cloud of gas, its main identifying feature. Underneath the dotted line of their route through space, he had printed "200,000,000,000, u".

Then followed a little table. The numeral "1" followed by a straight bar, then "2" followed by two bars, and so on up to ten. Ten was represented by ten bars and, in addition, an S-shaped sign. Twenty was next, followed by twenty bars and two S-shaped signs. Thus he had worked up to "100".

The system he used would make it clear to any reasoning creature that he had used a decimal system and that the zeroes meant ten times.

Next below, he had drawn the planetary system of the frozen world, and the distance from the planet they were on to the central sun he labeled "u". Thus, the finders could reason that they had come a distance of two hundred billion units, where a distance of three hundred million miles was taken as the unit; they had, then, come from another galaxy. Certainly any creature with enough intelligence to reach this frozen world would understand this!

"Since the year of this planet is approximately eight times our own," Arcot continued, "I am indicating that we came here approximately five hundred years after the catastrophe." He pointed at several of the other drawings.

They left the message in the tower, and Arcot closed the door, leaving the pyramid exactly as it had been before they had come.

"Say!" Morey commented, "how did you open and close that door, anyway?"

Arcot grinned. "Didn't you notice the jewel at the corner? It was the lens of a photoelectric cell. My flashlight opened the door. I didn't figure it out; it just worked accidentally."

Morey raised an eyebrow. "But if the darned thing is so simple, any creature, intelligent or not, might be able to get in and destroy the records!"

Arcot looked at him. "And where are your savages going to come from? There are none on this planet, and anyone intelligent enough to build a spaceship isn't going to destroy the contents of the tower."

"Oh." Morey looked a little sheepish.

They went into the airlock and took off their suits. Then they began packing the precious books in specimen cases that had been brought for the purpose of preserving such things.

When the last of them was carefully stowed, they returned to the control room. They looked silently out across this strange, dead world, thinking how much it must have been like Earth. It was dead now, and frozen forever. The low hills that stretched out beneath them were dimly lighted by the weak rays of a shrunken sun. Three hundred million miles away, it glowed so weakly that this world received only a little more heat than it might have received from a small coal fire a mile away.

So weakly it flared that in this thin atmosphere of hydrogen and helium, its little corona glowed about it plainly, and even the stars around it shone brilliantly. The men could see one constellation that grouped itself in the outlines of a dragon, with the sun of this system as its cold, baleful eye.

Gradually, Arcot lifted the ship, and, as they headed out into space, they could see the dim frozen plains fall behind. It was as if a load of oppressing loneliness parted from them as they flew out into the vast spaces of the eternal stars.

X

Arcot looked speculatively at the star field in the great broad window before him. "We'll want to find another G-O sun, naturally, but I don't think we ought to go directly from here. If we did, we'd have to do a lot of backtracking to get back to this dead star. I suggest we go back to the edge of this galaxy, taking pictures on the way out, so that any future investigators can come in directly. It'll only take a few hours."

"I think you're right," agreed Morey. "Besides, that will give us a wider choice of stars to pick our next G-O from. Let's get going."

Arcot moved the red switch, and the ship shot away at half speed. They watched the green image of the white dwarf fade and then suddenly flare up and become bright again as they outraced the light that had left it five centuries before.

They stopped and took more photographs so that the path could be marked. They stopped every light century until they reached a point where the star was merely a dim point, almost lost in the myriad of stars around it.

Then out to the edge of the galaxy they went, out toward their own universe.

"Arcot," Morey called, "let's go out, say one million light years into space, at an angle to this galaxy, and see if we can get both galaxies on one plate. It will make navigation between them easier."

"Good idea. We can get out and back in one day—and this 'time' won't count back on Earth, anyway." Since they would travel in the space-strain all the time, it would not count as Earth time.

Arcot pushed the red control all the way forward, and the ship began to move at its top velocity of twenty-four light years per second. The hours dragged heavily, as they had when they were coming in, and Arcot remained alone on watch while the others went to their rooms for some sleep, strapping their weightless bodies securely in the bunks.

It was hours later when Morey awoke with a sudden premonition of trouble. He looked at the chronometer on the wall—he had slept twelve hours! They had gone beyond the million light year mark! It didn't matter, except it showed that something had happened to Arcot.

Something had. Arcot was sound asleep in the middle of the library—exactly in the middle, floating in the room ten feet from each wall.

Morey called out to him, and Arcot awoke with a guilty start. "A fine sentry you make," said Morey caustically. "Can't even keep awake when all you have to do is sit here and see that we don't run into anything. We've gone more than our million light years already, and we're still going strong. Come on—snap out of it!"

"I'm sorry—I apologize—I know I shouldn't have slept, but it was so perfectly quiet here except for your deep-toned, musical snores that I couldn't help it," grinned Arcot. "Get me down from here and we'll stop."

"Get you down, nothing!" Morey snapped. "You stay right there while I call the others and we decide what's to be done with a sleeping sentry."

Morey turned and left to wake the others.

He had awakened Wade and told him what had happened, and they were on their way to wake up Fuller, when suddenly the air of the ship crackled around them! The space was changing! They were coming out of hyperspace!

In amazement, Morey and Wade looked at each other. They knew that Arcot was still floating helplessly in the middle of the room, but—

"Hold on, you brainless apes! We're turning around!" came Arcot's voice, full of suppressed mirth.

Suddenly they were both plastered against the wall of the ship under four gravities of acceleration! Unable to walk, they could only crawl laboriously toward the control room, calling to Arcot to shut off the power.

When Morey had left him stranded in the library, Arcot had decided it was high time he got to the floor. Quickly, he looked around for a means of doing so. Near him, floating in the air, was the book he had been reading, but it was out of reach. He had taken off his boots when he started to read, so the Fuller rocket method was out. It seemed hopeless.

Then, suddenly, came the inspiration! Quickly, he slipped off his shirt and began waving it violently in the air. He developed a velocity of about two inches a second—not very fast, but fast enough. By the time he had put his shirt back on, he had reached the wall.

After that, it was easy to shoot himself over to the door, out into the corridor and into the control room without being seen by Morey, who was in Wade's room.

Just as Wade and Morey reached the doorway to the control room, Arcot decided it was time to shut the power off. Both of the men, laboring under more than eight hundred pounds of weight, were suddenly weightless. All the strength of their powerful muscles were expended in hurling them against the far wall.

The complaints were loud, but they finally simmered down to an earnest demand to know how in the devil Arcot had managed to get off dead center.

"Why, that was easy," he said airily. "I just turned on a little power; I fell under the influence of the weight and then it was easy to get to the control room."

"Come on," Wade demanded. "The truth! How did you get here?"

"Why, I just pushed myself here."

"Yes; no doubt. But how did you get hold of anything to push?"

"I just took a handful of air and threw it away and reached the wall."

"Oh, of course—and how did you hold the air?"

"I just took some air and threw it away and reached the wall."

Which was all they could learn. Arcot was going to keep his system secret, it seemed.

"At any rate," Arcot continued, "I am back in the control room, where I belong, and you are not in the observatory where you belong. Now get out of my territory!"

Morey pushed himself back to the observatory, and after a

few minutes, his voice came over the intercom. "Let's move on a bit more, Arcot. We still can't get both galaxies on the same plate. Let's go on for another hour and take our pictures from that point."

Fuller had awakened and come in in the meantime, and he wanted to know why they didn't take some pictures from this spot.

"No point in it," said Morey. "We have the ones we took coming in; what we want is a wide-angle shot."

Arcot threw on the space-strain drive once more, and they headed on at top speed.

They were all in the control room, watching the instruments and joking—principally the latter—when it happened. One instant they were moving smoothly, weightlessly along. The next instant, the ship rocked as though it had been struck violently! The air was a snapping inferno of shooting sparks, and there came the sharp crash of the suddenly volatilized silver bar that was their main power fuse. Simultaneously, they were hurled forward with terrific force; the straps that held them in place creaked with the sudden strain, and the men felt weak and faint.

Consciousness nearly left them; they had been burned in a dozen places by the leaping sparks.

Then it was over. Except that the ghost ships no longer followed them, the *Ancient Mariner* seemed unchanged. Around them, they could see the dim glowing of the galaxies.

"Brother! We came near something!" Arcot cried. "It may be a wandering star! Take a look around, quick!"

But the dark of space seemed utterly empty around them as they coasted weightless through space. Then Arcot snapped off the lights of the control room, and in a moment his eyes had become accustomed to the dim lights.

It was dead ahead of them. It was a dull red glow, so dim it was scarcely visible. Arcot realized it was a dead star.

"There it is, Morey!" he said. "A dead star, directly ahead of us! Good God, how close are we?"

They were falling straight toward the dim red bulk.

"How far are we from it?" Fuller asked.

"At least several million—" Morey began. Then he looked at

the distance recorded on the meteor detector. "ARCOT! FOR
HEAVEN'S SAKE DO SOMETHING! THAT THING IS
ONLY A FEW HUNDRED MILES AWAY!"

"There's only one thing to do," Arcot said tightly. "We can
never hope to avoid that thing; we haven't got the power. I'm
going to try for an orbit around it. We'll fall toward it and give
the ship all the acceleration she'll take. There's no time to
calculate—I'll just pile on the speed until we don't fall into it."

The others, strapped into the control chairs, prepared themselves for the acceleration to come.

If the *Ancient Mariner* had dropped toward the star from an
infinite distance, Arcot could have applied enough power to put
the ship in a hyperbolic orbit which would have carried them
past the star. But they had come in on the space drive, and had
gotten fairly close before the gravitational field had drained the
power from the main coil, and it was not until the space field
had broken that they had started to accelerate toward the star.
Their velocity would not be great enough to form an escape
orbit.

Even now, they would fall far short of enough velocity to
get into an elliptical orbit unless they used the molecular drive.

Arcot headed toward one edge of the star, and poured power
into the molecular drive. The ship shot forward under an
additional five and a half gravities of acceleration. Their velocity
had been five thousand miles per second when they entered
hyperspace, and they were swiftly adding to their original velocity.

They did not, of course, feel the pull of the sun, since they
were in free fall in its field; they could only feel the five and
a half gravities of the molecular drive. Had they been able to
experience the pull of the star, they would have been crushed
by their own weight.

Their speed was mounting as they drew nearer to the star,
and Arcot was forcing the ship on with all the additional power
he could get. But he knew that the only hope they had was to
get the ship in a closed ellipse around the star, and a closed
ellipse meant that they would be forever bound to the star as a
planet! Helpless, for not even the titanic power of the *Ancient
Mariner* could enable them to escape!

As the dull red of the dead sun ballooned toward them,

Arcot said: "I think we'll make an orbit, all right, but we're going to be awfully close to the surface of that thing!"

The others were quiet; they merely watched Arcot and the star as Arcot made swift movements with the controls, doing all he could to establish them in an orbit that would be fairly safe.

It seemed like an eternity—five and a half gravities of acceleration held the men in their chairs almost as well as the straps of the antiacceleration units that bound them. When a man weighs better than half a ton, he doesn't feel like moving much.

Fuller whispered to Morey out of the corner of his sagging mouth. "What on Earth—I mean, what in Space is that thing? We're within only a few hundred miles, you said, so it must be pretty small. How could it pull us around like this?"

"It's a dead white dwarf—a 'black dwarf,' you might say," Morey replied. "As the density of such matter increases, the volume of the star depends less and less on its temperature. In a dwarf with the mass of the sun, the temperature effect is negligible; it's the action of the forces within the electron-nucleon gas which makes up the star that reigns supreme.

"It's been shown that if a white dwarf—or a black one—is increased in mass, it begins to decrease sharply in volume after a certain point is reached. In fact, no *cold* star can exist with a volume greater than about one and a half times the mass of the sun—as the mass increases and the pressure goes up, the star shrinks in volume because of the degenerate matter in it. At a little better than 1.4 times the mass of the sun—our sun, I mean: Old Sol—the star would theoretically collapse to a point.

"That has almost happened in this case. The actual limit is when the star has reached the density of a neutron, and this star hasn't collapsed that far by a long shot.

"But that star is only forty kilometers—*or less than twenty-five miles* in diameter!"

It took nearly two hours of careful juggling to get an orbit which Arcot considered reasonably circular.

And when they finally did, Wade looked at the sky above them and shouted: "Say, look! What are all those streaks?"

Arcing up from the surface of the dull red plain below them and going over the ship, were several dim streaks of light across the sky. One of them was brighter than the rest, a bright white streak. The streaks didn't move; they seemed to have been painted on the sky overhead, glowing bands of unwavering light.

"Those," said Arcot, "are the nebulae. That wide streak is the one we just left. The bright streak must be a nearby star.

"They look like streaks because we're moving so fast in so small an orbit." He pointed to the red star beneath them. "We're less than twenty miles from the center of that thing! We're almost exactly thirty kilometers from its center, or about ten kilometers from its surface! But, because of its great mass, our orbital velocity is something terrific!

"We're going around that thing better than three hundred times every second; our 'year' is three milliseconds long! Our orbital velocity is *seven hundred thousand kilometers per second!*

"We're moving along at about a fifth of the speed of light!"

"Are we safe in this orbit?" Fuller asked.

"Safe enough," said Arcot bitterly. "So damned safe that I don't see how we'll ever break free. We can't pull away with all the power on this ship. We're trapped!

"Well, I'm worn out from working under all that gravity; let's eat and get some sleep."

"I don't feel like sleeping," said Fuller. "You may call this safe, but it would only take an instant to fall down to the surface of that thing there." He looked down at their inert, but titanically powerful enemy whose baleful glow seemed even now to be burning their funeral pyre.

"Well," said Arcot, "falling into it and flying off into space are two things you don't have to worry about. If we started toward it, we'd be falling, and our velocity would increase; as a result, we'd bounce right back out again. The magnitude of the force required to make us fall into that sun is appalling! The gravitational pull on us now amounts to about five *billion* tons, which is equalized by the centrifugal force of our orbital velocity. Any tendency to change it would be like trying to bend a spring with that much resistance.

"We'd require a tremendous force to make us either fall into that star—or get away from it.

"To escape, we have to lift this ship out against gravity. That means we'd have to lift about five million tons of mass. As we get farther out, our weight will decrease as the gravitational attraction drops off, but we would need such vast amounts of energy that they are beyond human conception.

"We have burned up two tons of matter recharging the coils, and are now using another two tons to recharge them again. We need at least four tons to spare, and we only started out with twenty. We simply haven't got fuel enough to break loose from this star's gravitational hold, vast as the energy of matter is. Let's eat, and then we can sleep on the problem."

Wade cooked a meal for them, and they ate in silence, trying to think of some way out of their dilemma. Then they tried to sleep on the problem, as Arcot had suggested, but it was difficult to relax. They were physically tired; they had gone through such great strains, even in the short time that they had been maneuvering, that they were very tired.

Under a pull five times greater than normal gravity, they had tired in one-fifth the time they would have at one gravity, but their brains were still wide awake, trying to think of some way—*any way*—to get away from the dark sun.

But at last sleep came.

XI

Morey thought he was the first to waken when, seven hours later, he dressed and dove lightly, noiselessly, out into the library. Suddenly, he noticed that the telectroscope was in operation—he heard the low hum of its smoothly working director motors.

He turned and headed back toward the observatory. Arcot was busy with the telectroscope.

"What's up, Arcot?" he demanded.

Arcot looked up at him and dusted off his hands. "I've just been gimmicking up the telectroscope. We're going around this dead dwarf once every three milliseconds, which makes it awfully hard to see the stars around us. So I put in a cutoff which will shut the telectroscope off most of the time; it only looks at the sky once every three milliseconds. As a result, we can get a picture of what's going on around us very easily. It won't be a steady picture, but since we're getting a still picture three hundred times a second, it will be better than any moving picture film ever projected as far as accuracy is concerned.

"I did it because I want to take a look at that bright streak in the sky. I think it'll be the means to our salvation—if there is any."

Morey nodded. "I see what you mean; if that's another white dwarf—which it most likely is—we can use it to escape. I think I see what you're driving at."

"If it doesn't work," Arcot said coolly, "we can profit by the example of the people we left back there. Suicide is preferable to dying of cold."

Morey nodded. "The question is: How helpless are we?"

"Depends entirely on that star; let's see if we can get a focus on it."

At the orbital velocity of the ship, focussing on the star was indeed a difficult thing to do. It took them well over an hour to get the image centered in the screen without its drifting off toward one edge; it took even longer to get the focus close enough to a sphere to give them a definite reading on the instruments. The image had started out as a streak, but by taking smaller and smaller sections of the streak at the proper times, they managed to get a good, solid image. But to get it bright enough was another problem; they were only picking up a fraction of the light, and it had to be amplified greatly to make a visible image.

When they finally got what they were looking for, Morey gazed steadily at the image. "Now the job is to figure the distance. And we haven't got much parallax to work with."

"If we compute in the timing in our blinker system at opposite sides of the orbit, I think we can do it," Arcot said.

They went to work on the problem. When Fuller and Wade showed up, they were given work to do—Morey gave them equations to solve without telling them to what the figures applied.

Finally Arcot said: "Their period about the common center of gravity is thirty-nine hours, as I figure it."

Morey nodded. "Check. And that gives us a distance of two million miles apart."

"Just what are you two up to?" asked Fuller. "What good is another star? The one we're interested in is this freak underneath us."

"No," Arcot corrected, "we're interested in getting *away* from the one beneath us, which is an entirely different matter. If we were midway between this star and that one, the gravitational effects of the two would be canceled out, since we would be pulled as hard in one direction as the other. Then we'd be free of both pulls and could escape!

"If we could get into that neutral area long enough to turn on our space strain drive, we could get away between them fast. Of course, a lot of our energy would be eaten up, but we'd get away.

"That's our only hope," Arcot concluded.

"Yes, and what a whale of a hope it is," Wade snorted sarcastically. "How are you going to get out to a point halfway between these two stars when you don't have enough power to lift this ship a few miles?"

"If Mahomet can not go to the mountain," misquoted Arcot, "then the mountain must come to Mahomet."

"What are you going to do?" Wade asked in exasperation. "Beat Joshua? He made the sun stand still, but this is a job of throwing them around!"

"It is," agreed Arcot quietly, "and I intend to throw that star in such a way that we can escape between the twin fields! We can escape between the hammer and the anvil as millions of millions of millions of tons of matter crash into each other."

"And you intend to swing that?" asked Wade in awe as he thought of the spectacle there would be when two suns fell into each other. "Well, I don't want to be around."

"You haven't any choice," Arcot grinned. Then his face grew serious. "What I want to do is simple. We have the molecular ray. Those stars are hot. They don't fall into each other because they are rotating about each other. Suppose that rotation were stopped—stopped suddenly and completely? The molecular ray acts catalytically; we won't supply the power to stop that star, the star itself will. All we have to do is cause the molecules to move in a direction opposite to the rotation. We'll supply the impulse, and the star will supply the energy!

"Our job will be to break away when the stars get close enough; we are really going to hitch our wagon to a star!

"The mechanics of the job are simple. We will have to calculate when and how long to use the power, and when and how quickly to escape. We'll have to use the main power board to generate the ray and project it instead of the little ray units. With luck, we ought to be free of this star in three days!"

Work was started at once. They had a chance of life in sight, and they had every intention of taking advantage of it! The calculating machines they had brought would certainly prove worth their mass in this one use. The observations were extremely difficult because the ship was rocketing around the star in such a rapid orbit. The calculations of the mass and distance and orbital motion of the other star were therefore very difficult, but the final results looked good.

The other star and this one formed a binary, the two being of only slightly different mass and rotating about each other at a distance of roughly two million miles.

The next problem was to calculate the time of fall from that point, assuming that it would stop instantaneously, which would be approximately true.

The actual fall would take only seven hours under the tremendous acceleration of the two masses! Since the stars would fall toward each other, the ship would be drawn toward the falling mass, and since their orbit around the star took only a fraction of a second to complete, they had to make sure they were in the right position at the halfway point just before collision occurred. Also, their orbit would be greatly perturbed as the star approached, and it was necessary to calculate that in, too.

Arcot calculated that in twenty-two hours, forty-six minutes, they would be in the most favorable position to start the fall. They could have started sooner, but there were some changes that had to be made in the wiring of the ship before they could start using the molecular ray at full power.

"Well," said Wade as he finally finished the laborious computations, "I hope we don't make a mistake and get caught between the two! And what happens if we find we haven't stopped the star after all?"

"If we don't hit it exactly the first time," Morey replied, "we'll have to juggle the ray until we do."

They set to work at once, installing the heavy leads to the ray projectors, which were on the outside of the hull in countersunk recesses. Morey and Wade had to go outside the ship to help attach the cables.

Out in space, floating about the ship, they were still weightless, for they, too, were supported by centrifugal force.

The work of readjusting the projectors for greater power was completed in an hour and a quarter, which still left over twenty hours before they could use them. During the next ten hours, they charged the great storage coils to capacity, leaving the circuits to them open, controlled by the relays only. That would keep the coils charged, ready to start.

Finally, Wade dusted off his hands and said: "We're all ready to go mechanically, and I think it would be wise if we were ready physically, too. I know we're not very tired, but if we sit around in suspense we'll be as nervous as cats when the time comes. I suggest we take a couple of sleeping tablets and turn in. If we use a mild shock to awaken us, we won't oversleep."

The others agreed to the plan and prepared for their wait.

Awakened two hours before the actual moment of action, Wade prepared breakfast, and Morey took observations. He knew just where the star should be according to their calculations, and looked for it there. He breathed a sigh of relief—it was exactly in place! Their mathematics they had been sure of, but on such a rapidly moving machine, it was exceedingly difficult to make good observations.

The two hours seemed to drag interminably, but at last Acot signaled for the full power of the molecular rays. They waited, breathlessly, for some response. Nearly twenty seconds later, the other sun went out.

"We did it!" said Wade in a hushed voice. It was almost a shock to realize that this ship had power enough to extinguish a sun!

Arcot and Morey weren't awed; they didn't have time. There were other things to do and do fast.

They had checked the time required for them to see that the white dwarf had gone out. Half of this gave them the distance from the star in light seconds.

The screen had already been rigged to flash the information into a computer, which in turn gave a time signal to the robot pilot that would turn on the drive at precisely the right instant. There was no time for human error here; the velocities were too great and the time for error too small.

Then they waited. They had to wait for seven hours spinning dizzily around an improbably tiny star with an equally improbably titanic gravitational field. A star only a couple of dozens of miles across, and yet so dense that it weighed half a million times as much as the Earth! And they had to wait while another star like it, chilled now to absolute zero, fell toward them!

"I wish we could stay around to see the splash," Arcot said. "It's going to be something to see. All the kinetic energy of those two masses slamming into each other is going to be a blaze of light that will really be something!"

Wade was looking nervously at the telectroscope plate. "I wish we could see that other sun. I don't like the idea of a thing that big creeping up on us in the dark."

"Calm down," Morey said quietly. "It's out of our hands now; we took a chance, and it was a chance we *had* to take. If you want to watch something, watch Junior down there. It's going to start doing some pretty interesting tricks."

As the dense black sun approached them, Junior, as Morey had called it, did begin to do tricks. At first they seemed to be optical effects, as though the eye itself were playing tricks. The red, glowing ball beneath them began to grow transparent around its surface, leaving an opaque red core which seemed to be shrinking slowly.

"What's happening?" Fuller asked.

"Our orbit around the star is becoming more and more elliptical," Arcot replied. "As the other sun pulls us, the star beneath us grows smaller with the distance; then, as we begin to fall back toward it, it grows larger again. Since this is taking place many hundreds of times per second, the visual pictures all seem to blend in together."

"Watch the clock," Morey said suddenly, pointing.

The men watched tensely as the hand moved slowly around.

"Ten —nine —eight —seven —six —five —four —three —two —one —ZERO!"

A relay slammed home, and almost instantaneously, everyone on the ship was slammed into unconsciousness.

XII

Hours later, Arcot regained consciousness. It was quiet in the ship. He was still strapped in his seat in the control room. The relux screens were in place, and all was perfectly peaceful. He didn't know whether the ship was motionless or racing through space at a speed faster than light, and his first semiconscious impulse was to see.

He reached out with an arm that seemed to be made of dry dust, ready to crumble; an arm that would not behave. His nerves were jumping wildly. He pulled the switch he was seeking, and the relux screens dropped down as the motors pulled them back.

They were in hyperspace; beside them rode the twin ghost ships.

Arcot looked around, trying to decide what to do, but his brain was clogged. He felt tired; he wanted to sleep. Scarcely able to think, he dragged the others to their rooms and strapped them in their bunks. Then he strapped himself in and fell asleep almost at once.

Still more hours passed, then Arcot was waking slowly to insistent shaking by Morey.

"Hey! Arcot! Wake up! ARCOT! HEY!"

Arcot's ears sent the message to his brain, but his brain tried to ignore it. At last he slowly opened his eyes.

"Huh?" he said in a low, tired voice.

"Thank God! I didn't know whether you were alive or not. None of us remembered going to bed. We decided you must have carried us there, but you sure looked dead."

"Uhuh?" came Arcot's unenthusiastic rejoinder.

"Boy, is he sleepy!" said Wade as he drifted into the room. "Use a wet cloth and some cold water, Morey."

A brisk application of cold water brought Arcot more nearly awake. He immediately clamored for the wherewithal to fill an aching void that was making itself painfully felt in his midsection.

"He's all right!" laughed Wade. "His appetite is just as healthy as ever!"

They had already prepared a meal, and Arcot was promptly

hustled to the galley. He strapped himself into the chair so that he could eat comfortably, and then looked around at the others. "Where the devil are we?"

"That," replied Morey seriously, "is just what we wanted to ask you. We haven't the beginnings of an idea. We slept for two days, all told, and by now we're so far from all the Island Universes that we can't tell one from another. We have no idea where we are.

"I've stopped the ship; we're just floating. I'm sure I don't know what happened, but I hoped you might have an idea."

"I have an idea," said Arcot. "I'm hungry! You wait until after I've eaten, and I'll talk." He fell to on the food.

After eating, he went to the control room and found that every gyroscope in the place had been thrown out of place by the attractions they had passed through. He looked around at the meters and coils.

It was obvious what had happened. Their attempt to escape had been successful; they had shot out between the stars, into the space. The energy had been drained from the power coil, as they had expected. Then the power plant had automatically cut in, recharging the coils in two hours. Then the drive had come on again, and the ship had flashed on into space. But with the gyroscopes as erratic as they were, there was no way of knowing which direction they had come; they were lost in space!

"Well, there are lots of galaxies we can go to," said Arcot. "We ought to be able to find a nice one and stay there if we can't get home again."

"Sure," Wade replied, "but I like Earth! If only we hadn't all passed out! What caused that, Arcot?"

Arcot shrugged. "I'm sure I don't know. My only theory is that the double gravitational field, plus our own power field, produced a sort of cross-product that affected our brains.

"At any rate, here we are."

"We certainly are," agreed Morey. "We can't possibly back track; what we have to do is identify our own universe. What identifying features does it have that will enable us to recognize it?

"Our Galaxy has two 'satellites', the Greater and Lesser Magellanic Clouds. If we spent ten years photographing and studying and comparing with the photographs we already have, we might find it. We know that system will locate the Galaxy, but we haven't the time. Any other suggestions?"

"We came out here to visit planets, didn't we?" asked Arcot. "Here's our chance—and our only chance—of getting home, as far as I can see. We can go to any galaxy in the neighborhood— within twenty or thirty million light years—and look for a planet with a high degree of civilization.

"Then we'll give them the photographs we have, and ask them if they've any knowledge of a galaxy with two such satellites. We just keep trying until we find a race which has learned through their research. I think that's the easiest, quickest, and most satisfactory method. What do you think?"

It was the obvious choice, and they all agreed. The next proposition was to select a galaxy.

"We can go to any one we wish," said Morey, "but we're now moving at thirty thousand miles per second; it would take us quite a while to slow down, stop, and go in the other direction. There's a nice, big galactic nebula right in front of us, about three days away—six million light years. Any objections to heading for that?"

The rest looked at the glowing point of the nebula. Out in space, a star is a hard, brilliant, dimensionless point of light. But a nebula glows with a faint mistiness; they are so far away that they never have any bright glow, such as stars have, but they are so vast, their dimensions so great, that even across millions of light years of space they appear as tiny glowing discs with faint, indistinct edges. As the men looked out of the clear lux metal windows, they saw the tiny blur of light on the soft black curtain of space.

It was as good a course as any, and the ship's own inertia recommended it; they had only to redirect the ship with greater accuracy.

Setting the damaged gyroscopes came first, however. There were a number of things about the ship that needed readjustment and replacement after the strain of escaping from the giant star.

After they had made a thorough inspection Arcot said:

"I think we'd best make all our repairs out here. That flame that hit us burned off our outside microphone and speaker, and probably did a lot of damage to the ray projectors. I'd rather not land on a planet unarmed; the chances are about fifty-fifty that we'd be greeted with open cannon muzzles instead of open arms."

The work inside was left to Arcot and Fuller, while Morey and Wade put on spacesuits and went out onto the hull.

They found surprisingly little damage—far less than they had expected. True, the loudspeaker, the microphone, and all other instruments made of ordinary matter had been burned off clean. They didn't even have to clean out the spaces where they had been recessed into the wall. At a temperature of ten thousand degrees, the metals had all boiled away—even tungsten boils at seven thousand degrees, and all other normal matter boils even more easily.

The ray projectors, which had been adjusted for the high power necessary to stop a sun in its orbit, were readjusted for normal power, and the heat beams were replaced.

After nearly four hours work, everything had been checked, from relays and switch points to the instruments and gyroscopes. Stock had been taken, and they found they were running low on replacement parts. If anything more happened, they would have to stop using some of the machinery and break it up for spare parts. Of their original supply of twenty tons of lead fuel, only ten tons of the metal were left, but lead was a common metal which they could easily pick up on any planet they might visit. They could also get a fresh supply of water and refill their air tanks there.

The ship was in as perfect condition as it had ever been, for every bearing had been put in condition and the generators and gyroscopes were running smoothly.

They threw the ship into full speed and headed for the galaxy ahead of them.

"We are going to look for intelligent beings," Arcot reminded the others, "so we'll have to communicate with them. I suggest we all practice the telepathic processes I showed you—we'll need them."

The time passed rapidly with something to do. They spent a considerable part of it reading the books on telepathy that Arcot had brought, and on practicing it with each other.

By the end of the second day of the trip, Morey and Fuller,

who had peculiarly adaptable minds, were able to converse readily and rapidly, Fuller doing the projecting and Morey the receiving. Wade had divided his time about equally between projecting and reading, with the result that he could do neither well.

Early on the fourth day, they entered the universe toward which they were heading. They had stopped at about half a million light years and decided that a large local cluster of very brilliant suns promised the best results, since the stars were closer together there, and there were many of the yellow G-O type for which they were seeking.

They had penetrated into the galaxy as far as was safe, using half speed; then, at lower speeds, they worked toward the local cluster.

Arcot cut the drive several light years from the nearest sun. "Well, we're where we wanted to be; now what do we do? Morey, pick us out a G-O star. We await your royal command to move."

After a few minutes at the telectroscope, Morey pointed to one of the pinpoints of light that gleamed brightly in the sky. "That one looks like our best bet. It's a G-O a little brighter than Sol."

Morey swung the ship about, pointing the axis of the ship in the same direction as its line of flight. The observatory had been leading, but now the ship was turned to its normal position.

They shot forward, using the space-strain drive, for a full hour at one-sixteenth power. Then Arcot cut the drive, and the disc of the sun was large before them.

"We're going to have a job cutting down our velocity; we're traveling pretty fast, relative to that sun," Arcot told the others. Their velocity was so great that the sun didn't seem to swerve them greatly as they rushed nearer. Arcot began to use the molecular drive to brake the ship.

Morey was busy with the telectroscope, although greatly hampered by the fact that it was a feat of strength to hold his arm out at right angles to his body for ten seconds under the heavy acceleration Arcot was applying.

"This method works!" called Morey suddenly. "The Fuller System For Finding Planets has picked another winner! Circle the sun so that I can get a better look!"

Arcot was already trying vainly to decrease their velocity to a figure that would permit the attraction of the sun to hold them in its grip and allow them to land on a planet.

"As I figure it," Arcot said, "we'll need plenty of time to come to rest. What do you think, Morey?"

Morey punched figures into the calculator. "Wow! Somewhere in the neighborhood of a hundred days, using all the acceleration that will be safe! At five gravities, reducing our present velocity of twenty-five thousand miles per second to zero will take approximately twenty-four hundred hours—one hundred days! We'll have to use the gravitational attraction of that sun to help us."

"We'll have to use the space control," said Arcot. "If we move close to the sun by the space control, all the energy of the fall will be used in overcoming the space-strain coil's field, and thus prevent our falling. When we start to move away again, we will be climbing against that gravity, which will aid us in stopping. But even so, it will take us about three days to stop. We wouldn't get anywhere using molecular power; that giant sun was just too damned generous with his energy of fall!"

They started the cycles, and, as Arcot had predicted, they took a full three days of constant slowing to accomplish their purpose, burning up nearly three tons of matter in doing so. They were constantly oppressed by a load of five gravities except for the short intervals when they stopped to eat and when they were moving in the space control field. Even in sleeping, they were forced to stand the load.

The massive sun was their principal and most effective brake. At no time did they go more than a few dozen million miles from the primary, for the more intense the gravity, the better effect they got.

Morey divided his time between piloting the ship while Arcot rested, and observing the system. By the end of the third day, he had made very creditable progress with his map.

He had located only six planets, but he was certain there were others. For the sake of simplicity, he had assumed circular orbits and calculated their approximate orbital velocities from their distance from the sun. He had determined the mass of the sun from direct weighings aboard their ship. He soon had a fair diagram of the system constructed mathematically, and experimental observation showed it to be a very close approximation.

The planets were rather more massive than those of Sol. The innermost planet had a third again the diameter of Mercury and was four million miles farther from the primary. He named it Hermes. The next one, which he named Aphrodite, the Greek goddess corresponding to the Roman Venus, was only a little larger than Venus and was some eight million miles farther from its primary—seventy-five million miles from the central sun.

The next, which Morey called Terra, was very much like Earth. At a distance of a hundred and twenty-four million miles from the sun, it must have received almost the same amount of heat that Earth does, for this sun was considerably brighter than Sol.

Terra was eight thousand two hundred miles in diameter, with a fairly clear atmosphere and a varying albedo which indicated clouds in the atmosphere. Morey had every reason to believe that it might be inhabited, but he had no proof because his photographs were consistently poor due to the glare of the sun.

The rest of the planets proved to be of little interest. In the place where, according to Bode's Law, another planet, corresponding to Mars, should have been, there was only a belt of asteroids. Beyond this was still another belt. And on the other side of the double asteroid belt was the fourth planet, a fifty-thousand-mile-in-diameter methane-ammonia giant which Morey named Zeus in honor of Jupiter.

He had picked up a couple of others on his plates, but he had not been able to tell anything about them as yet. In any case, the planets Aphrodite and Terra were by far the most interesting.

"I think we picked the right angle to come into this system," said Arcot, looking at Morey's photographs of the wide bands of asteroids. They had come into the planetary group at right angles to the plane of the ecliptic, which had allowed them to miss both asteroid belts.

They started moving toward the planet Terra, reaching their objective in less than three hours.

The globe beneath them was lit brightly, for they had approached it from the daylight side. Below them, they could see wide, green plains and gently rolling mountains, and in a great cleft in one of the mountain ranges was a shimmering lake of clearest blue.

The air of the planet screamed about them as they dropped down, and the roar in the loudspeaker grew to a mighty cataract of sound. Morey turned down the volume.

The sparkling little lake passed beneath them as they shot on, seventy-five miles above the surface of the planet. When they had first entered the atmosphere, they had the impression of looking down on a vast, inverted bowl whose edge rested on a vast, smooth table of deep violet velvet. But as they dropped and the violet became bluer and bluer, they experienced the strange optical illusion of "flopping" of the scene. The bowl seemed to turn itself inside out, and they were looking down at its inner surface.

They shot over a mountain range, and a vast plain spread out before them. Here and there, in the far distance, they could see darker spots caused by buckled geological strata.

Arcot swung the ship around, and they saw the vast horizon swing about them as their sensation of "down" changed with the acceleration of the turn. They felt nearly weightless, for they were lifting again in a high arc.

Arcot was heading back toward the mountains they had passed over. He dropped the ship again, and the foothills seemed to rise to meet them.

"I'm heading for that lake," Arcot explained. "It seems absolutely deserted, and there are some things we want to do. I haven't had any decent exercise for the past two weeks, except for straining under high gravity. I want to do some swimming, and we need to distill some water for drink; we need to refill the tanks in case of emergencies. If the atmosphere contains oxygen, fine; if it doesn't, we can get it out of the water by electrolysis.

"But I hope that air is good to breathe, because I've been wanting a swim and a sun bath for a long time!"

XIII

The *Ancient Mariner* hung high in the air, poised twenty-five miles above the surface of the little lake. Wade, as chemist, tested the air while the others readied the distillation and air condensation apparatus. By the time they had finished, Wade was ready with his report.

"Air pressure about 20 psi at the surface; temperature around ninety-five Fahrenheit. Composition: eighteen percent oxygen, seventy-five percent nitrogen, four-tenths of one percent carbon dioxide, residue—inert gases. That's not including water vapor, of which there is a fair amount.

"I put a canary into the air, and the bird liked it, so I imagine it's quite safe except for bacteria, perhaps. Naturally, at this altitude the air is germ-free."

"Good," said Morey, "then we can take our swim and work without worrying about spacesuits."

"Just a minute!" Fuller objected. "What about those germs Wade mentioned? If you think I'm going out in my shorts where some flock of bacteria can get at my tender anatomy, you've got another think coming!"

"I wouldn't worry about it," Wade said. "The chances of organisms developing along the same evolutionary line is quite slim. We may find the inhabitants of the same shape as those of another world, because the human body is fairly well constructed anatomically. The head is in a place where it will be able to see over a wide area and it's in a safe place. The hand is very useful and can be improved upon but little. True, the Venerians have a second thumb, but the principle is the same.

"But chemically, the bodies are probably very different. The people of Venus are widely different chemically; the bacteria that can make a Venerian deathly ill is killed the instant it enters our body, or else it starves to death because it can't find the kind of chemical food it needs to live. And the same thing happens when a Venerian is attacked by an Earthly microorganism.

"Even on Earth, evolution has produced such widely varying types of life that an organism that can feed on one is totally incapable of feeding on another. You, for instance, couldn't catch tobacco mosaic virus, and the tobacco plant can't catch the measles virus.

"You couldn't expect a microorganism to evolve here that was capable of feeding on Earth-type tissues; they would have starved to death long ago."

"What about bigger animals?" Fuller asked cautiously.

"That's different. You would probably be indigestible to an alien carnivore, but he'd probably kill you first to find out. If he ate you, it might kill him in the end, but that would be small consolation. That's why we're going to go out armed."

Arcot dropped the ship swiftly until they were hovering a bare hundred feet over the waters of the lake. There was a little stream winding its way down the mountainside, and another which led the clear overflow away.

"I doubt if there's anything of great size in that lake," Arcot said slowly and thoughtfully. "Still, even small fish might be deadly. Let's play safe and remove all forms of life, bacterial and otherwise. A little touch of the molecular motion ray, greatly diffused, will do the trick."

Since the molecular ray directed the motion of the molecules of matter, it prevented chemical reactions from taking place, even when greatly diffused; all the molecules tend to go in the same direction to such an extent that the delicate balance of chemical reactions that is life is upset. It is too delicate a thing to stand any power that upsets the reactions so violently. All things are killed instantly.

As the light haze of the ionized air below them glowed out in a huge cone, the water of the lake heaved and seemed to move in its depths, but there was no great movement of the waters; they lost only a fraction of their weight. But every living thing in that lake died instantly.

Arcot turned the ship, and the shining hull glided softly over to one side of the lake where a little sandy beach invited them. There seemed no indication of intelligent life about.

Each of them took a load of the supplies they had brought, and carried them out under the shade of an immense pine-like tree—a gigantic column of wood that stretched far into the sky to lose its green leaves in a waving sea of foliage. The mottled sunlight of the bright star above them made them feel very much at home. Its color, intensity, and warmth were all exactly the same as on Earth.

Each of the men wore his power suit to aid in carrying the things they had brought, for the gravity here was a bit higher than that of Earth. The difference in air pressure was so little as to be scarcely noticeable; they even adjusted the interior of the ship to it.

They had every intention of staying here for a while. It was pleasant to lie in the warm sun once more; so pleasant that it became difficult to remember that they were countless trillions of long miles from their own home planet. It was hard to realize that the warm, blazing star above them was not Old Sol.

Arcot was carrying a load of food in a box. He had neutralized his weight until, load and all, he weighed about a hundred pounds. This was necessary in order to permit him to drag a length of hose behind him toward the water, so it could be used as an intake for the pumps.

Morey, meanwhile, was having trouble. He had been carrying a load of assorted things to use—a few pneumatic pillows, a heavy iron pot for boiling the water, and a number of other things.

He reached his destination, having floated the hundred or so feet from the ship by using his power suit. He forgot, momentarily, and dropped his load. Immediately, he too began to "drop"—upward! He had a buoyancy of around three hundred pounds, and a weight of only two fifty. In dropping the load, the sudden release had caused the power unit to jerk him upward, and somehow the controlling knob on the power pack was torn loose.

Morey shot up into the air, showing a fair rate of progress toward his late abode—space! And he had no way to stop himself. His hand power unit was far too weak to overcome the pull of his power-pack, and he was rising faster and faster!

He realized that his friends could catch him, and laughingly called down: "Arcot! Help! I'm being kidnaped by my power suit! To the rescue!"

Arcot looked up quickly at Morey's call and realized immediately that his power control had come off. He knew there was twenty miles or so of breathable air above, and long before Morey rose that far, he could catch him in the *Ancient Mariner*, if necessary.

He turned on his own power suit, using a lift of a hundred pounds, which gave him double Morey's acceleration. Quickly he gathered speed that shot him up toward his helpless friend, and a moment later, he had caught up with him and passed him. Then he shut off his power and drifted to a halt before he began to drop again. As Morey rose toward him, Arcot adjusted the power in his own suit to match Morey's velocity.

Arcot grabbed Morey's leg and turned his power down until he had a weight of fifty pounds. Soon they were both falling again, and when their rate of fall amounted to approximately twenty miles per hour, Arcot cut their weight to zero and they continued down through their momentum. Just short of the ground, he leaped free of Morey, who, carried on by momentum, touched the ground a moment later. Wade at once jumped in and held him down.

"Now, now! Calm yourself," said Wade solicitously. "Don't go up in the air like that over the least little thing."

"I won't, if you'll get busy and take this damned thing off—or fasten some lead to my feet!" replied Morey, starting to unstrap the mechanism.

"You'd better hold your horses there," said Arcot. "If you take that off now, we sure will need the *Ancient Mariner* to catch up with it. It will produce an acceleration that no man could ever stand—something on the order of five thousand gravities, if the tubes could stand it. And since that one is equipped with the invisibility apparatus, you'd be out one good invisibility suit. Restrain yourself, boy, and I'll go get a new knob control.

"Wade, get the boy a rock to hold him down. Better tie it around his neck so he won't forget it and fly off into space again. It's a nuisance locating so small an object in space and I promised his father I'd bring the body back if there was anything left of it." He released Morey as Wade handed him a large stone.

A few minutes later, he returned with a new adjustment dial and repaired Morey's apparatus. The strain was released when he turned it, and Morey parted with the rock with relief.

Morey grunted in relief, and looked at the offending pack.

"You know, that being stuck with a sky-bound gadget that you can't turn off is the nastiest combination of feeling stupid, helpless, comical, silly and scared I've hit yet. It now—somewhat late—occurs to me that this is powered with a standard power coil, straight off the production line, and that it has a standard overload cut-out for protection of associated equipment. I want to install an emergency cut-off switch, in case a knob, or something else, goes sour. But I want to have the emergency overload where I can decide whether or not an emergency overload is to be accepted. I'd feel a sight more than silly if that overload relay popped while I was a couple thousand feet up.

"Trouble with all this new stuff of ours is that we simply haven't had time to find out all the 'I never thought of that' things that can go wrong. If the grid resistor on that oscillator went out, for instance, what would it do?"

Arcot cocked an eye at the power pack, visualizing the circuits. "Full blast, straight up, and no control. But modern printed resistors don't fail."

"That's what it says in all the books." Wade nodded wisely. "And you should see the stock of replacement units every electronics shop stocks for purposes of replacing infallible units, too. You've got a point, my friend."

"I can see four ways we can change these things to fail-safe operation, if we add Morey's emergency cut-off switch. If it did go on-full then, you could use intermittent operation and get down," Arcot acknowledged.

"Anybody know what silly fail-unsafe tricks we overlooked in the *Ancient Mariner*?" Fuller asked.

"That," said Wade with a grimace, "is a silly question. The 'I didn't think of that' type of failure occurs because I didn't think of that, and the reason I didn't think of it is because it never occurred to me. If we'd been able to think of 'em, we would have. We'll probably get stuck with a few more yet, before we get back. But at least we can clean up a few bugs in these things now."

"Forget it for now, Wade, and get that chow on," suggested Fuller. He was lying on his back, clad only in a pair of short trunks, completely relaxed and enjoying life. "We can do that when it's dark here."

"Fuller has the right idea," said Morey, looking at Fuller with a judicious eye. "I think I'll follow his example."

"Which makes three in favor and one on the way," said Arcot, as he came out of the ship and sank down on the soft sand of the beach.

They lay around for a while after lunch, and then decided to swim in the cool waters of the lake. One of them was to stand guard while the others went in swimming. Standing guard consisted of lying on his back on the soft sand, and staring up at the delightful contrast of lush green foliage and deep blue sky.

It was several hours before they gathered up their things and returned to the ship. They felt more rested than they had before their exercise. They had not been tired before, merely restless, and the physical exercise had made them far more comfortable.

They gathered again in the control room. All the apparatus had been taken in; the tanks were filled, and the compressed oxygen replenished. They closed the airlock and were ready to start again.

As they lifted into the air, Arcot looked at the lake that was shrinking below them. "Nice place for a picnic; we'll have to remember that place. It isn't more than twenty million light years from home."

"Yes," agreed Morey, "it is handy. But suppose we find out where home is first; let's go find the local inhabitants."

"Excellent idea. Which way do we go to look?" Wade asked.

"This lake must have an outlet to the sea," Morey answered. "I suggest we follow it. Most rivers of any size have a port near the mouth, and a port usually means a city."

"Let's go," said Arcot, swinging the shining ship about and heading smoothly down along the line of the little stream that had its beginning at the lake. They moved on across the mountains and over the green foothills until they came to a broad, rolling plain.

"I wonder if this planet *is* inhabited," Arcot mused. "None of this land seems to be cultivated."

Morey had been scanning the horizon with a pair of powerful binoculars. "No, the land isn't cultivated, but take a look over there—see that range of little hills over to the right? Take a look." He handed the binoculars to Arcot.

Arcot looked long and quietly. At last he lowered the binoculars and handed them to Wade, who sat next to him.

"It looks like the ruins of a city," Arcot said. "Not the ruins that a storm would make, but the ruins that high explosives would make. I'd say there had been a war and the people who once lived here had been driven off."

"So would I," rejoined Morey. "I wonder if we could find the conquerors?"

"Maybe—unless it was mutual annihilation!"

They rose a bit higher and raised their speed to a thousand miles an hour. On and on they flew, high above the gently rolling plain, mile after mile. The little brooklet became a great river, and the river kept growing more and more. Ahead of them was a range of hills, and they wondered how the river could thread its way among them. They found that it went through a broad pass that twisted tortuously between high mountains.

A few miles farther on, they came to a great natural basin in the pass, a wide, level bowl. And in almost the exact center, they saw a looming mass of buildings—a great city!

"Look!" cried Morey. "I told you it was inhabited!"

Arcot winced. "Yes, but if you shout in my ear like that again, you'll have to write things out for me for ever after." He was just as excited as Morey, nevertheless.

The great mass of the city was shaped like a titanic cone that stood a half mile high and was fully a mile and a half in radius. But the remarkable thing about it was the perfect uniformity with which the buildings and every structure seemed to conform to this plan. It seemed as though an invisible, but very tangible line had been drawn in the air.

It was as though a sign had been posted: "Here there shall be buildings. Beyond this line, no structure shall extend, nor any vehicle go!"

The air directly above the city was practically packed with slim, long, needle-like ships of every size—from tiny private ships less than fifteen feet long to giant freighters of six hundred feet and longer. And every one of them conformed to the rule perfectly!

Only around the base of the city there seemed to be a slight deviation. Where the invisible cone should have touched the ground, there was a series of low buildings made of some dark metal, and all about them the ground appeared scarred and churned.

"They certainly seem to have some kind of ray screen over

that city," Morey commented. "Just look at that perfect cone effect and those low buildings are undoubtedly the projectors."

Arcot had brought the ship to a halt as he came through the pass in the mountain. The shining hull was in the cleft of the gorge, and was, no doubt, quite hard to see from the city.

Suddenly, a vagrant ray of the brilliant sun reached down through a break in the overcast of clouds and touched the shining hull of the *Ancient Mariner* with a finger of gold. Instantly, the ship shone like the polished mirror of a heliograph.

Almost immediately, a low sound came from the distant city. It was a pulsing drone that came through the microphone in a weird cadence; a low, beating drone, like some wild music. Louder and stronger it grew, rising in pitch slowly, then it suddenly ended in a burst of rising sound—a terrific whoop of alarm.

As if by magic, every ship in the air above the city shot downward, dropping suddenly out of sight. In seconds, the air was cleared.

"It seems they've spotted us," said Arcot in a voice he tried to make nonchalant.

A fleet of great, long ships was suddenly rising from the neighborhood of the central building, the tallest of the group. They went in a compact wedge formation and shot swiftly down along the wall of the invisible cone until they were directly over the low building nearest the *Ancient Mariner*. There was a sudden shimmer in the air. In an instant, the ships were through and heading toward the *Ancient Mariner* at a tremendous rate.

They shot forward with an acceleration that was astonishing to the men in the spaceship. In perfect formation, they darted toward the lone, shining ship from far-off Earth!

XIV

The four earthmen watched the fleet of alien ships roar through the air toward them.

"Now how shall we signal them?" asked Morey, also trying to be nonchalant, and failing as badly as Arcot had.

"Don't try the light beam method," cautioned Arcot. The last time they had tried to use a light beam signal was when they first contacted the Nigrans. The Nigrans thought it was some kind of destruction ray. That had started the terrible destructive war of the Black Star.

"Let's just hang here peaceably and see what they do," Arcot suggested.

Motionless, the *Ancient Mariner* hung before the advancing attack of the great battle fleet. The shining hull was a thing of beauty in the golden sunlight as it waited for the advancing ships.

The alien ships slowed as they approached and spread out in a great fan-shaped crescent.

Suddenly, the *Ancient Mariner* gave a tremendous leap and hurtled toward them at a terrific speed, under an acceleration so great that Arcot was nearly hurled into unconsciousness. He would have been except for the terrific mass of the ship. To produce that acceleration in so great a mass, a tremendous force was needed, a force that even made the enemy fleet reel under its blow!

But, sudden as it was, Arcot had managed to push the power into reverse, using the force of the molecular drive to counteract the attraction the aliens had brought to bear.

The whole mighty fabric of the ship creaked as the titanic load came upon it. They were using a force of a million tons!

The mighty lux beams withstood the stress, however, and the ship came to a halt, then was swiftly backing away from the alien battle fleet.

"We can give them all they want!" said Arcot grimly. He noticed that Wade and Fuller had been knocked out by the sudden blow, but Morey, though slightly groggy, was still in possession of his senses.

"Let's not," Morey remonstrated. "We may be able to make friends with them, but not if we kill them off."

"Right!" replied Arcot, "but we're going to give them a little demonstration of power!"

The *Ancient Mariner* leaped suddenly upward with a speed that defied the eyes of the men at the rays of the enemy ships. Then, as they turned to follow the sudden motion of the ship— *it was not there!*

The *Ancient Mariner* had vanished!

Morey was startled for an instant as the ship and his companions disappeared around him, then he realized what had happened. Arcot had used the invisibility apparatus!

Arcot turned and raced swiftly far off to one side, behind the strange ships, and hovered over the great cliff that made the edge of the cleft that was the river bed. Then he snapped the ship into full visibility.

Wade and Fuller had recovered by now, and Arcot started barking out orders. "Wade—Fuller—take the molecular ray, Wade, and tear down that cliff—throw it down into the valley. Fuller, turn the heat beams on with all the power you can get and burn that refuse he tears down into a heap of molten lava!

"I'm going to show them what we can do! And, Wade—after Fuller gets it melted down, throw the molten lava high in the air!"

From the ship, a long pencil of rays, faintly violet from the air they ionized, reached out and touched the cliff. In an instant, it had torn down a vast mass of the solid rock, which came raining down into the valley with a roaring thunder and threw the dirt of the valley into the air like splashed mud.

Then the violet ray died, and two rays of blinding brilliance reached out. The rock was suddenly smoking, steaming. Then it became red, dull at first, then brighter and brighter. Suddenly it collapsed into a great pool of white-hot lava, flowing like water under the influence of the beams from the ship.

Again the pale violet of the molecular beams touched the rock—which was now bubbling lava. In an instant, the great mass of flaming incandescent rock was flying like a glowing meteor, up into the air. It shot up with terrific speed, broke up in mid-air, and fell back as a rain of red-hot stone.

The bright rays died out, but the pale fingers of the molecular beams traced across the level ground. As they touched it, the solid soil spouted into the air like some vast fountain, to fall back as frost-covered powder.

The rays that had swung a sun into destruction were at work! What chance had man, or the works of man against such? What mattered a tiny planet when those rays could hurl one mighty sun into another, to blaze up in an awful conflagration that would light up space for a million light years around with a mighty glare of light!

As if by a giant plow, the valley was torn and rent in great streaks by the pale violet rays of the molecular force. Wade tore loose a giant boulder and sent it rocketing into the heavens. It came down with a terrific crash minutes later, to bury itself deep in the soil as it splintered into fragments.

Suddenly the *Ancient Mariner* was jerked violently again. Evidently undaunted by their display of power, the aliens' rays had gripped the Earthmen's ship again and were drawing it with terrific acceleration. But this time the ship was racing toward the city, caught by the beam of one of the low-built, sturdy buildings that housed the protective ray projectors.

Again Arcot threw on the mighty power units that drove the ship, bracing them against the pull of the beam.

"Wade! Use the molecular ray! Stop that beam!" Arcot ordered.

The ship was stationary, quivering under the titanic forces that struggled for it. The enemy fleet raced toward them, trying to come to the aid of the men in the tower.

The pale glow of the molecular beam reached out its ghostly finger and touched the heavy-walled ray projector building. There was a sudden flash of discharging energy, and the tower was hurled high in the air, leaving only a gaping hole in the ground.

Instantly, with the collapse of the beam that held it, the *Ancient Mariner* shot backward, away from the scene of the battle. Arcot snapped off the drive and turned on the invisibility apparatus. They hung motionless, silent and invisible in the air, awaiting developments.

In close formation, one group of ships blocked the opening in the wall of rays that the removal of one projector building had caused. Three other ships went to investigate the wreck of the building that had fallen a mile away.

The rest of the fleet circled the city, darting around, searching frantically for the invisible enemy, fully aware of the danger of collision. The unnerving tension of expecting it every second made them erratic and nervous to the nth degree.

"They're sticking pretty close to home," said Arcot. "They don't seem to be too anxious to play with us."

"They don't, do they?" Morey said, looking angry. "They might at least have been willing to see what we wanted. I want to investigate some other cities. Come on!" He had thoroughly enjoyed the rest at the little mountain lake, and he

was disappointed that they had been driven away. Had they
wanted to, he knew, they could easily have torn the entire city
out by the roots!

"I think we ought to smash them thoroughly," said Wade.
"They're certainly inhospitable people!"

"And I, for one, would like to know what that attraction ray
was," said Fuller curiously.

"The ray is easily understood after you take a look at the
wreck it made of some of these instruments," Arcot told him. "It
was projected magnetism. I can see how it might be done if
you worked on it for a while. The ray simply attracted everything in its path that was magnetic, which included our lux
metal hull.

"Luckily, most of our apparatus is shielded against magnetism.
The few things that aren't can be repaired easily. But I'll bet
Wade finds his gear in the galley thrown around quite a bit."

"Where do we go from here, then?" Wade asked.

"Well, this world is bigger than Earth," said Morey. "Even
if they're afraid to go out of their cities to run farms, they must
have other cities. The thing that puzzles me, though, is how
they do it—I don't see how they can possibly raise enough for a
city in the area they have available!"

"'People couldn't possibly live in hydrogen instead of oxygen',"
Arcot quoted, grinning. "That's what they told me when I made
my little announcement at the meeting on the Black Star
situation. The only trouble was—they did. That suggestion of
yours meets the same fate, Morey!"

"All right, you win," agreed Morey. "Now let's see if we can
find the other nations on this world more friendly."

Arcot looked at the sun. "We're now well north of the
equator. We'll go up where the air is thin, put on some speed,
and go into the south temperate zone. We'll see if we can't
find some people there who are more peaceably inclined."

Arcot cut off the invisibility tubes. Instantly, all the enemy
ships in the neighborhood turned and darted toward them at
top speed. But the shining *Ancient Mariner* darted into the
deep blue vault of the sky, and a moment later was lost to their
view.

"They had a lot of courage," said Arcot, looking down at the
city as it sank out of sight. "It doesn't take one-quarter as

much courage to fight a known enemy, no matter how deadly, as it does to fight an unknown enemy force—something that can tear down mountains and throw their forts into the air like toys."

"Oh, they had courage, all right," Morey conceded, "but I wish they hadn't been quite so anxious to display it!"

They were high above the ground now, accelerating with a force of one gravity. Arcot cut the acceleration down until there was just enough to overcome the air resistance, which, at the height they were flying, was very low. The sky was black above them, and the stars were showing around the blazing sun. They were unfamiliar stars in unfamiliar constellations— the stars of another universe.

In a very short time, the ship was dropping rapidly downward again, the horizontal power off. The air resistance slowed them rapidly. They drifted high over the south temperate zone. Below them stretched the seemingly endless expanse of a great blue-green ocean.

"They don't lack for water, do they?" Wade commented.

"We could pretty well figure on large oceans," Arcot said. "The land is green, and there are plenty of clouds."

Far ahead, a low mass of solid land appeared above the blue of the horizon. It soon became obvious that it was not a continent they were approaching, but a large island, stretching hundreds of miles north and south.

Arcot dropped the ship lower; the mountainous terrain had become so broken that it would be impossible to detect a city from thrity miles up.

The green defiles of the great mountains not only provided good camouflage, but kept any great number of ships from attacking the sides, where the ray stations were. The cities were certainly located with an eye for war! Arcot wondered what sort of conflict had lasted so long that cities were designed for perpetual war. Had they never had peace?

"Look!" Fuller called. "There's another city!" Below them, situated in a little natural bowl in the mountains, was another of the cone cities.

Wade and Fuller manned the ray projectors again; Arcot dropped the ship toward the city, one hand on the *reverse* switch in case the inhabitants tried to use the magnetic beam again.

At last, they had come quite low. There were no ships in the air, and no people in sight.

Suddenly, the outside microphone picked up a low, humming sound. A long, cigar-shaped object was heading toward the ship at high speed. It had been painted a dark, mottled green, and was nearly invisible against background of foliage beneath the ship.

"Wade! Catch that on the ray!" Arcot commanded sharply, moving the ship to one side at the same time. Instantly, the guided missile turned and kept coming toward them.

Wade triggered the molecular beam, and the missile was suddenly dashing toward the ground with terrific speed. There was a terrific flash of flame and a shock wave of concussion. A great hole gaped in the ground.

"They sure know their chemistry," remarked Wade, looking down at the great hole the explosion had torn in the ground. "That wasn't atomic, but on the other hand, it wasn't dynamite or TNT, either! I'd like to know what they use!"

"Personally," said Arcot angrily, "I think that was more or less a gentle hint to move on!" He didn't like the way they were being received; he had wanted to meet these people. Of course, the other planet might be inhabited, but if it wasn't—

"I wonder—" said Morey thoughtfully. "Arcot, those people were obviously warned against our attack—probably by that other city. Now, we've come nearly halfway around this world; certainly we couldn't have gone much farther away and still be on the planet. And we find this city in league with the other! Since this league goes halfway around the world, and they expected us to do the same, isn't it fair to assume, just on the basis of geographical location, that all this world is in one league?"

"Hmmm—an interplanetary war," mused Arcot. "That would certainly prove that one of the other planets is inhabited. The question is—which one?"

"The most probable one is the next inner planet, Aphrodite," replied Morey.

Arcot fired the ship into the sky. "If your conclusions are correct—and I think they are—I see no reason to stay on this planet. Let's go see if their neighbors are less aggressive!"

With that, he shot the ship straight up, rotating the axis until it was pointing straight away from the planet. He increased the acceleration until, as they left the outer fringes of the atmosphere, the ship was hitting a full four gravities.

"I'm going to shorten things up and use the space control," Arcot said. "The gravitational field of the sun will drain a lot of our energy out, but so what? Lead is cheap, and before we're through, we'll have plenty or I'll know the reason why!"

Dr. Richard Arcot was angry—boiling all the way through!

XV

There was the familiar tension in the air as the space field built up and they were hurled suddenly forward; the star-like dot of the planet suddenly expanded as they rushed forward at a speed far greater than that of light. In a moment, it had grown to a disc; Arcot stopped the space control. Again they were moving forward on molecular drive.

Very shortly, Arcot began to decelerate. Within ten minutes, they were beginning to feel the outermost wisps of the cloud-laden atmosphere. The heat of the blazing sun was intense; the surface of the planet was, no doubt, a far warmer place than Earthmen would find comfortable. They would have been far better suited to remain on the other planet, but they very evidently were not wanted!

They dropped down through the atmosphere, sinking for miles as the ship slowed to the retarding influence of the air and the molecular power. Down they went, through mile after mile of heavy cloud layer, unable to see the ground beneath them.

Then, suddenly, the thick, all-enveloping mists that held them were gone. They were flying smoothly along under leaden skies —perpetual, dim, dark clouds. Despite the brightness of the sun above them, the clouds made the light dim and gray. They reflected such an enormous percentage of the light that struck them that the climate was not as hot as they had feared.

The ground was dark under its somber mantle of clouds; the hills, the rivers that crawled across wide plains, and the oddly stunted forests all looked as though they had been modeled in a great mass of greenish-gray putty. It was a discouraging world.

"I'm glad we didn't wait for our swim here," remarked Wade. "It sure looks like rain."

Arcot stopped the ship and held it motionless at ten miles

while Wade made his chemical analysis of the air. The report looked favorable; plenty of oxygen and a trace of carbon dioxide mixed with nitrogen.

"But the water vapor!" Wade said. "The air is saturated with it! It won't be the heat, but the humidity that'll bother us—to coin a phrase."

Arcot dropped the ship still farther, at the same time moving forward toward a sea he had seen in the distance. Swiftly, the ground sped beneath them. The low plain sloped toward the sea, a vast, level surface of gray, leaden water.

"Oh, brother, what a pleasant world," said Fuller sarcastically.

It was certainly not an inspiring scene. The leaden skies, the heavy clouds, the dark land, and the gray-green of the sea, always shaded in perpetual half-light, lest the burning sun heat them beyond endurance. It was a gloomy world.

They turned and followed the coast. Still no sign of inhabitants was visible. Mile after mile passed beneath them as the shining ship followed up the ragged shore. Small indentations and baylets ran into a shallow, level sea. This world had no moon, so it was tideless, except for the slight solar tides.

Finally, far ahead of them, and well back from the coast, Arcot spotted a great mountain range.

"I'm going to head for that," he told the others. "If these people are at war with our very inimical friends of the other planet, chances are they'll put their cities in the mountains, too."

They had such cities. The *Ancient Mariner* had penetrated less than a hundred miles along the twisted ranges of the mountains before they saw, far ahead, a great, cone-shaped city. The city was taller, larger than those of the other planet, and the cone ran up farther from the actual city buildings, leaving the aircraft more room.

Arcot stopped and watched the city a long time through the telescope. It seemed similar to the others in all respects. The same type of needle-like ships floated in the air above it, and the same type of cone ray projectors nestled in the base of the city's invisible protection."

"We may as well take a chance," said Arcot. He shot the ship forward until they were within a mile of the city, in plain sight of the inhabitants.

Suddenly, without any warning signal, apparently, all the air traffic went wild—then it was gone. Every ship seemed to have ducked into some unseen place of refuge.

Within a few minutes, a fleet of battleships was winging its way toward the invisible barrier. Then it was out, and, in a great semi-cylinder a quarter of a mile high, and a quarter of a mile in radius, they advanced toward the *Ancient Mariner*.

Arcot kept the ship motionless. He knew that their only weapon was the magnetic ray; otherwise they would have won the war long ago. And he knew he could cope with magnetism.

Slowly the ships advanced. At last, they halted a quarter of a mile from the Earth ship. A single ship detached itself from the mass and advanced to within a few hundred feet of the *Ancient Mariner*.

Quickly, Arcot jumped to his feet. "Morey, take the controls. Evidently they want to parley, not fight. I'm going over there."

He ran the length of the corridor to his room and put on his power suit. A moment later, he left the airlock and launched himself into space, flying swiftly toward the ship. He had come alone, but armed as he was, he was probably more than a match for anything they could bring to bear on him.

He went directly toward the broad expanse of glass that marked the control room of the alien ship and looked in curiously.

The pilot was a man much like Arcot; quite tall, and of tremendous girth, with a huge chest and great powerful arms. His hands, like those of the Venerians, had two thumbs.

With equal curiosity, the man stared at Arcot, floating in the air without apparent means of support.

Arcot hung there a moment, then motioned that he wished to enter. The giant alien motioned him around to the side of the ship. Halfway down the length of the ship, Arcot saw a port suddenly open. He flew swiftly forward and entered.

The man who stood there was a giant as tall as Wade and even more magnificently muscled, with tremendous shoulders and giant chest. His thighs, rounded under a close-fitting gray uniform, were bulging with smooth muscle.

He was considerably larger than the man in the pilot room, and whereas the other had been a pale yellow in color, this man was burned to a more healthy shade of tan. His features were regular and pleasing; his hair was black and straight; his high forehead denoted a high degree of intelligence, and his clear black eyes, under heavy black eyebrows, seemed curious, but friendly.

His nose was rather thin, but not sharp, and his mouth was curved in a smile of welcome. His chin was firm and sharp, distinct from his face and neck.

They looked each other over, and Arcot smiled as their eyes met.

"Torlos," said the alien, pointing to his great chest.

"Arcot," replied the Earthman, pointing to himself. Then he pointed to the stranger. "Torlos." He knew he hadn't pronounced it exactly as the alien had, but it would suffice.

The stranger smiled in approval. "Ahcut," he said, pointing to the Earthman.

Then he pointed to the comparatively thin arms of the Earthman, and to his own. Then he pointed to Arcot's head and to the mechanism he wore on his back, then to his own head, and went through the motions of walking with great effort.

Again he pointed at Arcot's head, nodding his own in approval.

Arcot understood immediately what was meant. The alien had indicated that the Earthman was comparatively weak, but that he had no need for muscle, for he made his head and his machines work for him. And he had decided that the head was better!

Arcot looked at the man's eyes and concentrated on the idea of friendship, projecting it with all his mental power. The black eyes suddenly widened in surprise, which quickly turned to pleasure as he tried to concentrate on one thought.

It was difficult for Arcot to interpret the thoughts of the alien; all his concepts were in a different form. At last, he caught the idea of location—but it was location in the interrogative! How was he to interpret that?

Then it hit him. Torlos was asking: "Where are you from?"

Arcot pulled a pad of paper and a pencil from his pocket and began to sketch rapidly. First, he drew the local galaxy, with dots for stars, and swept his hand around him. He made one of the dots a little heavier and pointed at the bright blur in the cloudy sky above them. Then he drew a circle around that dot and put another dot on it, at the same time indicating the planet beneath them.

Torlos showed that he understood.

Arcot continued. At the other end of the paper, he drew another galaxy, and indicated Earth. Then he drew a dotted line from Earth to the planet they were now on.

Torlos looked at him in incredulous wonder. Again he indicated his respect for Arcot's brain.

Arcot smiled and indicated the city. "Can we go there?" he projected into the other's mind.

Torlos turned and glanced toward the end of the corridor. There was no one in sight, so he shouted an order in a deep, pleasant voice. Instantly, another giant man came striding down the corridor with a lithe softness that indicated tremendous muscular power, excellently controlled. He saluted by placing his left hand over the right side of his chest. Arcot noted that for future reference.

Torlos spoke to the other alien for a moment. The other left and returned a minute later and said something to Torlos. Torlos turned to Arcot indicating that he should return to his ship and follow them.

Arcot suddenly turned his eyes and looked directly into the black eyes of the alien. "Torlos," he projected, "will you come with us on our ship?"

"I am commander of this ship. I can not go without the permission of my chief. I will ask my chief."

Again he turned and left Arcot. He was back in a few minutes carrying a small handbag. "I can go. This keeps me in communication with my ship."

Arcot adjusted his weight to zero and floated lightly out the doorway. He rose about six feet above the landing, then indicated to Torlos that he was to grasp Arcot's feet, one in each hand. Torlos closed a grip of steel about each ankle and stepped off the platform.

At once, they dropped, for the power suit had not been adjusted to the load. Arcot yelped in pain as Torlos, in his surprise at not floating, involuntarily gripped tighter. Quickly, Arcot turned on more power and gasped as he felt the weight mount swiftly. He had estimated Torlos' weight at two hundred seventy or so—and it was more like three hundred and fifty! Soon, however, he had the weight adjusted, and they floated easily up toward the *Ancient Mariner*.

They floated in through the door of the ship, and, once inside, Torlos released his hold. Arcot was immediately slammed to the roof with a weight of three hundred and fifty pounds!

A moment later, he was again back on the floor, rubbing his back. He shook his head and frowned, then smiled and pretended to limp.

"Don't let go so suddenly," he admonished telepathically.

"I did not know. I am sorry," Torlos thought contritely.

"Who's your friend?" asked Wade as he entered the corridor. "He certainly looks husky."

"He is," Arcot affirmed. "And he must be weighted with lead! I thought he'd pull my legs off. Look at those arms!"

"I don't want to get him mad at me," Wade grinned. "He looks like he'd make a mean opponent. What's his name!"

"Torlos," replied Arcot, just as Fuller stepped in.

Torlos was looking curiously at a crowbar that had been lying in a rack on the wall. He picked it up and flexed it a bit, as a man might flex a rapier to test its material. Then he held it far out in front of him and proceeded to tie a knot in the inch-thick metal bar! Then, still frowning in puzzlement, he untied it, straightened it as best he could, and put it back in the rack.

The Earthmen were staring in utter astonishment to see the terrific strength the man displayed.

He smiled as he turned to them again.

"If he could do that at arm's length," Wade said thoughtfully, "what could he do if he really tried?"

"Why don't you try and see?" Fuller asked sweetly.

"I can think of easier—but probably no quicker—ways of committing suicide," Wade replied.

Arcot laughed and, looking at Torlos, projected the general meaning of the last remarks. Torlos joined them in the laugh.

"All my people are strong," he thought. "I can not understand why you are not. That was a tool? We could not use it so; it is too weak."

Wade and the others picked up the thought, and Wade laughed. "I suppose they use old I-beams to tie up their Christmas presents."

Arcot held a moment of silent consultation with Torlos, then turned to the others. "We are supposed to follow these men to their city to have some kind of an audience with their ruler, according to Torlos. Let's get started; the rest of the fleet is waiting."

Arcot led Torlos through the main engine room, and was going into the main coil room when Torlos stopped him.

"Is this all your drive apparatus?" he thought.

"Yes, it is," Arcot projected.

"It is smaller than the power equipment of a small private machine!" His thoughts radiated surprise. "How could you make so great a distance?"

"Power," said Arcot. "Look!" He drew his molecular ray pistol. "This alone is powerful enough to destroy all your battle fleet without any danger on our part. And, despite your strength, you are helpless against me!"

Arcot touched a switch on his belt and vanished.

In amazement, Torlos reached out a hand to the spot where Arcot had stood. There was nothing there. Suddenly, he turned, touching the back of his head. Something had tugged at his hair!

He looked all around him and moved his arms around—to no avail. There was nothing there.

Then, in the blink of an eye, Arcot was floating in the air before him. "What avails strength against air, Torlos?" he asked, smiling.

"For safety's sake," Torlos thought, "I want to be your friend!" He grinned widely.

Arcot led the way on into the control room, where Morey had already started to follow the great fleet toward the city.

"What are we going to do at the city?" Arcot asked Torlos telepathically.

"This is the capital of the world, Sator, and here is the commander-of-all-military-and-civil-forces. It is he you will see. He has been summoned," Torlos replied carefully.

"We visited the third world of this system first," Arcot told the alien, "and they repulsed us. We tried to be friendly, but they attacked us at once. In order to keep from being damaged, we had to destroy one of their city-protecting ray buildings." This last thought was hard to transmit; Arcot had pictured mentally a scene in which the ray building was ripped out of the ground and hurled into the air.

In sudden anxiety and concern, Torlos stared into Arcot's eyes. And in that look, Arcot read what even telepathy had hidden heretofore.

"Did you destroy the city?" asked Torlos anxiously. But it was not the question of a man hoping for the destruction of his enemies' cities; Arcot got the mental picture of the city, but with it, he picked up the idea of "home"! Of course, the ideas of "city" and "home" might be synonymous with these people; they never seemed to leave their cities. But why this feeling of worry?

"No, we didn't want to hurt them," Arcot thought. "We destroyed the ray building only in self defense."

"I understand." Despite obvious mental efforts, Torlos positively radiated a feeling of relief!

"Are you at war with that world?" Arcot asked coolly.

"The two worlds have been at war for many generations," Torlos said, then quickly changed the subject. "You will soon meet the leader of all the forces of Sator. He is all-powerful here. His word must be absolutely obeyed. It would be wise if you did not unnecessarily offend him. I see from what your mind tells me that you have great power, but there are many ships on Sator, more than Nansal can boast.

"Our commander, Horlan, is a military commander, but since every man is necessarily a soldier, he is a true ruler."

"I understand," Arcot thought. He turned to Morey and spoke in English, which Torlos could not understand. "Morey, we're going to see the top man here. He rules the army, which runs everything. You and I will go, and leave Wade and Fuller behind as a rear guard. It may not be dangerous, but after being chased off one world, we ought to be as careful as possible.

"We'll go fully armed, and we'll stay in radio contact at all times. Watch yourselves; we don't want them even to touch this ship until we know what kind of people they are."

They had followed the Satorian ships toward the city. The giant magnetic ray barrier opened for them, and the *Ancient Mariner* followed. They were inside the alien city.

XVI

Below the *Ancient Mariner,* the great buildings of the alien city jutted up in the gray light of this gray world; their massiveness seemed only to accentuate the depressing light.

On the broad roofs, they saw hundreds of people coming out to watch them as they moved across the city. According to Torlos, they were the first friendly strangers they had ever seen. They had explored all the planets of this system without finding friendly life.

The buildings sloped up toward the center of the city, and the mass of the great central building loomed before them.

The fleet that was leading the Earth ship settled down to a wide courtyard that surrounded the building. Arcot dropped the *Ancient Mariner* down beside them. The men from Torlos' ship formed into two squads as they came out of the airlocks and marched over to the great shining ship of Earth. They formed two neat rows, one on each side of the airlock.

"Come on, Morey," said Arcot. "We're wanted, Wade, keep the radio going at full amplification; the building may cut out some of the power. I'll try to keep you posted on what's going on, but we'll probably be busy answering questions telepathically."

Arcot and Morey followed Torlos out into the dim light of the gray sky, walking across the courtyard between the ranks of the soldiers from Torlos' ship.

Before them was a heavy gate of solid bronze which swung on massive bronze hinges. The building seemed to be made of a dense, gray stone, much like granite, which was depressing in its perfectly unrelieved front. There were no bright spots of color as there were on all Earthly and Venerian structures. Even the lines were grimly utilitarian; there seemed to be no decoration.

Through the great bronze door they walked, and across a small vestibule. Then they were in a mighty concourse, a giant hallway that went completely through the structure. All around them great granite pillars rose to support the mighty building above. Square cut, they lent but little grace to the huge room, but the floor and walls were made of a hard, light green stone, almost the same color as foliage.

On one wall there was a giant tablet, a great plaque fifteen feet high, made of a deep violet stone, and inlaid with a series of characters in the language of this world. Like English letters, they seemed to read horizontally, but whether they read from left to right or right to left there was no way of knowing. The letters themselves were made of some red metal which Arcot and Morey didn't recognize.

Arcot turned to Torlos and projected a thought: "What is that tablet?"

"Ever since the beginning of the war with the other planet, Nansal, the names of our mighty leaders have been inscribed on that plaque in the rarest metal."

The term "rarest metal" was definite to Torlos, and Arcot decided to question him further on the meaning of it when time permitted.

They crossed the great hall and came to what was evidently an elevator. The door slid open, and the two Earthmen followed Torlos and his lieutenant into the cubicle. Torlos pushed a small button. The door slid shut, and a moment later, Arcot and Morey staggered under the sudden terrific load as the car shot upward under an acceleration of at least three gravities!

It continued just long enough for the Earthmen to get used to it, then it snapped off, and they went flying up toward the ceiling as it continued upward under its own momentum. It slowed under the influence of the planet's gravitation and came to a stop exactly opposite the doorway of a higher floor.

"Wow! Some elevator!" exclaimed Morey as he stepped out, flexing his knees as he tried to readjust himself. "That's what I call a violent way of getting upstairs! It wasn't designed by a lazy man or a cripple! I prefer to walk, thanks! What I want to know is how the old people get upstairs. Or do they die young from using their elevators?"

"No," mused Arcot. "That's the funny thing. They don't seem to be bothered by the acceleration. They actually jumped a little off the floor when we started, and didn't seem to experience much difficulty when we stopped." He looked thoughtful for a moment. "You know, when Torlos was bending that crowbar back there in the ship, I picked up a curious thought—I wonder if—" He turned to the giant alien. "Torlos, you once gave me the thought-idea 'bone metal'; what is that?"

Torlos looked at him in surprise and then pointed mutely to a heavy belt he wore—made of closely woven links of iron wire!

"I was right, Morey!" Arcot exclaimed. "These men have *iron bones!* No wonder he could bend that crowbar! It would be as easy as it would for you or me to snap a human arm bone!"

"But, wait a minute!" Morey objected. "How could iron grow?"

"How can stone grow?" countered Arcot. "That's what your

bones are, essentially—calcium phosphate rock! It's just a matter of different body chemistry. Their body fluids are probably alkaline, and iron won't rust in an alkaline solution." Arcot was talking rapidly as they followed the aliens down the long corridor.

"The thing that confirms my theory is that elevator. It's merely an iron cage in a magnetic beam, and it's pulled up with a terrific acceleration. With iron bones, these men would be similarly influenced, and they wouldn't notice the acceleration so much."

Morey grinned. "I'll be willing to bet they don't use cells in their prisons, here! Just magnetize the floor, and the poor guy could never get away!"

Arcot nodded. "Of course, the bones must be pure iron; their bones evidently don't retain any of the magnetism when they leave the field."

"We seem to be here," Morey interrupted. "Let's continue the discussion later."

Their party had stopped just outside a large, elaborately carved door, the first sign of ornamentation the Earthmen had seen. There were four guards armed with pistols, which, they discovered later, were powered by compressed air under terrific pressure. They hurled a small metal slug through a rifled barrel, and were effective over a distance of about a mile, although they could only fire four times without reloading.

Torlos spoke briefly with the guard, who saluted and opened the door. The two Earthmen followed Torlos into a large room.

Before them was a large, crescent-shaped table, around which were seated several men. At the center of the crescent curve sat a man in a gray uniform, but he was so bedecked with insignia, medals, ribbons, and decorations that his uniform was scarcely visible.

The entire assemblage, including the leader, rose as the Earthmen entered. Arcot and Morey, taking the hint, snapped to attention and delivered a precise military salute.

"We greet you in the name of our planet," said Arcot aloud. "I know you don't understand a word I'm saying, but I hope it sounds impressive enough. We salute you, O High Muckymuck!"

Morey, successfully keeping a straight face, raised his hand and said sonorously: "That goes double for me, bub."

In his own language, the leader replied, putting his hands to his hips with a definite motion, and shaking his head from side to side at the same time.

Arcot watched the man closely while he spoke. He was taller than Torlos, but less heavily built, as were all the others here. It seemed that Torlos was unusually powerful, even for this world.

When the leader had finished, Arcot smiled and turned to project this thought at Torlos.

"Tell your leader that we come from a planet far away across the vast depths of space. We come in peace, and we will leave in peace, but we would like to ask some favors of him, which we will repay by giving him the secret of our weapons. With them, he can easily conquer Nansal.

"All we want is some wire made from the element lead and some information from your astronomers."

Torlos turned and spoke to his leader in a deep, powerful voice.

Meanwhile, Morey was trying to get in communication with the ship. The walls, however, seemed to be made of metal, and he couldn't get through to Wade.

"We're cut off from the ship," he said quietly to Arcot.

"I was afraid of that, but I think it'll be all right. Our proposition is too good for them to turn down."

Torlos turned back to Arcot when the leader had finished speaking. "The Commanding One asks that you prove the possibilities of your weapons. His scientists tell him that it is impossible to make the trip that you claim to have made."

"What your scientists say is true, to an extent," Arcot thought. "They have learned that no body can go faster than the speed of light—is that not so?"

"Yes. Such, they say, is the fact. To have made this trip, you must, of necessity, be not less than twenty million years old!"

"Tell them that there are some things they do not yet know about space. The velocity of light is a thing that is fixed by the nature of space, right?"

Torlos consulted with the scientists again, then turned back to Arcot. "They agree that they do not know all the secrets of the Universe, but they agree that the speed of light is fixed by the nature of space."

"How fast does sound travel?" Arcot asked.

"They ask in what medium do you mean?"

"How fast does light travel? In air? In glass? The speed of light is as variable as that of sound. If I can alter the nature of space, so as to make the velocity of light greater, can I not then go faster than in normal space?"

"They say that this is true," Torlos said, after more conversation with the men at the table, "but they say that space is unalterable, since it is emptiness."

"Ask them if they know of the curvature of space." Arcot was becoming worried for fear his explanation would be unintelligible; unless they knew his terms, he could not explain, and it would take a long time to teach them.

"They say," Torlos thought, "that I have misunderstood you. They say space could not possibly be curved, for space is emptiness, and how could empty nothingness be curved."

Arcot turned to Morey and shrugged his shoulders. "I give up, Morey; it's a bad case. If they insist that space is nothing, and can't be curved, I can't go any further."

"If they don't know of the curvature of space," said Morey, "ask them how they learned that the velocity of light is the limiting velocity of a moving body."

Torlos translated and the scientists gave their reply. "They say that you do not know more of space than they, for they know that the speed of light is ultimate. They have tested this with spaceships at high speeds and with experiments with the smallest particles of electricity."

The scientists were looking at Arcot now in protest; they felt he was trying to foist something off on them.

Arcot, too, was becoming exasperated. "Well, if they insist that we couldn't have come from another star, where do they think I come from? They have explored this system and found no such people as we, so I must have come from another star. How? If they won't accept my explanations, let them think up a theory of their own to explain the facts!" He paused for Torlos to translate, then went on. "They say I don't know any more than they do. Tell them to watch this."

He drew his molecular ray pistol and lifted a heavy metal chair into the air. Then Morey drew his heat beam and turned it on the chair. In a few seconds, it was glowing white hot, and then it collapsed into a fiery ball of liquid metal. Morey shut off the heat beam, and Arcot held the ball in the air while it cooled rapidly under the influence of the molecular ray. Then he lowered it to the floor.

It was obvious that the scientists were impressed, and the Emperor was talking eagerly with the men around him. They talked for several minutes, saying nothing to the Earthmen. Torlos stood quietly, waiting for a message to relay.

The Emperor called out, and some of the guards moved inside the door.

Torlos turned to Arcot. "Show no emotion!" came his telepathic warning. "I have been listening to them as they spoke. The Commanding One wants your weapons. Regardless of what his scientists tell him about the possibility of your trip, he knows those weapons work, and he wants them.

"You see, I am not a Satorian at all. I'm from Nansal, sent here many years ago as a spy. I have served in their fleets for many years, and have gained their trust.

"I am telling you the truth, as you will soon see.

"These people are going to follow their usual line of action and take the most direct way toward their end. They are going to attack you, believing that you, despite your weapons, will go down before superior numbers.

"And you'd better move fast; he's calling the guards already!"

Arcot turned to Morey, his face calm, his heart beating like a vibrohammer. "Keep your face straight, Morey. Don't look surprised. They're planning to jump us. We'll rip out the right wall and—"

He stopped. It was too late! The order had been given, and the guards were leaping toward them. Arcot grabbed at his ray pistol, but one of the guards jumped him before he had a chance to draw it.

Torlos seized the man by one leg and an arm and, tensing his huge muscles, hurled him thirty feet against the Commanding One with such force that both were killed instantly! He turned and grabbed another before his first victim had landed and hurled him toward the advancing guards. Arcot thought fleetingly that here was proof of Torlos' story of being from Nansal; the greater gravity of the third planet made him a great deal stronger than the Satorians!

One of the guards was trying to reach for Arcot. Acting instinctively, the Earthman lashed out with a hard jab to the point of the Satorian's jaw. The iron bones transmitted the shock beautifully to the delicate brain; the man's head jerked back, and he collapsed to the floor. Arcot's hand felt as though he'd hit it with a hammer, but he was far too busy to pay any attention to the pain.

Morey, too, had realized the futility of trying to overcome the guards by wrestling. The only thing to do was dodge and punch. The guards were trying to take the Earthmen alive, but, because of their greater weight, they couldn't move quite as fast as Arcot and Morey.

Torlos was still in action. He had seen the success of the Earthmen who, weak as they were, had been able to knock a man out with a blow to the jaw. Driving his own fists like pistons, he imitated their blows with deadly results; every man he struck went down forever.

The dead were piling around him, but through the open door he could see reinforcements arriving. Somehow, he had to save these Earthmen; if Sator got their secrets, Nansal would be lost!

He reached down and grabbed one of the fallen men and hurled him across the room, smashing back the men who struggled to attack. Then he picked up another and followed through with a second projectile. Then a third. With the speed and tirelessness of some giant engine of war, he slammed his macabre ammunition against the oncoming reinforcements with telling results.

At last Arcot was free for a moment, and that was all he needed. He jerked his molecular ray pistol from its holster and beamed it mercilessly toward the door, hurling the attackers violently backwards. They died instantly, their chilled corpses driving back against their comrades with killing force.

In a moment, every man in the room was dead except for the two Earthmen and the giant Torlos.

Outside the room, they could hear shouted orders as more of the Satorian guards were rallied.

"They'll try to kill us now!" Arcot said. "Come on, we've got to get out of here!"

"Sure," said Morey, "but which way?"

XVII

"Morey, pull down the wall over that door to block their passage," Arcot ordered. "I'll get the other wall."

Arcot pointed his pistol and triggered it. The outer wall flew outward in an explosion of flying masonry. He switched on his radio and called the *Ancient Mariner*.

"Wade! We were cut off because of the metal in the walls! We've been doublecrossed—they tried to jump us. Torlos warned us in time. We've torn out the wall; just hang outside with the airlock open and wait for us. Don't use the rays, because we'll be invisible, and you might hit us."

Suddenly the room rocked under an explosion, and the debris Morey's ray had torn down over the door was blasted away. A score of men leaped through the gap before the dust had settled. Morey beamed them down mercilessly before they could fire their weapons.

"In the air, quick!" Arcot yelled. He turned on his power suit and rose into the air, signaling Torlos to grab his ankles as he had done before. Morey slammed another parting shot toward the doorway as he lifted himself toward the ceiling. Then both Earthmen snapped on their invisibility units. Torlos, because of his direct contact with Arcot, also vanished from sight.

More of the courageous, but foolhardy Satorians leaped through the opening and stared in bewilderment as they saw no one moving. Arcot, Morey, and Torlos were hanging invisible in the air above them.

Just then, the shining bulk of the *Ancient Mariner* drifted into view. They drew back behind the wall and sought shelter. One of them began to fire his compressed air gun at it with absolutely no effect; the heavy lux walls might as well have been hit by a mosquito.

As the airlock swung open, Arcot and Morey headed out through the breach in the wall. A moment later, they were inside the ship. The heavy door hissed closed behind them as they settled to the floor.

"I'll take the controls," Arcot said. "Morey, head for the rear; you take the moleculars and take Torlos with you to handle the heat beam." He turned and ran toward the control room, where

Wade and Fuller were waiting. "Wade, take the forward molecular beams; Fuller, you handle the heat projector."

Arcot strapped himself into the control chair.

Suddenly, there was a terrific explosion, and the titanic mass of the ship was rocked by the detonation of a bomb one of the men in the building had fired at the ship.

Torlos had evidently understood the operation of the heat beam projector quickly; the stabbing beam reached out, and the great tower, from floor to roof, suddenly leaned over and slumped as the entire side of the building was converted into a mass of glowing stone and molten steel. Then it crashed heavily to the ground a half mile below.

But already there were forty of the great battleships rising to meet them.

"I think we'd better get moving," Arcot said. "We can't let a magnetic ray touch us now; it would kill Torlos. I'm going to cut in the invisibility units, so don't use the heat beams whatever you do!"

Arcot snapped the ship into invisibility and darted to one side. The enemy ships suddenly halted in their wild rush and looked around in amazement for their opponent.

Arcot was heading for the magnetic force field which surrounded the city when Torlos made a mistake. He turned the powerful heat beam downwards and picked off an enemy battleship. It fell, a blazing wreck, but the ray touched a building behind it, and the ionized air established a conducting path between the ship and the planet.

The apparatus was not designed to make a planet invisible, but it made a noble effort. As a result one of the tubes blew, and the *Ancient Mariner* was visible again. Arcot had no time to replace the tube; the Satorian fleet kept him too busy.

Arcot drove the ship, shooting, twisting upward; Wade and Morey kept firing the molecular beams with precision. The pale rays reached out to touch the battleship, and wherever they touched, the ships went down in wreckage, falling to the city below. In spite of the odds against it, the *Ancient Mariner* was giving a good account of itself.

And always, Arcot was working the ship toward the magnetic wall and the base of the city.

Suddenly, giant pneumatic guns from below joined in the battle, hurling huge explosive shells toward the Earthship. They managed to hit the *Ancient Mariner* twice, and each time the ship was staggered by the force of the blast, but the foot-thick armor of lux metal ignored the explosions.

The magnetic rays touched them a few times, and each time Torlos was thrown violently to the floor, but the ship was in the path of the beams for so short a time that he was not badly injured. He more than made up for his injuries with the ray he used, and Morey was no mean gunner, either, judging from the work he was doing.

Three ships attempted to commit suicide in their efforts to destroy the Earthmen. They were only semi-successful; they managed to commit suicide. In trying to crash into the ship, they were simply caught by Morey's or Wade's molecular beam and thrown away. Morey actually developed a use for them. He caught them in the beam and used them as bullets to smash the other ships, throwing them about on the molecular ray until they were too cold too move.

Arcot finally managed to reach the magnetic wall.

"Wade!" he called. "Get that projector building!"

A molecular beam reached down, and the black metal dome sailed high into the sky, breaking the solidity of the magnetic wall. An instant later, the *Ancient Mariner* shot through the gap. In a few moments, they would be far away from the city.

Torlos seemed to realize this. Moving quickly, he pushed Morey away from the molecular beam projector, taking the controls away from him.

He did not realize the power of that ray; he did not know that these projectors could move whole suns out of their orbits. He only knew that they were destructive. They were several miles from the city when he turned the projector on it, after twisting the power control up.

To his amazement, he saw the entire city suddenly leap into the air and flash out into space, a howling meteor that vanished into the cloudbank overhead. Behind it was a deep hole in the planet's surface, a mighty chasm lined with dark granite.

Torlos stared at it in amazement and horror.

Arcot turned back slowly, and they sailed over the spot where the city had been. They saw a dozen or so battleships racing away from them to spread the news of the disaster; they were the few which had been fortunate enough to be outside the city when the beam struck.

Arcot maneuvered the ship directly over the mighty pit and sank slowly down, using the great searchlights to illuminate the dark chasm. Far, far down, he could see the solid rock of the bottom. The thing was miles deep.

Then Arcot lifted the ship and headed up through the cloud layer and into the bright light of the great yellow sun, above the sea of gray misty clouds.

Arcot signaled Morey, who had come into the control room, to take over the controls of the ship. "Head out into space, Morey. I want to find out why Torlos pulled that last stunt. Wade, will you put a new tube in the invisibility unit?"

"Sure," Wade replied. "By the way, what happened back there? We were surprised as the very devil to hear you yelling for help; everything seemed peaceful up to then."

Arcot flexed his bruised hands and grinned ruefully. "Plenty happened." He went on to explain to Wade and Fuller what had happened in their meeting with the Satorian Commander.

"Nice bunch of people to deal with," Wade said caustically. "They tried to get everything and lost it all. We would have given them plenty if they'd been decent about it. But what sort of war is this that the people of these two planets are carrying on, anyway?"

"That's the question I intend to settle," replied Arcot. "We haven't had an opportunity to talk to Torlos yet. He had just admitted to me that he was a spy for Nansal when the fun began, and we've been too busy to ask questions ever since. Come on, let's go into the library."

Arcot indicated to Torlos that he was to go with him. Wade and Fuller followed.

When they had all seated themselves, Arcot began the telepathic questioning. "Torlos, why did you force Morey to leave the ray and then destroy the city? You certainly had no reason to kill all the non-combatant women and children in that city, did you? And why, after I told you absolutely not to use the heat beam while we were invisible, did you use the rays on that battleship? You made our invisibility break down and destroyed a tube. Why did you do this?"

"I am sorry, man of Earth," replied Torlos. "I can only say that

I did not fully understand the effect the rays would have. I did not know how long we would remain invisible; the thing has been accomplished in our laboratories, but only for fractions of a second, and I feared we might become visible soon. That was one of their latest battleships equipped with a new, secret, and very deadly weapon. I do not know exactly what the weapon is, but I knew that ship could be deadly against us, and I wanted to make sure we were not attacked by it. That is why I used the beam while your ship was invisible.

"And I did not intend to destroy the city. I was only trying to tear up the factory that builds these battleships; I only wanted to destroy their machines. I had no conception of the power of that ray. I was as horrified to see the city disappear as you were; I only wanted to protect my people." Torlos smiled bitterly. "I have lived among these treacherous people for many years, and I cannot say that I had no provocation to destroy their city and everyone in it. But I had no intention of doing it, Earthman."

Arcot knew he was sincere. There could be no deception when communicating telepathically. He wished he had used it when communicating with the Commanding One of Sator; the trouble would have been stopped quickly!

"You still do not have any conception of the magnitude of the power of that beam, Torlos," Arcot told him. "With the rays of this ship, we tore a sun from its orbit and threw it into another. What you did to that city, we could do to the whole planet. Do not tamper with forces you do not understand, Torlos.

"There are forces on this ship that would make the energies of your greatest battleship seem weak and futile. We can race through space a billion times faster than the speed of light; we can tear apart and destroy the atoms of matter; we can rip apart the greatest of planets; we can turn the hurtling stars and send them where we want them; we can curve space as we please; we can put out the fires of a sun, if we wish.

"Torlos, respect the powers of this ship, and do not release its energies unknowingly; they are too great."

Torlos looked around him in awe. He had seen the engines—small, apparently futile things, compared with the solid might of the giant engines in his ship—but he had seen explosive charges that he knew would split any ship open from end to end bounce harmlessly from the smooth walls of this ship. He had seen it destroy the fleet of magnetic ships that had formed a supposedly impregnable guard around the mightiest city of Sator.

Then he himself had touched a button, and the giant city had shot off into space, leaving behind it only a screaming tornado and a vast chasm in the crust of the blasted planet.

He could not appreciate the full significance of the velocities Arcot had told him about—he only knew that he had made a bad mistake in underrating the powers of this ship! "I will not touch these things again without your permission, Earthman," Torlos promised earnestly.

The *Ancient Mariner* drove on through space, rapidly eating up the millions of miles that separated Nansal from Sator. Arcot sat in the control room with Morey discussing their passenger.

"You know," Arcot mused, "I've been thinking about that man's strength; an iron skeleton doesn't explain it all. He has to have muscles to move that skeleton around."

"He's got muscles, all right," Morey grinned. "But I see what you mean; muscles that big should tire easily, and his don't seem to. He seems tireless; I watched him throw those men one after another like bullets from a machine gun. He threw the last one as violently as the first—and those men weighed over three hundred pounds! Apparently his muscles felt no fatigue!"

"There's another thing," pointed out Arcot. "The way he was breathing and the way he seemed to keep so cool. When I got through there, I was dripping with sweat; that hot, moist air was almost too much for me. Our friend? Cool as ever, if not more so.

"And after the fight, he wasn't even breathing heavily!"

"No," agreed Morey. "But did you notice him *during* the fight? He was breathing heavily, deeply, and swiftly—not the shallow, panting breath of a runner, but deep and full, yet faster than I can breathe. I could hear him breathing in spite of all the noise of the battle."

"I noticed it," Arcot said. "He started breathing *before* the fight started. A human being can fight very swiftly, and with tremendous vigor, for ten seconds, putting forth his best effort, and only breathe once or twice. For another two minutes, he breathes more heavily than usual. But after that, he can't just slow down back to normal. He has used up the surplus oxygen in his system, and that has to be replaced; he has run into 'oxygen debt'. He has to keep on breathing hard to get back the oxygen surplus his body requires.

"But not Torlos! No fatigue for him! Why? *Because he doesn't use the oxygen of the air to do work, and therefore his body is not a chemical engine!*"

Morey nodded slowly. "I see what you're driving at. His body uses the heat energy of the air! His muscles turn heat energy into motion the same way our molecular beams do!"

"Exactly—he lives on heat!" Arcot said. "I've noticed that he seems almost cold-blooded; his body is at the temperature of the room at all times. In a sense, he is reptilian, but he's vastly more efficient and greatly different than any reptile Earth ever knew. He eats food, all right, but he only needs it to replace his body cells and to fuel his brain."

"Oh, *brother*," said Morey softly. "No wonder he can do the things he did! Why, he could have kept up that fight for hours without getting tired! Fatigue is as unknown to him as cold weather. He'd only need sleep to replace worn parts. His world is warm and upright on its axis, so there are no seasons. He couldn't survive in the Arctic, but he's obviously the ideal form of life for the tropics."

As the two men found out later, Morey was wrong on that last point. The men of Torlos' race had a small organ, a mass of cells in the lower abdomen which could absorb food from the bloodstream and oxidize it, yielding heat, whenever the temperature of the blood dropped below a certain point. Then they could live very comfortably in the Arctic zones; they carried their own heaters. Their vast strength was limited then, however, and they were forced to eat more and were more subject to fatigue.

Wade and Fuller had been trying to speak with Torlos telepathically, and had evidently run into difficulty, for Fuller called into the control room: "Hey, Arcot, come here a minute! I thought telepathy was a universal language, but this guy doesn't get our ideas at all! And we can't make out some of his. Just now, he seemed to be thinking of 'nourishment' or 'food', and I found out he was thinking of 'heat'!"

"I'll be right down," Arcot told him, heading for the library.

As he entered, Torlos smiled at him; Arcot picked up his thought easily: "Your friends do not seem to understand my thoughts."

"We are not made as you are," Arcot explained, "and our thought forms are different. To you, 'heat' and 'food' are practically the same thing, but we do not think of them as such."

He continued, explaining carefully to Torlos the differences between their bodies and their methods of using energy.

"Stone bones!" Torlos thought in amazement. "And chemical engines for muscles! No wonder you seem so weak. And yet, with your brains, I would hate to have to fight a war with your people!"

"Which brings me to another point," Arcot continued. "We would like to know how the war between the people of Sator and the people of Nansal began. Has it been going on very long?"

Torlos nodded. "I will tell you the story. It is a history that began many centuries ago; a history of persecution and rebellion. And yet, for all that, I think it an interesting history.

"Hundreds of years ago, on Nansal . . ."

XVIII

Hundreds of years ago, on Nansal, there had lived a wise and brilliant teacher named Norus. He had developed an ideal, a philosophy of life, a code of ethics. He had taught the principles of nobility without arrogance, pride without stubbornness, and humility without servility.

About him had gathered a group of men who began to develop and spread his ideals. As the new philosophy spread across the planet, more and more Nansalians adopted it and began to raise their children according to its tenets.

But no philosophy, however workable, however noble, can hope to convert everyone. There always remains a hard core of men who feel that "the old way is the best way". In this case, it was the men whose lives had been based on cunning, deceit, and treachery.

One of these men, a brilliant, but warped genius, named Sator, had built the first spaceship, and he and his men had fled Nansal to set up their own government and free themselves from the persecution they believed they suffered at the hands of the believers of Norus.

They fled to the second planet, where the ship crashed and the builder, Sator, was killed. For hundreds of years, nothing was heard of the emigrants, and the people of Nansal believed them dead. Nansal was at peace.

But the Satorians managed to live on the alien world, and they built a civilization there, a civilization based on an entirely different system. It was a system of cunning. To them, cunning was right. The man who could plot most cunningly, gain his ends by deceiving his friends best, was the man who most deserved to live. There were a few restrictions; they had loyalty, for one thing—loyalty to their country and their world.

In time, the Satorians rediscovered the space drive, but by this time, living on the new planet had changed them physically. They were somewhat smaller than the Nansalians, and lighter in color, for their world was always sunless. The warm rays of the sun had tanned the skins of the Nansalians to a darker color.

When the Satorians first came to Nansal, it was presumably in peace. After so many hundreds of years without war, the Nansalians accepted them, and trade treaties were signed. For years, the Satorians traded peacefully.

In the meantime, Satorian spies were working to find the strengths and weaknesses of Nansal, searching to discover their secret weapons and processes, if any. And they rigorously guarded their own secrets. They refused to disclose the secrets of the magnetic beam and the magnetic space drive.

Finally, there were a few of the more suspicious Nansalians who realized the danger in such a situation. There were three men, students in one of the great scientific schools of Nansal, who realized that the situation should be studied. There was no law prohibiting the men of Nansal from going to Sator, but it seemed that Nature had raised a more impenetrable barrier.

All Nansalians who went to Sator died of a mysterious disease. A method was found whereby a man's body could be sterilized, bacteriologically speaking, so he could not spread the disease, and this was used on all Satorians entering Nansal. But you can't sterilize a whole planet. Nansalians could not go to Sator.

But these three men had a different idea. They carefully studied the speech and the mannerisms and customs of the Satorians. They learned to imitate the slang and idioms. They went even further; they picked three Satorian spaceship navigators and studied them minutely every time they got a chance, in order to learn their habits and their speech patterns. The three Satorians were exceptionally large men, almost perfect doubles of the three Nansalians—and, one by one, the Nansalians replaced them.

They had bleached their faces, and surgeons, working from photographs, changed their features so that the three Nansalians were exact doubles of the three astrogators. Then they acted. On three trips, one of the men that went back as navigator was a Nansalian.

It was six years before they returned to Nansal, but when they finally did, they had learned two things.

In the first place, the 'disease' which had killed Nansalians who had come in contact with Satorians on Nansal was nothing but a poison which acted on contact with the skin. The Nansalians who had gone to Sator had simply been murdered. There was no disease; it had simply been a Satorian plot to keep Nansalians from going to Sator.

The second thing they had learned was the secret of the Satorian magnetic space drive.

It was common knowledge on Sator that their commander would soon lead them across space to conquer Nansal and settle on a world of clear air and cloudless skies, where they could see the stars of space at night. They were waiting only until they could build up a larger fleet and learned all they could from the Nansalians.

They attacked three years after the three Nansalian spies returned with their information.

During those three years, Nansal had secretly succeeded in building up a fleet of the magnetic ships, but it went down quickly before the vastly greater fleet of the Satorians. Their magnetic rays were deadly, killing everyone they struck. They could lift the iron-boned Nansalians high into the air, then drop them hundreds of feet to their death.

The buildings, with their steel and iron frames, went down, crushing hundreds of others. They practically depopulated the whole planet.

But the warnings of the three spies had been in time. They had enlarged some of the great natural caverns and dug others out of solid rock. Here they had built laboratories, factories, and dwelling places far underground, where the Satorians could never find them.

Enough men reached the caverns before the disaster struck to carry on. They had been chosen from the strongest, healthiest, and most intelligent that Nansal had. They lived there for over a century, while the planet was overrun by the conquerors and the cities were rebuilt by the Satorians.

During this century, the magnetic ray shield was developed by the hidden Nansalians. Daring at last to face their conquerors, they built a city on the surface and protected it with the magnetic force screen.

By the time the Satorians found the city, it was too late. A battle fleet was mobilized and rushed to the spot, but the city was impregnable. The great domed power stations were already in operation, and they were made of nonmagnetic materials, so they could not be pulled from the ground. The magnetic beams were neutralized by the shield, and no ship could pass through it without killing every man aboard.

That first city was a giant munitions plant. The Nansalians built factories there and laughed while the armies of Sator raged impotently at the magnetic barrier. They tried sending missiles through, but the induction heating in every metal part of the bombs either caused them to explode instantly or to drop harmlessly and burn.

In the meantime, the men of Nansal were building their fleet. The Satorians stepped up production, too, but the Nansalians had developed a method of projecting the magnetic screen. Any approaching Satorian ship had its magnetic support cut from under it, and it crashed to the ground.

It took nearly thirty years of hard work and harder fighting for the Nansalians to convince the people of Sator that Nansal and the philosophy of Norus had not only not been wiped out, but was capable of wiping out the Satorians.

With their screened and protected fleet, the followers of Norus smashed the Satorian cities, and drove their enemy back to Sator.

There were only three enemy cities left on Nansal when, somehow, they managed to learn the secret of the magnetic screen.

By this time, the forces of Nansal had increased tremendously, and they developed the next surprise for the Satorians. One after another, the three remaining cities were destroyed by a barrage of poison gas.

The fleet of Sator tried to retaliate, but the Nansalians were prepared for them. Every building had been sealed and filters had been built into the air conditioning systems.

Shortly, the men of Nansal were again in control of their planet, and the fleet stood guard over the planet.

The Satorians, beaten technologically, were still not ready to give up. Falling back on their peculiar philosophy of life, they pulled a trick the Nansalians would never have thought of. They sued for peace.

The government of Nansal was willing; they had had enough of bloodshed. They permitted a delegation to arrive. The ship was escorted into the city and the parleying began.

The Satorian delegation asked for absolutely unreasonable terms. They demanded fleet bases on Nansal; they demanded an unreasonable rate of exchange between the two powers, one which would be highly favorable to Sator; they wanted to impose fantastic restrictions on Nansalian travel and none whatsoever on their own.

Month followed month and months became years as the diplomats of Nansal tried, patiently and logically, to show the Satorians how unreasonable their demands were.

Not once did they suspect that the Satorians had no intention of trying to get the conditions they asked for. Their sole purpose was to drag the parleying on and on, bickering, quarreling, demanding, and conceding just enough to give the Nansalians hope that a treaty might eventually be consummated.

And during all that time, the factories of Sator were working furiously to build the greatest fleet that had ever crossed the space between the two planets!

When they were ready to attack, the Satorian delegation told Nansal frankly that they would not treaty with them. The day the delegation left, the Satorian fleet swept down upon Nansal!

The Nansalians were again beaten back into their cities, safe behind their magnetic screens, but unable to attack. But the forces of Sator had not won easily—they had, in fact, not won at all. Their supply line was too long and their fleet had suffered greatly at the hands of the defenders of Nansal.

For a long while, the balance of power was so nearly equal that neither side dared attack.

Then the balance again swung toward Nansal. A Nansalian scientist discovered a compact method of storing power. Oddly enough, it was similar to the method Dr. Richard Arcot had discovered a hundred thousand light centuries away! It did not store nearly the power, and was inefficient, but it was a great improvement over their older method of generating energy in the ship itself.

The Nansalian ships could be made smaller, and lighter, and more maneuverable, and at the same time could be equipped with heavier, more powerful magnetic beam generators.

Very shortly, the Satorians were again at the mercy of Nansal. They could not fight the faster, more powerful ships of the Nansalians, and again they went down in defeat.

And again they sued for peace.

This time, Nansal knew better; they went right on developing their fleet while the diplomats of Sator argued.

But the Satorians weren't fools; they didn't expect Nansal to swallow the same bait a second time. Sator had another ace up her sleeve.

Ten days after they arrived, every diplomat and courier of the Satorian delegation committed suicide!

Puzzled, the government of Nansal reported the deaths to Sator at once, expecting an immediate renewal of hostilities; they were quite sure that Sator assumed they had been murdered. Nansal was totally unprepared for what happened; Sator acknowledged the message with respects and said they would send a new commission.

Two days later, Nansal realized it had been tricked again. A horrible disease broke out and spread like wildfire. The incubation period was twelve days; during that time it gave no sign. Then the flesh began to rot away, and the victim died within hours. No wonder the ambassadors had committed suicide!

Millions died, including Torlos' own father, during the raging epidemic that followed. But, purely by lucky accident, the Nansalian medical research teams came up with a cure and a preventive inoculation before the disease had spread over the whole planet.

Sator's delegation had inoculated themselves with the disease and, at the sacrifice of their own lives, had spread it on Nansal. Although the Satorians had developed the horribly virulent strain of virus, they had not found a cure; the diplomats knew they were going to die.

Having managed to stop the disease before it swept the planet, the Nansalians decided to pull a trick of their own. Radio communication with Sator was cut off in such a way as to lead the Satorian government to believe that Nansal was dying of the disease.

The scientists of Sator knew that the virus was virulent; in fact, too virulent for its own good. It killed the host every time, and the virus could not live outside a living cell. They knew that shortly after every Nansalian died, the virus, too, would be dead.

Their fleet started for Nansal six months after radio contact had broken off. Expecting to find Nansal a dead planet, they were totally unprepared to find them alive and ready for the attack. The Satorian fleet, vastly surprised to find a living, vigorous enemy, was totally wiped out.

Since that time, both planets had remained in a state of armed truce. Neither had developed any weapon which would enable them to gain an advantage over their enemy. Each was so spy-infested that no move could pass undiscovered.

Stalemate.

XIX

Torlos spread his hands eloquently. "That is the history of our war. Can you wonder that my people were suspicious when your ship appeared? Can you wonder that they drove you away? They were afraid of the men of Sator; when they saw your weapons, they were afraid for their civilization.

"On the other hand, why should the men of Sator fear? They knew that our code of honor would not permit us to make a treacherous attack.

"I regret that my people drove you away, but can you blame them?"

Arcot had to admit that he could not. He turned to Morey. "They were certainly reasonable in driving us from their cities;

experience has taught them that it's the safest way. A good offense is always the best defense.

"But experience has taught me that, unlike Torlos, I have to eat. I wonder if it might not be a good idea to get a little rest too —I'm bushed."

"Good idea," agreed Morey. "I'll ask Wade to stand guard while we sleep. If Torlos wants company, he can talk to Wade as well as anyone. I'm due for some sleep myself."

Arcot, Morey, and Fuller went to their rooms for some rest. Arcot and Morey were tired, but after an hour, Fuller rose and went down to the control room where Wade was communicating telepathically with Torlos.

"Hello," Wade greeted him. "I thought you were going to join the Snoring Chorus."

"I tried to, but I couldn't get in tune. What have you been doing?"

"I've been talking with Torlos—and with fair success. I'm getting the trick of thought communication," Wade said enthusiastically. "I asked Torlos if he wanted to sleep, and it seems they do it regularly, one day in ten. And when they sleep, they sleep soundly. It's more of a coma, something like the hibernation of a bear or a possum.

"If you want to do business with Mr. John Doe, and he happens to be asleep, your business will have to wait. It takes something really drastic to wake these people up.

"I remember a remark one of my classmates made while I was going to college. He was totally unconscious of the humor in the thing. He said: 'I've got to go to more lectures. I've been losing a lot of sleep.'

"He intended them to be totally disconnected thoughts, but the rest of us knew his habits, and we almost knocked ourselves out laughing.

"I was just wondering what would happen if a Nansalian were to drop off in class. They'd probably have to call an ambulance or something to carry him home!"

Fuller looked at the giant. "I doubt it. One of his classmates would just tuck him under his arm and take him on home—or to the next lecture. Remember, they only weigh about four hundred pounds on Nansal, which is no more to them than fifty pounds is to us."

"True enough," Wade agreed. "But you know, I'd hate to have him wrap those arms of his about me. He might get excited, or sneeze or something, and—*squish!*"

"You and your morbid imagination." Fuller sat down in one of the seats. "Let's see if we can't get a three-way conversation going; this guy is interesting."

Arcot and Morey awoke nearly three hours later, and the Earthmen ate their breakfast, much to Torlos' surprise.

"I can understand that you need far more food than we do," he commented, "but you only ate a few hours ago. It seems like a tremendous amount of food to me. How could you possibly grow enough in your cities?"

"So *that's* why they don't have any farms!" Fuller said.

"Our food is grown out on the plains outside the cities, where there is room," Arcot explained. "It's difficult, but we have machines to help us. We could never have developed the cone type of city you have, however, for we need huge huge quantities of food. If we were to seal ourselves inside our cities as your people have to protect themselves from enemies, we would starve to death very quickly."

"You know," Morey said, "I'll have to admit that Torlos' people are a higher type of creation than we are. Man, and all other animals on Earth, are parasites of the plant world. We're absolutely incapable of producing our own foods. We can't gather energy for ourselves. We're utterly dependent on plants.

"But these men aren't—at least not so much so. They at least generate their own muscular energy by extracting heat from the air they breathe. They combine all the best features of plants, reptiles, and mammals. I don't know where they'd be classified biologically!"

After the meal, they went to the control room and strapped themselves into the control seats. Arcot checked the fuel gauge.

"We have plenty of lead left," he said to Morey, "and Torlos has assured me that we will be able to get more on Nansal. I suggest we show him how the space control works, so that he can tell the Nansalian scientists about it from personal experience.

"In this sun's gravitational field, we'll lose a lot of power, but as long as it can be replaced, we're all right."

Turning to the Nansalian, Arcot pointed out toward the little spark of light that was Torlos' home planet. "Keep your eyes on that, Torlos. Watch it grow when we use our space control drive."

Arcot pushed the little red switch to the first notch. The air around them pulsed with power for an instant, then space had readjusted itself.

The point that was Nansal grew to a disc, and then it was swiftly leaping toward them, welling up to meet them, expanding its bulk with awesome speed. Torlos watched it tensely.

There was a sudden splintering crash, and Arcot jerked open the circuit in alarm. They were almost motionless again as the stars reeled about them.

Torlos had been nervous. Like any man so affected, he had unconsciously tightened his muscles. His fingers had sunk into the hard plastic of the arm rest on his chair, and crushed it as though it had been put between the jaws of a hydraulic press!

"I'm glad we weren't holding hands," said Wade, eyeing the broken plastic.

"I am very sorry," Torlos thought humbly. "I did not intend to do that. I forgot myself when I saw that planet rushing at me so fast." His chagrin was apparent on his face.

Arcot laughed. "It is nothing, Torlos. We are merely astonished at the terrific strength of your hand. Wade wasn't worried; he was joking!"

Torlos looked relieved, but he looked at the splintered arm rest and then at his hand. "It is best that I keep my too-strong hands away from your instruments."

The ship was falling toward Nansal at a relatively slow rate, less than four miles a second. Arcot accelerated toward the planet for two hours, then began to decelerate. Five hundred miles above the planet's surface, their velocity cut the ship into a descending spiral orbit to allow the atmosphere to check their speed.

The outer lux hull began to heat up, and he closed the relux screens to cut down the radiation from it. When he opened them again, the ship was speeding over the broad plains of the planet.

Torlos told Arcot that by far the greater percentage of the surface of Nansal was land. There was still plenty of water, for their seas were much deeper than those of Earth. Some of the seas were thirty miles deep over broad areas—hundreds of square miles. As if to compensate, the land surfaces were covered with titanic mountain ranges, some of them over ten miles above sea level.

Torlos, his eyes shining, directed the Earthmen to his home city, the capital of the world-nation.

"Is there no traffic between the cities here, Torlos?" Morey asked. "We haven't seen any ships."

"There's continuous traffic," Torlos replied, "but you have come in far to the north, well away from the regularly scheduled routes. The commerce must be densely populated with warships as well, and both warships and commercial craft are made to look as much alike as possible so that the enemy cannot know when ships of war are present and when they are not, and their attacks are more easily beaten off. They are forced to live off our commerce while they are here. Before we invented the magnetic storage device, they were forced to get fuel from our ships in order to make the return journey; they could not carry enough for the round trip."

Suddenly his smile broadened, and he pointed out the forward window. "Our city is behind the next range of mountains!"

They were flying at a height of twenty miles, and the range Torlos indicated was far off in the blue distance, almost below the horizon. As they approached them, the mountains seemed to change slowly as their perspective shifted. They seemed to crawl about on one another like living things, growing larger and changing from blue to blue-green, and then to a rich, verdant emerald.

Soon the ship was rocketing smoothly over them. Ahead and below, in the rocky gorge of the mountains, lay a great cone city, the largest the Earthmen had yet seen. As they approached, they could see another cone behind it—the city was a double cone! They resembled the circus tents of two centuries earlier, connected by a ridge.

"Ah—home!" smiled Torlos. "See—that twin cone idea is new. It was not thus when I left it, years ago. It is growing, growing—and in that new section! See? They have bright colors on all the buildings! And already they are digging foundations out to the left for a third cone!" He was so excited that it was difficult for Arcot to read his thoughts coherently.

"But we won't have to build more fortifications," Torlos continued, "if you will give us the secret of the rays you use!

"But, Arcot, you must hide in the hills now; drop down and deposit me in the hills. I will walk to the city on foot.

"I will be able to identify myself, and I will soon be inside the city, telling the Supreme Three that I have salvation and peace for them!"

"I have a better idea," Arcot told him. "It will save you a long walk. We'll make the ship invisible, and take you close to the city. You can drop, say ten feet from the ship to the ground, and continue from there. Will that be all right?"

Torlos agreed that it would.

Invisible, the *Ancient Mariner* dove down toward the city, stopping only a few hundred feet from the base of the magnetic wall, near one of the gigantic beam stations.

"I will come out in a one-man flier, slowly, and at low altitude, toward that mountain there," Torlos told Arcot, pointing. "Then you may become visible and follow me into the city.

"You need fear no treachery from my people," he assured them. Then, smiling: "As if you need fear treachery from the hands of any people! You have certainly proven your ability to defend yourselves!"

"Even if my people were treacherously inclined, they would certainly have been convinced by your escape from the Satorians. And they have undoubtedly heard all about it by now through the secret radios of our spies. After all, I was not the only Nansalian spy there, and some of the others must surely have escaped in the ships that ran away after I destroyed the city." Arcot could feel the sadness in his mind as he thought of the fact that his inadvertent destruction of the city had undoubtedly killed some of his own people.

Torlos paused a moment, then asked: "Is there any message you wish me to give the Supreme Council of Three?"

"Yes," replied Arcot. "Repeat to them the offer we so foolishly made to the Commanding One of Sator. We will give them the molecular ray which tore the city out of the ground, and, as your people have seen, also tore a mountain down. We will give them our heat beam, which will melt anything except the material of which this ship is made. And we will give them the knowledge to make this material, too.

"Best of all, we will give them the secret of the most terrific energy source known to mankind; the energy of matter itself. With these in your hands, Sator will soon be peaceful.

"In return, we ask only two things. They will cost you almost nothing, but they are invaluable to us. We have lost our way. In the vastness of space, we can no longer locate our own galaxy. But our own Island Universe has features which could be distinguished on an astronomical plate, and we have taken photographs of it which your astronomers can compare with their own to help us find our way back.

"In addition, we need more fuel—lead wire. Our space control drive does not use up energy except in the presence of a strong gravitational field; most of it is drained back into our storage coils, with very little loss. But we have used it several times near a large sun, and the power drainage goes up exponentially. We would not have enough to get back home if we happened to run into any more trouble on the way."

Arcot paused a moment, considering. "Those two things are all we really need, but we would like to take back more, if your Council is willing. We would like samples of your books and photographs and other artifacts of your civilization to take back home to our own people."

"That, and peace, are all we ask."

Torlos nodded. "The things you ask, I am sure the Council will readily agree to. It seems little enough payment for the things you intend to do for us."

"Very well, then. We will wait for you. Good luck!"

Torlos turned and jumped out of the airlock. The ship rose high above him as he suddenly became visible on the plain below. He was running toward the city in great leaps of twenty feet —graceful, easy leaps that showed his tremendous power.

Suddenly, a ship was darting down from the city toward him. As it curved down, Torlos stopped and made certain signals with his arms, then he stood quietly with his hands in the air.

The ship hovered above him, and two men dropped thirty feet to the ground and questioned him for several minutes.

Finally, they motioned to the ship, which dropped to ten feet, and the three men leaped lightly to its door and entered. The door snapped shut, and the ship shot toward the city. The magnetic wall opened for a moment, and the ship shot through.

Within seconds, it was out of sight, lost in the busy air traffic above the city.

"Well," said Arcot, "now we go back to the hills and wait."

XX

For two days, the *Ancient Mariner* lay hidden in the hills. It was visible all that time, but at least two of the men were watching the sky every hour of the day. Torlos himself was, they knew, perfectly trustworthy, but they did not know whether his people were as honorable as he claimed them to be.

Arcot and Wade were in the control room on the afternoon of the second day—not Earth days, but the forty-hour Nansalian days —and they had been quietly discussing the biological differences between themselves and the inhabitants of this planet.

Suddenly, Wade saw a slowly moving speck in the sky.

"Look, Arcot! There's Torlos!"

They waited, ready for any hostile action as the tiny ship approached rapidly, circling slowly downward as it came nearer. It landed a few hundred feet away, and Torlos emerged, running rapidly toward the Earth ship. Arcot let him in through the airlock.

Torlos smiled broadly. "I had difficulty in convincing the Council that my story was true. When I told them that you could go faster than light, they strongly objected. But they had to admit that you had certainly been able to tear down the mountain very effectively, and they had received reports of the destruction of the Satorian capitol.

"It seems you first visited the city of Thanso when you came here. The people were nearly panic-stricken when they saw you rip that mountain down and uproot the magnetic ray station. No one ship had ever done that before!

"But the fact that several guards had seen me materialize out of thin air, plus the fact that they knew you could make yourselves invisible, convinced them that my story was true.

"They want to talk to you, and they say that they will gladly grant your requests. But you must promise them one thing—you must stay away from any of our people, for they are afraid of disease. Bacteria that do not bother you very much might be deadly to us. The Supreme Council of Three is willing to take the risk, but they will not allow anyone else to be exposed."

"We will keep apart from your people if the Council wishes," Arcot agreed, "but there is no real danger. We are so vastly different from you that it will be impossible for you to get our diseases, or for us to contract yours. However, if the Council wants it, we will do as they ask."

Torlos at once went back to his ship and headed toward the city.

Arcot followed in the *Ancient Mariner*, keeping about three hundred feet to the rear.

When they reached the magnetic screen of the city, one of the beam stations cut its power for a few moments, leaving a gap for the two ships to glide smoothy through.

On the roofs of the buildings, men and women were collected, watching the shining, polished hull of the strange ship as it moved silently above them.

Torlos led them to the great central building and dropped to the huge landing field beside it. All around them, in regular rows, the great hulls of the Nansal battleships were arranged. Arcot landed the *Ancient Mariner* and shut off the power.

"I think Wade is the man to go with me this time," Arcot said. "He has learned to communicate with Torlos quite well. We will each carry both pistols and wear our power suits. And we'll be in radio communication with you at all times.

"I don't think they'll start anything we don't like this time, but I'm not as confident as I was, and I'm not going to take any useless chances. This time I'm going to make arrangements. If I die here, there's going to be a very costly funeral, and these men are going to pay the costs!

"I'll call you every three minutes, Morey. If I don't, check up on me. If you still don't get an answer, take this place apart because you won't be able to hurt us then.

"I'm going to tell Torlos about our precautions. If the building shields the radio, I'll be listening for you and I'll retrace my steps until I can contact you again. Right? Then come on, Wade!" Arcot, fully equipped, strode down the corridor to the airlock.

Torlos was waiting for them with another man, whom Torlos explained was a high-ranking officer of the fleet. Torlos, it seemed, was without official rank. He was a secret service agent without official status, and therefore an officer had been assigned to accompany the Earthmen.

Torlos seemed to be relaxing in the soft, warm sunlight of his native world. It had been years since he had seen that yellow sun except from the windows of a space flier. Now he could walk around in the clear air of the planet of his birth.

Arcot explained to him the precautions they had taken against trouble here, and Torlos smiled. "You have certainly learned greater caution. I can't blame you. We certainly seem little different from the men of Sator; we can only stand on trial. But I know you will be safe."

They walked across the great court, which was covered with a soft, springy turf of green. The hot sun shining down on them, the brilliant colors of the buildings, the towering walls of the magnificent edifice they were approaching, and, behind them, the shining hull of the *Ancient Mariner* set among the dark, needle-shaped Nansalian ships, all combined to make a picture that would remain in their minds for a long time.

Here, there were no guards watching them as they were conducted to the meeting of the Supreme Council of Three.

They went into the main entrance of the towering government building and stepped into the great hall on the ground floor. It was like the interior of an ancient Gothic cathedral, beautiful and dignified. Great pillars of green stone rose in graceful, fluted columns, smoothly curving out like the branches of some stylized tree to meet in arches that rose high in pleasing curves to a point midway between four pillars. The walls were made of a dark green stone as a background; on them had been traced designs in colored tile.

The whole hall was a thing of colored beauty; the color gave it life, as the yellow sunlight gave life to the trees of the mountains.

They crossed the great hall and came at last to the elevator. Its door was made of narrow strips of metal, so bound together that the whole made a flexible, but strong sheet. In principle, the doors worked like the cover of an antique roll-top desk. The idea was old, but these men had made their elevator doors very attractive by the addition of color. In no way did they detract from the dignified grace of the magnificent hall.

Torlos turned to Arcot. "I wonder if it would not be wise to shut off your radio as we enter the elevator. Might not the magnetic force affect it?"

"Probably," Arcot agreed. He contacted Morey and told him that the radio would be cut off for a short while. "But it won't be more than three minutes," Arcot finished. "If it is—you know what to do."

As they entered the elevator, Torlos smiled at the two Earthmen. "We will ascend more gradually this time, so that the acceleration won't be so tiring to you." He moved the controls carefully, and by gentle steps they rose to the sixty-third floor of the giant building.

As they stepped out of the elevator, Torlos pointed toward an open window that stretched widely across one wall. Below them, they could see the *Ancient Mariner*.

"Your radio contact should be good," Torlos commented.

Wade put in a call to Morey, and to his relief, he made contact immediately.

The officer was leading them down a green stone corridor toward a simple door. He opened it, and they entered the room beyond.

In the center of the room was a large triangular table. At a place at the center of each side sat one man on a slightly raised chair, while on each side of him sat a number of other men.

Torlos stopped at the door and saluted. Then he spoke in rapid, liquid syllables to the men sitting at the table, halting once or twice and showing evident embarrassment as he did so.

He paused, and one of the three men in command replied rapidly in a pleasant voice that had none of the harsh command that Arcot had noticed in the voice of the Satorian Commanding One. Arcot liked the voice and the man.

Judging by Earth standards, he was past middle age—whatever that might be on Nansal—with crisp black hair that was bleaching slightly. His face showed the signs of worry that the making of momentous decisions always leaves, but although the face was strong with authority, there was a gentleness that comes with a feeling of kindly power.

Wade was talking rapidly into the radio, describing the scene before them to Morey. He described the great table of dark wood, and the men about it, some in the blue uniform of the military, and some in the loose, soft garments of the civilian. Their colored fabrics, individually in good taste and harmony, were frequently badly out of harmony with the costume of a neighbor, a difficulty accompanying this brightly tinted clothing.

Torlos turned to Arcot. "The Supreme council asks that you be seated at the table, in the places left for you." He paused, then quickly added: "I have told them of your precautions, and they have said: 'A wise man, having been received treacherously once, will not again be trapped.' They approve of your policy of caution.

"The men who sit at the raised portions of the table are the Supreme Three; the others are their advisors who know the details of Science, Business, and War. No one man can know all the branches of human endeavor, and this is but a meeting place of those who know best the individual lines. The Supreme Three are elected from the advisors in case of the death of one of the Three, and they act as co-ordinators for the rest.

"The man of Science is to your left; directly before you is the man of Business, and to your right is the Commander of the Military.

"To whom do you wish to speak first?"

Arcot considered for a moment, then: "I must first tell the Scientist what it is I have, then tell the Commander how he can use it, and finally I will tell the Businessman what will be needed."

Arcot had noticed that the military officers all wore holsters for their pneumatic pistols, but they were conspicuously empty. He was both pleased and embarrassed. What should he do—he, who carried two deadly pistols. He decided on the least conspicuous course and left them where they were.

Arcot projected his thoughts at Torlos. "We have come a vast distance across space, from another galaxy. Let your astronomer tell them what distance that represents."

Arcot paused while Torlos put the thoughts into the words of the Nansalian language. A moment later, one of the scientists, a tall, powerfully built man, even for these men of giant strength, rose and spoke to the others. When he was seated, a second rose and spoke also, with an expression of puzzled wonder.

"He says," Torlos translated, "that his science has taught him that a speed such as you say you have made is impossible, but the fact that you are here proves his science wrong.

"He reasoned that since your kind live on no planet of this system, you must come from another star. Since his science says that this is just as impossible as coming from another galaxy, he is convinced of the fallacy in the theories."

Arcot smiled. The sound reasoning was creditable; the man did not label as "impossible" something which was proven by the presence of the two Earthmen.

Arcot tried to explain the physical concepts behind his space-strain drive, but communication broke down rapidly; Torlos, a warrior, not a scientist, could not comprehend the ideas, and was completely unable to translate them into his own language.

"The Chief Physicist suggests that you think directly at him," Torlos finally told Arcot. "He suggests that the thoughts might be more familiar to him than to me." He grinned. "And they certainly aren't clear to me!"

Arcot projected his thoughts directly toward the physicist; to his surprise, the man was a perfect receiver. He had a natural gift for it. Quickly, Arcot outlined the system that had made his intergalactic voyage possible.

The physicist smiled when Arcot was finished, and tried to reply, but he was not a good transmitter. Torlos aided him.

"He says that the science of your people is far ahead of us. The conceptions are totally foreign to his mind, and he can only barely grasp the significance of the idea of bent emptiness that you have given him. He says, however, that he can fully appreciate the possibility that you have shown him. He has given your message to the Three, and they are anxious to hear of the weapons you have."

Arcot drew the molecular pistol, and holding it up for all to see, projected the general theory of its operation toward the physicist.

To the Chief Physicist of Nansal, the idea of molecular energy was an old one; he had been making use of it all his life, and it was well known that the muscles used the heat of air to do their work. He understood well how it worked, but not until Arcot projected into his mind the mental impression of how the Earthmen had thrown one sun into another did he realize the vast power of the ray.

Awed, the man translated the idea to his fellows.

Then Arcot drew the heat pistol and explained how the annihilation of matter within it was converted into pure heat by the relux lens.

"I will show you how they work," Arcot continued. "Could we have a lump of metal of some kind?"

The Scientist spoke into an intercom microphone, and within a few minutes, a large lump of iron—a broken casting—was brought in. Arcot suspended it on the molecular beam while Wade melted it with the heat beam. It melted and collapsed into a ball that glowed brilliantly and flamed as its surface burned in the oxygen of the air. Wade cut off his heat ray, and the ball quickly cooled under the influence of the molecular beam until Arcot lowered it to the floor, a perfect sphere crusted with ice and frost.

Arcot continued for the better part of an hour to explain to the Council exactly what he had, how they could be used, and what materials and processes were needed to make them.

When he was finished, the Supreme Three conferred for several minutes. Then the Scientist asked, through Torlos: "How can we repay you for these things you have given us?"

"First, we need lead to fuel our ship." Arcot gave them the exact specifications for the lead wire they needed.

He received his answer from the man of Business and Manufacturing. "We can give you that easily, for lead is cheap. Indeed, it seems hardly enough to repay you."

"The second thing we need," Arcot continued, "is information. We became lost in space and are unable to find our way home. I would like to explain the case to the Astronomer."

The Astronomer proved to be a man of powerful intelligence as well as powerful physique, and was a better transmitter than receiver. It took every bit of Arcot's powerful mind to project his thoughts to the man.

He explained the dilemma that he and his friends were in, and told him how he could recognize the Galaxy on his plates. The Astronomer said he thought he knew of such a nebula, but he would like to compare his own photographs with Arcot's to make sure.

"In return," Arcot told him, "we will give you another weapon —a weapon, this time, to defeat the Astronomer's greatest enemy, distance. It is an electrical telescope which will permit you to see life on every planet of this system. With it, you can see a man at a distance ten times as great as the distance from Nansal to your sun!"

Eagerly, the Astronomer questioned Arcot concerning the telectroscope, but others were clamoring for Arcot's attention.

The Biologist was foremost among the contenders; he seemed worried about the possibility of the alien Earthmen carrying pathogenic bacteria.

"Torlos has told us that you have an entirely different internal organization. What is it that is different? I can't believe that he has correctly understood you."

Arcot explained the differences as carefully as possible. By the time he was finished, the Biologist felt sure that any such creature was sufficiently far removed from them to be harmless biologically, but he wanted to study the Man of Earth further.

Arcot had brought along a collection of medical books as a possible aid in case of accident. He offered to give these to Nansal in exchange for a collection of Nansalian medical texts. The English would have to be worked out with the aid of a dictionary and a primary working aid which Arcot would supply. Arcot also asked for a skeleton to take with him, and the Biologist readily agreed.

"We'd like to give you one in return," Arcot grinned, "but we only brought four along, and, unfortunately, we are using them at the moment."

The Biologist smiled back and assured him that they would not think of taking a piece of apparatus so vitally necessary to the Earthmen.

The Military Leader was the man who demanded attention next. Arcot had a long conference with him, and they decided that the best way for the Military Leader to learn the war potential of the *Ancient Mariner* was to personally see a demonstration of its powers.

The Council decided that the Three would go on the trip. The Military Commander picked two of his aides to go, and the Scientist picked the Astronomer and the Physicist. The head of Business and Manufacturing declined to bring any of his advisors.

"We would learn nothing," he told Arcot, "and would only be

in the way. I, myself, am going only because I am one of the Three."

"Very well," said Arcot. "Let's get started."

XXI

The party descended to the ground floor and walked out to the ship. They filed into the airlock, and in the power room they looked in amazement at the tiny machines that ran the ship. The long black cylinder of the main power unit for the molecular drive looked weak and futile compared to the bulky machines that ran their own ships. The power storage coils, with their fields of intense, dead blackness, interested the Physicist immensely.

The ship was a constant source of wonder to them all. They investigated the laboratory and then went up to the second floor. Morey and Fuller greeted them at the door, and each of the four Earthmen took a group around the ship, explaining as they went.

The library was a point of great interest, exceeded only by the control room. Arcot found some difficulty in taking care of all his visitors; there were only four chairs in the control room. The Three could sit down, but Arcot needed the fourth chair to pilot the ship. The rest of the party had to hold on as best they could, which was not too difficult for men of such physical strength; they were accustomed to high accelerations in their elevators.

Morey, Wade, and Fuller strapped themselves into the seats at the ray projectors at the sides and stern.

Arcot wanted to demonstrate the effectiveness of the ship's armament first, and then the maneuverability. He picked a barren hillside for the first demonstration. It was a great rocky cliff, high above the timber line, towering almost vertically a thousand feet above them.

Wade triggered his molecular projector, and a pale beam reached out toward the cliff. Instantly, the cliff leaped ten miles into the air, whining and roaring as it shot up through the atmosphere. Then it started to fall. Heated by its motion through the air, it struck the mountaintop as a mass of red hot rock which shattered into fragments with a terrific roar! The rocks rolled and bounced down the mountainside, their path traced by a line of steam clouds.

Then, at Arcot's order, the heat beams were all turned on the mountain at full power. In less than a minute, the peak began to melt, sending streamers of lava down the sides. The beams began to eat out a crater in the center, where the rock began to boil furiously under the terrific energy of the heat beams.

Then Arcot shut off the heat beams and turned on the molecular ray.

The molecules of the molten rock were traveling at high velocities—the heat was terrific. Arcot could see that the rock was boiling quite freely. When the molecular beam hit it, every one of those fast moving molecules shot upward together! With the roar of a meteor, it plunged toward space at five miles a second!

It had dropped to absolute zero when the beam hit it, but at that speed through the air, it didn't stay cold long! Arcot followed it up in the *Ancient Mariner*. It was going too slowly for him. The air had slowed it down and heated it up, so Arcot hit it with the molecular ray again, converting the heat back into velocity.

By the time they reached free space, Arcot had maneuvered the lump of rock into an orbit around the planet.

"Tharlano," he thought at the Astronomer, "your planet now has a new satellite!"

"So I perceive!" replied Tharlano. "Now that we are in space, can we use the instrument you told me of?"

Arcot established the ship in an orbit twenty thousand miles from the planet and led them back to the observatory, where Morey had already trained the telectroscope on the planet below. There wasn't much to see; the amplification showed only the rushing ground moving by so fast that the image blurred.

He turned it to Sator. It filled the screen as they increased the power, but all they could see was billowing clouds. Another poor subject.

Morey showed Tharlano, the Astronomer, how to use the controls, and he began to sweep the sky with the instrument, greatly pleased with its resolving ability and tremendous magnification.

The Military Leader of the Three pointed out that the Satorians still had a weapon that was reported deadly, and they were in imminent danger unless Arcot's inventions were applied at once. All the way back to Nansal, they spent the time discussing the problem in the *Ancient Mariner's* Library.

It was finally agreed that the necessary plans and blueprints were to be given to the Nansalians, who could start production at once. The biggest problem was in the supply of lux and relux, which, because of their vast energy-content, required the atomic converters of the *Ancient Mariner* to make them. The Earthmen agreed to supply the power and the necessary materials to begin operations.

When the ship landed, a meeting of the manufacturers was called. Fuller distributed prints of the microfilmed plans for the equipment that he had packed in the library, and the factory engineers worked from them to build the necessary equipment.

The days that followed were busy days for Earthmen and Nansalians alike.

The Nansalians were fearful of the consequences of the weapon that the Satorians were rumored to have. The results of their investigations through their agents had, so far, resulted only in the death of the secret service men. All that was known was exactly what the Satorians wanted them to know; the instrument was new, and it was deadly.

On the other hand, the Satorians were not entirely in the dark as to the progress of Nansal, as Arcot and Morey discovered one day.

After months of work designing and tooling up the Nansalian factories, making the tools to make the tools to make the war material needed, and training the engineers of Nansal all over the planet to produce the equipment needed, Arcot and Morey finally found time to take a few days off.

Tharlano had begun a systematic search of the known nebulae, comparing them with the photographs the Earthmen had given him, and looking for a galaxy with two satellite star clouds of exactly the right size and distance from the great spiral.

After months of work, he had finally picked one which filled the bill exactly! He invited Arcot and Morey to the observatory to confirm his findings.

The observatory was located on the barren peak of a great mountain more than nine miles high. It was almost the perfect place for an astronomical telescope. Here, well above the troposphere, the air was thin and always clear. The solid rock of the mountain was far from disturbing influences which might cause any vibration in the telescope.

The observatory was accessible only from a spaceship or air flyer, and, at that altitude, had to be pressurized and sealed against the thin, cold air outside. Within, the temperature was kept constant to a fraction of a degree to keep thermal expansion from throwing the mirror out of true.

Arcot and Morey, accompanied by Tharlano and Torlos, settled the *Ancient Mariner* to the landing field that had been blasted out of the rock of the towering mountain. They went over to the observatory and were at once admitted to the airlock.

The floor was of smoothed, solid rock, and in this, the great clock which timed and moved the telescope was set.

The entire observatory was, of course, surrounded by a magnetic shield, and it was necessary to make sure there were no enemy ships around before using the telescope, because the magnetic field affected the light rays passing through it.

The mirror for the huge reflecting telescope was nearly three hundred inches in diameter, and was powerful enough to spot a spaceship leaving Sator. Its military usefulness, however, was practically nil, since painting the ships black made them totally invisible.

There were half a dozen assistants with Tharlano at the observatory at all times, one of them in charge of the great file of plates that were kept on hand. Every plate made was printed in triplicate, to prevent their being destroyed in a raid. The original was kept at the observatory, and copies were sent to two of the largest cities on Nansal. It was from this file that Tharlano had gathered the data necessary to show Arcot his own galaxy.

Tharlano was proudly explaining the telescope to Arcot, realizing that the telectroscope was far better, but knowing that the Earthmen would appreciate this triumph of mechanical perfection. Arcot and Morey were both intensely interested in the discussion, while Torlos, slightly bored by a subject he knew next to nothing about, was examining the rest of the observatory.

Suddenly, he cried out in warning, and leaped a full thirty feet over the rock floor to gather Arcot and Morey in his great arms. There was a sharp, distinct snap of a pneumatic pistol, and the thud of a bullet. Arcot and Morey each felt Torlos jerk!

Quick as a flash, Torlos pushed the two men behind the great tube of the telescope. He leaped over it and across the room, and disappeared into the supply room. There was the noise of a scuffle, another crack from a pneumatic pistol, and the sudden crash and tinkle of broken glass.

Suddenly, the figure of a man described a wide arc as it flew out of the supply room and landed with a heavy crash on the floor. Instantly, Torlos leaped at him. There was a trickle of blood from his left shoulder, but he gripped the man in his giant arms, pinning him to the floor. The struggle was brief. Torlos simply squeezed the man's chest in his arms. There was the faint creak of metal, and the man's chest began to bend! In a moment, he was unconscious.

Torlos pulled a heavy leather belt off of the unconscious man and tied his arms with it, wrapping it many times around the wrists, and was picking the man up when Tharlano arrived, followed by Arcot and Morey. Torlos smiled broadly.

"This is one Satorian spy that won't report. I could have finished him when I got my hold on him, but I wanted to take him before the Council for questioning. He'll be all right; I just dented his chest a little."

"We owe our lives to you again, Torlos," Arcot told him gravely. "But you certainly risked your life; the bullet might well have penetrated your heart instead of striking a rib, as it seems to have done."

"Rib? What is a rib?" The thought concept seemed totally unfamiliar to Torlos.

Arcot looked at him oddly, then reached out and ran an exploratory hand over Torlos' chest. It was smooth and solid!

"Morey!" Arcot exclaimed. "These men have no ribs! Their chest is as solid as their skulls!"

"Then how do they breathe?" Morey asked.

"How do you breathe? I mean most of the time. You use your diaphragm and your abdominal muscles. These people do, too!"

Morey grinned. "No wonder Torlos jumped in front of that bullet! He didn't have as much to fear as we do—he had a built-in bullet proof vest! You'd have to shoot him in the abdomen to reach any vital organ."

Arcot turned back to Torlos. "Who is this man?"

"Undoubtedly a Satorian spy sent to murder you Earthmen.

I saw the muzzle of his pistol as he was aiming and jumped in the way of the bullet. There is not much damage done."

"We'd better get back to the city," Arcot said. "Fuller and Wade might be in danger!"

They bundled the Satorian spy into the ship, where Morey tied him further with thin strands of lux cable no bigger than a piece of string.

Torlos looked at it and shook his head. "He will break that as soon as he awakens, without even knowing it. You forget the strength of our people."

Morey smiled and wrapped the cord around Torlos' wrists.

Torlos looked amused and pulled. His smile vanished. He pulled harder. His huge muscles bulged and writhed in great ridges along his arms. The thin cord remained complacently undamaged. Torlos relaxed and grinned sheepishly.

"You win," he thought. "I'll make no more comments on the things I see you do."

They returned to the capitol at once. Arcot shoved the speed up as high as he dared, for Torlos felt there might be some significance in the attempt to remove Arcot and Morey. Wade and Fuller had already been warned by radio, and had immediately retired to the Council Room of the Three. The members of the Investigation Board joined them to question the prisoner upon his arrival.

When they arrived, Arcot and Morey went in with Torlos, who was carrying the struggling, shackled spy over his shoulder.

The Earthmen watched while the expert interrogators of the Investigation Board questioned the prisoner. The philosophy of Norus did not permit torture, even for a vicious enemy, but the questioners were shrewd and ingenious in their methods. For hours, they took turns pounding questions at the prisoner, cajoling, threatening, and arguing.

They got nowhere. Solidly, the prisoner stuck by his guns. Why had he tried to shoot the Earthmen? He didn't know. What were his orders from Sator? Silence. What were Sator's plans? Silence. Did he know anything of the new weapon? A shrug of the shoulders.

Finally, Arcot spoke to the Chief Investigation Officer. "May I try my luck? I think I'm powerful enough to use a little combination of hypnosis and telepathy that will get the information out of him." The Investigator agreed to try it.

Arcot walked over as if to inspect the prisoner. For an instant, the man looked defiantly at Arcot. Arcot glared back. At the same time, his powerful mind reached out and began to work subtly within the prisoner's brain. Slowly, a helpless, blank expression came over the man's face as his eyes remained fixed on Arcot's own. The man was as helplessly bound mentally as the lux cable bound him physically.

For a full quarter of an hour, the two men, Earthman and Satorian, stood locked in a frozen tableau, staring into each other's eyes. The onlookers waited in watchful silence.

Finally, Arcot turned and shook his head, as if to clear it. As he did so, the spy slumped forward in his chair, unconscious.

Arcot rubbed his own temples and spoke in English to Morey. "Some job! You'll have to tell them what I found out; my head is splitting! With a headache like this, I can't communicate.

"Torlos was right; they were trying to get rid of all four of us. We're the only ones who can operate the ship, and that ship is the only defense against them.

"He knows several other spies here in the city, and we can, I think, practically wipe out the Satorian spy system all over the planet with the information he gave me and what we can get from others we arrest.

"Unfortunately, he doesn't know anything about the new weapon; the higher-ups aren't telling anyone, not even their own men. I get the idea that only those on board the ships using it will know about it before the attack.

"An attack is planned, and very soon. He didn't know when. We can only lie in readiness and do everything we can to help these people with their work."

While Morey relayed this information to the Investigating Board and the Council, Wade was talking in low tones to Arcot.

"They had a lot of workmen bring twenty tons of lead wire on board this evening, and the distilled water tanks are full. The tanks are full of oxygen, and they gave us some synthetic food which we can eat.

"They have it all over us in the field of chemistry. They've found the secret of catalysis, and can actually synthesize any catalytic agent they want. They can make any possible reaction go in either direction at any rate they desire.

"They took a slice of flesh from my arm and analyzed it down to the last detail. From that, they were able to predict what sort of food we would need to eat. They can actually synthesize living things!

"I've tried the food they made, and it has a very good flavor. They guaranteed it would have all the necessary ingredients, right down to the smallest trace element!

"We're fully stocked for a long trip. The Three said it was their first consideration that we should be able to return to our homes."

"How about their armament?" Arcot asked. He was holding his head in his hands to ease the throbbing ache within it.

"Each city has a projector supplied by the regular power station on top of their central building. The molecular ray, of course; they still don't have enough power to run a heat beam.

"We didn't have time to make more than one for each city, but this one will give the Satorians a nasty time if they come near it. It works nicely through the magnetic screen, so it won't be necessary for them to lower the barrier to shoot."

Morey had finished telling the Council what Arcot had discovered from the prisoner, and the Councilmen were leaving one by one to go to their duties in preparing for the attack.

"I think we had best go back to the *Ancient Mariner*," Arcot said. "I need an aspirin and some sleep."

"Same here," agreed Fuller. "These men make me feel as though I were lazy. They work for forty or fifty hours and think nothing of it. Then they snooze for five hours and they're ready for another long stretch. I feel like a lounge lizard if I take six hours out of every twenty-four."

They asked Torlos to stand guard on the ship while they got some much needed sleep, and Torlos consented readily after getting the permission of the Supreme Three. The Earthmen were returned to their ship under heavy guard to prevent further attempts at assassination.

It was seven hours after they had gone to sleep that it came.

Through the ship came the low hum that rose quickly to a screeching call of danger—the warning! The city was under attack!

XXII

The Nansalian fleet was already outside the city and hard at it. The fight was on! But Arcot saw that the fight was one-sided in the extreme. Ship after ship of the Nansalian fleet seemed to burst into sudden, inexplicable flame and fall blazing against another of their own ships! It seemed as though some irresistible attraction drew the ships together and smashed them against each other in a blaze of electric flame, while the ships of Sator did nothing but stay far off to one side and dodge the rays of the Nansalian ships.

Quickly, Arcot turned to Torlos. "Torlos, go out! Leave the ship! We can work better when you aren't here, since we don't have to worry about exposure to magnetic rays. I don't like to make you miss this, but it's for your world!"

Torlos showed his disappointment; he wanted to be in this battle. But he realized that what the Earthman said was true. Their weak, stone bones were completely immune to the effects of even the most powerful magnetic ray.

He nodded. "I'll go. Good Luck! And give them a few shots for me!"

He turned and ran down the corridor to the airlock. As soon as he was outside, Arcot lifted the ship.

It had taken less than a minute to get into the air, but in that minute, the Nansalian fleet had taken a terrific beating. Arcot noticed that the few ships of Sator that had been hit smashed into the ground with a terrible blaze of violet light that left nothing but a pile of fused metal.

"They've got something, all right," Arcot thought to himself as he drove the Ancient Mariner into battle.

It would be impossible for the Nansalians to lower their magnetic screen, even for a second, so Arcot simply aimed the ship toward it and turned on the power.

"Hold on!" he called as they struck it. The ship reeled and sank suddenly planetward, then it bounced up and outward. They were through the wall.

The rooms were suddenly oppressively hot, and the molecular cooler was struggling to lower it. "We made it," Morey said triumphantly, "but the eddy currents sure heated up the hull!"

They were out of the city now, speeding toward the battle. Following a prearranged system, the Nansalian ships retreated, leaving the Earthmen a free hand. They needed no help!

Wade, Fuller, and Morey began to lash out with the molecular beams, smashing the Satorian ships in on themselves, crushing them to the ground, where they exploded in violet flame.

Wade and Fuller began to work together. Wade caught one ship in the molecular ray, and Fuller hit with a heat beam. Like some titanic broom they swept it around at dozens of miles a second, leaping, twisting, smashing ship after ship. Like a snowball, the lump of glowing metal grew with each crash, till a dozen ships had fallen into it. It was a new broom, and it swept clean!

Then a magnetic beam caught the *Ancient Mariner*. With a shock, it slowed down at a terrific rate. Then Arcot turned on more power, and simply dragged the other ship along by its own magnetic beam! Wade tore the ship loose with his molecular beam, but the mighty mass of metal that had been his broom was gone, a glowing mass of metal on the ground.

"We haven't seen that new weapon yet," Morey called.

"Can't find us!" Arcot replied into the intercom. The sun was setting, and the blazing red star was lighting the ship, making it seem like a ball of fire when still and a flashing streak of red light when in motion.

Ship after ship of the Satorians was going down before the three beams of the Earth ship; the great fleet was dissolving like a lump of sugar in boiling water.

Suddenly, just ahead of them, an enemy ship drove toward them with obvious intent to ram; if his magnetic beam caught them, and drew them toward him, there would be a head-on collision.

Wade caught it with a molecular beam, and it became a blazing wreck on the ground.

"All rays off!" Arcot called. As soon as they were off, Arcot hit a switch, and the *Ancient Mariner* vanished.

Arcot drove the invisible ship high above the battle. Below, the Satorians were searching wildly for the ship. They knew it must be somewhere near, and feared that at any second it might materialize before them with its deadly rays.

Arcot stayed above them for nearly a minute while the ships

below twisted and turned, wildly seeking him. Then they went into formation again and started back for the city.

"That's what I wanted!" Arcot said grimly. "In formation, they're like sitting ducks!" He dropped the ship like a plummet while the ray operators prepared to sweep the formation with their beams.

Suddenly the *Ancient Mariner* was visible again. Simultaneously, three rays leaped down and bathed the formation in their pale radiance. The front ranks vanished, and the line broke, attacking the ship that hung above them now. Four magnetic beams hit the *Ancient Mariner* at once! Arcot couldn't pull away from all four, and his gunners couldn't tell which ships were holding them.

All at once, the men felt a violent electrical shock! The air about them was filled with the blue haze of the electric weapon they had seen!

Instantly, the magnetic beams left them, and they saw behind them a single Satorian ship heading toward them, surrounded by that same bluish halo of light. A suicide ship!

Arcot accelerated away from it as Fuller hit it with a molecular beam. The ship reeled and stopped, and the *Ancient Mariner* pulled away from it rapidly. Then, the frost-covered ship of the dead came on, still heading for them!

Arcot turned and went off to the right, but like a pursuing Nemesis, the strange ship came after them in the shortest, most direct route!

The molecular beams were useless now; there was no molecular energy left in the frozen hulk that accelerated toward them. Suddenly, the two envelopes of blue light touched and coalesed! A great, blinding arc leaped between the two ships as the speeding Satorian hull smashed violently against the side of the *Ancient Mariner!* The men ducked automatically, and were hurled against their seatstraps with tremendous force. There was a rending, crashing roar, a sea flame—and darkness.

They could only have been unconscious a few seconds, for when the fog went away, they could see the glowing mass of the enemy ship still falling far beneath them. The lux wall where it had hit was still glowing red.

"Morey!" Arcot called. "You all right? Wade? Fuller?"

"Okay!" Morey answered.

So were Wade and Fuller.

"It was the lux hull that saved us," Arcot said. "It wouldn't break, and the temperature of the arc didn't bother it. And since it wouldn't carry a current, we didn't get the full electrical effect.

"I'm going to convince those birds that this ship is made of something they can't touch! We'll give them a real show!"

He dived downward, back into the battle.

It was a show, all right! It was impossible to fight the Earth ship. The enemy had to concentrate four magnetic rays on it to use their electric weapon, and they could only do that by sheer luck!

And even that was of little use, for they simply lost one of their own ships without harming the *Ancient Mariner* in the least.

Ship after ship crumpled in on itself like crushed tinfoil or hurled itself violently to the ground as the molecular beams touched them. The Satorian fleet was a fleet no longer; it was a small collection of disorganized ships whose commanders had only one thought—to flee!

The few ships that were left spearheaded out into space, using every bit of acceleration that the tough bodies of the Satorians could stand. With a good head start, they were rapidly escaping.

"We can't equal that acceleration," said Wade. "We'll lose them!"

"Nope!" Arcot said grimly. "I want a couple of those ships, and I'm going to get them!"

At four gravities of acceleration, the *Ancient Mariner* drove after the fleeing ships of Sator, but the enemy ships soon dropped rapidly from sight.

Twenty five thousand miles out in space, Arcot cut the acceleration. "We'll catch them now, I think," he said softly. He pushed the little red switch for an instant, then opened it. A moment before, the planet Nansal had been a huge disc behind them. Now it was a tiny thing, a full million miles away.

It took the Satorian fleet over an hour to reach them. They appeared as dim lights in the telectroscope. They rapidly became larger. Arcot had extinguished the lights, and since they were on the sunward side of the approaching ships, the *Ancient Mariner* was effectively invisible.

"They're going to pass us at a pretty good clip," Morey said quietly. "They've been accelerating all this time."

Arcot nodded in agreement. "We'll have to hit them as they come toward us. We'd never get one in passing."

As the ships grew rapidly in the plate, Arcot gave the order to fire!

The molecular rays slashed out toward the onrushing ships, picking them off as fast as the beams could be directed. The rays were invisible in space, so they managed to get several before the Satorians realized what was happening.

Then, in panic, they scattered all over space, fleeing madly from the impossible ship that was firing on them. They knew they had left it behind, yet here it was, waiting for them!

"Let them go," Arcot said. "We've got our specimens, and the rest can carry the word back to Sator that the war is over for them."

It was several hours later that the *Ancient Mariner* approached Nansal again, bringing with it two Satorian ships. By careful use of the heat beam and the molecular beam, the Earthmen had managed to jockey the two battle cruisers back to Nansal.

It was nighttime when they landed. The whole area around the city was illuminated by giant searchlights. Men were working recovering the bodies of the dead, aiding those who had survived, and examining the wreckage.

Arcot settled the two Satorian ships to the ground, and landed the *Ancient Mariner*.

Torlos sprinted over the ground toward them as he saw the great silver ship land. He had been helping in the examination of the wrecked enemy ships.

"Have they attacked anywhere else on the planet?" Arcot asked as he opened the airlock.

Torlos nodded. "They hit five other cities, but they didn't use as big a fleet as they did here. The plan of battle seems to have been for the ships with the new weapons to hit here first and then hit each of the other cities in turn. They didn't have enough to make a full-scale attack; evidently, your presence here made them desperate.

"At any rate, the other cities were able to beat off the magnetic beam ships with the projectors of molecular beams."

"Good," Arcot thought. "Then the Nansal-Sator war is practically over!"

XXIII

Richard Arcot stepped into the open airlock of the *Ancient Mariner* and walked down the corridor to the library. There, he found Fuller and Wade battling silently over a game of chess and Morey relaxed in a chair with a book in his hands.

"What a bunch of loafers," Arcot said acidly. "Don't you ever *do* anything?"

"Sure," said Fuller. "The three of us have entered into a lifelong pact with each other to refrain from using a certain weapon which would make this war impossible for all time."

"What war?" Arcot wondered. "And what weapon?"

"This war," Wade grinned, pointing at the chess board. "We have agreed absolutely never to read each other's minds while playing chess."

Morey lowered his book and looked at Arcot. "And just what have you been so busy about?"

"I've been investigating the weapon on board the Satorian ships we captured," Arcot told them. "Quite an interesting effect. The Nansalian scientists and I have been analyzing the equipment for the past three days.

"The Satorians found a way to cut off and direct an electrostatic field. The energy required was tremendous, but they evidently separated the charges on Sator and carried them along on the ships.

"You can see what would happen if a ship were charged negatively and the ship next to it were charged positively! The magnitude of electrostatic forces is terrific! If you put two ounces of iron ions, with a positive charge, on the north pole, and an equivalent amount of chlorine ions, negatively charged, on the south pole, the attraction, even across that distance, would be three hundred and sixty tons!

"They located the negative charges on one ship and the positive charges on the one next to it. Their mutual attraction pulled them toward each other. As they got closer, the charges arced across, heating and fusing the two ships. But they still had enough motion toward each other to crash.

"They were wrecked by less than a tenth of an ounce of ions which were projected to the ship and held there by an automatic field until the ships got close enough to arc through it.

"We still haven't been able to analyze that trick field, though."

"Well, now that we've gotten things straightened out," Fuller said, "let's go home! I'm anxious to leave! We're all ready to go, aren't we?"

Arcot nodded. "All except for one thing. The Supreme Three want to see us. We've got a meeting with them in an hour, so put on your best Sunday pants."

In the Council of Three, Arcot was officially invited to remain with them. The fleet of molecular motion ships was nearing completion—the first one was to roll off the assembly line the next day—but they wanted Arcot, Wade, Morey, and Fuller to remain on Nansal.

"We have a large world here," the Scientist thought at them. "Thanks to you people, we can at last call it our own. We offer you, in the name of the people, your choice of any spot in this world. And we give you—this!" The Scientist came forward. He had a disc-shaped plaque, perhaps three inches in diameter, made of a deep ruby-red metal. In the exact center was a green stone which seemed to shine of its own accord, with a pale, clear, green light; it was transparent and highly refractive. Around it, at the three points of a triangle, were three similar, but smaller stones. Engraved lines ran from each of the stones to the center, and other lines connected the outer three in a triangle. The effect was as though one were looking down at the apex of a regular tetrahedron.

There were characters in Nansalese at each point of the tetrahedron, and other characters engraved in a circle around it.

Arcot turned it in his hand. On the back was a representation of the Nansalian planetary system. The center was a pale yellow, highly-faceted stone which represented the sun. Around this were the orbits of planets, and each of the eleven planets was marked by a different colored stone.

The Scientist was holding in the palm of his hand another such disc, slightly smaller. On it, there were three green stones, one slightly larger than the others.

"This is my badge of office as Scientist of the Three. The stone marked Science is here larger. Your plaque is new. Henceforth, it shall be the Three and a Coordinator!

"Your vote shall outweigh all but a unanimous vote of the Three. To you, this world is answerable, for you have saved our civilization. And when you return, as you have promised, you shall be Coordinator of this system!"

Arcot stood silent for a moment. This was a thing he had never thought of. He was a scientist, and he knew that his ability was limited to that field.

At last, he smiled and replied: "It is a great honor, and it is a great work. But I cannot spend my time here always; I must return to my own planet. I cannot be fairly in contact with you.

"Therefore, I will make my first move in office now, and suggest that this plaque signify, not the Coordinator, and first power of your country, but Counselor and first friend in all things in which I can serve you.

"The tetrahedron you have chosen; so let it be. The apex is out of the plane of the other points, and I am out of this galaxy. But there is a relationship between the apex and the points of the base, and these lines will exist forever.

"We have been too busy to think of anything else as yet, but our worlds are large, and your worlds are large. Commerce can develop across the ten million light years of space as readily as it now exists across the little space of our own system. It is a journey of but five days, and later machines will make it in less! Commerce will come, and with it will come close communication.

"I will accept this plaque with the understanding that I am but your friend and advisor. Too much power in the hands of one man is bad. Even though you trust me completely, there might be an unscrupulous successor.

"And I must return to my world.

"Your first ship will be ready tomorrow, and when it is completed, my friends and I will leave your planet.

"We will return, though. We are ten million light years apart, but the universe is not to be measured in space anymore, but in time. We are five days apart. I will be nearer to you at all times than is Sator!

"If you wish, others of my race shall come, too. But if you do not want them to come, they will not. I alone have Tharlano's photographs of the route, and I can lose them."

For a moment, the Three spoke together, then the Scientist was again thinking at Arcot.

"Perhaps you are right. It is obvious your people know more than we. They have the molecular ray, and they know no wars; they do not destroy each other. They must be a good race, and we have seen excellent examples in you.

"We can realize your desire to return home, but we ask you to come again. We will remember that you are not ten million light years, but five days, from our planet."

When the conference was ended, Arcot and his friends returned to their ship. Torlos was waiting for them outside the airlock.

"Abaout haow saon you laive?" he asked in English.

"Why—tomorrow," Arcot said, in surprise. "Have you been practicing our language?"

Torlos reverted to telepathy. "Yes, but that is not what I came to talk to you about. Arcot—can a man of Nansal visit Earth?" Anxiously, hopefully, and hesitatingly, he asked. "I could come back on one of your commercial vessels, or come back when you return. And—and I'm sure I could earn my living on your world! I'm not hard to feed, you know!" He half smiled, but he was too much in earnest to make a perfect success.

Arcot was amazed that he should ask. It was an idea he would very much like to see fulfilled. The idea of metal-boned men with tremendous strength and strange molecular-motion muscles would inspire no friendship, no feeling of kinship, in the people of Earth. But the man himself—a pleasant, kindly, sincere, intelligent giant—would be a far greater argument for the world of Nansal than the most vivid orator would ever be.

Arcot asked the others, and the vote was unanimous—let him come!

The next day, amid great ceremony, the first of the new Nansalian ships came from the factories. When the celebration was over, the four Earthmen and the giant Torlos entered the *Ancient Mariner*.

"Ready to go, Torlos?" Arcot grinned.

"Pearfactly, Ahcut. Tse soonah tse bettah!" he said in his oddly accented English.

Five hours saw them out of the galaxy. Twelve hours more, and they were heading for home at full speed, well out in space.

The Home Galaxy was looming large when they next stopped for observation. Old Tharlano had guided them correctly!

They were going home!

INVADERS FROM THE
INFINITE

CHAPTER I

INVADERS

Russ Evans, Pilot 3497, Rocket Squad Patrol 34, unsnapped his seat belt, and with a slight push floated "up" into the air inside the weightless ship. He stretched himself, and yawned broadly.

"Red, how soon do we eat?" he called.

"Shut up, you'll wake the others," replied a low voice from the rear of the swift little patrol ship. "See anything?"

"Several million stars," replied Evans in a lower voice. "And—" His tone became suddenly severe. "Assistant Murphy, remember your manners when addressing your superior officer. I've a mind to report you."

A flaming head of hair topping a grinning face poked around the edge of the door. "Lower your wavelength, lower your wavelength! You may think you're a sun, but you're just a planetoid. But what I'd like to know, Chief Pilot Russ Evans, is why they locate a ship in a forlorn, out of the way place like this—three-quarters of a billion miles, out of planetary plane. No ships ever come out here, no pirates, not a chance to help a wrecked ship. All we can do is sit here and watch the other fellows do the work."

"Which is exactly why we're here. Watch—and tell the other ships where to go, and when. Is that chow ready?" asked Russ looking at a small clock giving New York time.

"Uh—think she'll be on time? Come on an' eat."

Evans took one more look at the telectroscope screen, then snapped it off. A tiny, molecular towing unit in his hand, he pointed toward the door to the combined galley and lunch room, and glided in the wake of Murphy.

"How much fuel left?" he asked, as he glided into the dizzily spinning room. A cylindrical room, spinning at high speed, causing an artificial "weight" for the foods and materials in it, made eating of food a less difficult task. Expertly, he maneuvered himself to the guide rail near the center of the room, and caught the spiral. Braking himself into motion, he soon glided down its length, and landed on his feet. He bent and flexed his muscles, waiting for the now-busied assistant to get to the floor and reply.

"They gave us two pounds extra. Lord only knows why. Must expect us to clean up on some fleet. That makes four pound rolls left, untouched, and two-thirds of the original pound. We've been here fifteen days, and have six more to go. The main driving power rolls have about the same amount left, and three pound rolls in each reserve bin," replied Red, holding a curiously moving coffee pot that strove to adjust itself to rapidly changing air velocities as it neared the center of the room.

"Sounds like a fleet's power stock. Martian lead or the terrestrial isotope?" asked Evans, tasting warily a peculiar dish before him. "Say, this is energy food. I thought we didn't get any more till Saturday." The change from the energy-less, flavored pastes that made up the principal bulk of a space-pilot's diet, to prevent over-eating, when no energy was used in walking in the weightless ship, was indeed a welcome change.

"Uh-huh. I got hungry. Any objections?" grinned the Irishman.

"None!" replied Evans fervently, pitching in with a will.

Seated at the controls once more, he snapped the little switch that caused the screen to glow with flashing, swirling colors as the telectroscope apparatus came to life. A thousand tiny points of flame appeared scattered on a black field with a suddenness that made them seem to snap suddenly into being. Points, tiny dimensionless points of light, save one, a tiny disc of blue-white flame, old Sol from a distance of close to one billion miles, and under slight reverse magnification. The skillful hands at the controls were turning adjustments now, and that disc of flame seemed to leap toward him with a hundred light-speeds, growing to a disc as large as a dime in an instant, while the myriad points of the stars seemed to scatter like frightened chickens, fleeing from the growing sun, out of the screen. Other points, heretofore invisible, appeared, grew, and rushed away.

The sun shifted from the center of the screen, and a smaller reddish-green disc came into view—a planet, its atmosphere coloring the light that left it toward the red. It rushed nearer, grew larger. Earth spread as it took the center of the screen. A world, a portion of a world, a continent, a fragment of a continent as the magnification increased, boundlessly it seemed.

Finally, New York spread across the screen; New York seen from the air, with a strange lack of perspective. The buildings did not seem all to slant toward some point, but to stand vertical, for, from a distance of a billion miles, the vision lines were practically parallel. Titanic shafts of glowing color in the early summer sun appeared; the hot rays from the sun, now only 82,500,000 miles away, shimmering on the colored metal walls.

The new Airlines Building, a mile and a half high, supported at various points by actual spaceship driving units, was a riot of shifting, rainbow hues. A new trick in construction had been used here, and Evans smiled at it. Arcot, inventor of the ship that carried him, had suggested it to Fuller, designer of that ship, and of that building. The colored berylium metal of the wall had been ruled with 20,000 lines to the inch, mere scratches, but nevertheless a diffraction grating. The result was amazingly beautiful. The sunlight, split up to its rainbow colors, was reflected in millions of shifting tints.

In the air, supported by tiny packs strapped to their backs, thousands of people were moving, floating where they wished, in any direction, at any elevation. There were none of the helicopters of even five years ago, now. A molecular power suit was far more convenient, cost nothing to operate, and but $50 to buy. Perfectly safe, requiring no skill, everyone owned them. To the watcher in space, they were mere moving, snaky lines of barely distinguishable dots that shivered and seemed to writhe in the refractions of the air. Passing over them, seeming to pass almost through them in this strange perspectiveless view, were the shadowy forms of giant space liners, titanic streamlined hulls. They were streamlined for no good reason, save that they looked faster and more graceful than the more efficient spherical freighters, just as passenger liners of two centuries earlier, with their steam engines, had carried four funnels and used two. A space liner spent so minute a portion of its journey in the atmosphere that it was really inefficient to streamline them.

"Won't be long!" muttered Russ, grinning cheerily at the familiar, sunlit city. His eyes darted to the chronometer beside him. The view seemed to be taken from a ship that was suddenly scudding across the heavens like a frightened thing, as it ran across from Manhattan Island, followed the Hudson for a short way, then cut across into New Jersey, swinging over the great woodland area of Kittatiny Park, resting finally on the New Jersey suburb of New York nestled in the Kittatinies, Blairtown. Low apartment buildings, ten or twelve stories high, nestled in the waving green of trees in the old roadways. When ground traffic ceased, the streets had been torn up, and parkways substituted.

Quickly the view singled out a single apartment, and the great smooth roof was enlarged on the screen to the absolute maximum clarity, till further magnification simply resulted in worse stratospheric distortion. On the broad roof were white strips of some material, making a huge V followed by two I's. Russ watched, his hand on the control steadying the view under the Earth's complicated orbital motion, and rotation, further corrections for the ship's orbital motion making the job one requiring great skill. The view held the center with amazing clarity. Something seemed to be happening to the last of the I's. It crumpled suddenly, rolled in on itself and disappeared.

"She's there, and on time," grinned Russ happily.

He tried more magnification. Could he—

He was tired, terribly, suddenly tired. He took his hands from the viewplate controls, relaxed, and dropped off to sleep.

"What made me so tired—wonder—GOD!" He straightened with a jerk, and his hands flew to the controls. The view on the machine suddenly retreated, flew back with a velocity inconceivable. Earth dropped away from the ship with an apparent velocity a thousand times that of light; it was a tiny ball, a pinpoint, gone, the sun—a minute disc—gone—then the apparatus was flashing views into focus from the other side of the ship. The assistant did not reply. Evans' hands were growing ineffably heavy, his whole body yearned for sleep. Slowly, clumsily he pawed for a little stud. Somehow his hand found it, and the ship reeled suddenly, little jerks, as the code message was flung out in a beam of such tremendous power that the sheer radiation pressure made it noticeable. Earth would be notified. The system would be warned. But light, slow crawling thing, would take hours to cross the gulf of space, and radio travels no faster.

Half conscious, fighting for his faculties with all his will, the pilot turned to the screen. A ship! A strange, glistening thing streamlined to the nth degree, every spare corner rounded till the resistance was at the irreducible minimum. But, in the great pilotport of the stranger, the patrol pilot saw faces, and gasped in surprise as he saw them! Terrible faces, blotched, contorted. Patches of white skin, patches of brown, patches of black, blotched and twisted across the faces. Long, lean faces, great wide flat foreheads above, skulls strangely squared, more box-like than man's rounded skull. The ears were large, pointed tips at the top. Their hair was a silky mane that extended low over the forehead, and ran back, spreading above the ears, and down the neck.

Then, as that emotion of surprise and astonishment weakened his will momentarily, oblivion came, with what seemed a fleeting instant of memories. His life seemed to flash before his mind in serried rank, a file of events, his childhood, his life, his marriage, his wife, an image of smiling comfort, then the years, images of great and near great men, his knowledge of history, pictures of great war of 2074, pictures of the attackers of the Black Star—then calm oblivion, quiet blankness.

The long, silent ship that had hovered near him turned, and pointed toward the pinhead of matter that glowed brilliantly in the flaming jewel box of the heavens. It was gone in an instant, rushing toward Sun and Earth at a speed that outraced the flying radio message, leaving the ship of the Guard Patrol behind, and leaving the Pilot as he leaves our story.

CHAPTER II

CANINE PEOPLE

"And that," said Arcot between puffs, "will certainly be a great boon to the Rocket Patrol, you must admit. They don't like dueling with these space-pirates using the molecular rays, and since molecular rays have such a tremendous commercial value, we can't prohibit the sale of ray apparatus. Now, if you will come into the 'workshop,' Fuller, I'll give a demonstration with friend Morey's help."

The four friends rose, Morey, Wade, and Fuller following Arcot into his laboratory on the thirty-seventh floor of the Arcot Research Building. As they went, Arcot explained to Fuller the results and principles of the latest product of the ingenuity of the "Triumvirate," as Arcot, Morey, and Wade had come to be called in the news dispatches.

"As you know, the molecular rays make all the molecules of any piece of matter they are turned upon move in the desired direction. Since they supply no new energy, but make the body they are turned upon supply its own, using the energy of its own random molecular motion of heat, they are practically impossible to stop. The energy necessary for molecular rays to take effect is so small that the usual type of filter lets enough of it pass. A ship equipped with filters is no better off when attacked than one without. The rays simply drove the front end into the rear, or *vice versa,* or tore it to pieces as the pirates desired. The Rocket Patrol could kill off the pirates, but they lost so many men in the process, it was a Phyrric victory.

"For some time Morey and I have been working on something to stop the rays. Obviously it can't be by means of any of the usual metallic energy absorption screens.

"We finally found a combination of rays, better frequencies, that did what we wanted. I have such an apparatus here. What we want you to do, of course, is the usual job of rearranging the stuff so that the apparatus can be made from dies, and put into quantity production. As the Official Designer for the A.A.L. you ought to do that easily." Arcot grinned as Fuller looked in amazement at the apparatus Arcot had picked up from the bench in the "workshop."

"Don't get worried," laughed Morey, "that's got a lifting unit combined—just a plain ordinary molecular lift such as you see by the hundreds out there." Morey pointed through the great window where thousands of those lift units were carrying men, women and children through the air, lifting them hundreds, thousands of feet above the streets and through the doors of buildings.

"Here's an ordinary molecular pistol. I'm going to put the suit on, and rise about five feet off the floor. You can turn the pistol on me, and see what impression it makes on the suit."

Fuller took the molecular ray pistol, while Wade helped Arcot into the suit. He looked at the pistol dubiously, pointed it at a heavy casting of iron resting in one corner of the room, and turned the ray at low concentration, then pressed the trigger-button. The casting gave out a low, scrunching grind, and slid toward him with a lurch. Instantly he shut off the power. "This isn't any ordinary pistol. It's got seven or eight times the ordinary power!" he exclaimed.

"Oh yes, I forgot," Morey said. "Instead of the fuel battery that the early pistols used, this has a space-distortion power coil. This pistol has as much power as the usual A-39 power unit for commercial work."

By the time Morey had explained the changes to Fuller, Arcot had the suit on, and was floating five or six feet in the air, like a grotesque captive balloon. "Ready, Fuller?"

"I guess so, but I certainly hope that suit is all it is claimed to be. If it isn't—well I'd rather not commit murder."

"It'll work," said Arcot. "I'll bet my neck on that!" Suddenly he was surrounded by the faintest of auras, a strange, wavering blue light, like the hazy corona about a 400,000-volt power line. "Now try it."

Fuller pointed the pistol at the floating man and pushed the trigger. The brilliant blue beam of the molecular ray, and the low hum of the air, rushing in the path of the director beam, stabbed out toward Arcot. The faint aura about him was suddenly intensified a million times till he floated in a ball of blue-white fire. Scarcely visible, the air about him blazed with bluish incandescence of ionization.

"Increase the power," suggested Morey. Fuller turned on more power. The blue halo was shot through with tiny violet sparks, the sharp odor of ozone in the air was stifling; the heat of wasted energy was making the room hotter. The power increased further, and the tiny sparks were waving streamers, that laced across the surface of the blue fire. Little jets of electric flame reached out along the beam of the ray now. Finally, as full power of the molecular ray was reached, the entire halo was buried under a mass of writhing sparks that seemed to leap up into the air above the man's head, wavering up to extinction. The room was unbearably hot, despite the molecular ray coolers absorbing the heat of the air, and blowing cooled air into the room.

Fuller snapped off the ray, and put the pistol on the table beside him. The halo died, and went out a moment later, and Arcot settled to the floor.

"This particular suit will stand up against anything the ordinary commercial sets will give. The system now: remember that the rays are short electrical waves. The easiest way to stop them is to interpose a wave of opposite phase, and cause interference. Fine, but try to get in tune with an unknown wave when it is moving in relation to your center of control. It is impossible to do it before you yourself have been rayed out of existence. We must use some system that will automatically, instantly be out of phase.

"The Hall effect would naturally tend to make the frequency of a wave through a resisting medium change, and lengthen. If we can send out a spherical wave front, and have it lengthen rapidly as it proceeds, we will have a wave front that is, at all points, different. Any entering wave would, sooner or later, meet a wave that was half a phase out, no matter what the motion was, nor what the frequency, as long as it lies within the comparatively narrow molecular wave band. What this apparatus, or ray-screen, consists of, is a machine generating a spherical wave front of the nature of a molecular wave, but of just too great a frequency to do anything. A second part generates a condition in space, which opposes that wave. After traveling a certain distance, the wave has lengthened to molecular wave type, but is now beyond the machine which generated it, and no longer affects it, or damages it. However, as it proceeds, it continues to lengthen, till eventually it reaches the length of infra-light, when the air quickly absorbs it, as it reaches one of the absorption bands for air molecular waves, and any molecular wave must find its half-wave complement somewhere in that wedge of waves. It does, and is at once choked off, its energy fighting the energy of the ray screen, of course. In the air, however, the screen is greatly helped by the fact that before the half-wave frequency is met in the ray-narrow molecular wave band. What this apparatus, or ray-screen, little work to do.

"Now your job is to design the apparatus in a form that machines can make automatically. We tried doing it ourselves for the fun of it, but we couldn't see how we could make a machine that didn't need at least two humans to supervise."

"Well," grinned Fuller, "you have it all over me as scientists, but as economic workers—two human supervisors to make one product!"

"All right—we agree. But no, let's see you—Lord! What was that?" Morey started for the door on the run. The building was still trembling from the shock of a heavy blow, a blow that seemed much as though a machine had been wrecked on the armored roof, and a big machine at that. Arcot, a flying suit already on, was up in the air, and darting past Morey in an instant, streaking for the vertical shaft that would let him out to the roof. The molecular ray pistol was already in his hand, ready to pull any beams off unfortunate victims pinned under them.

In a moment he had flashed up through the seven stories, and out to the roof. A gigantic silvery machine rested there, streamlined to perfection, its hull dazzlingly beautiful in the sunlight. A door opened, and three tall, lean men stepped from it. Already people were collecting about the ship, flying up from below. Air patrolmen floated up in a minute, and seeing Arcot, held the crowd back.

The strange men were tall, eight feet or more in height. Great, round, soft brown eyes looked in curiosity at the towering multicolored buildings, at the people floating in the air, at the green trees and the blue sky, the yellowish sun.

Arcot looked at their strangely blotched and mottled heads, faces, arms and hands. Their feet were very long and narrow, their legs long and thin. Their faces were kindly; the mottled skin, brown and white and black, seemed not to make them ugly. It was not a disfigurement; it seemed oddly familiar and natural in some reminiscent way.

"Lord, Arcot—queer specimens, yet they seem familiar!" said Morey in an undertone.

"They are. Their race is that of man's first and best friend, the dog! See the brown eyes? The typical teeth? The feet still show the traces of the dog's toe-step. Their nails, not flat like human ones but rounded? The mottled skin, the ears—look, one is advancing."

One of the strangers walked laboriously forward. A lighter world than Earth was evidently his home. His great brown eyes fixed themselves on Arcot's. Arcot watched them. They seemed to expand, grow larger; they seemed to fill all the sky. Hypnotism! He concentrated his mind, and the eyes suddenly contracted to the normal eyes of the stranger. The man reeled back, as Arcot's telepathic command to sleep came, stronger than his own will. The stranger's friends caught him, shook him, but he slept. One of the others looked at Arcot; his eyes seemed hurt, desperately pleading.

Arcot strode forward, and quickly brought the man out of the trance. He shook his head, smiled at Arcot, then, with desperate difficulty, he enunciated some words in English, terribly distorted.

"Ahy wizz tahk. Vokle kohds ron. Tahk by breen."

Distorted as it was, Arcot recognized the meaning without difficulty. "I wish (to) talk. Vocal cords wrong. Talk by brain." He switched to communication by the Venerian method, telepathically, but without hypnotism.

"Good enough. When you attempted to hypnotize me, I didn't know what you wanted. It is not necessary to hypnotize to carry on communication by the method of the second world of this system. What brings you to our system? From what system do you come? What do you wish to say?"

The other, not having learned the Venerian system, had great difficulty in communicating his thoughts, but Arcot learned that they had machines which would make it easier, and the terrestrian invited them into his laboratory, for the crowd was steadily growing.

The three returned to their ship for a moment, coming out with several peculiar headsets. Almost at once the ship started to rise, going up more and more swiftly, as the people cleared a way for it.

Then, in the tiniest fraction of a second, the ship was gone; it shrank to a point, and was invisible in the blue vault of the sky.

"Apparently they intend to stay a while," said Wade. "They are trusting souls, for their line of retreat is cut off. We naturally have no intention of harming them, but they can't know that."

"I'm not so sure," said Arcot. He turned to the apparent leader of the three and explained that there were several stories to descend, and stairs were harder than a flying unit. "Wrap your arms about my legs, when I rise above you, and hold on till your feet are on the floor again," he concluded.

The stranger walked a little closer to the edge of the shaft, and looked down. White bulbs illuminated its walls down its length to the ground. The man talked rapidly to his friends, looking with evident distaste at the shaft, and the tiny pack on Arcot's back. Finally, smiling, he evinced his willingness. Arcot rose, the man grasped his legs, and then both rose. Over the shaft, and down to his laboratory was the work of a moment.

Arcot led them into his "consultation room," where a number of comfortable chairs were arranged, facing each other. He seated them together, and his own friends facing them.

"Friends of another world," began Arcot, "we do not know your errand here, but you evidently have good reason for coming to this place. It is unlikely that your landing was the result of sheer chance. What brought you? How came you to this point?"

"It is difficult for me to reply. First we must be *en rapport*. Our system is not simple as yours, but more effective, for yours depends on thought ideas, not altogether universal. Place these on your heads, for only a moment. I must induce temporary hypnotic coma. Let one try first if you desire." The leader of the visitors held out one of the several headsets they had brought, caplike things, made of laminated metal apparently.

Arcot hesitated, then with a grin slipped it on.

"Relax," came a voice in Arcot's head, a low, droning voice, a voice of command. "Sleep," it added. Arcot felt himself floating down an infinite shaft, on some superflying suit that did not pull at him with its straps, just floating down lightly, down and down and down. Suddenly he reached the bottom, and found to his surprise that it led directly into the room again! He was back. "You are awake. Speak!" came the voice.

Arcot shook himself, and looked about. A new voice spoke now, not the tonelessly melodious voice, but the voice of an individual, yet a mental voice. It was perfectly clear, and perfectly comprehensible. "We have traveled far to find you, and now we have business of the utmost import. Ask these others to let us treat them, for we must do what we can in the least possible time. I will explain when all can understand. I am Zezdon Fentes, First Student of Thought. He who sits on my right is Zezdon Afthen, and he beyond him, is Zezdon Inthel, of Physics and of Chemistry, respectively."

And now Arcot spoke to his friends.

"These men have something of the greatest importance to tell us, it seems. They want us all to hear, and they are in a hurry. The treatment isn't at all annoying. Try it. The man on the extreme right, as we face them, is Zezdon Fentes of Thought, Zezdon apparently meaning something like professor, or 'First Student of.' Those next to him are Zezdon Afthen of Physics and Zezdon Inthel of Chemistry."

Zezdon Afthen offered them the headsets, and in a moment everyone present was wearing one. The process of putting them *en rapport* took very little time, and shortly all were able to communicate with ease.

"Friends of Earth, we must tell our strange story quickly for the benefit of your world as well as ours, and others, too. We cannot so much as annoy. We are helpless to combat them.

"Our world lies far out across the galaxy; even with incalculable velocity of the great swift thing that bore us, three long months have we traveled toward your distant worlds, hoping that at last the Invaders might meet their masters.

"We landed on this roof because we examined mentally the knowledge of a pilot of one of your patrol ships. His mind told us that here we would find the three greatest students of Science of this Solar System. So it was here we came for help.

"Our race has arisen," he continued, "as you have so surely determined from the race you call canines. It was artificially produced by the Ancient Masters when their hour of need had come. We have lost the great science of the Ancient Ones. But we have developed a different science, a science of the mind."

"Dogs are far more psychic than are men. They would naturally tend to develop such a civilization," said Arcot judiciously.

CHAPTER III

A QUARTER OF A MILLION LIGHT YEARS

"Our civilization," continued Zezdon Afthen, "is built largely on the knowledge of the mind. We cannot have criminals, for the man who plots evil is surely found out by his thoughts. We cannot have lying politicians and unjust rulers.

"It is a peaceful civilization. The Ancient Masters feared and hated War with a mighty aversion. But they did not make our race cowards, merely peaceful intelligence. Now we must fight for our homes, and my race will fight mightily. But we need weapons.

"But my story has little to do with our race. I will tell the story of our civilization and of the Ancient Ones later when the time is more auspicious.

"Four months ago, our mental vibration instruments detected powerful emanations from space. That could only mean that a new, highly intelligent race had suddenly appeared within a billion miles of our world. The directional devices quickly spotted it as emanating from the third planet of our system. Zezdon Fentes, with my aid, set up some special apparatus, which would pick up strong thoughts and make them visible. We had used this before to see not only what an enemy looked upon, but also what he saw in that curious thing, the eye of the mind, the vision of the past and the future. But while the thought-amplification device was powerful, the new emanations were hard to separate from each other.

"It was done finally, when all but one man slept. That one we were unable to tune sharply to. After that we could reach him at any time. He was the commander. We saw him operate the ship, we saw the ship, saw it glide over the barren, rocky surface of that world. We saw other men come in and go out. They were strange men. Short, squat, bulky men. Their arms were short and stocky. But their strength was enormous, unbelievable. We saw them bend solid bars of steel as thick as my arm. With perfect ease!

"Their brains were tremendously active, but they were evil, selfishly evil. Nothing that did not benefit them counted. At one time our instruments went dead, and we feared that the commander had detected us, but we saw what happened a little later. The second in command had killed him.

"We saw them examine the world, working their way across it, wearing heavy suits, yet, for all the terrific gravity of that world, bouncing about like rubber balls, leaping and jumping where they wanted. Their legs would drive out like pistons, and they soared up and through the air.

"They were tired while they made those examinations, and slept heavily at night.

"Then one night there was a conference. We saw then what they intended. Before we had tried desperately to signal them. Now we were glad that we had failed.

"We saw their ship rise (in the thoughts of the second in command) and sail out into space, and rush toward our world. The world grew larger, but it was imperfectly sketched in, for they did not know our world well. Their telescopes did not have great power as your electric telescopes have.

"We saw them investigate the planet. We saw them plan to destroy any people they found with a ray which was as follows: 'the ray which makes all parts move as one.' We could not understand and could not interpret. Thoughts beyond our knowledge have, of course, no meaning, even when our mental amplifiers get them, and bring them to us."

"The Molecular ray!" gasped Morey in surprise. "They will be an enemy."

"You know it! It is familiar to you! You have it? You can fight it?" asked Zezdon Afthen excitedly.

"We know it, and can fight it, if that is all they have."

"They have more—much more I fear," replied Zezdon Afthen. "At any rate, we saw what they intended. If our world was inhabited, they would destroy every one on it, and then other men of their race were to float in on their great ships, and settle on that largest of our worlds.

"We had to stop them so we did what we could, We had powerful machines, which would amplify and broadcast our thoughts. So we broadcast our thought-waves, and implanted in the mind of their leader that it would be wise to land, and learn the extent of the civilization, and the weapons to be met. Also, as the ship drew nearer, we made him decide on a certain spot we had prepared for him.

"He never guessed that the thoughts were not his own. Only the ideas came to him, seeming to spring from his own mind.

"He landed—and we used our one weapon. It was a thing left to one group of rulers when the Ancient Masters left us to care for ourselves. What it was, we never knew; we had never used it in the fifteen thousand years since the Great Masters had passed—never had to. But now it was brought out, and concealed behind great piles of rock in a deep canyon where the ship of the enemy would land. When it landed, we turned the beam of the machine on it, and the apparatus rotated it swiftly, and a cone of the beam's ray was formed as the beam was swung through a small circle in the vertical plane. The machine leaped backward, and though it was so massive that a tremendous amount of labor had been required to bring it there, the push of the pencil of force we sent out hurled it back against a rocky cliff behind it as though it were some child's toy. It continued to operate for perhaps a second, perhaps two. In that time two great holes had been cut in the enemy ship, holes fifteen feet across, that ran completely through the hull as though a die had cut through the metal of the ship, cutting out a disc of metal.

"There was a terrific concussion, and a roar as the air blasted out of the ship. It did not take us long to discover that the enemy were dead. Their terrible, bloated corpses lay everywhere in the ship. Most of the men we were able to recognize, having seen them in the mentovisor. But the colors were distorted, and their forms were peculiar. Indeed, the whole ship seemed strange. The only time that things ever did seem normal about that strange thing, when the angles of it seemed what they were, when the machines did not seem out of proportion, out of shape, twisted, was when on a trial trip we ventured very close to our sun."

Arcot whistled softly and looked at Morey. Morey nodded. "Probably right. Don't interrupt."

"That you thought something, I understood, but the thoughts themselves were hopelessly unintelligible to me. You know the explanation?" asked Zezdon Afthen eagerly.

"We think so. The ship was evidently made on a world of huge size. Those men, their stocky, block legs and arms, their entire build and their desire for the largest of your planets, would indicate that. Their own world was probably even larger—they were forced to wear pressure suits even on that large world, and could jump all over, you said. On so huge a sphere as their native world seems to be, the gravity would be so intense as to distort space. Geometry, such as yours seems to be, and such as ours was, could never be developed, for you assume the existence of a straight line, and of an absolute plane surface. These things cannot exist in space, but on small worlds, far from the central sun's mass, the conditions approach that without sufficient discrepancy to make the error obvious. On so huge a globe as their world the space is so curved that it is at once obvious that no straight line exists, and that no plane exists. Their geometry would never be like ours. When you went close to your sun, the attraction was sufficient to curve space into a semblance of the natural conditions on their home planet, then your senses and the ship met a compromise condition which made it seem more or less normal, not so obviously strange to you.

"But continue." Arcot looked at Afthen interestedly.

"There were none left in their ship now, and we had been careful in locating the first hole, that it should not damage the propulsive machinery. The second hole was accidental, due to the shift of the machine. The machine itself was wrecked now, crushed by its own reaction. We forgot that any pencil of force powerful enough to do what we wanted, would tear the machine from its moorings unless fastened with great steel bolts into the solid rock.

"The second hole had been far to the rear, and had, by ill-luck, cut out a portion of the driving apparatus. We could not repair that, though we did succeed at last in lifting the great discs into place. We attempted to cut them, and put them back in sections. Our finest saws and machines did not nick them. Their weight was unbelievable, and yet we finally succeeded in lifting the things into the wall of the ship. The actual missing material did not represent more than a tiny cut, perhaps as wide as one of your credit-discs. You could slip the thin piece of metal in between them, but not so much as your finger.

"Those slots we welded tight with our best steel, letting a flap hang over on each side of the cut, and as the hot metal cooled, it was drawn against the shining walls with terrific force. The joints were perfectly airtight.

"The machines proper were repaired to the greatest possible extent. It was a heartbreaking task, for we must only guess at what machines should be connected together. Much damage had been done by the rushing air as it left, for it filled the machines, too, and they were not designed to resist the terrific air pressure that was on them when the pressure in the ship escaped. Many of the machines had been burst open, and these we could repair when we had the necessary elements and knew their construction from the remnants, or could find unbroken duplicates in the stock rooms.

"Once we connected the wrong things. This will show you what we dealt with. They were the wrong poles—two generators, connected together in the wrong way. There was a terrific crash when the switch was thrown, and huge sheets of electric flame leaped from one of them. Two men were killed, incinerated in an instant, even the odors one might expect were killed in that flash of heat. Everything save the shining metal and clear glass within ten feet of it was instantly wiped out. And there was a fuse link that gave. The generator was ruined. One was left, and several small auxiliary generators.

"Eventually, we did the job. We made the machine work. And we are here.

"We have come to warn you, and to ask aid. Your system also has a large planet, slightly smaller than the largest of our system, but yet attractive. There are approximately 50,000 planetary systems in this universe, according to the records of the Invaders. Their world is not of this system. It is the World Thett, sun Antseck, Universe Venone. Where that is, or even what it means, we do not know. Perhaps you understand.

"But they investigated your world, and its address, according to their records, was World 3769-8482730-3. This, I believe, means, Universe 3769, Sun 8482730, World 3. They have been investigating this system now for nearly three centuries. It was close to 200 years ago that they visited your world—two hundred years of your time."

"This is 2129—which makes it about the year 1929–30 that they

floated around here investigating. Why haven't they done anything?" Arcot asked him.

"They waited for an auspicious time. They are afraid now,
for recently they visited your world, and were utterly amazed to
find the unbelievable progress your people have made. They intend to make an immediate attack on all worlds known to be intelligently populated. They had made the mistake of letting one
race learn too much; they cannot afford to let it happen again.

"There are only twenty-one inhabited worlds known, and their
thousands of scouts have already investigated nearly all the central mass of this universe, and much of the outer rings. They
have established a base in this universe. Where I do not know.
That, alone, was never mentioned in the records. But of all peoples, they feared only your world.

"There is one race in the universe far older than yours, but
they are a sleeping people. Long ago their culture decayed. Still,
now they are not far from you, and perhaps it will be worth the
few days needed to learn more about them. We have their location and can take you there. Their world circles a dead star—"

"Not any more," laughed Morey grimly. "That's another surprise for the enemy. They had a little jog, and they certainly are
wide awake now. They are headed for big things, and they are
going to do a lot."

"But how do you know these things? You have ships that can
go from planet to planet, I know, but the records of the enemy
said you could not leave the system of your sun. They alone
knew that secret."

"Another surprise for them," said Morey. "We can—and we can
move faster than your ship, if not faster than they. The people
of the dead star have moved to a very live star—Sirius, the brightest in our heavens. And they are as much alive now as their new
sun. They can move faster than light, also. We had a little misun-
derstanding a while back, when their star passed close to ours.
They came off second best, and we haven't spoken to them since.
But I think we can make valuable allies there."

For all Morey's jocular manner, he realized the terrible import
of this announcement. A race which had been able to cross the
vast gulf of intergalactic space in the days when terrestrians
were still developing the airplane—and already they had mapped
Jupiter, and planned their colonies! What developments had

come? They had molecular rays, cosmic rays, the energy of matter, then—what else had they now? Lux and Relux, the two artificial metals, made of solidified light, far stronger than anything of molecular structure in nature, absolutely infusible, totally inert chemically, one a perfect conductor of light and of all radiation in space, the other a perfect reflector of all radiations—save molecular rays. Made into the condition of reflection by the action of special frequencies in its formation from light, molecular frequencies were, unfortunately, able to convert it into perfectly transparent lux metal, when the protective value was gone.

They had that. All Earth had, perhaps.

"There was one other race of some importance, the others were semi-civilized. They rated us in a position between these races and the high races—yours, those of the dead star, and those of World 3769-37, 478, 326, 894-6. Our science has been investigated two hundred or so years ago.

"This other race was at a great distance from us, greater than yours, and apparently not feared as greatly as yours. They cannot cross to other worlds, save in small ships driven solely by fire, which the Thessians have called a 'hopelessly inefficient and laughably awkward thing to ride in.'"

"Rockets," grinned Morey. "Our first ship was part rocket."

Zezdon Fentes smiled. "But that is all. We have brought you warning, and our plea. Can you help us?"

"We cannot answer that. The Interplanetary Council must act. But I am afraid that it will be all we can do to protect our own world if this enemy attacks soon, and I fear they will. Since they have a base in this universe, it is impossible to believe that all ships did not report back to the home world at stated intervals. That one is missing will soon be discovered, and it will be sought. War will start at once. Three months it took you to reach us—they should come soon.

"Those men who left will be on their way back from the home world from which they came. What do you call your planet, friend?"

"Ortol is our home," replied Zezdon Inthel.

"At any rate, I can only assure you that your world will be given weapons that will permit your people to defend themselves and I will get you to your home within twenty-four hours. Your ship—is it in the system?"

"It waits on the second satellite of the fourth planet," replied Zezdon Afthen.

"Signal them, and tell them to land where a beacon of intense light, alternating red and blue, reaches up from—this point on the map." Arcot pointed out the spot in Vermont where their private lake and laboratory were.

He turned to the others, and in rapid-fire English, explained his plans. "We need the help of these people as much as they need ours. I think Zezdon Fentes will stay here and help you. The others will go with us to their world. There we shall have plenty of work to do, but on the way we are going to stop at Mars and pick up that valuable ship of theirs and make a careful examination for possible new weapons, their system of speed-drive, and their regular space-drive. I'm willing to make a bet right now, that I can guess both. Their regular drive is a molecular drive with lead disintegration apparatus for the energy, cosmic ray absorbers for the heating, and a drive much like ours. Their speed-drive is a time-distortion apparatus, I'll wager. Time distinction offers an easy solution of speed. All speed is relative—relative to other bodies, but also to time-speed. But we'll see.

"I'm going to hustle some workmen to installing the biggest spare power board I can get into the storerooms of the *Ancient Mariner,* and pack in a ray-screen. It will be useful. Let's move."

"Our ship," said Zezdon Afthen, "will land in three of your hours."

CHAPTER IV

THE FIRST MOVE

The Ortolians were standing on a low, green-clad hill. Below them stretched the green flank of the little rise, and beyond lay ridge after ridge of the broad, smooth carpet of the beautiful Vermont hills.

"Man of Earth," said Zezdon Afthen, turning at last to Wade, who stood behind him. "It took us three months of constant flight at a speed unthinkable, through space dotted with the titanic gems of the Outer Dark, stars gleaming in red, and blue and orange, some titanic lighthouses of our course, others dim pinpoints of glowing color. It was a scene of unspeakable grandeur, but it was so awesomely mighty in its scope, one was afraid, and his soul shriveled within him as he looked at those inconceivable masses floating forever alone in the silence of the inconceivable nothingness of eternal cold and eternal darkness. One was awed, suppressed by their sheer magnitude. A magnificent spectacle truly, but one no man could love.

"Now we are at rest on a tiny pinpoint of dust in a tiny bit of a tiny corner of an isolated universe, and the magnitude and stillness is gone. Only the chirpings of those strange birds as they seek rest in darkness, the soft gurgling of the little stream below, and the rustle of countless leaves, break the silence with a satisfying existence, while the loneliness of that great star, your sun, is lost in its tintings of soft color, the fleeciness of the clouds, and the seeming companionship of green hills.

"The beauty of boundless space is awe-inspiring in its magnitude. The beauty of Earth is something man can love.

"Man of Earth, you have a home that you may well fight for with all the strength of your arms, all the forces of your brain, and all the energies of Space that you can call forth to aid you. It is a wondrous world." Silently he stood in the gathering dusk, as first Venus winked into being, then one by one the stars came into existence in the deepening color of the sky.

"Space is awesomely wonderful; this is—lovable." He gazed long at the heavens of this world so strange, so beautiful to him, looking at the unfamiliar heavens, as star after star flashed into the constellations so familiar to terrestrians and to those Venerians who had been above the clouds of Venus' eternal shroud.

"But somewhere off there in space are other races, and far beyond the power of our eyes to see is the star that is the sun of my world, and around it circles that little globe that is home to me. What is happening there now? Does it still exist? Are there people still living on it? Oh, Man of Earth, let us reach that world quickly, you cannot guess the pangs that attack me, for if it be destroyed, think—forever I am without home—without friends I knew. However kind your people may be to me, I would be forever lonely.

"I will not think of that—only it is time your ship was ready, is it not?"

"I think we had better return," replied Wade softly, his English words rousing thoughts in his mind intelligible to the Ortolians.

The three rose in the air on the molecular suits and drove quickly down toward the blue gem of the lake to the east, nestled among still other green hills. Lights were showing in the great shop, where the *Ancient Mariner* was being fitted with the ray-shields, and all possible weapons. Men streaming through her were hastily stocking her with vast quantities of foods, stocks of fuel, all the spare parts they could cram into her stock rooms.

When the men arrived from the hilltop, the work was practically done, and Wade stepped up to Morey, busily checking off a list of required items.

"Everything you ordered came through?" he asked.

"Yes—thanks to the pull of a two-billion-dollar private fortune. Who says credit-units don't have their value? This expedition never would have gotten through, if it hadn't been for that.

"But we have the main space-distortion power bank, and the new auxiliary coils full. Ten tons of lead aboard for fuel. There's one thing we are afraid of. If the enemy have a system of tubes that is able to handle more power than our last tube—we're sunk. These brilliant people that suggest using more tubes to a ray-power bank forget the last tube has to handle the entire output of all the others, and modulate it correctly. If the enemy has a better tube—it will be too bad for us." Morey was frankly worried.

"My end is all set, Morey. How soon will you be ready?" Arcot asked.

"'Bout ten-fifteen minutes." Morey lit a cigarette and watched as the last of the stuff was carried aboard.

At last they were ready. The *Ancient Mariner,* originally built for intergalactic exploration, was kept in working condition. New apparatus had been incorporated in it, as their research had led to improvements, and it was constantly in condition, ready for a trip. Many exploration trips to the nearer stars had already been made.

The ship was backed out from the hangar now, and rested on the great smooth landing field, its tremendous quarter-million-ton mass of lux and relux sinking a great, smooth depression in the turf of the field. They were waiting now for the arrival of the Ortolian ship. Zezdon Afthen assured them it would be there in a few minutes.

High in the sky, came the whining whistle of an approaching ship, coming at terrific velocity. It came nearer the field, darting toward the ground at an unheard of speed, flashing down at a speed of well over three thousand miles an hour, and, only in the last fifty feet slowed with a sickening deceleration. Even so it landed with a crash of fully two hundred miles of speed. Arcot gasped at the terrible landing the pilot had made, fully expecting to see the great hull dent somewhat, even though made of solid relux. And certainly the jar would kill every man on board. Yet the hull did not seem harmed by the crash, and even the ground under the ship was but slightly disturbed, though, at a distance of some thirty feet, the entire block of soil was crushed, and cracked by the terrific impact of hundreds of thousands of tons striking with terrific energy.

"Lord, it's a wonder they didn't kill themselves. I never saw such a rotten landing," exclaimed Morey with disgust.

"Don't be too sure. I think they landed gently, and at very low speed. Notice how little the soil directly under them was dented?" replied Arcot, walking forward. "They have time control, as I suspected. Ask them. They drifted in gently. Their time rate was speeded up tremendously, so that what was hundreds of miles per hour to us was feet per minute to them. But come on, get the handlers to bring that junk up to the door—they are coming out."

One of the tall, kindly-faced canine people was standing in the doorway now, the white light streaming out around him into the night, casting a grotesque shadow on the landing field, for all the flood lights bathing in it.

Zezdon Afthen came up and spoke quickly to the man evidently in command of the ship. The entire party went into the ship, and the cream of their laboratory instruments was brought in.

For hours Arcot, Morey and Wade worked at the apparatus in the ship, measuring, calculating, following electrical and magnetic and sheer force hook-ups of staggering complexity. They were not trying to find the exact method of construction, only the principles involved, so that they could perform calculations of their own, and duplicate the results of the enemy. Thus they would be far more thoroughly familiar with the machinery when done.

Little attention was paid to the actual driving plant, for it was a molecular drive with the same type of lead-fuel burner they used in their own ship. The tubes of the power bank were, however, a puzzle to them. They were made of relux, so that it was impossible to see the interior of the tube. To open one was to destroy it, but calculations made from readings of their instruments showed that they were more efficient, and could readily carry nearly half again the load that the best terrestrial tubes could sustain. This meant the enemy could send heavier rays and heavier ray-screens.

But finally they returned to the *Ancient Mariner,* and as the Ortolian ship whined its way out to space, the *Ancient Mariner* started, rising faster and faster through the atmosphere till it was in the night of space. Then the molecular power was shut off. The ship suddenly seemed to writhe, space was black and starless about them, then sparkling weirdly distorted stars, all before them. They were moving already. Almost before the Ortolians fully realized what was happening, a dozen stars had swung past the ship, driving on now at better than five light years in every second. At this speed, approximately fourteen hours would be needed to reach Ortol.

"Now, Arcot, perhaps you will explain to me the secret of this ship," said Zezdon Afthen at last, turning from the great lux pilot's window, to Arcot seated in the pilot's chair. "I know that only the broadest principles will be intelligible to me, for I could not understand that ship we captured, after almost four months of study. Yet it crept through space compared with this ship. Certainly no ship could outdistance this in a race!"

"As a matter of fact—watch!" Arcot pushed a little metal button along a slide to the extreme end. Again the ship seemed to writhe. Space was no longer black, but faintly gray, and beside them, on either side, floated two exact replicas of their ship! Zezdon Afthen stared. But in another moment, both were gone, and space was black, yet in but a few moments a grayness was showing, and light was appearing from all about, growing gradually in intensity. For three seconds Arcot continued thus, then he pulled the metal button down the slide, and flicked over another that he had pulled to cause the second change. The stars were again before them, their colors changed beyond all recognition at that speed. But the orientation of the stars behind them had been familiar. Now an entirely different set of constellation showed.

"I merely opened the ship out to her maximum speed for a moment. I was able to see any large star 2000 light years in our path, and there were none. Small stars do not bother us as I will explain. When I put on full power of the main power coils, I drove the ship up to a speed of 30 light years a second. When I turned in the full power of the auxiliary coils as well I doubled the power, and the speed was multiplied by eight. The result was that in the four seconds of racing, we made approximately 1000 light years!"

Zezdon Afthen gasped. "Two hundred and forty light years *per second!*" He paused in bewilderment. "Suppose we had struck a small sun, a dark star, even a meteor at that speed? What would have been the result?"

Arcot smiled. "The chances are excellent that we plowed through more than one meteor, more than one dark star, and more than one small sun.

"But this is the secret: the ship attains the speed only by going out of space. *Nothing in space can attain the speed of light, save radiation.* Nothing in normal space. But, we alter space, make space along patterns we choose, and so distort it that the natural speed of radiation is enormously greater. In fact, we so change space that nothing can go *slower* than a speed we fix.

"Morey—show Afthen the coils, and explain it all to him. I've got to stay here."

Morey rose, and diving through the weightless ship, went down to the power room, Zezdon Afthen following. Here, giant pots five feet high were in close packed rows. The "pots" contained specially designed coils storing tremendous energy, the energy of four tons of disintegrated lead, in the only form that energy may be stored, as a strain, or distortion in space. These charged coils distorted only the space within themselves, making a closed field entirely within themselves. But in the exact gravitational center of the quarter of a million ton ship was a single high coil of different design that distorted space around it as well as the space within it. This, as Morey explained, was the control that altered the constants of space to suit. The coils were charged, and the energy stored. Their energy could be pumped into the big coil, and then, when the ship slowed to normal space, could be pumped back to them. The pumping energy, as well as any further energy needed for recharging the coils could be supplied by three huge power generators.

"These energy-producers," Morey explained, "work on a principle known for hundreds of years on Earth. Lead, when reduced to a temperature approaching absolute zero as closely as, for instance, liquid helium, has *no* electrical resistance. In other words, no matter how great a current is sent through it, there is no resistance, and no heat is produced to raise the temperature. What we do is to send a powerful current through a lead wire. The wire has a current density so huge that the atoms are destroyed, and the protons and electrons coalesce into pure radiant energy. Relux, under the influence of a magnetic field, converts this directly into electrical potential. Electricity we can convert to the spatial strain in the power coils, and thus the ship is driven." Morey pointed out the huge molecular power cylinder overhead, where the main power drive was located in the inertial center of the ship, or as near as the great space coil would permit.

The smaller power units for vertical lift, and for steering, were in the side walls, hidden under heavy walls of relux.

"The projectors for throwing molecular and heat rays are on the outside of course. Both of these projectors are protected. The walls of the ship are made of an outer wall of heavy lux metal, a vacuum between, and an inner wall of heavy relux. The lux is stronger than relux, and is therefore used for an outer shell. The inner shell of relux will reflect any dangerous rays and serve to hold the heat in the ship, since a perfect reflector is a perfect non-radiator. The vacuum wall is to protect the occupants of the ship against any undue heat. If we should get within the atmosphere of a sun, it would be disastrous if the physical conduction of heat were permitted, for though the relux will turn out any radiated heat, it is a conductor of heat, and we would roast almost instantly. These artificial metals are both absolutely infusible and non-volatile. The ship has actually been in the limb of a star tremendously hotter than your sun or mine.

"Now you see why it is we need not fear a collision with a small sun, meteor or such like. Since we are in our own, artificial space, we are alone, and there is nothing in space to run into. But, if we enter a huge sun, the terrific gravitational field of the mass of matter would be enough to pull the energy of our coil away from us. That actually happened the time we made our first intergalactic exploration. But it is almost impossible to fall into a large star—they are too brilliant. We won't be worrying about it," grinned Morey.

"But how did the ship we captured operate?" asked Zezdon Afthen.

"It was a very ingenious system, very closely related to ours, really.

"We distort space and change the velocity characteristics; in other words, we distort the rate of motion through distance characteristics of normal space. The Thessian ships work on the principle of distorting the rate of progress through time instead of through space.

"*Velocity* is really 'units of travel through space per unit of travel through time.' Now if we make the time unit twice as great, and the units traveled through space are not changed, the *velocity* is twice as great. That is, if we are moving five light years per second, make the second twice as long and we are moving ten light years per double-second. Make it ten thousand times as long, and we are traveling fifty thousand light years per ten-thousand-seconds. This is the principle—but there is a drawback. We might increase the velocity by slowing time passage, that is, if it takes me a year for one heartbeat, two years to raise my arm thus, and six months to turn my head, if all my body processes are slowed down in this way, I will be able to live a tremendous length of time, and though it takes me two hundred years to go from one star to another, so low is my time rate that the two hundred years will seem but a few minutes. I can then make a trip to a distant star—one five light years distant, let us say, in three minutes to me. I then will say, looking at my chronometer (which has been similarly slowed) 'I have gone five light years in three minutes, or five thirds light years per minute. I have exceeded the speed of light.'

"But people back on Earth would say, he has taken two

hundred years to go five light years, therefore he has gone at a speed one fortieth of that of light, which would be true—for their time rate.

"But suppose I can also speed up time. That is, I can live a year in a minute or two. Then everyone else will be exceedingly slow. The ideal thing would be to combine these two effects, arranging that space about your ship will have a very rapid time rate, ten thousand times that of normal space. Then the speed of radiation through that space will be 1,860,000,000 miles per second, and a speed of 1,000,000,000 miles per second would be possible, but still you, too, will be affected, so that though the people back home will say you are going far faster than light, you will say 'No, I am going only 100,000 miles per second.'

"But now imagine that your ship and surrounding space for one mile is at a time rate 10,000 times normal, and you, in a space of one hundred feet within your ship, are affected by a time rate 1/10,000 that, or normal, due to a second, reversing field. The two fields will not fight, or be mutually antagonistic; they will merely compound their effects. Result: you will agree that you are exceeding the speed of light!

"Do you understand? That is the principle on which your ship operated. There were two time-fields, overlapping time-fields. Remember the terrible speed with which your ship landed, and yet there was no appreciable jar according to the men? The answer of course was, that their time rate had been speeded enough, due to the fact that one field had been completely shut off, the other had not.

"That is the principle. The system is so complex, naturally, that we have not yet learned the actual method of working the process. We must do a great deal of mathematical and physical research.

"Wish we had it done—we could use it now," mused the terrestrian.

"We have some other weapons, none as important, of course, as the molecular ray and the heat ray. Or none that have been. But, if the enemy have ray-shields, then perhaps these others also will be important. There are molecular motion guns, metal tubes, with molecular director apparatus at one end. A metal shell is pulling the power turned on, and the shell leaps out at a speed of about ten miles per second—since it has been superheated—and is very accurately aimed, as there is no terrific shock of recoil to be taken up by the gun.

"But a more effective weapon, if these men are as I expect them to be, will be a peculiarly effective magnetic field concentrator device, which will project a magnetic field as a beam for a mile or more. How useful it will be—I don't know. We don't know what the enemy will turn against *us!*"

CHAPTER V

ORTOL

After Morey's explanation of the ship was completed, Wade took Arcot's place at the controls, while Morey and Arcot retired to the calculating room to do some of the needed mathematics on the time-field investigation.

Their work continued here, while the Ortolians prepared a meal and brought it to them, and to Wade. When at last the sun of Ortol was growing before them, Arcot took over controls from Wade once more. Slowing their speed to less than fifty times that of light, they drove on. The attraction of the giant sun was draining the energy from the coils so rapidly now, that at last Arcot was forced to get into normal space, while the planet was still close to a million miles from them. Morey was showing the Ortolians the operation of the telectroscope and had it trained now on the rapidly approaching planet. The planet was easily enlarged to a point where the features of continents were visible. The magnification was increased till cities were no longer blurs, but truly cities.

Suddenly, as city after city was brought under the action of the machine, the Ortolians recognizing them with glad exclamations, one swept into view—and as they watched, it leapt into the air, a vast column of dust, then twisting, whirling, it fell back in utter, chaotic ruin.

Zezdon Fentes staggered back from the screen in horror.

"Arcot—drive down—increase your speed—the Thessians are

there already and have destroyed one city," called Morey sharply. The men secured themselves with heavy belts, as the deep toned hum of the warning echoed through the ship. A moment later they staggered under an acceleration of four gravities. Space was dark for the barest instant of time, and then there was the scream of atmosphere as the ship rocketed through the air of the planet at nearly fifteen hundred miles per second. The outer wall was blazing in incandescence in a moment, and the heavy relux screens seemed to leap into place over the windows as the blasting heat, radiated from the incandescent walls flooded in. The millions of tons pressure of the air on the nose of the ship would have brought it to a stop in an instant, and had it not been that the molecular drive was on at full power, driving the ship against the air resistance, and still losing. The ship slowed swiftly, but was shrieking toward the destroyed city at terrific speed.

"Hesthis—to the—right and ahead. That would be their next attack," said the Ortolian. Arcot altered the ship's course, and they shot toward the distant city of Hesthis. They were slowing perceptibly, and yet, though the city was half around the world, they reached it in half a minute. Now Arcot's wizardry at the controls came into play, for by altering his space field constants, he succeeded in reaching a condition that slowed the ship almost instantly to a speed of but a mile a second, yet without apparent deceleration.

High in the white Ortolian sky was a shining point bearing down on the now-visible city. Arcot slanted toward it, and the approaching ship grew like an expanding rubber balloon.

A ray of intense, blindingly brilliant light flashed out, and a gout of light appeared in the center of the city. A huge flame, bright blue, shot heavenward in roaring heat.

Seeing that a strange ship had arrived was enough for the Thessians, and they turned, and drove at Arcot instantly. The Thessian ship was built for a heavy world, and for heavy acceleration in consequence, and, as they had found from the captured ship, it was stronger than the *Ancient Mariner*. Now the Thessians were driving at Arcot with an acceleration and speed that convinced him dodging was useless. Suddenly space was black around them, the sunlit world was gone.

"Wonder what they thought of *that!*" grinned Arcot. Wade smiled grimly.

"It's not what they thought, but what they'll do, that counts."

Arcot came back to normal space, just in time to see the Thessian ship spin in a quick turn, under an acceleration that would have crushed a human to a pulp. Again the pilot dived at the terrestrian ship. Again it vanished. Twice more he tried these fruitless tactics, seeing the ship loom before him—bracing for the crash—then it was gone instantaneously, and though he sailed through the spot he knew it to have occupied, it was not there. Yet an instant later, as he turned, it was floating, unharmed, exactly where his ship had passed!

Rushing was useless. He stood, and prepared to give battle. A molecular ray reached out—and disappeared in flaring ions on a shield utterly impenetrable in the ionizing atmosphere.

Arcot meanwhile watched the instrument of his shield. The Thessian shield would have been impenetrable, but his shield, fed by less efficient tubes, was not, and he knew it. Already the terrific energy of the Thessian ray was noticeably heating the copper plates of the tube. The seal would break soon.

Another ray reached out, a ray of flaring light. Arcot, watching through the "eyes" of his telectroscope view-plates, saw it for but an instant, then the "eyes" were blasted, and the screen went blank.

"He won't do anything with that but burn out eyes," muttered the terrestrian. He pushed a small button when his instruments told him the rays were off. Another scanner came into action, and the viewplate was alive again.

Arcot shot out a cosmic ray himself, and swept the Thessian with it thoroughly. For the instant he needed the enemy ship was blinded. Immediately the *Ancient Mariner* dove, and the automatic ray-finders could no longer hold the rays on his ship. As soon as he was out of the deadly molecular ray he shut off his screen, and turned on all his molecular rays. The Thessian ship, their own ray on, had been unable to put up their screen, as Arcot was unable to use his ray with the enemy's ray forcing him to cover with a shield.

Almost at once the relux covering of the Thessian ship shone with characteristic iridescence as it changed swiftly to lux metal. The molecular ray blinked out, and a ray-screen flashed out instead. The Thessians were covering up. Their own rays were useless now. Though Arcot could not hope to destroy their ray-shield, they could no longer attack his, for their rays were useless, and already they had lost so much of the protective relux, that they would not be so foolhardy as to risk a second attack of the ray.

Arcot continued to bathe the ship in energy, keeping their "eyes" closed. As long as he could hold his barrage on them, they would not damage him.

"Morey—get into the power room, strap onto the board. Throw all the power-coil banks into the magnets. I may burn them out, but I have hopes—" Arcot already had the generators going full power, charging the power coils.

Morey dived. Almost simultaneously the Thessians succeeded in the maneuver they had been attempting for some time. There were a dozen rays flaring wildly from the ship, searching blindly over the sky and ground, hoping to stumble on the enemy ship, while their own ship dived and twisted. Arcot was busily dodging the sweeping rays, but finally one hit his viewplates, and his own ship was blind. Instantly he threw the ray-screen out, cutting off his own molecular ray. His own cosmics he set rotating in cones that covered the three dimensions—save below, where the city lay. Immediately the Thessian had retreated to this one segment where Arcot did not dare throw his own rays. The Thessian cosmics continued to make his relux screens necessary, and his ship remained blind.

His ray-screen was showing signs of weakening. The Thessians got a third ray into position for operation, and opened up. Almost at once the tubes heated terrifically. In an instant they would give way. Arcot threw his ship into space, and let the tubes cool under the water jacket. Morey reported the coils ready as soon as he came out of space.

Arcot cut in the new set of eyes, and put up his molecular ray-screen again. Then he cut the energy back to the coils.

Half a mile below the enemy ship was vainly scurrying around an empty sky. Wade laughed at the strange resemblance to a puppy chasing its tail. The *Ancient Mariner* was utterly lost to them.

"Well, here goes the last trick," said Arcot grimly. "If this doesn't work, they'll probably win, for their tubes are better than ours, and they can maneuver faster. By win I mean force us to let them attack Ortol. They can't really attack us; artificial space is a perfect defense."

Arcot's molecular ray apprized the Thessians of his presence. Their screen flared up once more. Arcot was driving straight toward their ship as they turned. He snapped the relux screens in front of his eyes an instant before the enemy cosmics reached his ship. Immediately the thud of four heavy relays rang through the ship. The quarter of a million ton ship leaped forward under a terrific acceleration, and then, as the four relays cut out again, the acceleration was gone. The screen regained life as Arcot opened the shutters. Before them, still directly in their path, was the huge Thessian ship. But now its screen was down, the relux iridescent in decomposition. It was falling, helplessly falling to the rocky plateau seven miles below. Its rays reached out even yet—and again the *Ancient Mariner* staggered under the terrific pull of some acceleration. The Thessian ship lurched upward, and a terrific concussion came, and the entire neighborhood of that projector disappeared in a flash of radiation.

Arcot drove the *Ancient Mariner* down beneath the Thessian ship in its long fall, and with a powerful molecular beam ripped a mighty chasm in the deserted plateau. The Thessian ship fell into a quarter-mile rift in the solid rock, smashing its way through falling débris. A moment later it was buried beneath a quarter mile of broken rock as Arcot swept a molecular beam about with the grace of a mine foreman filling breaks.

An instant later, a heat ray followed the molecular in dazzling brilliance. A terrific gout of light appeared in the barren rocks. In ten minutes the plateau was a white hot cauldron of molten rocks, glowing now against a darkening sky. Night was falling.

"That ship," said Arcot with an air of finality, "will never rise again."

CHAPTER VI

THE SECOND MOVE

"What happened to him, though?" asked Wade, bewildered. "I haven't yet figured it out. He went down in a heap, and he didn't have any power. Of course, if he had his power he could have pulled out again. He could just melt and burn all the excess rock off, and he would be all set. But his rays all went dead. And why the explosion?"

"The magnetic beam is the answer. In our boat we have everything magnetically shielded, because of the enormous magnetic flux set up by the current flowing from the storage coils to the main coil. But—with so many wires heavily charged with current, what would have happened if they had not been shielded?

"If a current cuts across a magnetic field, a side thrust is developed. What do you suppose happened when the terrific magnetic field of the beam and the currents in the wires of their power-board were mutually opposed?"

"Lord, it must have ripped away everything in the ship. It'd tear loose even the lighting wires!" gasped Wade in amazement.

"But if all the power of the ship was destroyed in this way, how was it that one of their rays was operating as they fell?" asked Zezdon Afthen.

"Each ray is a power plant in itself," explained Arcot, "and so it was able to function. I do not know the cause of the explosion, though it might well have been that they had light-bombs such as the Kaxorians of Venus have," he added, thoughtfully.

They landed, at Zezdon's advice, in the city that their arrival had been able to save. This was Ortol's largest city, and their industrial capital. Here, too, was the University at which Afthen taught.

They landed, and Arcot, Morey and Wade, with the aid of

Zezdon Afthen and Zezdon Fentes worked steadily for two of their days of fifty hours each, teaching men how to make and use the molecular ships, and the rays and screens, heat beams, and relux. But Arcot promised that when he returned he would have some weapon that would bring them certain and easy salvation. In the meantime other terrestrians would follow him.

They left the morning of their third day on the planet. A huge crowd had come to cheer them on their way as they left, but it was the "silent cheer" of Ortol, a telepathic well-wishing.

"Now," said Arcot as their ship left the planet behind, "we will have to make the next move. It certainly looks as though that next move would be to the still-unknown race that lives on world 3769-37, 478, 326, 894-6. Evidently we will have to have some weapon they haven't, and I think that I know what it will be. Thanks to our trip out to the Islands of Space."

"Shall we go?"

"I think it would be wise," agreed Morey.

"And I," said Wade. The Ortolians agreed, and so, with the aid of the photographic copies of the Thessian charts that Arcot had made, they started for world 3769-37, 478, 326, 894-6.

"It will take approximately twenty-two hours, and as we have been putting off our sleep with drugs, I think that we had better catch up. Wade, I wish you'd take the ship again, while Morey and I do a little concentrated sleeping. We have by no means finished that calculation, and I'd very much like to. We'll relieve you in five hours."

Wade took the ship, and following the course Arcot laid out, they sped through the void at the greatest safe speed. Wade had only to watch the view-screen carefully, and if a star showed as growing rapidly, it was proof that they were near, and nearing rapidly. If large, a touch of a switch, and they dodged to one side, if small, they were suddenly plunged into an instant of unbelievable radiation as they swept through it, in a different space, yet linked to it by radiation, not light, that were permitted in.

Zezdon Afthen had elected to stay with him, which gave him an opportunity he had been waiting for. "If it's none of my business, just say so," he began. "But that first city we saw the Thessians destroy—it was Zezdon Fentes' home, wasn't it? Did he have a family?"

The words seemed blunt as he said them, but there was no way out, once he had started. And Zezdon Afthen took the question with complete calm.

"Fentes had both wives and children," he said quietly. "His loss was great."

Wade concentrated on the screen for a moment, trying to absorb the shock. Then, fearing Zezdon Afthen might misinterpret his silence, he plunged on. "I'm sorry," he said. "I didn't realize you were polygamous—most people on Earth aren't, but some groups are. It's probably a good way to improve the race. But . . . Blast it, what bothers me is that Zezdon Fentes seemed to recover from the blow so quickly! From a canine race, I'd expect more affection, more loyalty, more . . ."

He stopped in dismay. But Zezdon Afthen remained unperturbed. "More unconcealed emotion?" he asked. "No. Affection and loyalty we have—they *are* characteristic of our race. But affection and loyalty should not be uselessly applied. To *forget* dead wives and children—that would be insulting to their memory. But to mourn them with senseless loss of health and balance would also be insulting—not only to their memory, but to the entire race.

"No, we have a better way. Fentes, my very good friend, has not forgotten, no more than you have forgotten the death of your mother, whom you loved. But you no longer mourn her death with a fear and horror of that natural thing, the Eternal Sleep. Time has softened the pain.

"If we can do the same in five minutes instead of five years, is is not better? That is why Fentes has *forgotten*."

"Then you have aged his memory of that event?" asked Wade in surprise.

"That is one way of stating it," replied Zezdon Afthen seriously.

Wade was silent for a while, absorbing this. But he could not contain his curiosity completely. *Well, to hell with it,* he decided. *Conventional manners and tact don't have much meaning between two different races.* "Are you—married?" he asked.

"Only three times," Zezdon Afthen told him blandly. "And to forestall your next question—no, our system does not create problems. At least, not those you're thinking of. I know my wives have never had the jealous quarrels I see in your mind pictures."

"It isn't safe thinking things around you," laughed Wade. "Just the same, all of this has made me even more interested in the 'Ancient Masters' you keep mentioning. Who were they?"

"The Ancient Ones," began Zezdon Afthen slowly, "were men such as you are. They descended from a primeval omnivorous mammal very closely related to your race. Evidently the tendency of evolution on any planet is approximately the same with given conditions.

"The race existed as a distinct branch for approximately 1,500,000 of your years before any noticeable culture was developed. Then it existed for a total of 1,525,000 years before extinction. With culture and learning they developed such marvelous means of killing themselves that in twenty-five thousand years they succeeded perfectly. Ten thousand years of barbaric culture—I need not relate it to you, five thousand years of the medieval culture, then five thousand years of developed science culture.

"They learned to fly through space and nearly populated three worlds; two were fully populated, one was still under colonization when the great war broke out. An interplanetary war is not a long drawn out struggle. The science of any people so far advanced as to have interplanetary lines is too far developed to permit any long duration of war. Selto declared war, and made the first move. They attacked and destroyed the largest city of Ortol of that time. Ortolian ships drove them off, and in turn attacked Selto's largest city. Twenty million intelligencies, twenty million lives, each with its aims, its hopes, its loves and its strivings—gone in four days.

"The war continued to get more and more hateful, till it became evident that neither side would be pacified till the other was totally subjugated. So each laid his plans, and laid them to wipe out the entire world of the other.

"Ortol developed a ray of light that made things not happen," explained Zezdon Afthen, his confused thoughts clearly indicating his own uncertainty.

"'A ray of light that made things not happen,'" repeated Wade curiously. "A ray, which prevented things, which caused processes to stop—*The Negrian Death Ray!*" he exclaimed as he suddenly recognized, in this crude and garbled description of its powers, the Negrian ray of anti-catalysis, a ray which tended to stop the processes of life's chemistry and bring instant, painless death.

"Ah, you know it, too?" asked the Ortolian eagerly. "Then you will understand what happened. The ray was turned first on Selto, and as the whirling planet spun under it, every square foot of it was wiped clean of every living thing, from gigantic Welsthan to microscopic Ascoptel, and every man, woman and child was killed, painlessly, but instantly.

"Then Thenten spun under it, and all were killed, but many who had fled the planets were still safe—many?—a few thousand.

"The day that Thenten spun under that ray, men of Ortol began to complain of disease—men by the thousands, hundreds of thousands. Every man, every woman, every child was afflicted in some way. The diseases did not seem all the same. Some seemingly died of a disease of the lungs, some went insane, some were paralyzed, and lay helplessly inactive. But most of them were afflicted, for it was exceedingly virulent, and the normal serums were helpless. Before any quantity of new serum was made, all but a slender remnant had died, either of starvation through paralysis, none being left to care for them, or from the disease itself, while thousands who had gone mad were painlessly killed.

"The Seltonians came to Ortol, and the remaining Ortolians, with their aid, tried to rebuild the civilization. But what a sorry thing! The cities were gigantic, stinking, plague-ridden morgues. And the plague broke among those few remaining people. The Ortolians had done everything in their power with the serums—but too late. The Seltonians had been protected with it on landing—but even that was not enough. Again the wild fires of that loathsome disease broke out.

"Since first those men had developed from their hairy forebears, they had found their eternal friends were the dogs, and to them they turned in their last extremity, breeding them for intelligence, hairlessness, and resemblance to themselves. The Deathless ones alone remained after three generations of my people, but with the aid of certain rays, the rays capable of penetrating lead for a short distance, and most other substances for considerable distances." X rays, thought Wade. "Great changes had been wrought. Already they had developed startling intelligence, and were able to understand the scheme of their Masters.

Their feet and hands were being modified rapidly, and their vocal apparatus was changing. Their jaws shortened, their chins developed, the nose retreated.

"Generation after generation the process went on, while the Deathless Ancient Ones worked with their helpers, for soon my race was a real helping organization.

"But it was done. The successful arousing of true love-emotion followed, and the unhappy days were gone. Quickly development followed. In five thousand years the new race had outstripped the Ancient Masters, and they passed, voluntarily, willingly joining in oblivion the millions who had died before.

"Since then our own race has risen, it has been but a short thousand years, a thousand years of work, and hope, and continuous improvement for us, continual accomplishment on which we can look, and a living hope to which we could look with raised heads, and smiling faces.

"Then our hope died, as this menace came. Do you see what you and your world was meant to us, Man of Earth?" Zezdon Afthen raised his dark eyes to the terrestrian with a look in their depths that made Wade involuntarily resolve that Thett and all Thessians should be promptly consigned to that limbo of forgotten things where they belonged.

CHAPTER VII

WORLD 3769-37,478,326,894,6, TALSO

Wade sat staring moodily at the screen for some time, while Zezdon Afthen, sunk in his own reveries, continued.

"Our race was too highly psychic, and too little mechanically curious. We learned too little of the world about, and too much of our own processes. We are a peaceful race, for, while you and the Ancient Masters learned the rule of existence in a world of strife, where only the fittest, the best fighters survived, we learned life in a carefully tended world, where the Ancient Masters taught us to live, where the one whose social instincts were best developed, where he who would most help the others, and the race, was permitted to live. Is it not natural that our race will not fight among themselves? We are careful to suppress tendencies toward criminality and struggle. The criminal and the maniac, or those who are permanently incurable as determined by careful examination, are 'removed' as the Leaders put it. Lethal gas.

"At any rate, we know so pitiably little of natural science. We were hopelessly helpless against an attacking science."

"I promise you, Afthen, that if Earth survives, Ortol shall survive, for we have given you all the weapons we know of and we will give your people all the weapons we shall learn of." Morey spoke from the doorway. Arcot was directly behind him.

They talked for a short while, then Wade retired for some needed sleep, while Morey and Arcot started further work on the time-fields.

Hour after hour the ship sped on through the dark of space, weirdly distorted, glowing spots of light before them, wheeling suns that moved and flashed as their awesome speed whirled them on.

They had to move slower soon, as the changing stars showed them near the space-marks of certain locating suns. Finally, still moving close to fifteen thousand miles per second, they saw the sun they knew was sun 3769-37,478,326,894, twice as large as Sol, two and a half times as massive and twenty-six times as brilliant.

Thirteen major planets they counted as they searched the system with their powerful telectroscope, the outermost more than ten billion miles from the parent sun, while planet six, the one indicated by the world number, was at a distance of five hundred million miles, nearly as far from the sun as Jupiter is from ours, yet the giant sun, giving more than twenty-five times as much heat and light in the blue-white range, heated the planet to approximately the same temperature Earth enjoys. Spectroscopy showed that the atmosphere was well supplied with oxygen, and so the inhabitants were evidently oxygen-breathing men, unlike those of the Negrian people who live in an atmosphere of hydrogen.

Arcot threw the ship toward the planet, and as it loomed swiftly larger, he shut off the space-control, and set the coils for full charge, while the ship entered the planet's atmosphere in a screaming dive, still at a speed of better than a hundred miles a second. But this speed was quickly damped as the ship shot high over broad oceans to the dull green of land ahead in the daylit zone. Observations made from various distances by means of the space-control, thus going back in time, show that the planet had a day of approximately forty hours, the diameter was nearly nine thousand miles, which would probably mean an inconveniently high gravity for the terrestrians and a distressingly high gravity for the Ortolians, used to their world even smaller than Earth, with scarcely 80 percent of Earth's gravity.

Wade made some volumetric analysis of the atmosphere, and with the aid of a mouse, pronounced it "Q.A.R." (quite all right) for human beings. It had not killed the mouse, so probably humans would find it quite all right.

"We'll land at the first city that comes into view," suggested Arcot. "Afthen, you be the spokesman; you have a very considerable ability with the mental communication, and have a better understanding of the physics we need to explain than has Zezdon Fentes."

They were over land, a rocky coast that shot behind them as great jagged mountains, tipped with snow, rose beneath. Suddenly, a shining apparition appeared from behind one of the neighboring hills, and drove down at them with an unearthly acceleration. Arcot moved just enough to dodge the blow, and turned to meet the ship. Instantly, now that he had a good view of it he was certain it was a Thessian ship. Waiting no longer to determine that it was not a ship of this world, he shot a molecular beam at it. The beam exploded into a coruscating panoply of pyrotechnics on the Thessian shield. The Thessian replied with all beams he had available, including an induction-beam, an intensely brilliant light-beam, and several molecular cannons with shells loaded with an explosive that was very evidently condensed light. This was no exploration ship, but a full-fledged battleship.

The *Ancient Mariner* was blinded instantly. None of the occupants were hurt, but the combined pressure of the various beams hurled the ship to one side. The induction beam alone was dangerous. It passed through the outer lux-metal wall unhindered, and the perfectly conducting relux wall absorbed it, and turned it into power. At once, all the metal objects in the ship began to heat up with terrific rapidity. Since there were no metallic conductors on the ship, no damage was done.

Arcot immediately hid behind his perfect shield—the space-distortion.

"That's no mild dose," he said in a tense voice, working rapidly. "He's a real-for-sure battleship. Better get down in the power room, Morey."

In a few moments the ship was ready again. Opening the shield somewhat, Arcot was able to determine that no rays were being played on it, for no energy-field disclosed as distorting the opened field, other than the field of the sun and planet.

Arcot opened it. The battleship was searching vainly about the mountains, and was now some miles distant. His last view of Arcot's ship had been a suddenly contracting ship, one that vanished in infinite distance, the infinite distance of another space, though he did not know it.

Arcot turned three powerful heat beams on the Thessian ship, and drove down toward it, accompanying them with molecular rays. The Thessian shield stopped the moleculars, but the heat had already destroyed the eyes of the ship. By some system of magnetic or electrostatic locating devices, the enemy guns and rays replied, and so successfully that Arcot was again blinded.

He had again been driving in a line straight toward the enemy, and now he threw in the entire power of his huge magnetic field-rays. The induction ray disappeared, and the heat, light and cannons stopped.

"Worked again," grinned Arcot. A new set of eyes was inserted automatically, and the screen again lighted. The Thessian ship was spinning end over end toward the ground. It landed with a tremendous crash. Simultaneously from the rear of the *Ancient Mariner* came a terrific crash, an explosion that drove the terrestrian ship forward, as though a giant hand had pushed it from behind.

The *Ancient Mariner* spun like a top, facing the direction of the explosion, though still traveling in the direction it had been pursuing, but backward now. Behind them the air was a gigantic pool of ionization. Tremendous fragments of what obviously had been a ship were drifting down, turning end over end. And those fragments of the wall showed them to be fully four feet of solid relux.

"Enemy got up behind somehow while the eyes were out, and was ready to raise merry hell. Somebody blew them up beautifully. Look at the ground down there—it's red hot. That's from the radiated heat of our recent encounter. Heat rays reflected, light bombs turned off, heat escaping from ions— nice little workout—and it didn't seriously bother our defenses of two-inch relux. Now tell me: what will blow up four-foot relux?" asked Arcot, looking at the fragments. "It seems to me those fellows don't need any help from us; they may decline it with thanks."

"But they may be willing to help us," replied Afthen, "and we certainly need such help."

"I didn't expect to come out alive from that battleship there. It was luck. If they knew what we had, they could insulate against it in an hour," added Arcot.

"Let's finish those fellows over there—look!" From the wreck of the ship they had downed, a stream of men in glistening relux suits were filing. Any men comparable to humans would have been killed by the fall, but not Thessians. They carried peculiar machines, and as they drove out of the ship in dive that looked as though they had been shot from a cannon, they turned and landed on the ground and proceeded to jump back, leaping at a speed that was bewildering, seemingly impossible in any living creature.

They busied themselves quickly. It took less than thirty seconds, and they had a large relux disc laid under the entire group and machines. Arcot turned a molecular ray down. The rock and soil shot up all about them, even the ship shot up, to fall back into the great pit its ray had formed. But the ionization told of the ray-shield over the little group of men. A heat ray reached down, while the men still frantically worked at their stubby projectors. The relux disc now showed its purpose. In an instant the soil about them was white hot, bubbling lava. It was liquid, boiling furiously. But the deep relux disc simply floated on it. The enemy ship began sinking, and in a moment had fallen almost completely beneath the white hot rock.

A fountain of the melted lava sprung up, and under Arcot's skillful direction, fell in a cloud of molten rock on the men working. The suits protected, and the white hot stuff simply rolled off. But it was sinking their boat. Arcot continued hopefully.

Meanwhile a signaling machine was frantically calling for help and sending out information of their plight and position.

Then all was instantly wiped out in a single terrific jolt of the magnetic beam. The machines jumped a little, despite their weight, and the ray-shield apparatus slumped suddenly in blazing white heat, the interior mechanism fused. But the men were still active, and rapidly spreading from the spot, each protected by a ray-shield pack.

A brilliant stab of molecular ray shot at each from either of two of the *Ancient Mariner*'s projectors as Morey aided Arcot. Their little packs flared brilliantly for an instant under the thousands of horsepower of energy lashing at the screen, then flashed away, and the opalescent relux yielded a moment later, and the figure went twisting, hurtling away. Meanwhile Wade was busy with the magnetic apparatus, destroying shield after shield, which either Arcot or Morey picked off. The fall from even so much as half a mile seemed not sufficient to seriously bother these supermen, for an instant later they would be up tearing away in great leaps on their own power as their molecular suits, blown out by the magnetic field, failed them.

It was but a matter of minutes before the last had been chased down either by the rays or the ship. Then, circling back, Arcot slowly settled beside the enemy ship.

"Wait," called Arcot sharply as Morey started for the door. "Don't go out yet. The friends who wrecked that little sweetheart who crept up behind will probably show up. Wait and see what happens." Hardly had he spoken, when a strange apparition rose from behind a rock scarcely a quarter of a mile away. Immediately Arcot intensified the vision-screen covering him. He seemed to leap near. There was one man, and he held what was obviously a sword by the blade, above his head, waving it from side to side.

"There they are—whatever they are. Intelligent all right— what more universally obvious peace sign than a primitive weapon such as a knife held in reverse position? You go with Zezdon Afthen. Try holding a carving knife by the blade."

Morey grinned as he got into his power suit, on Wade's

O.K. of the atmosphere. "They may mistake me for the cook out looking for dinner, and I wouldn't risk my dignity that way. I'll take the baseball bat and hold it wrong way instead."

Nevertheless, as he stepped from the ship, with Afthen close behind, he held the long knife by the blade, and Afthen, very awkwardly operating his still rather unfamiliar power suit, followed.

Into the intensely blue sunlight the men stepped. Their skin and clothing took on a peculiar tint under the strange sunlight.

The single stranger was joined by a second, also holding a reversed weapon, and together they threw them down. Morey and Zezdon Afthen followed suit. The two parties advanced toward each other.

The strangers advanced with a swift, light step, jumping from rock to rock, while Morey and Afthen flew part way toward them. The men of this world were totally unlike any intelligent race Morey had conceived of. Their head and brain case was so small as to be almost animalish. The nose was small and well formed, the ears more or less cup-shaped with a remarkable power of motion. Their eyes were seemingly huge, probably no larger than a terrestrian's, though in the tiny head they were necessarily closely placed, protected by heavy bony ridges that actually projected from the skull to enclose them. Tiny, childlike chins completed the head, running down to a scrawny neck.

They were short, scarcely five feet, yet evidently of tremendous strength for their short, heavy arms, the muscle bulging plainly under the tight rubber-like composition garments, and the short legs whose stocky girth proclaimed equal strength were members of a body in keeping with them. The deep, broad chest, wide, square shoulders, heavy broad hips, combined with the tiny head seemed to indicate a perfect incarnation of brainless, brute strength.

"Strangers from another planet, enemies of our enemies. What brings you here at this time of troubles?" The thoughts came clearly from the stocky individual before them.

"We seek to aid, and to find aid. The menace that you face, attacks not alone your world, but all this star cluster," replied Zezdon Afthen steadily.

The stranger shook his head with an evident expression of

hopelessness. "The menace is even greater than we feared. It was just fortune that permitted us to have our weapon in workable condition at the time your ship was attacked. It will be a day before the machine will again be capable of successful operation. When in condition for use, it is invincible, but—one blow in thirty hours—you can see we are not of great aid." He shrugged.

An enemy with evident resources of tremendous power, deadly, unknown rays that wiped out entire cities with a single brief sweep—and no defense save this single weapon, good but once a day! Morey could read the utter despair of the man.

"What is the difficulty?" asked Morey eagerly.

"Power, lack of power. Our cities are going without power, while every electric generator on the planet is pouring its output into the accumulators that work these damnable, hopeless things. Invincible with power—helpless without."

"Ah!" Morey's face shone with delight—invincible weapon—with power. And the *Ancient Mariner* could generate unthinkable power.

"What power source do you use—how do you generate your power?"

"Combining oxidizing agent with reducing agents releases heat. Heat used to boil liquid and the vapor runs turbines."

"We can give you power. What wattage have you available?"

Only Morey's thoughts had to translate "watts" to "How many man-weights can you lift through your height per time interval, equal to this." He gave the man some impression of a second, by counting. The man figured rapidly. His answer indicated that approximately a total of two billion kilowatts were available.

"Then the weapon is invincible hereafter, if what you say is true. Our ship alone can easily generate ten thousand times that power.

"Come, get in the ship, accompany us to your capital."

The men turned, and retreated to their position behind the rocks, while Morey and Zezdon Afthen waited for them. Soon they returned, and entered the ship.

"Our world," explained the leader rapidly, "is a single unified colony. The capital is 'Shesto,' our world we call 'Talso.'" His directions were explicit, and Arcot started for Shesto, on Talso.

you going to transmit the power? We can't possibly move any power anywhere near that amount. We couldn't touch it to our lines without having them all go up in one instantaneous blaze of glory.

"We cannot drain such a lake of power through our tiny power pipes of silver."

"This man is Stel Felso Theu," said Tho Stan Drel. "The greatest of our scientists, the man who has invented this weapon which alone seems to offer us hope. And I am afraid he is right. See, there is the University. For the power requirements of their laboratories, a heavy power line has been installed, and it was hoped that you could carry leads into it." His face showed evident despair greater than ever.

"We can always feed some power into the lines. Let us see just what hope there is. I think that it would be wiser to investigate the power lines at once," suggested Morey.

Ten minutes later, with but a single officer now accompanying them, Tho Stan Drel, the terrestrial scientist, and the Talsonian scientist were inspecting the power installation.

They had entered a large stone building, into which led numerous very heavy silver wires. The insulators were silicate glass. Their height suggested a voltage of well over one hundred thousand, and such heavy cables suggested a very heavy amperage, so that a tremendous load was expected.

Within the building were a series of gigantic glass tubes, their walls fully three inches thick, and even so, braced with heavy platinum rods. Inside the tubes were tremendous elements such as the tiny tubes of their machine carried. Great cables led into them, and now their heating coils were glowing a somberly deep red.

Along the walls were the switchboards, dozens of them, all sizes, all types of instruments, strange to the eyes of the terrestrians, and in practically all the lightbeam indicator system was used, no metallic pointers, but tiny mirrors directing a very fine line of brilliant light acted as a needle. The system thus had practically no inertia.

"Are these the changers?" asked Arcot gazing at the gigantic tubes.

"They are; each tube will handle up to a hundred thousand volts," said Stel Felso Theu.

"But I fear, Stel Felso Theu, that these tubes will carry power only one way; that is, it would be impossible for power to be pumped from here into the power house, though the process can be reversed," pointed out Arcot. "Radio tubes work only one way, which is why they can act as rectifiers." The same was true of these tubes. They could carry power one way only.

"True, of tubes in general," replied the Talsonian, "and I see by that that you know the entire theory of our tubes, which is rather abstruse."

"We use them on the ship, in special form," interrupted Arcot.

"Then I will only say that the college here has a very complete electric power plant of its own. On special occasions, the power generated here is needed by the city, and so we arranged the tubes with switches which could reverse the flow. At present they are operating to pour power into the city.

"If your ship can generate such tremendous power, I suspect that it would be wiser to eliminate the tubes from the circuit, for they put certain restrictions on the line. The main power plant in the city has tube banks capable of handling anything the line would. I suggest that your voltage be set at the maximum that the line will carry without breakdown, and the amperage can be made as high as possible without heat loss."

"Good enough. The line to the city power will stand what pressure?"

"It is good for the maximum of these tubes," replied the Talsonian.

"Then get into communication with the city plant and tell them to prepare for every work-unit they can carry. I'll get the generator." Arcot turned, and flew on his power suit to the ship.

In a few moments he was back, a molecular pistol in one hand, and suspended in front of him on nothing but a ray of ionized air, to all appearances, a cylindrical apparatus, with a small cubical base.

The cylinder was about four feet long, and the cubical box about eighteen inches on a side.

"What is that, and what supports it?" asked the Talsonian scientists in surprise.

"The thing is supported by a ray which directs the molecules of a small bar in the top clamp, driving it up," explained Morey, "and that is the generator."

"That! Why it is hardly as big as a man!" exclaimed the Talsonian.

"Nevertheless, it can generate a billion horsepower. But you couldn't get the power away if you did generate it." He turned toward Arcot, and called to him.

"Arcot—set it down and let her rip on about half a million horsepower for a second or so. Air arc. Won't hurt it—she's made of lux and relux."

Arcot grinned, and set it on the ground. "Make an awful hole in the ground."

"Oh—go ahead. It will satisfy this fellow, I think," replied Morey.

Arcot pulled a very thin lux metal cord from his pocket, and attached one end of a long loop to one tiny switch, and the other to a second. Then he adjusted three small dials. The wire in hand, he retreated to a distance of nearly two hundred feet, while Morey warned the Talsonians back. Arcot pulled one end of his cord.

Instantly a terrific roar nearly deafened the men, a solid sheet of blinding flame reached in a flaming cone into the air for nearly fifty feet. The screeching roar continued for a moment, then the heat was so intense that Arcot could stand no more, and pulled the cord. The flame died instantly, though a slight ionization clung briefly. In a moment it had cooled to white, and was cooling slowly through orange—red deep—red—

The grass for thirty feet about was gone, the soil for ten feet about was molten, boiling. The machine itself was in a little crater, half sunk in boiling rock. The Talsonians stared in amazement. Then a sort of sigh escaped them and they started forward. Arcot raised his molecular pistol, a blue green ray reached out, and the rock suddenly was black. It settled swiftly down, and a slight depression was the only evidence of the terrific action.

Arcot walked over the now cool rock, cooled by the action of the molecular ray. In driving the molecules downward, the work was done by the heat of these molecules. The machine was frozen in the solid lava.

"Brilliant idea, Morey," said Arcot disgustedly. "It'll be a nice job breaking it loose."

Morey stuck the lux metal bar in the top clamp, walked off some distance, and snapped on the power. The rock immediately about the machine was molten again. A touch of the molecular pistol to the lux metal bar, and the machine jumped free of the molten rock.

Morey shut off the power. The machine was perfectly clean, and extremely hot.

"And your ship is made of that stuff!" exclaimed the Talsonian scientist. "What will destroy it?"

"Your weapon will, apparently."

"But do you believe that we have power enough?" asked Morey with a smile.

"No—it's entirely too much. Can you tone that condensed lightning bolt down to a workable level?"

CHAPTER IX

THE IRRESISTIBLE AND THE IMMOVABLE

The generator Arcot had brought was one of the two spare generators used for laboratory work. He took it now into the sub-station, and directed the Talsonian students and the scientist in the task of connecting it into the lines; though they knew where it belonged, he knew *how* it belonged.

Then the terrestrian turned on the power, and gradually increased it until the power authorities were afraid of breakdowns. The accumulators were charged in the city, and the power was being shipped to other cities whose accumulators were not completely charged.

But, after giving simple operating instructions to the students, Arcot and Morey went with Stel Felso Theu to his laboratory.

"Here," Stel Felso Theu explained, "is the original apparatus. All these other machines you see are but replicas of this. How it works, why it works, even what it does, I am not sure of.

Perhaps you will understand it. The thing is fully charged now, for it is, in part, one of the defenses of the city. Examine it now, and then I will show its power."

Arcot looked it over in silence, following the great silver leads with keen interest. Finally he straightened, and returned to the Talsonian. In a moment Morey joined them.

The Talsonian then threw a switch, and an intense ionization appeared within the tube, then a minute spot of light was visible within the sphere of light. "The minute spot of radiance is the real secret of the weapon. The ball of fire around it is merely wasted energy.

"Now I will bring it out of the tube." There were three dials on the control panel from which he worked, and now he adjusted one of these. The ball of fire moved steadily toward the glass wall of the tube, and with a crash the glass exploded inward. It had been highly evacuated. Instantly the tiny ball of fire about the point of light expanded to a large globe.

"It is now in the outer air. We make the—thing, in an evacuated glass tube, but as they are cheap, it is not an expensive procedure. The ball will last in its present condition for approximately three hours. Feel the exceedingly intense heat? It is radiating away its vast energy.

"Now here is the point of greatest interest." Again the Talsonian fell to work on his dials, watching the ball of fire. It seemed far more brilliant in the air now. It moved, and headed toward a great slab of steel off to one side of the laboratory. It shifted about until it was directly over the center of the great slab. The slab rested on a scale of some sort, and as the ball of fire touched it, the scale showed a sudden increase in load. The ball sank into the slab of steel, and the scale showed a steady, enormous load. Evidently the little ball was pressing its way through as though it were a solid body. In a moment it was through the steel slab, and out on the other side.

"It will pass through any body with equal ease. It seems to answer only these controls, and these it answers perfectly, and without difficulty.

"One other thing we can do with it. I can increase its rate of energy discharge."

The Talsonian turned a fourth dial, well off to one side, and the brilliance of the spot increased enormously. The heat was unbearable. Almost at once he shut it off.

"That is the principle we use in making it a weapon. Watch the actual operation."

The ball of fire shot toward an open window, out the window, and vanished in the sky above. The Talsonian stopped the rotation of the dials. "It is motionless now, but scarcely visible. I will now release all the energy." He twirled the fourth dial, and instantly there was a flash of light, and a moment later a terrific concussion.

"It is gone." He left the controls, and went over to his apparatus. He set a heavy silver bladed switch, and placed a new tube in the apparatus. A second switch arced a bit as he drove it home. "Your generator is recharging the accumulators."

Stel Felso Theu took the backplate of the control cabinet off, and the terrestrians looked at the control with interest.

"Got it, Morey?" asked Arcot after a time.

"Think so. Want to try making it up? We can do so out of spare junk about the ship, I think. We won't need the tube if what I believe of it is true."

Arcot turned to the Talsonian. "We wish you to accompany us to the ship. We have apparatus there which we wish to set up."

Back to the ship they went. There Arcot, Morey and Wade worked rapidly.

It was about three quarters of an hour later when Arcot and his friends called the others to the laboratory. They had a maze of apparatus on the power bench, and the shining relux conductors ran all over the ship apparently. One huge bar ran into the power room itself, and plugged into the huge power-coil power supply.

They were still working at it, but looked up as the others entered. "Guess it will work," said Arcot with a grin.

There were four dials, and three huge switches. Arcot set all four dials, and threw one of the switches. Then he started slowly turning the fourth dial. In the center of the room a dim, shining mist a foot in diameter began to appear. It condensed, solidified without shrinking, a solid ball of matter a foot in diameter. It seemed black, but was a perfectly reflective surface —and luminous!

"Then—then you had already known of this thing? Then why did you not tell me when I tried to show it?" demanded the Talsonian.

Arcot was sending the globe, now perfectly non-luminous, about the room. It flattened out suddenly, and was a disc. He tossed a small weight on it, and it remained fixed, but began to radiate slightly. Arcot readjusted his dials, and it ceased radiating, held perfectly motionless. The sphere returned, and the weight dropped to the floor. Arcot maneuvered it about for a moment more. Then he placed his friends behind a screen of relux, and increased the radiation of the globe tremendously. The heat became intense, and he stopped the radiation.

"No, Stel Felso Theu, we do not have this on our world," Arcot said.

"You do not have it! You look at my apparatus fifteen minutes, and then work for an hour—and you have apparatus far more effective than ours, which required years of development!" exclaimed the Talsonian.

"Ah, but it was not wholly new to me. This ship is driven by curving space into peculiar coordinates. Even so, we didn't do such a hot job, did we, Morey?"

"No, we should have—"

"What—it was not a good job?" interrupted the Talsonian. "You succeeded in creating it in air—in making it stop radiating, in making a ball a foot in diameter, made it change to a disc, made it carry a load—what do you want?"

"We want the full possibilities, the only thing that can save us in this war," Morey said.

"What you learned how to do was the reverse of the process we learned. How you did it is a wonder—but you did. Very well—matter is energy—does your physics know that?" asked Arcot.

"It does; matter contains vast energy," replied the Talsonian.

"Matter has mass, and energy because of that! Mass *is* energy. Energy in any known form is a field of force in space. So matter is ordinarily a combination of magnetic, electrostatic and gravitational fields. Your apparatus combined the three, and put them together. The result was—matter!"

"You created matter. We can destroy it but we cannot create it.

"What we ordinarily call matter is just a marker, a sign that there are those energy-fields. Each bit is surrounded by a gravitational field. The bit is just the marker of that gravitational field."

"But that seems to be wrong. This artificial matter of yours seems also a sort of knot, for you make all three fields, combine them, and have the matter, but not, very apparently, like normal matter. Normal matter also holds the fields that make it. The artificial matter is surrounded by the right fields, but it is evidently not able to hold the fields, as normal matter does. That was why your matter continually disintegrated to ordinary energy. The energy was not bound properly.

"But the reason why it would blow up so was obvious. It did not take much to destroy the slight hold that the artificial matter had on its field, and then it instantly proceeded to release all its energy at once. And as you poured millions of horsepower into it all day to fill it, it naturally raised merry hell when it let loose."

Arcot was speaking eagerly, excitedly.

"But here is the great fact, the important thing: It is artificially created in a given place. It is made, and exists at the point determined by these three coordinated dials. It is not natural, and can exist only where it is made and nowhere else—obvious, but important. It cannot exist save at the point designated. Then, if that point moves along a line, the artificial matter must follow that moving point and be always at that point. Suppose now that a slab of steel is on that line. The point moves to it— through it. To exist, that artificial matter *must* follow it through the steel—if not, it is destroyed. Then the steel is attempting to destroy the artificial matter. If the matter has sufficient energy, it will force the steel out of the way, and penetrate. The same is true of any other matter, lux metal or relux—it will penetrate. To continue in existence it must. And it has great energy, and will expend every erg of that energy of existence to continue existence.

"It is, as long as its energy holds out, absolutely irresistible!

"But similarly, if it is at a given point, it must stay there, and will expend every erg staying there. It is then immovable!

It is either irresistible in motion, or immovable in static condition. It is the irresistible and the immovable!

"What happens if the irresistible meets the immovable? It can only fight with its energy of existence, and the more energetic prevails."

CHAPTER X

IMPROVEMENTS AND CALCULATIONS

"It is still incredible. But you have done it. It is certainly successful!" said the Talsonian scientist with conviction.

Arcot shook his head. "Far from it—we have not realized a thousandth part of the tremendous possibilities of this invention. We must work and calculate and then invent.

"Think of the possibilities as a shield—naturally if we can make the matter we should be able to control its properties in any way we like. We should be able to make it opaque, transparent, or any color." Arcot was speaking to Morey now. "Do you remember, when we were caught in that cosmic ray field in space when we first left this universe, that I said that I had an idea for energy so vast that it would be impossible to describe its awful power?* I mentioned that I would attempt to liberate it if ever there was need? The need exists. I want to find that secret."

Stel Felso Theu was looking out through the window at a group of men excitedly beckoning. He called the attention of the others to them, and himself went out. Arcot and Wade joined him in a moment.

"They tell me that Fellsheh, well to the poleward of here has used four of its eight shots. They are still being attacked," explained the Talsonian gravely.

"Well, get in," snapped Arcot as he ran back to the ship. Stel Felso hastily followed, and the *Ancient Mariner* shot into the air, and darted away, poleward, to the Talsonian's directions. The

_____
* Islands of Space.

ground fled behind them at a speed that made the scientist grip the hand-rail with a tenseness that showed his nervousness.

As they approached, a tremendous concussion and a great gout of light in the sky informed them of the early demise of several Thessians. But a real fleet was clustered about the city. Arcot approached low, and was able to get quite close before detection. His ray-screen was up and Morey had charged the artificial matter apparatus, small as it was, for operation. He created a ball of substance outside the *Ancient Mariner,* and thrust it toward the nearest Thessian, just as a molecular hit the *Ancient Mariner's* ray-screen.

The artificial matter instantly exploded with terrific violence, slightly denting the tremendously strong lux metal walls. The pressure of the light was so great that the inner relux walls were dented inward. The ground below was suddenly, instantaneously fused.

"Lord—they won't pass a ray-screen, obviously," Morey muttered, picking himself from where he had fallen.

"Hey—easy there. You blinked off the ray-screen, and our relux is seriously weakened," called Arcot, a note of worry in his voice.

"No artificial matter with the ray-screen up. I'll use the magnet," called Morey.

He quickly shut off the apparatus, and went to the huge magnet control. The power room was crowded, and now that the battle was raging in truth, with three ships attacking simultaneously, even the enormous power capacity of the ship's generators was not sufficient, and the storage coils had been thrown into the operation. Morey looked at the instruments a moment. They were all up to capacity, save the ammeter from the coils. That wasn't registering yet. Suddenly it flicked, and the other instrument dropped to zero. They were in artificial space.

"Come here, will you, Morey," called Arcot. In a moment Morey joined his much worried friend.

"That artificial matter control won't work through ray-screens. The Thessians never had to protect against moleculars here, and didn't have them up—hence the destruction wrought. We can't take our screen down, and we can't use our most deadly weapon with it up. If we had a big outfit, we might throw a screen around the whole ship, and sail right in. But we haven't.

"We can't stand ten seconds against that fleet. I'm going to find their base, and make them yell for help." Arcot snapped a tiny switch one notch further for the barest instant, then snapped it back. They were several million miles from the planet. "Quicker," he explained, "to simply follow those ships back home—go back in time."

With the telectroscope, he took views at various distances, thus quickly tracing them back to their base at the pole of the planet. Instantly Arcot shot down, reaching the pole in less than a second, by carefully maneuvering of the space device.

A gigantic dome of polished relux rose from rocky, icy plains. The thing was nearly half a mile high, a mighty rounded roof that covered an area almost three-quarters of a mile in diameter. Titanic—that was the only word that described it. About it there was the peculiar shimmer of a molecular ray-screen.

Morey darted to the power room and set his apparatus into operation. He created a ball of matter outside the ship and hurled it instantly at the fort. It exploded with a terrific concussion as it hit the wall of the ray-screen. Almost instantly a second one followed. The concussion was terrifically violent, the ground about was fused, and the ray-screen was opened for a moment. Arcot threw all his moleculars on the screen, as Morey sent bomb after bomb at it. The coils supplied the energy, cracked the rock beneath. Each energy release disrupted the ray-screen for a moment, and the concentrated fury of the molecular beams poured through the opened screen, and struck the relux behind. It glowed opalescent now in a spot twenty feet across. But the relux was tremendously thick. Thirty bombs Morey hurled, while they held their position without difficulty, pouring their bombs and rays at the fort.

Arcot threw the ship into space, moved, and reappeared suddenly nearly three hundred yards further on. A snap of the eyes, and he saw that the fleet was approaching now. He went again into space, and retreated. Discretion was the better part of valor. But his plan had worked.

He waited half an hour, and returned. From a distance the telectroscope told him that one lone ship was patrolling outside the fort. He moved toward it, creeping up behind the icy mountains. His magnetic beam reached out. The ship lurched and fell. The magnetic beam reached out toward the fort, from which a molecular ray had flashed already, tearing up the icy waste which had concealed him. The ray-screen stopped it, while again Morey turned the magnetic beam on—this time against the fort. The ray remained on! Arcot retreated hastily.

"They found the secret, all right. No use, Morey, come on up," called the pilot. "They evidently put magnetic shielding around the apparatus. That means the magnetic beam is no good to us any more. They will certainly warn every other base, and have them install similar protection."

"Why didn't you try the magnetic ray on our first attack?" asked Zezdon Afthen.

"If it had worked, their sending apparatus would have been destroyed, and no message could have been sent to call their attackers off Fellsheh. By forcing them to recall their fleet I got results I couldn't get by attacking the fleet," Arcot said.

"I think there is little more I can do here, Stel Felso Theu. I will take you to Shesto, and there make final arrangements till my return, with apparatus capable of overthrowing your enemies. If you wish to accompany me—you may." He glanced around at the others of his party. "And our next move will be to return to Earth with what we have. Then we will investigate the Sirian planets, and learn anything they may have of interest, thence—to the real outer space, the utter void of intergalactic space, and an attempt to learn the secret of that enormous power."

They returned to Shesto, and there Arcot arranged that the only generator they could spare, the one already in their possession, might be used till other terrestrial ships could bring more. They left for Earth. Hour after hour they fled through the void, till at last old Sol was growing swiftly ahead of them, and finally Earth itself was large on the screens. They changed to a straight molecular drive, and dropped to the Vermont field from which they had taken off.

During the long voyage, Morey and Arcot had both spent much of the time working on the time-distortion field, which would give them a tremendous control over time, either speeding or slowing their time rate enormously. At last, this finished, they had worked on the artificial matter theory, to the point where they could control the shape of the matter perfectly, though as yet they could not control its exact nature. The possibility of such control was, however, definitely proven by the results the machines had given them. Arcot had been more immediately interested in the control of form. He could control the nature as to opacity or transparency to all vibrations that normal matter is opaque or transparent to. Light would pass, or not as he chose, but cosmics he could not stop nor would radio or moleculars be stopped by any present shield he could make.

They had signaled, as soon as they slowed outside the atmosphere, and when they settled to the field, Arcot's father and a number of very important scientists had already arrived.

Arcot senior greeted his son very warmly, but he was tremendously worried, as his son soon saw.

"What's happened, Dad—won't they believe your statements?"

"They doubted when I went to Luna for a session with the Interplanetary Council, but before they could say much, they had plenty of proof of my statements," the older man answered. "News came that a fleet of Planetary Guard ships had been wiped out by a fleet of ships from outer space. They were huge things—nearly half a mile in length. The Guard ships went up to them—fifty of them—and tried to signal for a conference. The white ship was instantly wiped out—we don't know how. They didn't have ray-screens, but that wasn't it. Whatever it was— slightly luminous ray in space—it simply released the energy of the lux metal and relux of the ship. Being composed of light energy simply bound by photonic attraction, it let go with terrible energy. They can do it almost instantly from a distance. The other Guards at once let loose with all their moleculars and cosmics. The enemy shunted off the moleculars, and wiped out the Guard almost instantly.

"Of course, I could explain the screen, but not the detonation ray. I am inclined to believe from other casualties that the destruction, though reported as an instantaneous explosion, was not that. Other ships have been destroyed, and they seemed to catch fire, and burn, but with terrific speed, more like gun powder than coal. It seems to start a spreading decomposition, the ship lasts perhaps ten minutes. If it went instantly, the shock of such a tremendous energy release would disrupt the planet.

"At any rate, the great fleet separated, twelve went to the

North Pole of Earth, twelve to the south, and similarly twelve to each pole of Venus. Then one of them turned, and went back to wherever it had come from, to report. Just turned and vanished. Similarly one from Venus turned and vanished. That leaves twelve at each of the four poles, for, as I said, there were an even fifty.

"They all followed the same tactics on landing, so I'll simply tell what happened in Arctica. In the North they had to pick one of the islands a bit to the south of the pole. They melted about a hundred square miles of ice to find one.

"The ships arranged themselves in a circle around the place, and literally hundreds of men poured out of each and fell to work. In a short time, they had set up a number of machines, the parts coming from the ships. These machines at once set to work, and they built up a relux wall. That wall was at least six feet thick; the floor was lined with thick relux as well as the roof, which is simply a continuation of the wall in a perfect dome. They had so many machines working on it, that within twenty-four hours they had it finished.

"We attacked twice, once in practically our entire force, with some ray-shield machines. The result was disastrous. The second attack was made with ray shielded machines only, and little damage was done to either side, though the enemy were somewhat impeded by masses of ice hurled into their position. Their relux disintegration ray was conspicuous by its absence.

"Yesterday—and it seems a lot longer than that, son—they started it again. They'd been unloading it from the ship evidently. We had had ray-shielded machines out, but they simply melted. They went down, and Earth retreated. They're in their fortress now. We don't know how to fight them. Now, for God's sake, tell us you have learned of some weapon, son!"

The older man's face was lined. His iron gray head showed his fatigue due to hours of concentration on his work.

"Some," replied Arcot briefly. He glanced around. Other men had arrived, men whom he met in his work. But there were Venerians here, too, in their protective suits, insulated against the cold of Earth, and against its atmosphere.

"First, though, gentlemen, allow me to introduce Stel Felso

Theu of the planet Talso, one of our allies in this struggle, and Zezdon Afthen and Fentes of Ortol, one of our other allies.

"As to progress, I can say only that it is in a more or less rudimentary stage. We have the basis for great progress, a weapon of inestimable value—but it is only the basis. It must be worked out. I am leaving with you today the completed calculations and equations of the time field, the system used by the Thessian invaders in propelling their ships at a speed greater than that of light. Also, the uncompleted calculations in regard to another matter, a weapon which our ally, Talso, has given us, in exchange for the aid we gave in allowing them the use of one of our generators. Unfortunately the ship could not spare more than the single generator. I strongly advise rushing a number of generators to Talso in intergalactic freighters. They badly need power—power of respectable dimensions.

"I have stopped on Earth only temporarily, and I want to leave as soon as possible. I intend, however, to attempt an attack on the Arctic base of the Thessians, in strong hopes that they have not armored against one weapon that the *Ancient Mariner* carries—though I sadly fear that old Earth herself has played us false here. I hope to use the magnetic beam, but Earth's polar magnetism may have forced them to armor, and they may have sufficiently heavy material to block the effects."

Morey already had a ground crew servicing the ship. He gave designs to machinists on hand to make special control panels for the large artificial matter machines. Arcot and Wade got some badly needed equipment.

In six hours, Arcot had announced himself ready, and a squadron of Planetary Guard ships were ready to accompany the refitted *Ancient Mariner*.

They approached the pole cautiously, and were rewarded by the hiss and roar of ice melting into water which burst into steam under a ray. It was coming from an outpost of the camp, a tiny dome under a great mass of ice. But the dome was of relux. A molecular reached down from a Guard ship—and the Guard ship crumbled suddenly as dozens of moleculars from the points hit it.

"They know how to fight this kind of a war. That's their biggest advantage," muttered Arcot. Wade merely swore.

"Ray-screens, no moleculars!" snapped Arcot into the transmitter. He was not their leader, but they saw his wisdom, and the squadron commander repeated the advice as an order. In the meantime, another ship had fallen. The dome had its screen up, allowing the multitudes of hidden stations outside to fight for it.

"Hmm—something to remember when terrestrians have to retire to forts. They will, too, before this war is over. That way the main fort doesn't have to lower its ray-screen to fight," commented Arcot. He was watching intensely as a tiny ship swung away from one of the larger machines, and a tremendously powerful molecular started biting at the fort's ray-screen. The ship seemed nothing but a flying ray projector, which was what it was.

As they had hoped, the deadly new ray stabbed out from somewhere on the side of the fort. It was not within the fort.

"Which means," pointed out Morey, "that they can't make stuff to stand that. Probably the projector would be vulnerable."

But a barrage of heat rays which immediately followed had no apparent effect. The little radio-controlled molecular beam projector lay on the rock under the melted ice, blazing incandescent with the rapidly released energy of the relux.

"Now to try the real test we came here for," Morey clambered back to the power room, and turned on the controls of the magnetic beam. The ship was aligned, and then he threw the last switch. The great mass of the machine jerked violently, and plunged forward as the beam attracted the magnetic core of the Earth.

Morey could not see it, but almost instantly the shimmer of the molecular screen on the fort died out. The deadly ray sprang out from the Thessian projector—and went dead. Frantically the Thessians tried weapon after weapon, and found them dead almost as soon as they were turned on—which was the natural result in the terrific magnetic field.

And these men had iron bones, their very bones were attracted by the beam; they plunged upward toward the ship as the beam touched them, but, accustomed to the enormous gravitation accelerations of an enormous world, most of them were not killed.

"Ah—!" exclaimed Arcot. He picked up the transmitter and spoke again to the Squadron Commander. "Squadron Commander Tharnton, what relux thickness does your ship carry?"

"Inch and a quarter," replied the surprised voice of the commander.

"Any of the other ships carry heavier?"

"Yes, the special solar investigator carries five inches. What shall we do?"

"Tell him to lower his screen, and let loose at once on all operating forts. His relux will stand for the time needed to shut them down for their own screens, unless some genius decides to fight it out. As soon as the other ships can lower their screens, tell them to do so, and tell them to join in. I'll be able to help then. My relux has been burned, and I'm afraid to lower the screen. It's mighty thin already."

The squadron commander was smiling joyously as he relayed the advice as a command.

Almost at once a single ship, blunt, an almost perfect cylinder, lowered its screen. In an instant the opalescence of the transformation showed on it, but its dozen ray projectors were at work. Fort after fort glowed opalescent, then flashed into protective ionization of screening. Quickly other ships lowered their screens, and joined in. In a moment more, the forts had been forced to raise their screens for protection.

A disc of artificial matter ten feet across suddenly appeared beside the *Ancient Mariner*. It advanced with terrific speed, struck the great dome of the fort, and the dome caved, bent in, bent still more—but would not puncture. The disc retreated, became a sharp cone, and drove in again. This time the point smashed through the relux, and made a small hole. The cone seemed to change gradually, melting into a cylinder of twenty-foot diameter, and the hole simply expanded. It continued to expand as the cylinder became a huge disc, a hundred feet across, set in the wall.

Suddenly it simply dissolved. There was a terrific roar, and a mighty column of white rushed out of the gaping hole. Figures of Thessians caught by the terrific current came rocketing out. The inside was at last visible. The terrific pressure was hurling the outside line of ships about like thistledown. The *Ancient Mariner* reeled back under the tremendous blast of expanding gas. The snow that fell to the boiling water below was not water, *in toto;* some was carbon dioxide—and some oxygen chilled in the expansion of the gas. It was snowing within the dome. The falling forms of Thessians were robbed of the life-giving air pressure to which they were accustomed. But all this was visible for but an instant.

Then a small, thin sheet of artificial matter formed beside the fort, and advanced on the dome. Like a knife cutting open an orange, it simply went around the dome's edge, the great dome lifted like the lid of a teapot under the enormous gas pressure remaining—then dropped under its own weight.

The artificial matter was again a huge disc. It settled over the exact center of the dome—and went down. The dome caved in. It was crushed under a load utterly inestimable. Then the great disc, like some monstrous tamper, tamped the entire works of the Thessians into the bed-rock of the island. Every ship, every miniature fort, every man was caught under it—and annihilated.

The disc dissolved. A terrific barrage of heat beams played over the island, and the rock melted, flowed over the ruins, and left only the spumes of steam from the Arctic ice rising from a red-hot mass of rock, containing a boiling pool.

The Battle of the Arctic was done.

CHAPTER XI

"WRITE OFF THE MAGNET"

"Squadron commander Tharnton speaking: Squadron 73-B of Planetary Guard will follow orders from Dr. Arcot directly. Heading south to Antarctica at maximum speed," droned the communicator. Under the official tone of command was a note of suppressed rage and determination. "And the squadron commander wishes Dr. Arcot every success in wiping out Antarctica as thoroughly and completely as he destroyed the Arctic base."

The flight of ships headed south at a speed that heated them white in the air, thin as it was at the hundred-mile altitude, yet going higher would have taken unnecessary time, and the white heat meant no discomfort. They reached Antarctica in about ten minutes. The Thessian ships were just entering through great locks in the walls of the dome. At first sight of the terrestrial ships they turned, and shot toward the guard-ships. Their screens were down, for, armored as they were with very heavy relux they expected to be able to overcome the terrestrial thin relux before theirs was seriously impaired.

"Ships will put up screens." Arcot spoke sharply—a new plan had occurred to him. The moleculars of the Thessians struck glowing screens, and no damage was done. "Ships, in order of number, will lower screen for thirty seconds, and concentrate all moleculars on one ship—the leader. Solar investigator will not join in action."

The flagship of the squadron lowered its screen, and a tremendous bombardment of rays struck the leading ship practically in one point. The relux glowed, and the opalescence shifted with bewildering, confusing colors. Then the terrestrial ship's screen was up, before the Thessians could concentrate on the one unprotected ship. Immediately another terrestrial ship opened its screen and bombarded the same ship. Two others followed—and then it was forced to use its screen.

But suddenly a terrestrial ship crashed. Its straining screen had been overworked—and it failed.

Arcot's magnetic beam went into action. The Thessian ray did not go out—it flickered, dimmed, but was apparently as deadly as ever.

"Shielded—write off the magnet, Morey. That is one asset we lose."

Arcot, protected in space, was thinking swiftly. Moleculars—useless. They had to keep their own screens up. Artificial matter —bound in by their own molecular screen! And the magnet had failed them against the protected mechanism of the dome. The ships were not as yet protected, but the dome was.

"Guess the only place we'd be safe is under the ground—way under!" commented Wade dryly.

"Under the ground—Wade, you're a genius!" Arcot gave a shout of joy, and told Wade to take over the ship.

"Take the ship back into normal space, head for the hill over behind the Dome, and drop behind it. It's solid rock, and even their rays will take a moment or so to move it. As soon as you get there, drop to the ground, and turn off the screen. No—here, I'll do it. You just take it there, land on the ground, and shut off the screen. I promise the rest!" Arcot dived for the artificial matter room.

The ship was suddenly in normal space; its screen up. The dog-fight had been ended. The terrestrial ships had been completely defeated. The *Ancient Mariner's* appearance was a signal for all the moleculars in sight. Ten huge ships, half a dozen small forts and now the unshielded Dome, joined in. Their screen tubes heated up violently in the brief moment it took to dive behind the hill, a tube fused, and blew out. Automatic devices shunted it, another tube took the load—and heated. But their screen was full of holes before they were safe for the moment behind the hill.

Instantly Wade dropped the defective screen. Almost as quickly as the screen vanished, a cylinder of artificial matter surrounded the entire ship. The cylinder was tipped by a perfect cone of the same base diameter. The entire system settled into the solid rock. The rock above cracked and filled in behind them. The ship was suddenly pushed by the base of the cylinder behind them, and drove on through the rock, the cone parting the hard granite ahead. They went perhaps half a mile, then stopped. In the light of the ship's windows, they could see the faint mistiness of the inconceivably hard, artificial matter, and beyond the slick, polished surface of the rock it was pushing aside. The cone shape was still there.

There was a terrific roar behind them, the rock above cracked, shifted and moved about.

"Raying the spot where we went down," Arcot grinned happily.

The cone and cylinder merged, shifted together, and became a sphere. The sphere elongated upward and the *Ancient Mariner* turned in it, till it, too, pointed upward. The sphere became an ellipsoid.

Suddenly the ship was moving, accelerating terrifically. It plowed through the solid rock, and up—into a burst of light. They were *inside* the dome. Great ships were berthed about the floor. Huge machines bulked here and there—barracks for men— everything.

The ellipsoid shrank to a sphere, the sphere grew a protuberance which separated and became a single bar-like cylinder. The cylinder turned, and drove through the great dome wall. A little hole but it whirled rapidly around, sliced the top off neatly and quickly. Again, like a gigantic teapot lid, the whole great structure lifted, settled, and stayed there. Men, scrambling wildly toward ships, suddenly stopped, seemed to blur and their features ran together horribly. They fell—and were dead in an instant as the air disappeared. In another instant they were solid blocks of ice, for the temperature was below the freezing point of carbon dioxide.

The giant tamper set to work. The Thessian ships went first. They were all crumpled, battered wrecks in a few seconds of work of the terrible disc.

The dome was destroyed. Arcot tried something else. He put on his control machine the equation of a hyperboloid of two branches, and changed the constants gradually till the two branches came close. Then he forced them against each other. Instantly they fought, fought terribly for existence. A tremendous blast of light and heat exploded into being. The energy of two tons of lead attempted to maintain those two branches. It was not, fortunately, explosive, and it took place over a relux floor. Most of the energy escaped into space. The vast flood of light was visible on Venus, despite the clouds.

But it fused most of Antarctica. It destroyed the last traces of the camp in Antarctica.

"Well—the Squadron was wiped out, I see." Arcot's voice was flat as he spoke. The Squadron: twenty ships—four hundred men.

"Yes—but so is the Arctic camp, and the Antarctic camp, as well," replied Wade.

"What next, Arcot. Shall we go out to intergalactic space at once?" asked Morey, coming up from the power room.

"No, we'll go back to Vermont, and have the timefield stuff I ordered installed, then go to Sirius, and see what they have. They moved their planets from the gravitation field of Negra, their dead, black star, to the field of Sirius—and I'd like to know how they did it.* Then—Intergalactia." He started the ship toward Vermont, while Morey got into communication with the field, and gave them a brief report.

* "The Black Star Passes."

CHAPTER XII

SIRIUS

They landed about half an hour later, and Arcot simply went into the cottage, and slept—with the aid of a light soporific. Morey and Wade directed the disposition of the machines, but Dr. Arcot senior really finished the job. The machines would be installed in less than ten hours, for the complete plans Arcot and Morey had made, with the modern machines for translating plans to metal and lux had made the actual construction quick, while the large crew of men employed required but little time.

When Arcot and his friends awoke, the machines were ready.

"Well, Dad, you have the plans for all the machines we have. I expect to be back in two weeks. In the meantime you might set up a number of ships with very heavy relux walls, walls that will stand rays for a while, and equip them with the rudimentary artificial matter machines you have, and go ahead with the work on the calculations. Thett will land other machines here—or on the moon. Probably they will attempt to ray the whole Earth. They won't have concentration of ray enough to move the planet, or to seriously chill it. But life is a different matter—it's sensitive. It is quite apt to let go even under a mild ray. I think that a few exceedingly powerful ray-screen stations might be set up, and the Heavyside Layer used to transmit the vibrations entirely around the Earth. You can see the idea easily enough. If you think it worthwhile—or better, if you can convince the thickheaded politicians of the Interplanetary Defense Commission that it is—

"Beyond that, I'll see you in about two weeks," Arcot turned, and entered the ship.

"I'll line up for Sirius and let go." Arcot turned the ship now, for Earth was well behind, and lined it on Sirius, bright in the utter black of space. He pushed his control to "½," and the space closed in about them. Arcot held it there while the chronometer moved through six and a half seconds. Sirius was at a distance almost planetary in its magnitude from them. Controlling directly now, he brought the ship closer, till a planet loomed large before them—a large world, its rocky continents, its rolling oceans and jagged valleys white under the enormous energy-flood from the gigantic star of Sirius, twenty-six times more brilliant than the sun they had left.

"But, Arcot, hadn't you better take it easy?" Wade asked. "They might take us for enemies—which wouldn't be so good."

"I suppose it would be wise to go slowly. I had planned, as a matter of fact, on looking up a Thessian ship, taking a chance on a fight, and proving our friendship," replied Arcot.

Morey saw Arcot's logic—then suddenly burst into laughter. "Absolutely—attack a Thessian. But since we don't see any around now, we'll have to make one!"

Wade was completely mystified, and gave Morey a doubtful, sarcastic look. "Sounds like a good idea, only I wonder if this constant terrific mental strain—"

"Come along and find out!" Arcot threw the ship into artificial space for safety, holding it motionless. The planet, invisible to them, retreated from their motionless ship.

In the artificial matter control room, Arcot set to work, and developed a very considerable string of forms on his board, the equations of their formations requiring all the available formation controls.

"Now," said Arcot at last, "you stay here, Morey, and when I give the signal, create the thing back of the nearest range of hills, raise it, and send it toward us."

At once they returned to normal space, and darted down toward the now distant planet. They landed again near another city, one which was situated close to a range of mountains ideally suited to their purposes. They settled, while Zezdon Afthen sent out the message of friendship. He finally succeeded in getting some reaction, a sensation of skepticism, of distrust— but of interest. They needed friends, and only hoped that these were friends. Arcot pushed a little signal button, and Morey began his share of the play. From behind a low hill a slim, pointed form emerged, a beautifully streamlined ship, the lines obviously those of a Thessian, the windows streaming light, while the visible ionization about the hull proclaimed its molecular ray-screen. Instantly Zezdon Afthen, who had carefully refrained from learning the full nature of their plans, felt the intense emotion of the discovery, called out to the others, while his thoughts were flashed to the Sirians below.

From the attacking ship, a body shot with tremendous speed, it flashed by, barely missing the *Ancient Mariner,* and buried itself in the hillside beyond. With a terrific explosion it burst, throwing the soil about in a tremendous crater. The *Ancient Mariner* spun about, turned toward the other ship, and let loose a tremendous bombardment of molecular and cosmic rays. A great flame of ionized air was the only result. A new ray reached out from the other ship, a fan-like spreading ray. It struck the *Ancient Mariner,* and did not harm it, though the hillside behind was suddenly withered and blackened, then smoking as the temperature rose.

Another projectile was launched from the attacking ship, and exploded terrifically but a few hundred feet from the *Ancient Mariner.* The terrestrial ship rocked and swayed, and even the distant attacker rocked under the explosion.

A projectile, glowing white, leaped from the Earthship. It darted toward the enemy ship, seemed to barely touch it, then burst into terrific flames that spread, eating the whole ship, spreading glowing flame. In an instant the blazing ship slumped, started to fall, then seemingly evaporated, and before it touched the ground, was completely gone.

The relief in Zezdon Afthen's mind was genuine, and it was easily obvious to the Sirians that the winning ship was friendly, for, with all its frightful armament, it had downed a ship obviously of Thett. Though not exactly like the others, it had the all too familiar lines.

"They welcome us now," said Zezdon Afthen's mental message to his companions.

"Tell them we'll be there—with bells on or thoughts to that effect," grinned Arcot. Morey had appeared in the doorway, smiling broadly.

"How was the show?" he asked.

"Terrible—Why didn't you let it fall, and break open?"

"What would happen to the wreckage as we moved?" he asked sarcastically. "I thought it was a darned good demonstration."

"It was convincing," laughed Arcot. "They want us now!"

The great ship circled down, landing gently just outside of the city. Almost at once one of the slim, long Sirian ships shot up from a courtyard of the city, racing out and toward the *Ancient Mariner*. Scarcely a moment later half a hundred other ships from all over the city were on the way. Sirians seemed quite humanly curious.

"We'll have to be careful here. We have to use altitude suits, as the Negrians breathe an atmosphere of hydrogen instead of oxygen," explained Arcot rapidly to the Ortolian and the Talsonian who were to accompany him. "We will all want to go, and so, although this suit will be decidedly uncomfortable for you and Zezdon Afthen and Stel Felso Theu, I think it wise that you all wear it. It will be much more convincing to the Sirians if we show that people of no less than three worlds are already interested in this alliance."

A considerable number of Sirian ships had landed about them, and the tall, slim men of the 100,000,000-year-old race were watching them with their great brown eyes from a slight distance, for a cordon of men with evident authority were holding them back.

"Who are you, friends?" asked a single man who stood within the cordon. His strongly built frame, a great high brow and broad head designated him a leader at a glance.

Despite the vast change the light of Sirius had wrought, Arcot recognized in him the original photographs he had seen from the planet old Sol had captured as Negra had swept past. So it was he who answered the thought-question.

"I am of the third planet of the sun your people sought as a home a few years back in time, Taj Lamor. Because you did not understand us, and because we did not understand you, we fought. We found the records of your race on the planet our sun captured, and we know now what you most wanted. Had we been able to communicate with you then, as we can now, our people would never have fought.

"At last you have reached that sun you so needed, thanks, no doubt, to the genius that was with you.

"But now, in your new-found peace comes a new enemy, one who wants not only yours, but every sun in this galaxy.

"You have tried your ray of death, the anti-catalyst? And it but sputters harmlessly on their screens? You have been swept by their terrible rays that fuse mountains, then hurl them into space? Our world and the world of each of these men is similarly menaced.

"See, here is Zezdon Afthen, from Ortol, far on the other side of the galaxy, and here is Stel Felso Theu, of Talso. Their worlds, as well as yours and mine have been attacked by this menace from a distant galaxy, from Thett, of the sun Ansteck, of the galaxy Venone.

"Now we must form an alliance of far wider scope than ever has existed before.

"To you we have come, for your race is older by far than any race of our alliance. Your science has advanced far higher. What weapons have you discovered among those ancient documents, Taj Lamor? We have one weapon that you no doubt need; a screen, which will stop the rays of the molecule director apparatus. What have you to offer us?"

"We need your help badly," was the reply. "We have been able to keep them from landing on our planets, but it has cost us much. They have landed on a planet we brought with us when we left the black star, but it is not inhabited. From this as a base they have made attacks on us. We tried throwing the planet into Sirius. They merely left the planet hurriedly as it fell toward the star, and broke free from our attractive ray."

"The attractive ray! Then you have uncovered that secret?" asked Arcot eagerly.

Taj Lamor had some of his men bring an attractive ray projector to the ship. The apparatus turned out to be nearly a thousand tons in weight, and some twenty feet long, ten feet wide and approximately twelve feet high. It was impossible to load the huge machine into the *Ancient Mariner*, so an examination was conducted on the spot, with instruments whose reading was intelligible to the terrestrians operating it. Its principal fault lay in the fact that, despite the enormous energy of matter given out, the machine still gobbled up such titanic amounts of energy before the attraction could be established, that a very large machine was needed. The ray, so long as maintained, used no more power than was actually expended in moving the planet or other body. The power used while the ray was in action corresponded to the work done, but a tremendous power was needed to establish it, and this power could never be recovered.

Further, no reaction was produced in the machine, no matter what body it was turned upon. In swinging a planet then, a spaceship could be used as the base for the reaction was not exerted on the machine.

From such meager clues, and the instruments, Arcot got the hints that led him to the solution of the problem, for the documents, from which Taj Lamor had gotten his information, had been disastrously wiped out, when one of their cities fell, and Taj Lamor had but copied the machines of his ancestors.

The immense value of these machines was evident, for they would permit Arcot to do many things that would have been impossible without them. The explanation as he gave it to Stel Felso Theu, foretold the uses to which it might be put.

"As a weapon," he pointed out, "its most serious fault is that it takes a considerable time to pump in the power needed. It has here, practically the same fault which the artificial matter had on your world.

"As I see it, the ray is actually a directed gravitational field.

"Now here is one thing that makes it more interesting, and more useful. It seems to defy the laws of mechanics. It acts, but there is no apparent reaction! A small ship can swing a world! Remember, the field that generates the attraction is an integral, interwoven part of the mesh of Space. It is created by something outside of itself. Like the artificial matter, it exists there, and there alone. There is reaction on that attractive field, but it is created in Space at that given point, and the reaction is taken by all Space. No wonder it won't move.

"The work considerations are fairly obvious. The field is built up. That takes energy. The beam is focused on a body, the body falls nearer, and immediately absorbs the energy in acquiring a velocity. The machine replenishes the energy, because it is set to maintain a certain energy-level in the field. Therefore the machine must do the work of moving the ship, just as though it were a driving apparatus. After the beam has done what is wanted, it may be shut off, and the energy in the field is now available for any work needed. It may be drained back into power coils such as ours for instance, or one might just spend that last iota of power on the job.

"As a driving device it might be set to pull the entire ship along, and still not have any acceleration detectable to the occupants.

"I think we'll use that on our big ship," he finished, his eyes far away on some future idea.

"Natural gravity of natural matter is, luckily, not selective. It goes in all directions. But this artificial gravity is controlled so that it does not spread, and the result is that the mass-attraction of a mass of matter does not fall off as the inverse square of the distance, but like the ray from the parallel beam spotlight, continues undiminished.

"Actually, they create an exceedingly intense, exceedingly small gravitational field, and direct it in a straight line. The building up of this field is what takes time."

Zezdon Afthen, who had a question which was troubling him, looked anxiously at his friends. Finally he broke into their thoughts which had been too cryptically abbreviated for him to follow, like the work of a professor solving some problem, his steps taken so swiftly and so abbreviated that their following was impossible to his students.

"But how is it that the machine is not moved when exerting such force on some other body?" he asked at last.

"Oh, the ray concentrates the gravitational force, and projects it. The actual strain is in space. It is space that takes the strain, but in normal cases, unless the masses are very large, no considerable acceleration is produced over any great distance. That law operates in the case of the pulled body; it pulls the gravitational field as a normal field, the inverse-square law applying.

"But on the other hand, the gravity-beam pulls with a constant force.

"It might be likened to the light-pressure effects of a spotlight and a star. The spotlight would push the sun with a force that was constant, no matter what the distance, while the light pressure of the sun would vary as the inverse square of the distance.

"But remember, it is not a body that pulls another body, but a gravitational field that pulls another. The field is in space. A normal field is necessarily attached to the matter that it represents, or that represents it as you prefer, but this artificial field has no connection in the form of matter. It is a product of a machine, and exists only as a strain in space. To move it you must move all space, since it, like artificial matter, exists only where it is created in space.

"Do you see now why the law of action and reaction is apparently flouted? Actually the reaction is taken up by space."

Arcot rose, and stretched. Morey and Wade had been looking at him, and now they asked when he intended leaving for the intergalactic spaces.

"Now, I think. We have a lot of work to do. At present we have the mathematics of the artificial matter to carry on, and the math of the artificial gravity to develop. We gave the Sirians all we had on artificial matter and on moleculars.

"They gave us all they had—which wasn't much beyond the artificial gravity, and a lot of work. At any rate, let's go!"

CHAPTER XIII

ATTACKED

The *Ancient Mariner* stirred, and rose lightly from its place beside the city. Visible over the horizon now, and coming at terrific speed, was a fleet of seven Thessian ships.

They must do their best to protect that city. Arcot turned the ship and called his decision to Morey. As he did so, one of the Thessian ships suddenly swerved violently, and plunged downward. The attractive ray was in action. It struck the rocks of Neptune, and plunged in. Half buried, it stopped. Stopped—and backed out! The tremendously strong relux and lux had withstood the blow, and these strange, inhumanly powerful men had not been injured!

Two of the ships darted toward him simultaneously, flashing out molecular rays. The rays glanced off of Arcot's screen already in place, but the tubes were showing almost at once that this could not be sustained. It was evident that the swiftly approaching ships would soon break down the shields. Arcot turned the ship and drove to one side. His eyes went dead.

He cut into artificial space, waited ten seconds, then cut back.

The scene before him changed. It seemed a different world. The light was very dim, so dim he could scarcely see the images on the view-plate. They were so deep a red that they were very near to black. Even Sirius, the flaming blue-white star was red. The darting Thessian ships were moving quite slowly now, moving at a speed that was easy to follow. Their rays, before ionizing the air brilliantly red, were now dark. The instruments showed that the screen was no longer encountering serious loading, and, further, the load was coming in at a frequency harmlessly far down the radio spectrum!

Arcot stared in wide-eyed amazement. What could the Thessians have done that caused this change? He reached up and increased the amplification on the eyes to a point that made even the dim illumination sufficient. Wade was staring in amazement, too.

"Lord! What an idea!" suddenly exclaimed Arcot.

Wade was staring at Arcot in equally great amazement. "What's the secret?" he asked.

"Time, man, time! We are in an advanced time plane, living faster than they, our atoms of fuel are destroyed faster, our second is shorter. In one second of our earthly time our generators do the same amount of work as usual, but they do many, many times more work in one second, of the time we were in! We are under the advanced time-field."

Wade could see it all. The red light—normal light seen through eyes enormously speeded in all perceptions. The change, the dimness—dim because less energy reached them per second of their time. Then came this blue light, as they reached the X-ray spectrum of Sirius, and saw X-rays as normal light—shielded, tremendously shielded by the atmosphere, but the enormous amplification of the eyes made up for it.

The remaining Thessians seemed to get the idea simultaneously, and started for Arcot in his own time field. The Thessian ship appeared to be actually leaping at him. Suddenly, his speed increased inconceivably. Simultaneously, Arcot's hand, already started toward the space-control switch, reached it, and pushed it to the point that threw the ship into artificial space. The last glimmer of light died suddenly, as the Thessian ship's bow loomed huge beside the *Ancient Mariner*.

There was a terrific shock that hurled the ship violently to one side, threw the men about inside the ship. Simultaneously the lights blinked out.

Light returned as the automatic emergency incandescent lights in the room, fed from an energy store coil, flashed on abruptly. The men were white-faced, tense in their positions. Swiftly Morey was looking over the indicators on his remote-reading panel, while Arcot stared at the few dials before the actual control board.

"There's an air pressure outside the ship!" he cried out in surprise. "High oxygen, very little nitrogen, breathable apparently, provided there are no poisons. Temperature ten below zero C."

"Lights are off because relays opened when the crash short circuited them." Morey and the entire group were suddenly shaking.

"Nervous shock," commented Zezdon Afthen. "It will be an hour or more before we will be in condition to work."

"Can't wait," replied Arcot testily, his nerves on edge, too.

"Morey, make some good strong coffee if you can, and we'll waste a little air on some smokes."

Morey rose and went to the door that led through the main passage to the galley. "Heck of a job—no weight at all," he muttered. "There is air in the passage, anyway." He opened the door, and the air rushed from the control room to the passage till the pressure was equalized. The door to the power room was shut, but it was bulged, despite its two-inch lux metal, and through its clear material he could see the wreckage of the power room.

"Arcot," he called. "Come here and look at the power room. Quintillions of miles from home, we can't shut off this field now."

Arcot was with him in a moment. The tremendous mass of the nose of the Thessian ship had caught them full amidship, and the powerful ram had driven through the room. Their lux walls had not been touched; only a sledge-hammer blow would have bent them under any circumstances, let alone breaking them. But the tremendously powerful main generator was split wide open. And the mechanical damage was awful. The prow of the ship had been driven deep into the machine, and the power room was a wreck.

"And," pointed out Morey, "we can't handle a job like that. It will take a tremendous amount of machinery back on a planet to work that stuff, and we couldn't bend that bar, let alone fix it."

"Get the coffee, will you please, Morey? I have an idea that's bound to work," said Arcot looking fixedly at the machinery.

Morey turned and went to the galley.

Five minutes later they returned to the corridor, where Arcot stood still, looking fixedly at the engine room. They were carrying small plastic balloons with coffee in them.

They drank the coffee and returned to the control room, and sat about, the terrestrians smoking peacefully, the Ortolian and the Talsonian satisfying themselves with some form of mild narcotic from Ortol, which Zezdon Afthen introduced.

"Well, we have a lot more to do," Arcot said. "The air-apparatus stopped working a while back, and I don't want to sit around doing nothing while the air in the storage tanks is used up. Did you notice our friends, the enemy?" Through the great pilot's window the bulk of the Thessian ship's bow could be seen. It was cut across with an exactitude of mathematical certainty.

"Easy to guess what happened," Morey grinned. "They may have wrecked us, but we sure wrecked them. They got half in and half out of our space field. Result—the half that was in, stayed in. The half that was out stayed out. The two halves were instantaneously a billion miles apart, and that beautifully exact surface represents the point our space cut across.

"That being decided, the next question is how to fix this poor old wreck." Morey grinned a bit. "Better, how to get out of here, and down to old Neptune."

"Fix it!" replied Arcot. "Come on; you get in your space suit, take the portable telectroscope and set it up in space, motionless, in such a position that it views both our ship and the nose of the Thessian machine, will you, Wade? Tune it to—seven-seven-three." Morey rose with Arcot, and followed him, somewhat mystified, down the passage. At the airlock Wade put on his space suit, and the Ortolian helped him with it. In a moment the other three men appeared bearing the machine. It was practically weightless, though it would fall slowly if left to itself, for the mass of the *Ancient Mariner* and the front end of the Thessian ship made a considerable attractive field. But it was clumsy, and needed guiding here in the ship.

Wade took it into the airlock, and a moment later into space with him. His hand molecular-driving unit pulling him, he towed the machine into place, and with some difficulty got it practically motionless with respect of the two bodies, which were now lying against each other.

"Turn it a bit, Wade, so that the *Ancient Mariner* is just in its range," came Arcot's thoughts. Wade did so. "Come on back and watch the fun."

Wade returned. Arcot and the others were busy placing a heavy emergency lead from the storeroom in the place of one of the broken leads. In five minutes they had it fixed where they wanted it.

Into the control room went Arcot, and started the power-room teleview plate. Connected into the system of view-plates, the scene was visible now on all the plates in the ship. Well off to one side of the room, prepared for such emergencies, and equipped with individual power storage coils that would run it for several days, the view-plate functioned smoothly.

"Now, we are ready," said Arcot. The Talsonian proved he understood Arcot's intentions by preceding him to the laboratory.

Arcot had two view-plates operating here. One was covering the scene as shown by the machine outside, and the other showed the power room.

Arcot stepped over to the artificial-matter machine, and worked swiftly on it. In a moment the power from the storage coils of the ship was flowing through the new cable, and into the machine. A huge ring appeared about the nose of the Thessian ship, fitting snugly over it. A terrific wrench—and it was free of the *Ancient Mariner*. The ring contracted and formed a chunk of the stuff free of the broken nose of the ship.

It was carried over to the wall of the *Ancient Mariner*, a smaller piece snipped off as before, and carried inside. A piece of perhaps half a ton mass. "I hope they use good stuff," grinned Arcot. The piece was deposited on the floor of the ship, and a disc formed of artificial matter plugged the hole in its side. Another took a piece of the relux from the broken Thessian ship, pushed it into the hole on the ship. The space about the scene of operation was a crackling inferno of energy breaking down into heat and light. Arcot dematerialized his tremendous tools, and the wall of the *Ancient Mariner* was neatly patched with relux smoothed over as perfectly as before. A second time, using some of the relux he had brought within the ship, and the inner wall was rebuilt. The job was absolutely perfect, save that now, where there had been lux, there was an outer wall of relux.

The main generator was crumpled up, and torn out. The auxiliary generators would have to carry the load. The great cables were swiftly repaired in the same manner, a perfect cylinder forming about them, and a piece of relux from the store Arcot had sliced from the enemy ship, welding them perfectly under enormous pressure, pressure that made them flow perfectly into one another as heat alone could not.

In less than half an hour the ship was patched up, the power room generally repaired, save for a few minor things that had to be replaced from the stores. The main generator was gone, but that was not an essential. The door was straightened and the job done.

In an hour they were ready to proceed.

CHAPTER XIV

INTERGALACTIC SPACE

"Well, Sirius has retreated a bit," observed Arcot. The star was indeed several trillions of miles away. Evidently they had not been motionless as they had thought, but the interference of the Thessian ship had thrown their machine off.

"Shall we go back, or go on?" asked Morey.

"The ship works. Why return?" asked Wade. "I vote we go on."

"Seconded," added Arcot.

"If they who know most of the ship vote for a continuance of the journey, then assuredly we who know so little can only abide by their judgment. Let us continue," said Zezdon Afthen gravely.

Space was suddenly black about them. Sirius was gone, all the jewels of the heavens were gone in the black of swift flight. Ten seconds later Arcot lowered the space-control. Black behind them the night of space was pricked by points of light, the infinite multitude of the stars. Before them lay—nothing. The utter emptiness of space between the galaxies.

"Thlek Styrs! What happened?" asked Morey in amazement, his pet Venerian phrase rolling out in his astonishment.

"Tried an experiment, and it was overly successful," replied Arcot, a worried look on his face. "I tried combining the Thessian high speed *time* distortion with our high *speed* space distortion—both on low power. 'There ain't no such animals,' as the old agriculturist remarked of the giraffe. God knows what speed we hit, but it was plenty. We must be ten thousand light years beyond the galaxy."

"That's a fine way to start the trip. You have the old star maps to get back however, have you not?" asked Wade.

"Yes, the maps we made on our first trip out this way are in the cabinet. Look 'em up, will you, and see how far we have to go before we reach the cosmic fields?"

Arcot was busy with his instruments, making a more accurate determination of their distance from the "edge" of the galaxy. He adopted the figure of twelve thousand five hundred light years as the probable best result. Wade was back in a moment with the information that the fields lay about sixteen thousand light years out. Arcot went on, at a rate that would reach the fields in two hours.

Several hours more were spent in measurements, till at last Arcot announced himself satisfied.

"Good enough—back we go." Again in the control room, he threw on the drive, and shot through the twenty-seven thousand light years of cosmic ray fields, and then more leisurely returned to the galaxy. The star maps were strangely off. They could follow them, but only with difficulty as the general configuration of the constellations that were their guides were visibly altered to the naked eye.

"Morey," said Arcot softly, looking at the constellation at which they were then aiming, and at the map before him, "there is something very, very rotten. The Universe either 'ain't what it used to be' or we have traveled in more than space."

"I know it, and I agree with you. Obviously, from the degree of alteration off the constellations, we are off by about 100,000 years. Question: how come? Question: what are we going to do about it?"

"Answer one: remembering what we observed *in re* Sirius, I suspect that the interference of that Thessian ship, with its time-field opposing our space-field did things to our time-frame. We were probably thrown off then.

"As to the second question, we have to determine number one first. Then we can plan our actions."

With Wade's help, and by coming to rest near several of the stars, then observing their actual motions, they were able to determine their time-status. The estimate they made finally was of the order of eighty thousand years in the past! The Thessian ship had thrown them that much out of their time.

"This isn't all to the bad," said Morey with a sigh. "We at least have all the time we could possibly use to determine the things we want for this fight. We might even do a lot of exploring for the archeologists of Earth and Venus and Ortol and Talso. As to getting back—that's a question."

"Which is," added Arcot, "easy to answer now, thank the good Lord. All we have to do is wait for our time to catch up with us. If we just wait eighty thousand years, eight hundred centuries, we will be in our own time.

"Oh, I think waiting so long would be boring," said Wade sarcastically. "What do you suggest we do in the intervening eighty millenniums? Play cards?"

"Oh, cards or chess. Something like that," grinned Arcot. "Play cards, calculate our fields—and turn on the time rate control."

"Oh—I take it back. You win! Take all! I forgot all about that," Wade smiled at his friend. "That will save a little waiting, won't it."

"The exploring of our worlds would without doubt be of infinite benefit to science, but I wonder if it would not be of more direct benefit if we were to get back to our own time, alive and well. Accidents always happen, and for all our weapons, we might easily meet some animal which would put an abrupt and tragic finish to our explorations. Is it not so?" asked Stel Felso Theu.

"Your point is good, Stel Felso Theu. I agree with you. We will do no more exploring than is necessary, or safe."

"We might just as well travel slowly on the time retarder, and work on the way. I think the thing to do is to go back to Earth, or better, the solar system, and follow the sun in its path."

They returned, and the desolation that the sun in its journey passes through is nothing to the utter, oppressive desolation of empty space between the stars, for it has its family of planets —and it has no conscious thought.

The Sun was far from the point that it had occupied when the travelers had left it, billions on billions of miles further on its journey around the gravitational center of our galactic universe, and in the eighty millenniums that they must wait, it would go far.

They did not go to the planets now, for, as Arcot said in reply to Stel Felso Theu's suggestion that they determine more accurately their position in time, life had not developed to an extent that would enable them to determine the year according to our calendar.

So for thirty thousand years they hung motionless as the sun moved on, and the little spots of light, that were worlds, hurled about it in a mad race. Even Pluto, in its three-hundred-year-long track seemed madly gyrating beneath them; Mercury was a line of light, as it swirled about the swiftly moving sun.

But that thirty thousand years was thirty days to the men of the ship. Their time rate immensely retarded, they worked on their calculations. At the end of that month Arcot had, with the help of Morey and Wade, worked out the last of the formulas of artificial matter, and the machines had turned out the last graphical function of the last branch of research that they could discover. It was a time of labor for them, and they worked almost constantly, stopping occasionally for a game of some sort to relax the nervous tension.

At the end of that month they decided that they would go to Earth.

They speeded their time rate now, and flashed toward Earth at enormous speed that brought them within the atmosphere in minutes. They had landed in the valley of the Nile. Arcot had suggested this as a means of determining the advancement of life of man. Man had evidently established some of his earliest civilizations in this valley where water and sun for his food plants were assured.

"Look—there *are* men here!" exclaimed Wade. Indeed, below them were villages, of crude huts made of timber and stone and mud. Rubble work walls, for they needed little shelter here, and the people were but savages.

"Shall we land?" asked Arcot, his voice a bit unsteady with suppressed excitement.

"Of course!" replied Morey without turning from his station at the window. Below them now, less than half a mile down on the patchwork of the Nile valley, men were standing, staring up, collecting in little groups, gesticulating toward the strange thing that had materialized in the air above them.

"Does everyone agree that we land?" asked Arcot.

There were no dissenting voices, and the ship sank gently toward a road below and to the left. A little knot of watchers broke, and they fled in terror as the great machine approached, crying out to their friends, casting affrighted glances at the huge, shining monster behind them.

Without a jar the mighty weight of the ship touched the soil of its native planet, touched it fifty millenniums before it was made, five hundred centuries before it left!

Arcot's brow furrowed. "There is one thing puzzles me— I can't see how we can come back. Don't you see, Morey, we have disturbed the lives of those people. We have affected history. This must be written into the history that exists.

"This seems to banish the idea of free thought. We have changed history, yet history is that which is already done!

"Had I never been born, had—but I *was* already—I existed fifty-eighty thousand years before I was born!"

"Let's go out and think about that later. We'll go to a psych hospital, if we don't stop thinking about problems of space and time for a little while. We need some kind of relaxation."

"I suggest that we take our weapons with us. These men may have weapons of chemical nature, such as poisons injected into the flesh on small sticks hurled either by a spring device or by pneumatic pressure of the lungs," said Stel Felso Theu as he rose from his seat unstrapping himself.

"Arrows and blow-guns we call 'em. But it's a good idea, Stel Felso, and I think we will," replied Arcot. "Let's not all go out at once, and the first group to go out goes out on foot, so they won't be scared off by our flying around."

Arcot, Wade, Zezdon Afthen, and Stel Felso Theu went out. The natives had retreated to a respectful distance, and were now standing about, looking on, chattering to themselves. They were edging nearer.

"Growing bold," grinned Wade.

"It is the characteristic of intelligent races manifesting itself —curiosity," pointed out Stel Felso Theu.

"Are these the type of men still living in this valley, or who will be living there in fifty thousand years?" asked Zezdon Afthen.

"I'd say they weren't Egyptians as we know them, but typical Neolithic men. It seems they have brains fully as large as some of the men I see on the streets of New York. I wonder if they have the ability to learn as much as the average man of—say about 1950?"

The Neolithic men were warming up. There was an orator among them, and his grunts, growls, snorts and gestures were evidently affecting them. They had sent the women back (by the simple and direct process of sweeping them up in one arm and heaving them in the general direction of home). The men were brandishing polished stone knives and axes, various instruments of war and peace. One favorite seemed to be a large club.

"Let's forestall trouble," suggested Arcot. He drew his ray pistol, and turned it on the ground directly in front of them, and about halfway between them and the Neoliths. A streak of the soil about two feet wide flashed into intense radiation under the impact of millions on millions of horsepower of radiant energy. Further, it was fused to a depth of twenty feet or more, and intensely hot still deeper. The Neoliths took a single look at it, then turned, and raced for home.

"Didn't like our looks. Let's go back."

They wandered about the world, investigating various peoples, and proved to their own satisfaction that there was no Atlantis, not at this time at any rate. But they were interested in seeing that the polar caps extended much farther toward the equator; they had not retreated at that time to the extent that they had by the opening of history.

They secured some fresh game, an innovation in their larder, and a welcome one. Then the entire ship was swept out with fresh, clean air, their water tanks filled with water from the cold streams of the melting glaciers. The air apparatus was given a new stock to work over.

Their supplies in a large measure restored, thousands of aerial photographic maps made, they returned once more to space to wait.

Their time was taken up for the most part by actual work on the enormous mass of calculation necessary. It is inconceivable to the layman what tremendous labor is involved in the development of a single mathematical hypothesis, and a concrete illustration of it was the long time, with tremendously advanced calculating machines, that was required in their present work.

They had worked out the problem of the time-field, but there they had been aided by the actual apparatus, and the possibilities of making direct tests on machines already set up. The problem of artificial matter, at length fully solved, was a different matter. This had required within a few days of a month (by their clocks; close to thirty thousand years of Earth's time), for they had really been forced to develop it all from the beginning. In the small improvements Arcot had instituted in Stel Felso Theu's device, he had really merely followed the particular branch that Stel Felso Theu had stumbled upon. Hence it was impossible to determine with any great variety, the type of matter created. Now, however, Arcot could make any known kind of matter, and many unknown kinds.

But now came the greatest problem of all. They were ready to start work on the data they had collected in space.

"What," asked Zezdon Afthen, as he watched the three terrestrians begin their work, "is the nature of the thing you are attempting to harness?"

"In a word, energy," replied Arcot, pausing.

"We are attempting to harness energy in its primeval form, in the form of a space-field. Remember, mass is a measure of energy. Two centuries ago a scientist of our world proposed the idea that energy could be measured by mass, and proceeded to prove that the relationship was the now firmly intrenched formula $E=Mc^2$.

"The sun is giving off energy. It is giving off mass, then, in the form of light photons. The field of the sun's gravity must be constantly decreasing as its mass decreases. It is a collapsing field. It is true, the sun's gravitational field does decrease, by a minute amount, despite the fact that our sun loses a thousand million tons of matter every four minutes. The percentage change is minute, but the energy released is—immeasurable.

"But, I am going to invent a new power unit, Afthen. I will call it the 'sol,' the power of a sun. One sol is the rating of our sun. And I will measure the energy I use in terms of sunpowers, not horsepower. That may tell you of its magnitude!"

"But," Zezdon Afthen asked, "while you men of Earth work on this problem, what is there for us? We have no problems, save the problem of the fate of our world, still fifty thousand years of your time in the future. It is terrible to wait, wait, wait and think of what may be happening in that other time. Is there nothing we can do to help? I know our hopeless ignorance of your science. Stel Felso Theu can scarcely understand the thoughts you use, and I can scarcely understand his explanations! I cannot help you there, with your calculations, but is there nothing I can do?"

"There is, Ortolian, decidedly. We badly need your help, and as Stel Felso Theu cannot aid us here as much as he can by working with you, I will ask him to do so. I want your knowledge of psycho-mechanical devices to help us. Will you make a machine controlled by mental impulses? I want to see such a system and know how it is done that I may control machines by such a system."

"Gladly. It will take time, for I am not the expert worker that you are, and I must make many pieces of apparatus, but I will do what I can," exclaimed Zezdon Afthen eagerly.

So, while Arcot and his group continued their work of determining the constants of the space-energy field, the others were working on the mental control apparatus.

CHAPTER XV

ALL-POWERFUL GODS

Again there was a period of intense labor, while the ship drifted through time, following Earth in its mad careening about the sun, and the sun as it rushed headlong through space. At the end of a thirty-day period, they had reached no definite position in their calculations, and the Talsonian reported, as a medium between the two parties of scientists, that the work of the Ortolian had not reached a level that would make a scientific understanding possible.

As the ship needed no replenishing, they determined to finish their present work before landing, and it was nearly forty thousand years after their first arrival that they again landed on Earth.

It was changed now; the ice caps had retreated visibly, the Nile delta was far longer, far more prominent, and cities showed on the Earth here and there.

Greece, they decided would be the next stop, and to Greece they went, landing on a mountainside. Below was a village, a small village, a small thing of huts and hovels. But the villagers attacked, swarming up the hillside furiously, shouting and shrieking warnings of their terrible prowess to these men who came from the "shining house," ordering them to flee from them and turn over their possession to them.

"What'll we do?" asked Morey. He and Arcot had come out alone this time.

"Take one of these fellows back with us, and question him. We had best get a more or less definite idea of what time-age we are in, hadn't we? We don't want to overshoot by a few centuries, you know!"

The villagers were swarming up the side of the hill, armed with weapons of bronze and wood. The bronze implements of murder were rare, and evidently costly, for those that had them were obviously leaders, and better dressed than the others.

"Hang it all, I have only a molecular pistol. Can't use that, it would be a plain massacre!" exclaimed Arcot.

But suddenly several others, who had come up from one side, appeared from behind a rock. The scientists were wearing their power suits, and had them on at low power, leaving a weight of about fifty pounds. Morey, with his normal weight well over two hundred, jumped far to one side of a clumsy rush of a peasant, leaped back, and caught him from behind. Lifting the smaller man above his head, he hurled him at two others following. The three went down in a heap.

Most of the men were about five feet tall, and rather lightly built. The "Greek God" had not yet materialized among them. They were probably poorly fed, and heavily worked. Only the leaders appeared to be in good physical condition, and the men could not develop to large stature. Arcot and Morey were giants among them, and with their greater skill, tremendous jumping ability, and far greater strength, easily overcame the few who had come by the side. One of the leaders was picked up, and trussed quickly in a rope a fellow had carried.

"Look out," called Wade from above. Suddenly he was standing beside them, having flown down on the power suit. "Caught your thoughts—rather Zezdon Afthen did." He handed Arcot a ray pistol. The rest of the Greeks were near now, crying in amazement, and running more slowly. They didn't seem so anxious to attack. Arcot turned the ray pistol to one side.

"Wait!" called Morey. A face peered from around the rock toward which Arcot had aimed his pistol. It was that of a girl, about fifteen years old in appearance, but hard work had probably aged her face. Morey bent over, heaved on a small boulder, about two hundred pounds of rock, and rolled it free of the depression it rested in, then caught it on a molecular ray, hurled it up. Arcot turned his heat ray on it for an instant, and it was white hot. Then the molecular ray threw it over toward the great rock, and crushed it against it. Three children shrieked and ran out from the rock, scurrying down the hillside.

The soldiers had stopped. They looked at Morey. Then they looked at the great rock, three hundred yards from him. They looked at the rock fragments.

"They think you threw it," grinned Arcot.

"What else—they saw me pick it up, saw me roll it, and it flew. What else could they think?"

Arcot's heat ray hissed out, and the rocks sputtered and cracked, then glowed white. There was a dull explosion, and chips of rock flew up. Water, imprisoned, had been turned into steam. In a moment the whistle and crackle of combined heat and molecular rays stabbing out from Arcot's hands had built a barrier of fused rocks.

Leisurely Arcot and Morey carried their now revived prisoner back to the ship, while Wade flew ahead to open the locks.

Half an hour later the prisoner was discharged, much to his surprise, and the ship rose. They had been able to learn nothing from him. Even the Greek Gods, Zeus, Hermes, Apollo, all the later Greek Gods, were unknown, or so greatly changed that Arcot could not recognize them.

"Well," he said at length, "it seems all we know is that they came before any historical Greeks we know of. That puts them back quite a bit, but I don't know how far. Shall we go see the Egyptians?"

They tried Egypt, a few moments across the Mediterranean, landing close to the mouth of the Nile. The people of a village nearby immediately set out after them. Better prepared this time, Arcot flew out to meet them with Zezdon Afthen and Stel Felso Theu. Surely, he felt, the sight of the strange men would be no more terrifying than the ship or the men flying. And that did not seem to deter their attack. Apparently the proverb that "Discretion is the better part of valor," had not been invented.

Arcot landed near the head of the column, and cut off two or three men from the rest with the aid of his ray pistol. Zezdon Afthen quickly searched his mind, and with Arcot's aid they determined he did not know any of the Gods that Arcot suggested.

Finally they had to return to the ship, disappointed. They had had the slight satisfaction of finding that the Sun God was Ralz, the later Egyptian Ra might well have been an evolved form of that name.

They restocked the ship, fresh game and fruits again appearing on the menu, then once again they launched forth into space to wait for their own time.

"It seems to me that we must have produced some effect by our visit," said Arcot, shaking his head solemnly.

"We did, Arcot," replied Morey softly. "We left an impress in history, an impress that still is, and an impress that affected countless thousands.

"Meet the Egyptian Gods with their heads strange to terrestrians, the Gods who fly through the air without wings, come from a shining house that flies, whose look, whose pointed finger melts the desert sands, and the moist soil!" he continued softly, nodding toward the Ortolian and the Talsonian.

"Their 'impossible' Gods existed, and visited them. Indubitably some genius saw that here was a chance for fame and fortune and sold 'charms' against the 'Gods.' Result: we are carrying with us some of the oldest deities. Again, we did leave our imprint in history."

"And," cried Wade excitedly, "meet the great Hercules, who threw men about. I always knew that Morey was a brainless brute, but I never realized the marvelous divining powers of those Greeks so perfectly—now, the Incarnation of Dumb Power!" Dramatically Wade pointed to Morey, unable even now to refrain from some unnecessary comments.

"All right, Mercury, the messenger of the Gods speaks. The little flaps on Wade's flying shoes must indeed have looked like the winged shoes of legend. Wade was Mercury, too brainless for anything but carrying the words of wisdom uttered by others.

"And Arcot," continued Morey, releasing Wade from his condescending stare, "is Jove, hurling the rockfusing, destroying thunderbolts!"

"The Gods that my friends have been talking of," explained Arcot to the curious Ortolians, "are legendary deities of Earth. I can see now that we did leave an imprint on history in the only way we could—as Gods, for surely no other explanation could have occurred to those men."

The days passed swiftly in the ship, as their work approached completion. Finally, when the last of the equation of Time, artificial matter, and the most awful of their weapons, the unlimited Cosmic Power, had been calculated, they fell to the last stage of the work. The actual appliances were designed. Then the completed apparatus that the Ortolian and the Talsonian had been working on, was carefully investigated by the terrestrial physicists, and its mechanism studied. Arcot had great plans for this, and now it was incorporated in their control apparatus.

The one remaining problem was their exact location in time. Already their progress had brought them well up to the nineteenth century, but, as Morey sadly remarked, they couldn't tell what date, for they were sadly lacking in history. Had they known the real date, for instance, of the famous battle of Bull Run, they could have watched it in the telectroscope, and so determined their time. As it was, they knew only that it was one of the periods of the first half of the decade of 1860.

"As historians, we're a bunch of first-class kitchen mechanics. Looks like we're due for another landing to locate the exact date," agreed Arcot.

"Why land now? Let's wait until we are nearer the time to which we belong, so we won't have to watch so carefully and so long," suggested Wade.

They argued this question for about two hundred years as a matter of fact. After that, it was academic anyway.

CHAPTER XVI

HOME AGAIN

They were getting very near their own time, Arcot felt. Indeed, they must already exist on Earth. "One thing that puzzles me," he commented, "is what would happen if we were to go down now, and see ourselves."

"Either we can't or we don't want to do it," pointed out Morey, "because we didn't."

"I think the answer is that nothing can exist two times at the same time-rate," said Arcot. "As long as we were in a different time-rate we could exist at two times. When we tried to exist simultaneously, we could not, and we were forced to slip through time to a time wherein we either did not exist or wherein we had not yet been. Since we were nearer the time when we last existed in normal time, than we were to the time of our birth, we went to the time we left. I suspect that we will find we have just left Earth. Shall we investigate?"

"Absolutely, Arcot, and here's hoping we didn't overshoot the mark by much." As Morey intimated, had they gone much beyond the time they left Earth, they might find conditions very serious, indeed. But now they went at once toward Earth on the time control. As they neared, they looked anxiously for signs of the invasion. Arcot spotted the only evident signs, however; two large spheres, tiny points in appearance on the telectroscope screen, were circling Earth, one at about 1000 miles, moving from east to west, the other about 1200 miles moving from north to south.

"It seems the enemy have retreated to space to do their fighting. I wonder how long we were away."

As they swept down at a speed greater than light, they were invisible till Arcot slowed down near the atmosphere. Instantly half a dozen fast ships darted toward them, but the ship was very evidently unlike the Thessian ships, and no attack was made. First the occupants would have an opportunity to prove their friendliness.

"Terrestrians Arcot, Morey, and Wade reporting back from exploration in space, with two friends. All have been on Earth with us previously," said Arcot into the radio vision apparatus.

"Very well, Dr. Arcot. You are going to New York or Vermont?" asked the Patrol commander.

"Vermont."

"Yes, Sir. I'll see that you aren't stopped again."

And, thanks to the message thus sent ahead, they were not, and in less than half an hour they landed once more in Vermont, on the field from which they had started.

The group of scientists who had been here on their last call had gone, which seemed natural enough to them, who had been working for three months in the interval of their trip, but to Dr. Arcot senior, as he saw them, it was a misfortune.

"Now I never will get straight all you'll have ready, and I didn't expect you back till next week. The men have all gone back to their laboratories, since that permits of better work on the part of each, but we can call them here in half an hour. I'm sure they'll want to come. What did you learn, Son, or haven't you done any calculating on your data as yet?"

"We learned plenty, and I feel quite sure that a hint of what we have would bring all those learning-hounds around us pretty quickly, Dad," laughed Arcot junior, "and believe it or not, we've been calculating on this stuff for three months since we left yesterday!"

"What!"

"Yes, it's true! We were on our time-field, and turn on the space-control—and a Thessian ship picked that moment to run into us. We cut the ship in half as neatly as you please, but it threw us eighty thousand years into the past. We have been coasting through time on retarded rate while Earth caught up with itself, so to speak. In the meantime—three months in a day!

"But don't call those men. Let them come to the appointment, while we do some work, and we have plenty of work to do, I assure you. We have a list of things to order from the standard supply houses, and I think you better get them for us, Dad." Arcot's manner became serious now. "We haven't gotten our Government Expense Research Cards yet, and you have. Order the stuff, and get it out here, while we get ready for it. Honestly, I believe that a few ships such as this apparatus will permit, will be enough in themselves to do the job. It really is a pity that the other men didn't have the opportunity we had for crowding much work into little time!

"But then, I wouldn't want to take that road to concentration again myself!

"Have the enemy amused you in my absence? Come on, let's sit down in the house instead of standing here in the sun."

They started toward the house, as Arcot senior explained what had happened in the short time they had been away.

"There is a friend of yours here, whom you haven't seen in some time, Son. He came with some allies."

As they entered the house, they could hear the boards creak under some heavy weight that moved across the floor, soundlessly and light of motion in itself. A shadow fell across the hall floor, and in the doorway a tremendously powerfully-built figure stood.

He seemed to overflow the doorway, nearly six and a half feet tall, and fully as wide as the door. His rugged, bronzed face was smiling pleasantly, and his deep-set eyes seemed to flash; a living force flowed from them.

"Torlos! By the Nine Planets! Torlos of Nansal! Say, I didn't expect you here, and I will not put my hand in that meatgrinder of yours," grinned Arcot happily, as Torlos stretched forth a friendly, but quite too powerful hand.

Torlos of Nansal, that planet Arcot had discovered on his first voyage across space, far in another Island of Space, another Island Universe, was not constructed as are human beings of Earth, nor of Venus, Talso, or Ortol, but most nearly resembled, save in size, the Thessians. Their framework, instead of being stone, as is ours, was iron, their bones were pure metallic iron, far stronger than bone. On these far stronger bones were great muscles of an entirely different sort, a muscle that used heat of the body as its fuel, a muscle that was utterly tireless, and unbelievably powerful. Not a chemical engine, but a molecular motion engine, it had no chemical fatigue-products that would tire it, and needed only the constant heat supply the body sucked from the air to work indefinitely. Unlimited by waste-carrying considerations, the strength was enormous.

It was one of the commercial space freighters plying between Nansal, Sator, Earth and Venus that had brought the news of this war to him, Torlos explained, and he, as the Trade Coordinator and Fourth of the Four who now ruled Nansal, had suggested that they go to the aid of the man who had so aided them in their great war with Sator. It was Arcot's gift of the secret of the molecular ray and the molecular ship that had enabled them to overcome their enemy of centuries, and force upon them an unwelcome peace.

Now, with a fleet of fifty interstellar, or better, intergalactic battleships, Nansal was coming to Earth's aid.

The battleships were now on patrol with all of Earth's and Venus' fleet. But the Nansalian ships were all equipped with the enormously rapid space-distortion system of travel, of course, and were a shock troop in the patrol. The terrestrial and Venerian patrols were not so equipped in full.

"And Arcot, from what I have learned from your father, it seems that I can be of real assistance," finished Torlos.

"But now, I think, I should know what the enemy has done. I see they built some forts."

"Yes," replied Arcot senior, "they did. They decided that the system used on the forts of North and South poles was too effective. They moved to space, and cut off slices of Luna, pulled it over on their molecular rays, and used some of the most magnificent apparatus you ever dreamed of. I have just started working on the mathematics of it.

"We sent out a fleet to do some investigating, but they attacked, and stopped work in the meantime. Whatever the ray is that can destroy matter at a distance, they are afraid that we could find its secret too easily, and block it, for they don't think it is a weapon, and it is evidently slow in action."

"Then it isn't what I thought it was," muttered Arcot.

"What did you think it was?" asked his father.

"Er—tell you later. Go on with the account."

"Well, to continue. We have not been idle. Following your suggestion, we built up a large ray screen apparatus, in fact, several of them, and carried them in ships to different parts of the world. Also some of the planets, lest they start dropping worlds on us. They are already in operation, sending their defensive waves against the Heaviside layer. Radio is poor, over any distance, and we can't call Venus from inside the layer now. However, we tested the protection, and it works—far more efficiently than we calculated, due to the amazing conductivity of the layer.

"If they intend to attack in that way, I suspect that it will be soon, for they are ready now, as we discovered. An attack on their fort was met with a ray-screen from the fort.

"They fight with a wild viciousness now. They won't let a ship get near them. They destroy everything on sight. They seem tremendously afraid of that apparatus of yours. Too bad we had no more."

"We will have—if you will let me get to work."

They went to the ship, and entered it. Arcot senior did not follow, but the others waited, while the ship left Earth once more, and floated in space. Immediately they went into the time-field.

They worked steadily, sleeping when necessary, and the giant strength of Torlos was frequently as great an asset as his indefatigable work. He was learning rapidly, and was able to do a great deal of the work without direction. He was not a scientist, and the thing was new to him, but his position as one of the best of the secret intelligence force of Nansal had proven his brains, and he did his share.

The others, scientists all, found the operations difficult, for work had been allotted to each according to his utmost capabilities.

It was still nearly a week of their time before the apparatus was completed to the extent possible, less than a minute of normal time passing.

Finally the unassembled, but completed apparatus, was carried to the laboratory of the cottage, and word was sent to all the men of Earth that Arcot was going to give a demonstration of the apparatus he hoped would save them. The scientists from all over Earth and Venus were interested, and those of Earth came, for there was no time for the men of Venus to arrive to inspect the results.

CHAPTER XVII

POWER OF MIND

It was night. The stars visible through the laboratory windows winked violently in the disturbed air of the Heaviside layer, for the molecular ray-screen was still up.

The laboratory was dimly lighted now, all save the front of the room. There, a mass of compact boxes were piled one on another, and interconnected in various and indeterminate ways. And one table lay in a brilliant path of illumination. Behind it stood Arcot. He was talking to the dim white group of faces beyond the table, the scientists of Earth assembled.

"I have explained our power. It is the power of all the universe —Cosmic Power—which is necessarily vaster than all others combined.

"I cannot explain the control in the time I have at my disposal but the mathematics of it, worked out in two months of constant effort, you can follow from the printed work which will appear soon.

"The second thing, which some of you have seen before, has already been partly explained. It is, in brief, artificially created matter. The two important things to remember about it are that it *is*, that it *does exist*, and that it exists *only where it is determined to exist by the control there, and nowhere else.*

"These are all coordinated under the new mental relay control. Some of you will doubt this last, but think of it under this light. Will, thought, concentration—they are efforts, they require energy. Then they can exert energy! That is the key to the whole thing.

"But now for the demonstration."

Arcot looked toward Morey, who stood off to one side. There was a heavy thud as Morey pushed a small button. The relay had closed. Arcot's mind was now connected with the controls.

A globe of cloudiness appeared. It increased in density, and was a solid, opalescent sphere.

"There is a sphere, a foot in diameter, ten feet from me," droned Arcot. The sphere was there. "It is moving to the left." The sphere moved to the left at Arcot's thought. "It is rising." The sphere rose. "It is changing to a disc two feet across." The sphere seemed to flow, and was a disc two feet across as Arcot's toneless voice of concentration continued.

"It is changing into a hand, like a human hand." The disc changed into a human hand, the fingers slightly bent, the soft, white fingers of a woman with the pink of the flesh and the wrinkles at the knuckles visible. The wrist seemed to fade gradually into nothingness, the end of the hand was as indeterminate as are things in a dream, but the hand was definite.

"The hand is reaching for the bar of lux metal on the floor." The soft, little hand moved, and reached down and grasped the half-ton bar of lux metal, wrapped dainty fingers about it and lifted it smoothly and effortlessly to the table, and laid it there.

A mistiness suddenly solidified to another hand. The second hand joined the first, and fell to work on the bar, and pulled. The bar stretched finally under an enormous load. One hand let go, and the thud of the highly elastic lux metal bar's return to its original shape echoed through the soundless room. These men of the twenty-second century knew what relux and lux metals were, and knew their enormous strength. Yet it was putty under these hands. The hands that looked like a woman's!

The bar was again placed on the table, and the hands disappeared. There was a thud, and the relay had opened.

"I can't demonstrate the power I have. It is impossible. The power is so enormous that nothing short of a sun could serve as a demonstration-hall. It is utterly beyond comprehension under any conditions. I have demonstrated artificial matter, and control by mental action.

"I'm now going to show you some other things we have learned. Remember, I can control perfectly the properties of artificial matter, by determining the structure it shall have.

"Watch."

Morey closed the relay. Arcot again set to work. A heavy ingot of iron was raised by a clamp that fastened itself upon it, coming from nowhere. The iron moved, and settled over the table. As it approached, a mistiness that formed became a crucible. The crucible showed the gray of pure iron, but it was artificial matter. The iron settled in the crucible, and a strange process of flowing began. The crucible became a ball, and colors flowed across its surface, till finally it was glowing richly silvery. The ball opened, and a great lump of silvery stuff was within it. It settled to the floor, and the ball disappeared, but the silvery metal did not.

"Platinum," said Morey softly. A gasp came from the audience. "Only platinum could exist there, and the matter had to rearrange itself as platinum." He could rearrange it in any form he chose, either absorbing or supplying energy of existence and energy of formation.

The mistiness again appeared in the air, and became a globe, a globe of brown. But it changed, and disappeared. Morey recognized the signal. "He will now make the artificial matter into all the elements, and many nonexistent elements, unstable, atomic figures." There followed a long series of changes.

The material shifted again, and again. Finally the last of the natural elements was left behind, all 104 elements known to man were shown, and many others.

"We will skip now. This is element of atomic weight 7000."

It was a lump of soft, oozy blackness. One could tell from the way that Arcot's mind handled it that it was soft. It seemed cold, terribly cold. Morey explained:

"It is very soft, for its atom is so large that it is soft in the molecular state. It is tremendously photoelectric, losing electrons very readily, and since its atom has so enormous a volume, its electrons are very far from the nucleus in the outer rings, and they absorb rays of very great length; even radio and some shorter audio waves seem to affect it. That accounts for its blackness, and the softness as Arcot has truly depicted it. Also, since it absorbs heat waves and changes them to electrical charges, it tends to become cold, as the frost Arcot has shown indicates. Remember, that that is infinitely hard as you see it, for it is artificial matter, but Arcot has seen natural matter forced into this exceedingly explosive atomic figuration.

"It is so heavily charged in the nucleus that its X-ray spectrum is well toward the gamma! The inner electrons can scarcely vibrate."

Again the substance changed—and was gone.

"Too far—atom of weight 20,000 becomes invisible and nonexistent as space closes in about it—perhaps the origin of our space. Atoms of this weight, if breaking up, would form two or more atoms that would exist in our space, then these would be unstable, and break down further into normal atoms. We don't know."

"And once more substance," continued Morey as he opened the relay once more. Arcot sat down and rested his head in his hands. He was not accustomed to this strain, and though his mind was one of the most powerful on Earth, it was very hard for him.

"We have a substance of commercial and practical use now. Cosmium. Arcot will show one method of making it."

Arcot resumed his work, seated now. A formation reached out, and grasped the lump of platinum still on the floor. Other bars of iron were brought over from the stack of material laid ready, and piled on a broad sheet that had formed in the air, tons of it, tens of tons. Finally he stopped. There was enough. The sheet wrapped itself into a sphere, and contracted, slowly, steadily. It was rampant with energy, energy flowed from it, and the air about was glowing with ionization. There was a feeling of awful power that seeped into the minds of the watchers, and held them spellbound before the glowing, opalescent sphere. The tons of matter were compressed now to a tiny ball! Suddenly the energy flared out violently, a terrific burst of energy, ionizing the air in the entire room, and shooting it with tiny, burning sparks. Then it was over. The ball split, and became two planes. Between them was a small ball of a glistening solid. The planes moved slowly together, and the ball flattened, and flowed. It was a sheet.

A clamp of artificial matter took it, and held the paper-thin sheet, many feet square, in the air. It seemed it must bend under its own enormous weight of tons, but thin as it was it did not.

"Cosmium," said Morey softly.

Arcot crumpled it, and pressed it once more between artificial matter tools. It was a plate, thick as heavy cardboard, and two feet on a side. He set it in a holder of artificial matter, a sort of frame, and caused the controls to lock.

Taking off the headpiece he had worn, he explained, "As Morey said, Cosmium. Briefly, density, 5007.89. Tensile strength, about two hundred thousand times that of good steel!" The audience gasped. That seems little to men who do not realize what it meant. An inch of this stuff would be harder to penetrate than three miles of steel!

"Our new ship," continued Arcot, "will carry six-inch armor." Six inches would be the equivalent of eighteen miles of solid steel, with the enormous improvement that it will be concentrated, and so will have far greater resistance than any amount of steel. Its tensile strength would be the equivalent of an eighteen-mile wall of steel.

"But its most important properties are that it reflects everything we know of. Cosmics, light, and even moleculars! It is made of cosmic ray photons, as lux is made of light photons, but the inexpressibly tighter bond makes the strength enormous. It cannot be handled by any means save by artificial matter tools.

"And now I am going to give a demonstration of the theatrical possibilities of this new agent. Hardly scientific—but amusing."

But it wasn't exactly amusing.

Arcot again donned the headpiece. "I think," he continued, "that a manifestation of the supernatural will be more interesting. Remember that all you see is real, and all effects are produced by artificial matter generated by the cosmic energy, as I have explained, and are controlled by my mind."

Arcot had chosen to give this demonstration with definite reason. Apparently a bit of scientific playfulness, yet he knew that nothing is so impressive, nor so lastingly remembered as a theatrical demonstration of science. The greatest scientist likes to play with his science.

But Arcot's experiment now—it was on a level of its own!

From behind the table, apparently crawling up the leg came a thing! It was a hand. A horrible, disjointed hand. It was withered and incarmined with blood, for it was severed from its wrist, and as it hunched itself along, moving by a ghastly twitching of fingers and thumb, it left a trail of red behind it. The papers to be distributed rustled as it passed, scurrying suddenly across the table, down the leg, and racing toward the light switch! By some process of writhing jerks it reached it, and suddenly the room was plunged into half-light as the lights winked out. Light filtering over the transom of the door from the hall alone illuminated the hall, but the hand glowed! It glowed, and scurried away with an awful rustling, scuttling into some unseen hole in the wall. The quiet of the hall was the quiet of tenseness.

From the wall, coming through it, came a mistiness that solidified as it flowed across. It was far to the right, a bent stooped figure, a figure half glimpsed, but fully known, for it carried in its bony, glowing hand a great, nicked scythe. Its rattling tread echoed hollowly on the floor. Stooping walk, shuffling gait, the great metal scythe scraping on the floor, half seen as the gray, luminous cloak blew open in some unfelt breeze of its ephemeral world, revealing bone; dry, gray bone. Only the scythe seemed to know Life, and it was red with that Life. Slow running, sticky lifestuff.

Death paused, and raised his awful head. The hood fell back from the cavernous eyesockets, and they flamed with a greenish radiance that made every strained face in the room assume the same deathly pallor.

"The Scythe, the Scythe of Death," grated the rusty Voice. "The Scythe is slow, too slow. I bring new things," it cackled in its cracked voice, "new things of my tools. See!" The clutching bones dropped the rattling Scythe, and the handle broke as it fell, and rotted before their eyes. "Heh, heh," the Thing cackled as it watched. "Heh—what Death touches, rots as he leaves it." The grinning, blackened skull grinned wider, in an awful, leering cavity, rotting, twisted teeth showed. But from under his flapping robe, the skeletal hands drew something—ray pistols!

"These—these are swifter!" The Thing turned, and with a single leering glance behind, flowed once more through the wall.

A gasp, a stifled, groaning gasp ran through the hall, a half sob.

But far, far away they could hear something clanking, dragging its slow way along. Spellbound they turned to the farthest corner

—and looked down the long, long road that twined off in distance. A lone, luminous figure plodded slowly along it, his half human shamble bringing him rapidly nearer.

Larger and larger he loomed, clearer and clearer became the figure, and his burden. Broken, twisted steel, or metal of some sort, twisted and blackened.

"It's over—it's over—and my toys are here. I win, I always win. For I am the spawn of Mars, of War, and of Hate, the sister of War, and my toys are the things they leave behind." It gesticulated, waving the twisted stuff and now through the haze, they could see them—buildings. The framework of buildings and twisted liners, broken weapons.

It loomed nearer, the cavernous, glowing eyes under low, shaggy brows, became clear, the awful brutal hate, the lust of Death, the rotting flesh of Disease—all seemed stamped on the Horror that approached.

"Ah!" It had seen them! "Ahh!" It dropped the buildings, the broken things, and shuffled into a run, toward them! Its face changed, the lips drew back from broken, stained teeth, the curling, cruel lips, and the rotting flesh of the face wrinkled into a grin of lust and hatred. The shaggy mop of its hair seemed to writhe and twist, the long, thin fingers grasped spasmodically as it neared. The torn, broken fingernails were visible—nearer—nearer—nearer—

"Oh, God—stop it!" A voice shrieked out of the dark as someone leaped suddenly to his feet.

Simultaneously with the cry the Thing puffed into nothingness of energy from which it had sprung, and a great ball of clear, white glowing light came into being in the center of the room, flooding it with a light that dazzled the eyes, but calmed broken nerves.

CHAPTER XVIII

EARTH'S DEFENSES

"I am sorry, Arcot. I did not know, for I see I might have helped, but to me, with my ideas of horror, it was as you said, amusement," said Torlos. They were sitting now in Arcot's study at the cottage; Arcot, his father, Morey, Wade, Torlos, the three Ortolians and the Talsonian.

"I know, Torlos. You see, where I made my mistake, as I have said, was in forgetting that in doing as I did, picturing horror, like a snowball rolling, it would grow greater. The idea of horror, started, my mind pictured one, and it inspired greater horror, which in turn reacted on my all too reactive apparatus. As you said, the things changed as you watched, molding themselves constantly as my mind changed them, under its own initiative and the concentrated thoughts of all those others. It was a very foolish thing to do, for that last Thing—well, remember it *was*, it existed, and the idea of hate and lust it portrayed was caused by my mind, but my mind could picture what it would do, if such were its emotions, and it would do them because my mind pictured them! And *nothing* could resist it!" Arcot's face was white once more as he thought of the danger he had run, of the terrible consequences possible of that 'amusement.'

"I think we had best start on the ship. I'll go get some sleep now, and then we can go."

Arcot led the way to the ship, while Torlos, Morey and Wade and Stel Felso Theu accompanied him. The Ortolians were to work on Earth, aiding in the detection of attacks by means of their mental investigation of the enemy.

"Well—good-bye, Dad. Don't know when I'll be back. Maybe twenty-five thousand years from now, or twenty-five thousand years ago. But we'll get back somehow. And we'll clean out the Thessians!"

He entered the ship, and rose into space.

"Where are you going, Arcot?" asked Morey.

"Eros," replied Arcot laconically.

"Not if my mind is working right," cried Wade suddenly. All the others were tense, listening for inaudible sounds.

"I quite agree," replied Arcot. The ship turned about, and dived toward New York, a hundred thousand miles behind now, at a speed many times that of light as Arcot snapped into time. Across the void, Zezdon Fentes' call had come—New York was to be attacked by the Thessians, New York and Chicago next. New York because the orbits of their two forts were converging over that city in a few minutes!

They were in the atmosphere, screaming through it as their relux glowed instantaneously in the Heaviside layer, then was through before damage could be done. The screen was up.

Scarcely a minute after they passed, the entire heavens blazed into light, the roar of tremendous thunders crashing above them, great lightning bolts rent the upper air for miles as enormous energies clashed.

"Ah—they are sending everything they have against that screen, and it's hot. We have ten of our biggest tube stations working on it, and more coming in, to our total of thirty, but they have two forts, and Lord knows how many ships.

"I think me I'm going to cause them some worrying."

Arcot turned the ship, and drove up again, now at a speed very low to them but as they had the time-field up, very great. They passed the screen, and a tremendous bolt struck the ship. Everything in it was shielded, but the static was still great enough to cause them some trouble as the time-field and electric field fought. But the time-field, because of its very nature, could work faster, and they won through undamaged, though the enormous current seemed flowing for many minutes as they drifted slowly past it. Slowly—at fifty miles a second.

Out in space, free of the atmosphere, Arcot shot out to the point where the Thessians were congregating. The shining dots of their ships and the discs of the forts were visible from Earth save for the air's distortion.

They seemed a miniature Milky Way, their deadly beams concentrated on Earth.

Then the Thessians discovered that the terrestrial fleet was in action. A ship glowed with the ray, the opalescence of relux un-

der moleculars visible on its walls. It simply searched for its opponent while its relux slowly yielded. It found it in time, and the
terrestrial ship put up its screen.

The terrestrial fleet set to work, everything they had flying at
the Thessian giants, but the Thessians had heavier ships, and
heavier tubes. More power was winning for them. Inevitably, when the Sun's interference somewhat weakened the ray-
shield—

About that time Arcot arrived. The nearest fort dived toward
the further with an acceleration that smashed it against no less
than ten of its own ships before they could so much as move.

When the way was clear to the other fort—and that fort had
moved, the berserk fort started off a new tack—and garnered six
more wrecks on its side.

Then Thett's emissaries located Arcot. The screen was up, and
the Negrian attractive ray apparatus which Arcot had used was
working through it. The screen flashed here and there and collapsed under the full barrage of half the Thessian fleet, as Arcot
had suspected it would. But the same force that made it collapse
operated a relay that turned on the space-control, and Thett's
molecular ray energy steamed off to outer space.

"We worried them, then dug our hole and dragged it in after
us, as usual, but damn it, we can't hurt them!" said Arcot disgustedly. "All we can do is tease them, then go hide where it's
perfectly safe, in artificial—" Arcot stopped in amazement. The
ship had been held under such space-control that space was
shut in about them, and they were motionless. The dials had
reached a steady point, the current flow had become zero, and
they hung there with only the very slow drain of the Sun's gravitational field and that of the planet's field pulling on the ship.
Suddenly the current had leaped, and the dials giving the charge
in the various coil banks had moved them down toward zero.

"Hey—they've got a wedge in here and are breaking out our
hole. Turn on all the generators, Morey." Arcot was all action
now. Somehow, inconceivable though it was, the Thessians had
spotted them, and got some means of attacking them, despite
their invulnerable position in another space!

The generators were on, pouring enormous power into the
coils, and the dials surged, stopped, and climbed ever so slowly.
They should have jumped back under that charge, ordinarily

dangerously heavy. For perhaps thirty seconds they climbed, then they started down at full speed!

Arcot's hand darted to the timefield, and switched it on full. The dial jerked, swung, then swung back, and started falling in unison with the dials, stopped, and climbed. All climbed swiftly, gaining ever more rapidly. With what seemed a jerk, the time dial flew over, and back, as Arcot opened the switch. They were free, and the dial on the space-control coils was climbing normally now.

"By the Nine Planets, did they drink out our energy! The energy of six tons of lead just like that!"

"How'd they do it?" asked Wade.

Torlos kept silent, and helped Morey replace the coils of lead wire with others from stock.

"Same way we tickled them," replied Arcot, carefully studying the control instruments, "with the gravity ray! We knew all along that gravitational fields drank out the energy—they simply pulled it out faster than we could pump it in, and used four different rays on us doing it. Which speaks well for a little ship! But they burned off the relux on one room here, and it's a wreck. The molecs hit everything in it. Looks like something bad," called Arcot. The room was Morey's, but he'd find that out himself. "In the meantime, see if you can tell where we are. I got loose from their rays by going on both the high speed time-field and the space-control at full, with all generators going full blast. Man, they had a stranglehold on us that time! But wait till we get that new ship turned out!"

With the telectroscope they could see what was happening. The terrific bombardment of rays was continuing, and the fleets were locked now in a struggle, the combined fleets of Earth and Venus and of Nansal, far across the void. Many of the terrestrian, or better, Solarian ships, were equipped with space-distortion apparatus, now, and had some measure of safety in that the attractive rays of the Thessians could not be so concentrated on them. In numbers was safety; Arcot had been endangered because he was practically alone at the time they attacked.

But it was obvious that the Solarian fleet was losing. They could not compete with the heavier ships, and now the frequent flaming bursts of light that told of a ship caught in the new deadly ray showed another danger.

"I think Earth is lost if you cannot aid it soon, Arcot, for other Thessian ships are coming," said Stel Felso Theu softly.

From out of the plane of the planetary orbits they were coming, across space from some other world, a fleet of dozens of them. They were visible as one after another leapt into normal time-rates.

"Why don't they fight in advanced time?" asked Morey, half aloud.

"Because the genius that designed that apparatus didn't think of it. Remember, Morey, those ships have their time apparatus connected with their power apparatus so that the power has to feed the time continuously. They have no coils like ours. When they advance their time, they're weakened every other way.

"We need that new ship. Are we going to make it?" demanded Arcot.

"Take weeks at best. What chance?" asked Morey.

"Plenty; watch." As he spoke, Arcot pulled open the time controls, and spun the ship about. They headed off toward a tiny point of light far beyond. It rushed toward them, grew with the swiftness of an exploding bomb, and was suddenly a great, rough fragment of a planet hanging before them, miles in extent.

"Eros," explained Wade laconically to Torlos. "Part of an ancient planet that was destroyed before the time of man, or life on Earth. The planet got too near the sun when its orbit was irregular, and old Sol pulled it to pieces. This is one of the pieces. The other asteroids are the rest. All planetary surfaces are made up of great blocks; they aren't continuous, you know. Like blocks of concrete in a building, they can slide a bit on each other, but friction holds them till they slip with a jar and we have earthquakes. This is one of the planetary blocks. We see Eros from Earth intermittently, for when this thing turns broadside it reflects a lot of light; edge on it does not reflect so much."

It was a desolate bit of rock. Bare, airless, waterless rock, of enormous extent. It was contorted and twisted, but there were no great cracks in it for it was a single planetary block.

Arcot dropped the ship to the barren surface, and anchored it with an attractive ray at low concentration. There was no gravity of consequence on this bit of rock.

"Come on, get to work. Space suits, and rush all the apparatus out," snapped Arcot. He was on his feet, the power of the ship in neutral now. Only the attractor was on. In the shortest possible time they got into their suits, and under Arcot's direction set up the apparatus on the rocky soil as fast as it was brought out. In all, less than fifteen minutes were needed, yet Arcot was hurrying them more and more. Torlos' tremendous strength helped, even on this gravitationless world, for he could accelerate more quickly with his burdens.

At last it was up for operation. The artificial matter apparatus was operated by cosmic power, and controlled by mental operation, or by mathematical formula as they pleased.

Immediately Arcot set to work. A giant hollow cylinder drilled a great hole completely through the thin, curved surface of the ancient planetary block, through twelve miles of solid rock—a cylinder of artificial matter created on a scale possible only to cosmic power. The cylinder, half a mile across, contained a huge plug of matter. Then the artificial matter contracted swiftly, compressing the matter, and simultaneously treating it with the tremendous fields that changed its energy form. In seconds it was a tremendous mass of cosmium.

A second smaller cylinder bored a plug from the rock, and worked on it. A huge mass of relux resulted. Now other artificial matter tools set to work at Arcot's bidding, and cut pieces from his huge masses of raw materials, and literally, quick as thought, built a great framework of them, anchored in the solid rock of the planetoid.

Then a tremendous plane of matter formed, and neatly bisected the planetoid, two great flat pieces of rock were left where one had been—miles across, miles thick—planetary chips.

On the great framework that had been constructed, four tall shafts of cosmium appeared, and each was a hollow tube, up the center of which ran a huge cable of relux. At the peak of each mile-high shaft was a great globe. Now in the framework below things were materializing as Arcot's flying thoughts arranged them—great tubes of cosmium with relux element—huge coils of relux conductors, insulated with microscopic but impenetrable layers of cosmium.

Still, for all his swiftness of mind and accuracy of thought, he had to correct two mistakes in all his work. It was nearly an hour before the thing was finished. Then, two hundred feet long, a hundred wide, and fifty in height, the great mechanism was completed, the tall columns rising from four corners of the greater framework that supported it.

Then, into it, Arcot turned the powers of the cosmos. The stars in the airless space wavered and danced as though seen through a thick atmosphere. Tingling power ran through them as it flowed into the tremendous coils. For thirty seconds—then the heavens were as before.

At last Arcot spoke. Through the radio communicators, and through the thought-channels, his ideas came as he took off the headpiece. "It's done now, and we can rest." There was a tremendous crash from within the apparatus. The heavens reeled before them, and shifted, then were still, but the stars were changed. The sun shone weirdly, and the stars were altered.

"That is a time shifting apparatus on a slightly larger scale," replied Arcot to Torlos' question, "and is designed to give us a chance to work. Come on, let's sleep. A week here should be a few minutes of Earthtime."

"You sleep, Arcot. I'll prepare the materials for you," suggested Morey. So Arcot and Wade went to sleep, while Morey and the Talsonian and Torlos worked. First Morey bound the *Ancient Mariner* to the frame of the time apparatus, safely away from the four luminous balls, broadcasters of the time-field. Then he shut off the attractive ray, and bound himself in the operator's seat of the apparatus of the artificial matter machine.

A plane of artificial matter formed, and a stretch of rock rose under its lift as it cleft the rock apart. A great cleared, level space resulted. Other artificial matter enclosed the rock, and the fragments cut free were treated under tremendous pressure. In a few moments a second enormous mass of cosmium was formed.

For three hours Morey worked steadily, building a tremendous reserve of materials. Lux metal he did not make, but relux, the infusible, perfect conductor, and cosmium in tremendous masses, he did make. And he made some great blocks of oxygen from the rock, transmuting the atoms, and stored it frozen on the plane, with liquid hydrogen in huge tanks, and some metals that would be needed. Then he slept while they waited for Arcot.

Eight hours after he had lain down, Arcot was up, and ate his breakfast. He set to work at once with the machine. It didn't suit him, it seemed, and first he made a new tool, a small ship that could move about, propelled by a piece of artificial matter, and the entire ship was a tremendously greater artificial-matter machine, with a greater power than before!

His thoughts, far faster than hands could move, built up the gigantic hull of the new ship, and put in the rooms, and the brace members in less than twelve hours. A titanic shell of eight-inch cosmium, a space, with braces of the same non-conductor of heat, cosmium, and a two-inch inner hull. A tiny space in the gigantic hull, a space less than one thousand cubic feet in dimension was the control and living quarters.

It was held now on great cosmium springs, but Arcot was not by any means through. One man must do all the work, for one brain must design it, and though he received the constant advice and help of Morey and the others, it was his brain that pictured the thing that was built.

At last the hull was completed. A single, glistening tube, of enormous bulk, a mile in length, a thousand feet in diameter. Yet nearly all of that great bulk would be used immediately. Some room would be left for additional apparatus they might care to install. Spare parts they did not have to carry—they could make their own from the energy abounding in space.

The enormous, shining hull was a thing of beauty through stark grandeur now, but obviously incomplete. The ray projectors were not mounted, but they were to be ray projectors of a type never before possible. Space is the transmitter of all rays, and it is in space that those energy forms exist. Arcot had merely to transfer the enormously high energy level of the space-curvature to any form of energy he wanted, and now, with the complete statistics on it, he was able to do that directly. No tubes, no generators, only fields that changed the energy already there—the immeasurable energy available!

The next period of work he started the space-distortion apparatus. That must go at the exact center of the ship. One tremendous coil, big enough for the *Ancient Mariner* to lie in easily! Minutes, and flying thoughts had made it—then came thousands of the individual coils, by thinking of one, and picturing it many times! In ranks, rows, and columns they were piled into a great block, for power must be stored for use of this tremendous machine, while in the artificial space when its normal power was not available, and that power source must be tremendous.

Then the time apparatus, and after that the driving apparatus.

Not the molecular drive now, but an attraction ray focused on their own ship, with projectors scattered about the ship that it might move effortlessly in every direction. And provision was made for a force-drive by means of artificial matter, planes of it pushing the ship where it was wanted. But with the attraction-drive they would be able to land safely, without fear of being crushed by their own weight on Thett, for all its enormous gravity.

The control was now suspended finally, with a series of attraction-drives about it, locking it immovably in place, while smaller attraction devices stimulated gravity for the occupants.

Then finally the main apparatus—the power plant—was installed. The enormous coils which handled, or better, caused space to handle as they directed, powers so great that whole suns could be blasted instantaneously, were put in place, and the field generators that would make and direct their rays, their ray-screen if need be, and handle their artificial matter. Everything was installed, and all but a rather small space was occupied.

It had been six weeks of continuous work for them, for the mind of each was aiding in this work, indirectly or directly, and it neared completion now.

"But, we need one more thing, Arcot. That could never land on any planet smaller than Jupiter. What is its mass?" suggested Morey.

"Don't know, I'm sure, but it is of the order of a billion tons. I know you are right. What are we going to do?"

"Put on a tender."

"Why not the *Ancient Mariner?*" asked Wade.

"It isn't fitting. It was designed for individual use anyway," replied Morey. "I suggest something more like this on a small scale. We won't have much work on that, merely think of every detail of the big ship on a small scale, with the exception of the control cube furnishings. Instead of the numerous decks, swimming pool and so forth, have a large, single room."

"Good enough," replied Arcot.

As if by magic, a machine appeared, a "small" machine of two-hundred-foot length, modified slightly in some parts, its bottom flattened, and equipped with an attractor anchor. Then they were ready.

"We will leave the *Mariner* here, and get it later. This apparatus won't be needed any longer, and we don't want the enemy to get it. Our trial trip will be a fight!" called Arcot as he leaped from his seat. The mass of the giant ship pulled him, and he fell slowly toward it.

Into its open port he flew, the others behind him, their suits still on. The door shut behind them as Arcot, at the controls, closed it. As yet they had not released the air supplies. It was airless.

Now the hiss of air, and the quickening of heat crept through it. The water in the tanks thawed as the heat came, soaking through from the great heaters. In minutes the air and heat were normal throughout the great bulk. There was air in power compartments, though no one was expected to go there, for the control room alone need be occupied; vision-screens here viewed every part of the ship, and all about it.

The eyes of the new ship were set in recesses of the tremendously strong cosmium wall, and over them, protecting them, was an infinitely thin, but infinitely strong wall of artificial matter, permanently maintained. It was opaque to all forms of radiation known from the longest Hertzian to the shortest cosmics, save for the very narrow band of visible light. Whether this protection would stop the Thessian beam that was so deadly to lux and re-lux was not, of course, known. But Arcot hoped it would, and, if that beam was radiant energy, or material particles, it would.

"We'll destroy our station here now, and leave the *Ancient Mariner* where it is. Of course we are a long way out of the orbit this planetoid followed, due to the effect of the time apparatus, but we can note where it is, and we'll be able to find it when we want it," said Arcot, seated at the great control board now. There were no buttons now, or visible controls; all was mental.

A tiny sphere of artificial matter formed, and shot toward the control board of the time machine outside. It depressed the main switch, and space about them shifted, twisted, and returned to normal. The time apparatus was off for the first time in six weeks.

"Can't fuse that, and we can't crush it. It's made of cosmium, and trying to crush it against the rock would just drive it into it. We'll see what we can do though," muttered Arcot. A plane of artificial matter formed just beneath it, and sheared it from its bed on the planetoid, cutting through the heavy cosmium anchors. The framework lifted, and the apparatus with it. A series of planes, a gigantic honeycomb formed, and the apparatus was cut across again and again, till only small fragments were left of it. Then these were rolled into a ball, and crushed by a sphere of artificial matter beyond all repair. The enemy would never learn their secret.

A huge cylinder of artificial matter cut a great gouge from the plane that was left where the apparatus had been, and a clamp of the same material picked up the *Ancient Mariner*, deposited it there, then covered it with rubble and broken rock. A cosmic flashed on the rock for an instant, and it was glowing, incandescent lava. The *Ancient Mariner* was buried under a hundred feet of rapidly solidifying rock, but rock which could be fused away from its infusible walls when the time came.

"We're ready to go now—get to work with the radio, Morey, when we get to Earth."

The gravity seemed normal here as they walked about, no accelerations affected them as the ship darted forward, for all its inconceivably great mass, like an arrow, then flashed forward under time control. The sun was far distant now, for six weeks they had been traveling with the section of Eros under time control. But with their tremendous time control plant, and the space control, they reached the solar system in very little time.

It seemed impossible to them that that battle could still be waging, but it was. The ships of Earth and Venus, battling now as a last, hopeless stand, over Chicago, were attempting to stop the press of a great Thessian fleet. Thin, long Negrian, or Sirian ships had joined them in the hour of Earth time that the men had been working. Still, despite the reinforcements, they were falling back.

CHAPTER XIX

THE BATTLE OF EARTH

It had been an anxious hour for the forces of the Solar System.

They were in the last fine stages of Earth's defense when the general staff received notice that a radio message of tremendous power had penetrated the ray screen, with advice for them. It was signed "Arcot."

"Bringing new weapon. Draw all ships within the atmosphere when I start action, and drive Thessians back into space. Retire as soon as a distance of ten thousand miles is reached. I will then handle the fleet," was the message.

"Gentlemen: We are losing. The move suggested would be eminently poor tactics unless we are sure of being able to drive them. If we don't, we are lost in any event. I trust Arcot. How vote you?" asked General Hetsar Sthel.

The message was relayed to the ships. Scarcely a moment after the message had been relayed, a tremendous battleship appeared in space, just beyond the battle. It shot forward, and planted itself directly in the midst of the battle, brushing aside two huge Thessians in its progress. The Thessian ships bounced off its sides, and reeled away. It lay waiting, making no move. All the Thessian ships above poured the full concentration of their moleculars into its tremendous bulk. A diffused glow of opalescence ran over every ship—save the giant. The moleculars were being reflected from its sides, and their diffused energy attacked the very ships that were sending them!

A fort moved up, and the deadly beam of destruction reached out, luminous even in space.

"Now," muttered Morey, "we shall see what cosmium will stand."

A huge spot on the side of the ship had become incandescent. A vapor, a strange puff of smokiness exploded from it, and disappeared instantly. Another came and faster and faster they followed each other. The cosmium was disintegrating under the ray, but very slowly, breaking first into gaseous cosmic rays, then free, and spreading.

"We will not fight," muttered Morey happily as he saw Arcot shift in his seat.

Arcot picked the moleculars. They reached out, touched the heavy relux of the fort, and it exploded into opalescence that was hazily white, the colors shifted so quickly. A screen sprang into being, and the ray was chopped off. The screen was a mass of darting flames as energies of stupendous magnitude clashed.

Arcot used a bit more of his inconceivable power. The ray struck the screen, and it flashed once—then died into blackness. The fort suddenly crumpled in like a dented can, and rolled clumsily away. The other fort was near now, and started an attack of its own. Arcot chose the artificial matter this time. He was not watching the many attacking ships.

The great ship careened suddenly, fell over heavily to one side. "Foolish of me," said Arcot. "They tried crashing us."

A mass of crumpled, broken relux and lux surrounded by a haze of gas lying against a slight scratch on the great sides, told the story. Eight inches of cosmium does not give way.

Yet another ship tried it. But it stopped several feet away from the real wall of the ship. It struck a wall even more unyielding—artificial matter.

But now Arcot was using this major weapon—artificial matter. Ship after ship, whether fleeing or attacking, was surrounded suddenly by a great sphere of it, a sudden terrific blaze of energy as the sphere struck the ray shield, the control forces now backed by the energy of all the millions of stars of space shattered it in an instant. Then came the inexorable crush of the artificial matter, and a ball of matter alone remained.

But the pressing disc of the battle-front which had been lowering on Chicago, greatest of Earth's metropolises, was lifted. This disc-front was staggering back now as Arcot's mighty ship weakened its strength, and destroyed its morale, under the steady drive of the now hopeful Solarians.

The other gigantic fort moved up now, with twenty of the largest battleships. The fort turned loose its destructive ray—and Arcot tried his new "magnet." It was not a true magnet, but a transformed space field, a field created by the energy of all the universe.

The fort was gigantic. Even Arcot's mighty ship was a small thing beside it, but suddenly it seemed warped and twisted as space curved visibly in a magnetic field of such terrific intensity as to be immeasurable.

Arcot's armory was tested and found not wanting.

Suddenly every Thessian ship in sight ceased to exist. They disappeared. Instantly Arcot threw on all time power, and darted toward Venus. The Thessians were already nearing the planet, and no possible rays could overtake them. An instantaneous touch of the space control, and the mighty ship was within hundreds of miles of the atmosphere.

Space twisted about them, reeled, and was firm. The Thessian fleet was before them in a moment, visible now as they slowed to normal speed. Startled, no doubt, to find before them the ship they had fled, they charged on for a space. Then, as though by some magic, they stopped and exploded in gouts of light.

When space had twisted, seconds before, it was because Arcot had drawn on the enormous power of space to an extent that had been appreciable even to it—ten sols. That was forty million tons of matter a second, and for a hundredth part of a second it had flowed. Before them, in a vast plane, had been created an infinitesimally thin film of artificial matter, four hundred thousand tons of it, and into this invisible, infinitely hard barrier, the Thessian fleet had rammed. And it was gone.

"I think," said Arcot softly, as he took off his headpiece, "that the beginning of the end is in sight."

"And I," said Morey, "think it is now out of sight. Half a dozen ships stopped. And they are gone now, to warn the others."

"What warning? What can they tell? Only that their ships were destroyed by something they couldn't see." Arcot smiled. "I'm going home."

CHAPTER XX

DESTRUCTION

Some time later, Arcot spoke. "I have just received a message from Zezdon Fentes that he has an important communication to make, so I will go down to New York instead of to Chicago, if you gentlemen do not mind. Morey will take you to Chicago in the tender, and I can find Zezdon Fentes."

Zezdon Fentes' message was brief. He had discovered from the minds of several who had been killed by the magnetic field Arcot had used, and not destroyed, that they had a base in this universe. Thett's base was somewhere near the center of the galaxy, on a system of unusually large planets, circling a rather small star. But what star their minds had not revealed.

"It's up to us then to locate said star," said Arcot, after listening to Zezdon Fentes' account: "I think the easiest way will be to follow them home. We can go to your world, Zezdon Fentes, and see what they are doing there, and drive them off. Then to yours, Stel Felso. I place your world second as it is far better able to defend itself than is Ortol. It is agreeable?"

It was, and the ship which had been hanging in the atmosphere over New York, where Zezdon Afthen, Fentes and Inthel had come to it in a taxi-ship, signaled for the crowd to clear away above. The enormous bulk of the shining machine, the savior of Earth, had attracted a very great amount of attention, naturally, and thousands on thousands of hardy souls had braved the cold of the fifteen mile height with altitude suits or in small ships. Now they cleared away, and as the ship slowly rose, the tremendous concentrated mental well-wishing of the thousands reached the men within the ship. "That," observed Morley, "is one thing cosmium won't stop. In some ways I wish it would—because the mental power that could be wielded by any great number of those highly advanced Thessians, if they know its possibilities, is not a thing to neglect."

"I can answer that, terrestrian," thought Zezdon Afthen. "Our instruments show great mental powers, and great ability to concentrate the will in mental processes, but they indicate a very slight development of these abilities. Our race, despite the fact that our mental powers are much less than those of such men as Arcot and yourself, have done, and can do many things your greater minds cannot, for we have learned the direction of the will. We need not fear the will of the Thessians. I feel confident of that!"

The ship was in space now, and as Arcot directed it toward Ortol, far far across the Island, he threw on, for the moment, the combined power of space distortion and time fields. Instantly the sun vanished, and when, less than a second later, he cut off the space field, and left only the time, the constellations were instantly recognizable. They were within a dozen light years of Ortol.

"Morey, may I ask what you call this machine?" asked Torlos.

"You may, but I can't answer," laughed Morey. "We were so anxious to get it going that we didn't name it. Any suggestions?"

For a moment none of them made any suggestions, then slowly came Arcot's thoughts, clear and sharp, the thoughts of carefully weighed decision.

"The swiftest thing that ever was *thought!* The most irresistible thing, *thought,* for nothing can stop its progress. The most destructive thing, *thought.* Thought, the greatest constructor, the greatest destroyer, the product of mind, and producer of powers, the greatest of powers. Thought is controlled by the mind. Let us call it *Thought!*"

"Excellent, Arcot, excellent. The *Thought,* the controller of the powers of the cosmos!" cried Morey.

"But the *Thought* has not been christened, save in battle, and then it had no name. Let us emblazon its name on it now," suggested Wade.

Stopping their motion through space, but maintaining a time field that permitted them to work without consuming precious time, Arcot formed some more cosmium, but now he subjected it to a special type of converted field, and into the cosmium, he forced some light photons, half bound, half free. The fixture he formed into the letters, and welded forever on the gigantic prow of the ship, and on its huge sides. *Thought,* it stood in letters ten feet high, made of clear transparent cosmium, and the golden light photons, imprisoned in it, the slowly disintegrating lux metal, would cause those letters to shine for countless aeons with the steady golden light they now had.

The *Thought* continued on now, and as they slowed their progress for Ortol, they saw that messengers of Thett had barely arrived. The fort here too had been razed to the ground, and now they were concentrating over the largest city of Ortol. Their rays were beating down on the great ray screen that terrestrial engineers had set up, protecting the city, as Earth had been protected. But the fleet that stood guard was small, and was rapidly being destroyed. A fort broke free, and plunged at last for the ray screen. Its relux walls glowed a thousand colors as the tremendous energy of the ray-screen struck them—but it was through!

A molecular ray reached down for the city—and stopped halfway in a tremendous coruscating burst of light and energy. Yet there was none of the sheen of the ray screen. Merely light.

The fort was still driving downward. Then suddenly it stopped, and the side dented in like the side of a can someone has stepped on, and it came to sudden rest against an invisible, impenetrable barrier. A molecular reached down from somewhere in space, hit the ray screen of Ortol, which the Thessians had attacked for hours, and the screen flashed into sudden brilliance, and disappeared. The ray struck the Thessian fort, and the fort burst into tremendous opalescence, while the invisible barrier the ray had struck was suddenly a great sheet of flaming light. In less than half a second the opalescence was gone, the fort shuddered, and shrieked out of the planet's atmosphere, a mass of lux now, and susceptible to the moleculars. And everything that lived within that fort had died instantly and painlessly.

The fleet which had been preparing to follow the leading fort was suddenly stopped; it halted indecisively.

Then the *Thought* became visible as its great golden letters showed suddenly, streaking up from distant space. Every ship turned cosmic and moleculars on it. The cosmic rebounded from the cosmium walls, and from the artificial matter that protected the eyes. The moleculars did not affect either, but the invisible protective sheet that the *Thought* was maintaining in the Ortolian atmosphere became misty as it fought the slight molecular rebounds.

The *Thought* went into action. The fort which remained was the point of attack. The fort had turned its destructive ray on the cosmium ship with the result that, as before, the cosmium slowly disintegrated into puffs of cosmic rays. The vapor seemed to boil out, puff suddenly, then was gone. Arcot put up a wall of artificial matter to test the effect. The ray went right through the matter, without so much as affecting it. He tried a sheet of pure energy, an electromagnetic energy stream of tremendous power. The ray bent sharply to one side. But in a moment the Thessians had realigned it.

"It's a photonic stream, but of some type that doesn't affect ordinary matter, but only artificial matter such as lux, relux, or cosmium. If the artificial matter would only fight it, I'd be all right." The thought running through Arcot's mind reached the others.

A tremendous burst of light energy to the rear announced the fact that a Thessian had crashed against the artificial matter wall that surrounded the ship. Arcot was throwing the Thessian destructive beam from side to side now, and twice succeeded in misdirecting it so that it hit the enemy machines.

The *Thought* sent out its terrific beam of magnetic energy. The ray was suddenly killed, and the fort cruised helplessly on. Its driving apparatus was dead. The diffused cosmic reached out, and as the magnetic field, the relux and the cosmics interacted, the great fort was suddenly blue-white—then instantly a dust that scattered before an enormous blast of air.

From the *Thought* a great shell of artificial matter went, a visible, misty wall, that curled forward, and wrapped itself around the Thessian ships with a motion of tremendous speed, yet deceptive, for it seemed to billow and flow.

A Thessian warship decided to brush it away—and plowed into inconceivable strength. The ship crumpled to a mass of broken relux.

The greater part of the Thessian fleet had already fled, but there remained half a hundred great battleships. And now, within half a million miles of the planet, there began a battle so weird that astronomers who watched could not believe it.

From behind the *Thought,* where it hung motionless beyond the misty wall, a Thing came.

The Thessian ships had realized now that the misty sphere that walled them in was impenetrable, and their rays were off, for none they now had would penetrate it. The forts were gone.

But the Thing that came behind the *Thought* was a ship, a little ship of the same misty white, and it flowed into, and through the wall, and was within their prison. The Thessian ships turned their rays toward it, and waited. What was this thing?

The ovaloid ship which drifted so slowly toward them suddenly seemed to jerk, and from it reached pseudopods! An amoeba on a titanic scale! It writhed its way purposefully toward the nearest ship, and while that ship waited, a pseudopod reached out, and suddenly drove through the four foot relux armor! A second pseudopod followed with lightning rapidity, and in an instant the ship had been split from end to end!

Now a hundred rays were leaping toward the thing, and the rays burst into fire and gouts of light, blackened, burned pseudopods seemed to fall from the thing and hastily it retreated from the enclosure, flowing once more through the wall that stopped their rays.

But another Thing came. It was enormous, a mile long, a great, shining scaly thing, a dragon, and on its mighty neck was mounted an enormous, distorted head, with great flat nose and huge flapping nostrils. It was a Thessian head! The mouth, fifty feet across, wrinkled into an horrific grin, and broken, stained teeth of iron showed in the mouth. Great talons upraised, it rent the misty wall that bound them, and writhed its awful length in. The swish of its scales seemed to come to the watchers, as it chased after a great battleship whose pilot fled in terror. Faster than the mighty spaceship the awful Thing caught it in mighty talons that ripped through solid relux. Scratching, fluttering enormous, blood-red wings, the silvery claws tore away great masses of relux, sending them flying into space.

Again rays struck at it. Cosmic and moleculars with blinding pencils of light. For now in the close space of the Wall was an atmosphere, the air of two great warships, and though the space was great, the air in the ships was dense.

The rays struck its awful face. The face burst into light, and black, greasy smoke steamed up, as the thing writhed and twisted horribly, awful screams ringing out. Then it was free, and half the face was burned away, and a grinning, bleeding, half-cooked face writhed and screamed in anger at them. It darted at the nearest ship, and ripped out that ray that burned it—and quivered into death. It quivered, then quickly faded into mist, a haze, and was gone!

A last awful thing—a thing they had not noticed as all eyes watched that Thing—was standing by the rent in the Sphere now, the gigantic Thessian, with leering, bestial jaws, enormous, squat limbs, the webbed fingers and toes, and the heavy torso of his race, grinning at them. In one hand was a thing—and his jaws munched. Thett's men stared in horror as they recognized that thing in his hand—a Thessian body! He grinned happily and reached for a battleship—a ray burned him. He howled, and leaped into their midst.

Then the Thessians went mad. All fought, and they fought each other, rays of all sorts, their moleculars and their cosmics, while in their midst the Giant howled his glee, and laughed and laughed—

Eventually it was over, and the last limping Thessian ship drove itself crazily against the wreck of its last enemy. And only wreckage was left.

"Lord, Arcot! Why in the Universe did you do that—and how did you conceive those horrors?" asked Morey, more than a little amazed at the tactics Arcot had displayed.

Arcot shook himself, and disconnected his controls. "Why— why I don't know. I don't know what made me do that, I'm sure. I never imagined anything like that dragon thing—how did—"

His keen eyes fixed themselves suddenly on Zezdon Fentes, and their tremendous hypnotic power beat down the resistance of the Ortolian's trained mind. Arcot's mind opened for the others the thoughts of Zezdon Fentes.

He had acted as a medium between the minds of the Thessians, and Arcot. Taking the horror-ideas of the Thessians, he had imprinted them on Arcot's mind while Arcot was at work with the controls. In Arcot's mind, they had acted exactly as had the ideas that night on Earth, only here the demonstration had been carried to the limit, and the horror ideas were compounded to the utmost. The Thessians, highly developed minds though they were, were not resistant and they had broken. The Allies, with their different horror-ideas, had been but slightly affected.

"We will leave you on Ortol, Zezdon Fentes. We know you have done much, and perhaps your own mind has given a bit. We hope you recover. I think you agree with me, Zezdon Afthen and Inthel?" thought Arcot.

"We do, heartily, and are heartily sorry that one of our race has acted in this way. Let us proceed to Talso, as soon as possible. You might send Fentes down in a shell of artificial matter," suggested Zezdon Afthen.

"Which," said Arcot, after this had been done, and they were on their way to Talso, "shows the danger of a mad *Thought!*"

CHAPTER XXI

THE POWER OF "THE THOUGHT"

But it seemed, or must have seemed to any infinite being capable of watching it as it moved now, that the *Thought* was a mad thought. With the time control opened to the limit, and a touch of the space control, it fled across the Universe at a velocity such as no other thing was capable of.

One star—it flashed to a disc, loomed enormous—overpowering—then suddenly they were flashing *through* it! The enormous coils fed their current into the space-coils and the time field, and the ship seemed to twist and writhe in distorted space as the gravitational field of a giant star, and a giant ship's space field fought for a fraction of time so short as to be utterly below measurement. Then the ship was gone—and behind it a star, the center of which had suddenly been hurled into another space forever, as the counteracting, gravitational field of the outer layers was removed for a moment, and only its own enormous density affected space, writhed and collapsed upon itself, to explode into a mighty sea of flames. Planets it formed, we know, by a process such as can happen when only this man-made accident happens.

But the ship fled on, its great coils partly discharged, but still far more charged than need be.

It was minutes to Talso where it had been hours with the *Ancient Mariner,* but now they traveled with the speed of *Thought!*

Talso too was the scene of a battle, and more of a battle than Ortol had been, for here where more powerful defensive forces had been active, the Thessians had been more vengeful. All their remaining ships seemed concentrated here. And the great molecular screen that terrestrian engineers had flung up here had already fallen. Great holes had opened in it, as two great forts, and a thousand ships, some mighty battleships of the intergalactic spaces, some little scout cruisers, had turned their rays on the struggling defensive machines. It had held for hours, thanks to the tremendous tubes that Talso had in their power-distribution stations, but in the end had fallen, but not before many of their largest cities had been similarly defended, and the people of the others had scattered broadcast.

True, wherever they might be, a diffused molecular would find them and destroy all life save under the few screens, but if the Thessians once diffused their rays, without entering the atmosphere, the broken screen would once more be able to hold.

No fleet had kept the Thessian forces out of this atmosphere, but dozens of more adequately powered artificial matter bomb stations had taught Thett respect for Talso. But Talso's own ray-screen had stopped their bombs. They could only send their bombs as high as the screen. They did not have Arcot's tremendous control power to maintain the matter without difficulty even beyond a screen.

At last the screen had fallen, and the Thessian ships, a hole once made, were able to move, and kept that hole always under them, though if it once were closed, they would again have the struggle to open it.

Exploding matter bombs had twice caused such spatial strains and ionized conditions as to come near closing it, but finally the Thessian fleet had arranged a ring of ships about the hole, and opened a cylinder of rays that reached down to the planet.

Like some gigantic plow the rays tore up mountains, oceans, glaciers and land. Tremendous chasms opened in straight lines as it plowed along. Unprotected cities flashed into fountains of rock and soil and steel that leaped upwards as the rays touched, and were gone. Protected cities, their screens blazing briefly under the enormous ray concentrations as the ships moved on, unheeding, stood safe on islands of safety amidst the destruction. Here in the lower air, where ions would be so plentiful, Thett did not try to break down the screens, for the air would aid the defenders.

Finally, as Thett's forces had planned, they came to one of the ionized layer ray-screen stations that was still projecting its cone of protective screening to the layer above. Every available ray was turned on that station, and, designed as it was for protecting part of a world, the station was itself protected, but slowly, slowly as its already heated tubes weakened their electronic emission, the disc of ions retreated more and more toward the station, as, like some splashing stream, the Thessian rays played upon it forcing it back. A rapidly accelerating retreat, faster and faster, as the disc changed from the dull red of normal defense to the higher and bluer quanta of failing, less complete defense, the disc of interference retreated.

Then, with a flash of light, and a roar as the soil below spouted up, the station was gone. It had failed.

Instantly the ring of ships expanded as the great screen was weakened by the withdrawal of this support. Wider was the path of destruction now as the forces moved on.

But high, high in the sky, far out of sight of the naked eye, was a tiny spot that was in reality a giant ship. It was flashing forward, and in moments it was visible. Then, as another deserted city vanished, it was above the Thessian fleet.

Their rays were directed downward through a hole that was even larger. A second station had gone with that city. But, as by magic, the hole closed up, and chopped their rays off with a decisiveness that startled them. The interference was so sharp now that not even the dullest of reds showed where their beams touched. The close interference was giving off only radio! In amazement they looked for this new station of such enormous power that their combined rays did not noticeably affect it. A world had been fighting their rays unsuccessfully. What single station could do this, if the many stations of the world could not? There was but one they knew of, and they turned now to search for the ship they knew must be there.

"No horrors this time; just clean, burning energy," muttered Arcot.

It was clean, and it was burning. In an instant one of the forts was a mass of opalescence that shifted so swiftly it was purest white, then rocketed away, lifeless, and no longer relux.

The other fort had its screen up, though its power, designed to withstand the attack of a fleet of enormous intergalactic, matter-driven, fighting ships lasted but an instant under the driving power of half a million million suns, concentrated in one enormous ray of energy. The sheer energy of the ray itself, molecular ray though it was, heated the material it struck to blinding incandescence even as it hurled it at a velocity close to that of light into outer space. With little sparkling flashes battleships of the void after giant cruisers flashed into lux, and vanished under the ray.

A tremendous combined ray of magnetism and cosmic ray energy replaced the molecular, and the ships exploded into a dust as fine as the primeval gas from which came all matter.

Sweeping energy, so enormous that the defenses of the ships did not even operate against it, shattered ship after ship, till the few that remained turned, and, faster than the pursuing energies could race through space, faster than light, headed for their base.

"That was fair fight; energy against energy," said Arcot delightedly, for his new toy, which made playthings of suns and fed on the cosmic energy of a universe, was behaving nicely, "and as I said, Stel Felso Theu, at the beginning of this war, the greater Power wins, always. And in our island here, I have five hundred thousand million separate power plants, each generating at the rate of decillions of ergs a second, backing this ship.

"Your world will be safe now, and we will head for our last embattled ally, Sirius." The titanic ship turned, and disappeared from the view of the madly rejoicing billions of Talso below, as it sped, far faster than light, across a universe to relieve another sorely tried civilization.

Knowing their cause was lost, hopeless in the knowledge that nothing known to them could battle that enormous force concentrated in one ship, the *Thought*, the Thessians had but one aim now, to do all the damage in their power before leaving.

Already their tremendous, unarmed and unarmored transports

were departing with their hundreds of thousands from that base system for the far-off Island of Space from which they had come. Their battlefleets were engaged in destroying all the cities of the allies, and those other helpless races of our system that they could. Those other inhabited worlds, many of which were completely wiped out because Arcot had no knowledge of them, were relieved only when the general call for retreat to protect the mother planet was sent out.

But Sirius was looming enormous before them. And its planets, heavily defended now by the combined Sirian, Terrestrial and Venerian fleets and great ray-screens as well as a few matter-bomb stations, were suffering losses none the less. For the old Sixth of Negra, the Third here, had fallen. Slipping in on the night side of the planet, all power off, and so sending forth no warning impulses till it actually fell through the ray-screen, a small fleet of scouts had entered. Falling still under simple gravity, they had been missed by the rays till they had fallen to so small a distance, that no humans or men of our allied systems could have stopped, but only their enormous iron boned strength permitted them to resist the acceleration they used to avert collision with the planet. Then scattering swiftly, they had blasted the great protective screen stations by attacking on the sides, where the ray-screen projectors were not mounted. Designed to protect above, they had no side armor, and the Sixth was opened to attack.

Two and one-half billion people lost their lives painlessly and instantaneously as tremendous diffused moleculars played on the revolving planet.

Arcot arrived soon after this catastrophe. The Thessians left almost immediately, after the loss of three hundred or more ships. One hundred and fifty wrecks were found. The rest were so blasted by the forces which attacked them, that no traces could be found, and no count made.

But as those ships fled back to their base, Arcot, with the wonderfully delicate mental control of his ship, was able to watch them, and follow them; for, invisible under normal conditions, by twisting space in the same manner that they did he was able to see them flee, and follow.

Light year after light year they raced toward the distant base. They reached it in two hours, and Arcot saw them from a distance sink to the various worlds. There were twelve gigantic worlds, each far larger than Jupiter of Sol, and larger than Stwall of Talso's sun, Renl.

"I think," said Arcot as he stopped the ship at a third of a light year, "that we had best destroy those planets. We may kill many men, and innocent non-combatants, but they have killed many of our races, and it is necessary. There are, no doubt, other worlds of this Universe here that we do not know of that have felt the vengeance of Thett, and if we can cause such trouble to them by destroying these worlds, and putting the fear of our attacking their mother world into them, they will call off those other fleets. I could have been invisible to Thett's ships as we followed them here, and for the greater part of the way I was, for I was sufficiently out of their time-rate, so that they were visible only by the short ultra-violet, which would have put in their infra-red, and, no photo-electric cell will work on quanta of such low energy. When at last I was sure of the sun for which they were heading, I let them see us, and they know we are aware of their base, and that we can follow them.

"I will destroy one of these worlds, and follow a fleet as it starts for their home nebula. Gradually, as they run, I will fade into invisibility, and they will not know that I have dropped back here to complete the work, but will think I am still following. Probably they will run to some other nebula in an effort to throw me off, but they will most certainly send back a ship to call the fleets here to the defense of Thett.

"I think that is the best plan. Do you agree?"

"Arcot," asked Morey slowly, "if this race attempts to settle another Universe, what would that indicate of their own?"

"Hmmm—that it was either populated by their own race or that another race held the parts they did not, and that the other race was stronger," replied Arcot. "The thought idea in their minds has always been a single world, single solar system as their home, however."

"And single solar systems cannot originate in this Space," replied Morey, referring to the fact that in the primeval gas from which all matter in this Universe and all others came, no condensation of mass less than thousands of millions of times that of a sun could form and continue.

"We can only investigate—and hope that they do not inhabit

the whole system, for I am determined that, unpleasant as the idea may be, there is one race that we cannot afford to have visiting us, and it is going to be permanently restrained in one way or another. I will first have a conference with their leaders and if they will not be peaceful—the *Thought* can destroy or make a Universe! But I think that a second race holds part of that Universe, for several times we have read in their minds the thought of the 'Mighty Warless Ones of Venone.'"

"And how do you plan to destroy so large a planet as these are?" asked Morey, indicating the telectroscope screen.

"Watch and see!" said Arcot.

They shot suddenly toward the distant sun, and as it expanded, planets came into view. Moving ever slower on the time control, Arcot drove the ship toward a gigantic planet at a distance of approximately 300,000,000 miles from its primary, the sun of this system.

Arcot fell into step with the planet as it moved about in its orbit, and watched the speed indicator carefully.

"What's the orbital speed, Morey?" asked Arcot.

"About twelve and a half miles per second," replied the somewhat mystified Morey.

"Excellent, my dear Watson," replied Arcot. "And now does my dear friend know the average molecular velocity of ordinary air?"

"Why, about one-third of a mile a second, average."

"And if that planet as a whole should stop moving, and the individual molecules be given the entire energy, what would their average velocity be? And what temperature would that represent?" asked Arcot.

"Good— Why, they would have to have the same kinetic energy as individuals as they now have as a whole, and that would be an average molecular velocity in random motion of 12.5 miles a second—giving about—about—about—twelve thousand degrees centigrade!" exclaimed Morey in surprise. "That would put it in the far blue-white region!"

"Perfect. Now watch." Arcot donned the headpiece he had removed, and once more took charge. He was very far from the planet, as distances go, and they could not see his ship. But he wanted to be seen. So he moved closer, and hung off to the sunward side of the planet, then moved to the night side, but stayed in the light. In seconds, a battlefleet was out attempting to destroy him.

Surrounding the ship with a wall of artificial matter, lest they annoy him, he set to work.

Directly in the orbit of the planet, a faint mistiness appeared, and rapidly solidified to a titanic cup, directly in the path of the planet.

Arcot was pouring energy into the making of that matter at such a rate that space was twisted now about them. The meter before them, which had not registered previously, was registering now, and had moved over to three. Three sols—and was still climbing. It stopped when ten were reached. Ten times the energy of our sun was pouring into that condensation, and it solidified quickly.

The Thessians had seen the danger now. It was less than ten minutes away from their planet, and now great numbers of ships of all sorts started up from the planet, swarming out like rats from a sinking vessel.

Majestically the great world moved on in its orbit toward the thin wall of infinite strength and infinite toughness. Already Thessian battleships were tearing at that wall with rays of all types, and the wall sputtered back little gouts of light, and remained. The meters on the *Thought* were no longer registering. The wall was built, and now Arcot had all the giant power of the ship holding it there. Any attempt to move it or destroy it, and all the energy of the Universe would rush to its defense!

The atmosphere of the planet reached the wall. Instantly, as the pressure of that enormous mass of air touched it, the wall fought, and burst into a blaze of energy. It was fighting now, and the meter that measured sun-powers ran steadily, swiftly up the scale. But the men were not watching the meter; they were watching the awesome sight of Man stopping a world in its course! Turning a world from its path!

But the meter climbed suddenly, and the world was suddenly a tremendous blaze of light. The solid rock had struck the giant cup, 110,000 miles in diameter. It was silent, as a world pitted its enormous kinetic energy against the combined forces of a universe. Soundless—and as hopeless. Its strength was nothing, its energy pitted unnoticed against the energy of five hundred thousand million suns—as vain as those futile attempts of the Thessian battleships on the invulnerable walls of the *Thought*.

What use is there to attempt description of that scene as 2,500,000,000,000,000,000,000,000 tons of rock and metal and matter crashed against a wall of energy, immovable and inconceivable. The planet crumpled, and split wide. A thousand pieces, and suddenly there was a further mistiness about it, and the whole enormous mass, seeming but a toy, as it was from this distance in space, and as it was in this ship, was enclosed in that same, immovable, unalterable wall of energy.

The ship was as quiet and noiseless, as without indication of strain as when it hummed its way through empty space. But the planet crumpled and twirled, and great seas of energy flashed about it.

The world, seeming tiny, was dashed helpless against a wall that stopped it, but the wall flared into equal and opposite energy, so that matter was raised not to the twelve thousand Morey had estimated but nearer twenty-four thousand degrees. It was over in less than half an hour, and a broken, misshapen mass of blue incandescence floated in space. It would fall now, toward the sun, and it would, because it was motionless and the sun moved, take an eccentric orbit about that sun. Eventually, perhaps, it would wipe out the four inferior planets, or perhaps it would be broken as it came within the Roches limit of that sun. But the planet was now a miniature sun, and not so very small, at that.

And from every planet of the system was pouring an assorted stream of ships, great and small, and they all set panic-stricken across the void in the same direction. They had seen the power of the *Thought*, and did not contest any longer its right to this system.

CHAPTER XXII

THETT

Through the utter void of intergalactic space sped a tiny shell, a wee mite of a ship. Scarcely twenty feet long, it was one single power plant. The man who sat alone in it, as it tore through the void at the maximum speed that even its tiny mass was capable of, when every last twist possible had been given to the distorted time fields, watched a far, far galaxy ahead that seemed unchanging.

Hours, days sped by, and he did not move from his position in the ship. But the ship had crossed the great gulf, and was speeding through the galaxy now. He was near the end. At a reckless speed, he sat motionless before the controls, save for slight movements of supple fingers that directed the ship at a mad pace about some gigantic sun and its family of planets. Suns flashed, grew to discs, and were left behind in the briefest instant.

The ship slowed, the terrific pace it had been holding fell, and dull whine of overworked generators fell to a contented hum. A star was looming, expanding before it. The great sun glowed the characteristic red of a giant as the ship slowed to less than a light-speed, and turned toward a gigantic planet that circled the red sun. The planet was very close to 50,000 miles in diameter, and it revolved at a distance of four and one half billions of miles from the surface of its sun, which made the distance to the center of the titanic primary four billion, eight hundred million miles, in round figures, for the sun's diameter was close to six hundred and fifty million miles! Greater even than Antares, whose diameter is close to four hundred million miles, was this star of another universe, and even from the billions of miles of distance that its planet revolved, the disc was enormous, a titanic disc of dull red flame. But so low was its surface temperature, that even that enormous disc did not overheat the giant planet.

The planet's atmosphere stretched out tens of thousands of miles into space, and under the enormous gravitational acceleration of the tremendous mass of that planet, it was near the surface a blanket dense as water. There was no temperature change upon it, though its night was one hundred hours long, and its day the same. The centrifugal force of the rapid rotation of this enormous body had flattened it when still liquid till it seemed now more of the shape of a pumpkin than of an orange. It was really a double planet, for its satellite was a world of one hundred thousand miles diameter, yet smaller in comparison to its giant primary than is Luna in comparison to Earth. It revolved at a distance of five million miles from its primary's center, and it, too, was swarming with its people.

But the racing ship sped directly toward the great planet, and shrieked its way down through the atmosphere, till its outer shell was radiating far in the violet.

Straight it flew to where a gigantic city sprawled in the heaped, somber masonry, but in some order yet, for on closer inspection the appearance of interlaced circles came over the edge of the giant cities. Ray-screens were circular and the city was protected by dozens of stations.

The scout was going well under the speed of light now, and a message, imperative and commanding, sped ahead of him. Half a dozen patrol boats flashed up, and fell in beside him, and with him raced to a gigantic building that reared its somber head from the center of the city.

Under a white sky they proceeded to it, and landed on its roof. From the little machine the single man came out. Using the webbed hands and feet that had led the Allied scientists to think them an aquatic race, he swam upward, and through the water-dense atmosphere of the planet toward the door.

Trees overtopped the building, for it had but four stories, above ground, though it was the tallest in the city. The trees, like seaweed, floated most of their enormous weight in the dense air, but the buildings under the gravitational acceleration, which was more than one hundred times Earth's gravity, could not be built very high ere they crumple under their own weight. Though one of these men weighed approximately two hundred pounds on

Earth, for all their short stature, on this planet their weight was more than ten tons! Only the enormously dense atmosphere permitted them to move.

And such an atmosphere! At a temperature of almost exactly 360 degrees centrigrade, there was no liquid water on the planet, naturally. At that temperature water cannot be a liquid, no matter what the pressure, and it was a gas. In their own bodies there was liquid water, but only because they lived on heat, their muscles absorbed their energy for work from the heat of the air. They carried in their own muscles refrigeration, and, with that aid, were able to keep liquid water for their life processes. With death, the water evaporated. Almost the entire atmosphere was made up of oxygen, with but a trace of nitrogen, and some amount of carbon dioxide.

Here their enormous strength was not needed, as Arcot had supposed, to move their own bodies, but to enable them to perform the ordinary tasks of life. The mere act of lifting a thing weighing perhaps ten pounds on Earth, here required a lifting force of more than half a ton! No wonder enormous strength had been developed! Such things as a man might carry with him, perhaps a ray pistol, would weigh half a ton; his money would weigh near to a hundred pounds!

But—there were no guns on this world. A man could throw a stone perhaps a short distance, but when a gravitational acceleration of more than a half a mile per second acted on it, and it was hurled through an atmosphere dense as water—what chance was there for a long range?

But these little men of enormous strength did not know other schemes of existence, save in the abstract, and as things of comical peculiarity. To them life on a planet like Earth was as life to a terrestrial on a planetoid such as Ceres, Juno or Eros would have seemed. Even on Thettsost, the satellite planet of Thett, life was strange, and they used lux roofs over their cities, though their weight there was four tons!

As the scout swam through the dense atmosphere of his world toward the entrance way to the building, guards stopped him, and examined his credentials. Then he was led through long halls, and down a shaft ten stories below the planet's surface, to where a great table occupied a part of a low ceilinged, wide room. This room was shielded, interference screens of all known kinds lined the hollow walls, no rays could reach through it to the men within. The guard changed, and new men examined the scout's credentials, and he was led still deeper into the bowels of the planet. Once more the guard changed, and he entered a room guarded not by single shields but by triple, and walled with six foot relux, and ceiled with the same strong material. But here, under the enormous gravity, even its great strength required aid in the form of pillars.

A giant of his race sat before a low table. The table ran half the length of the room, and beside it sat four other men. But there were places for more than two dozen.

"A scout from the colony? What news?" demanded the leader. His voice was a growl, deep and throaty.

"Oh mighty Sthanto, I bring news of resistance. We waited too long, in our explorations, and those men of World 3769-8482730-3 have learned too much. We were wrong. They had found the secret of exceeding the speed of light, and can travel through space fully as rapidly as we can, and now, since by some means we cannot fathom, they have learned to combine both our own system and theirs, they have one enormous engine of destruction that travels across their huge universe in less time than it takes us to travel across a planetary system.

"Our cause is lost, which is by far the least of our troubles. Thett is in danger. We cannot hope to combat that ship."

"Thalt—what means have we. Can we not better them?" demanded Sthanto of his chief scientist.

"Great Sthanto, we know that such a substance can be made when pressure can be brought to bear on cosmic rays under the influence of field 24-7649-321, but that field cannot be produced, because no sufficient concentration of energy is available. Energy cannot be released rapidly enough to replace the losses when the field is developing. The fact that they have that material indicates their possession of an unguessed and terrific energy source. I would have said that there was no energy greater than the energy of matter, but we know the properties of this material and that the triple ray which has at last been perfected, can be produced providing your order for all energy sources is given, will release its energy at a speed comparable to the rate of energy relux in a twin ray, but that the release takes place only in the path of the ray."

"What more, Scout?" asked Sthanto smoothly.

"The ship first appeared in connection with our general attack on world 3769-8482730-3. The attack was near success, their screens were already failing. They have devised a new and very ionized layer as a conductor. It was exceedingly difficult to break, and since their sun had been similarly screened, we could not throw masses of that matter upon them.

"In another sthan of time, we would have destroyed their world. Then the ship appeared. It has molecular rays, magnetic beams and cosmic rays, and a fourth weapon we know nothing of. It has molecular screens, we suspect, but has not had occasion to use them.

"Our heaviest molecular screens flash under their molecular rays. Ordinary screens fall instantly without momentary defense. The ray power is incalculable.

"Their magnetic beams are used in conjunction with cosmics. The action of the two causes the relux to induce current, and due to reaction of currents on the magnetic field—"

"And the resistance due to the relux, the relux is first heated to incandescence and then the ship opens out as the air pressure bends the magnetically softened relux?" finished Thalt.

"No, the effect is even more terrific. It explodes into powder," replied the scout.

"And what happens to worlds that the magnetic ray touches?" inquired the scientist.

"A corner of it touched the world we fought over, and the world shook," replied the colonist.

"And the last weapon?" asked Sthanto, his voice soft now.

"It seems a ghost. It is a mistiness that comes into existence like a cloud, and what it touches is crushed, what it rams is shattered. It surrounds the great ship, and machines crashing into it at a speed of more than six times that of light are completely destroyed, without in the slightest injuring the shield.

"Then—what caused my departure from the colony—it showed once more its unutterable power. The mistiness formed in the path of our colonial world, number 3769-1-5, and the planet swept against that wall of mistiness, and was shattered, and turned in less than five sthan to a ball of blue-white fire. The wall stopped the planet in its motion. We could not fight that machine, and we left the worlds. The others are coming," finished the scout.

The ruler turned his slightly smiling face to the commander of his armies, who sat beside him.

"Give orders," he said softly, almost gently, "that a triple ray station be set up under the direction of Thalt, and further notice that all power be made instantly available to it. Add that the colonists are returning defeated, and bringing danger at their heels. The triple ray will destroy each ship as it enters the system." His hand under the table pushed an invisible protuberance, and from the perfectly conducting relux floor to the equally perfectly conducting ceiling, and between four pillars grouped around the spot where the scout stood, terrific arcs suddenly came into being. They lasted for the thousandth part of a second, and when they suddenly died away, as swiftly as they had come, there was not even ash where the scout had been.

"Have you any suggestions, Thalt?" he asked of the scientist, his voice as soft as before.

"I quite agree with your conduct so far, but the future conduct you had planned is quite unsatisfactory," replied the scientist. The ruler sat motionless in his great seat, staring fixedly at the scientist. "I think it is time I take your place, therefore." The place where the ruler had been was suddenly seen as through a dark cloud, then the cloud was gone, and with it the king, only his relux chair, and the bits of lux or relux that had been about his garments remained.

"He was a fool," said the scientist softly, as he rose, "to plan on removing his scientist. Are there any who object to my succession?"

"No one objects" said Faslar the ex-king's Prime Minister and councilor.

"Then I think, Phantal, Commander of planetary forces, that you had best see Ranstud, my assistant, and follow out the plan outlined by my predecessor. And you Tastal, Commander of Fleets, had best bring your fleets near the planets for protection. Go."

"May I suggest, mighty Thalt," said Faslar after the others had left, "that my knowledge will be exceedingly useful to you. You have two commanders, neither of whom loves you, and neither of whom is highly capable. The family of Thadstil would be glad to learn who removed that honored gentleman, and the family of Datstir would gladly support him who brought the remover of their head to them.

"This would remove two unwelcome menaces, and open places for such as Ranstud and your son Warrtil.

"And," he said hastily as he saw a slight shift in Thalt's eyes, "I might say further that the bereaved ones of Parthel would find great interest in certain of my papers, which are only protected by my personal constant watchfulness."

"Ah, so? And what of Kelston Faln, Faslar?" smiled the new Sthanta.

Thalt's hand relaxed and they started a conversation and discussion on means of defense.

CHAPTER XXIII

VENONE

Up from Earth, out of its clear blue sky, and into the glare and dark of space and near a sun the ship soared. They had been holding it motionless over New York, and now as it rose, hundreds of tiny craft, and a few large excursion ships followed it until it was out of Earth's atmosphere. Then—it was gone. Gone across space, racing toward that far Universe at a speed no other thing could equal. In minutes the great disc of the Universe had taken form behind them, as they took their route photographs to find their way back to Earth after the battle, if still they could come.

Then into the stillness of the Intergalactic spaces.

"This will be our first opportunity to test the full speed of this ship. We have never tried its velocity, and we should measure it now. Take a sight on the diameter of the Island, as seen from here, Morey. Then we will travel ten seconds, and look again."

Half a million light years from the center of the Island now, the great disc spread out over the vast space behind them, apparently the size of a dinner plate at about thirty inches distance, it was more than two hundred and fifty thousand light years across. Checking carefully, Morey read their distance as just shy of five hundred thousand light years.

"Hold on—here we go," called Arcot. Space was suddenly black, and beside them ran the twin ghost ships that follow always when space is closed to the smallest compass, for light leaving, goes around a space whose radius is measured in miles, instead of light centuries and returns. There was no sound, no slightest vibration, only Torlos' iron bones felt a slight shock as the inconceivable currents flowed into the gigantic space distortion coil from the storage fields, their shielded magnetic flux leaking by in some slight degree.

For ten seconds that seemed minutes Arcot held the ship on the course under the maximum combined powers of space distortion and time field distortion. Then he released both simultaneously.

The velvet black of space was about them as before, but now the disc of the Nebula was tiny behind them! So tiny was it, that these men, who knew its magnitude, gasped in sudden wonder. None of them had been able to conceive of such a velocity as this ship had shown! In seconds, Morey announced a moment later, they had traveled *one million, one hundred thousand light years!* Their velocity was six hundred and sixty quadrillion miles per second!

"Then it will take us only a little over one thousand seconds to travel the hundred and fifty million light years, at 110,000 light years per second—that's about the radius of our galaxy, isn't it!" exclaimed Wade.

They started on now, and one thousand and ten seconds, or a little more than eighteen minutes later, they stopped again. So far behind them now as to be almost lost in the far scattered universes, lay their own Island, and carefully they photographed the Universe that now lay less than twenty million light years ahead. Still, it was further, even after crossing this enormous gulf, than are many of those nebulae we see from Earth, many of which lie within that distance. They must proceed cautiously now, for they did not know the exact distance to the Nebula. Carefully, running forward in jumps of five million light years, forty-five second drives, they worked nearer.

Then finally they entered the Island, and drove toward the denser center.

"Good Lord, Arcot, look at those suns!" exclaimed Morey in amazement. For the first time they were seeing the suns of this system at a range that permitted observation, and Arcot had stopped to observe. The first one they had chosen had been a blue-white giant of enormous mass, nearly one hundred and fifty times as heavy as our own sun, and all the enormous surface was radiating power into space at a rate of nearly thirty thousand horsepower per square inch! No planets circled it, however, in its journey through space.

"I've been noticing the number of giants here. Look around."

The *Thought* moved on, on to other suns. They must find one that was inhabited.

They stopped at last near a great orange giant, and examined it. It had indeed planets, and as Arcot watched, he saw in the telectroscope a line of gigantic freighters rise from the world, and whisk off to nothingness as they exceeded the speed of light! Instantly he started the *Thought* searching in time fields for the freighters. He found them, and followed them as they raced across the void. He knew he was visible to them, and as he suspected, they soon stopped, slowing down and signaling to him.

"Morey—take the *Thought*. I'm going to visit them in the *Banderlog* as I think we shall name the tender," called Arcot, stripping off the headset, and leaving the control seat. The other fleet of ships was now less than a hundred thousand miles away, clearly visible in the telectroscope. They were still signaling, and Arcot had set an automatic signaling device flashing an enormously powerful searchlight toward them in a succession of dots and dashes, an obvious signal, though also, obviously, unintelligible to those others.

"Is it safe, Arcot?" asked Torlos anxiously. To approach those enormous ships in the relatively tiny *Banderlog* seemed unwise.

"Far safer than they'll believe. Remember, only the *Thought* could stand up against such weapons as even the *Banderlog* carries, run as they are by cosmic energy," replied Arcot, diving down toward the little tender.

In a moment it was out through the lock, and sped away from them like a bullet, reaching the distant stranger fleet in less than ten seconds.

"They are communicating by thought!" announced Zezdon Afthen presently. "But I cannot understand them, for the impulses are too weak to be intelligently received."

For nearly an hour the *Banderlog* hung beside the fleet, then it turned about, and raced once more to the *Thought.* Inside the lock, and a moment later Arcot appeared again on the threshold of the door. He looked immensely relieved.

"Well, I have some good news," he said and smiled, sitting down. "Follow that bunch, Morey, and I'll tell you about it. Set it and she'll hold nicely. We have a long way to go, and those are slow freighters, accompanied by one Cruiser.

"Those men," he began, "are men of Venone. You remember Thett's records said something of the Mighty Warless Ones of Venone? Those are they. They inhabit most of this universe, leaving the Thessians but four planets of a minor sun, way off in one corner. It seems the Thessians are their undesirable exiles, those who have, from generation to generation, been either forced to go there, or who wanted to go there.

"They did not like the easier and more effective method of disposing of undesirables, the instantaneous death chamber they now use. Thett was their prison world. No one ever returned and his family could go with him if they desired, but if they did not, they were carefully watched for outcroppings of undesirable traits—murder, crime of any sort, any habitual tendency to injustice.

"About six hundred years ago of our time, Thett revolted. There were scientists there, and their scientists had discovered a thing that they had been seeking for generations—the Twin-ray. I don't know what it is, and the Venonians don't either. It is the ray that destroys relux and lux, however, and can be carried only on a machine the size of their forts, due to some limitations. Just what those limitations are the Venonians don't know. Other than that ray they had no new weapons.

"But it was enough. Their guard ships which had circled the worlds of the prison system, Antseck, were suddenly destroyed, so suddenly that Venone received no word of it till a consignment ship, bringing prisoners, discovered their absence. The consignment ship returned without landing. Thett was now independent. But they were bound to their system, for although they had the molecular ships, they had never been permitted to have time apparatus, nor to see it, nor was any one who knew its principles ever consigned there. The result was that they were as isolated as ever.

"This was for two centuries. Two centuries later it was worked out by one of their scientists, and the Warless Ones had a War of defense. Their small fleet of cruisers, designed for rescue work and for clearing space lanes of wrecks and asteroids, was destroyed instantly, their world was protected only by the ray screen, which the Thessians did not have, and by the fact that they could build more cruisers. In less than a year Thett was defeated, and beaten back to her world, though Venone could not overcome Thett, now, for around their planets they had so many forts projecting the deadly rays, that no ship could approach.

"Then Thett learned how to make the screen, and came again. Venone had planetoid stations, that projected molecular rays of an intensity I wonder at, with their system of projecting. It seems these people have force-power feeds that operate through space, by which an entire solar system can tie in for power, and they fed these stations in that way. Lord only knows what tubes they had, but the Thessians couldn't get the power to fight.

"They've been let alone since then, they did not know why. I told them what their dear friends had been doing in that time, and the Venonians were immensely surprised, and very evidently sorry. They begged my pardon for letting loose such a menace, quite sincerely feeling that it was their fault. They offered any help they could give, and I told them that a chart of this system would be of the greatest use. They are going now to Venone, and we are to go with them, and see what they have to offer. Also, they want a demonstration of this 'remarkable ship that can defeat whole fleets of Thessians, and destroy or make planets at will,'" concluded Arcot.

"I do not in the least blame them for wanting to see this ship in operation, Arcot, but they are, very evidently, a much older race than yours," said Torlos, his thoughts coming clear and sharp, as those of a man who has thought over what he says carefully. "Are you not running danger that their minds may be more powerful than yours, that this story they have told you is but a ruse to get this ship on their world where thousand, millions can concentrate their will against you and capture the ship by mind where they cannot capture it by force?"

"That," agreed Arcot, "is where 'the rub' comes in as an ancient poet of Earth put it. I don't know and I did not have a chance to see. Wherefore I am about to do some work. Let me have the controls, Morey, will you?"

Arcot made a new ship. It was made entirely, perforce, of cosmium, lux and relux, for those were the only forms of matter he could create in space permanently from energy. It was equipped with gravity drive, and time distortion speed apparatus, and his far better trained mind finished this smaller ship with his titanic tools in less than the two days that it took them to reach Venone. In the meantime, the Venonian cruiser had drawn close, and watched in amazement as the ship was fashioned from the energy of space, became a thing of glistening matter, materializing from the absolute void of space, and forming under titanic tools such as the commander could not visualize.

Now, this move was partly the reason for this construction, for while the Venonian was busy, absorbed in watching the miraculous construction, his mind was not shielded, and it was open for observation of two such wonderfully trained minds as those of Zezdon Afthen and Zezdon Inthel. With their instruments and wonderfully developed mind-science, aided at times by Morey's less skillful, but more powerful mind of his older race, and powerful too, both because of long concentration and training, and because of his individual inheritance, they examined the minds of many of the officers of the ship without their awareness.

As a final test, Arcot, having finished the ship, suggested that the Venonian officer and one of the men of his ship have a trial of mental powers.

Zezdon Afthen tried first, and between the two ships, racing along side by side at a speed unthinkable, the two men struggled with those forces of will.

Quickly Zezdon Afthen told Arcot what he had learned.

The sun of Venone was close, now, and Arcot prepared to use as he intended the little space machine he had made. Morey took it, and went away from the *Thought* flying on its time field. The ship had been stocked with lead fuel for its matter-burning generators from the supply that had been brought on the *Thought* for emergencies, and the air had come from the *Thought's* great tanks. Morey was going to Venone ahead of the *Thought* to scout—"to see many of the important men of Venone and find out from them what I can of the relationship between Venone and Thett."

Hours later Morey returned with a favorable report. He had seen many of the important men of Venone, and conversed with them mentally from the safety of his ship, where the specially installed gravity apparatus had protected him and the ship against the enormous gravity of this gigantic world. He did not describe Venone; he wanted them to see it as he had first seen it.

So the little ship, which had served its purpose now, was destroyed, nearly a light year from Venone, and left a crushed wreck when two plates of artificial matter had closed upon it, destroying the apparatus, lest some unwelcome finder use it. There was little about it, the gravity apparatus alone perhaps, that might have been of use to Thett, and Thett already had the ray—but why take needless risk?

Then once more they were racing toward Venone. Soon the giant star of which it was a planet loomed enormous. Then, at Morey's direction, they swung, and before them loomed a planet. Large as Thett, near a half million miles in diameter, its mass was very closely equal to that of our sun. Yet it was but the burned-out sweepings of the outermost photospheric layers of this giant sun, and the radioactive atoms that made a sun active were not here; it was a cold planet. But its density was far, far higher than that of our sun, for our sun is but slightly denser than ordinary sea water. This world was dense as copper, for with the deeper sweepings of the tidal strains that had formed it, more of the heavier atoms had gone into its making, and its core was denser than that of Earth.

About it swept two gigantic satellite Worlds, each larger than Jupiter, but satellites of a satellite here! And Venone itself was inhabited by countless millions, yet their low, green tile and metal cities were invisible in the aspect of rolling lands with tiny hillocks, dwarfed by gigantic bulbous trees that floated their enormous weight in the water-dense atmosphere.

Here, too, there were no seas, for the temperature was above the critical temperature of water, and only in the self-cooling bodies of these men and in the trees which similarly cooled themselves, could there be liquid.

The sun of the world was another of the giant red stars, close to three hundred and fifty times the mass of our sun. It was circled by but three giant planets. Its enormous disc was almost invisible from the surface of the world as the *Thought* sank slowly through fifteen thousand miles of air, due to the screening effect on light passing through so much air. Earth could have rested on this planet and not extended beyond its atmosphere! Had Earth been situated at this planet's center, the Moon could have revolved about it, and would not have been beyond the planet's surface!

In silent wonder the terrestrians watched the titanic world as they sank, and their friends looked on amazed, comprehending even less of the significance of what they saw. Already within the titanic gravitational field, they could see that indescribable effects were being produced on them, and on the ship. Arcot alone could know the enormous gravitation, and his accelerometer told him now that he was subject to a gravitational acceleration of three thousand four hundred and eighty-seven feet per second, or almost exactly one hundred and nine times Earth's pull.

"The *Thought* weighs one billion, two hundred and six million, five hundred thousand tons, with tender, on Earth. Here it weighs approximately one hundred and twenty-one billion tons," said Arcot softly.

"Can you set it down? It may crush under this load if the gravity drive isn't supporting it," asked Torlos anxiously.

"Eight inches cosmium, and everything else supported by cosmium. I made this thing to stand any conceivable strain. Watch—if the planet's surface will take the load," replied Arcot.

They were still sinking, and now a number of small marvelously streamlined ships were clustered around the slowly settling giant. In a few moments more people, hundreds, thousands of men were flying through the air up to the ship.

A cruiser had appeared, and was very evidently intent on leading them somewhere, and Arcot followed it as it streaked through the dense air. "No wonder they streamline," he muttered as he saw the enormous force it took to drive the gigantic ship through this air. The air pressure outside their ship now was so great, that the sheer crushing effect of the air pressure alone was enormous. The pressure was well over nine tons to the square inch, on the surface of that enormous ship!

They landed approximately fifty miles from a large city which was the capital. The land seemed absolutely level, and the horizon faded off in distance in an atmosphere absolutely clear. There was no dust in the air at their height of nearly three hundred feet, for dust was too heavy on this world. There were no clouds. The mountains of this enormous world were not large, could not be large, for their sheer weight would tear them down, but what mountains there were were jagged, tortured rock, exceedingly sharp in outline.

"No rain—no temperature change to break them down," said Wade looking at them. "The zone of fracture can't be deep here."

"What, Wade, is the zone of fracture?" asked Torlos.

"Rock has weight. Any substance, no matter how brittle, will flow if sufficient pressure is brought to bear from all sides. A thing which can flow will not break or fracture. You can't imagine the pressure to which the rock three hundred feet down is subject to. There is the enormous mass of atmosphere, the tremendous mass of rock above, and all forced down by this gravitation. By the time you get down half a mile, the rock is under such an inconceivably great pressure that it will flow like mud. The rock there cannot break; it merely flows under pressure. Above, the rock can break, instead of flowing. That is the zone of fracture. On Earth the zone of fracture is ten miles deep. Here it must be of the order of only five hundred feet! And the planetary blocks that made a planet's surface float on the zone of flowage— they determine the zone of fracture."

The gigantic ship had been sinking, and now, suddenly it gave a very unexpected demonstration of Wade's words. It had landed, and Arcot shut off the power. There was a roaring, and the giant ship trembled, rocked, and rolled along a bit. Instantly Arcot drove it into the air.

"Whoa—can't do it. The ship will stand it, and won't bend under the load—but the planet won't. We caused a Venone-quake. One of those planetary blocks Wade was talking about slipped under the added strain."

Quickly Wade explained that all the planetary blocks were floating, truly floating, and in equilibrium just as a boat must be. The added load had been sufficiently great, so that, with an already extant overload on this particular planetary block, this "boat" had sunk a bit further into the flowage zone, till it was once more at rest and balanced.

"They wish us to come out that they may see us, strangers and friends from another Island," interrupted Zezdon Afthen.

"Tell them they'd have to scrape us up off the ground, if we attempted it. We come from a world where we weigh about as much as a pebble here," said Wade, grinning at the thought of terrestrians trying to walk on this world.

"Don't—tell them we'll be right out," said Arcot sharply. "All of us."

Morey and the others all stared at Arcot in amazement. It was utterly impossible!

But Zezdon Afthen did as Arcot had asked. Almost immediately, another Morey stepped out of the airlock wearing what was obviously a pressure suit. Behind him came another Wade, Torlos, Stel Felso Theu, and indeed all the members of their party save Arcot himself! The Galactians stared in wonder—then comprehended and laughed together. Arcot had sent artificial matter images of them all!

Their images stepped out, and the Venonian crowd which had collected, stared in wonder at the giants, looming twice their height above them.

"You see not us, but images of us. We cannot withstand your gravity nor your air pressure, save in the protection of our ship. But these images are true images of us."

For some time then they communicated, and finally Arcot agreed to give a demonstration of their power. At the suggestion of the cruiser commander who had seen the construction of a spaceship from the emptiness of space, Arcot rapidly constructed a small, very simple, molecular drive machine of pure cosmium, making it entirely from energy. It required but minutes, and the Venonians stared in wonder as Arcot's unbelievable tools created the machine before their eyes. The completed ship Arcot gave to an official of the city who had appeared. The Venonian looked at the thing skeptically, and half expecting it to vanish like the tools that made it, gingerly entered the port. Powered as it was by lead burning cosmic ray generators, the lead alone having been made by transmutation of natural matter, it was powerful, and speedy. The official entered it, and finding it still existing, tried it out. Much to his amazement it flew, and operated perfectly.

Nearly ten hours Arcot and his friends stayed at Venone, and before they left, the Venonians, for all their vast differences of structure, had proved themselves true, kindly honest men, and a race that our Alliance has since found every reason to respect and honor. Our commerce with them, though carried on under difficulties, is none the less a bond of genuine friendship.

CHAPTER XXIV

THETT PREPARES

Streaking through the void toward Thett was again a tiny scout ship. It carried but a single man, and with all the power of the machine he was darting toward distant Thett, at a speed insanely reckless, but he knew that he must maintain such a speed if his mission were to be successful.

Again a tiny ship entered Thett's far-flung atmosphere, and slowed to less than a light speed, and sent its signal call ahead. In moments the patrol ship, less than three hundred miles away, had reached it, and together they streaked through the dense air in a screaming dive toward Shatnsoma, the capital city. It was directly beneath, and it was not long before they had reached the great palace grounds, and settled on the upper roof. Then the scout leaped out of his tiny craft, and dove for the door. Flashing his credentials, he dove down, and into the first shielded room. Here precious seconds were wasted while a check was made of the credentials the man carried, then he was sent through to the Council Room. And he, too, stood on that exact spot where the other scout, but a few weeks before, had stood—and vanished. Waiting, it seemed, were four councilors and the new Sthanto, Thalt.

"What news, Scout?" asked the Sthanto.

"They have arrived in the Universe to Venone, and gone to the planet Venone. They were on the planet when I left. None

of our scouts were able to approach the place, as there were in-
numerable Venonian watchers who would have recognized our
deeper skin-color, and destroyed us. Two scouts were rayed,
though the Galactians did not see this. Finally we captured two
Venonians who had seen it, and attempted to force the information we needed from them. A young man and his chosen mate.

"The man would tell nothing, and we were hurried. So we
turned to the girl. These accursed Venonians are courageous for
all their pacifism. We were hurried, and yet it was long before
we forced her to tell what we needed to know so vitally. She had
been one of the notetakers for the Venonian government. We
got most of their conversation, but she died of burns before she
finished.

"The Galactians know nothing of the twin-ray beyond its action, and that it is an electro-magnetic phenomenon, though they
have been able to distort it by using a sheet of pure energy. But
their walls are impregnable to it, and their power of creating matter from the pure energy of space, as we saw from a distance,
would enable them to easily defeat it, were it not that the twin-
ray passes through matter without harming it. Any ray which will
destroy matter of the natural electrical types, will be stopped.

"The girl was damnably clever, for she gave us only the things
we already knew, and but few new facts; knowing that she
would inevitably die soon, she talked—but it was empty talk.
The one thing of import we have learned is that they burn no
fuel, use no fuel of any sort but in some inconceivable manner
get their energy from the radiations of the suns of space. This
could not be great—but we know she told the truth, and we
know their power is great. She told the truth, for we could determine when she lied, by mental action, of course.

"But more we could not learn. The man died without telling
anything, merely cursing. He knew nothing anyway, as we already had determined," concluded the scout.

Silently the Sthanto sat in thought for some moments. Then he
raised his head, and looked at the scout once more.

"You have done well. You secured some information of import,
which was more than we had dared hope for. But you managed
things poorly. The woman should not have died so soon. We can
only guess.

"The radiation of the suns of space—hmmm—" Sthanto Thalt's

brow wrinkled in thought. "The radiation of the *suns* of space. Were his power derived from the sun near which he is operating, he would not have said *suns*. It was more than one?"

"It was, oh Sthanto," replied the scout positively.

"His power is unreasonable. I doubt that he gave the true explanation. It may well have been that he did not trust the Venonians. I would not, for all their warless ways. But surely the suns of space give very little power at any given point at random. Else space would not be cold.

"But go, Scout, and you will be assigned a position in the fleet. The Colonial fleet, the remains of it, have arrived, and the colonists been removed. They failed. We will use their ships. You will be assigned." The scout left, and was indeed assigned to a ship of the colonists. The incoming colonial transports had been met at the outposts of the system, and rayed out of existence at once—failures, and bringing danger at their heels. Besides— there was no room for them on Thett without Thessians being crowded uncomfortably.

As their battleships arrived they were conducted to one of the satellites, and each man was "fumigated," lest he bring disease to the mother planet. Men entered, men apparently emerged. But they were different men.

"It seems," said the Sthanto softly, after the scout had left, "that we will have little difficulty, for they are, we know, vulnerable to the triple-ray. And if we can but once destroy their driving units they will be helpless on our world. I doubt that wild tale of their using no fuel. Even if that be true they will be helpless with their power apparatus destroyed, and—if we miss the first time, we can seek it out, or drive them off!

"All of which is dependent on the fact that they attack at a point where we have a triple-ray station to meet them. There are but three of these, actually, but I have had dummy stations, apparently identical with our other real stations, set up in many places.

"This gibberish we hear of creating matter—it is impossible, and surely unsuitable as a weapon. Their misty wall—that may be a force plane, but I know of no such possibility. The artificial substance though—why should any one make it? It but consumes energy, and once made is no more dangerous than ordinary matter, save that there is the possibility of creating it in dangerous position. Remember, we have heard already of the mental suggestions planes—mere force planes—*plus* a wonderfully developed power of suggestion. They do most of their damage by mental impression. Remember, we have heard already of the mental suggestions of horrible things that drove one fleet of the weak-minded colonists mad.

"And that, I think, we will use to protect ourselves. If we can, with the apparatus which you, my son, have developed, cause them to believe that all the other forts are equally dangerous, and that this one on Thett is the best point of attack— It will be easy. Can you do it?"

"I can, Oh Sthanto, if but a sufficient number of powerful minds may be brought to aid me," replied the youngest of the four councilmen.

"And you, Ranstud, are the stations ready?" asked the ruler.

"We are ready."

CHAPTER XXV

WITH GALAXIES IN THE BALANCE

The *Thought* arose from Venone after long hours, and at Arcot's suggestion, they assumed an orbit about the world, at a distance of two million miles, and all on board slept, save Torlos, the tireless molecular motion machine of flesh and iron. He acted as guard, and as he had slept but four days before, he explained there was really no reason for him to sleep as yet.

But the terrestrians would feel the greatest strain of the coming encounter, especially Arcot and Morey, for Morey was to help by repairing any damage done, by working from the control board of the *Banderlog*. The little tender had sufficient power to take care of any damage that Thett might inflict, they felt sure.

For they had not learned of the triple-ray.

It was hours later that, rested and refreshed, they started for Thett. Following the great space-chart that they had been given by the Venonians, a series of blocks of clear lux metal, with tiny points of slowly disintegrating lux, such as had been used to illuminate the letters of the *Thought's* name representing suns, the colors and relative intensity being shown. Then there was a more manageable guide in the form of photographs, marked for route by constellations formations as well, which would be their actual guide.

At the maximum speed of the time apparatus, for thus they could better follow the constellations, the *Thought* plunged along in the wake of the tiny scout ship that had already landed on Thett. And, hours later, they saw the giant red sun of Antseck, the star of Thett and its system.

"We're about there," said Arcot, a peculiar tenseness showing in his thoughts. "Shall we barge right in, or wait and investigate?"

"We'll have to chance it. Where is their main fort here?"

"From the direction, I should say it was to the left and ahead of our position," replied Zezdon Afthen.

The ship moved ahead, while about it the tremendous Thessian battlefleet buzzed like flies, thousands of ships now, and more coming with each second.

In a few moments the titanic ship had crossed a great plain, and came to a region of bare, rocky hills several hundred feet high. Set in those hills, surrounded by them, was a huge sphere, resting on the ground. As though by magic the Thessian fleet cleared away from the *Thought*. The last one had not left, when Arcot shot a terrific cosmic ray toward the sphere. It was relux, and he knew it, but he knew what would happen when that cosmic ray hit it. The solometer flickered and steadied at three as that inconceivable ray flashed out.

Instantly there was a terrific explosion. The soil exploded into hydrogen atoms, and expanded under heat that lashed it to more than a million degrees in the tiniest fraction of a second. The terrific recoil of the ray-pressure was taken by all space, for it was generated in space itself, but the direct pressure struck the planet, and that titanic planet reeled! A tremendous fissure opened, and the section that had been struck by the ray smashed its way suddenly far into the planet, and a geyser of fluid rock rolled over it, twenty miles deep in that world. The relux sphere had been struck by the ray, and had turned it, with the result that it was pushed doubly hard. The enormously thick relux strained and dented, then shot down as a whole, into the in-candescent rock.

For miles the vaporized rock was boiling off. Then the fort sent out a ray, and that ray blasted the rock that had flowed over it as Arcot's titanic ray snapped out. In moments the fort was at the surface again—and a molecular hit it. The molecular did not have the energy the cosmic had carried, but it was a single concentrated beam of destruction ten feet across. It struck the fort—and the fort recoiled under its energy. The marvelous new tubes that ran its ray-screen flashed instantly to a temperature inconceivable, and, so long as the elements embedded in the infusible relux remained the metals they were, those tubes could not fail. But they were being lashed by the energy of half a sun. The tubes failed. The element cannot exist—and broke to other elements that did not resist. The relux flashed into blinding iridescence—

And from the fort came a beam of pure silvery light. It struck the *Thought* just behind the bow, for the operator was aiming for the point where he knew the control room and pilot must be. But Arcot had designed the ship for mental control, which the enemy operator could not guess. The beam was a flat beam, perhaps an inch thick, but it fanned out to fifty feet width. And where it touched the *Thought*, there was a terrific explosion, and inconceivably violent energy lashed out as the cosmium instantaneously liberated its energy.

A hundred feet of the nose was torn off the ship, and the enormously dense air of Thett rushed in. But that beam had cut through the very edge of one of the ray projectors, or better, one of the ray feed apparatus. And the ray feed released it without control; it released all the energy it could suck in from space about it, as one single beam of cosmic energy, somewhat lower than the regular cosmics, and it flashed out in a beam as solid matter.

There was air about the ship, and the air instantly exploded into atoms of a different sort, threw off their electrons, and were raised to the temperature at which no atom can exist, and became protons and electrons. But so rapidly was that coil sucking energy from space that space tended to close in about it, and in enormous spurts the energy flooded out. It was directed almost straight up, and but one ship was caught in its beam. It was made of relux, but the relux was powdered under the inconceivable blow that countless quintillions of cosmic ray photons struck it. That ray was in fact, a solid mass of cosmium moving with the velocity of light. And it was headed for that satellite of Thett, which it would reach in a few hours time.

The *Thought*, due to the spatial strains of the wounded coil, was constantly rushing away to an almost infinite distance, as the ship approached that other space toward which the coil tended with its load, and rushing back, as the coil, reaching a spatial condition which supplied no energy, fell back. In a hundredth of a second it had reached equilibrium, and they were in a weirdly, terribly distorted space. But the triple-ray of the Thessians seemed to sheer off, and miss, no matter how it was directed. And it was painfully weak, for the coil sucked up the energy of whatsoever matter disintegrated in the neighborhood.

Then suddenly the performance was over. And they plunged into artificial space that was black and clean, and not a thing of wavering, struggling energies. Morey, from his control in the *Banderlog*, had succeeded in getting sufficient energy, by using his space distortion coils, to destroy the great projector mechanism. Instantly Arcot, now able to create the artificial space without the destruction of the coils by the struggling ray-feed coil, had thrown them to comparative safety.

Space writhed before they could so much as turn from the instruments. The Thessians had located their artificial space, and reached it with an attraction ray. They already had been withstanding the drain of the enormous fields of the giant planet and the giant sun; the attractive ray was an added strain. Arcot looked at his instruments, and with a grim smile set a single dial. The space about them became black again.

"Pulling our energy—merely let 'em pull. They're pulling on an ocean, not a lake this time. I don't think they'll drain those coils very quickly." He looked at his instruments. "Good for two and a half hours at this rate.

"Morey, you sure did your job then. I was helpless. The controls wouldn't answer, of course, with that titanic thing flopping its wings, so to speak. What are we going to do?"

Morey stood in the doorway, and from his pocket drew a cigarette, handed it to Arcot, another to each of the others who smoked, and lit them, and his own. "Smoke," he said, and puffed.

"Smoke and think. From our last experience with a minor tragedy, it helps."

"But—this is no minor tragedy, they have burst open the wall of this invulnerable ship, destroyed one of those enormous coils, and can do it again," exclaimed Zezdon Afthen, exceedingly nervous, so nervous that the normal courage of the man was gone. His too-psychic breeding was against him as a warrior.

"Afthen," replied Stel Felso Theu calmly, "when our friends have smoked, and thought, the *Thought* will be repaired perfectly, and it will be made invulnerable to that weapon."

"I hope so, Stel Felso Theu," smiled Arcot. He was feeling better already. "But do you know what that weapon is, Morey?"

"Got some readings on it with the *Banderlog's* instruments, and I think I do. Twin-ray is right," replied Morey.

"Hmhm—so I think. It's a super-photon. What they do is to use a field somewhat similar to the field we use in making cosmium, except that in theirs, instead of the photons lying side by side, they slide into one another, compounding. They evidently get three photons to go into one. Now, as we know, that size photon doesn't exist for the excellent reason that it can't in this space. Space closes in about it. Therefore they have a projected field to accompany it that tends to open out space—and they are using that, not the attractive ray, on us now. The result is that for a distance not too great, the triple-ray exists in normal space—then goes into another. Now the question is how can we stop it? I have an idea—have you any?"

"Yes, but my idea can't exist in this space either," grinned Morey.

"I think it can. If it's what I think, remember it will have a terrific electric field."

"It's what you think, then. Come on." Arcot and Morey went to the calculating room, while Wade took over the ship. But one of the ray-feeds had been destroyed, and they had three more in action, as well as their most important weapon, artificial matter. Wade threw on the time field, and started the emergency lead burner working to recharge the coils that the Thessians were constantly draining. Being in their own peculiar space, they could not draw energy from the stars, and Arcot didn't want to return to normal space to discharge them, unless necessary.

"How's the air pressure in the rest of the ship?" asked Wade.

"Triple normal," replied Morey. "The Thessian atmosphere leaked in and sent it up terrifically, but when we went into our own space, at the halfway point, a lot leaked out. But the ship is full of water now. It was a bit difficult coming up from the *Banderlog*, and I didn't want to breathe the air I wasn't sure of. But let's work."

They worked. For eight hours of the time they were now in they continued to work. The supply of lead metal gave out before the end of the fourth hour, and the coils were nearing the end of their resistance. It would soon be necessary for Arcot to return to normal space. So they stopped, their calculations very nearly complete. Throwing all the remaining energy into the coils, they a little more than held the space about them, and moved away from Thett at a speed of about twice that of light. For an hour more Arcot worked, while the ship plowed on. Then they were ready.

As Arcot took over the controls, space reeled once more, and they were alone, far from Thett. The suns of this space were flashing and glowing about them, and the unlimited energy of a universe was at Arcot's command. But all the remaining atmosphere in the ship had either gone instantaneously in the vacuum, or solidified as the chill of expansion froze it.

To the amazement of the extra-terrestrians, Arcot's first move was to create a titanic plane of artificial matter, and neatly bisect the *Thought* at the middle! He had thrown all of the controls thus interrupted into neutral, and in the little more than half of the ship which contained the control cabin, was also the artificial matter control. It was busy now. With bewildering speed, with the speed of thought trained to construct, enormous masses of cosmium were appearing beside them in space as Arcot created them from pure energy. Cosmium, relux and some clear cosmium-like lux metal. Ordinary cosmium was reflective, and he wanted something with cosmium's strength, and the clearness of lux.

In seconds, under Arcot's flying thought manipulation, a great tube had been welded to the original hull, and the already gigantic ship lengthened by more than five hundred feet! Immediately great artificial matter tools gripped the broken nose-section, clamped it into place, and welded it with cosmium flowing under the inconceivable pressure till it was again a single great hull.

Then the Thessian fleet found them. The coils were charged now, and they could have escaped, but Arcot had to work. The Thessians were attacked with moleculars, cosmics, and a great twin-ray. Arcot could not use his magnet, for it had been among those things severed from the control. He had two ray feeds, and the artificial matter. There were nearly three thousand ships attacking him with a barrage of energy that was inconceivably great, but the cosmium walls merely turned it aside. It took Arcot less than ten seconds to wipe out that fleet of ships! He created a wall of artificial matter at twenty feet from the ship—and another at twenty thousand miles. It was thin, yet it was utterly impenetrable. He swept the two walls together, and forced them against each other until his instruments told him only free energy remained between them. Then he released the outer wall, and a terrific flood of energy swept out.

"I don't think we'll be attacked again," said Morey softly. They were not. Thett had only one other fleet, and had no intention of losing the powers of their generators at this time when they so badly needed them. The strange ship had retired for repairs— very well, they could attack again—and maybe—

Arcot was busy. In the great empty space that had been left, he installed a second collector coil as gigantic as the main artificial matter generator. Then he repaired the broken ray feed, and it, and the companion coil which, with it, had been in the severed nose section, were now in the same relative position to the new collector coil that they had had with relation to the artificial matter coil. Next Arcot built two more ray feeds. Now in the gigantic central power room there loomed two tremendous power collectors, and six smaller ray feed collectors.

His next work was to reconnect the severed connectors and controls. Then he began work on the really new apparatus. Nothing he had constructed so far was more than a duplicate of existing apparatus, and he had been able to do it almost instantly, from memory. Now he must vision something new to his experience, and something that was forced to exist in part in this space, and partly in another. He tried four times before the apparatus had been completed correctly, and the work occupied ten hours. But at last it was done. The *Thought* was ready now for the battle.

"Got it right at last?" asked Wade. "I hope so."

"It's right—tried it a little. I don't think you noticed it. I'm going down now to give them a nice little dose," said Arcot grimly. His ship was repaired—but they had caused him plenty of trouble.

"How long have we been out here, their time?" asked Wade.

"About an hour and a half." The *Thought* had been on the time field at all times save when the Thessian fleet attacked.

"I think, Earthman, that you are tired, and should rest, lest you make a tired thought and do great harm," suggested Zezdon Afthen.

"I want to finish it!" replied Arcot, sharply. He was tired.

In seconds the *Thought* was once more over that fortified station in the mountains—and the triple-ray reached out—and suddenly, about the ship, was a wall of absolute, utter blackness. The triple-ray touched it, and exploded into coruscating, blinding energy. It could not penetrate it. More energy lashed at the wall of blackness as the operators within the sphere-fort turned in the energy of all the generators under their control. The ground about the fort was a great lake of dazzling lava as far as the eye could see, for the triple-ray was releasing its energy, and the wall of black was releasing an equal, and opposing energy!

"Stopped!" cried Arcot happily. "Now here is where we give them something to think about. The magnet and the heat!"

He turned the two enormous forces simultaneously on the point where he knew the fort was, though it was invisible behind the wall of black that protected him. From his side, the energy of the spot where all the system of Thett was throwing its forces, was invisible.

Then he released them. Instantly there was a terrific gout of light on that wall of blackness. The ship trembled, and space turned gray about them. The black wall dissolved into grayness in one spot, as a flood of energy beyond comprehension exploded from it. The enormously strong cosmium wall dented as the pressure of the escaping radiation struck it, and turned X-ray hot under the minute percentage it absorbed. The triple-ray bent away, and faded to black as the cosmic force playing about it, actually twisted space beyond all power of its mechanism to overcome. Then, in the tiniest fraction of a second it was over, and again there was blackness and only the brilliant, blinding blue of the cosmium wall testified to its enormous temperature, cooling now far more slowly through green to red.

"Lord—you're right, Zezdon Afthen. I'm going to sleep," called Arcot. And the ship was suddenly far, far away from Thett. Morey took over, and Arcot slept. First Morey straightened the uninjured wall and ironed out the dents.

"What, Morey, is the wall of Blackness?" asked Stel Felso Theu.

"It's solid matter. A thing that you never saw before. That wall of matter is made of a double layer of protons lying one against the other. It absorbs absolutely every and all radiation, and because it is solid matter, not tiny sprinklings of matter in empty space, as is the matter of even the densest star, it stops the triple-ray. That matter is nothing but protons; there are no electrons there, and the positive electrical field is inconceivably great, but it is artificial matter, and that electrical field exerts its strain not in pulling and electrifying other bodies, but in holding space open, in keeping it from closing in about that concentrated matter, just as it does about a single proton, except that here the entire field energy is so absorbed.

"Arcot was tired, and forgot. He turned his magnet and his heat against it. The heat fought the solid matter with the same energy that created it, and with an energy that had resources as great. The magnet curved space about it, and about us. The result was the terrific energy release you saw, and the hole in the wall. All Thett couldn't make any impression on it. One of the rays blasted a hole in it," said Morey with a laugh. For he, too, loved this mighty thing, the almost living ideas of his friend's brain.

"But it is as bad as the space defense. It works both ways. We can't send through it but neither can they. Anything we use that attacks them, attacks it, and so destroys it—and it fights."

"We're worse off than ever!" said Morey gloomily.

"My friend, you, too, are tired. Sleep, sleep soundly, sleep till I call—sleep!" And Morey slept under Zezdon Afthen's will, till Torlos carried him gently to his room. Then Afthen let the sleep relax to a natural one. Wade decided he might as well follow under his own power, for now he knew he was tired, and could not overcome Zezdon Afthen, who was not.

On Thett, the fort was undestroyed, and now floating on its power units in a sea of blazing lava. Within, men were working quickly to install a second set of the new tubes in the molecular motion ray screen, and other men were transmitting the orders of the Sthanto who had come here as the place of actually greatest safety.

"Order all battleships to the nearest power-feed station, and command that all power available be transmitted to the station attacked. I believe it will be this one. There is no limit on the power transmission lines, and we need all possible power," he commanded his son, now in charge of all land and spatial forces.

"And Ranstud, what happened to that molecular ray-screen?"

"I do not know. I cannot understand such power.

"But what most worries me is his wall of darkness," said Ranstud seriously.

"But he was forced to retire for all his wall of darkness, as you saw.

"He can maintain it but a short time, and it was full of holes when he fled."

"Old Sthanto is much too confident, I believe," said an assistant working at one of the great boards in the enemy's fort, to one of his friends. "And I think he has lost his science-knowledge. Any power-man could tell what happened. They tried to use their own big rays against us, and their screen stopped them from going out, just as it stopped ours on the way in. Ours had been working at it for seconds, and hadn't bothered them. Then for a bare instant their ray touched it—and they retired. That shield of blackness is absolutely new."

"They have many men on that ship of theirs," replied his friend, helping to lift the three hundred ton load of a vacuum tube into place, "for it is evident that they built new apparatus, and it is evident their ship was increased in size to contain it. Also the nose was repaired. They probably worked under a time field, for they accomplished an impossible amount of work in the period they were gone."

Ranstud had come up behind them, and overheard the later part of this conversation. "And what," he asked suddenly, "did your meters tell you when our ray opened his ship?"

"Councilor of Science-wisdom, they told us that our power diminished, and our generators gave off but little power when his power was exceedingly little, we still had much."

"Have you heard the myth of the source of his power, in the story that he gets it from all the stars of the Island?"

"We have, Great Councilor. And I for one believe it, for he sucked the power from our generators. So might he suck the power from the inconceivably greater generators of the Suns. I believe that we should treat with them, for if they be like the peace-loving fools of Venone, we might win a respite in which to learn their secret."

Ranstud walked away slowly. He agreed, in his heart, but he loved life too well to tell the Sthanto what to do, and he had no intention of sacrificing himself for the possible good of the race.

So they prepared for another attack of the *Thought*, and waited.

CHAPTER XXVI

MAN, CREATOR AND DESTROYER

"What we must find," said Arcot, between contented puffs, for he had slept well, and his breakfast had been good, "is some weapon which will attack them, but won't attack us. The question is, what is it? And I think, I think—I know." His eyes were dreamy, his thoughts so cryptically abbreviated that not even Morey could follow them.

"Fine—what is it?" asked Morey after vainly striving to deduce some sense from the formulas that were chasing through Arcot's thoughts. Here and there he recognized them: Einstein's energy formula, Planck's quantum formulas, Nitsu Thansi's electron interference formulas, Stebkowfski's proton interference, Williamson's electric field, and his own formulas appeared, and others so abbreviated he could not recognize them.

"Do you remember what Dad said about the way the Thessians made the giant forts out in space—hauled matter from the moon and transformed it to lux and relux. Remember, I said then I thought it might be a ray—but found it wasn't what I thought? I want to use the way I was thinking of. The only question in my mind is—what is going to happen to us when I use it?"

"What's the ray?"

"Why is it, Morey, that an electron falls through the different quantum energy levels, falls successively lower and lower till it reaches its 'lowest energy level,' and can radiate no more. Why can't it fill another step, and reach the proton? Why has it no more quanta to release? We know that electrons tend to fall aways to lower energy level orbits. Why do they stop?"

"And," said Morey, his own eyes dreamily bright now, "what would happen if it did? If it fell all the way?"

"I cannot follow your thoughts, Earthmen, beyond a glimpse of an explosion. And it seems it is Thett that is exploding, and that Thett is exploding itself. Can you explain?" asked Stel Felso Theu.

"Perhaps—you know that electrons in their planetary orbits, so called, tend to fall away to orbits of lower energy, till they reach the lowest energy orbit, and remain fixed till more energy comes and is absorbed, driving them out again. Now we want to know why they don't fall lower, fall all the way? As a matter of fact, thanks to some work I did last year with disintegrating lead, we do know. And thanks to the absolute stability of artificial matter, we can handle such a condition.

"The thing we are interested in is this: Artificial matter has no tendency to radiate, its electrons have no tendency to fall into the proton, for the matter is created, and remains as it was created. But natural matter does have a tendency to let the electron fall into the proton. A force, the 'lowest energy wall,' over which no electron can jump, caused by the enormous space distorting of the proton's mass and electrical attraction, prevents it. What we want to do is to remove that force, iron it out. Requires inconceivable power to do so in a mass the size of Thett— but then—!

"And here's what will happen: Our wall of protonic material won't be affected by it in the least, because it has no tendency to collapse, as has normal matter, but Thett, beyond the wall, *has* that tendency, and the ray will release the energy of every planetary electron on Thett, and every planetary electron will take with it the energy of one proton. And it will take about one one-hundred-millionth of a second. Thett will disappear in one instantaneous flash of radiation, radiation in the high cosmics!"

"Here's the trouble: Thett represents a mass as great as our sun. And our sun can throw off energy at the present rate of one sol for a period of some ten million years, three and a half million tons of matter a second for ten million years. If all of that went up in *one one-hundred-millionth of a second,* how many sols?" asked Morey.

"Too many, is all I can say. Even this ship couldn't maintain its walls of energy against that!" declared Stel Felso Theu, awed by the thought.

"But that same power would be backing this ship, and helping it to support its wall. We would operate from—half a million miles."

"We will. If we are destroyed—so is Thett, and all the worlds of Thett. Let that flood of energy get loose, and everything within a dozen light years will be destroyed. We will have to warn the Venonians, that their people on nearby worlds may escape in the time before the energy reaches them," said Arcot slowly.

The *Thought* started toward one of the nearer suns, and as it went, Arcot and Morey were busy with the calculators. They finished their work, and started back from that world, having given their message of warning, with the artificial matter constructors. When they reached Thett, less than a quarter of an hour of Thessian time had passed. But, before they reached Thett, Arcot's viewplates were blinded for an instant as a terrific flood of energy struck the artificial matter protectors, and caused them to flame into defense. Thett's satellite was sending its message of instantaneous destruction. That terrific ray had reached it, touched it, and left it a shattered, glowing ball of hydrogen.

"There won't be even that left when we get through with Thett!" said Arcot grimly. The apparatus was finished, and once more they were over the now fiery-red lava sea that had been mountains. The fort was still in action. Arcot had cut a sheet of sheer energy now, and as the triple-ray struck it, he knew what would happen. It did. The triple-ray shunted off at an angle of forty-five degrees in the energy field, and spread instantly to a diffused beam of blackness. Arcot's molecular reached out. The lava was instantly black, and mountains of ice were forming over the struggling defenses of the fort. The molecular screen was working.

"I'd like to know how they make tubes that'll stand that, Morey," said Arcot, pointing to an instrument that read .01 millisols. "They have tubes now, that would have wiped us out in minutes, seconds before this."

The triple-ray snapped off. They were realigning it to hit the ship now, correcting for the shield. Arcot threw out his protonic shield, and retreated to half a million miles, as he had said.

"Here goes." But before even his thoughts could send Thett to radiation, the entire side of the planet blazed suddenly incandescent. Thett was learning what had happened when their ray had wounded the *Thought*.

And then, in the barest instant of time, there was no Thett. There was an instant of intolerable radiation, then momentary blackness, and then the stars were shining where Thett had been. Thett was utterly gone.

But Arcot did not see this. About him there was a tremendous roar, titanic generator-converters that had not so much as hummed under the impact of Thett's greatest weapons, whined and shuddered now. The two enormous generators, the blackness of the protonic shield, and the great artificial matter generator, throwing an inner shield impervious to the cosmics Thett gave off as it vanished, both were whining. And the six smaller machines, which Arcot had succeeded in interconnecting with the protonic generator, were whining too. Space was weirdly distorted, glowing gray about them, the great generators struggling to maintain the various walls of protecting power against the surge of energy as Thett, a world of matter, disintegrated.

But the very energy that fought to destroy those walls was absorbed in defending it, and by that much the attacking energy was lessened. Still, it seemed hours, days that the battle of forces continued.

Then it was over, and the skies were clear once more as Arcot lowered the protonic screen silently. The white sky of Thett was gone, and only the black starriness of space remained.

"*It's gone!*" gasped Torlos. He had been expecting it—still, the disappearance of a world—

"We will have to do no more. No ships had time to escape, and the risk we run is too great," said Morey slowly. "The escaping energy from that world will destroy the others of this system as completely, and it will probably cause the sun itself to blow up—perhaps to form new planets, and so the process repeats itself. But Venone knows better now, and their criminals will not populate more worlds.

"And we can go—home. To our little dust specks."

"But they're wonderfully welcome dust specks, and utterly important to us, Earthman," reminded Zezdon Afthen.

"Let us go then," said Arcot.

It was dusk, and the rose tints of the recently-set sun still hung on the clouds that floated like white bits of cotton in the darkening blue sky. The dark waters of the little lake, and the shadowy tree-clad hills seemed very beautiful. And there was a little group of buildings down there, and a broad cleared field. On the field rested a shining, slim shape, seventy-five feet long, ten feet in diameter.

But all, the lake, the mountains even, were dwarfed by the silent, glistening ruby of a gigantic machine that settled very, very slowly, and very, very gently downward. It touched the rippled surface of the lake with scarcely a splash, then hung, a quarter submerged in that lake.

Lights were showing in the few windows the huge bulk had, and lights showed now in the buildings on the shore. Through an open door light was streaming, casting silhouettes of two men. And now a tiny door opened in the enormous bulk that occupied the lake, and from it came five figures, that floated up, and away, and toward the cottage.

"Hello, Son. You have been gone long," said Arcot, senior, gravely, as his son landed lightly before him.

"I thought so. Earth has moved in her orbit. More than six months?"

His father smiled a bit wryly. "Yes. Two years and three

months. You got caught in another time field and thrown the other way this time?"

"Time and force. Do you know the story yet?"

"Part of it—Venone sent a ship to us within a month of the time you left, and said that all Thett's system had disappeared save for one tremendous gas cloud—mostly hydrogen. Their ships were met by such a blast of cosmic rays as they came toward Thett that the radiation pressure made it almost impossible to advance. There were two distinct waves. One was rather slighter, and was more in the gamma range, so they suspected that two bodies had been directly destroyed; one small one, and one large one were reduced completely to cosmics. Your warning to Sentfenn was taken seriously, and they have vacated all planets near. It was the force field created when you destroyed Thett that threw you forward? Where are the others?"

"Zezdon Afthen and Zezdon Inthel we took home, and dropped in their power suits, without landing. Stel Felso Theu as well. We will visit them later."

"Have you eaten? Then let us eat, and after supper we'll tell you what little there is to tell."

"But Arcot," said Morey slowly, "I understand that Dad will be here soon, so let us wait. And I have something of which I have not spoken to you as yet. Worked it out and made it on the back trip. Installed in the *Thought* with the *Banderlog's* controls. It is—well, will you look?—Fuller! Come and see the new toy you designers are going to have to work on!"

They had all been depressed by the thought of their long absence, by the scenes of destruction they had witnessed so recently. They were beginning to feel better.

"Watch." Morey's thoughts concentrated. The *Thought* outside had been left on locked controls, but the apparatus Morey had installed responded to his thoughts from this distance.

Before them in the room appeared a cube that was obviously copper. It stayed there but a moment, beaming brightly, then there was a snapping of energies about them—and it dropped to the floor and rang with the impact!

"It was not created from the air," said Morey simply.

"And now," said Arcot, looking at it, "Man can do what never before was possible. From the nothingness of Space he can make anything.

"Man alone in this space is Creator and Destroyer.

"It is a high place.

"May he henceforth live up to it."

And he looked out toward the mighty starlit hull that had destroyed a solar system—and could create another.